Amarillo

ISBN 978-1450539517

Acknowledgements

The idea for this novel began in Mona Lee's acting class in Austin, Texas, and it is with much gratitude that I thank all those fine actors.

Appreciation must also go to E.L. Doctorow, who told me that I needed to write a contemporary western novel.

Through the years many people kindly listened to me talk about the story, and some read it and gave comments. Thank you for your kindness and patience.

I would not have finished the book without the loving encouragement of my wife, Susan. She and Taylor make my life worth living. It is to them that I dedicate this book, along with my late boon companions Tom Ramsay, Bailey, and Rocky, whom I will never cease to miss.

Praise for Amarillo

The characters are right on the money, and the plot twists that constantly surprise and delight the reader come straight out of the interactions of the people who bring this book to life. From cowboys to dust storms to Palo Duro Canyon at dawn, Bill Durham nails the West Texas setting and makes that setting relevant to the nailbiter that comes at the end. Highly recommended!

--Andrew Geyer, author of *Siren Songs from the Heart of Austin*

Bill Durham has managed to shatter the [familiar mystery] patterns and yet create characters that seem like the people next door. The story that unfolds is amazing - and unlike any other thriller that I've ever read. I recommend this book highly.

--Mary Devlin, author of *Murder on the Canterbury Pilgrimage* and *The Legend of Good Women*

AMARILLO is as dusty and desolate, diverse and delightful, searing hot, windy, wondrous, bone- numbing cold and tightlipped laugh-out-loud hilarious as the real place.

Brad Leland, star of TV's *Friday Night Lights*

Be assured, readers will be unwilling to set this book aside, no matter what the hour, primarily because they become emotionally invested in these characters. Some, they may dislike. Others, however, do touch their hearts, to the point that readers will wonder, at times, just how much tragedy Durham thinks they can stand. Indeed, there are moments when tears arrive with the speed of a trigger being pulled.

"Amarillo" is an unpredictable story — the best kind — and one well told. It is a tale in which victims turn up where and when least expected, and memories, if left unchecked, also can carry a destructive weight.

-- William Kerns, *Lubbock Avalanche Journal*

Part One

Chapter 1

Max Friedman's fingers clenched the steering wheel of his ancient Toyota. Was it the arctic wind or the rapid deterioration of something under the hood that was causing his car to buck and shake? Whichever it was, he knew it didn't bode well for him. It was all he could do to stay on the road.

Max had no idea where he had made the wrong turn. It must have been somewhere past Oklahoma City, he decided, where he found the road that had led him into this gut-churning, roiling, sandstorm underworld.

The map said that I-40 would take him across the Texas Panhandle into New Mexico. Although the interstate signs said that he was still on the right road, he knew better. That fear was confirmed forty miles outside of Amarillo. Just past an exit announcing the presence of a town called Groom, he had encountered a gigantic, starkly silver cross almost 200 feet tall, looming up over the four-lane, illuminated by spotlights. Max first saw it from three miles away, a tiny bright spot on the horizon, but as he got closer, it grew to frightening dimensions. He expected the cross to catch fire at any moment, a present from the Ku Klux Klan set expressly for him, as if the local chapter knew he was coming and had prepared a warm welcome.

It had been eleven years, seven months, and fifteen days since his last drink, and at that moment Max would have sold his soul for one—would have offered up his car, his clothing, or the soft skin of his skull to the perpetrators of the gigantic cross for just one shot of scotch. Even bourbon would have served his needs.

Just after he drove into Amarillo on Interstate 40, his car began to do strange things. It sounded strained—choking and chugging—emitting ratcheting noises, and suddenly began to decelerate at an alarming rate. Max pulled off on an exit marked "Georgia Street," hoping to find a motel. He would have bet his NYU Law diploma that his chances of finding an open mechanic's shop at 10:00 p.m. on a Saturday night were nil, even in this state that seemed to have raised cars and trucks to the level of religion.

The wind buffeted his Toyota, rocking it from side to side, until he was afraid it would go slamming up over the sidewalk into one of the storefronts lining the street. The traffic lights were almost parallel with the pavement, so hard was the wind blowing. Fine grains of sand hissed across his windshield like cockroaches. He remembered walking across Washington Square on a January night, on his way home to the East Village after a literature class; the sleet skittering across the sidewalks had sounded just like this, except now it was brown instead of white, and tumbleweeds were maniacally hopping down the street and up onto the sidewalks. Max had never seen a tumbleweed outside of a western movie, and until this moment had thought them a corny invention of Hollywood hacks.

The night was tinted yellow. At first he had thought the source of the color was the streetlights but soon realized it was the storm itself, the monstrous sand storm that had been following him when he left Oklahoma City four hours ago and had slowly caught up with him. Could a storm travel faster than a car on the interstate? Apparently this one could.

Texas was supposed to be hotter than hell, but this night, although only late September, was freezing cold. He had cranked up the heater to the highest setting, and still the insidious wind crept and crawled and whistled through every nook and cranny and froze his feet. He cursed himself for a Yankee fool.

By now his car was barely moving, and he made a right turn off Georgia onto a small street bordering a K-Mart parking lot as big as two football fields laid side by side. With a frightening metallic sigh, his car died in the middle of the street.

Max sat in the car while the wind rocked them back and forth. If it took a mind to flip them over and over into the K-Mart's front windows, there was nothing he could do to stop it. He glanced at the storefront directly to his right. A sign on the mirrored windows read Bailey's Billiards, in a fluid red script that seemed to be fashioned out of a lariat. As Max looked at the front of the joint, the door slammed open and two men dressed like cowboys came blasting out as if they had been fired from cannons. One of them leaned against the wall like a fighter up against the ropes. His partner rubber-legged out into the street in front of Max's car, peering wildly through the windshield as if Max were an exhibit in the Brooklyn Aquarium. Apparently satisfied with what he saw, he grabbed his crotch with his left hand and thrust his right fist up toward where the moon would be if it were visible through the screen of dusty grit. He howled, a sound that chilled Max even more than the invading cold wind. "Happy New Year!" he screamed, then staggered to the curb, where he vomited into the gutter, an alcohol-filled explosion that reminded Max of the floating oil slicks that appear on the streets of Manhattan after a rain.

Max slammed down the locks, pumped the gas, and turned the key. Nothing. The car was still dead, as dead as the ancient Jews who had spawned him, who would now be rolling over in their tombs to see their descendant, an NYU history major, a law graduate, a magna cum laude, stranded on a street in the middle of some hell-hole of a cowboy outpost in the middle of a sandstorm that should never have happened outside of the Arabian desert.

He hadn't wanted a drink this badly in years. He wanted to open his glove box and take out an old, familiar friend like Jack Daniel's or Wild Turkey, to feel their warm, soothing handshake sliding down his parched throat, to ease into a smoky dream of comfort and love and woody alcohol. That's what Southerners can do, he thought. They're not shit for making weather, but whiskey they can do; everyone should be able to do something well and— knock knock went the glass next to his face.

Max realized his forehead was resting against the wheel, and he could feel a killer of a headache coming on. He looked through the smudged window and saw the vomiting cowboy; thankfully his juices were no longer flowing. His face was pressed up against the glass so that he looked like that idiot TV pitchman a few years back, who had gone on to make all those stupid movies.

The cowboy was trying to talk to Max, so he reluctantly rolled down the window a few inches. The cowboy stuck his mouth up to the window and began to speak, his breath fragrant with a bouquet of cheap alcohol.

"Name's Frank Vaughn. I was saying you best get it off the street. Need some help?" Max nodded assent and put the car in neutral. The cowboy yelled at his friend, "Larry, get your goddamn useless ass over here. We gonna push this feller's car into the parking lot. Come on, let's do a good deed!"

"I look like a Boy Scout?" Larry hollered back, but relinquished his place at the wall and weaved over to the back of the car. They pushed while Max steered, and in seconds he was parked in the K-mart lot, next to the street.

He stepped out of his car and was shocked at the ferocity of the sandstorm. Instantly his mouth was coated with a film of grit, and when he moved his teeth the grit ground against the surfaces like a mortar and pestle. His winter clothes were packed into the back of the car, too deep to dig for, so he stood vaguely in the stream of dirt, trying to find its direction so he could turn his back to it.

Frank stopped to catch his breath. "I'm too fucked up," he said, with the penchant for the obvious many drunks seem to possess.

"You need a tow truck?" he offered. "Old Larry here, he's got one, could probably go home and come back. Might cost you extra, though." He belched loudly.

Max studied Larry's drunken grin. "No, thanks. I guess I just need a phone. There a hotel close by?"

"*Ho*tel I don't know," Frank said. "*Mo*tel's not so far, though. You need a ride?"

"Just a phone."

"Go on into Bailey's. Angel's got one in there. We'd show you, but we can't go back in on account of that dog."

"Excuse me?" Max asked, then decided ignorance, if not exactly bliss, would be preferable to knowledge.

He squinted at the building across the street. The mirrored windows made it impossible to see in, but the amount of light it leaked made it seem busy and almost friendly.

They crossed the street, heads ducked against the frigid blast. Max opened the door, which was no easy task with the wind applying sixty miles an hour of effort to shut it again. He wedged his shoulder against it, his cowboy companions backing him up. Their three bodies prevailed against the wind, and as Max stepped into the place he was confronted by an enormous gray dog, the biggest, most vicious animal he had ever seen in his life.

The creature stood two feet back from the doorway, its hackles raised, leaning forward, ears back, yellow eyes narrowed to mere slits, lips pulled back from a set of teeth that were so big you could have constructed a grand piano from them. The dog was monstrously big, and as Max looked into the hostile eyes gleaming out of its gray and tan body, he knew he was seeing the last sight he would ever be allowed on God's green earth. From deep in its throat issued growls that turned his marrow into popsicles.

Miraculously, the dog didn't lunge at him. Still Max, mindful of Falstaff's philosophy of valor, twisted his body out of the doorway and let the wind slam the door shut.

"Jesus Christ," he panted, back pressed firmly against the door, "there's a fucking *wolf* in there!"

"Hell," Frank said, "she ain't but half wolf. And it's us that pissed her off, not you. Go on in. I ain't gonna try it, cause I'm kind of used to having only one asshole."

Larry laughed, and they both pulled the door open again. The dog was still poised to leap, and when it saw the cowboys it started growling again. But Max saw that its eyes were fixed on them and managed to slip by it into the pool hall.

"Shut that goddamn door!" a woman's voice commanded. It slammed shut, and when the dog seemed sure that Frank and Larry weren't intent on returning, it gathered its haunches and launched itself onto the counter, then dropped quietly to the floor behind it.

Max cringed at the acrid smell of cigarette smoke. The sharp clack of balls and the periodic explosion of a hard break were comforting, however. The jukebox cranked out a hideous, harrowing, country music song, the kind Max was sure caused Texas rednecks to gleefully kick the shit out of ponytailed Yankee lawyers who, through their own stupidity, had driven a broken-down Japanese car into this hell-blown corner of the globe.

This place called Bailey's was a world removed from the fern-bar pool halls surrounding N.Y.U., with their no-smoking sections and waitresses delivering cappuccino to the patrons. Max didn't like cigarette smoke, but he thought that any pool hall that had a no-smoking policy was an aberration in nature; it should stick its tail between its legs and slink away, lay on its back with its belly in the air.

Neon beer signs were scattered around the walls amid sports posters and— Max could barely believe his eyes—an actual, for real, velvet print of dogs playing pool, lovingly cradled by a heavy wooden frame. The bulldog wore a visor over his Edward G. Robinson forehead, a cigar wedged between two stubby toes as he surveyed a shot. A Golden Lab chalked his cue as a Dalmatian, an Irish Setter, and a Great Dane leaned on their sticks, good-naturedly hoping the bulldog would miss. Underneath the table, a Chihuahua wearing an apron swept up the floor with a whisk broom. Maybe, just maybe, Max thought, there might be some redeeming value in this city.

His eyes patrolled the room, searching for the phone Frank had promised him was on the premises.

The same voice that had earlier commanded the door be shut asked, "Help you?"

Max focused on the woman behind the counter. She had a willowy body, strawberry blonde hair, and steely green eyes that challenged him without the barest ounce of warmth. They were eyes that he would not want to face in a courtroom. A judge with those eyes, he mused, would give no quarter. She would give a defendant the needle for running a stop sign.

The woman wore Levi's faded almost white and a pair of plain, round-toed cowboy boots. Her flannel shirt looked much warmer than his own cotton, ill-prepared for the cold weather as he was, and he knew if he looked at her a second longer she would pull a gun from behind the counter and shoot him down. "Phone?" he asked.

She nodded her chin toward the back of the room and drew a beer for a customer at the counter, expertly stopping the flow a second before the head boiled over the rim in a cascade of foam. Max could almost taste the beer as he wound his way to the back of the hall, wishing he had tucked his hair underneath his collar. Like that would have made him seem a native. He felt like the deer in that "Far Side" cartoon, the one named Hal who had a bull's eye birthmark. "Hell, Mr. Lawyer, you're the one had a 'Kick Me' sign on your butt. All we's doing was following orders."

Max reached the pay phone without incident and found a 24-hour towing service. Half an hour, they said. He weighed his options. Outside was the sandstorm blowing straight from the North Pole; inside was a pool hall filled with pitchers of beer and drunk Texans. When he was working on his undergrad and law degrees, Max had hustled extra spending money in the pool halls of Manhattan. Somehow, this seemed the wrong place and time to start honing his skills again, but the thought of waiting for the wrecker out in the sand storm was too daunting.

Aimlessly, Max drifted up to the front where he could keep an eye out for the truck and settled onto a wooden stool that was gouged, burned, and nicked from years of abuse. Leaning his head against the wall, he tried to examine his options, which at the moment seemed to be precious few. His eyelids drifted down while he tried to shut out the smoke and noise.

He must have fallen asleep, because the next thing he was aware of, the minute hand on the Coors Light clock had advanced ten minutes. It was 11:15 p.m. Max felt like crying but knew that of the few options he had, breaking down in tears in this place would mark him even more as an outsider than sporting a ponytail and a New York accent. If he could just hold out until the truck came and try to get a lift to a motel, then in forty minutes or so he could cry all he wanted to.

A growl emanated from behind the counter, and Max looked up in time to see the wolf leap down to the floor and pad toward the door. It was open a foot, and Frank and Larry were peeking in. The wolf's growling grew lower and more threatening, coming from somewhere down deep in its chest.

The red-headed woman behind the counter finished up with a customer. "Hey," she said to the two men at the door, "didn't Bailey already throw your sorry asses out once tonight? You want to try for twice?"

"C'mon, Angel," Frank said. "It's goddamn cold out there. You let us back in and we ain't gonna cause no more shit."

"It's not up to me," Angel said. "You want back in, you talk to the bouncer."

Max looked around for a gentleman sizable enough to fill that role. He saw no one.

"Well shit, we didn't mean nothing by it. I mean, goddamn!"

Angel turned her back and took a rack of balls from a middle-aged Mexican couple who were leaving for the night. She totaled up their bill and gave them change. "See you next time," she said, ignoring the two cowboys huddled in the doorway.

The couple walked past Bailey, who stood staring at Frank and Larry, rumbling deep in its chest.

"Say looky here, we ain't going to do nothing else," Larry said to the wolf. "I mean, you let us back in, we'll be on our best behavior for the rest of the night, and I guarantee it. Frank does too."

"Oh hell yeah," Frank said. "Absolute best."

Bailey continued to stare at them for a long moment, golden eyes narrowed to slits, then turned and walked back to the bar. In one instant the wolf gathered its powerful legs and launched itself up onto the counter, now a head taller than any man in the room, staring at Frank and Larry as they gingerly walked by. Bailey surveyed the rest of the place before flowing down onto the floor behind the counter without a sound.

Max watched all this, trying to decide whether he was dreaming. A wolf bouncer, an owner who deferred all rules of decorum to the terrifying creature, and two drunken cowboys who actually talked to the wolf as if it understood. Of the whole bizarre sequence of events, that was the only one he could understand. Max himself, when drunk, had done things that would make talking to a wolf seem the very essence of rational behavior.

Larry grinned at Max triumphantly. "Made it back, pardner," he said. "Set us up, Angel." They raised their hands in a high-five and came close to connecting.

She handed Larry a tray of balls with two cubes of chalk nestled in among them. "I ain't warning you two hoo-rahs again. You slip up once more, Bailey'll take your goddamn heads off."

"No worry about that," Frank said. "We done told Bailey we'll be on our best behavior."

Max closed his eyes again. He prayed that the tow truck would be early.

"Hey," he heard a voice say. "You okay?"

He opened his eyes and focused on the woman named Angel. "You okay?" she repeated.

"Compared to what?"

"You gonna be a smartass?"

"Sorry. I think I'll be all right. I'm just waiting for a tow truck. Is that okay?"

"Yeah," she said, the first warmth he'd felt from her all night.

"Thanks."

She studied him, her head at an odd, contemplative angle. She drew a beer for a customer. "You want one? On the house."

He thought for a moment. "Do you have whiskey?"

"This is a pool hall, not a bar. Draft is the strongest thing we got. You want it?"

Max closed his eyes and nodded. She reached for a clean glass.

"You're gonna have to come get it," Angel said.

Max slid off his stool and picked up the glass of beer. The yeasty smell, although not as satisfying as the scent of grain alcohol, sent a thrill through him. He raised it to his lips, savoring the foam. It gave him a faint mustache before his hand began to tremble, and he knew that one would be too many and a hundred not enough. He set the glass down on the bar.

"On second thought, how about some water?" Wahtuh, he heard himself say.

Her eyes drilled a hole through him, but she poured out the beer. "Sure." She fizzed the water out of a hose head with buttons on it, an apparatus that always reminded him of some cousins who had moved from the Lower East Side to Syosset, on Long Island. They had a hose that looked like that on their new kitchen faucet and considered themselves only a step down from the Rockefellers because of it. For years they'd shown it to any new visitors, as if it were the height of sophisticated living.

Max drank deeply from the glass of water. "Is the weather always this bad here? I thought it was supposed to be hot in Texas."

"You know what they say."

"I do?"

"You don't like the weather in Texas, stick around for a half hour. It's sure to change."

"Do they say that?"

"Yeah. I always thought it was pretty stupid. What's wrong with your car?"

"Everything probably. It sleeps with the fishes, I'm afraid."

"Like Luca Brasi?"

Max focused on her to see if it were possible that she was trying to be friendly. "Hey, you're good."

"We're not all hicks in here, like your pals Frank and Larry."

Max started feeling a little better. He leaned his elbow on the counter and peered over it. Bailey, relaxed on the floor with front paws crossed right over left, stared at him.

"You own this place?" he asked either one of them.

"Yeah, I do," Angel replied.

"So why is it called Bailey's?"

"My name may be on the papers, but you just start any shit in here and you'll find out who makes the rules."

Max leaned over the counter and addressed the dog. "Bailey, my name is Max Friedman and I'm an attorney. You touch me and I'll sue your balls off."

"She doesn't have any," Angel said.

"So I guess you're in charge of the balls around here, huh?"

Angel stared at him, and Bailey began growling deep in her chest.

"Pool balls, I meant." Oh, shit. "Look, do I get a second chance?"

Angel turned her back to him while Bailey continued to stare. Frank weaved his way to the counter. "Hey Angel, what's the chance of me getting a beer?"

"None at all."

"Just checking." He turned to Max. "Did you say you're a man of the law?"

"Why?"

"Well see, I got about eight hundred jillion dollars worth of traffic warrants outstanding. If they ever catch me, my ass is grass." He smiled brilliantly at Max, waiting for a reply.

"And?"

"And I can't step into that court unless I have the money, or they'll arrest me on the spot. What I need is a fast-talking lawyer who'll at least get me out of some of them."

"If you can't pay the tickets, how are you going to pay a lawyer?"

"Oh hell, I can always come up with money for a good cause. So how 'bout it?"

"Look, I'm licensed in New York. If I try to practice law in Texas, we'll be sharing a cell. Plus I'm on my way to Phoenix."

Frank draped his arm over Max's shoulder and lowered his voice. "If your car's as bad off as it sounds, it may take you a while to get down to Phoenix. Look, in case you stick around a while, can I at least give you my number?"

What would it hurt, Max thought. He shrugged.

Frank looked at Angel and made a scribbling motion which accompanied by raised eyebrows, served as a request for a pencil. She stared at him. He patted his pockets and finally came out with a stubby pencil. Max handed him a gas receipt, and Frank wrote down his number. "All right! I got a feeling this is going to work out just fine. I knew when your engine died out in the street that there was more to it than meets the eye."

"Oh yeah," Max said. "It feels like a match made in heaven to me."

The door opened and a big man sporting a flattop haircut and a wool-lined suede jacket opened the door.

"Goddamn, it's cold out there! Hey, how you doing?" he asked Angel. "You know if anybody in here called for a tow?"

"That would be me," Max said.

"It would, huh? Well, that would be me that's come to tow you off."

Max turned to Angel. "Thanks for the water, miss. And about that comment I made, I'm sorry. I was just trying to make a joke."

Angel nodded at him. He had no idea what it meant. It could be Texas shorthand for "no problem," or it could mean "If I see you again my dog will take your head off at the shoulders."

Max stepped out onto the sidewalk, and the freezing wind slammed him against the wall. Grains of sand drove straight into his mouth and his eyes. He turned his back to the onslaught.

"That it over there?" the driver asked. Max nodded. "Yeah, I figured it was. What's wrong with her?"

"Well," said Max, "she's lived a long and loyal life, and she has 248,000 miles on her."

"Jesus Christ! You thought about maybe you might not be able to revive her?"

"It's crossed my mind a couple of times."

The man threw back his head and laughed. It was not unkind. "Yeah, I guess it has. Any special garage you want her towed to?"

"I'm just passing through." I hope and pray, Max thought. "Do you know a good place?"

"I know a fellow who'll treat you right."

"You know a good motel?"

"Yeah, I can find you one somewhere."

By the time Max got his car dropped off and the tow truck man delivered him to a motel, he was so tired he didn't even want a drink anymore. He slipped between the sheets and found to his amazement that the urge to cry had passed. So he nestled into the pillow, serenaded by the soothing drone of the heater, and dropped off to sleep instead.

Chapter 2

George Strait blared from the speakers. The lights were low over the dance floor, which was filled with couples two-stepping, the men's enormous belt buckles caressing the women's as their boots glided smoothly over the polished floor, expertly weaving in and out of each other's way, passing slower couples, allowing faster ones to pass them. A man in a big gray hat slid his hand from his date's shoulder blade up to the back of her neck. Her eyes closed as she smiled, bending her neck sensuously backward to receive his hand, which dropped down to the back of her tight western jeans and squeezed. Her eyes popped open and her eyebrows shot up. He laughed and returned his hand to her back. She giggled at him, and they never broke from the beat of music.

Tina wiggled uncomfortably on her seat in a corner of the club. "You think I'd learn," she said to her best friend Beverly. "I come out here and we start ordering pitchers, and before you can say Rocky Mountain High I've got to pee every ten minutes." They were with a group of their friends from Amarillo National Bank, celebrating a birthday.

"I know, don't it just burn you up?" Beverly said. "I'm glad I wasn't born a man, but I have to say I do envy them their bladder control. I swear Ricky's already drunk two pitchers by himself and four shots of tequila, and I don't think he's peed once. Well, I guess we can sit here complaining about it or get up and make room for more. You ready, girlfriend?"

They pushed away from the table, aware as they swayed around the perimeter of the dance floor that men were watching them in their cowgirl jeans that clung to their butts and their legs, fitting snugly over their round-toed roper boots. Five days a week they sat at their tellers' windows at the bank, smiling at customer after customer, until they thought their mouths would freeze that way, but on Friday and Saturday they spent their evenings at the Midnight Rodeo, gloriously young and single, drinking beer and dancing backwards around the dance floor, sometimes to a live band but usually to canned music. It didn't matter to them which kind. They rewarded the guys who were cute with a four-minute dance, and the ones who weren't, they politely turned down.

To reach the ladies' room they passed by the game area, where men in hats and jeans stared belligerently at the video screens, slapping at the controls; others slammed their hands against anchored speed bags, trying to see who was more manly than whom.

Tina nudged Beverly's elbow and said, "Check out the pool table." Beverly turned her head, searching. Tina hissed at her "Don't *look*, girl!"

Two tables over, playing by himself, Joe Wagner lined up a shot and saw the girls checking him out. They were ten years younger than him, but that was the way he liked them. Young, just out of college or maybe in it, he didn't give a shit. He didn't care if they was in high school, except most of the girls in here were at least twenty-one, 'cause of the goddamn law. He knew they were looking him over, thinking how they'd like to go home with him, maybe go out to his truck and suck his dick right there, not even wait until they got somewhere, just do him right there in the parking lot, and then he could pull the pants off those smooth butts and fuck them right there in his truck but hell, as good as he was, even he couldn't fuck both of them at once. Maybe he'd make one of them wait outside, or fuck that, no, she could just sit on the driver's side wetting her little panties just waiting to get to him, watching.

He straightened up as they passed by and holding his cue stick in front of him stepped over it, letting it stand up between his legs. He slid his hand up and down on it as he stared at them. "You girls sure are looking pretty tonight," he said.

Tina's eyes got wider and wider and she picked up speed, trying to put as much distance as possible between herself and the cowboy. "Oh my god, did you see that?"

"He doesn't leave much to the imagination, does he?" Beverly said. Her head craned back at him and he kept smiling at them. "But he is cute, isn't he?"

"So was Ted Bundy."

They reached the restroom with a little wooden cutout of a cowgirl in a skirt hanging on the door. Beverly gave him a last look. He was almost six feet, and his faded jeans looked like they were painted onto his butt. He had on one of those old-fashioned cowboy shirts like her dad wore, with the pearl snaps instead of buttons. He smiled at her, a kind of sideways grin that reminded her of Dennis Quaid when he'd played that cop in New Orleans in an old movie she'd rented when she was sick one Saturday night and hadn't felt like competing with the light and sound of the Rodeo.

"Beverly, come on!" She came back to the present, almost running into a fat woman coming out of the bathroom. She wished they wouldn't wear those tight jeans when they were so big. You'd never catch her getting all swollen up like that.

"Can you believe that guy?" Tina said. "God, he was just completely gross! Does he think that works with women?"

"Maybe it does with some," Beverly said. He was awful cute, she thought. A little old, but real cute.

Joe watched her go into the bathroom. He could tell her girlfriend didn't like him. She was one of them women who thought she was too goddamn good, that's what it was. Wiggled their little butts and got your dick good and hard, then crossed their legs when it came down to it. Well, he knew how to deal with them. He'd had plenty of experience. He leaned over the table, lined up his shot again and cracked the white cue ball against the nine, banking it against the rail so it shot into the left side pocket. He smiled. Them fuckers at Bailey's wouldn't know what hit them. He didn't like to practice there. Bailey's was for serious pool playing. By the time he stepped in through that doorway he wanted to be practiced, knowing anybody who put a bill on his table was in for a hell of a fight.

Joe liked Bailey's as well as any place he'd ever played, except that bitch that ran it and her ugly dog got on his nerves. She was kind of old for him, had to be close to forty, but she wasn't bad looking. But he knew she was one of them bitches that thought they were better than him. You could tell from the way she looked at him with her eyes half open. When she saw him come in she'd get that look on her face like somebody had stepped in shit and she was trying to figure out who. He'd seen that look all his life, seen it in the eyes of women, the asshole bosses he'd worked for, those fuckers at home, his old man and his mother, his sister Evvy. He sees it on Darlene, his wife. She's either scared, looking at him with those big brown eyes like a dog that someone's just kicked, or like he's a bug under a microscope, something that's less than human. When she gives him either of those looks it's all he can do to keep from balling his fist up and smashing it into her face, hitting her like a sledge hammer. And sometimes he does just that.

Joe continued playing, and when someone flushed with beer and taking a break from the dance floor laid a bill on his table, he accepted and won every time.

Tina looked at her watch. Eleven thirty. She knew she should probably go home. She wanted to get up and dress for church tomorrow. She hadn't been in a month of Sundays—Tina giggled at that—and she really should. Maybe she'd at least meet somebody nice. And if she got really ambitious and didn't have a headache, she could go to that singles Bible Study class they had. But she was having such a good time here, and the birthday group didn't seem close to shutting down. Hell, she thought, one more beer wouldn't hurt anything. She just needed to remember to take some aspirin and drink a glass of water before she went to bed tonight. Then she'd be fine.

"I'm making a bar run," she yelled above the blare of the speakers. "Y'all need anything?"

A chorus of approval greeted her, and the consensus was that she should bring back another pitcher. "All right then, pony up," she said. They threw bills down on the table indiscriminately until she yelled "That's enough! I could buy a whole keg with that."

She gathered the bills and walked up front to the bar. The bartender grinned at her. "Back for more, huh?"

"Yeah, they don't let us drink on the job, so we have to make up for lost time," she said.

"Ain't it the truth." He filled the pitcher for her and she paid him, leaving a generous tip in the jar.

She was barely halfway back to her table when she almost ran into a man who suddenly stepped in front of her. It was all she could do to keep from spilling the beer. "Oh, I'm sorry," she began, and then stopped as she looked up into the man's face. It was the gross cowboy from the pool table.

A finger of fear touched the back of her neck, making the hair stand up. "Excuse me," she said.

"Why, honey? You done something wrong?"

"Let me by, please." She looked across the club for her friends, but there were too many people in the way for them to see her. And how would they know?

"Look, I'm sorry for what I done before," he said. "Sometimes, I don't know, I just do dumb stuff. That was pretty dumb, I guess, but I'm not like that at all."

"I don't care what you're like, and I have no intention of finding out. Let me by." She shifted to move past him, but he blocked her way again.

"You 'have no intention?' Look baby, I just thought maybe you and me could talk a little bit. Hey, I'll buy you a beer. Take that one to your friends, and come on back. I'll get you one."

"I'm not going to drink a beer with you. And don't call me honey or baby. Don't call me anything at all." She started to move past him again, but he stepped in front of her.

"Come on, now—"

"Get out of my way, or I swear to God I'll scream bloody murder."

"Hey, who the fuck do you think you are, bitch? You ain't a goddamn bit better than me, and I don't care how you act, you're—"

Tina tried to get around him again and almost succeeded. He grabbed her arm and whirled her around to face him, pulling her close. Some of the beer sloshed onto her hand. She could smell his sweat, and the whiskey on his breath.

Tina didn't think about what she did next, and when she told the whole story to Beverly and their friends it almost seemed funny. But it wasn't when it happened. It was a purely instinctual reaction, acting out of her fear. She grabbed the pitcher in both hands and sloshed the entire thing onto his crotch.

Joe's face froze into shock, and then rage crawled up from his neck onto his cheeks. He brushed at his pants with his hand, but he was soaked all the way down to his knees. "Why you goddamn, fucking cunt—"

"Hey, what's going on here?" A couple passing by on their way out of the club stopped. "What's the matter, pal?" the man asked. "You pee on yourself? Pisser too far away for you?"

"Excuse me," Tina said. She hurried back to her table. There was no way she would make another run to the bar alone tonight. By the time she got back to her friends and told the story, she had turned it into a tale of her own heroism against some drunken asshole. But what she remembered most was the look on the man's face as she glanced over her shoulder at him. He caught her eyes, and the dark rage she saw there, like a bloody bruise, made her shiver and walk faster. When she got back to the table she saw the man scurrying out of the club, the handful of couples near enough to have witnessed the scene obviously laughing at him.

Tina stayed until her friends were ready to leave; it was much too late for her, but she didn't want to walk to her car by herself. When she got home she hurried into her apartment and checked the locks on the door and all the windows three times before she finally was able to fall asleep on the couch, with a light and the television still on. She didn't make it to church.

Chapter 3

The convenience store squatted in the northwest corner of the Panhandle, past Clayton, New Mexico, and Texline, Texas, halfway between Dalhart and nowhere. Two gas pumps, regular and super, stood out in front like sentinels. Built of military-green cinder blocks, the store barely broke the monotony of the flat plains. Inside, the cashier had total control of the cigarette packs behind her, keeping a close eye on the Mr. Frostee machine and the glass case where a red heating lamp shone on burritos, corn dogs, and hot dogs all hours of the day and night.

Loralene, the night cashier, slid a finger under the shoulder strap of her bra. She watched the sun rise through the window toward the east and dreamed of the time ten years ago when she had lived in Tulsa, a place imminently more interesting and lively than this desolate pocket of Texas. She daydreamed about watching Oklahoma beat Texas next month, until the tinkling of bells broke her reverie and announced a visitor.

"Hey, good looking. Whatcha got cookin'?"

"Just sitting here thinking about you, Darrell. Wondering when you was gonna come by in that big bread truck and sweep me off my feet."

Darrell, a red-cheeked young man wearing a gray uniform with a blue and white oval sign on the back that read "Aunt Mae's Bread," expertly maneuvered a rack of loaves from his shoulder onto the counter.

"I couldn't do that, Loralene. That's what I like about you; your feet are always solid on the ground."

"How much do I owe you today, Hon?" she asked.

"Thirty two dollars and forty one cents."

He started lining up the loaves and the snack cakes expertly, barely looking at them.

"How's that little one of yours doing?" Loralene asked as she took the money from the register.

"Oh, she has what the doctors call attention deficit disease, or some shit like that. We're getting her looked at, but I think it's just a chance for all of them quacks to buy another Mercedes. But Kimberly says we gotta give her the best chance in life, so you know what we're doing. I was hoping to go deer hunting up in Colorado next month, but I think it's them doctors'll be bringing home a ten-point buck instead."

"No news to me. If I could have all the money back I've given them bastards and their cohorts the insurance agents through the years, I guarantee you I wouldn't be working here today."

An old, white Ford LTD coasted into the parking lot and pulled up on the side of the building away from Darrell's truck. Neither of them saw it.

"Don't I know it? Well honey, as much as I love talking to you and soaking up the heater, I gotta get back on the road. Them folks in Clayton is getting hungry for their morning toast."

"All right baby, see you on Saturday. Give Kimberly a hug for me."

"Will do."

Loralene slid a Salem Light out of her half empty pack and lit it up. I'd give these up, she thought, if they didn't taste so damned good. She closed her eyes and leaned against the counter, imagining Darrell peeling his clothes off piece by piece, like those Chippendale boys, except he'd look even sillier in a bow tie than they did. She didn't give a shit that he was 12 years younger than her and married. Let those bastards in Congress just try to outlaw daydreaming. She felt a burning that was hotter than the cigarette start in her crotch and crawl upwards. Darrell's face shifted into Roy Parnham, the man she had lived with in Tulsa before he two-timed her. Two-timer or not, he had known how to set her on fire. Roy stepped right up to her and slid his warm, rough hands down into the back of her unbuttoned jeans. "Oh baby," he said, "you got what I need."

He slowly worked the buttons on her blouse loose and slid her bra straps down her arms. He put his fingers under the edge of the cups, and with infinite patience drew them down, revealing her nipples. She moaned, and he put his lips on her—

The door opened and the bell jingled, signaling a customer. Loralene awoke with a start from her reverie. Her customer walked in and went back to where the magazines and chips were. She barely saw his back. The balloon of her daydream popped, and she sighed. At those moments when she told herself the truth—and right now was one of them—Loralene remembered that the fire in her relationship with Roy Parnham had lasted about two months. Then it had been just about the way it was with all the other men she'd dated, and the two she'd married. Roy would roll on top of her, make like a rocking chair for about a minute, than finish his messy business and roll off of her. If she was lucky she'd get to sleep before he started snoring, and that didn't happen often.

She started cleaning up behind the counter. The boy they had hired last week for the evening shift had left it a mess. Half the cigarette brands were in the wrong slots, the floor hadn't been swept up, and guess who had to do it? Probably staring at those high school girls' boobs while the shit just piled up. And in a storm like this it was hard enough to keep things clean anyway. Three or four times during her shift she was compelled to sweep up the sand. She'd give that kid hell when he relieved her at the end of her shift—if he even showed up, the sneaky little bastard.

She forgot about her sole customer, and when she heard the bell again she looked toward the door expectantly. There was no one in the store. She glimpsed the customer's back as he walked toward the corner of the building. That's a funny place to park, she thought. I guess he's too good to park out here in front like everybody else. She looked out the window toward the east and watched the sunrise. It would sure be a beautiful day, if it weren't so goddamn cold and windy.

Smith Dixon sat in his car, his head back against the seat, breathing loudly through his mouth. The object in the back of his pants dug into his spine, but he didn't feel it. The corduroy jacket he wore was too light for the cold wind, but he wasn't aware of it. Sweat poured down his face. He had promised himself he would never do it again, that the time in Denver had been his last, and for the past three weeks he had kept to that promise, as difficult as it had been. But this morning he had almost done it again, and he knew as he sat slumped in his car that in some dark corner of his heart he would have taken delight in seeing the look of abject terror on that woman's face. He had imagined how her hands would shake, and as he did he somehow grew taller and stronger.

"Goddamn," he whispered, and suddenly felt the pain in the small of his back. He lifted up his butt and dug into the back of his pants, pulling out the .38 revolver and a black ski mask. He punched the release on the glove compartment, jammed them into it with the maps, and turned the ignition. As he pulled back onto the highway, he saw the woman behind the counter look searchingly at his car.

Loralene wondered again why the man in the old Ford had parked around the corner, why he had entered the store and left without buying anything or asking even one damn question. As she looked at the car her sharp eyes saw that the license plate was smeared over with mud. She couldn't have read it if she had been three feet away. The truth swept over her colder than the wind outside. She wondered briefly whether to call the sheriff, when her second customer of the day came in, and then the third. By the time they left, she had forgotten all about Smith Dixon and he was well on his way to Amarillo, his big white Ford eating up the miles and the gasoline, taking him home.

On Sunday morning when he opened his eyes, Max had to search his surroundings for a few moments. Then he remembered: he was in the Quality Inn near Interstate 40 in Amarillo, Texas. He remembered the night before like it was an etching from *The Rake's Progress*. The two drunken cowboys, the wolf who wouldn't allow them into the bar until they apologized, the red-haired owner whose eyes were colder than this wind could ever be. He sighed.

The tow truck driver had dropped his car off at a little broken-down repair shop. Max didn't mind; he trusted it more than he would have one of the slick outfits with sixteen bays. Like his pool halls, Max liked his mechanics to have character.

"Gil'll take good care of you," the driver had said. "And he don't give a shit that tomorrow's Sunday. I'll give him a call in the morning. Probably by ten or so he'll know something." The driver had dropped him off at the motel, even though it was only a few blocks away. "Wouldn't be too nice to make you walk in this weather, would it?"

Max stirred under the heavy blanket. The pillow under his mouth was wet where he had slobbered on it during the night, and his feet were freezing. He could hear the wind still blowing outside as the sandstorm entered its second day. He hopped out of bed, teeth chattering, the air assaulting his naked skin. He dove for the heater on the wall under the window, and turned up the temperature dial. He glanced at the curtain, which had a three-inch gap he had tried for five minutes to close the night before. A woman passing by on the balcony, head bent to the side against the wind, glanced in. She jumped, then quickly turned her eyes away. Max knew he looked a sight to the unsuspecting eye: uncombed long hair gone wild, eyes bloodshot from all the sand the night before—not to mention the fact that he was entirely naked. Well, he thought, this could be the high point of her day, fodder for a good story over the lunch table.

In the shower, he scrubbed himself with the washcloth, so thin it could have passed for onion paper. No matter that he had showered the night before. The sand was insidious; it could creep in through crevices in windows and under the doors. If the wind could bring in the cold, Max surmised, it could certainly bring in sand. He toweled his hair and shaved, eyeing his hairline anxiously. For the past several years it had been slowly receding. Intellectually, Max knew that baldness was something he could not change, but at this point accepting it was beyond his comprehension.

He pulled his hair back into a ponytail and dug through his suitcases for some warm clothes. At least, thank God, he had some. "What do you need warm clothes for?" his friends had whined before he left New York. "You're moving to Phoenix, for chrissake. What do they knew from cold? It gets below eighty there, they think it's a blizzard! Leave the clothes with us." But Max, who always believed that no matter how bad things were, they could always get worse, refused to discard his wool overcoat. He made it a habit to be ready for any emergency, for any catastrophic pit God dug in front of him, and today he had reason to be thankful for it.

Max donned a plain white tee-shirt and a long-sleeved flannel, a pair of jeans, and his overcoat. His snow boots were the only footwear that would be of any use in today's weather, but he still hesitated to wear them. But if I'm trying to look inconspicuous here, he thought, it's a little too late.

The repair shop was a little one-man operation, but it was as neat and orderly as a garage could get. Warm in his wool and flannel, with hands stuck deep into his pockets, Max pushed his way against the wind up to the bay. The mechanic emerged from under the hood of Max's car. He wore black glasses, which were held together with electrician's tape on the right stem. Over his greasy coveralls was a fleece-lined denim jacket. He kept his right hand tucked into his jacket pocket, and extended his left toward Max. "Morning," he said.

Max, who had learned how to talk from a culture of people to whom speech was a fine art, was learning that brevity was the law of the land. "Morning."

"I reckon you're Mr. Friedman."

"That would be me."

"Name's Gil. I have good news and bad news for you."

Uh-oh. "Which do I want first?"

"Good news is, your car's not a horse."

Max was mystified. Even someone with his credentials, born and reared in New York City, could tell the difference. But he was curious enough to follow when led. "And the bad news?"

"If it was, we'd have to shoot it."

Ah. "Is it that bad?"

"Yep."

"How much would it cost to fix it?"

"About the cost of a decent used car."

"Jeez."

"I hate to deliver bad news. Guess that's why I never became a doctor. Telling somebody their car's dead is a lot easier."

"Well, there is that."

"Actually, I could probably fix it for you, but it would cost over a thousand. Timing belt broke, and stripped the valves. Car's not worth that much. I wish I had better news for you. If you need a reliable used car, I can probably put you into one. I'm always hearing about something or other."

"Thank you."

"Let me give you my phone number." He pulled the right hand out of his jacket pocket, and Max saw that there were only two fingers on it.

"Another reason I wouldn't have made a good brain surgeon," Gil said. "Got it caught in a corn picker when I was sixteen. Tell you the truth, it's made it a little hard to repair cars too, but I guess I've done okay."

"Looks like it," Max said.

Gil handed him a scrap of paper with his number written on it. "Sorry I couldn't help you," he said.

"Oh, I knew it was coming."

"Small comfort, I guess, but I've come to believe that things happen to us for a purpose."

"Yeah, me too. I've just learned to take life a day at a time."

"Sounds like a good idea to me."

"How much do I owe you for looking at it?"

"Nada. What was I going to do at home, anyway?"

Max extended his left hand, and they shook. "Well," he said, "thank you again."

Max had almost cleared the door of the shop when Gil called his name. He turned back.

Gil squinted at him and shuffled his feet. "This may seem like a strange question, but are you a friend of Bill W.?" he asked, a question by which alcoholics the world over identify each other.

Max smiled. "Yeah," he said, "as a matter of fact I am."

"Well, it looks like we have something in common. You want to grab a bite of breakfast and go to a meeting?"

"I think right at this moment, I need a meeting more than I've ever needed one."

"I kind of figured." Gil grinned and clapped him on the back. "I'll even give you a ride."

Chapter 4

Nina Puente didn't know what to do. When the phone rang her mom was out in the garage, switching the laundry, and Dad was sitting in the living room in front of the TV like he always did on Sunday afternoons, watching a football game. Nina didn't like to be in the room with him when the game was on, because he started to yell really loud sometimes, and if his Cowboys team lost, sometimes he was really hard to be around for the rest of the day. Sometimes Mom just took her over to Grandma's or Aunt Regina's house. But that wasn't good either, because a lot of times Uncle Freddie would be drinking and that scared Nina worse than Daddy's yelling. She liked her cousins Travis and Maggie, though sometimes they'd fight. But they always made up. Not like Daddy and Uncle Freddie.

And now she was standing by the phone on its little table in the hallway between the living room and the kitchen, not knowing what to do. She didn't want to tell Daddy who it was, because he'd get even worse upset. But it wasn't polite just to hang up on someone, and besides, the man would probably just call back.

"Dolores? Who's that on the phone?" Nina heard her daddy holler from the living room. She took a big breath and stepped around the corner where he could see her.

"Daddy?"

"Yeah, honey, what is it?"

"It's uh, it's—"

"What? Didn't I hear the phone ring just now?"

"Uh huh. It's that man again, the one who called yesterday, the one you didn't want to talk to."

"Oh. Nina, honey, could you—look, would you tell him Daddy's not at home right now, and that I'll call him back?"

Tears started welling in his daughter's eyes. "Daddy, I don't want to do that; it doesn't feel good to me to lie."

Nina felt a hand on her shoulder and looked up to see her mother standing over her, a look on her face like she got sometimes when Daddy made her mad, her eyes squinting and her eyebrows pulled down.

"Nina, why don't you go into your room for a few minutes? I'll take care of it."

Nina turned and walked down the hall to her room, looking over her shoulder at her parents. She so badly wanted to do something to make it all right, but she knew that if she tried it would even be worse. She went into her room and shut the door, but even with her head scrunched down and hugging her favorite doll close to her chest, she could hear their voices.

Carl sat in the chair leaning forward, his forearms resting on his knees. He wanted to watch the game and forget about what Dolores said, but he knew if he even flicked an eye at the screen or picked up the can of Coors sitting on a coaster beside the chair, her anger and volume would increase proportionally.

"I can't believe you did that," she was saying. Carl tried to listen, but her voice sounded like the adults on *Peanuts*; it was garbled, like it was coming from a tin can and didn't make any sense to him.

"Dolores—" he tried.

"No," she said. "Don't even. I don't want to listen to a thing you have to say right now. I can't believe that you asked your daughter, who if you need to be reminded, is only seven years old, to tell that man you aren't at home."

"I'm getting the money together."

"You don't even know what I'm talking about, do you? I don't care about what money you're getting together. I am concerned about my daughter. Can you understand that? Have you gambled away so much of your soul that you don't even care that you asked her to lie to a man who is dangerous? Who could potentially kill you? Or her?"

"Dolores, don't be ridiculous. They don't kill people. It's just a business. You've watched too many movies."

"No Carl, it's you who's got his head stuck in that television all day long. I want you to come in here and hang up the phone, and then I'm going to call

Mama and tell her we're coming over. I'm afraid if I have to look at you for five more seconds, I'll do something I'll really regret."

Carl sat looking at her, yearning to see the score on the screen.

"Well? Are you going to hang it up?"

"Yeah." He got up from his chair and she stepped back away from the phone table. The receiver was making that horrible ratcheting sound that signaled it was off the hook. He hung it up.

"Look," he said. "Why don't we talk about this? I mean—"

"Oh, we're going to talk about it," she said. "You're damned right about that. But we'll do it tonight, after we get home."

Carl shook his head, not sure what to do. Walking back to his chair might unleash another barrage. Moving to touch her could be even worse. So Carl did what he always did—nothing. He stood there while she looked at him, her eyes laced with contempt.

Dolores picked up the phone and after a few seconds said, "Hi mama. Is it okay if Nina and I come over? Oh yes. Yep. I'll tell you about it when we get— well sure, we can just meet you over at Regina's. He didn't? Oh Lord, not again. When did he leave? Well, we sure know how to pick them, don't we?" She looked at Carl, even angrier than before. "All right, I'll see you in a few minutes."

She hung up the phone. "Freddie didn't come home again last night. Regina hasn't seen him. I'm sure he'll be great at work tomorrow. Maybe by then he'll even be half sober."

Dolores turned and walked down the hall. "Nina, honey, get your coat. We're going over to Aunt Regina's."

Carl turned back to his chair, feeling twenty years older than he had five minutes before. He remembered his father in the years before he'd died, shuffling around the house in a pair of slippers and an undershirt, just barely able to turn on the television or put a frozen dinner in the oven, barely able to keep his drapery business going. Carl had sworn he'd never become like that, yet right now he knew if he looked in the mirror he'd be the image of the old man, down to his dead eyes and the black hair bristling out of his ears.

When he looked back at the screen, Dallas had gone from a 13-13 tie to being down by 7. He had bet on the game, even though he couldn't pay back any of what he already owed. And that was forgetting the credit card bills he tried to keep from Dolores, and the hospital bills they still owed from when Nina had gone in with asthma last year, and the goddamn insurance company barely covered any of it.

Dolores walked down the hall, not glancing in at him in the living room. Nina followed her and stopped in the doorway. She gave him a small smile and a wave, and then walked out to the garage behind her mother.

A few minutes after they left, he heard the phone ring again. His beer was gone, and he wanted to get up for another one, but it was just so hard to get up from the chair that he stayed there as the phone rang a dozen times, then stopped. As soon as it ceased he began to feel a little better, and when half-time started he went into the kitchen and came back with two cold cans.

"Why are you mad at Daddy?" Nina asked.

She and her mom were in their Taurus, which was showing a little wear and tear after five years, but still, thank God, in good condition. Nina was bundled up in a bright blue coat and a stocking cap as they drove toward Regina's house, four miles away.

"It's kind of hard to talk about, honey."

"I don't like for you to yell at each other," Nina said.

"I know you don't. I don't like it either. But sometimes people do things that just aren't right, and we have to stand up to them. And Daddy did something I didn't like for him to do. And that's why I'm angry at him."

"Oh." She pulled the cuffs of her coat down over her slender wrists. "Are you going to get a divorce?"

"Nina! Where did you get that idea?"

Nina shrugged and looked out the window. "Becky Wolfforth's parents got divorced. She says it's okay."

Dolores put her hand on Nina's head. "Daddy and I are going to talk, later tonight. But we're not going to get a divorce. We're just going to fix what's wrong."

"Okay."

Dolores drove on in silence, trying to convince herself that what she'd told her daughter was true.

Smith Dixon slid his old white Ford to the front of the house and turned off the ignition. The street was quiet but for the howling of the wind; a few leaves bravely clung to the trees, but the wind was stripping most of them away. The house was more run down than when he had last seen it. It was more gray than blue, and what paint was left peeled away from the boards. The shrubs were wild and spindly, and the grass needed mowing. He wondered how long it had been since the old man had tended them, or anything else. He noticed that some of the shingles were coming loose, and the trellis where his mother had grown her brilliant tapestry of roses each year was gone.

God, had it been twenty-seven years now? Twenty-seven years since he had woken up before dawn and thrown a few clothes—all he had, really—into a bag and slipped out through the front door into a future that he could not have predicted and would not have chosen. Smith pulled his jacket tight around him, as much against his childhood ghosts as the wind that whirled the leaves outside.

He got out of the car and walked up onto the porch, hesitating before ringing the doorbell. There was no response, and after a few moments he knocked on the door and then looked through the windows, cupping his hands against the glass. No lights appeared to be on, and he only got a faint impression of furniture. The door was locked; probably the old man was gone off somewhere. Smith stood on the porch, looking one way and the other, trying to decide what to do.

He heard what sounded like a voice a block away. But the wind was playing tricks on him, he realized. The man calling was just across the street, coming out of his house, pulling on a jacket much too light for this weather.

"Hey," the man called. Smith crossed down to the sidewalk to meet him.

"He ain't here no more." The man was tall and skinny, the skin on his nose broken in a mosaic of red veins. "They came for him in an ambulance oh, about a month ago, I guess. Took him off, and I ain't seen him since."

Smith took a moment before he spoke. "Dead?"

"Don't really know. I reckon if he was, they'd have told somebody, wouldn't you think? I haven't heard a word. I've cut the grass a couple of times, but not in the last oh, two weeks. Trying to make it look like he's still here, so nobody'll break in. Paper ran out a couple of weeks ago, and the mail's been stopped."

"Obliged to you."

"You kin to him?"

"Yeah. I'm his son."

"You don't say. Well, I didn't know there was anybody. I've lived here three years, and I doubt I've seen any visitors more than half a dozen times. I guess you could call around the hospitals, see if you can find him. You gonna stay here?"

"Don't have a key."

"Well, I don't mean to be unfriendly, but this goddamn wind is about to freeze my balls off. I gotta get in the house. Look, anything I can do, let me know. Name's Bob Mortimer."

"Obliged."

"No problem." Bob scurried off across the street, into his house.

Smith took another long look at the house, and then bent into his car. He leaned his head back against the seat. A headache was coming on, and he needed to get some aspirin. He cranked the engine and slowly drove down the street.

Darlene Wagner vacuumed the carpet in the living room slowly and methodically. Although left handed, she used her right arm to push the vacuum because the left hurt so much. When Darlene was hurt or angry she cleaned the house. It had been much cleaner in the last two years than it had ever been before. Although anger was an emotion she could ill afford, pain was a constant state she lived in.

Darlene had been married to Joe five years. She had met him at a dance club, a tall good-looking cowboy with a lopsided grin, and he was the best thing she'd seen in a long time. He had swept her off her feet and onto the dance floor, and two months later they were married. Her parents didn't like him and didn't think it was right, getting married at twenty-one to a man who was thirty. You could find someone closer to your own age, her mother said. How about Larry Parker, he always thought you were so cute. Oh mama, she'd said, Larry's okay, but he just don't excite me the way Joe does. And he's just not any fun, either. Joe's a lot of fun, and he treats me good.

That was then. For the first six months or so Joe did treat her well. Then he started to get strange—listening to her phone calls, not standing right over her, but always in the room, and then he took out the phone in the bedroom, saying it cost too much, but Darlene knew good and well it didn't cost extra. She wasn't stupid. It was just his excuse to eavesdrop. Then Joe started to get impatient with her a lot, and when she couldn't understand something he had said or just didn't hear it, he would repeat it in a real loud voice, like talking to a baby or something. He'd done it a couple of times at the Midnight Rodeo in front of her friends, but that didn't happen anymore because Darlene didn't go. After a while Joe just started to go out by himself, and when she said she wanted to go he'd just look at her with a light in his eyes that scared the shit out of her, a light that said, you just go ahead and say one more goddamn thing, and see where it gets you. Just do it. So Darlene stopped going out much.

It was two years ago before Joe first hit her. He was watching a re-run of *Walker, Texas Ranger* one Saturday night and called out to her to bring him a beer. In a minute, Darlene had said, because right then she was cooking and didn't want it to burn. A few seconds later Joe was right behind her, and she turned around, startled. He grabbed her face in his hand, squeezing her cheeks between his fingers and said when I tell you to get me something, I mean right now, you hear?

Darlene nodded her head, terrified. Now how would it feel, Joe said, if I took and stuck your goddamn hand in that fucking skillet? You think that would be as good as a piece of string wrapped around your finger? That help you remember who you are? Would it? Huh? She nodded again, and he let go of her face but quick as lightning brought his hand up and slapped her across the cheek. That was the first bruise she got from him, but it sure wasn't the last. Darlene mostly stayed home now, except for work. She didn't really have any friends anymore, because there's only so many times they can hear her say no before they'll give up on her.

She didn't know what had happened to Joe last night except that it must have been real bad. He went out most nights, usually playing pool downtown or at the Rodeo; she wasn't sure because asking could get dangerous for her. Last night Joe had come home while she was watching TV, some old movie and getting sleepy, and she could tell from the look in his eyes that she was in trouble.

Joe was in a rage. She didn't know why, and she knew better than to ask. Hi honey, she had said to him, and he didn't say anything back, just went into the kitchen and got a bottle of beer from the fridge. He drank it in there, and then he came back into the living room, picked up the remote, and turned the TV off. He reached down and grabbed her left arm and yanked her out of the chair. It felt like her arm would come straight out of its socket. Joe put his face right into hers. Get in the goddamn bedroom he said, his voice hissing like tires on wet asphalt. When she hesitated he raised his arm like he was going to slap her in the face, so she scurried down the hall into their small bedroom. She heard him in the kitchen again, and two minutes later he came in. Darlene was sitting on the bed with her clothes on, arms crossed in front of her. You ain't going to bed with your clothes on are you, he said, and she said I guess not, afraid to say anything at all. Well get them off then, he said. She pulled her jeans off and carefully folded and laid them on the cedar chest that her momma had given her when they got married. Then she pulled her blouse up over her head, and during the moment that she was blind he pushed her down on the bed and ripped her panties down around her knees and off her legs. She felt him enter her but she was dry and God, it burned and hurt, and it felt like he was killing her, like he was going to tear all the skin out of her. There was KY in the nightstand next to the bed; she had bought it and told him it was there, but he never would use it. He didn't say anything, just pounded himself into her like he wanted to kill her. She struggled, trying to get the blouse off, trying to get away from him, trying to die, but her movements seemed to make him more angry and excited. Darlene could feel that his pants were still on; he must have only unbuttoned. Her blouse was still over her head and her arms were pinned together. Joe raged on top of her, squeezing and biting her nipples, hurting her more until finally he shuddered and grew still. He pulled out of her and sat on the side of the bed. After a minute, he said "You look stupid like that. Why don't you go to bed?" She did, curling into a ball as tight as she could get, her tears dampening the pillow. Her arm hurt and her insides hurt, but she was afraid to get up and go to the bathroom, to get something for the pain. Later Darlene subsided into sleep, and when Joe came to bed she woke up afraid, but he didn't touch her again. She didn't know what time it was when she awoke again, startled out of sleep by him jerking and twitching, mumbling. Then she fell asleep again, and when she woke up he was already gone.

Now Darlene vacuumed the carpet in the living room, and realized that she hadn't moved in a while, but she didn't know how long. It might have been two minutes, or it might have been an hour that she was running the vacuum over the same strip of carpet. She switched it off and sat on the couch, her head down on her chest, her hands clasped between her legs, and rocked gently back and forth.

Freddie Odom sat in his car with his hands jammed between his legs to fend off the cold and looked at the front door of the house. He had known it would be bad, coming in this late. Freddie had thought at first that he would make it back home by about two or three the morning, could sneak into the house and slip into bed without waking Regina, maybe with his sneakers in his hand, the way Dagwood always did after those poker parties with his comic strip buddies. Freddie wished his friends from the night before had been comic strip characters, so he could just wad them up and stick them in the trash can. But they weren't, and he hadn't made it back by two or three. He hadn't made it back by nine or ten this morning, either. The later it got, the harder it would be to just come walking into his house. He thought of waiting until tonight, when they'd all be asleep again, but he knew by then Regina would have called the police and reported him missing. So he finally came home at 3:00 p.m. But he couldn't pull into the driveway because Bernice, his nosy mother-in-law, was already parked there, and so was Dolores, Regina's sister, and now he had to walk into the house and face all three of them plus the kids. He'd known it was going to be hard, but he hadn't thought it would be this hard, and he just didn't know what he had done in his life to deserve this kind of shit. Freddie was only twenty-six years old, and he already had two kids and an asshole boss who happened to be his brother-in-law. Or brother-in-law-in-law, he guessed. His head wasn't working well enough to figure out exactly what Carl and he were. Fucker and fuckee ought to cover it well enough.

He sat in the car a few more minutes and finally opened the door. The cold wind blew fine grains of sand into his hair and eyes. He tripped on the curb and almost fell down, racing through the yard that was trying fiercely to hold onto a few measly sprigs of grass. The rocking chair on the bungalow's porch was furiously rocking, as if inhabited by a ghost, perhaps old Charles Goodnight himself. Freddie leaped onto the porch; each step made the hangover pound his head with increasing fervor. He unlocked the door and pushed in on it, but it was caught by the night chain, which almost snapped.

"Goddamn! Regina, what the hell are you doing? Let me in!"

There was no response. "Come on, already. Will you just—I mean, just open the fucking door, will you please?"

Still there was silence, although he knew they couldn't be far enough away from the door that they couldn't hear him. "I said please, will you? What the hell more do you want?"

He heard a noise behind the door, then Bernice's voice. "You think saying 'please' makes you sober?"

"What are you talking about? I'm not drunk."

"Maybe now you're not. But if I bet that you couldn't walk a straight line two hours ago, I'd be a rich woman."

Freddie knew that he was beat. He slumped against the wall next to the door and slid down it until he was sitting flat on the porch with his head in his hands. Right now Freddie was having less fun than he'd ever had in his life. He knew that when he went inside he'd be stared at by all three of them like he had dog shit on his shoe, or more to the point like he was the dog shit on their shoes, and his kids would be afraid to talk to him for fear of getting yelled at. He could remember when Bernice and Dolores used to like him, but that was before he and Regina got married, when they were still at Tascosa High, and he came over for dinner on Sundays and picked up Regina before the game on Friday night. That was when he played football and she was head cheerleader, flashing enticing views of her panties whenever she jumped up in the air. That was before they had Maggie and Travis, before he had gotten fired from three jobs and Bernice had talked Carl into hiring him at the upholstery shop, "for the sake of the family." Freddie looked down at his shoes, and there was something crusted on the left one. It could have been mud or one of several other things, and he had no idea of what it was or how it had gotten there.

Now they were undoing the night chain, and Bernice was standing looking at him. He didn't have to see her face to know what it looked like. Disgusted. Regina was standing behind her. He knew he ought to say something. "It won't happen again, Gina, I swear to God it won't."

"That's a song I've heard before," Bernice said. "Now get up, Freddie. I don't want the neighbors to see any more of this than they have to."

He struggled to his feet, pushing his hands up the wall behind him. All of a sudden he didn't feel nearly as sober or as brave as he had a few minutes earlier. He hoped that he would be able to make it into the bathroom before he threw up. Regina put her hand under his arm, but Bernice didn't touch him. She just stood looking at him, hands on her hips and shaking her head, while the sand swirled around them on the porch in tiny dust devils. He went through the door and saw Dolores and the kids watching him. Maggie and Travis, looking a little nervous, said "Hi Daddy."

"Hey guys," he said. "Come give Daddy a hug." Maggie, with her straight dark hair, looking like a clone of the other women in the room and Travis, his curly blonde hair just like his dad's, hugged him around the waist. When they pulled away he sat down on the couch, knowing it was going to be a very long evening.

Chapter 5

After counting his traveler's checks and cash, Max discovered that he had a grand total of $865.72. It was plenty enough, he had thought, to find an apartment in Phoenix. But now, 750 miles away and with a car that needed a decent burial, Arizona seemed halfway around the globe.

After breakfast Gil had taken Max to a meeting at the Fresh Air Club, and Max couldn't help but laugh when he saw that it was only a block and a half down the street from Bailey's. It was just like him to have his car die practically next door to an AA club.

At the meeting Max had shared his story of the night before. When he told it, his cowboy friends Larry and Frank became Frank and Jesse, and the hilarity with which his words were greeted helped him forget, for a few minutes, that his ass was in a crack. After the meeting several of the members talked to him. Gil had offered to loan him a car for a few weeks, and someone else had given him some leads on an apartment if he needed one. He had said no thanks, that he really needed to get on to Phoenix, but lurking in the back of his mind was the knowledge that his plans were most likely about to take a sudden turn. Now, sitting cross-legged on a motel bed with his meager coffer spread out in front of him, what was a suspicion earlier had become a cold reality. He didn't have enough money to buy a car and find an apartment in Phoenix. In fact there wasn't enough for a car that would be much better than the one now sitting in Gil's garage. An apartment seemed a little more possible, but the thought of staying in this city, with its incessant sand storm, was more than he could stand. He leaned his head back against the wall and closed his eyes. God, he thought, let me know. He tried to clear his mind of all extraneous shit. The move to Phoenix wasn't fixed, exactly. There was no one waiting for him there; it was simply a town that was not New York. He had grown tired of the speed and the dirt, the senseless lack of caring that defined the city. Phoenix was an idea to him, a place at the geographically opposite corner of the country that he had idealized as something not New York. He did not exactly have to move there, but the realization did not make Amarillo any more attractive. It did not make the storm abate, or the temperature rise. God, he prayed, grant me the serenity to accept the things I cannot change, the courage to change the things I can, and the wisdom to know the difference. God, give me a sign. Give me a fucking sign.

Max started to undress, and cleared out the contents of his pockets. With his wallet came a slip of paper that read "Frank Vaughn, 346-7812." He stared at it for a few moments then laughed, his first real laugh since he had driven into this city almost twenty-four hours ago. It sounded good to him. Well, I asked for a sign, Max thought. He put the gas receipt back with his wallet, then pulled out the phone book and looked up the number for the local chapter of the State Bar. He wrote it down, slid between the cool sheets, and fell asleep almost instantly.

Max woke up and looked at the alarm clock. It was 3:28 a.m. He knew something was wrong, or at least different, but couldn't quite put his finger on what it was. He fell back asleep before he realized that the strangeness was the absence of the wind. It had stopped, the sandstorm moving on south to Lubbock and Post, on down to Abilene.

At 2:00 a.m. Angel threw everybody out. With Bailey patrolling between the tables, it wasn't very hard. She sat at attention by the door as the last customers filed out. Angel locked up and left the straightening for the next afternoon when she opened again. Once a week she had a crew come in and clean, but only when she was there to let them in. She didn't feel comfortable with a key in any hand but her own.

She drew herself a beer and sipped it while she checked the bathrooms for passed-out drunks. There was no one; she and Bailey were by themselves. She hiked herself up on the counter and reached behind it to turn down the tape that fed through the speakers. While Garth Brooks sang about friends in low places, she and Bailey talked. Angel told her how it felt to have a decent income from owning her own business, to have a nice house and her own horses and a warm bed for her wolf, but nothing better to do at night than work at the pool hall as if she were, after all, just a salaried employee who was doing it to make ends meet. She sighed and sipped her beer. Bailey rumbled her commiseration deep in her chest, never taking her eyes from the face of her best friend as she listened.

By now Garth had given way to Annie Lennox and George Jones and then to Joe Ely, who sang a love song to the city of angels. Angel smiled at that, and slid down from the counter, knowing this was as good a time as any to lock up and go home. She dug her fingers through the fur at the back of Bailey's neck, and the wolf closed her eyes in ecstasy. For a few moments she was more the puppy she had once been than the fierce wolf who could bounce anyone from the club at the first hint of trouble. The moment Angel's hand released her Bailey snapped to attention, eyes narrowing, looking for any potential threats to the life the two of them had hewn together. Angel unlocked the front door and Bailey went through first, nosing the air for the slightest scent of danger that despite the sand storm she could have smelled in an instant. Satisfied, she stepped aside and Angel shut the door behind them and locked it. They ran for her truck.

Later Angel sat in bed reading, her legs tented in front of her, a cup of hot cocoa on the nightstand. Bailey curled in her own bed deep in REM sleep, her eyes, nose, paws, and ears twitching. Angel re-read her favorite novel, Michael Malone's *Time's Witness*. When her eyes closed too often to keep reading, she laid the book on the nightstand and turned off the lamp. From the small barn behind her house she heard the nicker of her Appaloosa mare, Summerlea, and the black and white mustang she had named Nightfall. At the last moment before Angel slid into sleep, she realized that she felt something intangible, a change, moving toward her. She didn't know why or how, and before she could reach out and grasp the knowledge, touch it, she was heading toward her dreams. She and Bailey slept through the cessation of the storm.

The next morning, as Max Friedman awoke to find out that there was more to Amarillo than blowing sand, while he called the State Bar to find out about becoming licensed to practice law in Texas, the people of Amarillo crept out after the storm. They removed the towels that were stuffed under the doors and windows to keep the sand out of their homes. The white dust masks were rinsed and put back into garages and tool sheds; the bandanas men wrapped around their mouths went into the wash.

In the Palo Duro Canyon, southeast of town, the deer and roadrunners, the lizards and birds emerged again to the delight of tourists and souvenir sellers.

Smith Dixon sat in a room on the fifth floor of High Plains Hospital. On the opposite side of the curtain, the room's other patient rattled a magazine and cleared his throat. From the side on which Smith sat there was no noise and no movement. The man in the bed breathed slowly in and out, his eyes shut, his frail chest barely raising the sheet. Smith sat staring, wondering at the irony of life. Smith didn't believe in God, but if he did, he would believe in the presence of a big hand that very slowly was turning up the heat on the skillet of hot grease in which he swam. It seemed to Smith that his life had been one problem after another, one long painful skid mark.

He had left Amarillo long ago, just a short jog ahead of the law, and spent many years on the road. Sometimes he stayed ahead of the law, but there were too many years that he found himself behind the bars of county or state institutions. He had tired of this life and eventually decided that he had to make his way back to Amarillo, the city which had birthed him, and where his only family member lived.

And now he sat in the hospital watching and listening for any sign of consciousness while his father lay in a coma. The old man had managed to call 911 before he succumbed to the stroke. Thank God, because there was no one, anymore, to report him missing. He lived alone. His wife was long dead, and his only son had answered the call of the road almost thirty years before.

Smith had called the city's hospitals until he found the one the old man lay in. He had talked to the doctors, identified himself as the only kin, and listened to their prognosis. It doesn't look good, Mr. Dixon, one had droned. Your father is in a coma from which he will not awaken. He may pass away while we're talking, or he might last years. There's never a way to tell until it happens. Yeah, Smith had said. Kind of like life, ain't it? The doctor had stared at him and then left the room.

So Smith sat, not moving, not picking up one of the magazines in the lounge to make his vigil smoother. Instead, he just sat and thought. Years of staying in the shadows away from the law had taught him the value of a poker face, and as he sat next to his father's bed no one could have guessed what passed through his mind.

I didn't mean it to be this way, he thought. I wanted to come back, maybe sit down with you and talk, tell you I was sorry for what I done and the way I done it. Sorry I let you down. Maybe you thought I never came back because I didn't want to see you anymore. That's not true. I was just too goddamn ashamed to. I didn't want to face you again. But this time I was ready to. I was going to come back and ask you to forgive me, try to make a new life for myself here, settle down. And instead, I find you laying up in this bed, and you ain't ever going to know if I'm here or not.

Smith balled his fist up and pounded it onto the table next to him. "You okay over there?" the man in the other bed asked from beyond the curtain.

"Yeah," Smith said. "Hand slipped getting me a glass of water."

"All right."

Smith closed his eyes and leaned his head against the back of the chair. It wasn't supposed to turn out this way, he thought. No, it wasn't supposed to be like this at all.

After a few moments he fell into a light sleep, and when a nurse gently shook his shoulder and told him visiting hours were over, he was surprised to see that it was dark.

Chapter 6

On a Saturday night two weeks later, Angel had to turn up the music to hear it herself. Bailey's was more crowded than usual for a Saturday, and what was good for business was not always good for her peace of mind. She preferred Tuesdays, when the crowd was the lightest of the week, and more polite too. The Tuesday night crowd was many of the same people who came on Saturday; there were just fewer of them. But although the faces were the same, they acted differently. On Saturdays the beer taps flowed faster, people talked louder, and Angel often had to turn the stereo's volume all the way up to ten. Newcomers to Bailey's were often surprised that there wasn't a jukebox. There had been one during the first year of Angel's ownership, but she had soon yanked it out and sold it. She preferred her own mix of songs, which might find George Jones crooning "He Stopped Loving Her Today" followed by Helen Reddy's "I Am Woman," which preceded Carl Douglas singing "Kung-Fu Fighting." Angel had never been accused of playing boring music.

Bailey lay quietly behind the counter, one foreleg delicately crossed over the other, her eyes looking half-asleep—a look that was deceptive. Even when Bailey was relaxed, she could see what she needed to. Her nose was constantly alert for the smells of fear and anger; her ears were always pricked for the sound of an altercation or the raising of angry voices. She never personally took the initiative of inviting someone to leave; she always waited for the signal from Angel, although she felt that Angel often took far too long to give it. Bailey preferred to keep a clean house and would rather let someone know at the first sign of trouble that his patronage was no longer appreciated.

Angel worked the counter herself, and she always knew exactly who was in the club and whether they were old-timers, newcomers, or somewhere in between. Tonight she kept a careful eye on two men who played at a table in the back corner. One of them was brand new and looked almost as wary as Bailey. He was not drunk and not wired; instead there was a stillness to him. His eyes were constantly in motion, even as he lined up his shots, surveying the room, registering all actions. It was not him who concerned Angel, but the man he was sharing a table with.

This man had the arrogant male strut that Angel had grown weary of years ago, the kind of strut that her father had, that had driven her out of the Panhandle and north over the state line when she was seventeen years old. He was slender and not bad looking as that kind go, but he faced life leading with his crotch, always aware of his effect on people, particularly women. He wore blue jeans and boots and a cowboy shirt and looked to be in his 30's. The man had been in several times over the course of the summer, but in the last few weeks he had showed up at least ten times. He was a good player, and Angel surmised he was either new to town or had been eighty-sixed from another club and had chosen Bailey's as his new base of operations. From her familiarity with the type, she suspected the latter. If he was from out of town, he hadn't moved far. His kind was peculiar to the Panhandle.

Tonight he had shown up a little later than usual, about 8:00, and all the tables were filled. His partner, the quiet watchful one, had occupied the corner table by himself for an hour, carefully moving around the felt surveying his shots before inevitably sinking the one he sought. The cowboy had asked if he could share the table. His partner spoke little while the cowboy talked on and on, looking at the door whenever it opened. When a man walked in he watched for a moment like an alpha male assessing the competition. When a woman entered, he dismissed the overweight ones and the very few over fifty; the rest he devoured with his eyes. Yes, Angel knew the type. He would bear watching.

"So you just come into town, huh?" Joe asked Smith.

"Couple weeks ago. I used to live here, but it's been a while."

"Welcome back, partner. It's a hell of a town. All the goddamn wind you can handle, and pussy just for the taking. They're dying for it; you hear what I'm saying?"

"My ears work fine." Smith leaned over, lined up the cue ball with the nine, and gently urged it into a corner pocket.

"Yeah, seems like half the guys today are fags anyway. You imagine that? Fags right here in Amarillo. Shit, you'd think it was Dallas. In fact, in here just the other night I saw—"

"Your shot." After Smith put the nine in there were no shots left, and he had effectively cut Joe off from scoring. There were two added bonuses in Joe having a turn. For one, it would shut him up for a few moments, and two, there was a good chance he would leave Smith set up with a good shot.

Sure enough, Joe managed to leave a shot that most pool players, even the best, would have missed. But Smith thought he could make it. He squatted down and eyed it, then smoothly moved around the table, assessing the shot from all directions.

Joe smirked. "Ain't a shot on that table you can make," he said. "I couldn't sink one, but I damn sure fixed it so you couldn't neither."

Smith smiled. He knew for a fact that Joe, although a decent player, very seldom thought about anything beyond whatever shot he was making at the moment. He arrived back where he had started, at the far corner pocket. "I'm going to put the seven ball there."

"Never happen," Joe said.

Smith leaned over and in one graceful stroke hit the cue ball, which rapped against the seven, bouncing it against two rails of the table and inching between two other balls before rolling slowly into the designated pocket.

"Goddamn," Joe said. "Is this how you make your living?"

"I've done it before, but the work's a little slow and it doesn't pay too well."

"So what are you doing for work?"

"Nothing yet."

"You must be rich."

"I have some money saved up from my last job."

"I wish I did. I sweat ever goddamn day over a welding torch, and it ain't gonna make me rich."

"Eight ball."

"Shit. I'm starting to think I picked the wrong guy to partner with."

"Maybe next game your luck will turn."

"You know what kind of job I'd like to have? I'd like to get paid for fucking women. You know what I mean? You hear about them little guys out in New York and L.A., young guys that women hire to just fuck them, cause they can't get no one else to? That wouldn't be bad, even if they are ugly, cause they're all rich. Then with all that money you made from them old bitches, you could get any young girl you wanted, you know, a girl with tits out to here."

Smith began to regret saying yes when Joe approached his table. It was going to be a long night. It was possible that a table would open up and Joe would take it, but judging from the line at the counter it would be a while before one was free. And even if there were, he figured that Joe had found something even better than a woman with big tits—a man with ears.

Angel was surprised when the door opened and the lawyer walked in. What was his name? Max, that was it. She hadn't expected to see him again and found herself strangely pleased when she did. She gave him a nod when he caught her eye and turned to face her next customers, a pair of regulars named Carl and Freddie. Carl was the older one, a quiet man who played, drank, and paid up without giving her any shit. Freddie, the young guy with sandy-colored curly hair that was seldom combed, was another matter. He played poorly, got drunk fast, and got loud even quicker.

Carl stepped up to the counter, and when Angel said "Help you?" directly to him, Freddie planted his elbow on the counter and leaned straight toward her. "Hell yes, we need help. Last time we played, you charged us for ten minutes past an hour. You ain't gonna do that tonight, are you honey?"

Angel's green eyes drilled straight into him. "Hell yes I am. And if you ever call me 'honey' again, I'll give you open-heart surgery with a cue stick."

"Freddie, goddamn it shut up," Carl said. "Look, we just need a table."

"Be a few minutes. But don't wait at the counter. Wait somewhere else. I'll let you know when it's ready. And the next time you bring your friend, he'd better have either some manners or a muzzle."

"He's not my friend, he's my brother-in-law, almost." Embarrassed, Carl looked around for somewhere to take Freddie.

"Hey," Freddie said slowly, as Carl's words worked their way through the cloud of alcohol in his brain. "What the fuck's that supposed to mean?"

Lying on the floor near Angel's feet, Bailey began to issue a soft rumble from her throat. "It's okay," Angel said.

"Who the hell does she think she is, anyway?" Freddie asked.

"The owner of this place, that's who she is," Carl said. "She makes the rules here. I don't even know why I let you come with me. You're going to get us thrown out of here, you know that?"

"Hey, I ain't scared of her goddamn dog. And I can go any place I want to, I ain't gotta wait for you to—"

"Come on," Carl said and grabbed him by the arm. They moved off to a corner and watched a college-age couple aimlessly shooting a rack of balls.

Max stepped up to the counter after Carl and Freddie left. "Hello again," Angel said. "I guess I didn't expect to see you back here. You walk?"

Before Max could say anything, Frank Vaughan slapped him on the back. "I just want you to know, Angel, that this man's money is absolutely no goddamn good in this place tonight. This old hippie boy may not look like it, but he's the best lawyer in the town of Amarillo—hell, he's the best goddamn lawyer in the whole state of Texas, and whoever says he ain't gets a free ass-whippin' courtesy of me."

"Any asses you whip, you better do it off my property," Angel said.

"How's that car working out, Max?"

"Pretty good, Frank. It has four wheels, couple of doors, a gas tank. That's about all I need."

"You're a stitch, you know that man? Hey Angel, set Max up with—what do you want, partner? Bud? Coors?"

"No really, thanks but you've already paid me with the car. You don't need to—"

"C'mon, let me buy you a beer. That damn car ain't worth all the tickets you got me out of. So what'll it be?"

"Well, just a Coke would be fine."

"You sure you don't want a glass of horse-piss?"

"Absolutely. My doctor advises me to reduce my intake of equine urine."

Frank snorted. "He's quick, ain't he? All right then, but Angel? If he wants a damn thing, remember, his money's no good tonight." He slapped a ten-dollar bill on the counter. Angel eyed it suspiciously, as if it might be counterfeit.

"Yeah, yeah, I heard," she said, and waved him away. Frank went back to the table where he and Larry were playing, weaving uncertainly in his cowboy boots, a mug of golden beer sporting a foamy head clasped in his hand.

Max still didn't feel completely comfortable, but the hall had the same ambiance of some of his favorite hangouts in Manhattan. He played pool at real pool halls, his favorite being one on the second floor of a building on 14th Street, right across from Union Square. He hated the yuppie clubs that had popped up in the last few decades all over the Village: ferny places with no regular clientele, catering to the oily crowds that slid about the sidewalks of Manhattan throwing their money at whatever amusement *New York* magazine listed as new and trendy that week.

When he drank, Max had taken up space in pool halls all over Brooklyn and Manhattan, playing for fun and money. He won a little money when he was sober enough to shoot straight, and after he stopped drinking he still found the atmosphere comforting. It was a link to his past that he enjoyed. After he finished law school there was a cop and lawyer club downtown near City Hall where he played. His fellow players soon discovered that he was one of those rare lawyers who didn't drink and eventually stopped urging him to share a pitcher of beer.

So although the accents were all wrong, and the cowboy boots were a far cry from the Florsheims, Guccis, and Wing Tips that wore down the floors of his former haunts, he found Bailey's a comforting place to be on a Saturday night.

From the speakers mounted in each corner of the room, the sound of a frantically pounding piano emanated. A gravely voice growled over the chords, and Max caught the words "Amarillo highway" in the lyrics.

"You here to play?" Angel asked.

"What, you show movies too?" Max answered Angel.

He might have been mistaken, but there was almost a flicker at the corner of her mouth that could have been a smile. "It'll be a few minutes before I can get you a table."

"Time is something I have a lot of right now."

"If you're such a great lawyer as your friend Frank here brags you up as, why did you end up at the ass-end of nowhere in a car that's dying?"

"Because I'm an honest lawyer. You ever meet an honest lawyer who was rich?"

"I've never met an honest lawyer."

"A hit, a very palpable hit." Max clutched at his chest.

"So who are you, Hamlet or Laertes?"

Max had been scanning the room, bandying with her in an offhand way, but now he turned and studied her more seriously.

"Well, I'm Jewish, not Danish, and I don't know how tragic I am, but my life sure is crazy, so I'll choose Hamlet. You want to play Ophelia?"

"She's a little passive. How about Laertes?"

"How about if we just sheath our swords? Truce."

She shrugged and drew two pitchers of beer for a customer. Max watched the room again. He hadn't meant to be sarcastic; he liked Angel more than anyone else he'd met so far in Amarillo outside of the A.A. rooms. He had just tried to have fun with her, but in some way she seemed to take offense. It was a problem that Max had often had in his life. He could cause offense without having the slightest idea that he'd said anything wrong. Sometimes he thought it was just the nature of a trial attorney, always fencing with words, trying to find an exposed patch of nerves. Maybe he'd become so used to it that he no longer knew how to have a regular conversation.

Angel rapped her knuckles on the bar next to him. "What?" he said, startled.

"I asked what you what happened to Phoenix."

"Oh. After I paid for a few nights in a motel and some meals, the towing charge, there wasn't enough left to get set up there. So I got temporary certification to practice in Texas and lowered the level of shit from Frank's neck to his ankles, for which he kindly gave me a car."

"Yeah, kindness is his big forté, I'm sure."

"He's an okay guy."

"So what were you doing driving to Phoenix, anyway?"

"I guess I'd burned out on New York. I was sick of the dirt and the crime, trying to jam myself into a subway car. One morning a couple of months ago I was on a train headed downtown to the courthouse, when I saw this woman— probably 55 or 60. She was running ass over teakettle for the train, just as the doors were closing. There was no room at all. I mean, we could have formed a band and called ourselves the Sardines. She gets up to the door, and tries to cram herself onto the train, but there just wasn't enough room. Didn't faze her. She just stands there letting the door open and close on her head. And whenever the door closes, it makes this little bell noise—'bing bong.' She's pushing herself in, killing the people standing next to the door, the door's closing on her head, bing bong, and she's railing at all of us. 'There's room in the middle, could you move in closer, you there in the middle, move closer.'" Max acted out her role with all the skill of an experienced courtroom thespian, contorting his face into an expression of narcissistic angst.

He took a sip of his Coke and looked out over the room. Angel waited a few moments and said "Well?"

"Well what?"

"Don't fuck with me. What happened?"

"There was a young woman, 19 or 20, standing next to the door. She was one of the people the older woman was mashing. Finally, just when the door's open, she swivels her hip right into the older one. Boom. Out the woman goes onto the platform, the door closes, and we're on our way to work. The whole car erupted with applause."

There was no one at the counter needing beer. Angel wiped the dark wood surface with a damp rag, then hung it over a beer spigot. "You just made that up, right? I mean, it's just some bullshit story you came up with."

Max raised his right hand, the first three fingers extended up, his thumb crossed over the pinky. "On my honor."

"And people live like that?"

"Some would call it living."

Angel turned her green eyes on him and tucked a strand of her red hair behind her right ear.

"And that's why you left?"

"Part of it. The biggest thing is that I didn't fit anymore. The whole island of Manhattan, or at least the parts I lived and worked in, have been taken over by the yuppies. You know, the guys with greasy hair and cell phones, the women with their smart suits, walking to work in sneakers, then switching to the shoes they keep in their desk drawers. I lived in the East Village, which used to be a neat old European neighborhood, and now, you know what they got on the corner where my favorite deli was? A Gap. When they put that thing in, I knew it was the beginning of the end. What would be next, a goddamn Planet Hollywood, the Hard Rock Cafe East Village? I swear this is the truth, but there's a place near where I lived where you can see three Starbucks without moving your body. All you have to do is turn your head. And apartments that used to rent for a couple hundred a month are a couple thousand. The people who used to live in them, you know where they are? If they're not dead, they're on the street eating from the dumpster."

"Well gee," Angel said, "this is an uplifting conversation. So that still doesn't explain Phoenix."

"I just decided New York wasn't for me anymore. I had heard some good things about Phoenix from another lawyer. I figured it's far enough away from New York, it would be okay. When I finally realized I was serious about moving, I decided that I wanted to wake up somewhere else on January 1, 2000."

"Well, you made it by three months. And here you are in Amarillo."

"Yeah, but it's not so bad. I like this place, met a couple of nice people. And this is the Wild West, for Christ's sake. I mean, there can't be any yuppies here. Any of those little vermin stick their greasy heads above the ground in Amarillo, they're liable to get them shot off. Am I right?"

Max heard the chirp of a phone. He glanced at Angel, who didn't move to answer it. "You need to get that?" he said.

She shook her head, a slight movement. "Not mine."

The chirp came again, and a man at a table four feet away from Max made a shot, then straightened up and in the same motion pulled a telephone from a holster on his belt. He wore a cotton button-down shirt and khaki pants. His hair glistened in the light.

"This is Whit, talk to me," he said. "Yeah Charlie, how's it hanging, big guy? It what? Went down? Well hell, just sell it now. Don't wait for them to make a killing on it. Soon as New York opens Monday a.m., get on the phone and dump it. Okay, babe. You too. Catch you later."

He slid his phone back in its holster. "My broker," he said to the others playing at the table. "Don't know what I'd do without him."

Max closed his eyes and lifted the cold glass of Coke to his forehead. "Looks like you fucked up," Angel said, not unkindly.

"So it would seem."

Two couples weaved from the back of the room toward the counter, holding racks of balls. "I think your luck's about to change, Max." She cashed the couples out and handed him a rack of balls and a cube of chalk.

Max wound his way through the crowd, avoiding jabbing elbows and thrusting sticks. He set up the balls, chalked his cue, leaned over and smoothly stroked the stick into the cue ball. With a satisfying crack, the balls scattered like a crowd of Brooklyn schoolgirls when a homeless man enters their subway car. It wasn't as satisfying as the first drink of the night or the last one of the morning used to be, but it would do. He started to work the table. In a strange way, playing pool at Bailey's felt the same as his first meeting at the Fresh Air AA club: he felt like he was home.

Angel searched the crowd for Carl and Freddie. She raised her voice. "Hey! You two! Got a table." When they made it back to the counter, she handed the balls and chalk to Carl, ignoring Freddie.

When Smith first noticed the man across the room, it did not immediately register who he was. He was concentrating on his shots and listening with half an ear to Joe's monologue about his sexual exploits, like dirty water running down a drainpipe after a rain. Joe occasionally changed his theme, relating a story about a fight he had been in. Smith nodded appropriately, periodically letting Joe win a game. He was not only a sharp winner; he was an astute loser as well, having practiced this skill through his years of hustling pool. A hustler who wins every game will soon find himself out of playing partners.

He continued searching the room with his eyes, always aware of who was playing and how they played. When his eyes lit on the man, he was touched with the feeling that he should know who this was. At first he dismissed it. He had been born in Amarillo and had run away at 19. During those years he had known many people: hundreds of schoolmates, customers in his father's butcher shop, teenagers and adults he hung out with in the downtown pool halls where he learned his skills. As an adolescent he played air hockey and foosball as he watched the older teens and adults at the pool tables. Eventually he proved himself a pool prodigy, easily taking the one and five dollar bills the grown men laid down on the green felt. The familiar looking man could have been any of these former acquaintances, but somehow he felt more important than that.

"Hey Joe," he said. "You know that guy over there?"

Joe interrupted his story long enough to look. "Which guy?"

Smith pointed him out.

"Man, I don't know. I've maybe seen him here a couple of times. Where was I? Oh yeah. Anyway, she must have known she could get into deep shit about it, if anybody ever found out, her being a teacher and all. But you know, the way I fucked her she didn't have time to think about it. This one night I met her behind the bus barn at the school. She didn't want anybody to see us, but I think she got off on doing it right there on the school grounds. It was warm, like in April, and I had this Firebird with a big-ass hood on it, so I just fucked her right there on that—"

Smith was staring down the stick at the cue ball, in his mind's eye seeing the dotted lines that would connect it to the 3 ball then to the pocket, when the knowledge of who the man suddenly was cut through his mind like hi-beam headlights in a dense fog. He slowly stood erect and for the first time actually saw the man across the hall from him.

"Goddamn, Carl. Look at you," he said.

When Smith was at Amarillo High, he spent most of his time cutting class, appearing often enough to take tests occasionally. His teachers complained and the principal periodically threatened to expel him, but all that usually happened was that he would be sent to the guidance counselor's office. The counselor, Mr. Perkins, wore prim glasses, and his hair was carefully combed and oiled. He was fond of bow ties, and the set of his mouth reminded Smith of the woman in that old painting of the farm couple. On his desk was a penholder that had a diamondback rattler and head glued on it. The mouth was spread open, exposing its fangs. Rampant in the school was a rumor that Mr. Perkins had been seen one night crawling drunk around the floor of a local bar, calling for his cat.

He never seemed overly concerned to see Smith in his office. "Now Smith, you seem like a bright boy," he'd say. "Test scores are good when you take them. But it's clear you're not cut out for college. Why don't you settle down and pay attention in your auto mechanics class? Just come to that one class every day, and try to get passing marks in English and History. Then when you graduate you can set up as a mechanic. Work for someone else for a while, develop a clientele, then open up your own shop. I think that's something you could do real well at."

Smith always pretended to be listening. He would nod and say "uh-huh" at the appropriate places, leaving Mr. Perkins with the impression that he had been heard. The next day Smith would spend most of the morning at a pool hall, then show up for one or two afternoon classes. His father would get angry at him for skipping school, but feeling guilty for his wife leaving them when Smith was 11, he was afraid to be too hard on his son. Instead he worked harder, thinking that if he could bring home more money, he could make up for the fact that the boy had no mother.

Smith had been vaguely aware of Carl all the way from elementary school through junior high, but it was in their sophomore year of high school, on the first day of Coach Tankersley's World History class, that they started to become friends.

The coach wore a very short, very wide, mustard colored tie, and the buttons on his white shirt threatened to jump ship whenever he sat up straight. "Now most of y'all kids probably don't know much about the world," he said that day, "but there ain't no shame in that. How many of you, for instance, know that the Rock of Gibraltar sits smack dab between the coasts of Africa and Italy?"

Carl had tried to stifle his laugh but it came out anyway, and he disguised it as a sneeze. "Gesundheit!" the coach bawled out, and Smith, sitting behind Carl, started to laugh. The coach had a wooden paddle in his desk with which he would give three whacks on the ass to any boy he felt was disturbing the peace of his classroom, so Smith prudently pretended to have a coughing fit. The coach stood up and maneuvered his body, with its tight shirt and sagging black pants, around the desk to the row where they sat. "Y'all boys all right?" he asked. "I'd hate to have to call out the ambulance. Now see, if y'all went out for the ball team, wouldn't be none of this coughing. You can't be a ballplayer and be in poor health." The snickers behind him at that statement were also covered as coughs, and he hurried back up the front of the classroom, afraid to catch whatever contagious virus his students were carrying.

Occasionally the coach came out with other bits of interesting historical trivia, like the time he said that King Henry VIII had eight wives and killed them all. By that time Carl and Smith were practiced enough that they contained their mirth. But most of the time during class the coach gave a reading assignment and hurried to the library, where he spent the remainder of the period asleep in one of the deep leather chairs.

Smith and Carl's friendship grew, and they began playing pool together. After they graduated, Smith almost at the bottom of the class, Carl began working at his father's drapery shop, and they saw less of one another. Then there came the day when they stopped seeing each other completely, and two days later Smith left town.

Now, looking at Carl across the pool hall through a curtain of cigarette smoke and time, he could barely recognize his old friend. Carl's face was lined, and his hairline was much farther back than the boy's who had laughed at the ignorant coach. In fact, he bore a startling resemblance to his father. Smith thought of all he had lost in the past 27 years and hoped that life had been kinder to his old friend.

"That's ten bucks you owe me, Freddie." Carl had just sunk his second eight ball in as many games. Never a good player at his best, Freddie drunk was like a kindergartner trying to play Minnesota Fats.

"Okay," Freddie said, pushing a curl of his dirty blond hair out of his eyes. "I'll buy you lunch."

"No you won't. You owe me ten. You work for me anyway, so I'd be buying lunch for myself. I want the cash." Goddamn Freddie, always trying to get away with squelching.

Freddie's mouth curled up in a half smile. He looked around, as if Carl were talking to someone else. "You're kidding, right?"

"Do I look like I'm kidding? A bet's a bet. You owe me ten bucks. Pay up."

Freddie shook his head and turned away from Carl, reaching for the chalk. He mumbled something, but Carl couldn't hear it. "What did you say?"

Freddie moved away down the table, still rubbing more and more chalk on his stick. "Nothing. I mean, you know. You really think that's going to help?"

Carl watched him with the chalk, and when Freddie realized where he was looking he put it down, a slight red burning his cheeks. "Like help with the groceries is what I meant."

Carl's voice was quiet. He thought of an old black and white Robert Mitchum movie he had seen on AMC a few nights ago, after Dolores and Nina had gone to bed. "Don't bullshit me, Freddie. You're no good at it. What'd you mean? Help with what?"

"Shit. I just—if I wanted a third degree, I'd go piss on the sidewalk and get arrested! Christ!" Embarrassed, he started to arrange the balls in the rack. "Hey, whose break is it, anyway?"

Carl felt a moment of smug satisfaction. "It's yours," he said. He waited for

Freddie to make his shot, and it took him a moment to realize that his brother-in-law was staring across the room.

"Hey," Freddie said, almost in a whisper. "There's some guy over there staring at us." Carl started to turn his head. "Don't look!" Freddie whispered.

"Christ Freddie, this isn't a spy movie. What do you think you're—"

He turned and searched the room. When he found the man Freddie was talking about, for the first time he understood what people meant when they said that their blood ran cold. He could feel his temperature suddenly lower, could feel five skeletal fingers lightly brush the skin on his neck below his freshly cut hair. It had been several years since that face had appeared in his mind's eye and 27 since he had actually seen it, but he would never forget it. As Carl looked at him Smith smiled, shaking his head back and forth slowly.

Smith looked toward the counter and caught Angel's eye. He motioned in the direction of Carl and Freddie's table, indicating that he and Joe were going to double up with them. Angel looked at him hard, the little wrinkles between her eyes showing a harsh V against her freckled skin. Then she slowly nodded and motioned at a couple who were standing at the counter waiting for a table. The couple moved up and she handed them a rack of balls and two cubes of chalk.

"Who the hell is this guy, anyway? Why're we giving up our table?" Joe strutted between the other players, avoiding their sticks.

"Friend of mine from the old days," Smith said. "I'll introduce you."

Joe wasn't looking where he was going when he veered too close to a table and got nudged in the stomach by a pool cue. The man who held it turned around immediately. "Sorry, chief. You okay?"

Joe looked down at the player, a small man who wore his hair pulled back into a ponytail. "Why don't you look the fuck where you're waving that thing?" he said. "I guess you got an excuse, though. Maybe all that hair got in your eyes." He turned around to see who was watching him and smiled his crooked grin. Smith was still working his way through the players toward Carl.

Max looked back at Joe. "Like I said, I'm sorry."

"Well," Joe said, "sorry don't get it. We don't appreciate little longhaired hippies coming in here and not minding their manners. We—"

"Look, you've already gotten two apologies," Max said. "You want something more than that, you're shopping at the wrong store." He saw the light go cold in Joe's eyes and wrapped his hand tighter around the stick, drawing on long-ago memories of barroom fights, hoping that his instincts would still serve him well if they were needed.

Joe stared at him. His eyes became unsure, as if he didn't quite know what to do next. He wasn't used to people who stood up to his bullying. He said, "Just watch yourself next time," and turned to follow Smith.

Max softly blew out a sigh and turned back to his game, checking very carefully behind him to make sure no one was in range of his stick. He banked the cue ball against the left side rail and neatly sank the 3 ball. When he looked up again he saw that Angel was watching him from across the room. Her eyes lingered for a moment, and then she turned her back to him and drew a beer for a customer. Not for the first time he wondered about her, about why she was running this place by herself and if she was as tough as she wanted everyone to think.

When Smith was in junior high school, a kid named Ray Street told him that the father of a classmate named Doyle Benson had died. Smith was upset by the death, because Doyle's father had been kind to him several different times, going out of his way to pay attention to a boy he could tell was lonely. Smith grieved the death, and several days later as he was riding his bike, he looked up to see Doyle's father passing by in his car. It turned out that Ray Street had gotten it wrong and it was Doyle's uncle, not his father, who had died. When Smith saw the father behind the wheel of the big blue Chevrolet station wagon, he was for a moment shocked. Then he felt a rush of joy, and for several moments both emotions shared his face.

As he approached the table where Carl and Freddie were staring at them, he wore the same expression. Smith slowed down when he reached the table. For the first time in many years he felt happiness, some glint that maybe life wasn't all bad, that there was something gleaming on the ground in front of him, and if he were careful he could reach down and pick it up, brush it off and put it into his pocket.

"Goddamn, Carl. It has been just too many goddamn years. How are you?"

"Since when have you given a shit how I am?"

Smith was taken aback. He had hoped for a warm greeting from his old friend, for the same kind of enthusiasm that he felt. He was not a man who hugged, but if he were, he would have thrown his arms around Carl, pounded his back. Instead, feeling puzzled, he offered his hand.

Carl reluctantly extended his, but when Smith gripped it there was no warmth from Carl, who had obviously shaken hands only to avoid an embarrassing situation. Several of the players at tables around them had paused when they heard Smith's words, anticipating the reunion of two old friends. Like revelers at a birthday surprise at a restaurant when the waiters group together to bring the cake and sing, they wore expressions composed half of embarrassment and half of delight.

Smith looked around, aware of the eyes on him, and shook his shoulders as if to shrug them off.

"Carl, this is a hell of a greeting for an old buddy."

"You're a hell of an old 'buddy,' Smith. I mean it's been what, 27 years? A lot of things can happen in that time, can't they?" He flicked his eyes at Freddie, across the table, and lowered his voice. "Tell you the truth, buddy," hitting the word very hard, "I never thought I'd ever see you again. And you want some more truth? You're about the last goddamn person on this earth I'd *want* to see. So why don't you just go back to your table and leave me alone?"

Smith was lost. "Jesus Christ, Carl. I mean, I don't know what to say."

"Goodbye. That would be good. You want to try it out?"

Smith looked back to the table he and Joe had just vacated, but there was already a couple at it. Desperately he looked for another, but the hall was still packed.

"Hey man! Who's your pals here?" Joe strutted up to the table." I had to take care of some little asshole back there. Show him some manners."

Smith prided himself as someone who always knew what to do. He liked to have situations in hand, liked to know going in what the risk was, and liked to know coming out if the events that had transpired would have any effect on him. He played the odds and seldom lost.

And now, standing on the hardwood floor of an Amarillo pool joint, the place where he should have been most comfortable in the world, he felt as if he were standing on the beach at Galveston, when the tide was rushing back over his feet into the ocean, knowing that although he was firmly on the land, at any moment the shifting sand could knock him flat on his ass.

"Oh," he said. "Well, this is Joe Wagner. Joe, Carl Puente and—I'm sorry," he said to Freddie, "I didn't catch your name."

"Well shit," Freddie said. "That's because my brother-in-law forgot to introduce us. I'm Freddie Odom." He reached his hand toward Smith, who took it gingerly, still looking at Carl, who avoided his eyes.

Freddie gulped from his beer mug and pushed the hair out of his eyes with his other hand, and then offered it to Smith and Joe. The curl that came to Joe's lips wasn't a true smile; it was more like a look of malevolent amusement, as if he had just discovered some useful bit of information that he was planning to store away for future use.

"Carl, look—" Smith stepped toward him, his back to Joe and Freddie, his fingers wrapped around the top of his stick. "I don't know exactly what's going on here with you and me. I was happy to see you, and obviously you ain't. But look, Angel's already give away our table. So how about if we play a little while? Call it old time's sake."

"Funny thing about old times, Smith. You ever notice they're different for some people than others? Like two people can be standing six inches away from each other, and one of them takes a shot to the head and the other one doesn't even feel the wind?"

Smith shook his head. At the next table a young woman with an overbite and the slack jaw of someone well on her way to being drunk checked over her shoulder. She noticed Smith and said "Excuse me." He shifted his hips slightly to bring him out of the line of her stroke. "You're so sweet," she said, and slowly turned back to her shot. The cue ball skittered only a foot before stopping, making no contact with any ball near it. "I've gotta stop drinking so much," she said.

"Look Carl," Smith said. "I know I haven't always been the best guy to be around. And I'll be the first to say I've done a lot of bad shit before, but I ain't like that no more, that's why I—"

"All right, here's the deal," Joe broke in. "Me and Smith here will play old Carl and Freddie, eight ball with tournament rules. Two play, two set out, and we switch off each game. Best three out of five, losers buy a pitcher." He looked around slyly, cutting his eyes at the other three. "I ain't gonna play too late, though. I still want a chance to round up some pussy tonight. Aaooohhh!" He let out a rebel yell and rubbed his hand on his crotch.

Carl looked at Smith, his eyes dark. "I'm married, so I'll just concentrate on the game."

"Shit Carl, I am too," Joe said. "A wedding certificate ain't a barbed wire fence. Feels a hell of a lot better crossing it, you get my meaning."

"If we're playing, let's play," Carl said. "Quit dicking around."

Freddie laughed. "Old Carl, he's so used to being a boss he just can't quit at 5:00."

"Fuck you, Freddie. Come on, rack them up." Carl expertly set the balls in the rack. "Let's flip for the break. Heads."

Smith removed his corduroy jacket and neatly folded it on a bar stool. He took a quarter from the front pocket of his jeans and flipped it, turning it over onto his wrist. "Tails it is. Joe, you break."

"Wait a second," Carl said. "I want to see it."

Smith looked at him as if he were waiting for the punch line. "You serious?"

"Hell yeah, he's serious," Freddie said. "Comes to wagering, he don't trust nobody for shit."

Carl's head twisted viciously to him. "You know, Freddie, someday you'll learn that you're not nearly so cute as you think you are. And I hope to God I'm there to see it."

Smith turned his wrist to Carl and showed him the coin. "Tails. I ain't gonna cheat you at a game of pool, Carl."

"All right, go on and break."

Joe leaned over the table and lined up his body above the cue stick. He worked the stick back and forth in his right hand; it slid easily through the bridge formed by his fingers, almost kissing the white cue ball, then withdrawing eight inches away. After four such motions, he cracked the stick against the ball and scattered the other fifteen like crows on a wire at the sudden roar of a shotgun.

The phone at the counter rang and Angel yanked up the receiver, propping it beneath her ear and shoulder as she drew a pitcher of beer.

"Yeah, Bailey's."

"Is Carl Puente there, please?"

"Sorry, lady. I ain't an answering service or a lost and found." She set the pitcher on the counter, scooped up the twenty the customer had laid down, and made the change.

Angel could hear the woman's breath draw in. "Well, can you at least look?"

"Ma'am," Angel said, "do you have a driver's license? Then come down here and look for yourself."

"Can't you at least tell me if you see him?"

"No, I can't. I've gone blind. What a tragedy. Look, we got a pay phone here. 272-3438. Use it."

She dropped the phone onto its cradle and wrapped the counter cloth around the back of her neck. Bailey lay at Angel's feet, her left front paw crossed over the right. She opened her eyes and looked up at Angel, who knelt down and ran her fingers through Bailey's ruff. "Yeah, I know," she said. "Sometimes it's about more than a body can take, isn't it?" She straightened up again; for once there were no customers demanding her attention, and she leaned over the counter, watching the room. At a table by himself, Max Friedman moved slowly and thoughtfully around the table, carefully lining up each shot, chalking his cue as he strategized. Max wasn't a flashy player, one of those who strutted and said, "Hey, look at me," but Angel noticed that when he lined up a shot the ball usually went in.

Frank and Larry played like two drunken cowboys, which made sense, seeing as they were exactly that. They were fairly harmless; occasionally Bailey had to bounce them, like the night Max first showed up, but neither of them had ever caused any serious injury, never been so drunk they ripped the felt on a table, or poked anyone in the eye with a stick. Tonight there was the usual contingent of college students, cowboys, housewives on a girls' night out, yuppies from the banks and couples on dates, trying desperately to impress each other. There was no one besides Max with long hair, so his ponytail made him stand out from the rest of the crowd. One time there had been a transvestite—not a very good one—and when some of the Rexall wranglers got ugly Bailey was forced to take one of them down to the floor. Angel was fairly certain that at least half of her regular crowd packed a gun, either legally or otherwise. However, she also knew that Bailey was certainly quicker than a drunk digging around in his pants for his piece and so wasn't overly concerned.

She closed her eyes for a moment, tired of the routine of her life. In the mornings she slept late then fed the horses, and took one of them for a ride out in the country bordering the Palo Duro Canyon. In the early afternoons she did house work and read or worked on the books for the club. Before suppertime she was behind the counter at Bailey's and usually didn't get home until 2:00.

"Hi. Can I get another Coke?" Angel opened her eyes to see Max Friedman.

"If you keep up this big spending, I'm gonna close down and go to Mexico with all the profits I'm making."

"Sorry. If I drank, this would be my favorite watering spot, and my money would probably never reach my bank account. Of course if I drank, Bailey would have to evict me on a regular basis." At the mention of her name, Bailey opened her eyes and fixed Max with a wide yellow-orbed stare. "And you'd be very happy to do it, wouldn't you, my furry friend?" Bailey slit her eyes half closed and rumbled in her chest.

Angel scooped his glass full of ice and filled it from the hose. "And why would she do that?"

"When I drink, my size usually doubles, and I become invincible until my knuckles strike an object harder than they are. One time it took a knife to slow me down. I have the scar to prove it."

"I'll take your word for it. Showing off your scars in public lost its appeal when Lyndon died."

"So no, if the equilibrium and peace of your establishment—not to mention the health of your clients—are important to you, it's best to keep me away from the booze."

"You've got two out of three right," Angel said.

"You're a hard woman—something you've heard before, am I right?"

"Your table's getting cold, Max."

"Oh-kay," Max said, stretching the two syllables out. "That's fine. I can take a hint when I hear one." He started walking back to his table. He decided to turn back and see whether she was looking at him and if so, if she were smiling. The look could be a good sign. Actually, it could go either way. But the smile would definitely be a good sign. Taken together, they would most certainly constitute a run of good luck. He counted to three and suddenly turned his head to look at Angel. She was leaning against the counter, a smile on her lips. Her eyes were closed. Max sighed and returned to his table. Next to him, two guys in their early 20's were playing a half-hearted game of nine-ball. Their hairy, skinny legs stuck out of big shorts that ended just below their knees, and their hair looked like it had been subjected to a pint of Vitalis. Max looked at them and sighed, shaking his head. He decided that their names must be Biff and Graham. He briefly considered waiting until they left the club and running them down with his car. But he knew that with his luck his tires would slip and slide in the oil pool left by their hair and go crashing through the plate glass window of the K-Mart across the street. Why couldn't she just have had her eyes open?

Across the room, the pay phone mounted on the wall around the corner from the men's room started ringing. The two players closest to it looked at each other then back at it, as if playing a mental game of scissors and rock. One of them lost, because he reluctantly walked over and picked it up. "Yeah," he said wearily, as if answering the call were the greatest favor he had done in a decade. "Uh, hang on a second and I'll look." He pressed the receiver against his chest to cut off the sound of his voice. "Hey Carl," he called. "You here?"

Carl looked up from his shot. His cheeks turned ruddy. "No," he said.

The player put the phone back to his mouth. "No ma'am, he don't seem to be here. Sorry about that. Okay, I sure will." He hung up the phone. "She says if I should happen to see you sometime tonight on these premises, I should ask you to call your loan officer."

Carl lined up his shot and stroked the cue, but neither the cue ball nor the seven touched the rail. A scratch.

Joe smirked, and Carl's eyes snapped to him. Joe slapped Carl lightly on the back. "I used to have an old horse I had to keep a tight rein on," Joe said. "She thought she was in complete control, but all I had to do was just pull them reins up tight, and she'd do anything I'd tell her to. Just snapped straight to it."

"Is there supposed to be a point to that story?" Carl asked.

"What?" Joe asked innocently. "Nah, I'm just talking about a horse I kept under a tight rein. That's all."

Smith watched Joe thoughtfully. He hadn't caused any trouble all night, but Smith was disturbed by the cowboy's talk and manner. Joe was the closest thing Smith had to a friend so far in Amarillo, and that in itself was a depressing thought. He wished Carl hadn't been so unhappy to see him, but to tell the truth if he had been happy it would have put Smith out of sorts. It had been so long since he had a true friend that he wouldn't have known what to do with one. In the lines of work he had pursued for almost three decades, friends were more of a liability than an asset. For armed robbers and pool hustlers, the ability to leave a place quickly and without notice had a certain advantage. Tonight for the benefit of the other three he had dulled down his skills, sometimes missing shots that he could normally have made blindfolded with a mop handle. But now he was growing tired, and the brick wall between him and Carl was hurting more than he would have thought anything could. When his turn came he ran the table, putting the eight ball in.

"Now that's what I call a great goddamn shot," Freddie slurred. Smith had watched him grow drunker and drunker as the evening passed. Now it was a miracle he was still on his feet. His eyelids drooped, and it took him two or three seconds to register anything said to him. This was another reason Smith was pulling back his game, to give Carl and Freddie a chance to win occasionally. As Freddie grew drunker, it took all Smith's skill to lose games.

"Thanks," he said. "Fellows, I think this one's it for me."

"Yeah, me too," Carl said. "Come on, Freddie. Let's settle up with Angel and go home."

"Shit, man, I could play one or two—you know, fuck, it's too early to—" Freddie swayed on his feet. "I mean, hell, I could play another game or two. How about you, Joe? You ain't gonna pussy out on me, are you?"

Joe put his hand in the small of his back and stretched. "Sorry hoss," he said, "I think I'm going to call it a night."

"Heading for home?"

"Oh, eventually." He looked at Carl and then popped the pearl snap on the breast pocket of his denim shirt. He thumbed a cigarette from the pack he kept there and lit it with an old-fashioned lighter, the kind with a top that snapped open with a metallic click. He spun the wheel and the flame leapt up. He snapped the lid shut and sucked on the cigarette with his eyes closed. "First, though, I'm going over to this little motel I know about on the Dumas Highway. There's a little old Mexican whore there that sucks my dick like she's a fucking Hoover. Then I guess I'll head home to the little wife."

Silence settled over the table. Even Freddie realized that something uncomfortable was happening, although he couldn't exactly pin down what was wrong. He looked at the tip of his stick and rubbed some chalk on it. Smith glanced around at the other tables, checking out his options, deciding if he needed to leave. Joe stared straight into Carl's brown eyes, the right side of his mouth lifted in a smile that had no humor in it.

"Yeah," he said. "This little old wetback has titties like you've never seen, I mean just big as can be, and a narrow little ass like a girl's. I been telling her for months she ought to give it up for free cause I'm most definitely the best thing she's ever had up her snatch or in her mouth. But you know what she says?" Joe smiled directly at Carl now, moving closer to him, invading his space. "She says—" Joe put on a broad Mexican accent, the kind dubbed into the mouths of Italian actors in old spaghetti westerns. "She says 'no meester, I sharge you double cause you so focking beeg.'" He laughed and drew on his cigarette. "Yeah, I tell you what, time this little old whore turns eighteen, she's gonna be top of the line with a teacher like me." Joe stared at Carl, just two feet away, his eyes like a glove slapping against Carl's cheek, leaving a red slash.

Smith shifted his weight and moved closer to the two men. "Carl. Look, why don't you settle up, like you said? Just take it on home. Freddie too."

Joe reached out his hand and almost gently put the tips of his fingers on Smith's chest. "I think you need to stay out of this," he said.

"Who the fuck is this guy?" Carl asked Smith. "I mean, in what quarry did you find the rock that he crawled out from under?"

"Hey Carl, wasn't we leavin'?" Freddie asked.

"What are you talking about rocks? I hope you're not talking about me. I mean, that wouldn't be nice at all." Joe moved an inch closer to Carl, taking a tighter grip on the cue stick.

The players at two of the tables flanking them had stopped their games and were looking at their neighbors, the smell of fear and anger like the stench of cordite in the air after a gun is fired. Carl looked around at them. "I got better things to do with my time than to think about somebody like you."

"What's the matter with you, man?" Joe grinned, flicking his eyes at his audience. "You think there's something wrong with the way I get my pleasure? I ain't hurting nobody. This little spic likes to give up her pussy to me for a few dollars, who's to say there's anything wrong with that?"

Carl swallowed. Fear started to rise into his gorge along with the anger, and he could feel his balls pulling up into his body. He didn't think Joe was stupid enough to start a fight here in public, but the man was obviously a rabid dog, totally unpredictable. "I just think—"

"What? You just think what? You don't like what I'm saying, just say so. I hear it's a free country."

Completely against his will, Carl could feel a wetness start in his eyes, and suddenly he needed to urinate very badly. Don't show him any weakness, he thought. Don't do it!

"All right," he said. "I don't like it."

Joe laughed, a booming bark of derision. "Shit, boy, we can tell that. We're past that part. Question now is, what the fuck are you going to do about it? I mean, the question we all need an answer to," and he looked around at the growing number of people watching, "is how big a set of balls do you have? That's what we're all wondering about."

Behind the counter, Bailey's canine radar had already discerned a disturbance in her universe. She opened her eyes and unwound the muscular springs in her body, standing up and putting her front paws on the counter. It was four feet from the floor, and her shoulders and head easily cleared the top. When Bailey moved, Angel stopped what she was doing and focused on the group of four. She had felt nothing bad from either Carl or Smith, but she knew Freddie had a tendency to be a drunken fuck-up, and her eye had been on Joe since he had first crossed her threshold. She couldn't hear the exchange of words, but Angel could read bodies like a trucker reads a road map. The tension, she decided, had not yet reached dangerous proportions, and she hesitated to intervene until a situation was almost at the boiling point. She believed that most men had matured little since the first grade schoolyard, where they would bluster and bully each other then back away with snarled epithets, not once touching their opponents.

Bailey turned her head and looked at Angel, her eyes bright with anticipation, her eyebrows raised in a strangely human gesture. "I don't think so," Angel said. "Not just yet." Bailey chuffed through her lips.

Joe refused to let go of Carl's eyes. Every time the older man's eyes strayed Joe spoke, forcing them back to his face. "You know, the thing about it is, it's her job and I pay her for it. And she likes it. I mean, I'm a welder. That's not a job you can like. But how can you not like getting fucked for a living?" He smiled and looked around, as if what he said made perfect sense. "You got a job, don't you? You just probably don't have as much fun on yours as she does. What do you do, anyway?"

Don't answer, Carl thought. You don't have to talk to him. Just walk away. "I own my own business."

"Oh yeah, doing what?"

Carl looked away at Freddie, at Smith, at the players nearby. "Uh," he said. "Making draperies."

Jesus Christ, Smith thought.

Joe grinned broadly, pleasure written all over his face. "Making draperies! Man, it sounds like you probably like to suck dicks, too. I never heard of a man before that made drapes for a living."

His parents' company, Smith thought to himself. Goddamnit, Carl, why are you taking this?

"Look, back off, okay?" Carl could feel his eyes tearing up more.

"Oh look, honey, you don't have to cry about it. You want me to back off, why don't you just make me? I ain't that tough. Come on." He stepped closer to Carl until their faces were less than a foot apart.

Bailey growled and looked up at Angel, unwilling to move until she was given permission but nonetheless begging and pleading with her friend. Angel looked at the men, who had now captured the attention of most of her more sober patrons. From only a handful of tables could the sound of clicking balls still be heard. She nodded her head. "Okay," she said, her voice soft and low.

Immediately Bailey gathered her powerful legs and silently leapt up onto the counter then off onto the floor just as silently. Deliberately, very slowly, her eyes never wavering from her prey, she began stalking her way toward the cluster of men.

There was no smile on Joe's face now. The stick was held tighter in his hand, his eyes focused on Carl's with a pale green light that was frightening. "You want to fuck with me, do it," he said in a low voice. "Oh, but I better not use that word, huh? You might take me literal, drapery-hanging fellow like you. You might just take that as an invitation to suck my dick yourself. And we sure couldn't have that, could we?"

Carl's guts roiled. "Why don't you just quit? There's no point in this."

Joe's voice lowered almost to a whisper. "Says who? The point is, this is fun. I'm enjoying the hell out of it. It's almost as good as fucking that little girl, and the only thing that could make it better is—"

At first Joe didn't know exactly what was happening. He was aware that Carl was forced back away from him, surprise on his face. Joe could feel something next to his legs pushing on him, a sensation that was like a cat gliding its way around his boots, except it was much bigger and harder and not as flexible. He looked down to see what was interrupting his rhythm, what was spoiling his evening. At the level of his waist he stared into a pair of cold yellow eyes in a dark face, a face that was triangular in shape, covered with gray fur, a face that to Joe looked like it had come straight up through the floorboards from the gates of hell. As if in slow motion, the wolf's head started to rise up toward him, getting closer and closer until he could see every hair on its head, could see his own death reflected in its cold stare. At first he was struck with the improbable idea that it would reach for his crotch and rip his balls off, and his hand went to his pants to protect himself. Bailey's head pushed his arm aside as if it were nothing, of no more consequence than a mosquito. She seemed to put no effort into the movement, but his hand went flying away and hit the edge of the table, barking his knuckles painfully. She rose to her full height and placed her paws onto his chest, then very slowly pressed her face closer to his. As she did her lips curled back, revealing black gums and a set of teeth shocking in their number, length, and sharpness. Her nose a bare two inches away from his, she very softly began to growl.

When Bailey stood up Joe leaned back until his butt was pressed up against the rail of the table. Bailey pushed on his chest, and Joe was forced to lean one hand back to support himself. Smith and Carl had immediately given them room. Freddie, noticing several seconds later what was happening, staggered to a stool against the wall where he collapsed, the back of his neck against the shelf where drinkers put their beer mugs.

Joe very quietly, very carefully trying not to move his lips, said, "Get this fucking thing off of me!" By now there was no other noise in the pool hall. The final players had noticed what was happening and ceased their motion, afraid that the slightest movement would attract Bailey's attention and make them her next target.

Joe's eyes flicked from side to side, pleading for help. He was afraid to move his head. All he could see from the corners of his eyes were the wolf's paws on his chest, their black claws looking wickedly sharp. Straight in front of him Bailey's teeth and eyes were the only thing in his line of vision, the long whiskers on her snout trembling. He could feel her growls vibrating into his chest, spreading through his whole body. Her warm, meaty breath assaulted his nostrils.

"Is anybody listening to me?" he asked, slightly louder. "Get it off me!"

Angel stood calmly behind the counter, both hands resting on top of it. When she spoke her voice was low; the hall was absolutely silent but for Bailey's growling. "The last time I looked," she said, "it was Bailey's name on the window, and mine on the checks. I don't see anything that says 'Joe' on it. You don't give orders in here. You understand?"

Joe nodded slowly. "Get it off," he managed to say again, his voice choked.

Angel shook her strawberry blond hair out of her eyes. Despite the calm in her voice, the corners of her mouth were turned down in anger, and the lines on the outside of her eyes showed white. "The trouble with Bailey is, she's got a real sensitive nose. She can smell an asshole a mile off." She paused a moment. Bailey never moved away from Joe's face. "Now I want you to take your loud voice and your ugly manners and get out of my pool hall. And you'd better hope I don't see your face again." She paused before saying "Bailey."

At the sound of her name the wolf dropped her paws to the floor, turned her back on Joe, and padded back to the counter which she landed on in one smooth bound. She turned back to watch Joe, her hackles standing straight up.

Joe looked around at the other players, trying to gather up the remains of his dignity. He tucked his shirt in and brushed off his sleeves. Despite his show of arrogant indifference, his face was a mask of red rage and fear.

"We're all waiting," Angel said.

"Goddamn it, I didn't do nothing. This ain't legal!"

"There's the pay phone. I'm pretty sure 911's a free call, though."

Joe looked wildly around, trying to gather support for his cause, but no eyes would meet his except Smith's, who shrugged. Shaking with rage, Joe started to walk toward the door. "You're going to regret this," he said. "You and that fucking mutt."

Still standing on the counter, Bailey lowered her head and slit her eyes. She bared her teeth again and growled at Joe, her body ready to spring forward at his slightest motion in her direction.

"You'd better check my pulse," Angel said. "I think I just died of fright."

Walking sideways like a crab scuttling along the beach, Joe reached the door, his eyes never leaving the wolf. He pulled the door open and disappeared through it. Silence covered the pool hall like a blanket over a smoking fire. All eyes stared at the front, where Bailey still stood on the counter watching the door. Angel stretched her hand toward the wolf's neck. At her touch, Bailey dropped down to the floor behind the counter and gracefully lowered herself down as if nothing had happened.

Angel's eyes swept across her patrons. "It's your time you're paying for. I'd hate to see you waste it." She looked up to find Max Friedman staring at her, his cue stick relaxed in his hand. She looked back at him and raised her eyebrows as if to say, "You got a comment?" He shook his head and bent down for his shot.

The noise level began to rise again as the room turned its attention back to the games at hand, and Joe faded from the players' memories. At the tables near where he had been, a few curious players still glanced at Smith, Freddie, and Carl, trying to reconstruct what had happened, to figure out what had caused Bailey's wrath to come crashing down on Joe so suddenly.

Freddie stared around him uncomfortably. "Hey man, I got to take a leak," he said. "Hell, if Angel charged for that instead of beer, she could retire and move to Hawaii." He put his hand against the table to steady himself and walked slowly toward the men's room, moving with the forced dignity of someone desperately trying not to fall over.

"Nice friends you have these days," Carl said.

"I just met him here tonight, Carl. Look, what the hell was that all about when I came over here? The last time I saw you, we were friends."

"Yeah we were," Carl said bitterly. He kept his voice low. "But then, the last time I saw you, I wasn't sharing a cell in Abilene, either, was I? And that's exactly where I was three months after you skipped town. So that's what the hell it was all about."

"Oh, Jesus Christ. Was it—it was that gas station thing?"

Carl laughed bitterly, a short bark. "Oh yeah, that was it. 'That gas station thing.' Except to me it was two years of my goddamn life, hearing the bars slam shut every night, the moaning of guys beating off in the cells around me, the screams from the showers where some fish was getting raped. It was getting blood on me in the goddamn yard, when some cholo stuck another one cause they were arguing over a pack of cigarettes. That's what that little gas station thing meant to me."

"Carl, I didn't know. I mean—"

Carl leaned in to him, sneaking glances around to see if anyone was listening. "Of course you didn't know. Because you left town two days after we did it. Let the Mexican kid take the rap. My parents couldn't even hold up their heads in this town after that, their business dropped off by half for the next three years because their son let some punk talk him into taking off a gas station."

"The gun wasn't even loaded."

"You think they gave a shit? It was still armed robbery, and it was worth two years. And every single day of those two years I dreamed about loading that fucking gun and blowing your brains out."

"Shit Carl, I'm sorry. I—how are your parents?"

Carl smiled. "They're dead. I couldn't look my father in the eye until the day he died. The next time I looked him straight in the eyes, they were closed."

Smith blew the air out of his lungs. "Carl, I'm real sorry."

"The next time you say that I swear I'll crack your skull open with a stick, like your little pal was ready to do to me."

Smith squeezed his eyes shut. There was a pain behind them that was steadily increasing, showing no signs of going away. "All that stuff's behind me now. I'm not going to—"

"Good for you. Look, I'm leaving. And if you ever see me again, do me a favor. Just forget we ever met. My wife doesn't know about this, my daughter doesn't know, and that's the way it's going to stay. As far as I give a rat's ass, I've never seen you before in my life. Understand?"

"Yeah." There was nothing Smith could say. He knew Carl was right, knew that he had been a fuck-up, that he had used people. All he wanted was to apologize and make things right. But Carl obviously wanted nothing of it.

Carl pulled some bills out of his pocket and tossed them on the table. "You decided you wanted to come over here and play, so you can settle the bill. I am going to take my fuck-up brother-in-law, if he can still walk, and pour him into the car and drop his worthless ass off on his front porch for his wife to deal with." He hitched up his pants and stalked out the front door past Max, who watched him leave, past Angel, who glanced at him. A few minutes later Freddie Odom walked out of the men's room, his fly gaping open. He went back to the table and looked for Carl, his head slowly rotating.

"He already left," Smith said. Freddie's eyes fixed on the men's room door and he started listing in that direction. "Front door," Smith said, and gently turned him around.

"Oh yeah," Freddie said, and a minute later made it through the door after two attempts to pull instead of push.

Max watched him, thinking "there but for the grace of God," and racked his set of balls back into their homes, as cozy as eggs in a carton. He strolled to the counter.

"Have fun?" Angel asked.

"As a matter of fact, I did. Entertaining little floor show Bailey put on."

"Par for the course around here. Some little petty asshole tyrant forgets that he's not in his own kingdom anymore, and wants to make the rules here. That won't work."

"I can see that." He leaned his back to the counter and breathed deeply, surveying the surroundings. He took in the dogs playing pool, the wooden floor, the posters on the wall, and the proprietor. "I'll see you again." As he walked toward the door, he almost thought he heard her say "good." But he could have been mistaken.

He stood on the sidewalk and stretched his arms luxuriously under the full moon and banquet of stars. The freezing sand storm that had accompanied his entry to the town was only a memory. Since then the weather had been beautiful—dry and golden days where the warm sun gently teased through his shirt and bathed his skin. Whenever he left the courthouse he wanted to be stretched out on a beach somewhere, reading a good book. Wishful thinking; the nearest beach was 650 miles away. He had checked the map.

The wooden door behind him opened and a man came out. Max recognized him as one of the four who was at the table where Bailey had set matters straight. It wasn't the one who had tried to fuck with Max; he had already left, under the watchful golden eyes of the wolf. The other two had also left. In this man's carriage and eyes, Max recognized the demeanor of the professional criminal. Not the crack addicts who snatched chains and killed their grandmothers for chump change, the ones whom Max had watched entering the Manhattan courtrooms in a never-ending parade. No, this man had the look of one of the Mafia men in their thousand dollar suits who frequented the social clubs in Little Italy with far more frequency than the courtrooms. When on occasion they did land in front of a judge they were whisked quickly away by a cadre of lawyers.

This man, the one who now stood on the sidewalk outside Bailey's, was like the best of the mobsters. Some of them had the twitchy kind of energy which marked them as doomed in their chosen life style. The others, the old-timers, had a core of white flame inside them that was almost palpable. They kept their own secrets, exposing nothing. This was the kind of man who stood on the sidewalk outside Bailey's, instinctively moving away from the light leaking out of the windows. He saw Max, looked him over, assessed him, and nodded.

"How are you?" Max said.

The man nodded again, as if to say pretty good. "Yourself?"

"I think I'm doing well today. Who knows what tomorrow will bring?"

"You're not from around here, I guess." Smith wasn't asking a question.

"What, did my poorly disguised New York accent give me away?"

Smith smiled. "It's a little different, I'll say that."

"I like a man who appreciates good understatement."

They stood for a moment, absorbing the night. "How about you? Texan by birth, by heart?"

"Both, I guess. Come from Amarillo, but it's been a while since I was here. Just moved back." A raucous laugh from inside the pool hall broke the tranquil night. "I guess I'll head home," Smith said. "Good night now."

"Maybe I'll see you here again," Max said.

"It's likely." Smith nodded his head at Max and headed for his car. Max closed his eyes, drawing the already cooling air deep into his lungs, and did the same.

Chapter 7

Diane DiAngelo didn't know which she hated more: knee-jerk bleeding heart liberals; her ex-husband Michael, a worthless loafer if ever there was one, who might even now be lurking about some curtained booth scheming to vote a straight Democratic ticket; the scumbag criminals she spent every day sending to prison, and good riddance to them; or just plain old fashioned whiners. Actually, her hierarchy of whom she despised the most depended on who was closest to her at the moment with the exception of Michael, for whom she was convinced there already awaited a high-chair in hell with his name on it.

As she sat in the big chair behind her hopelessly piled-up desk, whiners were at the top of her shit list. She cradled the telephone receiver between her right shoulder and ear, her earring lying on the desk. The earring coordinated perfectly with the cautious blue suit she had bought on a shopping trip to Dallas the month before. It was conservative yet displayed the shapely legs that had helped her get elected head cheerleader her junior and senior years at Caprock High School. Several years later those legs, combined with her exquisite face, dark blonde hair, and a desire to win anything at any cost, had helped her land the title of Most Beautiful Coed at the University of Texas. The honor was bestowed by the members of the Texas Cowboys, a group of undergraduate boys whose ostensible reason for existence was to escort the school's mascot, a longhorn steer. Their primary occupation, however, was drinking, raising hell, and yelling loudly at football games—preferably all at the same time. When she graduated third in her class from UT's School of Law, she did it strictly on brains and discipline, realizing that her beauty would count for little in that competitive circus.

Diane played with the loose earring, spinning it one direction and then the other. She rolled her eyes back into their sockets, a childhood habit she had been unable to shake despite knowing that it momentarily made her look much less beautiful.

"Look," she finally said into the phone, "will you stop crying long enough to listen to me? No! Just stop it. In the first place, I don't give a damn if we did go to high school together; I said I'm not going to—"

A light tap sounded at her open office door. A tall man with graying hair and a bushy mustache stood in the doorway. Champ Phillips' gentle eyes gave him a slightly hound dog expression. He wore a white shirt with the long sleeves rolled up onto his muscular forearms. To the left of his belt buckle was clipped a badge, and on the right side just above his hip a pistol rode snugly in its holster. In one hand he held a white take-out bag from a coffee shop.

Diane impatiently waved him into her office. He sat down opposite her desk, stretching his long legs, and removed a takeout coffee cup from the bag which he set on the floor by the chair. He cracked the tab on the lid and blew through it gently and then put the cup on her desk.

Her face getting redder by the moment, Diane said "Childhood mischief? Beverly, let me clue you in on something. 'Childhood mischief' is when your kid makes skid marks on his neighbor's sidewalk with his bicycle. If you'd have put skid marks on his butt when he was smashing mail boxes with a baseball bat two years ago, you wouldn't be packing his little suitcase for the juvenile center now!"

Diane's voice was getting more and more strident, and her rich West Texas twang, by her preference often undetectable, began to sneak out. Champ's eyes traveled around her office walls, taking in the array of perfectly ordered books arranged by discipline and alphabetized by the author's last name. A photograph of her with U.S. Senator Kay Bailey Hutchison hung on the wall behind her desk; the senior senator was listening avidly, lips pursed, while Diane made a point—two former cheerleaders who had used their iron wills to climb the ladder of success.

"And let me tell you something else, Beverly. Joy-riding may sound cute to you, but the State of Texas calls it car theft, and you can wave goodbye to him for a year!" She slammed the phone back onto its cradle and carefully replaced her earring. Raising her hand to the back of her neck and her shoulders, Diane began massaging them. "God, I've got a headache coming. You bring me one?" she asked, nodding at his cup. Champ reached into the bag and placed a second cup on her desk. She pulled the lid off and threw it into the trashcan.

"Fine, thank you," Champ said. "And how 'bout yourself?"

Diane narrowed her eyes. "Don't start with me." She took a sip of the coffee and made a sour face. Reaching inside the drawer of her desk, she pulled out a half-full packet of Sweet 'n' Low and poured it into the coffee. She sipped again, closed her eyes and leaned backwards, resting her neck on the chair back. After a moment she opened her eyes and looked at him, an elusive smile playing across her lips.

"Sorry. This is just one of those bad—" She waved her hand in the air, palm up, her long fingernails painted a light blue.

"Days, cases, lifetimes?" Champ finished.

"Yeah, whatever."

"You really think busting his ass would have kept him out of the news?"

"Shit, probably not," Diane said. "Beverly would have got to liking it too much. She was mean as hell ever since she moved here from Plainview in the sixth grade."

Champ leaned back thoughtfully. "Could be she was too heavy on his hiney, and that's what did it in the first place."

Diane was searching in her desk drawer for something to stir her coffee with. She stopped and looked up directly at him, her eyes as cool a shade of blue as her suit. "Do you need a tourniquet, Champ? I can hear the drip drip drip of your bleeding heart all the way over here."

Champ sat quietly, blew on his coffee, and took another sip. He had twenty years on the police force, the last five as a lieutenant, and his quietly patient manner had led to more confessions than his colleagues who raged and threatened. Diane had been with the Potter County District Attorney's office for nine years; it was her first job after graduating from law school. It annoyed her that he always made her feel like a little girl throwing a tantrum.

"All right," she gave in, "this must be some kind of record for me. Two apologies in one day, and to the same person. God, humility's a bitch, isn't it? I'm sorry. Okay?"

Under his bushy mustache the outer corners of Champ's lips turned up slightly, and his eyebrows went up with them.

"Why is it," Diane said, "that you have the ability to make me feel like such an idiot sometimes? Don't answer that. I think I've been off kilter ever since we lost Kimbrough last week. God, that pissed me off! I thought we had him."

"So did I. Jury saw it different."

"Did they ever. Bunch of stupid—all right, all right. It's over. Get past it." She stood up and looked out the window. "How is it out there? Hot?"

"Sixty-five. One of those beautiful Amarillo days."

"That makes what, about ten of them this year? I think we're over our quota. How are you doing on that homeless guy got stabbed by the tracks?"

"Just him, getting colder every day."

"Shit. Guy who did it's probably out of state by now, if he's smart. Maybe we should forget it. What do you think?" She opened a file folder. Her blue shoes were underneath the desk, and she rubbed her silk-stockinged feet against each other.

Champ looked down at his hands, the forefinger of his right carefully tracing a vein on the back of his left. "I think that when this guy was a little boy, he probably had a momma who loved him. I think I'd like to find out who he is, and who killed him. I'd want somebody to do it for me."

Diane sighed. "All right, but just make sure you keep on the other cases. But you always do. So did you come by just to visit today?"

"Yeah, just social. You trying that Skeffington burglary case today? How's that going?"

Diane shook her head emphatically. "No problem. Won't take me long to slam the cell door on him."

Champ finished his coffee and tossed the cup into the trash. "Well, I guess if the county's gonna pay me, I'd better start working. Anything you need from me in the next couple of days?"

Diane was already buried in a file folder. Keeping her eyes on the paper, she waved her hand. "No, I'm fine. Don't sweat it."

Champ stood, adjusted his pistol, and headed for the door. "I'll try to stay calm."

Just before he disappeared, Diane's voice stopped him. "Hey Champ?"

He turned and looked at her.

"Thanks for the coffee," she said, and offered up a smile that would melt the hardest heart.

"My pleasure," he said, and walked out the door.

Judge Edna Gandy peered down from her bench, holding the verdict in her hand. She passed it back to the bailiff who returned it to the jury foreman. The judge was the only black woman on the bench in the Texas Panhandle, and she took not only her position but the honor of holding it quite seriously. The only time her job was difficult was on days that she saw a face in front of her that was so familiar it might have appeared in her family album.

"Mr. Foreman, would you please read your verdict?"

The foreman nervously swiped his hand across the twenty strands of hair that ineffectively hid his bald spot. "We the jury find the defendant guilty of burglary."

"Thank you," the judge said. "You are dismissed." She turned her attention to the young, slightly jittery white man standing at the defendant's table. "Mr. Skeffington, it would be nice if I didn't recognize you so readily. You've made more appearances in this courtroom than I have. Sentencing next Monday at 10:00 a.m."

Max Friedman turned to his client and attempted to get the young man's eyes focused on his face. "I'm sorry, Jeff," he said. "I did my best."

"Oh it's cool, man," Jeff said. "You're a hell of a lot better than that last public defender I had. That guy? What a dipshit! Hey, when I get out, maybe I'll give you a call."

"Only if you need to."

"Oh, it ain't no question of *if*, man. This is about *when*." Two deputies arrived at his side and snapped on a set of handcuffs. "How you boys doing?" Jeff said as they led him away. "Good to see you again." They led him out of the courtroom. Max picked up a notepad and several pens that he had scattered on the defense table, loading them back into the leather shoulder bag he used for a briefcase. He loosened his tie and bent his neck from side to side, trying to work out the cricks in it.

"You might send him a dictionary when he settles down into the Ellis unit. That way he can look up 'habitual criminal.' If he can read." Max took in the District Attorney in her blue suit and perfect blonde hair, which was almost as big as the girls' he used to see at the malls on Long Island. Beautiful women often made him nervous, and he wasn't quite sure what to do and where to look.

"Thanks for the advice," he said. "I'll sneak one into a cake with the file."

Diane swung her calfskin briefcase from her right to her left hand. "Don't feel bad. No one could have gotten him off."

There had been few observers in the courtroom; this was a case that had excited no interest. They were alone. Max finished putting his materials back into their proper places. "Do I look like I feel bad?"

"Well, I guess I took you for one of those civil rights types who wants them all out on the streets."

"Looks can be deceptive," Max said, as he pulled his hair out of its ponytail and shook it smoothly onto his shoulders.

Diane looked at his hair, a flicker of disgust briefly visiting her face. "Yes, well, I've had to fight that all my life, people not knowing there was more to me than meets the eye."

"What happened, they mistook you for someone with compassion?"

Diane stepped back from him, the shock in her face disappearing beneath a carefully studied mask of indifference. "You know," she said, "I don't think I like you very much."

"Good. Because that's not what my clients pay me for."

Diane slid her lower lip under the edge of her front teeth and thoughtfully squeezed a moment. "Well. I'll probably see you again, if you plan to stick around." She started walking down the center aisle between the benches toward the courtroom door and then turned and walked a few steps backward as she addressed him. "And by the way, that barber's strike y'all must have had up in New York? It never took hold down here. You want to play the game, it's best to wear the uniform." She went through the door, and Max was alone.

Amazing, he thought. I've just been told by the District Attorney to get a haircut. Maybe I'd better just go the whole nine yards, and take a shower before I see her again. He sat on the edge of the table and said a slow serenity prayer, praying that his anger would be removed. His eyes slowly surveyed the room, taking in the dark wood of the rail, the jury box, the bench. He loved the majestic courtrooms in Manhattan, hated the cold beige boxes in Brooklyn and Queens. You couldn't practice law in a space that had no respect for itself. This was a good room. Five minutes later, feeling centered once again, he left and went home.

Chapter 8

Smith Dixon locked the door of his cabin at the Ace Courts. The Ace was a run-down motel that had probably been around when the Dust Bowl immigrants passed through Amarillo on Route 66 and was most likely shabby even then. Several cars that had little chance of ever running again were scattered here and there throughout the horseshoe-shaped enclosure. At the Ace, there were no neighbors; most folks there kept their own company. As he locked the door, he wanted to laugh. The downside of living at the Ace was that security was a joke; the upside was that no one who lived there owned anything worth stealing.

Smith had thought of finding the key for his father's house and moving in there but finally decided against it. Since the old man was still alive, it didn't technically belong to Smith, and besides, he didn't like the thought of sleeping in the house. What was he going to do, stay in his old bedroom, if there was still a bed in it? Sleep in the room where his parents had conceived him? It didn't feel comfortable. He was used to the shabby anonymity of places like the Ace. For almost thirty years, he had practiced being so nondescript that no one would ever notice him, and his present home was a perfect complement. It was a place nobody noticed. He bet that not one out of ten natives of Amarillo would be even vaguely familiar with it.

Smith got into his LTD and made the trip to the hospital, as he did every morning. He passed through the lobby unnoticed, another concerned family member blending into the stream of visitors, a man in worn jeans and a corduroy jacket.

He sat next to his father's bed, this time reading a novel he had purchased in the gift shop, It was a simple mystery, but he sometimes had to read a page three or four times before it sunk in. He read it here at the hospital and at night in his room if he didn't go to Bailey's. Soon he would have to find another one.

And a job. He kept his meager savings, left over from a payroll truck he had robbed in Denver, in a safe deposit box in a downtown bank. It hadn't netted him as much as he hoped, and after he split it with two partners it hadn't seemed worth it. Smith had decided to go back to pulling jobs on his own after that, like he used to, even if they were smaller. One of his partners had been squirrely, and the other certifiably crazy, and he had been afraid to turn his back on them. Smith never got around to pulling a job on his own, however. He lived for a while on the payroll money, and one day as the sun rose above the horizon he looked through the window of his efficiency apartment and knew, somewhere deep down, that he had to leave the road and return to Amarillo. He had almost slipped once, at the little one-stop robbery shop up near Clayton. He hadn't needed the money; he was just so used to robbery that he could barely help himself. It was only a last moment gasp of courage that had kept him from taking off the cash register.

Smith shook his head to clear out these thoughts. They didn't do him any good and probably a lot of harm. His father lay in the bed, still not moving. Smith watched periodically for the slightest sign of life, hoping that one day the old man would suddenly open his eyes and start talking, like a cop he had read about in the paper, a man who after being shot in the forehead by a drunk didn't speak for 7 1/2 years. His father never moved. Occasionally he would twitch his eyes, but it seemed only a reflex. The doctors said that eventually, if he lived that long, he would start curling up into the fetal position.

The door opened and a nurse bustled in, an overweight woman in her late 40's. She smiled at Smith, checked his father's I.V., and arranged the bed sheets. "No matter how early I get here," she said, "I find you already just sitting here. So many of the older folks, they get dropped in on once or twice a week, if that even." Her voice was exasperated. "But not Mr. Dixon. Bless your heart. Holler if you need something, will you?"

"Sure will." She gave him a sweet smile and moved on to her next room.

Smith put the paperback carefully on the floor beside him, open with the spine facing up. Sometimes when he sat here he felt like crying, something he hadn't done since he was a little boy. He couldn't get over seeing his father so small and weak. The old man lay in the bed wasting away, the arms that had once swung a cleaver with such ease looking thin as an asthmatic child's. Before he started spending his spare time at the pool halls, Smith used to go to the butcher shop after school. He loved the old man, loved the rich meaty smell, the chains of sausage tightly rolled in the cooler. Trying to feel grown up, Smith had stood behind the counter struggling to put his elbows up on it.

The customers, mostly women doing their family's shopping, smiled when they watched the little boy busily helping his father, weighing the meat, wrapping it up, slapping the sticker on the white paper to hold it all together.

He wondered if he would have turned out better if his father had spent more time at home. After closing, the old man had worked in the store cutting up meat for the next day and cleaning up. Smith sat at home, reading comic books and watching *Bonanza* and *Gunsmoke* until he was old enough to hang out with his friends.

Probably not, he thought. Maybe he would have turned out like this anyway. Sometimes he thought maybe it was just hard for his father to be at home, where his momma lived until she ran off. Too many bad memories, maybe. He didn't know. He might've started hanging out anyway, talked Carl into taking off that Phillips 66.

Smith had been stunned to find out that Carl had done time for that. It seemed that nothing had ever turned out in Smith's life the way he had wanted it to. He hadn't meant to spend almost thirty years committing armed robbery, hustling drunks at pool tables in bowling alleys and dusty, back street snooker halls. He hadn't meant to stay away from home for so long, with no more than a birthday card or a telephone call every few years. It had been, as best he could count, eight years since he had called. He was surprised at how quickly the years seemed to accumulate. After what he would have thought was no more than two or three months, he would notice that the Christmas decorations were going up again over the streets of whatever town he was staying in at the moment. And then, too soon, they would come again, and in the meantime all he had done with his life was walk around a table with a pool stick in his hand, picking up five or ten dollar bills from the edge. All he had done was to enter stores with a mask over his face and a gun in his hand.

He thought about Carl again, about the anger in his face when he looked at Smith, and his mind summoned images of Carl in high school—laughing at Coach Tankersley, of the two of them at the rodeo their senior year jeering at the high school cowboys with their jug ears and short hair, the boys they had felt so superior to. Carl had changed, and Smith could not escape the feeling that it was his fault.

He leaned forward and put his face in his hands. He didn't know how long he had sat that way, maybe a minute, maybe an hour, when he heard a woman clear her throat. He looked up slowly and saw her standing in front of him, a young woman with a clipboard, one of those efficient people who have found a way they can function in the world for forty hours a week, working for someone else and liking it. He looked at her and tried to clear the cobwebs from his head.

She wore a lavender dress with shoulder pads, and her black hair was cut short on the sides and back and longer on top. The woman's expression was kindly solicitous, as if she were taking a moment to feel sympathy for the man whose father lay in the bed like one of the slabs of meat he used to cut up. She waited for Smith to greet her, but he kept his own counsel, waiting for her to deliver the message that she had so obviously brought. Finally she smiled a little stiffly. "You're Mr. Dixon?" she asked.

He nodded.

"Well," she said. "I want to say first that Panhandle Memorial Hospital shares your concern over your father's condition, and we're happy to make every effort that is within our ability to help you as much as possible."

I'm fucked, he thought.

"But in going through our records, we have discovered a disturbing situation, and it is imperative that we bring it to your attention immediately."

Smith wondered where a woman like this, who had probably not been to college, just graduated from high school and fell into this job, would learn a word like "imperative." Smith hadn't learned it in high school. Of course, maybe she had actually gone to class. That would make a difference, wouldn't it? Or maybe they had a book with little canned speeches in it, just for delivering bad news. Goddamn it, listen, he thought savagely. What is she saying?

"—and our projections show that the funds will only be sufficient for approximately one more week, at which point they will have to be replaced by private assets. Now this graph here will show you just how much is required both on a daily and a weekly basis. May I?" She indicated the chair next to him. He nodded numbly.

The woman sat down and pointed a lacquered fingernail at a series of figures on the paper. "This is the amount required each week to ensure that your father's upkeep is adequate." The figure $1,000 swam on the paper in front of his eyes, like ants caught in a sudden rain. "Because his insurance policy is exhausted, it will be necessary to find another source for his upkeep. Now, an alternative at this point is to admit him to an elder care facility."

"A nursing home?"

She smiled at him. "We prefer the term 'elder care facility.' That could be accomplished at approximately seven hundred dollars a week."

This was all going too fast for Smith to fathom. "And the insurance will pay for that?"

She smiled sweetly. "No sir, I'm sorry but it won't. However, the financial burden would be less significant." Another of those textbook phrases, he thought. Less significant.

"What do you recommend?" he asked.

"The elder care facility would see to his every need," she said.

"He don't seem to need too fucking much."

The woman hesitated, as if afraid he would suddenly start arguing with her, begin a scene here in the hospital room. He had an image of her hitting the bell for a security officer.

"Mr. Dixon, please understand that I'm trying to help here. That's all."

He nodded his head. "I know that. I'm sorry for what I said. That was out of line."

"Why don't you take a few days to think it over? We don't need an answer today." But by next Monday, he thought, she'll want one thousand dollars in the grasping hand of the hospital.

She stood up and smoothed down the back of her dress, then extended her hand to him. He shook it numbly. "Again," she said, "let me repeat our absolute dedication to working with you on this matter."

"All right."

"If you have any questions, please don't hesitate to call me." She handed him a card that read "Lori Butler, Finance Officer." She smiled at him again and walked efficiently out of the room, expending no more energy than necessary, glancing at the clipboard to see who her next victim was.

Smith massaged his eye sockets with his fingertips. He pictured himself inserting the key that opened his safe deposit box downtown, looking at the stack of bills in it. He thought it was approximately five thousand dollars but was unsure. That meant there was about enough for five more weeks of the hospital or almost two months at the nursing home. He had no job and no prospects that would bring in seven hundred a week, and that was before he bought food or paid his own rent. There was only one way he knew to make that kind of money that quickly. And that was no longer an option for him. At least he hadn't thought so until right now. As he sat and ticked off his alternatives, he realized that he had been right when Ms. Butler walked into the room. He was fucked.

Smith drove on automatic pilot, halfway listening to Joe's story, halfway ignoring it. It went in the right ear and straight out through the left. Smith's thoughts were on the hospital and the news brought by the very efficient, very cold Lori Butler. Ever since he had met her the day before he had been stunned, like a cow that had gotten a glancing blow to the head with a sledge hammer, not quite dead yet, but not really alive either. He kept ticking through the possible ways to make enough money to keep his father in a nursing home. Nothing that flashed into his head was even remotely possible. There was only one place he knew to get money, and that was from those who had it. And there was only one way he knew how to get it from them. The means lay in the trunk of his car, locked in a toolbox.

It had stopped raining only an hour before, leaving a silver patina on the streets. The shower had made the air feel remarkably clean, and Smith rolled down the driver's side window and breathed deeply. As he drove down Wolflin Boulevard, the neon signs from the strip-mall centers reflected off the wet streets, giving everything a surreal, mirrored look. The storm was rolling off to the east toward Fort Worth and Dallas. It was not yet completely dark, and Smith could see the purplish clouds in the sky like a herd of buffalo crossing the plains millions strong, the way they used to more than a century before.

He had no plans for tonight beyond reading a book at home, but when Joe called for some inexplicable reason he said yes. Perhaps he thought that he needed some human contact, to hear a voice other than the one in his head. His judgment had been faulty in that respect. Joe set him on edge. They couldn't go to Bailey's together, and when they tried Amarillo Slim's pool hall it was too full for Joe. He almost created an ugly scene at the counter when he found out the wait could be up to half an hour. Just as well we didn't stay, Smith thought. He would have gotten his ass thrown out of there too, and me along with him, the way my luck's been running.

Joe had an empty beer in his hand and a pinch of snuff tucked into his lip.

As he talked he gestured with his free hand, every few moments raising the bottle to his lips and dribbling his tobacco-laden saliva down the side of it.

"—and neither of us said word one, from the time she give me the come-on 'til I got back in my car. And I mean, right out there in the city park. Man, that was about the best piece of ass I ever had."

"Thought you said that about the housewife when you were a plumber."

"Shit man, which one? There was about a hundred of them. No, hell, they're all good."

Smith slowed for a red light, and on their right they passed slowly by Food Giant, a sprawling supermarket.

"Hey man, pull in here," Joe said.

"What for?"

"Beer and cigarettes, the major food groups. Maybe some Fritos, too."

Smith wheeled his LTD into an angle space in front of the store. They got out, and once again Smith breathed deeply of the damp air. It was at times like these that it felt so good to be home. He would have eaten the air if he could, served it up on a plate with a knife and fork.

"Hey, you coming in, or you going to stand there all night sniffing the air? Looks like you're a dog whuffing for a bitch in heat."

Smith slowly opened his eyes and followed Joe through the automatic doors into the store. A blast of frigid air whooshed out. Supermarkets were always too cold.

He automatically started casing the store, getting a sense of the entrances and exits, the size of the place, the effectiveness of the security system, trying to determine if there were video cameras, whether at this moment he and Joe were on someone's monitor, or if a silent tape were slowly gliding their images through its heads. He wasn't planning on taking off the place; it was just an occupational habit of his, the way that an architect will memorize the lines of a building or a guitar player will watch the way another fingers a chord.

To the right of the entrance was the office with its Plexiglas walls above a metal counter. The safe would be somewhere behind that barrier, either in the floor or a free-standing iron monster. Smith had no ability to crack a safe and had never used any explosives. Neither had been necessary as long as he had a shotgun or a revolver. Most humans were amazingly compliant when they had a round barrel stuck against the skin behind their ear.

Joe headed toward the cooler section and pulled down a six-pack of Pabst. "The working man's beer," he said with a grin. "How many little faggots you think are out there sucking this down right now? Not a goddamn one, I'll tell you that. Too busy sucking dicks. And when their mouths are empty, they're probably sipping one of them European beers."

"Give it a rest, will you?" Smith said.

"Shit, what's the matter with you? You ain't getting enough, are you? I could fix you up if you—hey, look at that!" He lowered his voice and grabbed Smith's elbow.

At the frozen foods section, a blonde woman wearing a red sweat suit was kneeling down on the floor getting a container of yogurt from the bottom shelf. A young girl, the very image of her mother, stood next to her. The sweats clung tightly to the woman's backside, and it was this sight that Joe found so exciting. Smith moved his arm away from Joe's hand. A headache was slowly starting to spider-web its way from his eyes up into the center of his forehead. By the time he went to bed he'd be lucky if he got any sleep.

"Now look at *this*," Joe said. Ahead of them an obese woman was pushing a shopping cart in their direction. She wore jeans and a sweatshirt; the fat on her legs and buttocks stuck out like slabs of meat beneath the jeans, and the roll of fat at her waist jiggled with each step.

"Ugh," Joe said, sticking his tongue out, and twisting his face. "Man, I wouldn't fuck her with *your* dick." He said this in a voice loud enough for the blonde woman with the little girl to hear. Her eyes snapped to him, outrage on her face.

"Watch your mouth," she said. Joe shrugged his shoulders and kept heading toward the snack aisle, the six-pack swinging from his fingers. "Little girl that age," he said to Smith, "she probably hears worse in the schoolyard every day. You know how it is."

Smith was sure he didn't know, at least didn't know how Joe thought things were. Joe grabbed a bag of Fritos. "I'll just get me my cigarettes, and that'll be it," he said. "I wonder who's working the register tonight. Hope she's good looking."

He pulled a wad of money out of the front left pocket of his jeans and counted out twenty dollars for the beer, snacks, and cigarettes. Smith took a small tin of aspirins off the display in front of the register and popped out two of them while Joe was paying. He gathered a mouthful of saliva and tossed them both back, praying that neither one would get stuck. They both slid down. Finally, a piece of luck.

There was only one register working; the other six were closed. The fluorescent light made Smith's head hurt worse, he thought. He was always aware of a slight buzz inside of his head when he was near them.

The cashier wore a red apron, but even through it Joe could see that she had a good-looking body. "How you doing there tonight, baby?"

"I'm just fine, and how are you doing?"

"Feeling a lot better since I seen you, I can tell you that right now."

She totaled up Joe's purchases. "Paper or plastic for you, sir?"

"Neither one." She gave him his change and he stepped away from the register, turning around so that he could still see her. Smith put a dollar in her hand for the aspirin.

The cashier turned to take a longer look at Joe. "I have this feeling that I know you from somewhere . . . ." Her voice trailed off, a question in it.

"Only in your dreams, honey." He winked at her and grinned. Smith joined him.

Joe stopped just in front of the door, pretending to check his receipt, and said in a low voice, "Hey. Look over there."

"What?" Smith said.

"That little prick in the manager's office?"

Smith glanced into the office thirty feet to their left. Behind the glass, a balding man in his early forties was busily performing some type of paperwork.

He looked up at the two of them, and Smith instinctively glanced away. The man immediately returned his eyes to his work.

"What about him?"

Joe stepped onto the mat that automatically opened the doors and out into the clean fresh air, Smith just behind him. "Got me fired, that's what about him."

Smith was surprised. He couldn't picture Joe working at a supermarket. Doing what? Bagging groceries? Testing beer? "You used to work here?" he said.

Joe popped the top off a beer can and took a long, satisfying sip. "Not for the store," he said, rapping the pack of cigarettes against the heel of his hand. He opened it, thumbed one between his lips, and lit it all in one motion. "Few years ago I was having a money squeeze—like I'm still not—and I moonlighted here as a rent-a-cop."

They reached the car and Joe leaned up against it, drawing the smoke deeply into his lungs. He found a fleck of tobacco on his tongue and flicked it away. "Wasn't much to it. Walk around and look like a bad ass." He offered one of the beers to Smith, who took it, pushed the tab in, and began to sip.

"So what happened?"

"Little shit I showed you in there got me canned, is what happened. He complained about me, and they let me go. Son of a bitch has got a lot to answer for someday, cause that was sweet money for just standing around." He put a hand on the car hood and hopped up onto it.

"What'd you do to get fired?"

Joe looked at him sharply, trying to determine if Smith was showing him disrespect. Satisfied, he went back to his story. "Not a goddamn thing, that's what I was doing. Now he said I was harassing women. Said a couple customers complained, and one of the check-out girls."

"That one in there?"

"Hell no. That gal was just starting there back then. I don't think she really remembered who I was. No, them complaints was just a fucking lie, I'll tell you that. That little check-out girl liked me a lot, I could tell from the way she was always looking at me. Them things I said was just fun, you know how that is."

Smith said nothing, just sipped his beer.

"I tell you," Joe said. "You remember about ten years back when that nigger couple up in Washington went on TV about all that shit? Sexual harassment and all that? Since then guys like you and me are having zero fun. They just blow everything up too much, you know what I mean?"

He looked back at the store, brooding. "Tell you what that fucker deserves, is a little midnight visit. Be easy as shit, too."

Smith's professional radar pricked up. He didn't look at Joe but deliberately made both his voice and demeanor casual. "What do you mean?"

Joe laughed. "Hell, what do you think I mean? Somebody could take this place off blindfolded. Get you a nice piece of cash. Now you ain't gonna get rich, but enough so you ain't searching your pockets for beer money for a while at least. Way I see it is, they owe me that money just for the pay I missed. Best thing, though, would be seeing that little fucker get his."

"Yeah," Smith said softly. "What, do they take the deposit at night?"

"No, not until the morning. Nighttime they just lock it into the safe."

"Security system?"

"Not when I was there." Smith's line of questioning sank in, and Joe looked at him with an expression halfway between suspicion and curiosity. "Hey, what're you so interested for?"

Smith pushed away from the car and shook his head. "Nothing," he said. "Idle thoughts. Forget it." He finished the beer. "Man, I think I'm about done for tonight. How about if I drop you back at the house?"

They got in the car and he drove Joe home then headed back to his cabin in the Ace Courts, his mind racing, thinking more quickly than it had in weeks.

Chapter 9

Freddie knew when he got up that it was destined to be a bad day. He wasn't psychic; it just wasn't that hard to guess. Most days weren't very good any more. It was true that sometimes Maggie or Travis did something to warm his heart, and sometimes after the kids were asleep he and Regina had a good time sitting together on the couch and watching Jay Leno. A few times a month they would carry that good feeling into the bedroom where they rocked together in the bed, the clock radio on low, trying to hush the frantic sounds of their lovemaking in such a small house. At times like that, it was almost as good as it had been in high school, when he was playing ball and still had some respect from certain parties, when he was someone who was looked up to as he strutted through the halls of Tascosa High, wearing his letter jacket. It was as good as when he and Regina steamed up the windows of his old '81 Chevy at the fairgrounds. Sometimes when Bernice was out playing bridge they had actually done it in Regina's own bed in the house where Bernice still lived, the house where he could now barely cross the threshold without being looked at like he had AIDS or something.

This morning Regina had smiled at him when he came in for breakfast like she usually did. Although Bernice and Dolores didn't like him, Regina still loved him. She remembered the boy in the letter jacket and how handsome he'd looked in his ivory colored tuxedo the day they got married. She knew he had some problems, but she still loved him. The kids were almost finished with their breakfast when he came in, and they gave him a hug and a kiss.

He hadn't drunk much the night before, so his head didn't feel very fuzzy at all. Regina buttered his toast and cooked him eggs the way he liked them best, scrambled with onions. Despite all this, the kids and Regina and the eggs, his head fairly clear, he just had a feeling that was hanging over him stronger than the aftermath of any drunken binge, that this would be a bad day. He already could feel that the moment he showed up at work, Carl would have some special kind of hell in store for him.

And sure enough, when he pulled into the small parking lot of Puente's Draperies the feeling of foreboding became even stronger. He doused his cigarette in the gravel because he had learned long ago that Carl would give him hell if he carried it into the shop. Carl kept a big sign that said "No

Smoking—Take It Outside!" in the work area, so Freddie slipped out to the side of the building six or seven times a day besides lunch to sneak a Winston.

He walked into the showroom area and Sharon, the cute little cowgirl who worked up front, gave him a quick smile that seemed to hold a heaping dose of pity. She looked away just as quickly as she had smiled.

"Hey sweetheart, what's up?" he said to her.

"S.O.S., darling, same old shit."

Freddie moved up the counter and lowered his voice. "He got a hair up his ass today?"

"Something's boiling, that's for sure. If he was a thermometer, he'd already have mercury spurting out his ears."

"Shit. You know what it's about?"

"No, he hasn't said and we haven't been able to find out anything."

"Bet you one damn thing, bet it's about me."

"Oh, you don't know that, Freddie. Maybe Dolores didn't give him any last night."

"Or maybe she did, that'd be even worse." Freddie tried valiantly not to believe that it was about him although he figured differently, and Sharon rewarded him with a giggle.

"Well," he said, "I guess I'd better go see about it." He lifted the hinged panel in the counter and passed through, entering the door to the workroom.

Carl had five full-time employees including Freddie. The two of them were the only men in the business. Sharon spent most of her time up front, and in the back were three young women who took measurements in homes, and sewed the drapes. Carl had tried Freddie at cutting material, but he had ruined several bolts of cloth and felt embarrassed at doing something he considered a woman's task. Measuring was bad enough, but he did well at it on the days when his head was clear and he didn't have a hangover.

Freddie walked into the work area and saw Carl looking over an order with one of the girls. When he saw Freddie he looked up at the clock. It was five past nine, earlier than when Freddie usually got there. The steady whirr of sewing machines filled the air, and overhead fans turned lazily. Freddie went to his desk and started looking over the orders he had to fill today. He was wishing he could have another cigarette and thinking about going to the communal coffee pot for a stiff cup when he heard Carl call his name. He glanced up, and as soon as he saw the look on Carl's face he knew he was in trouble. Carl jerked his head toward the glassed-in office in the back corner of the work area. "Yeah," Freddie said, "let me get some coffee."

"Get it fast," Carl yelled back and shut the door of the office.

Oh shit, Freddie thought. He knew that it was something big, knew that his intuition this morning was dead on target. He took his time stirring three packets of sugar and some white powder into his coffee, then gathered his balls and walked back to Carl's office, his head held high and his back straight.

He opened the door and stepped in. "Yeah, Carl?"

"Shut the door." Freddie shut it and Carl went on. "The Ekstrands. Remember them?"

"Not offhand, I—"

"Let me refresh your memory. They're the couple you measured last week, and when we went out there yesterday the fucking curtains looked like they were made for someone else's house. Sound familiar now?"

"C'mon, Carl—"

"No, I don't want any of your bullshit. Just tell me what happened. You went out there, you took the measurements, so why don't they fit? And don't tell me the windows moved."

Freddie sighed deeply. "I don't know. I couldn't tell you unless I went out there again. Look, I fucked up, okay? Is that what you want? I did it wrong."

Carl picked up his coffee cup and automatically tried to take a sip but found only a drop left. He looked at Freddie levelly. "You did it wrong *again*, you mean. How many times does this make? I've lost count. Were you drunk when you went out there? Mrs. Ekstrand said she could smell it on you."

"Oh man, I don't need this shit!" Freddie felt like he would cry if this took any longer.

"No," Carl said, "but you do need this job, don't you? So I'm giving you a warning. I don't care what Bernice says about 'family,' once more and you're gone. I'll bounce you straight out of this place for good. Watch yourself."

Freddie stood up and backed away from the desk a step. "Fuck you Carl—"

Carl stood up too and slammed his palm against the desk so hard that everything on it shook. "Don't talk to me like that in my own business! Don't you dare! This is only what, the sixth job you've had in four years?" Freddie stood with his head down, his cheeks red, hands hanging at his sides. "Freddie, I'm talking. Do you hear me?" Carl's voice was so loud that not only could Freddie hear him, but everyone in the workroom and probably down at Bailey's could have, if it had been open this early.

Freddie finally nodded his head. "Yeah. Yeah, I hear you."

Carl was breathing deeply, his chest heaving from the stress of yelling. "Good. Now get back to work. And keep an eye on your cigarette breaks. You're starting to take too many." Freddie didn't reply, just walked out of the office and back to his desk. The phone rang Carl answered it. "Yeah, this is him." He listened for a moment and said, "No, you don't have to do that. No. Look, I'll swing by after work. I can have a hundred for you. Will that be okay? Yeah, I know it's not all, but I mean for today, will it work? All right. I'll be there at six. Yeah, I know. I will." He hung up the phone and looked out into the workroom, where he saw four heads bent to their tasks. He put his head into his hands for several minutes and then went for another cup of coffee. It was all gone, so he had to make a new pot. He considered yelling at Freddie again but decided it wouldn't do as much good as he needed right now.

Chapter 10

The Snazzy Pig Cafe and Bistro was strictly a breakfast and lunch operation. It opened every day at 6:00 for the early birds, serving pancakes and eggs any style, juice and hot coffee, and a small list of hot and cold cereals for those who worried as much about heart attacks as convictions and acquittals.

In the front window was a red neon pig whose left eye winked; the curly tail wagged back and forth. The windows were slatted with blinds for when the sun cleared the tops of the courthouses, bank buildings, and bail bond offices in downtown Amarillo.

Like most cities where cars are the main method of transportation, the traditional downtown section of Amarillo was deserted but for a few buildings. Most of the commerce was contained in the malls or on the other main thoroughfares like Wolflin and Georgia. The civic center brought some traffic downtown, but the old elegant hotels were closed for good. Only pigeons and the homeless lived there; the classiest buildings in town were reduced to a collection of shattered glass covered with boards. Bail bondsmen and the Salvation Army shelter created the texture of the district more than the briefcase brigade that frequented the buildings during the daylight hours.

Breakfast at the Snazzy Pig was slow, a period of leisurely conversations, often between attorneys planning their side's strategies for the day. Half the booths and tables would fill by 7:00 a.m., and precisely an hour later the room would be deserted. The waitresses served coffee and an occasional omelet to the stragglers who wandered in between breakfast and lunch. As soon as lunch started, the aisles between the tables were pandemonium with waitresses carrying their orders to the kitchen window and swinging back again, their arms lined with plates.

At the stroke of noon it was as if someone had opened the gates on a surging river of men and women clad in suits and ties or natty scarves, all with briefcases swinging from their hands or hanging from their shoulders. Within five minutes a small group was waiting just inside the front door, and until 1:00 there was never a moment when attorneys were not waiting for a table. As soon as one was vacated, whoever had been waiting the longest moved to occupy it. There was no waiting list; everyone operated on the honor system. Four years earlier a defense attorney who was especially hungry and was due in court in forty-five minutes snuck to the front of the line and took a table out of turn. No one said anything to him, but he found that from then on not one Assistant District Attorney was willing to make a deal with him on any case. The last anyone had heard, he was doing well with his practice in San Angelo.

Bobby Turner and Jack Ogan had a standing date for lunch on Wednesday that they had seldom broken in the seven years since it had started. They had become good friends when they were both members of the Potter County District Attorney's office. They prosecuted cases together, bowled on the same team, and occasionally by accident swigged from the same bottle of beer. The fact that they now sat on opposite sides of the bench and had ever since Bobby quit the D.A.'s office and went into private practice three years before had not affected their friendship in the least.

"Hell, I don't know why I even bother looking," Jack said as he put down his menu. He loosened his tie and unnotched his belt by one. He was now on the fourth notch since he'd bought it two years ago. "I always get the damn double cheeseburger, fries, and a beer."

"Don't I know it," Bobby said. "It wouldn't hurt you to try something green on your plate once in a while, and I don't mean the pickle. You keep eating like this and you'll drop dead in the courtroom one day. I just hope you'll wait 'til the jury comes in. I'd hate to get a mistrial."

"You're all heart, Bobby." Jack grinned. "Look now, I'll tell you what. We'll let this clown you've got plead to a B and E if you'll—"

"Hell no, I'm not gonna plead," Bobby sputtered. "This is just despicable. It's worse than a Democrat turning Republican. Are you trying to spoil my salad? If you and Diane think you can send this poor boy down the river without a speck of evidence, I just—"

"Now Bobby, you know you don't have a chance in hell of saving this little bastard's—hey, did you hear about Donny Washington?"

Bobby's eyebrows drew together. "Now which way is this train headed? I thought we were talking about my client. And the last I checked, that phrase does not describe Donny Washington, and I hope it never does, either. No, what about him?"

Jack rubbed his hands together. "You're gonna love this. Ready? He beat a charge."

"We've been friends too long for you to lie to me, Jack."

"I kid you not. See that fellow over there by the door? Long hair?"

Bobby craned his neck around and glimpsed Max Friedman. "Oh yeah, I been seeing him around. You're not trying to tell me he convinced a jury that Donny was innocent of something? That boy was born guilty."

"Well I wasn't working the case, but the way I heard it, old Max there practically proved Donny was taking a naked nap at the North Pole when this burglary went down."

"Well I'll be a son of a senator," Bobby said. "This boy bears watching."

"Oh hell yeah. And look, this is just under the table, you got that?"

"Flat on the floor."

"When Diane heard about it, she practically had to go home and change whatever new outfit she was wearing that day."

"She's not a gal who likes being beat," Bobby said.

"She's sure not."

As Max stood waiting for a seat, he balanced a volume of the Texas State Criminal Statutes book in his left hand and took notes on a legal pad laid on the open book with his right. Familiarizing himself with the unusual and often arcane laws of Texas was almost a full time job in itself. He hated going anywhere without something to read, and the daily wait required at the Snazzy Pig had helped him get up to speed more quickly. He had learned to shut out the yelling of orders and the wheedling of deal making. He wasn't close enough to any of the other attorneys he saw walking the hallways to eat lunch with them. They all looked slightly askance at his hair, as if mere association with him would cause theirs to start accelerating its growth. The younger among the men and even some in their 50's groomed their hair stylishly over their ears, but Max noticed that several rules were observed: no one had hair completely covering their ears or touching their collars, and their sideburns all ended no lower than the bottoms of their earlobes.

He was still absorbed in his notes when a hand plopped down on his shoulder. He looked up to see a man he had come to think of as the Cowboy

Attorney. A defense lawyer of the old Southern Charm school, he always wore a polyester suit with a yoke on the back of the jacket and a pair of scuffed yellowish boots. They were made out of some type of exotic leather Max couldn't begin to identify. It was bumpy and looked to him like the original owner had had a case of acne it had never recovered from.

The man's shirts always were bunched around a belly that looked like it was carrying twenty pounds more than gravity could allow. Although he was probably no more than fifty, the florid lines on his cheeks and nose made him seem at least ten years older. Max recognized the look of a habitual drinker in the man and offered a silent prayer for him.

"Hey there," the lawyer said, like he was wheedling a bargain from an assistant D.A. "I hear you pulled a pretty good one yesterday, slick."

"And what might that be?"

"Well hell, Donny Washington. He's the sorriest small-time crook Potter County's ever had. We used to have a pool about if he'd ever get off or not, but it finally got so high we just split it up. Goddamn. He probably ain't gonna know what to do tonight, not being in jail. Whole courthouse is talking about it."

A waitress came by with her pad and barely glancing at Max, said "You're up."

Max looked apologetically at the Cowboy Attorney. "That's me. Well thanks, I guess. And you're—?"

The man quickly stuck out his hand. "Oh, yeah. Sonny Tarleton, that's me. Say, you ever get into anything you need some help on, make sure you give me a call. I'm your man."

"Oh, sure. Will do." Max weaved his way through the tables back to the one being cleared for him. He glanced over his shoulder at Tarleton. This place was getting weirder and weirder by the moment, but amazingly enough, he was beginning to like it. Maybe he was just getting weirder, too.

Max settled into his table and ordered a Reuben sandwich and a glass of iced tea. It had taken him a while to get used to iced tea as a year-round drink; in New York it was available only in the summer, but he had a sneaking suspicion that the citizens of Amarillo would drink it in the middle of a blizzard.

He concentrated on the criminal statutes book in front of him, studying the precedents, which were as familiarly serpentine as any he had memorized in New York. He managed to find a place of concentration inside his head where the clatter of dishes and drone of voices didn't bother him.

After a few minutes the waitress put the sandwich and check down in front of him with a clatter, and he returned to the reality of the diner. He picked up the sandwich and watched the flow of attorneys around his table. In the front, next to the window, was a table that was reserved only for judges. There was no official policy that specified it was only for them; rather, it was a tradition that had through the course of years become bound with iron bands.

Max watched that table for a while as he carefully chewed his sandwich. Periodically, one of the lawyers who had finished lunch would walk by the judges to kiss their butts. The speed and manner of their response to him let

Max know the esteem they held the attorney in. Some they recognized immediately, and some they took an agonizingly slow time to acknowledge, leaving the lawyer twisting in the wind. The other attorneys having lunch watched the table as they would a weather vane. As he chewed the sandwich, Max wondered idly if he would ever find himself walking up to that table, his metaphorical hat held in his hand, stepping and fetching for favor. In your dreams, he thought.

He glanced down the aisle and saw a tall man walking unhurriedly to a table in the back. He recognized him as Champ Phillips, a lieutenant in the Police Department and a chum of Diane DiAngelo.

Max had lost one case that Phillips had testified in, but he'd also won one. After both verdicts were delivered, he had caught Phillips' eyes on him in the corridor. The lieutenant seemed to be appraising him, and strangely enough Max had a sneaking suspicion that the policeman in some way approved of him. He didn't know exactly how he felt about a member of the prosecution holding him in esteem, but decided that a life spent making friends was better than one spent making enemies.

As Phillips strolled toward his table, Max thought that he looked like an Old West marshal. He decided that Phillips was more James Arness than John Wayne. He was not a bully or a braggart. In fact there was a kindness and humility to him; nonetheless, Max felt he would be dangerous when crossed, a man whose sense of right and wrong was strict and unimpeachable.

Phillips nodded at occupants of some of the tables. Others he ignored, and occasionally he reached down to shake a hand or pat a shoulder. When he came near Max, he slowed down just the slightest bit and under the thick mustache was the shadow of a smile.

"Howdy," he said.

Max considered a moment. "Not bad," he replied. "How about yourself?"

Champ paused, as if he were about to say something, and then started forward again. He got a foot past Max, then turned back and touched his shoulder gently, as if embarrassed. He cleared his throat.

"Let me give you a word of advice, partner," he said in a low voice. "Around here, 'howdy' ain't a question."

"Ah," Max said, as the color rose hotly to his cheeks. "All right, then. Howdy to you too, Lieutenant."

Champ smiled and winked at him, then walked to his table.

Max finished his sandwich and slowly sipped his iced tea. He picked up his pencil to continue making more notes and paused with the lead against the page. He squinted his eyes in the distance. "Howdy pardner," he said, in his unmistakable Brooklyn accent. Then he laughed harder than he had since he had arrived in Amarillo, laughed until iced tea spurted from his nose, and Sonny Tarleton hurried over as fast as his overweight body would allow and pounded him on the back.

Regina Odom pulled an oven mitt shaped like a spotted bass over her hand and slid a casserole dish of lasagna out of the oven. Lasagna was Regina's specialty, a favorite of her children and husband. She placed it on the burners.

The mixture of parmesan, ricotta, and mozzarella cheeses bubbled through the layers of tomato sauce, pasta, beef, and sausage. She had not yet answered her mother's question. She craned her neck so she could see into the living room. Maggie and Travis were sitting on the couch, quietly for once, watching *Sesame Street*. Regina tried to find something for her hands to do and settled on wiping them on the towel that hung from the handle of the oven door.

"I'm not sure what's wrong this time, Mama. He's just upset. I think Carl yelled at him again."

Bernice quickly and efficiently cut up vegetables. "Well, that's easy to fix. I'll talk to Dolores, and get it straightened out."

Regina took a quick breath and unwrapped the foil from around the bread. Steam rose into her face, carrying with it the delicious smell of yeast, butter, and garlic. "Mama, maybe we just ought to stay out of it. Let them work it out."

"And maybe he just ought to lose that job. Then where would you be?" She continued to cut the vegetables. Each cut was precise, each slice the same.

"Mama—"

"Don't 'Mama' me. I'll do whatever I have to do to take care of my family. If you don't know that about me, you just don't know me very well. And if that means straightening out problems between Freddie and Carl, so be it." She scraped the vegetables into a salad bowl with the edge of her knife. Bernice caught a glimpse of herself in the microwave window; she was still pretty at 64. Her hair was thinning just a bit, and she had to use more color than she did just five years ago, thanks largely to Freddie. Who would have ever dreamed that Regina would actually marry him?

"Is he coming home for dinner?" she asked.

Regina ducked her head and after a moment nodded. "He said he would."

"Well, let's hope so. Give it ten minutes, then call the children. They need to eat on a regular schedule, even if their father apparently doesn't."

Regina could feel the familiar pressure from behind her eyes and quickly excused herself to the bathroom. The tears started coming as she reached the door, which she quickly shut behind her. She turned on the water, sat on the toilet, and hugged her arms around her chest, rocking back and forth as the tears flowed down her cheeks, the same way she had done since she was a little girl, and her mother stabbed her in the chest with words that felt like a rusty icepick. The words still felt the same, as if she were only ten years old and not a mother in her own home. Regina had tried to tell Bernice how it felt to hear Freddie criticized; often she didn't even wait until the children were out of the room, and the pain and confusion Regina could see on their faces hurt her more than her own did.

After two minutes she turned off the faucet and flushed the toilet. It covered the last of her tears. As she was wiping her eyes with a tissue, trying to repair the smeared mascara, Bernice knocked on the door.

"It's not getting any warmer, Regina. Maggie and Travis are already starting."

"Okay, Mama. I'll be out in a second." She dabbed at her eyes once more and fixed a smile on her lips before opening the door.

The television glowed faintly in Joe and Darlene's bedroom. The room was too small, with barely enough room on each side of the bed to make a path to the closet, the dresser, and the doorway. The television sat on top of the dresser. The light flickered off the shapes their bodies made under the covers. On one of the sports channels, soccer players raced back and forth across the 12-inch screen.

Darlene hugged the edge of the bed, taking up just enough of it to keep from falling off. She lay on her side, her arms hugged around the pillow. Joe sprawled on his back, one arm covering his eyes, the other thrown over Darlene's hip. His mouth was open, and a snore came from deep in his throat. A light sheen of sweat glowed on his skin. The soccer players continued their silent game.

After several minutes Joe turned on his side, his back to Darlene, and pulled his knees close to his chest. He stayed that way for several minutes. Then his right foot began to jerk, and his right hand and forearm tensed until the muscles were as tight as the string of a hunting bow. His left leg began to twitch and then his mouth. He bared his teeth like a horse in pain. He shook his head and rubbed some of the sweat off onto the pillow. His head began turning from side to side, and from low in his throat there came guttural sounds which could have been the beginning of words. His right hand moved to his scrotum and gripped it, covering it. Joe's entire body began to shake, and the sound from his throat turned into "uh uh." His right leg shot out to the end of the bed and brought him abruptly out of sleep. Close to the edge of the bed by now, the sheet wrapped around him, he almost fell onto the floor and was caught by his instinctual fear of falling. As he awoke he sat up quickly, his arm out in front of him. A sharp "huh!" exploded from his mouth, and he realized where he was. He wiped the sweat from his face with the edge of the sheet.

Darlene had awoken, as she always did, when Joe first began to shake. She lay very quietly, warily, careful not to touch him, trying to hug her edge of the bed even more tightly. She had made the mistake of touching him once, early in their marriage. No one at work had asked about the sunglasses, but she knew they were all looking at her.

Slowly, carefully, she turned over in bed, still keeping her distance. "Joe? Are you okay?"

He didn't turn to look at her, just said, "Go back to sleep," and searched on the floor with his foot until he found his jeans. He slipped them on and left the bedroom, putting one hand against the wall to steady himself. He paused a moment in the doorway, looked back at Darlene in the bed, and shut the door.

Darlene lay until the tears came, silently as always, seeping into the pillow. She cried until she felt some comfort, then got up and turned off the television. Usually, turning off the television when Joe had turned it on, even five or six hours later, was an invitation to a beating for her. But she knew from experience that he would not come back to bed, and when he got dressed for work he would not remember that he had gone to sleep with the television on. She turned the portable fan up a speed and fell back into a soft, comforting sleep.

Joe opened the refrigerator and took out a bottle of Schlitz. He unscrewed the top and sat down at the kitchen table, his elbow propped on top of it. He took a long, slow sip and held the cool, sweating bottle against his forehead. He walked into the living room and turned on the television, idly surfing the channels, looking for something that would help him focus. He saw the sports channels, the politicians yammering at each other, all doing their best to personally screw him. He glanced at CNN, but as usual he had trouble figuring out just what the hell they were talking about. Sometimes Joe had the feeling that other people were participating in some big hoax, talking about things that didn't really exist, just to make him feel stupid. He found *Rio Bravo* and watched Dean Martin pretend to be a cowboy for a while, but he had seen it before, and he couldn't focus on it either. As he watched the movie he saw one cowboy riding a pinto horse, and for a moment remembered a brown and white spotted pony he had when he was just a little boy. He remembered with perfect clarity how it felt to ride it, the smell of its skin, and wondered why he had never thought of that pony or seemed to have any memory of it until now. And in the next moment he wasn't sure whether he had ever had such a pony at all.

Joe thumbed the remote, turning off the TV. He wandered back into the kitchen and took out three more beers. Walking through the living room, with its faded recliner and the green couch Darlene's parents had given them two years before, he padded across the braided rug to the front door.

Joe sat down on the top step of the two leading off the front porch and lined the three bottles of beer up beside him. He raised the bottle he was working on to his lips and took a long, slow drink, his eyes closed.

He was startled by a loud thump, and a whirring sound heading away from him. In the middle of the street was a boy on a bicycle, carrying a bag of newspapers. He had just scored a direct hit on the door of the house across the street from Joe and was delivering another to a house two doors down. The thump he had heard was the sound of the paper hitting the door. He realized that it was already dawn, and when he had sat down on the porch it was nowhere near that; it had been completely dark, yet he wasn't aware of any time passing. He reached out for a sip of beer and saw a line of four empty bottles beside him. He knew he hadn't drunk the other three, and he also knew that it shouldn't be close to dawn, yet the beers were gone and there was light in the sky. He put his face into his hands and came closer to crying than at any time since he was a boy.

Darlene heard him in the shower and got out of bed. She put on her robe and began to cook breakfast, knowing that Joe would be quiet this morning, that he would eat with barely a glance at her and head off to work. She felt pain inside her heart over what happened to Joe in the night, but could not help feeling relief that those nights signaled a rare sense of safety for her the next morning. This knowledge hurt her, too. It made her feel hard, a long way from the girl who had married a man for love and found less than she had expected.

When Joe left without speaking to her, as she had known he would, she got ready for work.

Chapter 11

Angel had theories why Wednesday was a quieter night at Bailey's. Not that she minded; after the noise and confusion of the weekend, she was always ready for a dose of calm. She thought it might have something to do with Wednesday being church night. It wasn't that most of her customers spent the evening dozing on the hard bench of some stodgy church. No, she just thought that a lot of the men (or their wives) felt that if so many others were in church, then the least they could do was stay home. It was just like Sunday morning. A lot of people stayed away from church, but they didn't venture out until after noon. For some reason, maybe just growing up in the Bible Belt, their consciences wouldn't allow them to have fun on Sunday mornings. It sounded perverse, but Angel felt that much of life is built on perversity. As a pool hall owner, she knew that better than most. Why else would people choose to pay her money to play a game that required physical dexterity and then pay her for beer that would slow down their reflexes and judgment?

At 8:00 this Wednesday night, the room was deader than usual. No more than thirty players were scattered around the seventeen tables, and the volume control on her stereo was set at three. On a typical Saturday night, ten was barely adequate. Reba McEntire sang that if she had only known this was the last walk in the rain, things would surely have been different. Isn't that the truth, Angel thought. She reached out her leg and touched Bailey's ruff with the round tip of her brown roper boot. The wolf's head rested on her paws. She did not raise it but turned her eyes up at Angel. A contented rumble bubbled up from deep in her chest.

Angel leaned her arms on the counter like a cowboy waiting for a shot of rye in an old movie. She could have sworn that she had seen Rory Calhoun in the same position not three evenings ago on a late-night horse opera.

Three tables away from the counter, Max Friedman played his usual game of focused eight-ball. In the month since the dust storm had blown Max in through the front door of Bailey's, she had never once seen him play a game of pool with anyone else. Max was always friendly, and sometimes she almost got the impression that, given half a signal, he might even be interested in flirting with her. And then again, maybe he already had been. It had been so long since Angel had gone out with a man, let alone been flirted with, that she thought she just might have forgotten what it felt like. She thoughtfully stroked Bailey with her boot and continued to watch Max. As he moved around to the side of his table facing the counter, he suddenly looked up at her and caught her glance. He looked straight into her eyes for a moment, slowly smiling. Embarrassed, she looked quickly away, an almost queasy feeling in the pit of her stomach. Suddenly she felt like she was sixteen years old again, worried whether the right boy was going to invite her to the dance. Jeez.

She glanced around the rest of the room, trying to avoid meeting Max's eyes again. In the far corner table on the left that he always chose was Smith. Since Bailey had eighty-sixed his partner, Smith had played his efficient games of eight-ball by himself.

In the opposite corner of the room were the men whose names she had learned were Carl and Freddie. Freddie was wearing his baseball cap backwards, a habit which convinced Angel that the percentage of morons in the world had increased dramatically in the past several years.

Since the altercation with Joe she had kept a wary eye on both of them. Although she had no idea if Carl caused the problem that night, she knew she didn't trust either him or his partner. For all she knew he might have provoked Joe, but it was obvious that taking Joe out would defuse the fight. Bailey had seemed to think so too, and that was good enough for Angel. Still, she kept an eye on Carl and Freddie as potential troublemakers.

The door opened, bringing with it a hint of a soft, cool evening breeze. Frank and Larry blew in, both wearing denim jackets and straw cowboy hats. They started to hoo-haw with another of their friends at a nearby table then slapped him on the back and made their way over to the counter.

"Set us up with a table, Red. We're gonna close this joint down."

"What did you call me?" Angel asked quietly.

From behind the counter, the cowboys heard Bailey's guttural growl.

"Oh hell, he's sorry, Angel. Ain't gonna happen again. Is it, Frank?" Larry asked as he punched his partner on the shoulder.

"Hell yeah, I'm sorry, Angel. This pretty weather is just making me a little frisky tonight. I ain't gonna cause no shit, scout's honor." He held up the appropriate fingers and placed them over his heart for good measure.

"Now, how about you draw us up a pitcher of Bud, and we'll quit bothering you."

"No," Angel said as she placed their rack of pool balls on the counter.

They looked at each other, utterly confused. "What?"

"You two've already been drinking. You want to start drinking here, you wait until you sober up."

"Well goddamn, that ain't fair, is it?" Larry turned and raised his arms, appealing to the crowd; unfortunately for him there wasn't one, and the closest player was bent over his stick.

"Who said life was fair?" Angel tapped her finger against the balls. "You want them, or you want to go play at Sticks or Clicks, or one of those stupid-ass sounding places?"

"All right, all right," Frank said, "but you mark my words, soon as we sober up, we'll be right back here for a pitcher!"

"I'm not going anywhere," Angel said. "Now go find your table, I'm tired of jawing with you."

They moved far away from the counter, throwing dagger glances back over their shoulders. Angel ignored them.

"I don't know why I keep letting their sorry asses back in here," she said. "Half the time you end up throwing them back out. But I guess it's okay."

Bailey rumbled in her chest.

Angel looked down at her. "Yes it is."

Bailey met her eyes and gave out a small "chuff." "Because I said so, that's why," Angel said. "Now is that good enough for you?"

Bailey stared at her a moment longer, never blinking her yellow eyes, and then laid her head back down on her paws.

Max had just sunk the eight ball and was starting to rerack when Frank Vaughan put his hand on his shoulder. He looked around to make sure no one was listening. "Hey Max, you got a second?"

"Sure. Is everything okay?"

"Step into my office here." He guided Max to an emptier section of the room. "Everything's okay, but I got a little problem."

"Something I can help with?"

"Yeah, that's what I was thinking. Man, they got me jacked up against a barb wire fence on this thing here."

"What is it?"

Frank licked his lips and scratched his nose with a forefinger. "Well, it's a DWI. I mean it's a load of bullshit, you know how the cops are."

"In what sense is it a load of bullshit?"

"Well, you know how they do, touch your nose, walk a straight line, ask you everything but how long your dick is, just to confuse you."

"Were you driving?"

"Was I—well hell yes, but that's got nothing to—"

"Had you been drinking?"

"Hell, well yeah, but you know, some beer is all—"

"Frank, I like you a lot, and I appreciate you trading with me for the car, but I have to say no. I can't defend you on this one."

Frank tipped his hat back and stroked his balding skull. "Hell, what for? You did a great job with them parking tickets; man, I need me a good lawyer."

"I appreciate that, Frank. But I don't get involved with alcohol or drug charges."

"Well shit, Max, come on, I—"

"I'm sorry. You ever need me for anything else, and I pray you don't, but if you do, come to me. I'll help you all I can. But not with this one." Max reached up and patted the cowboy on the shoulder. He walked back to his table and continued racking the balls. He glanced up at Frank and watched him walk back to where Larry had already broken. Frank's usual cockiness had deserted him for once; his head was down, his hat still pushed back, and he looked for the moment very sad. Exactly the same way Max felt when he watched him.

Smith Dixon was shooting on auto pilot. Although he sunk the balls with his usual precision and grace, his mind was not on the table at all. It was on money. He was two days closer to his deadline of the old man getting shut out and no closer to getting the money. He hustled a game here and there, but that was pocket money, twenty dollars or maybe fifty if he was lucky. He needed seven hundred dollars a week to keep his father going in some stale, death-smelling old age home. The thousand for the hospital was definitely out, but over the last two days he realized that it was all just a pipe dream. Hell, if he was going to dream, he might as well just rent a floor of the hospital and invite everybody from the Moodys to the Wittenbergs, all the people in their fucking mansions, and they all could dance around in black ties and tails while the old man—

All right, Smith thought, get a grip on it. You know what you have to do.

Quit dragging your balls. You ain't got no fucking choices here. There's only one thing you can do, so figure out where you can do it. He glanced briefly up at the counter, where he found Angel's eyes lingering on him. He knew that was impossible. He had never even considered it at all. She brought in pretty good money on a Saturday night, but with Bailey always around there was no chance of getting a dime. Most likely he'd get his head handed to him on a dog food plate. Besides, his honor forbade him from robbing friends, and although Angel was not exactly a friend, she was almost like a business associate. Also, he would almost surely be recognized, and he wanted to stay in Amarillo. That was his intention before Lori Butler had brought her smiling face and tailored suit into his life.

Despite his efficiency at his job, Smith had always been a small-time robber. It was never his way to take off an armored car, like he saw Robert DeNiro do in a movie one time. Nor was he the kind to breeze into a bank in the middle of the day, like the same gang had done in that same movie. He liked to move at night, when the risk of getting caught was lower and the likelihood of gunfire could be easily controlled.

The more he thought, the more he kept coming back to the supermarket that he had been in with Joe. Food Giant. It had the kind of set-up he liked. It was a big store, with no visible camera operations. Usually if a store like that had cameras they would be in the open, more as a deterrent to crime than as a way to catch criminals after the act. It also had large mirrors in the corners, the way older grocery stores used to. Most likely Amarillo's biggest problem with armed robbery was cracked-up punks taking off 7-11's with a pop gun, a little .22 they had traded crack for on Amarillo Boulevard. A big store wouldn't likely be looking for a professional to breeze in after closing and take off their day's proceedings. The more he thought about it, the more certain it seemed. The only problem with it was Joe. He needed at least two men to back him up: one as an enforcer inside the store and one in the car waiting for them the moment they got out. If he was going to do Food Giant, he almost certainly needed Joe to help him out. It was, after all, his tip that had put the idea into Smith's head in the first place. He knew the set-up from his experience as a security guard, he was willing to do it, and he was really the only person Smith knew to take along. Since he had decided to end his career as a hold-up man, there had been no reason to frequent the areas of town where he would find others who pursued that line of work.

Joe was a wild hair, there was no doubt about that. Yet this job was so simple that Smith could figure out no way that even he could fuck it up. He sank the eight ball and decided that taking Joe along was a calculated risk, but he thought it would work. The next problem was finding someone who could drive them. He set up the balls again and expertly broke them, letting his mind turn over the new problem as he settled into the rhythm of his game.

Carl and Freddie saw Smith playing at the table in the opposite corner of the room under the velvet pool-playing dogs. On the wall above their table was a poster from *Cape Fear*, featuring a leering, shirtless Robert Mitchum. This was the first time they had played at Bailey's since the night a week before when Joe had threatened to open Carl's head with a pool stick.

"Isn't that your friend over there?" Freddie asked, nodding at Smith. "You want to invite him over?"

"You're pushing it, Freddie. Someday you'll realize you're not nearly as goddamn cute as you may think."

"So who is he, anyway?"

"A guy I knew a long time ago. And that's all I want to say about it. All right?" Carl stared across the table at Freddie.

Freddie smirked at him. "Yeah, if you say so."

"Goddamn right I said so." He looked up to make sure Freddie had heard, but his brother-in-law was on his way to the counter for a beer.

After she drew Freddie his mug, Angel pondered for a little while. She could probably afford to take a few minutes away from the counter; the crowd tonight mostly consisted of people serious about their game, and the beer taps hadn't been flowing steadily. Besides, she wouldn't be more than twenty feet away, so she could see if anyone needed something. If there were any new customers she'd hear the door open.

"What do you think, Bailey?" She nudged the wolf with her boot; Bailey raised her head and slitted her eyes, which Angel tried to interpret. It could mean sure, go ahead, what have you got to lose, or it could mean be careful you don't get hurt, or it could mean leave me alone with your petty problems, I have sleeping to do.

Angel took another minute to half-heartedly try to talk herself out of it. Maybe it's stupid, she thought. It'll be obvious to everybody what I'm trying to do; maybe they'll laugh at me. Then she considered the chances of anyone laughing at her out loud, knowing that Bailey was right behind the counter.

Oh screw it, she thought. I'm just getting older standing here. So she lifted the hinged board on the far side of the counter and passed through the space, as unsure of her fate as if she were approaching the gates of heaven or hell.

Max had an ability to be aware of his surroundings no matter what he was doing; perhaps it came from his upbringing on the streets of Brooklyn. It was certainly beneficial later during his short career of trying to kill himself with alcohol, although during that period the only thing that really interested him was seeing the bottom of the last glass and the top of the next. But it did keep him from being blind-sided several times by drunks who imagined that some offense had issued from Max's mouth. Unfortunately, it didn't work the night someone he'd evidently pissed off had waited for him with a knife. Eventually his awareness paid off in the practice of law, where he found that there were always those who were interested in figuratively back-stabbing someone else on their way to the top of whichever ladder they were currently climbing. Max had tried that approach for a while, until he realized that whenever you got to the top of one ladder there was always a taller one close by just begging to be climbed, and the ladder you were on didn't look quite so good anymore.

From the corner of his eye he saw Angel make her way over to his table, pretending to check on the condition of the felt on the tables between his and the counter. Max knew what she was doing and decided to support her pretense, even though it was obvious that she was deliberately making her way over to him.

Max liked listening to the songs on Angel's sound system. At a generous estimate, he had probably heard only a score of country music songs in his life before his arrival in Amarillo, and he found them an interesting anthropological study. Not only that, but to his chagrin he actually found himself liking some of them. He stood up and leaned on his stick, then pretended that he had just become aware of her presence.

"So tell me," he said, nodding to the stereo speaker. "That song is about a man and woman, their filaments aren't glowing too brightly. So they decide to take off some drug dealers. The man gets caught by the police, but his girlfriend shows up with a shotgun, blows the cop away. The guy tells her to beat it and takes the rap for her. He gets the chair, she takes the money and goes back to her hometown, where she never received any respect, and peels out in the Mercedes she bought with the cash. Have I got it so far?"

Angel leaned her hip against the table, her arms crossed. "Right on target."

"Okay." Max leaned his stick against the table. It helped him to have his hands free when he thought out loud, and he needed some walking space, approximately the same size as the floor in front of a jury box. "What I can't figure out—and I've heard this song a couple of times here before—is what we're supposed to think of this pair. Are they like a new Bonnie and Clyde, beautiful young lovers? In that case, why didn't they go down together? Is the guy supposed to be showing some kind of innate nobility by taking the fall for her, knowing that even in the South, where guns are as common and as sacred as cows in India, he'll get the chair for a cop killing? Is she supposed to be pissing on the people in her hometown by driving around in a Mercedes? Didn't she hate it there in the first place?"

The clack of balls came from a nearby table. Angel's eyes flicked over to it. "In the first place, you've got to consider that the guy who wrote it got an English degree from Texas A&M. That's like learning how to repair tractors at Harvard. I'm not saying he's dumb, cause he's not. You just can't measure him by your regular yardstick. Second place, I don't think you can take it literally. It's all tied up in cultural mythology. It'd be like reading Jimmy Breslin, then trying to take all his bluster and bullshit literally. It's a smart guy reinterpreting a myth that's buried deep down in the dirt of West Texas. Or the sidewalks of Manhattan. I think the singer knows more than he's letting on."

"So the guy in the song probably thinks he's doing something noble, even if we know he isn't?"

"I think you got it." She pushed her hair behind her ear and found the courage to look right at him.

"'A smart guy reinterpreting a myth,'" he said. "I have to say I like that one."

"Thanks." She fought the urge to go back behind the counter, to once again become the boss, the tough woman who spoke softly and walked a big dog.

"So," she said, "don't you get a little rusty playing by yourself?"

"No, not really," Max said. "I think bored more than anything."

Angel nodded her head toward the sticks racked on the wall. "You mind?"

"No, I don't," Max said. "I don't at all." She walked over to pick out a cue, and he watched the way her fine red hair swayed from side to side, like silk on a warm day when a breeze kisses it.

When the pay phone rang, Carl and Freddie were the only players near it. Freddie, still sober after only one beer, picked it up on the fourth ring.

"Yeah, Bailey's. Bailey speaking. Arf arf!" He put the receiver to his chest and laughed at Carl, who shook his head and made a shot.

Freddie put the phone back to his ear and heard what was unmistakably Dolores's voice.

"Freddie, is that you?" she said, weariness flooding her voice.

"What? Hang on a second. I can't hear. Who?" He rubbed his sleeve against the mouth of the receiver, hoping it would make a good simulation of static.

When he put it back to his ear, he heard Dolores saying, "Freddie, stop that nonsense and put Carl on the phone."

"No, really, this is—"

"Freddie, damn it, now!"

Freddie dropped his hand, looking over at Carl, who he knew needed no more excuses than this to kill him. He brought the receiver back up to his mouth. "Hang on. Hey, Carl!"

Carl looked up from his shot and chalked his stick. "Yeah?"

Freddie gestured at him with the phone. "For you," he said apologetically.

"Goddamn it, is it Dolores?"

Freddie lifted his left shoulder and eyebrow in shame-faced assent.

Carl slammed his stick down on the table, then looked around for Angel. She was engrossed in a conversation with the pony-tailed lawyer. Her head snapped up and she looked around the room, too late to see what he had done. Bailey's head appeared above the counter, and she stared straight at him. Against his will, his knees began to tremble. After a moment she disappeared. He grabbed the phone from Freddie, wrapping his hand around the mouthpiece. "You should have said I wasn't here!"

"Really Carl, I did. I tried my—"

"Your best, right? I know. I've heard it before."

He put the phone to his mouth. "Yeah, this is Carl."

He heard Dolores's voice in his ear. "I want you to tell those men not to call you at home anymore. If I get one more call here, where Nina can hear me talking to them, the next time you come home from that pool hall, you'll find everything you own in a pile on the sidewalk."

Carl started to answer, but it was pointless. All he heard was the clunk of the phone disconnecting and the angry whine of the dial tone.

He hung up the phone, abandoning the desire to slam it back into its cradle. He knew that if he did, that crazy wolf with the golden eyes would come barreling over the counter straight for him.

Freddie stood by the table, inanely rubbing chalk on the end of his stick. Carl took it from him and slapped it down on the edge of the table. He reached out and took Freddie's cap and turned the bill forward. Freddie jumped when

Carl reached for him, afraid his brother-in-law had finally gone over the edge and was about to hurt him very badly. "Carl," he said, "I'm really—"

Carl put his hand out, the palm facing Freddie, doing nothing to hide his contempt for his brother-in-law. "Don't say a word to me, Freddie, I'm telling you. Not one."

He brooded, eyes open, seeing nothing but the projection of his own pain. He didn't see Freddie return to the game, didn't see Smith pass four feet away from him on his way into the men's room.

"So, how's business?" Max regretted the question the moment it escaped his lips. Despite degrees in history and law from New York University, at that moment he felt like a pathetic singles club denizen, the kind of guy who hangs out in Green Point, Brooklyn, still wearing his *Saturday Night Fever* chains and polyester. But he had felt that it was up to him to break the ice; since Angel had started playing eight-ball with him, she'd been as nervous as George Wallace at an NAACP convention.

"Okay. How's yours?"

This is your chance, Max thought. Think of something. Something witty, something that will impress her, make her giggle uncontrollably at my off-the-wall sense of humor. "It's like the guy who works the park with a nail pounded in a stick."

He loved the little furrow that appeared between her eyes when she said "How's that?"

"Picking up." Almost as much as the way her eyes rolled when she groaned at his joke. Almost as much as the slight smile that barely touched her lips when she said, "You want to make a wager?"

"I'm not much of a gambler."

"I'm not after your money. I get my share of that every week. Here's my wager: I put this eight ball in, we go out on Sunday, do what I choose. You win, it's your choice."

Max pretended to feel calm while his heart started to lift and do its own aerobic routine. Act as if, he thought. "So, win or not, we're going out."

"You have a problem with that?"

"Not at all. I'm just negotiating the terms."

The almost smile again. "Next time I go to the sign store, remind me to order one that says 'Lawyers must leave jargon at the door.' Now, are the terms negotiated?"

"I think we're in agreement."

She leaned gracefully over the felt. Max noticed that the shade of green was only slightly darker than her eyes and was instantly embarrassed for having such a thought. He had to remind himself that his sixteenth birthday was more than twenty years ago.

Angel carefully lined up her shot. It required that she nudge the eight past his five, ticking the left side so that it would turn into the far left corner pocket but not give it so much English that it would pop out. Max stood with both hands on his cue stick, watching the muscles in her upper arms. She was wearing a blue plaid cowboy shirt with the sleeves ripped off. Her bicep rippled as she slid the stick into the cue ball. It rolled into the eight, which turned like a ballerina and lilted its way into the pocket.

She stood up and looked him straight in the eyes, and this time she really did smile. It wasn't a neon smile, the kind that's like the sign on a rainy night when you haven't seen anything at all for a hundred miles. It was the smile of someone who was happy and scared at the same time.

"Where and when?" Max asked.

"Meet me out in front at 5:30. Bring a jacket. It might be cold."

Max was puzzled. "What? It's got to be at least seventy-five degrees during the day."

Still with that Mona Lisa smile, she tucked her hair behind her left ear. "I'm not talking about p.m., Max. I mean morning."

"Let's review for a second. You're asking me to meet you before the sun rises? Am I into this too far to back out already? Am I contractually bound?"

She put her stick into the wall rack and turned back to him. "Yeah," she said softly, "I think you're in too far. Me too. At least, I hope so."

The bell on the front door jingled as a customer came in. Angel looked at Max one last time and walked back to the counter, striding swiftly in her boots and jeans. Max leaned against the table and let out his breath. He looked after her and felt for a moment that he had never met someone with such sadness in her eyes. He wondered how it had gotten there and realized that, starting on Sunday, he had a good chance of finding out. He racked the balls and started another game.

A sign above the two urinals read "Stand Closer, It's Not As Long As You Think." Smith smiled at it but did not obey. Judging from the floor, neither did many of the other patrons. He stood with his feet wide, trying to avoid the moisture. Because the hall was quiet tonight, he could hear most of the action on the other side of the wall, which was decidedly thin. The light buzz of conversation, the throbbing of the country bass, the click of pool balls, a voice growing increasingly louder very close to the wall.

"Look, I already told you," the voice said, "never, never call me at home. Yeah, of course I know it's late. As soon as I can, goddamn it!"

It took a moment for Smith to recognize that the voice on the other side of the wall belonged to Carl Puente. He washed his hands, lingering as he dried them on the paper towels.

"Monday," Carl said. "You have my word. I'll have at least half. And look, I'm telling you again. Don't call me at my—"

There was silence for a moment. Smith heard the sound of the phone being slammed into its cradle.

"All right, all right," Carl said, even louder now, with a quaver of fear in his voice. Smith figured Bailey had made her presence known behind the counter. He tossed the paper towel into the trash can and pulled the door open. He was ready to walk straight by Carl with a poker face. But it wasn't even necessary, because one look at Carl told him that his old friend was seeing nothing at the moment. He was slumped against the wall by the pay phone, arms crossed over his chest. As Smith walked by Carl's table Freddie glanced at him for a moment, embarrassed, before his eyes stole away to the floor. Smith went back to his game, where the seed of an idea began to germinate. By the time he sank the eight ball, he felt better than he had in days.

Angel stood at the counter busily straightening up the cubes of chalk, arranging them as square as tiles on a bathroom floor. She didn't know what had come over her a few minutes earlier, but she felt like a high school girl getting ready for her prom. That was the first time in her life she'd had that feeling, because the night of her own prom she'd been out with her circle of friends smoking marijuana, drinking beer, and cruising down Wolflin in a red 1974 Ford Maverick.

Talking to Max made her want to smile, something Angel had done very seldom in her life and barely at all in the last seven years, since she moved from Boulder back to Amarillo. She felt about half silly when she was around him—afraid of giving something away, but she didn't really know what. Angel was afraid that playing and talking with Max would make her lose the intimidation factor that her job required, but with Bailey behind the counter there was little real chance of that. Maybe she was just afraid of letting someone into her life who walked on two legs. Right now all she had was a wolf and two horses; with the customers, she only listened enough to respond to what they said. She didn't really care about how their day had gone, if they were happy or not. But she now found that slowly, over the past month, she had come to want to ask those questions of Max. She wanted to let him into her life. And that was what really scared her.

Max unlocked the door to his apartment, gently pushing aside the cats with his feet. They rubbed up against him, mewling. He shut the door and picked up his longhaired calico Mayella, rubbing his chin against her head. She was about five years old and had been left at the animal shelter because her owners were moving to an apartment complex that wouldn't allow pets. So they had put her up for execution until Max chose her. Sometimes, understanding the human race was more than he had the energy for. His other cat, a three month-old black and white shorthair named Lord Asbury Park New Jersey, Jersey for short, butted his head against Max's ankle. Jersey, who had a peculiar black stripe down his white face, had arrived at the shelter with his litter mates covered with fleas, eyes swollen shut with infection. The shelter had nursed them to good health, and Jersey was the last to be adopted. When Max had opened the cage and pulled him out, he held the kitten to his chest. Jersey immediately climbed up onto his shoulders then to the top of his head where he perched, yowling. Max had plucked him down and taken his and Mayella's tickets to the adoption office.

Adopting the cats had made him realize, more than anything else, that he was in Amarillo for the long run. So he had used almost all the money he made from his first cases to buy furniture for his apartment. It was still a little bare, which was fine with Max. Sometimes he liked to stretch out on the floor with his criminal code books or a novel, lying on his back or his stomach on the thick carpet and digging his bare toes into it while the cats crawled over him.

He had bought a second hand frame and mattress and a wooden head- and footboard. He visited Sears at the mall and bought some kitchen appliances, and at a Target store found assemble-it-yourself bookshelves and a desk and chair. The apartment was cozy, a far cry from the streets he had periodically lived on when he was 20, and bigger and cheaper than the apartment he had rented in the East Village when he was practicing in New York.

Despite himself, he sometimes missed the bustle of St. Mark's Place. He missed being able to go around the corner to a deli at any time of the night and picking up blintzes and coffee in the morning at B&D Dairy. But he liked being in a city that actually seemed to recognize the night hours, that had a stretch of time when most people, except for the drunks and speed freaks, were actually in bed asleep. He liked being able to look up and see the sky, unimpeded by lofty buildings. He loved the horizon-to-horizon expanse of blue and the astounding sunsets with shades of gold and red he had never imagined. Once, while walking down Third Avenue in midtown Manhattan, he had heard a passerby say that she liked Third more than Lex because you could see more of the sky. Yeah, about two inches more, Max had thought to himself, and the breadth of sky he saw now in this barren but somehow beautiful land sometimes brought him to the edge of tears.

He poured some food for the cats. Mayella ran immediately to the bowl. Her name was Tinkerbelle when he found her at the shelter sitting forlornly in the center of her cage. He decided that Tinkerbelle was a name that didn't seem to fit the cat he saw that day, and after a couple days of her not responding to it, he decided that perhaps she herself had never been overly fond of it. So he tried several others, and her lack of response to them was not encouraging. When he hit on Mayella, she pricked up her ears and strolled over the couch to him, rubbing her head against his chest. Like her namesake, Mayella Violet Ewell, she was a horribly wronged innocent who was searching for someone to love her. Max hoped that his Mayella would come to less tragic circumstances. He thought that everyone and everything, even names, deserved a second chance for happiness.

He sat down on the couch and pulled off his shoes. Jersey stalked onto his lap, head down, bottle-brush tail straight in the air. A tiny, black and white fuzzy steamroller. As Jersey walked back and forth, his tail tickled Max's chin. Max rubbed between Jersey's ears while the kitten purred. He put his feet on the coffee table and thought of Angel, of their upcoming—date? He wasn't quite sure if it was that. Years ago, someone in a St. Mark's Place A.A. club had told him that when two people of coordinating sexual orientations go out with each other, and both of them are currently unattached, then it's a date whether they know it or not. More often than not, Max had found it to be true. He liked the idea of going out on a date with Angel. He hadn't gone out with a woman in Amarillo. After meetings, groups would usually drift away for coffee or dinner at one restaurant or another, and occasionally he would end up next to an attractive and interesting woman. He had vaguely felt that one or two were trying to make more than conversation, but the thought was dismissed as quickly as it had appeared in his mind. He hadn't felt ready, and if nothing else Max had learned to trust his instincts. But at this time, with this woman, he felt ready, if a date it was. He closed his eyes and felt the small weight of the kitten crossing him, rubbing against him, felt the warmth and vibration. When he woke up an hour later, both cats were curled up on him, sleeping soundly. He smiled.

Chapter 12

Until five minutes ago, Carl had felt better than he had in days. The air was whirring with the sound of orders being filled. Freddie had shown up on time and sober. There had been no news yet of any fuck-ups. Business had been picking up lately. At times like this, Carl actually believed, however briefly, that he would be able to pay off the debts that were burying him more deeply each day. Then reality blasted in like the daylight at the end of a vampire movie. He owed six thousand on bad football bets, four thousand he had borrowed from a loan shark to pay off more football bets, fourteen thousand to credit card companies, which as far as he was concerned were just legal versions of the sharks, and on and on and on. It never seemed to end. And a couple of orders here and there were never going to make a dent in all that when his money had to go to the mortgage, car payments, Nina's braces, food, clothes, the whole fucking thing. There was just no way to get ahead. None.

He realized it had been minutes since he had moved, caught up as he was in brooding, and his head snapped to attention. Good. No one was looking. Everyone was busy. Freddie was on the phone, but he was writing something down on a pad. Carl figured it must be a business call, because Freddie wasn't smart enough to cover up a personal call to make it look real.

"Hey boss!" A woman's voice called out and he looked around. Sharon, the woman who mostly worked the front counter, was walking toward him. Of the five people he employed, Sharon was his favorite, not just because she gave him the fewest headaches, but because she seemed to genuinely like and understand the business. She always dressed in cowgirl clothes—roper boots, jeans with no back pockets, frilly blouses or sleeveless T-shirts in the summer, and wide belts with buckles half as big as she was. She was petite, her makeup always immaculate, hair teased to a fault. But she had a lot more going for her than most of the others of that type he had met.

She thrust a cloth sample under his nose. "It may be me, I'll own to that right up front, but does this color look like homegrown puke, or does it not? I saw it written up on an order, and figured I'd better check it out with you. Maybe it got written up wrong."

Carl looked at the form she held in her other hand. "That's what it looks like to me. But I agree with you, I wouldn't have it up in my house."

Sharon sighed tragically. "Well, I guess as long as the customers have money, it ain't our business if they got taste to go along with it."

"You got it."

"Hey Carl!" Freddie's voice blared out from the front.

"What?"

"A guy wants to see you up here."

"Customer?"

Freddie looked back over his shoulder. Carl detected a note of nervousness in his posture, his movements, and an alarm went off in his head.

"Why don't you come on up," Freddie said.

"Okay. I think this is fine, Sharon, but thanks for being alert. That's more than I can say for some of the others here. I'm going to see what this guy wants."

"You want me to watch the front?"

Freddie walked by, deliberately avoiding his eyes. "No, I'll take care of it. Find something to keep you busy for a few minutes."

"Aye-aye, chief." She snapped him a smart salute and walked away.

Which one is it, Carl thought to himself. It can't be the credit cards, they don't come to your job. Their dirty work always happens over the phone, where they try to make you feel like a piece of shit for not paying them. It could be the football guys, the shark, could be anybody for that matter, anybody except Santa Claus or Publishers' Clearinghouse.

He walked behind the counter and saw a man standing with his back turned, looking out the windows at the street. Not much to see there, Carl thought, just sand blowing and bubbled asphalt that the cheap shits from the city won't fix no matter how many times I complain.

"Yes sir, may I help you?" he asked, in his most butt-kissing, "give me your business" voice.

The man turned, and as he did Carl recognized the familiar profile, knew in some way deep down in his heart that he was in trouble even before Smith Dixon had finished turning all the way around.

"What do you want?"

"Couple of minutes," Smith said. His face showed nothing to Carl. "Can we go outside?"

"You can go outside and keep going until you reach whatever shit hole you've been hiding in for the last 27 years."

Smith pursed his lips and rubbed his right hand against his thigh. It was too hot today for the corduroy jacket he usually wore to play pool in at Bailey's. He glanced out the windows and through the door into the workroom. Carl recognized the demeanor from his years in prison. It was the way the old timers looked, not the fish like Carl, but the ones who had been in ten years, always looking for an edge, trying to find the next trap before it snapped on their ankles. A goddamn jailbird.

"I think we need to go outside," Smith said.

"Do you have a hearing problem? I told you to get out of here. If I call the cops, do you think criminal trespass is enough to get your probation yanked?"

"I'm off it. Look Carl, I know you need money. I can help you get it."

A chill settled over Carl, like someone was massaging his heart with an ice cube. He lowered his voice almost to a whisper. "What are you talking about? I don't need—"

"I heard you on the phone at Bailey's last night. Five minutes, that's it."

If Carl had a baseball bat, he could have busted Smith's head like a Halloween pumpkin.

"There's a little bench out front," he said. "I'll be there in three minutes."

Smith nodded and pushed open the door. He sat down on the bench, leaned back against the wall, and waited until he heard the door open. Carl's shoes crunched toward him in the gravel, like a sound effect on an old radio show. He didn't sit down.

"Okay, let's hear it."

Smith opened his eyes and looked at Carl. "You know that place Food Giant?"

"Who doesn't? Used to be a Safeway when you lived here."

"I hear their security is real loose. It wouldn't take anything to get in there and—where are you going?" he said to Carl's back.

Carl turned to him, his face flushed with fury. "Did you not hear one word I said? I did two years in prison for listening to one of your bullshit schemes—"

"Carl, this is different, I—"

"You're goddamn right it's different, because this time I'm not going to—"

Smith stood up quickly and walked over to him, walked right up to his face. "What? What aren't you going to do? The only thing for sure you can't do now is pay them. I don't know what you're into or for how much, but the hole just gets deeper. If you've learned nothing else, you've gotta know that."

As Smith watched Carl's face, he saw its expression shift from rage to anger to uncertainty, and finally to the kind people get when the doctor comes from the I.C.U. looking at them and shaking his head. Carl sat down on the bench like his torso had increased in mass a thousand fold and his legs could not bear the weight. His face was suddenly gray. In a shaky voice, he said, "Jesus, Smith, it's not that bad."

"What is it?" Smith sat back down beside him. In the dirt on the shop's parking lot, a foot-high dust devil whirled around and around, a tiny tornado, before disappearing into the wind.

Carl glanced into the store window, then cradled his head in his hands. "Some football bets. That's a lot of it. I lost a few grand with that. And I could have paid it back, no sweat," he said, believing it, "but Nina, my kid, she has bad asthma problems. Insurance company doesn't pay jack on it. So I had to take a loan on this place, didn't tell her about that, and you know, credit cards. I'm getting calls at the house all the time, I'm afraid they'll start coming by next, threatening me. The cards are the only thing keeping me going now, but they're maxed out and I'm scared to use them anywhere. I don't want my wife to know about all this, and my kid. Jesus. I mean, she knows about the hospital, of course, and I'm making up fucking excuses about why they're calling. The check crossed the bill in the mail, that kind of thing. The thing is, none of my lies are working any more, and I don't think I have the energy to do it much longer." He stopped suddenly, realizing that he was spilling his most fearful secrets to a man who had betrayed him, to whom he swore he would never speak again. But somehow, he felt a faint hope at Smith's presence. Years ago, when they were in school and until the robbery, hadn't Carl depended on him? Didn't Smith always seem to have an answer? Hadn't they been friends? Smith hadn't ever let him down, until the day they stepped out of a raging rainstorm and stuck a gun into the face of a skinny, pimple-faced kid barely older than themselves. The kid had gone completely white, his pimples showing stark red against his face. Carl's stomach turned at the sight of the kid, turned at the thought of what he was doing, and he swore to God that if he got out of this okay, he would never do it again.

When they caught him two weeks later, he pled guilty and his attorney said the sentence was light. But to Carl, lying on his bunk at night, listening to the cell door slam, it seemed as heavy as melted lead poured into his ears and sitting there until it congealed. It didn't seem light at all.

Neither he nor Smith spoke. Carl thought of the promise he had made God 27 years ago. He hadn't made it out okay, so maybe that promise not to do it again was void. For months, Carl had tried to figure out ways to get himself out of debt. The loan sharks were worse than the bookies, with their high interest and threats. He had even gone to a credit counselor, but was too ashamed to tell about the bets. The guy had helped fix him up with a plan to pay off his credit cards, but when the next call came from a shark, in fear Carl had thrown him the two hundred dollars the credit place was supposed to get, and they canceled him. None of his plans to pay it off had worked. Finally, against his better judgment, against his own rational mind, he looked up at Smith, the friend who had betrayed him a quarter century ago. It was a sign of how bad off he was that Smith looked better at the moment than anything else. With a sinking feeling in his gut, he said "How much?"

Smith breathed out a sigh of relief. "This thing, do it right and it'll be sweet. Maybe twenty thousand each, maybe more. It's hard to say."

Carl leaned forward, not looking at Smith, his eyes flicking from side to side. "Forty for the two of us? Seems low, the kind of business that place does. I mean yeah, a lot of it's checks and credit cards, but even for the cash—I don't know. There has to be more than that."

Smith knew that this was the most delicate moment of all. He hadn't known if he could talk Carl into going along with him, but the tone of desperation in his voice the night before had given Smith hope that maybe, just maybe, he would do it. Smith needed Carl, needed someone he could trust.

"About the forty, yeah you're probably right, I think there'll be more than that. I'm thinking about sixty, based on what I know about that type of operation. The thing is, see, there's got to be another guy. We need three. Two to handle the personnel, and one to drive. We need a quick pickup, somebody waiting with the car the second we hit the door."

"Okay. I can see that. I don't know anybody for that kind of thing, I don't run in those circles—"

"No, I didn't figure you did. I have somebody for it."

"Who is it?"

"You know him, sort of. Joe, from the pool hall."

For the first time since he had sat down, Carl looked directly at Smith. He felt panic rising from his guts up into his chest. "Absolutely not. You're talking about the psycho? The guy that almost got his nuts ripped off by that dog?"

"He'll be okay. If you're asking is the guy an asshole? Absolutely. But can he be trusted? I think so, Carl. He's not so bad."

"He's a nut is what he is! Smith, that guy is not to be trusted. You let him in, we'll have casualties. No."

"Carl, look. He put me on to it. If we don't use him, we'll be twisting in the wind. He could go to the cops."

"Then stay the hell away from Food Giant. It's not the only place in Amarillo that deals in money, for Christ's sake."

"I don't have time to set up a plan anywhere else. This is slick, it'll go off without a hitch. Besides, he'll know I'm in charge."

"He'll know? Have you told him you're going to do it yet?"

"No, but—"

"Smith, use some sense. We can do it, and he'll never know."

"But we still need a third man. I don't have any connections here anymore, and goddamn it, I don't plan to get any! I'm out of all that. This is strictly a one-time deal."

Carl shook his head so hard he thought his ears would pop. "I can't believe I'm listening to all this shit. I'm a businessman, I'm not a criminal."

"Carl, this isn't a 19 year-old punk that's planning this. That gas station thing, I didn't think it out. That's why you got caught. But I've done stuff since the old days. I know how to pull this off. You can trust me."

"What have you done?"

"I've done about thirty in six states."

"Thirty what," Carl said bitterly. "Jobs, years?"

"I'm not going to lie to you. I've done a couple of years here and there. But not on this one. There's no way."

Carl stood. He glanced into the front of the store, where Sharon was looking through a stack of orders, making notes. "I'll tell you one thing right now, Smith. I'm not going down for any of this. I'm a family man, I have a respected business. My wife's been sick. I've got a kid. Any lawyer with half a brain will stick it to you. Drifter. Professional criminal. And I'll tell you one more thing, too. If you take off this time, you better bet I'll find your sorry ass. I won't quit. You understand me? *I will find you.*"

Smith thought of his father, the butcher with the arms of iron, now a husk in a hospital bed. Hopefully soon in an "elder care facility."

"I'm not going to run," he said.

"Yeah, I really believe that."

"I want to get this over with. I need the money soon. Let's look at Saturday. I'll talk to Joe."

"Fucking nut," Carl mumbled.

"He'll be fine."

"Look, I have to get back to work. They're probably wondering what the hell I'm doing."

"I'll look the place over again tonight, firm up the plan. We can meet tomorrow night, and I'll lay it all out for you. I'll call you."

Carl had already started to walk back inside. He reached the door, but dropped his hand from it like it was wired with a hundred thousand volts. He spun back to Smith, and stubbed his toe on a pot of cactus beside the door. "Shit! Not at my house! You have to call, do it here. And don't say your name. Make something up."

Smith sighed. The day was growing hotter, and his jacket was too much.

He took it off and draped it over his arm.

"Carl. I was thinking with this deal. If it helps you out, gets you back on level ground? Then maybe we'd be square with the gas station deal."

Carl's eyes teared from his stubbed toe. "You know what the worst part was? You were my best friend. But you hung me out to dry. You drove a knife into my heart." His eyes were still wet, but the pain in his foot was fading.

"Carl—"

"Do me a favor, Smith. Just get out of here. I don't want you on my property. It's not good for my business to have convicts loitering around my place." He went back into the building. Smith's eyes followed him. Carl went through the counter and into the back. Sharon saw Smith and smiled at him. He turned away and went back to his car.

Around the corner of the building, where he was hidden from the view of the bench, Freddie took one final drag on his cigarette. He watched Smith's car drive down toward Georgia Street, then flicked the butt down and ground it out into the gravel. He hurried around to the side entrance, the one the employees used.

Darlene tried not to listen to Joe as she cleaned up the kitchen. It was hard not to because he was sitting in the living room, and their house was small. She wiped down the stove, scratching at a particularly tough stain with her fingernail.

She could picture Joe sitting in his old easy chair, the one with the hole in the vinyl side, the hole they had covered with duct tape. He'd have his leg draped over the arm. She had bought a magic marker to try to make the tape brown, but it hadn't worked well and Joe didn't notice anyway. The chair had been a cast-off when her parents had bought matching recliners. Half of their furniture came from her folks.

She had never met Joe's parents, who she understood were long dead, and his sister only once, when they went out to eat at Whistler's restaurant. It was very awkward. Joe's sister came over to their table, and they exchanged a few words. Darlene thought his sister was relieved to get away from him. For the rest of the night Joe was in a particularly dark mood, and she was relieved when he left and didn't come back until late.

She was trying not to listen to Joe because early on in the conversation she began to suspect that something was not right with it. She heard him talking about the "job," and the only job she knew about that Joe had was welding, and this didn't sound like it was about welding. Joe started to get louder and angrier as the call went on, and she was getting scared.

"No, look," he was saying now. "I know the layout, you got the experience, what the fuck we need somebody else for?"

Darlene finished cleaning the kitchen. She edged to the archway into the living room and glanced in. Joe was wearing a T-shirt with sweat stains under the arms, faded jeans, and his old Red Wing work boots. He wasn't sitting with his leg draped over the arm of the chair, though. He was leaning forward, the phone gripped in his left hand, his right elbow on his knee. "I still don't like it," he said. "What if he pussies out?" His voice was getting louder, and his right hand was clenched into a fist.

Darlene pushed open the screen door that led from the kitchen into the small back yard. Most of the yard was bare dirt, and what grass there was grew long and spindly. It was starting to get cool in the evenings, and the sky was a deep, peaceful blue. She slid her hands into the hip pockets of her jeans and turned her face up to the sky. The sun was just disappearing over the horizon, and she could see it beyond their chain-link fence and the neighborhood. The other houses were old, but few were as run down as theirs. Darlene shook the hair from her face, and for a moment in the cool breeze, with the dry air caressing her forehead, she felt like she had in high school. It was only eight years since she had graduated, but it seemed like a hundred on most days. She walked to the fence and leaned her arms against it, rested her chin on them, and watched the sun say good-bye for the night.

Joe liked the sound of this less and less. "Look, this is not a good idea," he said. "What the fuck do we need him for?"

"I've already told you," Smith's voice said in his ear. The less he got through to Joe, the more exasperated he became. He tried not to show it in his voice. "The more of us, the less likely they'll be to pull a John Wayne. They'll have three guys in there, and it'll take two of us to cover them. We do it, and he drives."

"I still don't like it. What if he pussies out?" Joe rapped his heel against the rag rug. On the wall was a paint-by-number of a horse that Darlene had found at a garage sale and given him for a surprise on his birthday. He hated it. It didn't look like a real horse at all.

"—because he just won't," Smith was saying. "I told you, I did a job with him one time, and he was stand-up. Besides, he needs the money. He's motivated not to screw it up."

Joe stood up and looked into the kitchen. Where the fuck was Darlene? She'd better not be hearing any of this. He walked to the front door and looked out onto the porch, pulling the long phone cord behind him.

"You know what gets my motor vatin'? Seeing that little fucker pee his pants when we show up. That little manager cocksucker. Faggot. The money's just gravy."

Smith sighed. "My advice is, do it for the money. It lasts longer than revenge."

"All I got to say is, he better not fuck up. That's it."

"Don't worry about it. I'm going to look it over again tomorrow night, and we'll go in on Saturday. That's when they'll have the biggest bank bags."

"Yeah. Look, I have to go find my old lady. I don't know where the fuck she's got off to." He hung up the phone.

Darlene heard him yelling for her from inside the house, and her short reverie ended. The sun was already down anyway. She stood up and for one more moment closed her eyes, trying to recapture the feeling that she had found so fleetingly. But it was gone. She went back inside the house.

Carl stood at the door with the key, waiting for his staff to leave. "Hey

Freddie," he called, "make sure you—"

"Turn off the copier, the coffee machine, and the air conditioner. You don't know how much those things cost until you're paying the bills," Freddie intoned.

"Nobody likes a smartass, Freddie."

"So I've been told."

What the hell's up with him, Carl thought. He usually doesn't give me this much crap. He's too scared to.

Freddie made the circuit of the room, turning all the switches off, while Carl waited impatiently. The others trooped out one by one. Sharon passed through the door and stepped down, her size five red boots crunching into the gravel. "Hey Sharon," Freddie called to her, "you goin' dancing tonight?" He held his right hand to his stomach and his left at shoulder height, sliding his shoes across the floor, eyes closed, front teeth clenched down on his lower lip in mock ecstasy.

Sharon turned around. "I just might be," she said. "Why, you interested?"

Freddie hit the final switch and stepped out into the dying light. "Oh hell I would, but my wife would kill me."

Carl looked at his watch. They were the only three left; the others were already opening their cars or pulling out of the parking lot on the street, wheels spinning lightly in the gravel.

"That's why I got divorced," Sharon said. "Only thing waiting up for me is my coffee maker."

Carl looked at Sharon in her tight jeans and blouse; she was small but full-bodied. He realized his eyes were lingering on her breasts and turned away, embarrassed. "All right, let's go," he coughed. Sharon laughed and walked away to her little Nissan truck, swaying as each foot sunk down into the rocks.

"Jesus Christ, Freddie," Carl said as he locked the door. "What are you thinking of? Don't let Bernice hear you talking like that, or Regina either, for that matter."

"God, Carl, you know I don't mean it. It's just fun," Freddie said. "Hell, Bernice probably already heard it, big as her ears is. Hey, you want to shoot some stick?"

"No, I'm beat. I'll just go home." Carl pulled his keys out of his pocket, wanting to get to his car, get home to the TV, pull off his shoes, sit back in his lounger with a can of beer, and surf the sports channels.

Freddie followed him over to his white eight-year old Ford. Carl worried every day that the engine would crash, the timing belt would break while he was driving, then he'd have to get a valve job, or it would throw a rod, and that would be over a thousand bucks, and then where would he be? He opened the door, thinking that if he were obviously going home, Freddie would take the hint and do the same. Carl slid onto the warm vinyl seat. The back was littered with Nina's toys and books. He had his hand on the door, ready to shut it, but Freddie leaned one arm up on top of it, the other on the roof. He looked off into the distance, that maddening grin still on his face.

"So," he said, "I guess your money problems are about over, huh?" Then he sniffed as if proud of what he had said, the smile pasted on his lips.

Carl had no idea of what he was saying. "What are you talking about?"

"Bernice ain't the only one got big ears," Freddie said. Then he smiled his little smug smile again and glanced past the parking lot to where the early evening traffic was steadily finding its way back home.

It finally settled into Carl's mind just what Freddie was saying. He knew that he had to stay calm; if he let his impulses take him, he would grab Freddie by his little weasel throat and rattle him until he had a fatal case of whiplash. Instead, he patted his right hand on his leg, and blew out a breath. "It's the size of your mouth you should worry about, Freddie. And if you know what's good for you, you'll keep it shut."

"Oh, I don't think so. I guess it's too late for that."

Why does it always happen to me, Carl asked himself. "Okay, let's hear it."

Smith had spent the evening at the hospital quietly reading a paperback, his long legs stretched out in front of him, boots crossed at the ankles. At one point he thought he heard a noise from the old man, and said, "Pop?" But there was no response except the rattling breath that squeezed out of the creaking lungs. He went back to his reading.

Later he bought a six-pack of Cokes at Food Giant and strolled through the aisles. He went home and sketched a rough plan, working out the best point of entry, which was from the warehouse door. He had stripped to his boxer shorts and undershirt, planning to spend a half hour with the paperback before going to sleep, when the phone rang.

"Yeah." Every night he half expected, half hoped that the hospital would call telling him the old man was dead, and his guts churned in anticipation of the news.

"Smith, it's Carl."

"Yeah?"

He could hear Carl's nervousness over the phone line, could hear his dry throat swallowing. "Look, we have a problem."

"What do you mean, a problem?"

"My brother-in-law, you remember him?"

Smith's mind snapped to the image of Freddie, his shirt sticking out of his fly, his eyes glazed in a stupor, drunkenly trying to find the front door of Bailey's. "Yeah," he said warily.

"This afternoon while we were talking, he was having a cigarette around the corner, and he heard us. Jesus Christ. I can't believe this. He wants in, Smith. Says he wants part of the money."

"So tell him no, Carl. That's simple enough."

"You don't think I already did? That's the first thing I said. But he's a slimy little shit. I don't know if—I think he might do something if we take the place and don't include him."

"'Something' meaning what? What are you talking about, Carl?"

"Shit, I don't know. Maybe call it in. You know, the cops."

Smith rubbed his hand across his forehead. "Carl, this is your deal. You take care of it. No offense, but this guy's nothing to me—"

"Believe me, I—"

"—and I don't want to have to deal with it."

"We're going to have to! He knows, he heard us talking. I mean what are you going to do, kill him? Is that the way you are now?"

Smith stared at the wallpaper. It had once held a wagon wheel pattern but was now faded to an almost even gray. "You know better than that, Carl. I've done a lot of shit in my life, but I've never killed anyone, and you got no call to say something like that."

He heard Carl's exhalation. "This is getting worse and worse. I don't know what's—look, maybe we just should pull out of it."

Shit. "No," Smith said. "I'm not pulling out!" He twirled the phone cord around in his fingers. "I need the money."

"So do I."

"How about Freddie? Is he broke? Bottomed out? What?"

"I don't think so. I mean he's got a couple of kids, but I pay him decent wages." I wonder, Smith thought. "Regina works, too."

"So what's he want?"

"God, I don't know. Maybe—"

"Shut up for a second." Carl's breathing told Smith that he was angry at getting an order, but he did it. Smith sat on his bed and leaned against the wall. Think. He closed his eyes and concentrated.

"All right, look. Tell him he gets two thousand. That's it. I don't care what the total take is, that's all he gets. Can you depend on him to drive?"

Carl sighed. "I—yeah, I guess. I don't see how even he could fuck that up."

"All right. It won't hurt us to have three inside. There'll be a guard, a clerk, and the night manager. One on one. The split will be smaller, but I think we'll make out. Tell him—shit no, I have to fill him in. And I have to tell Joe." Smith grimaced at the thought of talking to Joe about it. He checked his watch. 9:00. "Look, can you do this now?"

"What?"

"I have to talk to him, tell him how it is. Maybe scare him a little so he'll stand up and do the job."

"What do you mean, scare him?"

"Nothing, Carl. I'm not going to hurt him, for Christ's sake. I just have to let him know this isn't anything he can dick around on, or show up slammed."

"I guess I can bring him, I think he's home. Where at? I don't know where you live."

"Not here." He thought a moment. "Hey, you remember that old drive-in we used to go to, up on the Borger highway?"

"The Comanche? Sure. It's all closed up now, though."

"Yeah, I know. Look, meet me there at—be there at nine-thirty. Bring him with you, and tell him how serious this is. It ain't a game of Candyland."

"Sure."

"It'll be a miracle if this goes off right. Look, I'll see you in a half-hour."

Smith hung up and wearily got dressed again. He was about to pull on his boots when there was a knock at the door.

"Hey," Joe said, "thought we might go out and shoot some—what the hell's the matter with you?"

Decades before, the Comanche Drive-In had crawled with cars every Friday and Saturday night. It was the best place in north Amarillo to see friends, to pick fights, to have sex, to perform all the functions so necessary to a teen-ager's life. Families knew that if they wanted to watch the movie undisturbed and unembarrassed, they should choose a speaker pole within the first ten rows of either screen; the back belonged to the younger crowd.

It had been years since films flickered on either of the Comanche's screens; like most of the other drive-ins across the country, they had bowed their heads to the convenience of cable and video. Slowly bits and pieces were sold off or stolen. Only one screen remained, glowing eerily white against the black sky. The snack shack had been destroyed by vandals through the years. The only evidence of the one-lane bowling alley it had contained was a scattered nest of wooden pins lying among the glass. A broken cash register lay beside a desiccated stack of popcorn boxes, almost unidentifiable after years of exposure to the rain and heat.

The speakers are the first items to be salvaged from an abandoned drive-in; their wires will make a few pennies from electronics dealers. The poles that served as pedestals for their speech are worthless, however. In country drive-ins, which sit on land that no one wants, they will eventually become invisible from the road, eclipsed by the growth of weeds, trees, and cactus.

In the Comanche the poles stood at skewed angles, like dragons' teeth sowed in the dirt, waiting to be watered. The marquee sign, topped by a stylized painting of Quanah Parker, his painted feathers faded and peeling, stood lonely against the starry sky. On the marquee, a handful of leftover letters spelled out "CL SED FOR SE ASON."

Carl turned off the lights on his car as he coasted by the sign, passed the ticket booth, and slowly braked to a stop among the poles. Freddie took out a cigarette, and Carl detected a slight shake in his hands as he pulled a lighter from his pocket. He wasn't quite as cocky as he had been that afternoon, and Carl took a small satisfaction from it.

"Not in the car," he said.

Freddie mumbled "Sorry," and opened the door. Carl felt a little more balanced again, seeing Freddie obey his order.

Freddie lit the cigarette; a light breeze was blowing, and he turned his back to it, cupping his hands around the lighter. "I figured he'd be here by now," he said.

"Soon," Carl said. He thought about his lounger in front of the TV, of the sports channels, and wished he were anywhere else right now. Then he thought of the bills he would be able to pay off when they finished the job, when their final count was made, and he felt some relief.

They stood for a few minutes, not talking, until the sound of a car crunching over gravel reached their ears.

"All right," Freddie said. "He's here."

They stepped back to allow the car to drive closer to them. The only lights were from the cars driving up and down on the Borger Highway. The drive-in was only fifty yards from the road, but it was wrapped in a wreath of mesquite trees. No one could see in.

Carl saw that there were two figures in the car, and he felt an acid burn start to rise from his stomach to his throat. The car stopped and Smith stepped out, pulling down the cuffs of his corduroy jacket. The other door opened and Carl's fear spiked as Joe got out wearing jeans and a faded old cowboy shirt.

Joe stared at Carl and Freddie, then turned his head and spit into the red dirt, his eyes never leaving them. "Well ain't this a nice welcome. The two pool hall pussies back again."

Carl turned to Smith. "Why'd you bring him?"

"What'd he bring me for?" Joe said. "I'm wondering the same thing about you two assholes. Wasn't you that come up with this deal. It was mine, and Smith and I could have done it without either of you."

Smith felt that he had to get control of this before it blew up in his face. "Listen," he said to Freddie, "you weren't supposed to be a part of this thing. I didn't invite you along, but we don't have time to screw around with you. We've got to do this thing quick. All you have to do is wait for us in the car outside the store. You see us come out, you hit the gas and that's it. In the meantime, you keep a watch out, and if anything doesn't look right, you drive right up to the door and hit the horn. And that's all you got to do. For that, you get two thousand dollars."

Joe kicked at the dirt with his boot heel, and broken glass scattered. "Man, this is so fucked," he said. "I ought to give it to somebody else!"

"It's still workable," Smith said.

"Oh, sure it is. Why don't we just invite everybody at Bailey's to come along? That mutt could be the watchdog. It's probably smarter than fuckhead here."

"Joe—"

"I should have just advertised in the high school newspapers. Three kids needed to fuck up a job. No references required."

When Carl saw Joe get out of the car, he had made a pact to say nothing to him, not to let his temper carry him somewhere he'd best not go. But against his better judgment, he blurted, "Wait a second. Who do you think—"

"Just shut up," Smith said. "Both of you!"

Joe turned to him, surprised. Then his eyes narrowed, and his right hand brushed against his crotch. "Hey man, you don't tell me to—"

"I am telling you! Look, I know what I'm doing. And this can work, just like I said."

Joe lowered his voice. "Goddamn, Smith, I can't believe you're gonna let this little punk blackmail us."

Freddie sucked deeply on his cigarette and snapped it away into the night. "I know as much about this as you do. I been around."

Joe rolled his eyes. "Oh right, the only thing you been around is somebody's dick, you little faggot."

"Don't call me that," Freddie said. "I'm giving you a warning."

"Or what?" Joe shoved Freddie with his right hand planted on his chest. "Just what do you think you can do, you little—"

Joe reached out to shove Freddie again, and found Smith in front of him, holding Joe's hand in his. He pushed it aside, and stepped in close to Joe. "This is how it works," he said. "I know what the hell I'm doing, and you don't. So I tell you what to do."

"Hey—"

"Shut up! I don't want to hear one word from you about who's a faggot or a punk or anything else. We're doing this for money. Not revenge, not fun, nothing else. You hear me? It's a job. I'm employing you. I will pay you. I plan it, we all execute it. There are four of us."

When Joe spoke, his voice was low; he tried to keep it from Carl and Freddie. "Smith, we don't need—"

Smith stepped closer; his voice was even softer than Joe's. "One more word from you—one, you hear me? And I will drag you down to Bailey's, and laugh when that dog turns you into hamburger." He stepped back. "Now, you got anything else to say?"

"Man," Joe said, "I thought you were okay."

"I am. But that doesn't mean I like you. When this thing's over, we don't see each other again, except for you two," he said, raising his voice and nodding at Freddie and Carl. "You're stuck with each other."

"Don't remind me," Carl said.

Freddie looked at him, genuinely hurt. "Hey!"

"Get out of here," Smith said. "Joe, get in the car. I'll drive you back. And I don't want to hear one goddamn word."

He took his keys from his pocket as the other three got in the cars. A breeze wafted through the drive-in, stirring the weeds and the mesquite branches. For an instant, Smith remembered a double date with Carl from high school. He didn't remember who they had been with, or to what movie; he just remembered that they had been laughing. Smith couldn't remember how long it had been since he had really laughed. He turned to the car and drove Joe back to the Ace Courts. Joe sulked, looking out the window. Smith took two aspirins for his headache, and then he went to sleep.

Chapter 13

Friday was October 30th, and Dolores Puente's classroom was decorated for Halloween. The windows and blackboards were covered with twenty-seven first-graders' ideas of what was scary; sometimes when she looked at them she didn't know whether to laugh or cry. Most of them ran to jagged toothed jack-o-lanterns, but there were a few real monsters. One little girl whose hair always seemed a few days past a washing, and whose eyes had circles darker than a raccoon's, had drawn a nightmarish figure that looked too much like her father. Dolores made a note to herself to talk to the school counselor.

It was just before lunch hour, and her students were wriggling with anticipation; they had heard the cafeteria was decorated even better than the classroom, and that there would be packets of candy corn for everyone.

"Is everybody ready for Halloween?" Dolores asked.

In a perfect chorus, their voices squeaked out "Yeah!"

"And when is it?"

At least half the class rolled their eyes, not believing she could be so stupid. Those not busy contorting their faces said "Tomorrow." God, their voices said, Mrs. Puente is *so* dumb.

"Very good," Dolores said. "Can you tell me what day of the week that's going to be?"

"Saturday!"

"Great! Now remember, if you go trick or treating, it's important that you stay with your parents, or your big brothers and sisters. Now, who wants to tell me what costume you're going to wear?"

Every hand in the room shot into the air.

Dolores laughed. "Everybody! Let's just go down the row, then. Maria, you go first." And Maria started to describe her witch costume, the first of six in the class who planned to dress that way.

Jack Ogan spotted Diane when she was forty yards away, down the hall of the county courthouse. He didn't want to start calling out her name and make a spectacle of himself, so he started hurrying faster and faster. Unfortunately for him, even on high heels her long, slender legs covered the tiles much more quickly than his short thick ones did. After ten yards he was wheezing; his asthma inhaler was in his briefcase, and he knew if he stopped to fish it out he would never overtake her. As fast as he moved, it was too slow, and when she was halfway up the stairs he finally resorted to calling her name. He himself was an elevator man, but she always used the stairs.

He tried calling quietly, but she had her head in a file folder while she walked and was oblivious until he finally raised his voice and yelled, "Diane! Goddamnit, Diane, slow down!" Two passing attorneys glanced at him with a smile; Diane's staff chasing her down the hall was a common sight. She paused to wait for him ten steps up, requiring him to climb up toward her. He knew his face was alarmingly red when he reached her.

On the seventh step he set his briefcase down and braced his hands against his knees. His face had passed red and was moving up quickly on purple. His lungs felt like two pieces of burnt toast, and he no longer cared if he embarrassed himself; now he was concerned with simple survival.

From above him came his boss' voice, containing more Texas twang than usual. "Jack, I read in the Globe-Times just this morning that High Plains Healthy and Happy is having a membership sale. You might look into it."

"Fat chance. Oh Jesus Christ, those stairs are steep," he wheezed. He tried to stand upright and almost made it. His heart was still pumping harder than an oil-rig at Spindletop. "Look Diane." He clutched his heart. "Oh shit."

"Jack, the color of your face is one that nature never intended it to be. I'm serious."

"Yeah, yeah." He fluttered his hand. "Look, I wanted to tell you—" He stopped again to catch his breath.

Diane looked at her watch. "I'm due in court in about three minutes, Jack."

"So am I." He finally was able to breathe again. "I've got to tell you that I might lose this one. I didn't want you to hear it from hallway scuttlebutt."

"Don't waste time telling me about it. Just get in there and dig!"

"You think I'm not? I'm doing the best I can."

"What's wrong with your case? Is he guilty?"

"Oh hell yes. Without a doubt. I just don't know if I'm proving it. It's a burglary rap, but none of the stuff was insured or registered. They didn't record serial numbers. This guy Billy Porter still had some of the pieces, but we can't prove for sure they belonged to the plaintiff. Porter's defense is pulling stuff out of the crack of his butt, muddying the water."

"Thank you Jack, that's so charming. Who is it?"

"You know him. That goddamn Max Friedman."

Jack could see the anger rise into her cheeks. "He's been winning too many lately. Get back in there and just hammer away at him with everything you can." She looked at her watch again. "I've got to go."

"Gotcha." His breath now stabilized, Jack picked up his briefcase and walked down the stairs to the elevator. He knew that no matter what artillery he produced, Max Friedman would win this battle. The holes in Jack's case were already there; Max was just revving up the truck and driving on through. If Diane fires me, he thought, maybe I'll ask Friedman if he's looking for a partner. Hell, worse things could happen.

Max preferred early meetings to late ones. It gave him a chance to start the day off on a good note, before anything had a chance to go wrong. As he leaned back in his chair at the Clean Air 9:30 meeting on Saturday morning, sipping a cup of coffee, he felt as happy as he had in months.

There were twenty-nine people in the forty-one circled chairs. Most of them were drinking coffee from mugs that they kept in the club for their own use. They didn't mind if anyone else used the cups when they weren't there, as long as they all got washed out and put away right.

Max's eyes shifted around the circle, matching names with faces. There was Connie, who worked in a bank downtown, near the courthouse. He had seen her one day when he was leaving court. He was so new then that in her eyes he saw a faint recognition, but she didn't realize where she knew him from until he reminded her at a meeting a few days later. Usually he saw her in tailored suits, but today she wore a big red t-shirt and jeans so faded they could have been a surgeon's scrubs.

Next to her was Keith, an insurance salesman whose weekend togs were the same as his work clothes, with the absence of a tie making the only difference. Both ran to polyester pants and short-sleeved cotton blend shirts that probably came from the K-Mart down the block. Max would never have given him a glance on the street, but the day he spoke about his father's alcoholism, and his own inheritance of the disease, starting at age twelve, Max had wept at his eloquence.

Gil, the mechanic who had first brought Max to Clean Air, sat across the circle from him, wearing coveralls and picking at the grease under the nails of his remaining fingers.

The rest of the alcoholics in the room could not have been more diverse if they had been chosen at random by a computer. There were two high school teachers, a math professor from West Texas A&M University, a radio announcer, a record store clerk with bright green hair who would have gone unnoticed in the East Village, but who in Amarillo was even more visible than Max with his ponytail. And there's a lawyer, Max thought. Mustn't forget him.

Today's meeting was being chaired by, amazingly enough to Max, a real live cowboy. Max had no idea there were any cowboys left outside of reruns of *Bonanza* on the cable channels, but shortly after his arrival in Amarillo he learned differently. It seemed to him that half the men walking or driving the streets wore cowboy boots and jeans, and a good number of them also wore western hats, or baseball caps with the insignias of farm equipment companies on the front. He started to think of these men as cowboys, but soon learned they really weren't. They were, in the local lexicon, Drugstore Cowboys. Although some of them knew the back end of a horse from the front, most didn't.

He learned all this from Angel one slow night at the club, when he was taking a break from his game and trying to find an excuse to hang around at the counter. "Rexall Wranglers, is all they are. If you can find one out of ten of them that knows to tighten the cinch before he gets on, you'd be lucky," she said. "Ask them what the saddle horn's for, and they'll probably tell you it's to hang onto when the horse starts to trot." She put a glass of Coca-Cola on the counter in front of him and wiped down the bar, snorting in an unladylike way that he found lovely.

The first time he had seen Danny Gonzalez at a meeting, he knew instantly what Angel was talking about. The 5:30 Wednesday meeting had already started when the door opened and Danny entered, ducking to clear the doorway. He wore jeans and boots, like the other cowboys, and his green baseball cap had the insignia of John Deere tractors on it. But he also wore on his legs the strangest things Max had ever seen in his life. Max had known his way around the film emporiums of Brooklyn and Manhattan, and in his youth when they still made Westerns, he had seen the cowboys in them wearing chaps. But these were not the chaps John Wayne had worn. They came down only to Danny's knees, and he wondered if they had shrunk, or Danny had grown. He found out later that they were called "chinks," but having a name for them made them no less strange. The other giveaway that Danny was no soda-fountain hanger-on was that the moment he appeared in the doorway, Max heard the clink of small metal parts touching each other. Danny was wearing spurs, and besides the leather guys who hung around Christopher Street in the West Village, Max had never seen a real pair in his life. But Danny was obviously a world removed from those K-Y cowboys. Max knew instantly that here was the real thing.

He also learned that Danny was someone whose recovery was rock-solid, who had been through the earthquake of alcoholism and survived relatively intact.

On this Saturday morning he was clad as usual, in boots smelling distinctly of cow manure, a bandana around his neck, the chinks and spurs securely strapped on. He wore a long mustache, which he lovingly kept well oiled. A kitchen match stuck out of the corner of his mouth. He leaned back in his folding chair, hands crossed on his belly, long legs stretched out in front of him.

"So here I was sitting at that bar, lifting to my mouth what I believe was a shot glass of Jack Daniels, with the sure knowledge that I had the world by the balls. That bourbon went down warm and smooth, with just a slight little burn to let me know it wasn't Kool-Aid I was drinking, you know."

He paused for a few titters to work their way around the table. Danny was a natural storyteller, and this was not the first time he had told this one.

"Next thing I knew, what seemed at the time to be about a second later, I felt something uncomfortable between my legs, and it took me oh, say half a second longer to realize that it was about a ton of Brahma bull stuck up my ass. My eyes come to and focused a little bit, and the crud started to work its way out of them. I had just come out of a blackout sitting in a rodeo chute, my left hand already gripping that damn rope, the bull going crazy under me, slinging strings of snot ever which way. The noise of the crowd, the cowboys setting there on the fence around me, the goddamn loudspeaker blaring all around the place, kept me from doing any thinking I was capable of at the moment, which I guarantee you wasn't much. I was trying to sort it all out. See I didn't have any idea of what town I was in, what rodeo it was, what round, and most important what bull. I didn't know its name, how it bucked, whether it was gonna duck right and then go left, if it circled, I knew flat nothing.

"And just about the second all this was going through what was left of my mind, I accidentally nodded my head, and the gate opened. I hit the ground about two seconds later. Them bull fighters knew something was bad wrong with me, so they done a extra quick job of getting him out of there and away from me. Didn't tease the crowd at all. I dug into my pocket and found a motel key, went on back to my room, and sat there with the lights out swigging from a bottle until I did what in those days I referred to as falling asleep."

He picked up his coffee mug and took a sip. "Couple weeks later I was at a rodeo in Tucumcari, over in New Mexico, and I looked in the yellow pages book there to find a liquor store, 'cause I was real dry and there wasn't a 7-11 close. Now I don't know what I was doing looking under A for 'alcohol' instead of L for 'liquor, but damn if my eyes didn't by accident light on alcohol treatment instead. I set there for a few seconds, then I picked up the phone and called the number for the AA club. Old gal answered the phone said 'Hell, come on over, there's a few of us here and I guess if you can stand us we can stand you.' Good thing I wasn't drunk then, 'cause I probably wouldn't have gone. And I ain't had a drink since, and I'm real happy about it."

Danny opened up the meeting for sharing. Several people shared about the petty resentments they carried through their day-to-day lives, about how they'd be better off just letting them go. Connie said that she was having tension with her ex-husband about child visitation rights.

"If I'd been sober when I met the bastard I never would have married him," she said. "But then I wouldn't have my daughter either, and she's about the best thing ever happened to me."

When she finished there was a pause while everyone decided if they had anything to say. Max waved his hand at Danny, who nodded. "My name's Max, and I'm an alcoholic."

The others said, "Hi Max," in ragged unison. They focused their attention on him, and he saw a number of smiles as he surveyed the room.

"As you probably know, I'm from New York."

Someone, he didn't see who, said "Naw," and everyone laughed.

"About a month ago," Max continued, "my car broke down on the street about two blocks away. At first I thought that once again I was the fire hydrant and God was hiking up his leg. Later, I found out that I was right across the street from a pretty good pool hall, and pretty close to a damn good AA meeting. That's about as good a definition of 'security' as I can think of." A few of the members laughed.

"I haven't talked too much in here. At first I thought of Amarillo as a kind of way station, a resting place of sorts. But now I realize that God kind of wants me to stay here for a while. Who knows why. So here I am in this town, where you can see the sky, and people talk pretty funny." He was very aware that he pronounced the word "tawk," and an appreciative round of laughter swept through the room.

"So I thought it was about time to tell my story." The other members settled back to listen. "Or at least the part of it that matters here.

"I grew up in Brooklyn, New York, which is a place as vastly different from Amarillo as any of you can imagine. By that I mean the buildings, the customs, the way people talk." A few smiles ricocheted around the table. "But a lot of the stuff, the way that people raise their kids and the things those kids do because of it, well those are remarkably the same.

"When I was about fourteen years old, I did the same thing that most of you did—I stole drinks from my old man's whiskey, then poured in a jigger of water. I think he knew I was doing it, but he and my mother were too far gone themselves to do much about it. Then I started sneaking beers from the older kids, giving the neighborhood wino a buck to buy me something at the corner deli.

"And when I was sixteen, and the pain got too much for me, I stayed out one night and didn't go back. To John Jay High School or my parents' apartment. I slept on friends' couches, on the friendly streets of Manhattan sometimes, in empty buildings. I hustled pool, worked as a messenger, did a little of this and that. I started doing some bar fighting, an endeavor that I definitely was not cut out for. I finally figured that out when I was twenty-five years old. I'd been in jail three times during those years, on drunk and disorderly, and one night I ended up at the emergency room of Bellevue, which is where all the poor folks and crazies go. In New York, I'm sorry to say, those two are often the same. And I was definitely both that night. They put eighteen stitches in me. The doctor who treated me said if I didn't quit drinking right then, I'd never live to see twenty-six.

"I told him he was full of shit, and then I laid there for a couple of days and thought about it. I finally realized that I was really great at starting fights, but not so hot at finishing them. And the only way to change that was to do what the man said. So I asked the nurse casually, to show I didn't really need it because I was so cool, if there was a meeting in the hospital. And just as casually, because she knew I really did need it, and she didn't want to scare me off, she told me where it was, and when. So I went.

"And when I got out of the hospital, I kept going. I had a couple of slips, and then after a while, I didn't. I got my G.E.D., found a job at New York University and put myself through school there, then wonder of wonders, I managed to bullshit myself into their law school. I worked harder there than I ever hope to again in my life.

"I built a little practice defending people who were mostly too poor to pay me. That was okay for a while, then it wasn't. The walls in New York felt like they ever so slowly squeezing in on me. So I decided to move to Phoenix, and for some reason God saw fit to play mechanic, by fucking up my car so badly that it wouldn't run any more. And then he saw fit to have my car towed to a real mechanic who happened to be a grateful recovering alcoholic. Who said to me 'Hey how about a meeting?'

"So right now I'm grateful to be alive and sober. I don't really know why I'm in Amarillo, but one day at a time it's looking better to me. And you guys are a big part of that. Thanks for being here."

Danny nodded at him. "Thanks, Max. Anybody have any burning desires?" The math professor said that yes, he had a burning desire for a drink, and everyone laughed again. "In that case, I'll close it up. I got some calves that need to be herded." At least that was what Max thought he said. What Max's ears heard was "kevs." They all stood and joined hands. Danny said, "New York, why don't you kick us off on the prayer of your choice?" Then he winked at Max.

Max felt a warm glow in his chest as he led the others in the Serenity Prayer. They all stood milling around for a while. Danny clapped Max on the shoulder, and smiled, close-mouthed but warm. "Good to hear you, son," he said, even though he was probably younger than Max. "I was wondering when you was gonna open up. I heard you New Yorkers was notorious talkers, and here you was about to prove it wrong."

He shook Max's hand, and sauntered to the door, fringe swinging, spurs jingling, a walking Webster's entry for "mosey."

Max hurried after him, and asked for a private moment. They stepped outside.

"So," Max said," I was thinking it's about time I got a sponsor. And I wanted to ask you."

"I don't know," Danny said, his expression grave. "That sounds pretty permanent. More than just a stranger passing through. Think you're ready for it?"

"You know what I always say. Ride your horse in the direction it's going."

"That doesn't sound like something you'd say."

"Actually, it's not. I heard you say it once, and I've been waiting for the chance to use it."

"I think it's going to take a while before you make it your own. So are you asking me?"

"Yeah, that's the general idea."

"Well, like the gal told me that time—if you can stand me, I guess I can stand you."

Max squeezed Danny's arm. "Thanks."

"You got my number. All you got to do is use it."

"Yeah. I know."

Max smelled the aroma of a light perfume. Connie put her arms around both of them. "Hey you two, some of us are going for breakfast. You wanna come?"

"Too much work, girl." Danny said. "Maybe next time."

"Where are you going?" Max asked.

"Luby's, I think."

"And that would be what?" Max asked. "A place where they feed you breakfast while they change your oil?"

"Sounds like you need a crash course in Texas culture. And we're just the group to give it to you." She linked one arm through his. "I hope they got enough food left. Nobody eats like a bunch of boring, self-righteous drunks."

Chapter 14

"May I have your attention, please? Food Giant will close in fifteen minutes. Please bring all your selections to the register."

Earl Waddell put the microphone back in its slot and peered out through the window in the office to the check-out lanes. Business had been heavy earlier in the evening with people buying last minute Halloween treats. Then it had trickled down so much that he had let one of the last three checkers go home early. Now he had two lanes open, and it was just the two checkers, him, and Grady, the security guard left. Not that Grady was much of a guard. He was a twenty-four year-old kid who played bass guitar in a country band. The most important thing in his life seemed to be his intricately oiled hair, which he was always combing.

Earl had never been impressed with the quality of the guards the store had gotten. They'd used every service in town and never had a guard who looked like he would scare a mouse. Most of them were goof-offs, and one of them he'd even had to fire, because the guy was a real loose cannon. Off-duty cops would be best, Earl knew, and God knows he'd suggested it enough times at management meetings. But the big boys said they cost too much. Besides, they said, we'll probably never really need one. They're just for show. Earl told them that the way things were now, with gangs and crack junkies shooting innocent folks, they'd better take precautions or they'd be sorry. But he was just the night manager, and they had better things to do than to listen to him.

He picked up the microphone again. "Food Giant will close in ten minutes. Please bring your selections to the front for check-out."

Smith put a carton of milk into the basket dangling from one hand. He heard the door into the warehouse area whisk open and turned his back to it. An older woman and a teen-age boy passed through it. "Oh shit, I'm tired," he heard the kid say.

"What'd I tell you about that cussing?" the woman said as she poked his arm.

He yawned. "Sorry. I'm almost too tired to party, but hey, Halloween only comes once a year."

"Halloween's a pagan celebration," she said. "You'd be better off if you stayed home and read your Bible, and didn't go out on the street with all that trash. Oh, if I don't get home and soak these feet, they'll fall off!"

Neither of them noticed Smith at the dairy cooler. He waited until they were out of sight and slipped through the door into the warehouse. The lights were dim, and he stepped very carefully, very silently around the stacks of food, cleaning products, diapers. As he worked his way around an eight-foot stack of Tide, he thought idly that if it fell on him, it would be all she wrote.

He had spent several nights slumped in his car, watching the front door as the store closed. He knew there should be only the front crew left, but he'd had to make sure. He sat down behind a towering stack of toilet paper and made a snack out of the milk, a package of cheese, and a box of wheat crackers.

Grady locked the door behind the final customers. "That it?" Earl called.

"I think so," Grady said. "I'll do the patrol." Patrol my ass, Earl thought. He means strolling around the store and stealing a package of Oreos. "Annette, run me the tapes on those registers. Mindy, get the drawers and let's you and me start counting them."

Mindy carried the drawers to the office. She was a young wife, no children yet. Earl thought she was cute but got depressed whenever he realized that she was young enough to be his daughter. It seemed not that long ago that he was her age, but his class at Dimmitt High School had just held its 25 year reunion. He didn't go, because who would want to report that he was the night manager at a grocery store in Amarillo? He figured they would probably mouth niceties like "Boy, that sounds like good work," and secretly think "Oh, poor Earl, I knew he wouldn't amount to much."

He sat with one tray on his lap, while she counted the other one. Annette brought the tapes and started to count the proceeds they had dropped into the floor safe earlier in the day.

At fifteen minutes past midnight, Smith stood up and brushed the crumbs off his black denim shirt and pants. The dim light and the towering ceiling were eerie. He glanced around at them, and a shiver went through him. God, I must be getting old, he thought. For what seemed like the hundredth time in the last five days he wondered what the hell he was doing here, why was he even thinking about another stick-up, much less actually doing it. Then the picture of his father lying on his deathbed drifted into his mind.

He walked very softly to the back door, which led out onto a small loading zone. Against the alley at the back of the lot was a high board fence, and twenty yards down from that on the left hand side was a street. The exit door had a horizontal bar in the middle; it opened only from the inside. Smith put both hands on the bar and very slowly inched it until the door clicked. He opened it a foot. Carl and Joe were standing there waiting, exactly on time. He opened the door a few inches wider to let them in, and leaned out. On the street to his left, he could see the nose of his car. Although he could not see into it, he knew Freddie was at the wheel.

In all the years he spent on the road, living in one little apartment or another in one town or the next, sometimes with a lover, but never with friends, Smith had found himself more often than not in darkened movie theatres. Now he remembered a movie where Gary Busey had played a fuck-up who took off on his friends who were in the middle of a diamond heist. They hit the door of the place running hard, and he was simply gone. Smith prayed that Freddie would be there when they were finished tonight. He seemed sober; at least Smith had not smelled alcohol on him. That had been one of his stipulations for the job—that Freddie could drink as much as he wanted when the job was over. Smith didn't much care if he drank himself to death, as long as he showed up sober. Truth told, Smith was sick of all three of them and sometimes of himself too.

Carl held a paper sack with the top rolled down. He reached down into it and pulled out a revolver and a pistol. The grips were covered with electrician's tape. Smith nodded at him and Carl took out three black ski masks and three pairs of gloves. They pulled the masks over their heads, rolling them down over their faces like condoms. In Joe's right hand was a 12-gauge pump action Remington shotgun. He put the mask and gloves on and held the gun across his chest. Smith looked at each of them, and they gave him short nods. He could see sweat on Carl's lip where the mask didn't cover it.

He always preferred using ski masks. They lent even the least threatening countenance an air of insanity. Ski masks made the average person think of terrorists, of rapists, of the cruelest of people, those without a conscience, who struck in the night for the joy of it. They were even more effective than guns. Smith knew from experience that the more scared someone was, the less likely he would try to be heroic.

"Ready?" he asked.

Carl licked his lips and nodded.

"Hell yes," Joe said.

Smith nodded his head toward the swinging doors. They crept toward them. Smith inched his head up to one of the diamond-shaped windows and peered through it. He nodded to the others to let them know it was all clear. One of the slippery spots in his plan was that he didn't know just where the guard would be when they entered the store. He would take the aisle closest to the office; Carl would be in the middle and Joe on the opposite side of the store. Whoever found the guard first would take him down quickly and silently, so the other workers wouldn't know the trio was in the store until the right moment. Smith knew that in a robbery the element of surprise was as important as location in real estate.

He pushed open the door and let the others through. They quickly went to their positions. Smith breathed in and out slowly. Thank God. He had been afraid that Joe would get a wild hair up his ass and go barreling off to the front, blasting with his shotgun. Instead, he reached the far right aisle and looked back at Smith one more time before he disappeared behind a pyramid of Coca-Cola cans.

Mindy finished counting her drawer and handed the stacks of bills to Earl. "Here you go, Mr. Waddell. You need any help?"

He finished a stack of tens, counting silently to himself. He wrote down the number and shook his head at her. "No, I don't think so. We can handle it. Why don't you go on home?"

"I won't argue that. My weekend's coming up, so I'll see you on Tuesday."

"All right. Be careful getting to your car." For a moment he wished he could be escorting her out there. God, he thought, I need a vacation.

Mindy reached down and picked up her purse. "'Night, Annette."

Annette looked up and smiled at her. "See you, Mindy. Enjoy them days off." She walked with her to the door, twisted the key so Mindy could get out, and locked it after her.

Annette hated the counting worse than any part of her job, so she took her time getting back to the office. As she passed aisle six, where all the frozen foods sat in rows of gleaming metal freezers, she saw Grady walking from the back, wiping off his fingers on his pants. She knew he had just wolfed down a package of cookies and that Earl would have a cow if he saw him. Grady winked at her.

"Twelve-thirty and all is well," he said. He picked up a *People* magazine from a register rack and sat on the check-out belt.

"Don't wrinkle that magazine, Grady," Earl said.

"You bet." Grady looked over the top of the magazine to see if Earl was watching and gave him the finger behind it. He settled in to read an article about a starlet whose picture showed just enough of her breasts to still be respectable. He scooted down off the belt and wandered away a few feet down an aisle so Earl couldn't see him. He put the starlet down and started fingering the chords to a new song the band was learning. He never guessed that anyone was even close to him until he felt the cold metal gently nestle into his neck.

"Man, working Saturday night's a bitch," Annette said.

"So are starving kids."

"Yeah, ain't that the truth. I figured once Mike found another job I could quit and go back to school, but that hasn't happened yet. Here I am, spending another Saturday night at Food Giant. Makes you want to cry sometimes, don't it?"

"Well, I feel lucky I got a job at all and I—"

Earl's voice faltered before he actually heard anything. He was concentrating on the money stacked on the desk in front of him when out of the corner of his eye, over Annette's shoulder, he saw something that he knew just didn't belong there. It seemed to him that he just couldn't lift his head fast enough and that if he could everything would be okay. In the months following, he lost many nights of sleep trying to figure out what he could have done differently. If I had only, his thoughts began as he sat in his easy chair at three in the morning, the television playing old movies, sports, anything to get his mind off what he saw when he was finally able to look up.

"Gentlemen, I need your attention," the man in the mask said. Right at the door of the office stood three of them, the tallest one holding an arm around poor Grady's throat. In his other hand was a gray revolver that he held to the security guard's temple. Grady was trying very hard not to squirm, trying his very hardest to remain completely still, but his eyes rolled and his tongue kept squirming out to lick his lips.

There were two other men, dressed identically in black jeans and shirts, ski masks pulled down over their heads. One held a pistol, which was pointed straight at Earl's head. Earl started to sweat. The other man held a shotgun across his chest, and under the mask Earl could see a smirk on his lips.

"Here's the way it is," the tall man said. "You put everything green into those bank bags. Do it in 30 seconds, and maybe I won't I splatter your brains all over this store."

Earl sat at the desk, knees together, his hands still holding a stack of dollars. A single tear squeezed from Annette's right eye and rolled down her cheek. Her mouth was open, and her bottom lip trembled so slightly it couldn't be noticed from more than a foot away.

The man pressed the barrel gently but firmly against the soft skin of Grady's neck. "I suggest you start now," he said.

Earl and Annette snapped back into the real world. They furiously began stuffing bills into the bags. Every time they hesitated, or their fingers hung up on the zipper, they were afraid they would hear a metallic click and the sound of an explosion a moment before Grady's brains sprayed the air around them.

Earl had never played football in high school. He had not even been in the band. When the Dimmitt High Bobcats rushed down the field against the Muleshoe Mules or the Friona Chieftains, he had always sat in the stands, dreaming that he was the charging hero in the helmet, carrying the ball into the realm of eternal glory. He had never done one heroic thing in his life, but he knew that he must act now not just from heroism, but in protection of himself, Annette, and the proceeds of Food Giant which had been entrusted to him. As he continued to put bills in the bag on his lap, he very stealthily inched his foot toward a black button on the floor, a silent alarm which to his knowledge had never been used.

As he did, the man with the shotgun who until now had not spoken, pushed aside the tall masked man and Grady, throwing them both off balance. He took two steps that brought him straight to Earl and slammed his cowboy boot down onto Earl's ankle before his foot could trip the alarm.

Earl's whole leg caught fire like it had been splashed with gasoline and lit with a match. The man stuck the shotgun right in his face and growled, "Motherfucker, you try that again and I'll blow your head off."

Annette was crying in earnest now but didn't stop stuffing money in the bags.

Smith regained his balance and wrapped his arm tighter around the boy's neck. Fortunately for him, the guard was petrified. He could have no more made a move for the gun than he could have performed any other of his job's duties.

The woman went back to stuffing the bag, but the manager was still rubbing his ankle, his face strained with pain. "I want four hands working," Smith said. The man slowly started putting money into the bag. They finished with the money on the counter.

"The safe," Smith said.

"It's a, uh, it's a time lock safe. I can't—"

"Don't even try that, cocksucker," Joe broke in. "We ain't stupid."

Carl nudged Joe in the ribs with his elbow and shook his head at him. Behind the mask, Joe's eyes burned.

The manager reached into the safe and took out two bank bags already stuffed with money. "This is all there is."

Smith moved back, hauling Grady with him. "You two get out. Take a look," he said, nodding at Carl. Carl stepped into the office, glanced down into the floor safe and opened the drawers, all the time with his eyes flicking back to Earl and Annette. He nodded at Smith.

"All right, let's go," Smith said. He guided Grady down the first aisle, toward the back. The boy was still terrified. Smith could feel him trembling. "Each of you take one," he said to Joe and Carl. Joe immediately went to Annette. She looked at Earl, pleading. The six of them started toward the back.

Halfway down the aisle, Joe started to lag behind. Smith glanced to both sides, and when he couldn't see Joe and the woman, he found them five feet back. "Come on," he said.

Joe had his left arm around her waist, the right gripping the stock of the shotgun, with the barrel pointed toward the floor. "You go on back," he said. "This ain't gonna take a minute."

Shit, Smith thought. He's thinking with his dick again. He smoothly whirled Grady around and went back to Joe. Annette, realizing what Joe planned, was struggling against him. "Oh yeah, I like that," Joe said. "Just keep on, that'll make it better."

Smith let go of Grady's neck and pushed him against Joe, then grabbed the woman's belt, pulling her to him. Joe stumbled back a step before he recovered, jamming the shotgun into Grady's back. The guard winced in pain. "Let's go, shitface," Joe mumbled.

They reached the swinging doors into the storage room and Smith put his shoulder against them, still holding Annette. He entered the storeroom and reached for the paper bag Carl and Joe had brought in. He pulled out a roll of silver duct tape.

"Watch her," he told Carl. Carl motioned Annette to move over by him. Smith nodded to Earl. "Lay down on your stomach."

Earl's face turned even paler. "Mister, come on," he said. "I got people who care about me. I got a wife at home, and kids. Jesus Christ!"

Smith ripped a piece of tape with his teeth. "If you don't shut up, there won't be enough of you left for anybody to care about."

Earl lay down on his stomach. "Hands behind you, crossed at the wrists," Smith said. Earl complied instantly. Smith wrapped tape around his ankles, wrists, and mouth. He looked at Grady. "You're next." Grady lay down on the floor in the appropriate position. Smith glanced at Joe, who stood a few feet away from him. Jesus Christ, he thought, he's pouting like a kid who didn't get his way. He nodded at Annette. "Go ahead."

Annette glanced at Joe, fear feverish in her eyes. "Don't hurt me, please."

"Nobody's going to hurt you," Smith said. "Just lay down." Her face shone with a faint sheen of sweat. He taped her up. Lying on her stomach, face turned to the side, a patch of shiny silver over her mouth, she swiveled her eyes up at the three men.

"You ready?" Smith said. Carl, holding the bank bags, nodded. "Got everything you came in with?" Joe ignored him. "All right, let's go."

"I got one last piece of business to look after," Joe said. Before Smith or Carl could do anything to stop him, he pumped the shotgun and jammed the barrel into the back of Earl's neck. "You had this one coming." He grinned as Earl squeezed his eyes shut. "Say good-bye, prick."

Smith felt like he was wading through water as he thrust his hand toward the shotgun, desperately trying to pull it away from the manager's neck, trying to stop the disaster he knew he had invited by using Joe for this job.

His fingers were just grazing the stock of the shotgun when Joe pulled the trigger and the click of the pin striking on the empty chamber echoed through the warehouse. Joe's scowl slowly turned into a grin. The sound of spreading water reached their ears, and a moment later they smelled the acrid odor of urine as Earl wet his pants. The manager lay so still that at a glance the dark pool flowing from his middle looked like blood.

Joe stared straight into Smith's eyes. He stepped close and in a low voice said, "I told you I'd make that little fucker pee his pants. And I done it. Now I'm ready to go." He walked straight to the exit door. Smith looked at Carl, who shook his head and mumbled "Jesus Christ." They followed him out.

The moment the door opened the car began to roll, and in fifteen seconds it stopped beside the loading dock. Smith took a quick look around and got into the front seat. Carl and Joe slammed the back doors and Freddie smoothly accelerated, waiting until they were on the street driving away from the store before turning on his headlights. At least he didn't fuck this up, Smith thought. "You know how to get to my place?"

Freddie nodded. "Man, I thought you were never going to get out of there."

"It's always harder when you're the pick-up man. Seems like it's an hour for every minute of real time."

In the back seat, Joe and Carl were pressed against the doors as if trying to put every inch possible between them. "I'm just gonna say one thing," Joe said, looking at Carl. "Don't you ever put a hand on me again. You do, and they'll find you in an irrigation ditch."

Carl exploded in frustration. "You weren't supposed to say anything! What if that guy recognized your voice? You could have fucked it all up!"

Joe stared at Carl and shook his head. "Pussy," he said, and turned his face to stare out the window.

Freddie pulled off Amarillo Boulevard into the driveway of the Ace Courts and glided to a stop in front of Smith's cabin. Joe reached for the door. "Not yet," Smith said. He glanced around. Four doors down two men sat in lawn chairs in front of their unit, but the cabin's front light, like most of them, was burned out. There was no other sign of life. "Okay," he said. He picked up the paper bag where the masks, tape and handguns rested. "Let's go." He stepped out of the car and quickly but casually unlocked the door of the cabin. The other three followed him in.

"Throw the money on the bed," he ordered. Carl and Joe, carrying the bags, tossed them down. "You two count that one, Joe and I will split the other one. Let's get it done."

They unzipped the bags and upended them over the bed. Each man took stacks of bills and began counting. "You got any beer?" Freddie asked.

Smith shook his head. "Worry about that when we finish."

Fifteen minutes later Freddie counted the last of his stack. "Okay, what do we have?" Smith said. "Carl?"

"Twenty seven thousand, five forty one."

"Joe?"

"Four thousand four hundred eleven."

"Freddie?"

"Seven thousand seven eighty one."

"All right, I've got twenty three thousand one hundred sixteen. Add that up—" he quickly jotted down the numbers "—comes to sixty two thousand, eight hundred forty-nine. Freddie gets two thousand, that's sixty, eight forty nine. Three ways is," he said, doing the division, "twenty thousand two hundred and eight-three. I'll divide it up." He picked up four stacks of rubber-banded twenties and handed them to Freddie.

"All right!" Joe said. "Shit, I don't make much more than that in a year!"

Carl said nothing.

"I didn't have any idea it was going to be so much," Freddie said. "Shit! Look, I know you three did all the work and I don't mean to sound ungrateful, but I think I really deserve more than this. I mean I—"

Smith shut him down quickly. "Uh uh. We made an agreement, and you're two thousand dollars richer than you were an hour ago. So you take this money and shut the fuck up and that's the last we hear about it."

He quickly counted out the rest of it and handed Joe and Carl their stacks. They stuffed them into the pockets of their jackets.

"There it is," Smith said. "And I want to say this again. I see any of you on the street, I don't know you. We've never met. That's it. Use it in good health."

Joe stood up and nodded at Smith. He ignored Carl and walked out the door. Freddie gave him a second to get away, and said, "I'm going to smoke a butt." He stepped out onto the cement slab that passed for a front porch. They could hear the traffic from Amarillo Boulevard, the sounds and smells of neon and strip joints, of fast food and gasoline. Carl sat for a moment, forearms on his knees, looking at the floor. Then he raised his head and looked at Smith. "You know what's going to happen, don't you?" he said.

Smith shrugged his shoulders. "What?"

"Someday that guy's going to waste somebody. It's going to happen. No doubt. I'm just glad I won't be there when it does. I'm glad I'm never going to see that crazy fucker again."

Smith didn't say anything. Finally, he nodded his head.

"And to tell you the truth," Carl said, "I'm glad I won't see you again, either. Not at Bailey's or anywhere else." Smith nodded again. "And you know, this doesn't make us even. Not even close."

Carl turned and walked out the door, slamming it behind him. Freddie leaned against the wall, smoking. "Let's go," Carl said.

"Can we stop off and get some beer?"

Carl sighed. "Yeah. Sure." They walked to the car, which was parked on a side street.

Smith shoved his money and the paper bag under the bed. Tomorrow he would visit the hospital, and tomorrow night he would get rid of the guns, except for his own. For the first time in a week, he felt like he could breathe again. For a while.

Chapter 15

Max's hands were stuffed deep in the pockets of his jeans. He couldn't believe how cold it was. Lately the days were warm, sometimes hot, with the temperature creeping up close to ninety degrees in the mid-afternoons, and sometimes when he left home, usually between 8:00 and 9:00 a.m., there was a faint chill in the air. But this morning, at 5:30, it was downright freezing. He had put on a light jacket but hadn't thought to bring gloves. It also hadn't helped that he was here ten minutes early. He didn't want to be late and make a bad impression. Max danced around, trying to warm up his toes, wondering what Angel wanted to do that couldn't just as well be done at noon.

"Jesus, it's cold!" he called out to the stars overhead that were bright despite the lights of the city. He pulled his hands out of his pockets and breathed hard on them like he had seen people do in the movies, but that only made them feel colder. He stuck them under his arms. "Shit shit shit!" A breeze picked up and pierced straight through the jacket. Oh this is great, he thought. Just exactly what I needed.

He heard the roar of a powerful engine and looked toward Georgia. A white truck pulling a trailer was turning the corner and droning toward Bailey's. Max's first thought was that it was Danny Gonzalez, who more often than not showed up at meetings pulling a horse trailer. A saddled horse was Danny's briefcase, the most essential tool of his job. He glanced again at the truck. There was no reason for it to be Danny; the earliest meeting on a weekend was 9:30, and that was still four hours away. When it would almost be warm, Max reminded himself.

He leaned against the wall of Bailey's, trying to get out of the wind. The truck slowed down as it approached him and pulled to a stop directly in front of the pool hall. Fright seized his guts. Although no one with the exception of Joe Wagner had been overtly unpleasant to him in the six weeks he had been here, he was always afraid some crazed redneck type would suddenly take it into his head to put the boot to a Yankee Jew insurgent. He tried to look through the passenger's side window, but a heavy tint obscured his view. Shit, he thought. The truck sat for a moment like a growling white dragon, the trailer giving it twice the length of a normal truck, exhaust puffing ghost-like in the cold, dark air.

The passenger's window slid down, and Max imagined a fanatic wearing a

Confederate flag t-shirt with the sleeves ripped off emerging from the truck. Instead, a gray furry face peered out, and Bailey bounded to the ground. She paced up to him and stood looking at him solemnly, her gold eyes ablaze. Max heard the driver's door open and Angel's face appeared over the cab. From the trailer came the sound of a soft nicker and the ring of a hoof on metal.

"Hey," she said. "You want some coffee?"

"I think that might take some of the chill out, yeah."

"All right. Gonna have to come over here to get it." Angel raised a thermos up where he could see it.

Max pushed away from the wall and Bailey followed him. He could not hear her, so quiet was she, but he knew she was there, and to his surprise he found that knowledge reassuring.

Angel still stood on the running board of her big Dodge Ram. She poured coffee into the lid of the thermos, and the steam rose into the cold air like a ghostly wreath.

Bailey jumped through the still-open passenger window into the cab. Angel pushed the cup across the top of the truck toward Max. "Cold enough for you?"

"I'll be honest with you, it's a lot colder than I think it has any right to be. One thing you can say about the north, when it gets cold it tends to stay that way the whole frigging day, you know what I mean?"

"I don't mind this, to be honest. It keeps me challenged. I used to never want to stay in the same place for very long. Now I've found that I kind of like having a home. But when the weather's like this, it feels like the place is changing even though I'm staying settled. Does that make any sense?"

Amazingly enough to Max, it did. He nodded his head. What didn't make sense to him was why they were drinking coffee over the roof of a truck, as if it were a shoulder-high breakfast table. Apparently Bailey had that same thought, because they both heard a low rumble coming from inside the cab.

"Yeah, I guess maybe we should," Angel said. "How about it, Max? You ready to hit the road?"

"Yeah, we could do that. Is it going to sound dumb if I ask if the horses I assume are in that trailer are coming with us? And whether our morning's activity concerns me making physical contact with said horses?"

"Just one of them," Angel said. She shut her door and looked at him. She was wearing a red flannel shirt covered with a gray/blue down vest, her usual faded Levi's, and leather gloves. "Let's get you to riding one at a time before we start on two."

"Oh my God," said Max, as Angel put the truck in gear.

She drove them southeast of town, along narrow county roads, the truck's hi-beams sweeping along the dark and lonely pavement. They passed the thermos cup back and forth, occasionally refilling it. The dashboard seemed to have more lights on it than some jets Max had flown on. "Are all these for real? I mean, is consultation of them essential to driving this thing?"

"I don't know what most of them are, tell you the truth. And the ones I do, I don't need. Who the hell needs a tachometer? For what? I think they put all these whistles and farts on here for the benefit of those yuppies who think they need a 4-wheel even though they never leave the pavement. Makes them feel like they're important." She took a sip of coffee. "I guess it's one of the advantages of owning your own business. You have extra money to spend on toys. Doesn't it work that way for you?"

"Not really. I have a knack for finding clients who don't have what you would call stacks of ready cash."

"Well, it helps that I don't have too much to spend it on. Just me and my house and my dog and my horses. And the club. But I try not to put too much money into that. Destroys the ambiance."

Max glanced out the window in time to see a flash of white bounding away from the road. Bailey must have seen it too, because she chuffed softly to herself. Max turned to Angel, his face lit up like a little boy's. "Was that a deer?"

"I didn't see it, but probably. There're quite a few of them around here."

"You know, it's funny," Max said. "Lots of people up in New York, myself one of them until recently, think that Texas is all desert, and it's still the Wild West. I think we picture like saguaro cactus, the ones with the big arms stuck up like traffic cops on 42nd Street. It's not like that at all. I mean yeah, there are cowboys, but not riding up and down the streets shooting."

"I don't know," Angel said. "It's a lot wilder than you might think. We've got gangs—little kids who don't get any love at home, so they try to find it by being punks, shooting each other up. There's stuff happening along Amarillo Boulevard that would probably rival anything in New York, day or night. People still get drunk and shoot their wife or husband, or their neighbor just cause he kicked their dog. That's what today has in common with the old days of Amarillo. People shooting each other up cause they're too dumb to know any better."

"Or too drunk."

"Yeah." Her eyes flicked over to him and settled on the road again.

They drove for a mile in silence. "So is it a secret where we're going?" Max asked.

Angel turned to him and her mouth flirted with a smile. "More like a surprise." She reached her hand out and dug it into Bailey's ruff. The wolf closed her eyes rapturously. Angel kept her eyes on the road.

"You starting to like it here?"

Max thought for a moment. "You know, that first night, when I was at Bailey's"—the wolf flicked her ears—"I was scared to death. I just wanted to die, to cry, to disappear into a hole in the floor. But after a while, some things happened. I met some folks I had a lot in common with, I bartered with that guy Frank for a car, got some clients I didn't lose sleep over. And the more I stayed, the more I liked it. I never liked it that much in New York anyway. I mean, it was okay, I think it was me that didn't fit. I just always itched, you know how that goes? Feeling like you need to be somewhere else, do something else. Thinking if you can just find the right longitude and latitude, everything will just settle into place. I know that's the geographic cure. I think that's probably what I was doing with the Phoenix thing. So I guess the answer to your question is yes, I do."

"The people you were talking about having something in common with, is that the crowd at Bailey's?"

Max didn't answer for a moment. "Yeah, mostly. Some of the courthouse crowd. A few others." He didn't know how to tell her the others were a gang of coffee-guzzling sober drunks.

Angel slowed down and turned carefully onto a gravel road. After a while she turned again onto a dirt track and stopped. She poured the last of the coffee and drank a little bit, then handed it to him. "Finish it." He did.

She opened the door and got out. She stood stretching her back. "You ever see anything like that?" She nodded her head upward, and Max looked up at the sky.

"Oh my god," he said, and once again he felt like a little kid. The only thing he had even experienced like it was at the Hayden Planetarium on Central Park West. But as majestic as that was, it was just a faint imitation. Everywhere he looked, in all corners of the sky, were thousands and millions of stars. He never knew why the Milky Way was called that until he saw the almost pure whiteness of it. He slowly craned his neck around until he felt dizzy.

"Something, huh?" Angel said.

"It's beautiful. I don't think even Shakespeare could have found the words for it."

Already the air was just a touch warmer, and he started to find it almost pleasant. The brush a few feet away skittered, and he saw a jackrabbit explode from under a bush. He expected Bailey to go bounding after it, but she only glanced that way with faint disinterest.

Angel crossed over to the other side of the truck. "Hey, do me a favor, will you?"

"Sure, what it is it?"

He heard the brush of denim rubbing against something else. "Stay over there for a minute."

There was a trickle of water, and he realized that it was the sound of Angel peeing. Max felt his cheeks flush hot in the chilly air. After a few moments there was the sound of the brushing cloth again, and her voice. "I guess I should apologize, but I don't think I will. Coffee tends to go through me fast. It's going to be a while before we're back inside, and all we're going to have between us are two horses and a dog. If you need to go, you better do it now."

"Oh, I don't know."

"I think you might be more comfortable."

Max thought it over a moment. Maybe she was right. "Stay over there, okay?"

"I'm not moving."

Sheesh, he thought. The last time I did something like this I was drunk, and then it was probably on the sidewalk or in an alley. He unzipped his jeans and leaned his arm against the trailer. Oh my God, he thought, I can't believe I'm doing this. What if I get arrested? No, there aren't any cops out here. What about rats? That's New York. What if a snake bites me? Do snakes jump? It took him a minute to actually start peeing, and then it felt like he would never stop. He was afraid Angel was standing on the other side of the trailer, wondering the same thing. Max did a quick inventory of his life and decided that he had never been more embarrassed than he was right now.

Finally he finished and zipped up his jeans. He cleared his throat a couple of times and bumped his elbow against the trailer to let Angel know he was finished. It must have worked, because a few moments later he heard her unlatch the back gate on the trailer and make a soft clucking sound with her tongue and teeth. He walked around just in time to almost get run over by a horse's rear end as it backed out of the trailer. He jumped back as the horse's front legs touched the ground. Angel took hold of the halter. The horse was the color of milk chocolate, with white spots dappled across her rump.

"Hey, sugar. It's okay. This is our friend Max. Yeah, baby." Steam billowed from the animal's nostrils in the cold air. "You want to come over here, Max?"

He passed in back of the horse, giving its legs plenty of room, and approached its head with trepidation.

"You ever been around horses at all?"

"No, not really. Mostly down in the Village, they have cops who ride horses, and sometimes they'd tie them up by the basketball courts at Sixth Avenue and West Fourth. I'd go up and look at them, but that's about it."

"Come here, step closer." He did. "Put your hand on her nose." Max reached his hand up to the horse's nostrils, but when he was less than an inch away it blew warm air out onto his hand, and shuffled its front hooves in a tiny dance. Scared, Max stepped back quickly.

"No, it's okay," Angel said. "She's pretty big, but she won't hurt you. C'mon." She took Max's hand, and he realized it was the first time his skin had actually touched hers. He expected to feel an electric charge, the high that in the past he had often felt with women, a high almost as good as alcohol. But it didn't come; instead, he felt the strength in her hand, the calluses on her palms from many hours of holding pool sticks and leather reins, of lifting bales of hay and pushing a curry comb through a horse's mud-caked coat. Instead of making him high, the touch of her hand made him feel secure. The fear he had of the horse just moments before wisped away like its steaming breath.

Angel guided his hand up to the horse's nose. Once again he felt its warm breath on him, and then his fingers stroked the most brilliantly soft surface they had ever encountered. Max had touched silk before, and velvet, had felt the fur of a tiny kitten on his face, had laid his head on the breasts of lovers, had stroked the skin on the inside of their thighs, but never had he felt anything that was so soft or sensuous. His fingers lingered on the horse's nose. He tried to find a word for the touch, the feel of it, and simply could not. The breeze brushed the tears that were starting to escape from his eyes and cooled his face. It felt pleasant, and once again he felt more alive than he had in years.

He turned to find Angel watching him, and he thought he detected sadness in her eyes. Then she smiled, the first real smile he had ever seen from her beyond the slight turn the corners of her mouth sometimes took. Her lips opened, and her eyes laughed, and Max thought she was the most beautiful woman he had ever seen, standing there in the dark under the cornucopia of stars, wearing denim and flannel and down. He realized that he was living in an entirely new world, and he was in love with it.

"This is Summerlea," she said. "She's an Appaloosa. We've been together for six years. She was five when we found each other." She rubbed her face against the horse's head, and it nickered at her. "Yeah, baby. I know. Hold her, will you?" She handed Max the lead rope attached to the mare's halter. She walked to the back of the trailer and made a kissing noise with her lips. Another horse backed out. This one was smaller than Summerlea, and his coat was white, but splashed with patches that were so black they seemed to absorb the very night around them.

"What's her name?"

"His. This one's a gelding. He's called Nightfall."

"What's that color called?"

"He's a black and white paint. There are different names for different types of paints, but that'll do." She handed his lead rope to Max too, and went into the trailer, emerging with a saddle and pad hoisted over one shoulder, a bridle draped over the other. She set the saddle down on its horn, with the cantle sticking up in the air, and went back into the trailer. She returned in moments with another set of tack.

"You want to help?"

Max couldn't find the words to answer. "Well I, I mean, God, of course. Yes."

Angel tied the horses to the trailer and showed him how to touch them, to stroke their heads and backs and explain to them what he was going to do. She settled the blankets onto the horses' backs. Max picked up Nightfall's saddle and placed it carefully on the blanket. He only hesitated when he had to reach underneath the horse's belly to grab the cinch and pull it up to him. He was still a little scared of the horse's size, the strength in its legs. Angel talked him through it, showed him how to tighten the cinch, and told him how horses always blow out their bellies, so that it was necessary to walk them a few paces and retighten the cinch. She saddled Summerlea while Max stroked Nightfall's head and touched the smooth, shiny leather of the saddle. Once she looked at Max and saw him kiss the horse's nose, and rub his cheek against it, and she smiled.

When she finished with Summerlea, she showed Max how to put the bridle on, pushing her thumb between the horse's teeth and sliding the bit into its mouth. She adjusted the stirrups for his height and shut the doors to the trailer.

"You ready?"

"I think so, yeah."

"You know how to get on?"

"I've seen it in the movies."

"That'll work. Just put your left hand on the reins right in front of the saddle, on his neck. Then put your left foot into the stirrup, and swing your right leg up and over. Don't worry. He's pretty calm."

Max did as she said, amazed that at the age of thirty-six he was doing something for the first time that felt so affirming and so full of life. He took the reins, put his left foot into the stirrup, and swung his body up. In a moment he was astride Nightfall, his right foot searching until it found the stirrup. The feel of the horse's powerful body between his legs was so sensuous, so new to him.

He felt like he was being born again into a wonderful world. Nightfall walked a few paces forward, and Max pulled back on the reins like he had seen Gary Cooper, John Wayne, James Stewart do in the movies, and to his amazement it worked, exactly like it was supposed to. The horse stopped. He felt his cheeks flush, and he touched the horse's neck with the right rein. It turned to the left, toward Angel.

"What do you think, Nightfall?" she said. "Think we got a natural here? Sure seems like it to me." Max was pleased with the compliment. Then he watched as Angel did what seemed to him an amazing feat. She took the reins in her left hand, put both hands on the saddle horn, and jumped straight up from the ground. As she did, her left boot slid into the stirrup and she landed in the saddle in one swift movement. Without breaking her motion, she nudged Summerlea with her right leg and touched her with the right rein, and the horse danced in circles, with as much grace and beauty as Max had ever seen on the stage of any ballet company. She saw him looking at her.

"Don't worry. It won't take you long to be doing this, if you want to. Let's go. Just pick up a nice slow walk."

They headed away from the truck, and for the first few minutes all Max could hear was the creak of leather, the rustle of the horses' legs in the brush, and the soft sounds they made when they talked to each other. Occasionally Bailey would deliver a small "uff" sound when she found something interesting. The stars were still bright, but in the east Max detected the first sign of the sunrise.

"So how did you find these horses?" His voice sounded too loud in the cool air, a harsh intrusion.

"I bought Summerlea at an auction. She'd been seized by the Humane Society. Asshole who owned her didn't feed her right, didn't trim her hooves, basically ignored her. She was about 300 pounds underweight, and pretty skittish. But I could tell she was basically sound and a pretty good saddle horse under all those ribs. Nightfall started out life as a wild horse, a mustang, and I bought him for $25. Government program. Took a couple of years to train him, but he's good as gold."

"Yeah, I can tell."

"You want to trot?"

"Is that fast?"

"Not really. Just a little faster than a walk. When you're ready, just make a kissing sound, and squeeze him lightly with your legs. I'll let you go first, because if we start, he might just follow us. It'll feel a little funny at first, a little jarring, but just keep your heels down. You can grab the horn if you need to, but I don't think you will. Go ahead when you're ready."

Max closed his eyes and mouthed the Serenity Prayer, then gently squeezed Nightfall. The horse fell into a slow trot, and on his left Angel and Summerlea kept pace with them. He knew that with very much of this his body would get sore. His shoulders were shaking up and down, and his butt slapped against the saddle.

"Try to find the rhythm of the horse," Angel said. "You'll be able to balance better if you do. When it moves up, you can go with it. Settle your weight on the balls of your feet, and kind of gently rock with the horse."

She trotted alongside him, and Max watched how her body moved in the saddle. He started to copy her, and slowly he found a rhythm that matched the horse's. He still wasn't very comfortable, but he could feel them working together. He hadn't pulled his hair back this morning, and it whipped around his face.

"Looks like you're a natural, Max. Now all you have to do is pronounce 'horse' right."

"What, you think 'hoowas' doesn't sound right? Yo, dat's de way we say it in Brooklyn."

Angel laughed. "Up here you're likely to hear 'harse' as 'horse.' So I guess however you say it is ok."

She nudged Summerlea with her boot and the horse started to speed up. Nightfall kept up with her, and in moments Max found himself hanging onto the horn with his right hand, hoping fervently that Angel didn't see him.

"Are we still trotting?" he called out to her, hoping that the wind wouldn't carry his voice away.

"Sorry. This is called a lope. 'Canter' if you're one of those nose-in-the-air folks who ride English. It's faster than a trot, slower than a gallop."

"Could we maybe not try the gallop today?" Actually, the lope was smoother than the trot, and Max found himself getting used to it. It was probably no more dangerous than crossing between the cars of a subway train, something he had done thousands of times in his life.

They loped across the prairie, Bailey running to stay even with them, her tongue hanging out of her mouth. Max took his hand off the horn, and to his astonishment he didn't fall out of the saddle. He reached down, touched the horse's neck, and loosened the reins. After a few minutes Angel and Summerlea began to slow down, and Nightfall followed suit. They slowed to a trot, then to a walk, and finally they stopped. They stood side by side, Angel with her eyes closed, letting the breeze caress her face. It was no longer cold but delightfully cool, and Max unzipped his jacket.

"Are we just resting?" he asked.

Angel kept her eyes closed. "Yeah, kind of. Just wait for a few minutes. I want to show you something."

Max rubbed Nightfall's neck. The horse was blowing air in and out of its nostrils. Max didn't know what to call it. Panting didn't seem the right word. Too doggy. But he couldn't figure out anything else. He realized there was more to horses than meets the eye. Or the leg. He laughed at his own bad joke.

The songs of birds started to get louder. Max turned his head from horizon to horizon, and as he did he saw, or rather sensed, something that had not been there moments before. Thirty yards in front of them, he felt an absence of earth, a black maw that grew larger and deeper as it stretched away from them. As he watched, the eastern horizon grew pinker and pinker, and the clouds along it looked like an oil painting, so delicate were their details. Red and orange appeared in them, touching wisps of horizontal clouds, breaking through a hole like a spear of light. As the sun peeked closer and closer to the horizon, it began to illuminate the rim of the canyon. The top layers of it were a deep reddish brown, but as the light crept down the canyon wall, it revealed bands of yellow and black and red and brown, and the gray sticks of the mesquite tree branches became a rich green.

Max was captivated. His eyes couldn't move from the spectacular, awe-inspiring vision unfolding before his eyes. He nudged Nightfall with his foot and the horse took him closer to the rim. As the sun finally appeared over the edge of the world, it struck even deeper into the canyon. Max looked down into it, and saw rich vegetation dotting the floor, and a muddy river winding its way along the bottom. He knew that this tiny river had created the vision that was unfolding before him, yet he couldn't believe that even the millions of years it had taken was enough. Along one wall was a gentle slope of deep red rock with horizontal white stripes near the top.

"Those are called the Spanish Skirts," Angel said. She had ridden up beside him, but he had no idea how long she had been there. "When the Spaniards, the conquistadors, came here, they missed their homes so much that they were reminded of the women they loved. That's the way the story goes."

She pointed at a cliff face far in the distance, so far that Max had to strain his eyes to find it. "That's the Sad Monkey. They say that's what the face looks like, but I don't think so. I think it looks more like Quanah Parker, mourning for his land, or his mother after she was stolen back by the white people, before she starved herself to death."

Max looked up and down the canyon, knowing that what he was seeing could only be a small portion of the whole. He was dazzled by the immensity of it, by the brilliance of its colors and formations.

"They say that Manhattan is made of concrete canyons," he said, "but using the word that way feels wrong to me. I mean yeah, the buildings will suck your breath away, but they don't come anywhere to matching the beauty of this place. They can't hold a candle to it."

Angel shifted her weight onto her left leg and pulled the saddle a little so that it was more balanced. The creak of the leather was loud in the morning air. "I'm glad you like it," she said, and smiled again. She was not much older than Max, he knew, but when she smiled he suddenly felt ancient next to her. She could have been a teenager again, the way the years fled from her face. Her eyes were still mapped by a fine pattern of wrinkles, and her skin too dry from the ever-present wind and sun, but her little girl's soul shown from inside like a candle held by an angel. Max laughed, because he knew that her name was well-chosen.

He smiled back at her and on impulse reached out to touch the hand that she rested on the saddle horn. The smile started to fade from her lips, and she looked straight at him, so deep into his eyes that for a moment he wanted to hide. I don't know if I'm ready for this, he thought, but when she leaned toward him he took that hand from hers, keeping the other still on his saddle horn with the reins threaded through his fingers, and put it behind her head as he drew her face to him.

Her lips tasted like vanilla. She pressed them against his softly, and they stayed like that a moment before breaking apart. Her eyes were brilliantly green, like chips of jade warming in the sun.

"I liked that," she said, and caressed the line of his jaw with her palm. He could feel the rough calluses on it. Then she kissed him again, gently touching his teeth with her tongue. He pressed himself closer to her, and the horses danced closer as their riders leaned in and kissed so hard that they almost merged. Finally their mouths separated, and Max touched his forehead against hers. He reached out his forefinger and lightly touched the freckled skin in the V of her shirt, drawing circles on it, feeling the warmth of her.

It had been more than two years since his last relationship, and Max realized that he was skin-starved, that he missed the feeling of being held in another's arms. He had missed the touch of affection, as essential for life as food and water. Max touched her hair, lifting it away from her eyes and pushing it behind her ears. He kissed her again, touching her tongue with his, the horses stepping to each other, then broke away and brushed his lips against her cheek.

"Mmmm," she said, drawing her breath in as deeply as she could. Max looked at the canyon again, and in just the several minutes since he had last looked, more was revealed—more colors, formations, more joy and sadness clutched in the arms of the ancient rocks.

"Come on," she said, and touched her heel to Summerlea's flank. The horses started walking along the edge of the canyon with Bailey ranging ahead, ever vigilant.

"She likes you, you know."

"How can you tell?"

"Well, for one, if she didn't, she probably would have knocked you out of the saddle when we kissed."

"Thank God for small favors."

"But there are other ways to tell. I'm not sure exactly how. Guess it's the way I can read her mind. Body language."

"You mean like the way she doesn't tear my face off every chance she gets."

Angel tossed her head and looked at him. "She wouldn't do that unless I told her to, or unless I was in danger." She glanced down at his leg. "If you'll keep your heel down, it'll make it easier for you to balance. Don't put a lot of weight in your feet; keep most of it in your butt. Sit hard on your pockets, and brace yourself just a little in the stirrups."

Max pushed his heels down and tried to sit hard in the saddle. "I'm not quite sure I'm getting that."

"Here then," Angel said. "Take your feet out of the stirrups."

"Is it safe?"

"Yep. He won't run off." Max slipped his feet out of the stirrups, and immediately his rear went down deep into the saddle.

"Ah!" he said, childlike surprise in his eyes.

"You feel it?"

"Absolutely."

"Good. Stay like that for a while, until your butt memorizes the feeling. How is it, by the way?"

"And what would 'it' be?"

"'It' would be your butt."

Max thought about it for a moment. "I've been told it's pretty good," he said.

She laughed and slapped him lightly on the arm. "I meant, is it sore?"

"Well, right now it's kind of numb, actually."

"You'll get used to it. We keep this up, pretty soon you won't feel it at all."

Max thought about what she said, her belief that "after a while" they could still be riding horses together, and didn't know what he felt. Happy? Giddy? For so many years, his emotional range was about as much as a glass of whiskey would hold, and after all these years sometimes he still didn't know how to slap a label on his emotions. Happy, giddy, it didn't matter, he decided. It felt good.

They rode in silence for a while, watching the canyon change with every hundred yards.

"So can you drive down in there?"

"Yeah," she said. "In a little while you'll probably see some cars. That's what makes it different from the Grand Canyon—that and the size. It's easier to get into, which means there are lots of yahoos hollering and building fires, generally acting like buttholes. Mostly I prefer it from up here. Easier to imagine the way it used to be, a hundred years ago. Two hundred."

"What was it like? Were there what, Indians living here?"

"Yeah, they did. The Comanches, until they were forced out and onto the reservations. Their greatest chief, Quanah Parker, was half white. His mother was taken by the Comanches, then rescued years later and returned to her white family. She died of grief."

"I remember that story," Max said. "Studied it in college."

"If you're like me, it made you pretty sad."

"I was just about to say that it did," said Max. He wasn't just kissing up to her. It really had made him sad, and he kicked himself for not saying it before she did.

She touched her heels to Summerlea and made a clicking sound with her mouth. The mare started to trot, and Nightfall followed with no signal from Max. Who's in charge here, he thought, him or me? Then he laughed. What a silly question.

The wind blew the hair across his face and into his mouth. He marveled at the way Angel moved with her horse. Daylight never showed its face between her jeans and the saddle, and he knew that the Greeks had imagined centaurs by seeing someone as beautiful as her on a day like this. Max thought again about her belief that he would get better at this, and he prayed to God that he would be given that chance.

Eventually, when the sun was well above the canyon wall, Angel turned around and they headed back toward the truck. No longer interested in rabbits, Bailey trotted along between the horses. The breeze blowing through the brush, the squeak of leather, and the occasional snorting of the horses was like a symphony to Max's ears.

"So did you grow up doing this stuff? Were you a cowgirl? A rodeo queen?"

Angel laughed. "Not hardly. My daddy was a cowboy, kind of. Didn't make his living at it; not many do any more. He owned an appliance store, but he had a couple of horses, and I grew up learning how to ride them.

"I didn't care for him too much, and by the time I got to junior high I prioritized my to-do list according to what would piss him off the most. So riding horses was not high on my list of activities."

"So when did you start again?"

"About seven years ago, after I moved back to Amarillo."

"Where had you been in the meantime?"

"I'd managed to graduate from high school, mostly because I was too lazy to quit. I read a lot, but not what they wanted me to. I took off across the country, landed here and there."

Max glanced at Angel, about to say something else, and saw her looking across the prairie away from the canyon. Her eyes were unfocused. Then she turned back and looked right at him, right into his eyes.

"I did a lot of things I'm not proud of," she said, but from the set of her chin, she almost could have been.

Max shrugged. "Join the club. I'm not proud of most of what I've done in my life, and the rest of it I can't even remember."

"That's where you're luckier than me. I still can." After a moment she seemed to relax again. The tension drained from her body, and once more she was at one with the horse. "I ended up in Seattle for a while, when everybody was wearing their shirts wrapped around their waists and spending all their time talking about coffee. Boulder for a few years. Came back for visits here and there. My mother died. I got married, and that didn't turn out as well as I wanted it to. I got divorced. About the time I decided my father wasn't quite as bad as I thought, he died. I never got a chance to tell him. Left me everything, including the appliance store, which I needed like a new husband. So I moved back, sold off the appliances, turned it into a pool hall. After a while I figured the statute of limitations on being pissed off at him had given out, and I could take back those parts of myself that were too close to him for comfort when I was sixteen. Bought Summerlea."

Max glanced down at the bottom of the canyon, and just as Angel had said he could see a couple of cars on the road that wound through the bottom, crawling along like ants. He breathed deeply, and from somewhere far away caught the musty smell of a cattle feedlot.

"So how about you?" she asked "What's your story?"

"I thought I already told you. About the subways?"

"That's New York's story, not yours."

"What do you want to know?"

"The usual stuff, I guess. Where you grew up, if you've been married. Like that. If you're an alcoholic."

The question took Max by surprise, and he snapped his head around at her. Her eyes were focused across the prairie as if she were faintly embarrassed at having asked.

"Brooklyn, no, and yes," he answered. "In that order. How'd you know?"

She thought for a moment, then reached forward and patted Summerlea's neck. "Things you said that night we were talking. My dad was too, and I can recognize the style."

"What do you mean?"

"I'm not exactly sure. There's just some air about you that says it. I'm not sure what it is. Maybe it's being a bartender that does it. Recognizing that whether you're drinking or not, alcohol is more important in your life than in other people's."

Max thought about it a moment and realized she was right. Drunk or sober, he thought more about alcohol than someone without a problem. He nodded.

"You go to the meetings?"

"Got to."

"That little place just down the street from Bailey's?"

"Yeah. A guy took me over there my first day in town. I realized it was just a couple of blocks from where I broke down. Sometimes the irony in my life flies on automatic pilot. Did your father ever go?"

She shook her head quickly, and Max could tell there was no more she would say about it.

"So how come you never got married?"

Max lifted up on his toes and readjusted his butt. It really was starting to get sore. Not so much his butt really as the inside of his thighs.

"I'm not exactly sure. Scared, maybe. For a while I was afraid of letting anyone get too close. Later, I don't know. Maybe I just got used to being alone."

"Has there been anybody special?"

"I guess you could say so, here and there. Not for a couple of years."

Nightfall started to walk a little faster, and Max noticed a dot on the horizon. The truck and trailer. "Tell me he's not suddenly going to race for the truck."

She shook her head. "No, he won't. But let's pick up a trot. I don't want them to get lazy." She touched Summerlea with her heel, and the mare increased her speed. So did Nightfall, and Max's thighs began to throb. Then both horses hit a lope, and the smoother gait felt better to him.

In less than five minutes they were back at the truck. Angel pulled Summerlea to a walk before they got there to let the horses cool down. She showed Max how to unsaddle Nightfall, how to slip the bridle over his ears so the bit slid out of his mouth. Then she loaded them back into the trailer.

On the way back into town, Bailey seemed even more comfortable with him. She curled up on the seat between Max and Angel, mashing both of them against the doors. She was a big dog. He tentatively reached out his left hand and stroked the fur between her eyes, preparing for the possibility that he might lose some fingers. She closed her eyes and sighed.

"How long have you had her?" Max asked.

"I don't really think I do 'have' her. I think she stays with me because she wants to." She thought a moment. "Seven years. I got the phone call about my Dad. I was still in Boulder then, working as an insurance claims adjuster. I blew off work and drove up into the mountains. Got out of the car and walked a long ways. Finally I came to a clearing where the sun could peek through the pines, and I sat down on a rock. My eyes were closed. I was trying to will myself not to cry, but the tears wouldn't stop. It was October, already cool, but the sun warmed my skin. And as I sat there, I heard a strange sound. I guess I'd been in the city too long, but after a while I could tell it was a dog in pain. I searched around for a while, changing course when the sound got louder or weaker. Finally I found her, wedged between two rocks. She was just a puppy, maybe three months old. She had a big gash on her right front leg, infected. As soon as I touched her, she calmed down. She had a right to be scared, but somehow she knew I wanted her to be my friend. I pulled her out of the rocks, real careful, and cradled her in my arms. I could tell she had wolf in her.

"I never did find out where she came from. Lots of people up there breed dogs to wolves. I don't know if she got lost or dumped. Dumped wouldn't surprise me much. Sometimes it seems like there's no end to the meanness people do."

"I think that gives us something in common. I've been the last stop before the needle for a few cats in my life. I have a couple right now, in fact."

"I like that," Angel said.

They drove back into town, up Georgia Street to the club. Angel pulled her muscular white truck in front of Bailey's and put it in park. "You think you might be coming by tonight?"

"Geez I don't know, as busy as I am and everything, but I think I can probably free up a few minutes."

She reached out and, pulling his face to hers, kissed him again. He put his arms around her, feeling even through the down vest the muscles in her wiry back. Bailey let out a slight chuff.

"Hey, you feel like breakfast?" Max asked.

"Actually I feel like sleep. I closed up early last night, but early for us is midnight. Time I got home it was one, so I missed out on a few hours. I've been living on coffee this morning. So, how about a rain check?"

"That I can do."

He reached for the door handle, paused. "Hey," he said. "Why did you pick me? I mean, what was it about me that made you take that walk over to my table?"

She reached down and ran her fingers through Bailey's ruff. She looked out the windshield, where an old green Plymouth Fury crawled toward them. "It seemed like you had more brains, and a better sense of humor, than anybody I've met since I moved back here."

"Maybe you've been looking in the wrong places."

"Yeah. Amarillo." She put the truck into gear.

Max kissed her again and got out of the truck. She honked the horn at him as she pulled away, a real horn like cars had when he was a kid, not those little beep-beep things like today's cars had that sounded like bicycle horns. As the truck passed by, Bailey was sitting upright in the passenger's seat. She swiveled as they passed, as if he were an old friend whom she had seen on the street. He almost expected her to wave. He heard one of the horses stamping its hooves on the bottom of the trailer, the sound ringing out over the noise of Georgia's traffic.

Max checked his watch. It was 8:45, and there was time for him to grab a bite to eat before the 9:30 meeting. Then afterwards, if enough of the drunks hung out talking for long enough, it would be almost time for lunch. In the afternoon he would do a couple of hours of work preparing a brief and maybe catch a movie before he went to Bailey's.

It occurred to Max that it felt like his time had expanded here in Texas, as if it, like the horizon, seemed much wider than the one he had known in Manhattan. He seemed somehow able to do more work in less time than he had in New York.

A smile was in his heart as he got into his car which, thank God, was still working, and drove to Luby's for the breakfast buffet.

Chapter 16

Carl searched the TV grid in the Sunday *Globe-News*. He knew Dallas wouldn't play until tomorrow night, but he found himself obsessively checking the schedule. He clicked on the TV anyway, knowing that he would probably draw Dolores's ire like a red Trans-am draws a cop car. He kept the sound down low, hoping that it would attract no attention from the kitchen.

The newscaster, one of those guys who looked like an ex-college football player with a mouth full of teeth and a blonde coif, was reading an item. "Amarillo Police disclosed today the name of the homeless man found murdered last month in the railroad yard. Fifty-two year-old James Lee Gillette—"

The front door slammed open, and Nina came rushing through the living room and into the kitchen like a little steam train. Seconds later the door slammed again, and her cousin Travis blasted after her. "Aunt Regina," she yelled, "Travis hit me!"

"I did not!"

Regina caught Travis's arms. "Travis, what did I tell you about hitting?"

He rolled his eyes. "But Mom—"

"No buts, buddy. I said no. Now go see if you can't play nicer. Where's your sister?"

"I don't know, somewhere."

"Well go find her, okay? You're supposed to be looking out for her."

She and Dolores and Bernice had cleaned up the supper dishes while the kids went to play, and Carl had moved into the living room. Regina wished Freddie were here, but he said he didn't quite feel good enough to come. His stomach was upset, he said, and he thought he'd just lie on the couch and watch the game. He looked more worried to her than anything else. He and Carl had gone out to shoot pool last night, and it was almost one before he got in. Regina wished he wouldn't stay out that late, but it was better than not coming home at all. He had seemed giddy last night, but he was sober. Freddie didn't usually act like that unless he'd been drinking too much. And then today he wasn't giddy anymore, but kind of edgy. Like sometimes he wouldn't hear what she was saying, and sometimes he'd hear the wrong thing, and sometimes he just jumped at the sound of her voice. She shook her head.

"Some days, I swear Travis doesn't listen to a thing I say."

"You know what they say about that. It's a grandmother's revenge," Bernice said.

Dolores sighed. "Oh, Mama."

"What? You two just don't remember what you were like at that age. I think every parent should have a child just like they were."

"Look, forget I said anything."

"What are you mad about?"

"Did I say I was mad?"

Bernice shook her head. "Sometimes I wish I had a—"

"Tape recorder," Dolores said.

"That's right, so I could prove I've said the things I know good and well I—"

"Why don't both of you just be quiet!" Regina blurted out.

"Excuse me? I thought I brought my children up better than to—"

Carl leaned forward from his chair in the living room so he could see into the kitchen. "What are you arguing about?"

"We're not arguing," Bernice said. "Oh look, have you heard about this? It was in the paper."

She stood up and walked quickly into the living room. Regina and Dolores gave each other a weary look.

On the television, the football newscaster had adopted the serious look he always took when discussing crime news. "—a bold robbery that occurred just after midnight." The screen switched to a shot of the Food Giant. "In the early hours of the morning, three masked men entered Food Giant, on Georgia Street, just after it closed. The trio made off with more than seventy-five thousand dollars after tying up and brutalizing three store personnel, one of whom, night manager Earl Waddell, received an injury to his leg. He was treated and released from Panhandle Memorial Medical Center. The three robbers are still at large. WKYR will keep you updated on this brazen robbery as we receive more information."

The camera cut to the newscaster and his partner, an equally well-coifed brunette woman in a blue suit. The woman said, "If you think it's feeling a little chilly out there, that's because the temperature's been dropping over the last hour. Ernie will tell us all about the five day forecast when we return from these words." She and her partner looked down at their papers until the camera cut to the commercial.

Bernice stood with her arms crossed, lips pressed tightly together. "Um," she said. "Um, um, um. Why, I can remember the day when you didn't even have to lock your house."

Regina shrugged her shoulders. "Times have changed, Mama."

"Oh, don't tell me that. People still know the difference between right and wrong. When they find out who did this, they ought to string them up by their heels from a light pole downtown. Right?"

"Of course," Dolores said.

"I mean what if it had happened at your place, Carl?"

Carl rubbed the back of his neck. A single drop of sweat squeezed out of his right armpit and ran all the way down his side until it stopped at his tucked-in shirt. "They wouldn't get away with seventy-five grand, I promise you that."

"You know what I mean," Bernice said. "How would you feel?"

"You're right, it's terrible."

"Um. What's this world coming to?"

Carl leaned back in the chair and tried to look like he was watching the news.

At work on Monday morning, the robbery was the only thing anyone talked about until lunch. When Sharon came into the back to get a cup of coffee she asked her friend Jonice, one of the cutters, if she had heard about it.

Jonice bit through a length of thread. "Sure did. Probably the only person who hasn't is King Carl," she said, nodding her head at his closed office door.

Sharon rolled her eyes. "Hell, if I'd known they had that much cash in the place, I'd have taken it off myself."

"Wouldn't have been too hard to find you," Jonice said. "You'd have done the two-step gettin' away."

Sharon high-fived her. "You got that right, girl."

Carl's door swung open, and he stuck his head out. "If you two worked as much as you talked, we'd all be rich. Sharon, don't you have something to do?"

"Sorry," she said.

He slammed the door and she stuck her tongue out at him. "Hope he don't have this place wired for video," she said.

Freddie sat at his desk in the corner, looking at the same work order that had been in front of him for the last hour. He finally found the nerve to stand up, tuck in his shirt, and rap lightly on Carl's door.

"Yeah!" Carl barked from inside.

"Hey," Freddie said. "You got a minute?" He could tell that talking to him was the last thing Carl wanted to do.

"Shut the door," Carl said. Freddie stood in front of the desk, shifting from foot to foot.

"What?"

"Well," Freddie ran his hand through his hair. He couldn't ask the question that was on his mind. He glanced toward the door and lowered his voice to almost a whisper. "How come they said that, about it being seventy-five? It's a lie."

Jesus. Carl craned his head and looked through the window at the others. Their heads were all bent down to their work.

"It's called taking the insurance company for a ride. Juggling the books to get back more than they lost. Maybe they're giving those three a bonus or something, so they don't sue."

Freddie sat down on the edge of the chair facing Carl's desk. His knees jittered, and finally he found the question he wanted to ask. "Hey, Carl. You don't think there's any chance of them—you know, finding out?"

Carl stood up and yanked the blinds closed on his windows. Then he walked straight to Freddie and said, "Look at me." Freddie glanced up at him and away again. "Goddamn it, Freddie, it is too late for that." He spoke very slowly. "Do you understand me? Just shut up. I don't want to hear anything from you about it. It's over and done with."

Freddie stood up like the chair had sent a thousand volts through him. "Yeah. I got to get back to work. I got a lot to do."

He closed the office door behind him and went back to his desk, staring at the stack of papers that littered it. He had hoped that Carl would talk to him, would listen to what he had to say. But he had known, deep down, that it wasn't worth a try. He had known that, like always, he was on his own.

Joe wasted half a tank of gas just listening to the truck purr. Usually he tried to miss as many red lights as possible. He hated stopping at them, and whenever he could he hit the gas when he saw a yellow light and didn't give much of a shit how many people honked at him. Sometimes he flipped them off and sometimes he ignored them, but mostly he just didn't care.

Today, though, he didn't try to run the lights. He loved shifting down into first, loved the way he could gently rock the truck by letting up on the clutch and lightly kicking the accelerator, then letting it up and pressing down on the clutch. He watched the lights on the cross-street, waiting for that yellow light to hit so that as soon as he got a green, a split-second before, he let go of the clutch and hit the gas, tearing out before the other lanes even started to roll their tires.

He had seen the looks those assholes at the Ford place had given him when he pulled up in his old broken down piece of shit. He knew they were rolling their eyes behind their slick-haired, button-down good old boy bullshit, but when he pulled out the roll of hundreds and started peeling them off, their dicks got stiffer than if they'd seen Pamela Anderson naked.

He was flat broke after he bought the bright red Ford 350 pickup. Hell, he'd have to make a few payments on it, but it was worth it. He'd been wanting one for a while, with a CD player in it, a rack of spotlights on top, and a 5-speed transmission, but he knew that he'd never be able to afford it. And now, with only one night's work, he had his dream truck. And it had gone off smooth as grease sliding around a skillet. He had to admit that Smith had done a pretty decent job of planning the whole deal. He'd been pissed off when Smith wouldn't let him get closer to that little check-out girl, but later he had realized that he was out of line. There was a time for work and a time for play, and besides he could always go back there sometime if that gal hadn't quit. He'd work on her some night when she was about to get off duty. It wasn't like she'd recognize him or anything. Yeah, he might just head on back one of these nights.

He'd wanted to buy Darlene a little something, a ring or another piece of jewelry, but there was nothing left. Of course she'd be suspicious when he showed up with this much truck, but she knew better than to say anything about it by this time. Maybe someday soon he'd take a spin down to that little good for nothing hometown of his, take a spin down Main Street and show those sorry sons of bitches just what he was made of. Might go by and see his bitch sister, and see just how proud she'd carry herself once she saw that fiery red Ford. Yeah, he just might. When the red light turned to green, he hit the gas.

The doors of Panhandle Memorial whispered open, and a blast of cold air embraced Smith as he passed through them. It wasn't hot out, not at all, but it seemed like they always had the air cranked up to arctic levels in there. He shivered and stopped in front of the hospital's directory. He scanned the sign until "Financial Office" caught his eye and navigated the hallways until he found the door. A young red-haired woman with a splash of freckles across her nose sat behind the desk.

"May I help you sir?" she asked in a voice appropriately hushed for the serious concerns she had to attend to.

"I'd like to see—" and he glanced at the card in his hand "—Miss Butler, please."

"May I tell her your name?"

"Smith Dixon."

With a lacquered fingernail, she tapped out four numbers on the phone pad and after a moment said "There's a Mr. Dixon here to see you." She paused a moment. "Certainly."

She rested the receiver on the cradle. "Ms. Butler will be with you in a moment. Would you like to take a seat?"

Smith nodded at her and sat down on a plush blue chair. He closed his eyes, imagined himself writing out one of the checks in his pocket, imagined moving his father to a nursing home. Imagined the look of surprise on Ms. Butler's perfect face when he gave her the money. Finally, he felt back in control again. His conscience, or whatever passed for it after all these years, had told him not to do Food Giant, not to pick up a gun again. But maybe, just maybe, it had been wrong. When he heard the soft brush of Ms. Lori Butler's heels on the carpet, he was smiling.

So was Carl when he opened the shop the next day. He was smiling so much that everyone was suspicious right away.

"Wish I would have brought my camera," Sharon told Freddie when he walked in at a quarter past nine.

"What for?"

"Hell, so I could get this historic occasion on film. Probably the only time I've seen him happy in the two years I've been working here. Maybe I could show it to my grandkids or something. I'm sure it'll be the only time for fifty years. Wonder what's up?"

"I don't know," Freddie said, even though he did. He wished he was that happy. Before he came to work he had raced through the *Globe-News*, searching for an article that would begin "Amarillo Police are rapidly closing in on—"

Carl sat at his computer, going through the books for the company. This morning they didn't look quite so bad as they usually did; in fact, they didn't look bad at all. Last night he had made a visit over to Amarillo Boulevard, where he had paid off his gambling debts in full, every last cent. He wished he had a picture of the asshole's face when he did, laying the hundred dollar bills into his hand until there were enough. Then he made the minimum payments, plus a little more, just for spite, on all of his credit cards. When he paid off the medical bills, it would total sixteen thousand, five hundred and sixteen dollars, which meant he had about four thousand dollars left. With that he could buy Christmas presents for Dolores and Nina, even for Bernice and Regina and her kids, and that deadbeat husband of hers. He glanced out at the floor where Freddie, amazingly enough, was already at work. Or at least sitting at his desk. He felt his pulse start to work quicker and breathed in deeply. Yeah, maybe I'll have enough left over to fix that goddamn Ford. No, screw that, I'll use it as a down payment on a new car. A Chevy this time, a Suburban fully loaded. That'll be sweet. He leaned back in the chair, savoring it. Maybe get a new roof on the house, and finally let Dolores redo the bathroom the way she's always talking about. And from now on, football and basketball are going to be just games. Something to watch for fun. No more betting. That was so goddamn stupid anyway, wasn't it? Betting on games. So childish. Carl was glad he was beyond it. Yeah, life didn't look so bad after all.

Freddie settled deeply onto the couch and held the cold can of Budweiser to his forehead, rolling it back and forth. He had the sound turned low on the new TV. Freddie had bought it the day before, all forty-two inches of the screen and fifteen hundred dollars, and now he wasn't even sure what was playing. Some cop show, it sounded like, from the sound of the sirens. Usually he liked them, the real ones and the ones with the actors, it didn't really matter which. The ones with the actors were likely to show some bare skin, although it was often as not men as women, and he wasn't interested in that. They also used a lot of bad language, which he still found slightly scandalous. It was like saying "shit" when you were a little kid and wondering if you'd get away with it. Now they were saying "prick" and "asshole" on TV like it was nothing. It still gave Freddie a thrill and made him look around guiltily, like he was going to get in trouble for just having that channel on. But the real cop shows were okay too, the ones where they chased down real criminals, knocking them to the ground and snapping the cuffs on. Those were exciting because they were true-life, and Freddie liked them because he was glad it was those criminals who were getting it and not him. He could sit in his living room content in the knowledge that he was a working man, a father, a football star. Well, a former one. High school. Even if he was getting a little fat, he still had the trophies and knew he'd earned them. But in the last couple of days that line between him and the guys on the shows had begun to blur.

Helping with the robbery had been a lot of fun at the time; even sober he had felt drunk. The adrenaline had kept him going well after he and Carl had left Smith's place. They had picked up beer, but he only drank one can and when he got home a few minutes later, even though it was late, he and Regina had set the sheets on fire. That didn't happen too much anymore, since Maggie and Travis had come along. When they did have sex, it was quick and mechanical, not like it was in high school. For Freddie, nothing really seemed like it was in high school. Sometimes his mind started to hover in on that idea and its implications, but it usually wasn't too hard to distract himself.

The high he got from the robbery didn't last as long as a good beer buzz, when the truth was out. By the next day he was itchy, not feeling good enough to have dinner at Carl's. He wasn't really sick; he just didn't want to be with Carl that day. He was afraid that they'd look each other in the eyes too much, or not all. Bernice, with her eyes sharp as an owl on a mouse, would surely notice. Since then he'd jumped whenever the phone rang, started to sweat whenever a new customer came into the shop. He was convinced it was a cop undercover, or maybe even the FBI. He didn't think they got involved in stuff this small, but he was a little fuzzy on what they did and didn't do. There hadn't been a show on them in years.

As the days went by, Freddie realized that he'd never really gotten away with anything in his life. Sure, he and Regina had had sex in Bernice's house when they were kids. That was the exception. The one time they tried on the school bus coming back from a game with Lubbock Coronado, they got caught before much had happened. And when he was a little kid, all the intricate lies he was sure his mother would never see through disappeared like spider webs sucked up by the vacuum. He knew in his heart that he would never get away with this because he had never really gotten away with anything in his whole life. That thought depressed him worse than working for someone who hated him and begrudged every penny in his paycheck.

Freddie smelled Regina before she sat down next to him. It wasn't perfume; it was the soap that he got for her birthday and Christmas every year. It smelled of lilacs and wasn't very expensive, but she didn't seem to want a lot. That's what broke his heart sometimes, made him feel guilty every time he came home drunk or late. She didn't yell at him, like some women would. She cried usually, but that was just because he was home safe. Beyond that, what she wanted was more for the kids and him than herself.

Regina had just gotten the kids into bed. They'd kissed Freddie before they went in, and he hugged them a little harder than he did most nights. Sometimes it was hard to realize that he was a parent. It hadn't been that long since he was a kid himself, and sometimes he still felt like one. The knowledge that they looked to him for guidance was often baffling.

Regina folded her legs underneath her as she sat next to him and burrowed her face into his neck. He could feel her warm breath sweetening his skin. She stayed like that, her arms wrapped around his shoulders, for a few minutes. He slid his hand in between her thighs, which were still slender. Not like Dolores, who was gaining weight. Regina was slender like her mother, but for a different reason. Bernice wasn't fat because being that mean burned up a buttload of calories. No, Freddie knew that Regina was one of those women who was going to age gracefully and still be beautiful when she was 70.

She kissed his neck. "Are you okay, honey?"

"Yeah," Freddie said. "How come?"

"Well, you're just a little quiet tonight."

Freddie looked at the TV. It was one of those fake cop shows. The cops were beating up on a suspect, and Freddie knew before the next commercial he would give up the truth.

"I really like it," she said.

"Huh?"

"The TV." She ran her fingers underneath the collar of his white cotton shirt, smoothed it down. "Sure was nice of Carl to give you that bonus. I'm glad y'all are getting along better."

"Yeah, me too." He lowered his voice. "Hey Gina, don't say anything about this to Dolores, okay?"

Two little furrows popped up between her hazel eyes. "How come?"

"Oh," he stumbled, looking for a reason, "he did better than he thought for the third quarter, and he's going to surprise her."

"But isn't it funny that he's giving out bonuses this early? I mean, Christmas is over a month off."

"I think he just did this one to me for right now. Just cause of the problems we've been having, and—you know."

It took a few seconds before she nodded. They watched TV a few minutes before she said that she was going to bed. "Those two wear me out sometimes."

She got up from the couch, then quickly turned back and hugged him very hard. "I'm glad you take care of us, me and the kids," she said, so low he had to strain to hear. "I'm glad your family's important to you. I don't know what we'd do without you." She stood up abruptly and was down the hall to the bedroom before he could think.

Regina opened the door to the kids' room. They were sound asleep, or at least pulling off a good semblance of it. She closed the door noiselessly and went into the bathroom. She brushed her teeth and flossed them, making sure to rinse afterwards like the dentist told her to. She got ready for bed, the door open enough to let in a little light from the hallway or any noise from the children, closed enough that she couldn't hear the TV.

She slid between the sheets and turned on her side facing the wall. The glowing red digits on the clock radio told her it was 9:50. She closed her eyes.

Dear Savior, she thought, I ask that you will show me what it is that you want me to do, and how I may better serve you. Please help me to live a life worthy of your sacrifice to us. I pray that you will protect Maggie and Travis, just fold them in your arms and lift them up. She paused a moment, thinking. And dear Lord, please watch over Freddie, and lead him in your path, keeping him out of harm's way. She struggled for what she wanted to say next. Show him the difference between right and wrong? Yes, but that wasn't quite it. She started to drift away, and she tried to get it right before sleep took her. Hold him close to you, she prayed, but couldn't find the rest of the words. In your precious name I pray, Amen.

Regina didn't believe that Carl had given Freddie an early bonus. She might have, but she knew that however much that TV cost, it was a lot more than Carl would ever have given Freddie. That left her wondering just how he had gotten that much money, and where. She fell asleep before she could give it any more thought.

Freddie's thumb rested lightly on the channel button of the remote, his mind drifting like a leaf on a breezy day, until he heard the words "Food Giant" on the TV. Then he sat straight up on the couch, turned the sound down, and moved closer to the TV, his ear bent toward it to make sure he didn't miss anything. One of the newscasters, he didn't know which one because they all looked alike to him, was giving an update on the robbery. "No arrests have been made yet in the crime, in which the thieves netted $75,000. Our own Debbie Carstairs spoke today with APD Lieutenant Champ Phillips."

The camera cut to a blond woman holding a microphone, dressed casually in a denim shirt and blazer. When did they start dressing that way on TV, Freddie wondered. "Thank you," she said. "While it's true that none of the daring robbers have yet been captured, the police department is optimistic they will be able to make some arrests soon. Isn't that correct, Lieutenant Phillips?"

The camera pulled back to reveal a tall man with a dark mustache and wearing a cowboy hat. "That's right," he said in a slow drawl. "We haven't made an arrest in the case yet, but we feel like we're drawing closer and closer to it. We're running down some leads, and it's just a matter of time."

"Can you tell us who you're looking at?"

"No ma'am, not just yet." Someone off-camera caught his attention. He tipped his hat to her and walked out of the camera's range.

Debbie moved the microphone back underneath her mouth and said "Thank you, Lieutenant. As soon as the Amarillo Police do make the arrests, we'll be the first to inform you. Back to you, Doug."

The guy in the studio appeared again, and Freddie fumbled for a few seconds before he found the Off button on the remote.

Oh shit, he thought, shit shit shit. I knew this was going to happen. I shouldn't have said anything to Carl. I should have just kept my fat mouth shut. Then it would just be them, Carl and Smith and that crazy fucker, and I'd be okay, with nothing to worry about. Shit!

And how the hell did the cops find out? Probably Joe ran his mouth off somewhere. Didn't matter, really. All that really mattered was that there was no way in hell he was going to jail or prison. No way he was going to leave Regina and the kids. It was all Carl's fault, anyway, him and Smith and Joe. Freddie hadn't even gone into the goddamn place. How could they arrest him if he hadn't even gone in there? It could have been anybody driving the car.

He sank down onto the couch and closed his eyes. Just think. Figure it out. Even when you were a kid and got caught, you could sometimes talk your way out of it. Just think.

He sat on the couch for ten minutes, his head leaned back, until he came up with a plan. It maybe wasn't the best one, but it was the only one he could think of right then. And it might just work. It just might. He got up and checked on the kids, who were asleep. So was Regina. He slid between the sheets quietly, so he wouldn't wake her up. In a couple of days, everything would be okay. He was sure of it.

Freddie had avoided Bailey's in the four days since the robbery. He had driven by once, and his stomach felt so sick that he thought he was going to throw up. He pulled up into the K-Mart parking lot across the street with his back to the club, until his stomach settled down and he knew he wasn't going to lose it all. It wasn't that he held anything against the club. That wasn't it at all. It's just that, in his mind, Bailey's was where it all had started on that night he and Carl had played eight and nine-ball with Smith and Joe. The four of them had never been together before at all, and then suddenly they were, and the next thing that came out of it was that goddamn robbery, which Freddie seemed incapable of getting out of his mind. He could barely work for thinking about it; every morning he thumbed through the paper half expecting that he'd see his picture under the heading, "Robbery Suspect ID'd." He woke up at night and couldn't sleep. Usually he sat in the living room and drank a couple of cold beers until he felt sleepy again. He watched that giant screen TV and realized that when all was said and done it wasn't any better than their old 19-inch, just like all that Dolby stuff at the movies didn't make a shitty movie any better. It just made it louder.

At work he sat at his desk watching Carl's mood, trying to imagine what he would do if he knew what Freddie was thinking. It wouldn't be fun to watch, he knew that. In his mind he saw Carl running Freddie's hand through one of the sewing machines, stitching his fingers together like in the Three Stooges or something. At lunch he drove around in his car, listening to the radio, trying to find out if there was any news about the robbery. Freddie knew that he was falling apart, and he wasn't sure what he could do about it. But he had an idea.

After dinner he told Regina that he was going out to the Pac-n-Sac to get some beer. He'd be back in about twenty minutes, he said. Regina asked if that wasn't a little long for just some beer.

"I might go to the video store too, while I'm out," he said. "We haven't watched a movie in a while. It'll look good on that new TV." He hugged her while she was cleaning up the kitchen, put his arms around her and kissed her neck.

"Be careful," she said, like she usually did whenever he went anywhere.

"I'm just going to the store, Gina."

"I know. But you never can tell what's out there."

"I'll be all right."

Travis was doing his homework at the kitchen table. Maggie wasn't old enough for school yet. She wouldn't start kindergarten until next year. But she was sitting at the table with her brother, watching him painstakingly write a story for his second grade class. He tousled Travis's hair and leaned over to kiss Maggie on the head. Her soft brown hair stilled smelled like a baby's, warm and fresh, like bluebonnets on a spring day. "See you in a few minutes," he said.

When Freddie pushed aside the screen door and walked out on to the porch on his way to the car, it felt like an anvil had been lifted off his chest. He got into the car and pulled out of the driveway, reminding himself that he needed to actually get some beer and a video while he was out, so it would look okay when he came back.

It was already dark as he cruised down the silent streets of his neighborhood. Thanksgiving was just around the corner, and then Christmas right on its heels. He still had enough left from the two thousand to buy some nice gifts for Regina and the kids. He realized that there was an almost certain chance that they'd make him give everything back, all that was left after the TV, and wished he'd done the shopping before he did this. Well, too late now. There were other details that he hadn't thought about too much, either. Like where would he work if Carl went to jail. Freddie was sure that there was no way he would go; after all, he was being honest and he hadn't even walked into the store. He knew he was safe there. When the possibility of Carl going to jail entered his mind, he waved it away like a mosquito on his neck. Carl wasn't a criminal; it was Smith and Joe they'd go after. Carl was a good man. Not to Freddie; to Freddie he was an asshole, but to Dolores and Nina he was good. No, Freddie was sure Carl would be okay. The possibility that Carl might fire him never entered his mind.

He turned onto Western Boulevard on his way to the Pac-n-Sac he usually went to. In the middle of the second block he heard a growling roar behind him, and he glanced in the rearview mirror. At first he thought it was a fire engine behind him, but after a moment he realized it was just a big, bright red pickup. Goddamn rednecks, he thought. He'd never had any use for those bastards even when he was playing ball and half of the crowd seemed to be made up of them. The truck's lights glared too bright in his rearview, and he switched it to the night mode. He could see the big silver grill on the front and a row of big lights on top of the cab. Freddie shook his head, nervous and irritated.

He turned into the convenience store lot. The green and yellow sign seemed comforting to him; it offered salvation, a way to make sure he kept his family intact. He pulled into a slot at the right end of the store, away from the door, next to the pay phones on the corner of the building. Some boys about junior high size came out of the store right then, wearing those baggy jeans that were four sizes too big, where the pockets hung down by their knees and their underwear stuck six inches way out of the top. Stupid, he thought. Probably in a gang. I hope Travis never wants to do that. He got out of the car and stepped up to the phone. Good. There was a phone book. Some of the pages were ripped out, but he found the one he needed, and his eyes followed his finger down the column of tiny print until it reached the name he was looking for. He took a deep breath, gently slid a quarter into the slot, punched out the seven numbers, and held his breath.

Gary Ryan had always wanted their number to be unlisted. He knew that his partner's line of work would bring what he considered unwelcome attention from a certain segment of the population: lawyers wanting to talk to him about a case and criminals he put away who, lacking in courage, would call at home and try to scare him. Gary didn't know which was worse. Not that scaring Champ Phillips would be easy; Gary figured it was about as likely as finding enough Democrats in the Panhandle to fill a good-sized rowboat. Champ said with the number of times he gave out his home phone number, it was a moot point anyway. People needed to reach him when he wasn't at work. He compromised by not listing their address in the book, and over the years Gary had grown comfortable with it, as he had with Champ's long and erratic hours.

He knew Champ was in his study when the phone rang, reading on a new book about the Texas Rangers. Champ usually turned the ringer off on the phone when he was in there. The department required him to carry a cell phone anyway, but he liked to think that home was the only place he didn't have to be a slave to the phone. Of course, all that meant to Gary is that he would have to answer it instead.

On Wednesday, November 4, Gary was on the computer downloading his files of new houses for sale. The market was slow in Amarillo these days, and he was looking at other towns in the Panhandle: Perryton, Pampa, and Dalhart all showed some promise. Gary made more money as a real-estate salesman than Champ did with all his years on the force. It was a disgrace, but thank God he held no jealousy or bitterness. When the phone rang, Gary let it go three times before he picked it up in case Champ had forgotten to turn the ringer off. As soon as he heard the voice, he knew it wasn't a friend or colleague. There was a tone of fear that he had come to recognize over the years. No matter how innocent anyone may be, the tone was always the same. Calling a cop's house made people's mouths go dry.

"Yeah, is Champ Phillips there?" the man's voice asked when Gary answered.

"Let me check," Gary said, in case Champ didn't want to talk. "May I ask your name?"

"Can I just talk to him?"

Ah, he thought. One of those. Anonymous tip, threat, whatever.

"Just a moment."

Gary was working in his own study, just down the hall from Champ's, and he padded in his bare feet across the carpeting. He tapped lightly on the door before he opened it six inches. Champ glanced up at him, smoothing his thick salt and pepper mustache with one finger, raising his eyebrows.

"How's the book?" Gary asked.

"Pretty good. He's no Walter Prescott Webb, but he'll do."

"There's a call for you. Wouldn't give his name."

Champ sighed. "Thanks, baby."

Gary smiled at him and closed the door as he reached for the phone. "Yeah, this is Phillips."

"Hey," the voice said. "I got something you want."

"All right, I'll jump. Why don't you tell me about it?" Champ placed the book, still open, face down on his desk.

"I got to know the terms first, man."

"Terms are you tell me your name and what you got, and then we'll talk. I can't tell you anything 'til I know something."

"Man, you got to understand my position."

"Partner, I don't have to do anything. Now let me explain my position. If you're in a jam, and we can help each other, I'll go out on a limb for you. But I got to know what it's about."

"Oh, shit. Look, can you meet me?

"I'm hanging up this phone in five seconds."

"No, no, don't do that! Freddie! It's Freddie Odom," the man said, lowering his voice. Champ scrawled the name on a piece of note paper.

"All right," he said, "that's something. Now what's your situation, Freddie?"

"Look, I'm starting to get scared. I don't want to talk about it over the phone. Can you meet me at—" There was a click on the line, and in a moment

Champ heard the dull whine of the dial tone. He listened a moment longer before carefully replacing the phone on its cradle. He leaned back in his chair and stroked his mustache. He picked up the book again and read a few paragraphs. Then he dialed *69, call return. The phone rang ten times, and no one picked up. He pulled the white pages out of his desk drawer and looked up "Odom, Freddie." He dialed the number and on the second ring a woman's voice said, "Hello?"

"Yeah, is Freddie Odom there, please?"

"He's not here just this minute. Do you want him to call you?"

"No, that's all right. I'll reach him later on."

He hung up, turned the ringer on, and put the phone back. He closed his eyes, wondering if he would hear from Freddie Odom again.

Freddie had thought he was ready to make the call, that the issue was settled in his mind. But as soon as the guy answered the phone, he knew he wasn't. While he was waiting for Phillips he started to sweat, and the pressure on his bladder became acutely intense. He felt like if he didn't pee right then, he wouldn't be able to make it. Just a minute, he said to himself, and it'll all be over. Then I'll go inside. It was the same deal he'd made when he was a little boy, and he needed to go really badly. Just a second, he told himself. It was the only way he could keep from wetting his pants. Sweat leaked down from his forehead into his eyes, and he wiped his face on his sleeve. Is it really that hot? he asked himself.

Then a man's voice picked up and said, "Yeah, this is Phillips." It was the same voice he had heard on the TV the night before, a slow, deep, Texas drawl. Freddie trusted the voice. That guy will make it all okay. He started to talk, then realized he hadn't rehearsed this even once. He had no idea of what he was going to say.

"Hey," he said. "I got something you want." God, that sounds stupid!

As they talked, he began to sweat even more. A car pulled into a parking space and more of those kids got out, the ones with the baggy jeans and stupid underwear.

Phillips tried to get Freddie's name. This wasn't going the way Freddie wanted it to. He wanted to be in control of it. But when the cop said he was about to hang up, Freddie blurted out his name, and a wave of emotions almost knocked him down. Regret, fear, relief. It was too late to go back now.

"All right," Phillips said, "that's something. Now what's your situation, Freddie?"

"Look, I'm starting to get scared. I don't want to talk about it over the phone. Can you meet me at—" And suddenly the phone went dead. Son of a bitch, he thought. What is this? "Hello? Hello?"

He wasn't sure which happened first, whether he looked up at the pay phone and saw a finger holding down the cradle or heard the mocking voice behind him saying "What's the matter? He hang up?"

Freddie recognized the voice and his body froze. The night was suddenly cold, the sweat on his neck and face, under his arms, turning to ice. He slowly looked around, and there was Joe standing right behind him, that grin on his face, but his eyes were coals burning into Freddie. He was wearing an old pair of jeans and a t-shirt. Freddie could smell his sweat.

Joe took his finger from the cradle, plucked the receiver from Freddie's hand, and replaced it. "Who you talking to?"

"Oh, just my wife—I forgot what she wanted me to—you know, and I thought I'd call and see if uh—"

Joe blew air out of his nostrils. "You know what you are? You're just a lying little sack of shit. You wasn't on the phone with no wife. I heard every goddamn word you said. You was talking about fucking, all right, but it wasn't your wife you's fixing to fuck. It was me. And I ain't gonna stand for that."

"No, I swear it was my wife, I—"

"You little faggot, I followed you in my truck. Saw you in your car, and even through the windows of that piece of shit I could see you was up to something. I knew your little pecker was just shriveling up, and I figured well hell, I better see what you're up to, before it gets out of hand. And here you are on the phone with the fucking cops!" He spit the last words; Freddie could feel it spray his face, could smell Joe's fetid cigarette breath.

"I—"

"Don't you say a fucking word! Not one!" Joe looked up at the entrance to the store; no one was there. He grabbed Freddie's shirt collar and pulled him forward, a finger shaking in his face. "Nothing!" Then he let go of Freddie, pushing him back. "Now gimme a quarter."

Silently, so scared he could barely move, Freddie reached into his pocket and dug the coin out.

Joe lifted the receiver. "Put it in."

Trembling, Freddie's fingers barely found the slot. He thought he would drop the coin on the ground, prayed that he would and that he wouldn't. It rolled into the pay phone with a metallic thunk.

Joe waited a few seconds while the phone on the other end rang. Freddie's eyes flicked to the door, hoping someone would come out, even one of those punks with the pants, so he could get away. Even Joe wasn't crazy enough to do something to him in front of witnesses. He thought so, anyway. But there was no one at the door.

Joe saw his eyes. "Don't even think about it."

Then he said, "Yeah, it's me. Joe. Look, we got us a situation. I guess you call it a little squeaking rat asshole named Freddie. Yeah, no shit. I just found him on the phone to the cops, and this is something else you owe me for." He paused a moment, listening. "Meet me at the drive-in in twenty minutes, and we'll straighten this shit out."

He slammed the phone down and wiped his forehead on his sleeve. "You and me are going for a ride, little buddy." Freddie stood still, looking at the Pac-n-Sac sign that scarce minutes before had seemed to offer salvation. "Well what are you waiting for? Let's go." In a trance, Freddie walked toward his car. "Not that way, asshole," Joe said. "We're going in my truck." He shoved Freddie in the back. "Just don't pee on the seat. I don't want to have to clean it out." Freddie started toward the side of the store where he saw the gleaming grille of the monstrous truck peering around it. He glanced back at the door one last time. No one was there.

They were almost to the truck when the pay phone began to ring.

Chapter 17

Smith tried to drive smoothly, tried not to speed as he headed north toward the Borger highway. He breathed deeply, willing his head to be clear, making sure he signaled for lane changes, anything to keep himself grounded. When the phone rang he had only been back ten minutes from the nursing home. With his father's bills paid off and money still left in the safe deposit box, he finally felt like he could breathe a little easier.

And now this. Smith had hoped that he would never hear Joe's voice again. Through the years, Smith's line of work being what it was, he had met his share of psychotic assholes, but he'd never met one he'd less wanted to be around than Joe. Some people were just born shit magnets, and Joe was one of them. It was inevitable that something would go wrong when he was around, and Smith was distressed that he hadn't recognized it in time. He should have seen it immediately, should have steered clear of Joe after that first night at Bailey's. But he hadn't, and the fact that he had actually done a job with Joe continued to astound him. Smith knew he must be losing his edge, and he knew more certainly than ever that his days as a criminal were over. One more job and he would get caught or killed. Something. If he could only get through this one unscathed, never again would he walk into a store or bank for any reason other than to make a purchase or deposit money.

The traffic thinned out, and he increased the pressure on the accelerator. He had called Carl before he left, and if luck was in his corner one of them would get to the drive-in before Joe did anything that couldn't be fixed. If Freddie really had called the cops, maybe Joe got to him before he did anything really damaging. Smith tightened his grip on the steering wheel. Goddamn amateurs.

Freddie stared out the passenger's window all the way to the drive-in. At first he hoped maybe a cop car would pull up beside them at a light, and he would jump out before Joe could get to him. But after a few minutes he knew he wouldn't do that. It took more guts than he had, and there weren't any cops anyway. He tried to keep the tears that were streaming down his face from showing. He didn't want to wipe his face, afraid that the gesture would draw Joe's attention. Not that Joe was paying attention anyway. He was driving with his left arm out the window, occasionally flicking his cigarette ashes into the wind, shifting and steering with his right hand. He had some country music shit on the stereo. Freddie couldn't tell who it was; they all sounded alike to him. Every once in a while Joe smirked, as if at some private joke.

Freddie was terrified that before they got to the drive-in he would lose all control of his bladder and bowels. He didn't care what it would do to Joe's truck; he was scared of what it would do to his own mind.

By the time they reached the Borger Highway it was almost empty. Joe sped up to 70, and in a few minutes the skeleton of the drive-in appeared on their right. Barely slowing down, Joe swept past the broken-down ticket booth. He cut the lights and skidded to a stop, snapped the cigarette through the window, and opened the door. "Stay in the truck," he said to Freddie without looking at him.

Freddie watched him strut across the grass and stop. A red flick appeared when he lit another cigarette, and Freddie watched the glowing tip as it raised and lowered from his mouth. He heard the sound of water flowing and realized Joe was pissing in the weeds like a dog marking its territory.

The drive-in's one remaining screen glowed eerily silver in the moonlight. It was weathered, and patches of the white paint had been worn away by the rain and sand storms, making it look like a giant's jigsaw puzzle. Joe leaned his arm against a speaker pole and bent down into the grass. He came up with a bowling pin that some kids must have carried away from the snack shack. He tossed it in the air, end over end. Joe caught it three times, but the weight was too clumsy and the fourth time he dropped it. Then he toed it with his boot, as if to get in the last word. Freddie leaned his head back against the headrest, wondering what he was doing in this place, trying to remember how it all started. He wanted to figure out a way he could go back to that day at the store when he eavesdropped on Smith and Carl. He wanted to finish his cigarette and go back inside when he heard them talking, wanted to get in his car after work and go home to his family, and not wait to talk to Carl. For a few moments he imagined that scenario and felt some relief from the pressures raging through his guts. Then he felt the glare of headlights on the back of his head for an instant before they were doused. Someone was here.

Smith stepped out of the car and slowly shut the door. He surveyed the drive-in: Joe's truck, with a shadowed figure inside, facing him. Joe standing twenty yards away, sucking a cigarette, hanging onto a speaker pole. Joe seemed somehow more agitated than Smith had seen him before, and he didn't know if that was good or bad. He walked toward Joe warily, trying to appear casual, his hands hanging at his sides. He stumbled over something lying in the weeds and glanced down to see what it was. A wooden letter D from the marquee, its red paint stripped away by time and neglect.

He stopped fifteen feet away from Joe, facing him, and flicked his eyes toward the truck. Smith hooked his thumbs in his front pockets, trying to appear friendly and relaxed. "You want to tell me about it?"

"I was out driving around, breaking in my new truck."

"Nice one."

"And who do I see? Little pissant there." Joe jerked his chin toward the truck. "Something about him, I don't know. Just told me he was up to no good. So I pull in behind him, follow him. He gets on the pay phone at a store, and I track in around the corner. Walk up on him real quiet, and I hear him on the phone talking to that big fucking cop Phillips, the one's on the news about Food Giant. He's trying to tell him about it, except thank God for us, he pussies around too long. He gives the guy his name before I disconnect him. He was gonna spill the whole thing. If I hadn't come along, we'd all be in a squad car right now, next stop Huntsville Prison."

"Shit." Smith looked at the truck. A sliver of moonlight had crept into the cab, and he could see Freddie looking at them. "I called Carl. He'll get here in a few minutes, and maybe we can talk some sense into him."

Joe spit into the weeds. A shiver went through him, although the night was still warm. "I don't need no Carl to talk some sense into him." He snapped the cigarette away from him and started toward the truck, the muscles of his neck and back rigid.

"Joe, come on, don't—"

Joe turned and faced him, walking backward. "Just watch me, and maybe you'll learn you something." He turned back and in two strides reached the truck. He yanked open the passenger's door.

"Get out."

His face white as curdled milk, Freddie shook his head.

"I say get out of the fucking truck now!"

Joe grabbed Freddie's shirt collar and hauled him out. Freddie stumbled and went to his knees, then grabbed the truck door and pulled himself up, flailing his arms. "Let go of me! Leave me alone!" He pulled himself away from Joe and desperately searched for Smith. "Where's Carl, is he coming?"

"Yeah," Smith said. "He's on his way. Joe come on, calm down." He touched Joe on the shoulder, and Joe shook his hand away.

Freddie looked toward the highway, searching for the glow of headlights pulling in. He was praying that Carl would get here in the next three seconds. He would do something; he would help.

His head was still turned toward the road when he felt a sharp slap on his cheek, and his skin started to burn. He stumbled away from the truck and looked at Joe; he saw rage running through his face. "Smith, keep him away!"

"Now you listen to me," Joe said. "Ain't no Carl gonna come save you. You're dealing with me now, and there is no way that I'm going to prison for some little chickenshit asshole like you."

Smith moved in between them. "Joe back off. I can deal with this."

Freddie circled around, trying to keep Smith between him and Joe. "Man, on the news they said they were about to arrest somebody!"

"Jesus Christ, Freddie," Smith said, "that's just bullshit, they gotta say that. Is that what this is about? Look, they're not—"

Joe stopped and stared at Freddie. He spit out a fleck of tobacco that was on his tongue. "And you were ready to sell us because of that? Shit!"

Freddie was afraid he was about to cry again. He felt it in his throat, heard it in his voice. "Man, I got kids. I can't go to prison."

Quicker than Smith could even see, Joe reached around him and shoved Freddie. Freddie fell back onto his butt, his hands splayed. Joe stood over him. "And we can? Why you little motherfucker. I hope you do go to prison, so you can see what it's like to get fucked by a guy. But you'd probably like it wouldn't you, you little faggot."

Freddie felt a knifing pain in the heel of his hand, and when he looked at it he saw a green piece of glass the size of a dime sticking out of it, pooling up blood. A piece of an old Coke bottle. Now, against his will, he did start to cry. He tried to stop the tears, but they dripped from his eyes like the blood from his hand—thick, unstoppable, unwanted. He looked up at Joe; the adrenaline pumping through him was almost visible, like tracer bullets just under his skin.

Freddie's lip started to tremble. This wasn't the way it was supposed to be. I'm not supposed to be sitting here in a patch of weeds, away from Regina, with blood dripping from my hand, listening to some asshole call me names. I'm just not, I'm not!

He didn't realize he had actually spoken the words out loud until Joe said "What did you say?"

"I'm not."

"Ain't what?"

"I'm not—what you said I am."

Joe laughed, a loud grating sound that ended in a smoker's phlegmy ratchet. He smiled at Freddie, a shark's smile, and brushed his crotch with his right hand. "Who are you trying to kid? Why don't you just admit it?"

"You're crazy!"

"Yeah, I'd rather be crazy than a little dick-sucking—"

"Shut up!"

"—faggot."

Freddie squeezed his wrist, trying to stop the pain, but it just caused more blood to flow from his hand. Then he felt something else, besides the blood and the fear that he had felt since the phone call disconnected. He felt anger begin to pulse through him with each heartbeat. He struggled to his knees, even used his throbbing right hand to support himself. The pain felt like an old friend now, and not at all like the enemy it had been a moment before, coming like a thief in the night to steal away his manhood.

When Freddie played for Tascosa, he didn't have the arm to play quarterback; other boys better suited had filled that role on the team. He wasn't big enough to block, either. But he came out fast on the field, and he had a sure grip that could hang onto the ball, so more often than not it was his job to carry it. And when someone got through the guards and came for him, those players from Lubbock Coronado and Plainview were always in for a big surprise, because if Freddie Odom couldn't find his way around you he'd just go straight through. He wasn't big but he could hit hard, and it left a lot of those boys laying on their big butts wondering what had happened.

He looked up at Joe's face and the contempt on it made the anger in him grow wings and fly. Joe was sneering at him. Joe, who had probably never played football like he did, who sure didn't have a shelf full of trophies. Joe had his hands on his hips, laughing at him. Freddie thought back to Joe in the pool hall, the way he made fun of him and Carl, how he had called him a punk and a faggot and a loser. He pushed both his hands against the ground and rising from his crouch, flew at Joe, right arm folded in against his body like it was holding a ball, left shoulder and head tucked down. He slammed into Joe's gut and they both hit the ground, Freddie on top.

Joe felt his back almost crack in two; he had landed on something thick and hard. Freddie rolled off of him and got to his feet, his fists cocked. He felt hands on him and knew it must be Smith, but the feeling was inconsequential, like a breeze tugging at his shirt. Instead, he felt electricity surging through his veins and muscles. For the first time since high school he felt like he could accomplish something. No one was laughing at him now for being drunk or late or slow. Joe still lay on the ground, reaching around underneath himself with one hand. He came out with the bowling pin he'd been juggling earlier. His face was as red as that truck he was so proud of. Screw him, Freddie thought. No one talks like that about me and gets away with it. Too bad it didn't break his back.

Joe's mouth twisted in pain as he struggled to get to his feet. "That's it," he said. "It's all over."

Freddie stood over him with his fists balled up. "Yeah? You're the one that's down. Man, why are you always talking about faggots, calling everybody one? I've got kids! You're the faggot."

Smith took his arms and pushed him back, away from Joe. "Freddie, come on. Back off. Don't get him more pissed off."

He glanced over his shoulder. Joe was on his feet again, weaving like a sapling in a high wind. He said, "You're gonna pay for that. You can't call me a faggot and get away with it. You ain't gonna do it again." His voice started to whine.

Freddie jerked his arms away from Smith's grip. "You can't say that about me, man. What does that say about my kids? You're the one who's a homo. That's why you're always talking about sucking dicks. You're a queer, man. I don't know how you found somebody to marry you, 'cause—"

Smith's back was still turned to Joe, so it was too late when he heard the scuff of Joe's boots in the weeds, getting closer to him. He tried to turn, to ward him off, but Joe slammed into both of them. As Smith spun away his feet tangled up and he went down, his right arm pinned under himself at an angle, and he felt pain shoot from his elbow up to his shoulder and down to his wrist.

He could only watch as Joe grabbed Freddie's shirt and threw him to the ground, pulled back one heavy boot and slammed it into Freddie's ribs, then kicked him again. Freddie screamed and with one arm grabbed the boot, pulling him off balance. Joe teetered on one leg and fell back to the ground. Freddie got to his knees, holding his ribs, moaning. "Smith," he said. "God, this hurts."

"What do you expect! Fuck you!" Joe screamed.

Freddie struggled to his feet, holding his ribs with both arms. Joe pushed to his feet too, and at first Smith couldn't tell what the flash of white in his hands was. Then he saw that Joe had them wrapped around the neck of the bowling pin, like a baseball bat. As he wound up to swing it Smith lunged for him, but he was too far away; he saw Joe's arms make a dreadful arc, ending when the pin slammed into Freddie's left ear. Smith reached Joe just as it connected and grabbed the pin, flinging it end over end twenty yards away into the weeds.

He turned to look at Freddie, who was staring at Joe with a look of wonder on his face. Blood was streaming from his ear, and Smith could see the bones in his cheek were shattered. Freddie was wearing a blue pullover shirt with a tiny red man falling off a horse above the left pocket. He took a breath, as if to say something, and lifted his right forefinger into the air like he was a politician trying to make a point. His eyes left Joe and wandered to Smith, and his lips began to work. They pursed and his tongue came out to lick them, and finally, in a ragged whisper, he said "Smi—?" and then he was falling backward like a felled redwood, a straight line from his ankles to the crown of his head. Smith leapt for him and caught his head just before it hit the ground. He cradled the younger man in his arms. Freddie gave an involuntary shake, and as Smith watched he saw the open eyes glaze over, and the body went limp.

"Oh Jesus," Smith said, "where is that fucking dog when you really need it?"

He heard a scuffle of gravel. Joe was standing in the same spot as when he hit Freddie. He shook his head slowly, and Smith was surprised to see the glisten of tears on Joe's cheeks. Joe's eyes swiveled slowly until he found Smith. "He should have shut up," he said. "I didn't go to kill him. You saw that."

Then, as if his body had lost all sense of its own weight, he abruptly sat down with his back against one of the speaker poles, knees raised in front of him, lost on the wrong highway. He put his hands behind him and his head jerked backwards as if he were looking at the stars.

A bright light hit Joe's face, but he didn't move. The light went out after a second as Carl's old white Ford glided to a stop. The dome light came on when he opened the door and blinked off as he abruptly shut it. He was wearing an old T-shirt and a pair of jeans.

"All right, what the hell is this all about? Do you know how it looked, getting a call and rushing off at this time of—" Then he saw Freddie and stopped like he'd slammed into an invisible wall. "What is this shit?" he whispered. "Smith, what—" His eyes found Joe, still sitting with his face turned up and his mouth gaped open.

"God in heaven. What's wrong with him?" He ran to Freddie, knelt down beside him, and saw the blood still trickling from his ear. "Smith, he's dead. Who—" He stopped as the truth seeped into his mind. He looked at Joe, whose eyes were still turned to the stars. Carl shook his head. The breeze sifted his hair. "I knew this was going to happen. I told you it was. God damn it! Why did I let you talk me into this again? You motherfucker, you should have stopped him from doing this!"

"Carl, there's no way I could have known he was going to—"

"Just shut up, you hear me? I don't want to hear a goddamn word from you." He stood up abruptly. Smith heard his knees crack when they straightened out. "We've got to get to a phone."

"Carl, I don't think that's a good idea. We can't do that."

Carl stared at him and shook his head like he was trying to clear something from his ears. "What? He's lying there dead, and you're telling me not to call the police? I've listened to you too many goddamn times in my life. I listened to you once and I ended up in prison for two years. I listened to you again and now I end up here, looking at—at this, my employee dead because you trusted some crazy fucking lunatic asshole that anybody with a brain would've known not to get near. Shit! How dare you! How dare you tell me we're not going to call the police!" He kicked the ground savagely, gouging holes in it with his heels.

Smith waited until he was silent. "Carl, he's dead. Ain't no way to bring him back."

"Listen to me—"

Smith gently lifted Freddie's head and shoulders and slid him off his lap onto the ground, like putting a child into a cradle. He stood up and brushed off his jeans.

"Carl, listen to me. If we call this in, we're in a cell. All three of us."

"What are you talking about? This is my wife's brother-in-law. He's my employee!"

"God damn it, I know that! But there's nothing we can do to help him. He's gone. I'm sorry he is, but I can't change it. There's no chance for him, but for us, there still is. We've got to think about the future. Our future. Yours and mine." His eyes flicked at Joe, who was sitting on the ground silent and unmoving. "If we don't panic, we can come out of this okay."

Carl hugged his arms across his body, as if he felt a cold breeze creep around him. Smith felt hot; sweat dripped down from his forehead. "Oh man," Carl said. "I can't believe this."

Smith looked again at Joe, who wasn't moving, and showed no signs of hearing them. "You've got a wife and kid," he said to Carl. "And who's going to help Freddie's family if you go up?"

Carl walked over to where Freddie lay, eyes staring at the sky, blood pooling on the ground next to his ear. His cheekbone and the left side of his face seemed about a quarter of an inch thicker than they should have been. He looked at Joe, who now had his arms resting on his knees, his forehead leaning on his wrists. Carl's lower lip curled out. "That guy should be in a cage. Fuck him. There's no way I'm going to protect him."

"Carl, Jesus Christ, forget him! You and I are the ones who can think! So let's do it. If we report this, we're going down. They get a look at my sheet it'll be life for me and what? Ten years for you, minimum? Can you afford that?"

Carl looked at him straight in the eyes. "What are you proposing?"

Smith took a deep, long breath and slowly blew it out. "Nobody comes out to this place. There's mounds of dirt between the poles. It'll blend right in."

"You're asking me to bury him out here?"

"God no, I wouldn't ask you to—look, I'll dig the—"

"Yes you are. Let's just get our terms straight. You want to bury him out here, where the fucking coyotes and the—" He flung his hand in the air, palm up, in short jerks, trying to find the right words.

Smith rubbed his stubbled chin. "All right. What do you think we should do? What seems right to you?"

Carl dropped his chin to his chest. His hand still moved, gently, in its quest for a way to describe what was happening. He hung the thumb in his belt loop to stop it and ran his other hand through his hair. "What'll we do with his car?"

Smith sighed, a soft exhalation of breath. He had started to answer when he heard a voice say "I can take it apart. They'll never find the pieces."

Smith turned his head slowly. Joe was still sitting, leaning against the pole, but his head was up. His eyes still looked unfocused, but he was obviously back in the game. "When'd you get here?" he asked Carl.

Smith ignored him and looked back to Carl. "What about it?"

Carl pursed his lips, and shook his head back and forth. "I'm not going to help."

"Joe. You got a shovel in your truck?"

"Yeah."

"Start digging." Smith rubbed his hand on his jeans. "Carl, look. If I had any idea that something like this would happen—"

"I don't want to hear it."

Smith sighed. "I guess not." He heard Joe get to his feet, heard his boots shuffle through the dirt and the sound of the big tool box in the truck bed opening and closing.

"You 'guess,'" Carl said. "I don't know how I could have been so stupid." He looked up at the stars, which blanketed the sky like a field of fully loaded cotton stalks. "What are you going to do now, get out of town and leave me holding this sack of shit?"

"No. I'll be around for a while."

"Why? You spend all the money already? Well, don't ask me to help you with another job."

Joe was starting to move faster now, almost back to his normal self. A small hole had appeared in one of the speaker rows, the chunk of his shovel signaling another shifting of dirt and sand.

"Actually, a lot of it is gone. My old man's dying, but they don't know how long it'll be. I'm about all he's got left."

Carl laughed with no joy. "I feel sorry for him." He thought a moment. "What happened with Freddie and that asshole? And what was wrong with him when I got here? Why was he just sitting there?"

Smith shook his head. "I ain't a goddamn psychiatrist. You really want to know what happened?"

"Fuck it. No."

"All right, we got to come up with a story. Joe's out of it."

"That's the truth. Shit. I don't even know what I'll tell Dolores and Regina."

Smith picked up a stick and drew circles in the dirt for a few moments. "All right. Let's try this," he said, and started to talk.

The howl of a coyote on the prairie half a mile away accompanied the murmur of their voices and the sound of the shovel moving earth. When Joe finished digging the grave, he and Smith lifted Freddie by the shoulders and legs and lowered him into the hole, and Joe started shoveling the dirt back on top of him. He kept his back to the body, pitching each shovelful behind him in the general direction of the hole until it was full. He and Smith pulled some weeds randomly and put them on the grave, trying to make them look like they were growing there. Smith stepped back and looked at it. It would take a sharp eye to see that anything was wrong.

He looked at Joe, who was slowly getting color back in his face. Joe didn't look him in the eye.

"Where's his car?"

"Pac-n-Sac over on Western."

"You know what to do with it?"

"Shit yeah. I'll take it apart and scatter it all over the goddamn Panhandle."

"All right." Smith saw Carl leaning against his car, his back turned to them.

"Joe. Why'd you hit him like that? We could have talked to him."

Joe still wouldn't look at him. He lifted his left shoulder. "You couldn't tell what he'd do after we let him go. He was on the phone with that cop. I think you're forgetting I pulled your ass out of the fire. Besides, he called me a faggot. I couldn't let him get away with that, could I?"

Wherever Joe had gone, there was no doubt he was back, Smith thought.

"Look," he said. "You ever see me coming down the street, in my car, in the goddamn pool hall, do me a favor. Turn around and go the other way. If I could pray to God, I'd ask that this is the last time I ever have to see your face." He glanced one more time at the grave and strode toward his car. Carl stared a hole in him and slowly shook his head back and forth, like he was the mayor watching a wino piss on the sidewalk in front of City Hall. He got into his car and drove out past the derelict ticket booth. Smith dropped in behind him, and in his rear-view mirror he saw Joe's truck pull onto the highway. Smith deliberately put a half-mile between him and Carl. Joe crossed the double yellow line and with a roar kicked his huge red truck around Smith's LTD. Fuck him, Smith thought.

The breeze sifted the sand over where Freddie lay, and the weeds in the Comanche Drive-In swayed gently. The theatre rested in its cradle of mesquite trees. Another coyote joined the first in a mournful duet. Aside from that and the wind, there was no noise at all.

Part Two

Chapter 18

Max woke up wearing a warm, vibrating helmet of fur. Short hairs tickled his nose, and he sneezed. Jersey whirred at Max, telling him to stop moving. He was wrapped around Max's head, purring, and Mayella was sprawled across his chest, sleeping deeply. Max squinted and checked the blue digital numbers on his alarm clock. 3:15. He had spent a quiet evening shooting pool at Bailey's. It was church night again, and Angel left the counter long enough to shoot a game with him. She beat him at 8-ball while Bailey kept an eye on the counter. He had seen her at the club twice since their sunrise date on Sunday morning. No one who saw them would have noticed anything different, but Max could feel her eyes on him sometimes, and the smiles she gave him were much different than the ball-bearing stare he'd received the night of the big sand storm. They'd made a tentative plan to have breakfast on Sunday morning. He was trying not to be nervous about the thought of kissing her again, hoping he'd have the chance.

He slowly extracted his head from Jersey's embrace. The cat purred and stretched all four legs at once then relaxed, never truly waking up. He picked up Mayella and kissed the fur between her ears. She whirred at him and pushed her head up under his chin. He put her back on the bed and went into the kitchen. Max poured skim milk over a bowl of Cocoa Crispies and settled on the couch with the notes he had prepared for a child-custody case. His client was trying to gain sole custody of her four-year old, whose father currently had custody every other weekend. One Sunday night she had called the police when she saw bruises on her daughter's thighs. The little girl said her father had "pushed" her there. The doctor's office couldn't conclusively prove sexual abuse, and the husband was claiming the mother was accusing him falsely; he'd never touched the girl. Because there was nothing to take to a judge, the husband was out walking around.

Max had a good case; he knew he would win custody for his client, and it wouldn't be the first good thing he'd done in Amarillo. The parents both looked like teenagers, and in truth they almost were. The mother was 21 and the father a year older. He had a wispy mustache that he was obviously proud of; during the depositions, he had stroked it continually. Max was determined that the guy wouldn't see his child again, if there was anything he could do about it. He worked on his notes for another half hour and rejoined the cats in bed. He was not surprised to find them still sound asleep.

It took Regina most of the day before she knew she had to call the police. After all, there couldn't be anything wrong with Freddie, really, because she had prayed to God for him the night before, and wasn't God supposed to answer your prayers? He usually did hers.

She had slept soundly through the night, not waking up once. When she woke up in the morning she reached for Freddie, and that was the first time she realized that he wasn't there and hadn't been all night. She put on her robe and looked in the living room for him because there had been times that he fell asleep on the couch while he was watching TV. But he wasn't there.

She sank down onto the couch and leaned her head back. She figured that he had ended up at a bar or that pool hall again, although he hadn't seemed to have been hanging out there much lately. In the last month or so he'd been around home more, had been paying attention to the kids. Even Bernice had noticed it, although when she said it her mouth was pursed up like she had eaten a lemon.

It had been more than a month since Freddie had stayed out all night, and she thought that maybe, just maybe, God was answering her prayers. She had been praying that God would take away Freddie's desire for alcohol. Maybe not completely; she wasn't sure if God would go that far. What she wanted was for Freddie to know when he'd had enough and then be able to stop. The last time he had stayed out all night was when they had the big sand storm. He had come in that afternoon, and it was even worse because Bernice and Dolores had been there with her. It hurt her to have them see Freddie like that. She knew it embarrassed Freddie too, and was sure that was the reason—that plus her praying, of course—that he had seemed to change.

It wasn't that he had stayed out all night on a regular basis. Over the course of the nine years that they'd been married, it might have happened about a dozen times. Maybe twenty. No more than that. And more the first six years than the last three. At first Freddie had been hanging around a lot with his old high school football buddies, but when they got married and had kids it happened less frequently. In the last several years it hardly ever happened, except when he ran into one of them at the pool hall or a bar.

Regina figured that's what must have happened last night, too. He ran into Pete Blakemore or Bob Stone or one of those guys he'd played ball with. She glanced at her watch and saw that it was almost time to get the kids up and start cooking their oatmeal. A couple of more minutes. She pulled her legs up underneath her and tucked her robe around them. Amarillo weather was unpredictable at the best of times. It was November 5th, and although the temperature might well be in the 70's that afternoon, it felt like it was barely above freezing right then. That meant she'd have to put a warm coat on Travis, and when she picked him up he'd be carrying it, most likely dragging it in the dirt. It's not that Travis was careless or anything; he was like his father—good hearted, but sometimes he just didn't pay enough attention. In the corner of the room was a stack of shelves that was shaped like a triangle so it would fit right. There were some knick-knacks on it, things people had given to them over the years mostly, and five football trophies from Freddie's high school days. One was for being Tascosa's Most Valuable Player his junior year. That award almost always went to a senior, so he was doubly proud that he got it. Of course that was hard too, because when you got it your senior year, you didn't have to see anyone else get it the next year. You'd be working or in college. But they never gave it to the same person twice. She knew that hurt Freddie a little, seeing it go to someone else while he was still there. But he had done well that year anyway.

She knew that he missed playing a lot; he didn't even like to look at it on television, and she could tell it was because he was jealous of the ones who were still out there. He said he wouldn't watch because the players got too much money. She knew differently but didn't say anything.

Regina drifted a little while longer, thinking about Freddie the way he was in high school, and not about where he might be right now. She got the kids up and fed and dressed and their teeth brushed, and when Travis was gone she sat Maggie down in front of *Sesame Street* and started cleaning the house. It wasn't real big; just one bathroom and two bedrooms, but when she was nervous or upset Regina always seemed to clean the house more. She finished it around lunchtime and made grilled cheese sandwiches and tomato soup for her and Maggie. The little girl meticulously ate one small bite at a time. Sometimes Regina marveled at her. Travis was so much like Freddie, but Maggie didn't really seem like either of them as far as she could tell. Regina had always thought of herself as sort of timid, but Maggie wasn't like that at all. She always had to keep an eye on her at the supermarket, or she'd wander away and just start talking to strangers. Bernice joked and said Maggie would end up a politician if they weren't careful, but Regina could tell that secretly she was proud. That confused Regina too, and made her more than a little angry. When she was a little girl Bernice wouldn't let her say boo. The less Regina said, the better. Of course she didn't let her mother know how much this double standard upset her; old habits die hard.

At noon she gathered up her courage, called Puente Draperies, and asked for Freddie. Sharon answered the phone, and when she heard Regina's voice it sounded like she was a little embarrassed.

"Just a second, Hon" she said, and in a few moments Carl's voice came on the line.

When she asked to talk to Freddie, Carl too sounded like something was wrong.

"He didn't come in this morning, Gina," he said. "Haven't you heard anything from him?" Regina thought that was a stupid thing to ask, because if she had heard something from him she wouldn't be calling to see if he was at work, would she? She didn't say that to Carl, though. She just said to have him call home when he came in. Carl asked her the same thing. "I want to talk to him," he said. Regina hung up, but she had a funny thought. Carl sounded more worried than mad, and usually it seemed that where Freddie was concerned he was mostly mad. Where anybody was concerned, Carl was mostly mad.

At twelve-thirty she and Maggie took a walk to the park that was three blocks down from their house. She pushed her daughter on the swings and on the little crooked merry-go-round, the one with bars that looked like handrails in a public building. Other mothers from the neighborhood were there with their children. A toddler took three halting steps, her tiny fists holding on tightly to her mother's index fingers.

"That's so good!" the mother said.

"Mommy, can you push harder?" Maggie asked. Regina did, digging the toes of her sneakers into the ring of scruffy grass around the merry-go-round. A faint breeze crept by, ruffling Maggie's curls.

After an hour, Regina took Maggie's hand and led her back home. The girl picked up a rock on the sidewalk that seemed to have some magic for her and asked if she could add it to the collection on the shelf next to her bed. Regina said yes, and she pocketed it.

Back at home Maggie took a nap and Regina watched television for a while, although she never could concentrate on what was playing. She thought of calling someone, but Dolores was still teaching at Dawson Elementary, and she didn't want Bernice to know that Freddie hadn't come home.

At 2:00 she picked up the phone and started to look up the number for the police department in the phone book. Then she thought maybe she could just dial 911, but this wasn't an emergency, really. To her it was, but maybe not to the police department, and weren't they always talking in the newspapers and on TV about people dialing it when they weren't supposed to? She was sure they were. She put the phone back and made a pot of coffee. She had a big mug with Mickey and Minnie Mouse on the side that Freddie had given her one Christmas. She filled it up and sat on the front porch with it.

It wasn't until she heard Maggie say "Why are you crying, Mommy?" that she realized she was. Tears were trickling down her face, and the inch of coffee still left in the mug was cold. Maggie had gotten up from her nap, and Regina hadn't heard her whispered steps come down the hall into the living room, looking for her mother. She hadn't heard the screen door whine, hadn't heard anything until Maggie put her hand on her mother's arm and asked why she was crying.

Regina hugged her and said "It's okay, honey. Mommy's fine." She and Maggie walked down to the school bus stop to meet Travis, and when they got home the children settled down in front of the big television. Regina went into the bedroom and called Carl one more time to make sure Freddie wasn't there. She called Dolores, home from school by now, and told her. She asked Dolores to call Bernice. Then she called the police. She looked up the number in the blue pages instead of calling 911. It still felt like an emergency to her, but she didn't know how they would look at it. She wanted to do things the right way.

Cornelius Ross had seen all of this before. A worried family with no idea where their loved one was. So they called in the police. He's dead, they said. We're sure of it. Or maybe he's been kidnapped, abducted by spies from the federal government. That was one he'd actually worked. A woman's husband hadn't shown up for two days, and when she finally called she said the feds had more than a passing interest in him because he could prove that what had happened in Waco in 1993 was an experiment by U.S. storm troopers to see how far they could take their fight against religious freedom and still get away with it. Or maybe the guy had information about how the Oklahoma City bombing was actually committed by the President against his own people, so that God-loving American patriots would get blamed for it. Some shit like that.

The gal had seemed less than pleased when Ross called her two hours later with the news that her old man had temporarily set up shop in the county drunk tank. It hadn't actually taken Ross two hours to find him. Fifteen minutes was more like it. As soon as he got in his car he made the call, and sure enough in twenty minutes he knew where the old guy was, but he decided to let her sweat a while. When Champ found out, he said that Ross was just being plain cruel and that he'd unfairly prolonged the woman's agony. He said that around a toothpick inserted in the corner of his mouth, trying not to smile. Ross said he should go by and spend five minutes talking to the old crow, looking at the framed Confederate flag on the wall, at the pictures of a blue-eyed blonde Jesus all over the place, and just try to keep his hand off the butt of his service pistol. Champ finally smiled and said he'd pass on that one.

So whenever Ross, whose nickname was Cee, got called in on a missing person case he was immediately suspicious. The family was always convinced that foul play was evident, and he knew that in most cases the missing person wasn't missing at all. He was in Vegas or Corpus or shacked up or drunk, and in some way or other perpetually pissed off at or strung up by the world at large and his family in particular, and Cee knew he'd eventually lose his bankroll or get booted out or sober up and more likely than not he'd turn up.

All that was if the missing person was male. If it was female, the chances were still good that it was a temporary misplacement, but not quite as likely. Cee looked closer at those cases. Missing kids were another matter entirely. He jumped straight on those, and the first thing he did was look at what was going on in the home. Were the parents drinking? Was the old man an asshole on automatic pilot? Was a girl, and as much as he hated to say it, even a boy being forced to play the role of surrogate mother? One of those scenarios was the truth more often than not, and Cee, often teaming with Champ Phillips, came straight down hard on the family, which usually "knew" somewhere the runaway might be, and why.

So when Cee got this call he tried not to make any prejudgments, but it was hard. Freddie Odom, 32 years old, 5'10", 190 pounds, curly dark blonde hair. When he first got to the house he was surprised to see more than just the wife, who had made the call. There were also her mother and sister, who flanked her on the couch, and the sister's husband, who turned out to be the guy's boss.

As Cee sat on the edge of the chair sipping at a cup of coffee, which he had a policy of never refusing, it seemed to him that maybe this might not be the average case. These folks didn't seem crazy or mean; they just seemed nervous and scared.

Cee ran his hand over his shaved head. He'd worn it shaved since the early 1980's, when he realized that each day in front of the mirror he faced a hairline that had receded slightly from the day before. He was only 25 years old, a patrol cop, too young to go bald. He cursed his mother's genes. Then one night while flipping channels, he happened on the Tonight Show. Isaac Hayes was the guest, and within an hour Cee was going to work with a pair of scissors, a razor, and a can of Barbisol shaving cream.

He set down the empty cup of coffee and took out his notepad. He had heard the general story, and now he focused in on its particulars. "Now am I right in remembering that Mrs. Odom was the last one to see her husband?"

Regina nodded nervously. She knew she hadn't done anything wrong and neither had Freddie, but she didn't like having a police officer in her house. It was a little funny him being black too, because her knowledge of the police came mostly from the television, and there weren't many black policemen there. But that was okay, because she didn't care, really, if someone was black or white. She decided that she was okay with his color; it was just having him here that she wished wasn't necessary.

"And that was at what time again?"

Regina realized he was talking to her. "I think it was about 8:30 when he left."

Cee took a note of that. "Now the thing that I'm wondering about here," he said, "is why you didn't make a call last night when your husband didn't come home. Seems like that would have been the time to call, wouldn't it?"

Regina started to talk, and Bernice cut her off. "What are you trying to say, officer?"

"Detective," he gently corrected her. "And I'm not trying to say anything, ma'am—"

"Well it doesn't sound like it to me," she said. "What we all want here is to find Freddie, and insinuating anything about my daughter won't help to—"

"Ma'am, I'm sorry if you felt that I was insinuating anything," Cee said, thinking "old bitch." "I'm just trying to find out if there was any reason that Mrs. Odom wasn't worried that her husband didn't come home. Now ma'am," he said, looking straight at Regina, "is there any reason you can think of?"

Regina looked at Carl, standing against the arch leading from the living room into the kitchen. He glanced away. She looked at Bernice, who was trying to stare a cold hole through Cee. Dolores reached down and took her hand, gently squeezing it.

"Well, Detective," Regina said, "Freddie, like I told you, was going down to get some beer at the store, and then he said he'd go to the video store. And sometimes that takes a while."

"Oh I know, Mrs. Odom. Sometimes I go down there and can't figure out what movie to pick up, a new one that'll probably be bad or an old one that I know is good. I can spend a half hour down there. A miracle my wife doesn't call the police on me." Cee had been divorced for ten years, but it was an effective ploy. He chuckled, and everyone else's expression lightened.

"So you know, then. I waited up for him a while, but I was tired, and I thought maybe he'd run into some of his friends, or something."

Aha, Cee thought. "And what might have happened then?"

The mother-in-law breathed out an irritated puff of air from her nose. He made a mental note of it.

"Well, he might spend some time with them, or something."

"Like they might go over to Denny's and grab an omelette?"

"Well no, I mean there's nothing to say he wouldn't, but it would probably be more like going to Bailey's. That's a place where he plays pool sometimes."

"Played a few games there myself," Cee said, which was untrue; he'd never so much as broken up a fight there, and for a good reason. He'd heard the security in the place was so tight that a police presence was never required. "So you went to bed after a while because you figured Freddie might have hooked up with some friends and they were playing pool?"

"Yes."

"I see." Cee rubbed his left hand over his shining head then thoughtfully stroked his mustache with the forefinger of the same hand. "And you didn't know something was wrong until you woke up this morning?"

"That's right."

"Mr. Puente?" Carl, deep in thought and trying to appear nonchalantly worried at the same time, was caught off guard.

"Yes?" Be calm but concerned, he said to himself.

"Tell me again why it didn't bother you when Mr. Odom didn't show up at work this morning."

"Well, I thought he might be sick or something."

"Is that such a common occurrence for him, that you might suspect it right away?"

"No, but—" Carl shrugged "somebody doesn't show up, you suspect it. He was sick on Sunday afternoon, and I thought maybe he still was, you know."

"I'm not sure I do."

"I thought maybe he still hadn't gotten over it."

"But he was at work Monday, Tuesday, and yesterday, wasn't he?"

"Yeah."

"So he was sick then, not enough to skip work, but maybe got worse. But that doesn't explain why you didn't call and see what was up, when he didn't come in."

"Detective, I feel like you think I've done something wrong here. I mean, why are you asking me these questions?"

"Again, my apologies. I just want to ascertain the whole situation here." Lying my ass off, Cee thought. "I'm just trying to find out if there's anything you know that you may have forgotten about. Everybody's memory can use a little jogging. Just like my waistline." He got only a few mild smiles. Apparently his act was wearing thin.

"It's like I was trying to say, Detective," Carl said. "He didn't show up, and I knew he'd been sick. I didn't call because I figured Regina might have her hands full taking care of him and Maggie. If he hadn't shown up tomorrow, for sure I would have called."

"I'm sure you would have." Cee flipped his notebook shut. "I think I have what I need for now. Description, license plate, car, last seen. You think he would have gone to Pac-n-Sac over on Western for the beer?"

"That's what he said."

"Did he go over there a lot? I mean for groceries, snacks, that kind of thing. If I show them this picture you gave me, they might know him? Remember if he was there last night?"

"I feel pretty sure, yes."

"Good. I think that's all I need for now. I'll make some copies of this information and give it to the patrol officers. But to tell you honestly, I think you'll hear from him sometime soon. I know it'll seem like a long time, but it won't be. I have a hunch."

He started toward the door, and then did what he had come to think of as his Columbo #4 trick. He paused at the door and said "Oh yeah, one more thing. Does Mr. Odom keep regular hours?"

He could see the mother-in-law's face get cloudy. "What do you mean by that? He's a good father and husband."

A defensive response if he'd ever heard one, Cee thought. "Oh, yes ma'am, I know that. I was just wondering, Mr. Puente, if Mr. Odom ever shows up late to work. I mean, I myself am not an on the dot 8:00 a.m. kind of man. Time I stop off for a cup of coffee and a doughnut, it's maybe ten minutes past. I hate to say that, the way people talk about cops and doughnuts, but sometimes it's true. So Freddie, did he show up at work straight up the hour, or is he more of a five minute, ten minute kind of guy?"

Carl thought, trying to second-guess what he wanted. He decided the truth would harm no one. "Sometimes, maybe half the time, he's a little late. Maybe fifteen to thirty minutes."

"Okay. And coming home, Mrs. Odom. Would you say he's regular? Can you expect him home straight up five or six, ready for dinner?"

He noticed the pleading look in her eyes as she glanced at her mother and sister. "Freddie's always home," she said.

"Oh, I know. But his schedule. Would you say his hours were regular?" He glanced at the football trophies on the corner shelves. "Dependable?"

"Sometimes his hours weren't so regular."

"Okay. Like I say, same holds true for me sometimes. Anytime you ever worried about him? Maybe more than a couple of hours late?"

"Oh," she said, and Cee knew he had to get to this quick and back off before she started bawling. Right now he could see her eyes brimming. He hated this part of the job, asking shitty questions of decent people and pretending to be a good old boy.

"A few times," she said, and a tear lost its grip from each eye and went sliding down her pretty cheeks.

"Ever happen that he was late like the next day?"

The tears were really streaming now, little creeks of them cutting across the banks of her face. She started to answer, but he didn't really need it. Her tears said it all.

He turned on his best warm, fat police detective demeanor. "I know it's hard not to worry, but I really think he'll show up very soon. He'll come walking in that door. Or we'll find him, but I don't even think that'll be necessary. He'll come home in a little while. Just give me a call when he does," he said, handing a card to Regina, "or if you have any other questions. My office and cell phone numbers are on there. I'll call and check in with you real soon, just to let you know what I've come up with. Y'all take care now."

He pushed open the screen door with his right hand and gave them a little wave goodbye. He walked down to his car and with a sigh settled himself behind the wheel. I've got to drop some weight, he thought. He looked at the photograph the family had given him of Freddie. It must have been taken at a park. He was kneeling on the green grass, one arm around his little boy, the other resting on a football. There were dirt and grass stains on Freddie's shirt, as if he had by choice lost a gentle game of tackle ball. As he looked at the picture, an unexpected pang went through Cee's heart. He offered up a little prayer that this man would do what he thought of as an "S and S": sober up and show up. He placed the photo carefully on his clipboard and made the drive downtown.

They waited until the detective was gone, waited until his car had pulled away from the curb. Regina cleared her throat and looked around at the others. "Well, he seems to know what he's talking about. I think he's right, you know, I think Freddie will just—" She tried to finish the sentence, tried to envision Freddie coming through the door, but she couldn't say the words before she started sobbing.

"Of course he will, honey," Bernice said. "He'll show up. He'll be back soon. Shhh, it's okay." She put her arm around her younger daughter and leaned Regina's head against her shoulder while she cried. Dolores put her hand on her sister's shoulder and made comforting sounds. She smoothed Regina's bangs back, pulled her hair behind her ears. "It's okay, baby. Momma's right, it won't be long now."

Carl stood up from his chair and quietly opened the screen door onto the porch. He hiked himself up onto the stucco wall at the left side of the porch.

He thought about the shitty hands that life had dealt him through the years: the gas station job, the two years in prison, the debt that almost broke his spine, Nina's medical bills, the humiliation of having the sharks call him at home. Of them all, he decided, this was the worst. Sitting there in the living room listening to Regina's pain, to her limping, pathetic hope that Freddie was going to come back when Carl himself knew goddamn well that he wasn't going to, because he knew exactly where he was: rotting under a foot of sand and weeds at the Comanche Drive-In. Sitting there listening to her, answering her call at work and telling her that no, he didn't know where Freddie was, trying to keep from floating away in a torrent of sweat while the cop was there, was almost more than he could take.

This was definitely the worst thing that had ever happened. If he didn't get eaten away from inside by an ulcer, it would be a miracle. He wanted so bad to just give it up, to stand up and say to the cop, I know where Freddie is, and I'll take you there. But he knew if he did, he'd lose everything. Oh, he didn't think he'd go to prison. After all, he didn't plan the job and he didn't kill Freddie; that had been that asshole Smith and his pit bull Wagner. Sure, Carl was in the store with a gun, but he could make a deal by giving them up; he knew that. He felt sure the cops and the D.A., whoever makes those decisions, would go for it. But he would still lose the business. Who'd want to buy drapes from a criminal? His income, his livelihood, his father's legacy would be gone. And Nina. Dolores would take her away. She and her mother would do that the first thing. There was no way he could tell anybody. He didn't know how he could sit down at Christmas with the family while the kids wondered where their daddy was. Carl couldn't walk back into Regina's living room with those fucking football trophies of Freddie's. He didn't think there would be any way he could do it. But deep down in his guts he knew he had to. Because if he made one misstep, if he said or did the wrong thing at the wrong time, they could pop him for it. Shit.

The screen door screeched open and Dolores walked out onto the porch, glancing over her shoulder inside the house.

"I can't stand to see her like that."

"Yeah, I know."

"I feel like a shit for thinking this, much less saying it. But I always thought something like this might happen. That Freddie might not come back some day. I love him, but he's such a big kid in some ways."

Carl nodded and didn't say anything.

Dolores leaned against the porch wall that faced the street, diagonally from him.

"We haven't gotten any more of those calls at the house. I like that. Is there anything I should know about it?"

Carl plucked a spot of lint off his khaki pants. "No. It's cleared up. They won't call anymore."

"Good." She leaned her head against a porch support and closed her eyes. "Where did you go last night?"

Carl had already anticipated this question, and the answer rolled smoothly off his tongue. "Oh, the alarm went off at the store and I had to go over there. It was just a crank call. Kids screwing around, probably."

Dolores nodded. "You think he's going to come back, Carl?"

He didn't have an answer ready for this one, and he stumbled. But that was normal; it was to be expected. "God, Dolores. I hope so. I think he will. Freddie's not the best worker in the world, but most of the time he's okay. And he really loves Regina and the kids, I know that. Yeah, of course he'll be back. He probably went off somewhere and you know, went on a bender. He's done that before."

"But this time it feels different. I don't know why, but it does. What odds do you think your bookie friends would give you on it?"

There was no way he could have prepared for this one. "Jesus Christ, Dolores, that's low! Look, I said it's over with, okay?"

Dolores was embarrassed. "I'm sorry, Carl. I don't know why I—look, I'm sorry. Okay?"

"Yeah. But you know it's over with, right? I told you. Are we square on that?"

"Yes." She walked over to him and awkwardly hugged him. He patted her on the shoulder with one hand, his other arm around her waist.

"How's it going in there, with Regina?"

"She's scared. Like I said, this time feels different."

"Is there anything I can do?"

"I don't think so. Are you getting itchy?"

"No, not at all. I'm just not sure if there's anything I can do."

"Why don't you just go on home, and I'll catch a ride with Momma? And can you take Nina with you? I doubt she'll mind some pizza tonight."

She kissed him on the cheek. "I don't know what you did to stop the calls, and I don't want to. But thanks. Let me go get Nina."

They had let her play on the swing set in the back yard with Maggie and Travis while Ross was there. Carl stayed on the porch, and in a few minutes Nina came running out and wrapped her arms around his waist. Dolores was right; she didn't mind having pizza.

Chapter 19

Joe tried everything he knew to get rid of the pinto horse, but nothing worked. On Wednesday night after he got back from taking care of Freddie's car, Darlene was already in bed. He sat and channel surfed for a while. Everything was okay until he found TV Land. He liked it because there were always good cowboy shows on. The shows on nowadays weren't worth a shit. Just a bunch of smug young assholes saying things meant to be funny. He guessed they were supposed to be, at least, because all those stupid fucking laugh tracks were turned on high. But they weren't funny at all, and sometimes they drove him crazy because they all had good looking women on them, beautiful blonde and brunette women with big tits and tight asses, and he hated it because the men on those shows all seemed like such little faggots, but they were supposed to be fucking those women. Oh, he knew it was just television, and that the women weren't really fucking those actors, or most of them weren't anyway, but he knew that somewhere out there in California those women were fucking somebody, closing their eyes and spreading their legs for some little fake-blond fucker in a fancy car, a BMW or Mercedes, who'd never done a day's work in his life, who'd never had a callus on his hands. The more Joe thought about that the more he hated it, so he never watched those shows. He stuck to sports and the old cowboy shows, like they had in the 1960's. That was when TV made sense to him, when they had shows like *Gunsmoke* and *Bonanza* and some of the others back then. Sometimes on cable he saw even older ones from before he was born, like Paladin, that badass with the mustache. He was just a little kid when the westerns ended, but they ran on TV Land all the time now.

On Wednesday night Joe sat on the sofa and tried to figure out what exactly had happened at the drive-in and why. He remembered seeing Freddie in his car on Georgia Street and listening to him on the pay phone. Then he had called Smith and driven out to the Comanche with the little rat. He remembered Smith getting there, and then for some reason he started having trouble. He did remember Freddie calling him a faggot, and he knew that they had fought with each other. Joe's back was hurting him really bad where he had fallen on the bowling pin. But everything else around that time was like it was swimming in fog. After he fought with Freddie he didn't really remember anything clearly until he was sitting on the ground. Carl was there, talking with Smith, and that was funny because Joe didn't know when he got there. And the scariest part of it all was that he didn't remember killing Freddie. He knew he must have, because Smith wouldn't have done it, and after all he was the one Freddie was fighting with. But all he remembered was sitting there and dimly hearing Carl and Smith arguing about what to do with Freddie. He pretended that he knew exactly what was going on. But he didn't. He dug the hole with Smith's help and they put Freddie in it. He took the bowling pin to a construction site he knew about where they were ready to pour the basement, and he buried it there, where it would be covered with concrete in a day at the outside. He went back to the Pac-n-Sac where he'd left Freddie's car and he moved it first, then arranged for some folks he knew to strip it down so that by morning the parts would be heading all over Texas and Mexico, piece of shit junk heap that it was, and there was no chance anyone would ever find enough of it to identify.

Then he went home and sat on the couch and tried to figure out what had happened that night. There was no way he could, though, and it gave him a headache so he took some aspirins and drank a beer. Finally he quit trying to figure it out. He flipped channels until he found *Bonanza*, one of the good episodes, before Adam left. He liked Adam best, with his bad-ass black clothes. Hoss was a dumb fuck and Little Joe was too much of a faggot, although beautiful girls were always falling in love with him. Same as those stupid-ass new shows. This was a good one though, an episode he'd seen before, and it was all going fine until Little Joe got on that pinto horse of his and rode into town. Then Joe, sitting there on the couch with his legs stretched out and a beer in his hand, started to feel sick to his stomach a little bit. Not like he had to throw up or anything, but his guts just started to churn and his throat began to get a little tight. He couldn't figure it out. After a while the show was over; the Cartwright boys had shot up all the bad guys again, and the show went off, replaced by an old episode of *Lancer*. It was good too, with another sissy and a bad ass in black, that actor who later got his leg and arm cut off in a motorcycle accident. But all Joe could think about was that pinto horse of Little Joe's. He flipped channels, and for some reason he just couldn't get that horse out of his head. It was stuck there hard as Chinese arithmetic, so he kept drinking more and more until finally he got so sick he did have to throw up. He staggered into the bathroom and knelt for five minutes with his head over the bowl, throwing his guts up. Finally he quit. Tears were streaming from his eyes, all down his cheeks, and he felt weak like a little boy. He stood up and rinsed his mouth out with a handful of water. His head was pounding, and his throat burned like he'd been gargling acid. The pressure in his bladder was intense too, so he unbuttoned his jeans and pissed, and when he looked down he saw that the stream of urine was a dark pink, and it felt like a giant hand was squeezing his insides. He threw his hand out against the wall to support himself. Joe had been in enough fights and thrown from enough horses to recognize that he had a kidney injury. Landing on that bowling pin must have bruised it. He knew that in a few days the blood would go away, but it would take longer than that for the pain to disappear. He pulled his shirt off and turned so that he could see his back; already ugly purple bruises were starting to appear.

He looked at his face in the mirror; it was white and red at the same time, and his eyes were all bloodshot. He ran water onto a washcloth and scrubbed his face then went back out into the living room and watched TV until he fell asleep on the couch. In the morning when he woke up Darlene was already gone to work. He'd give her shit for not waking him up, because now he'd be late for work and whose fault would that be?

He showered quickly and drank a cup of instant coffee. Usually he had a beer when he got up, but after getting sick last night he figured it wasn't maybe such a good idea this morning.

He did okay at work. His boss didn't give him any shit for being late, because he was a good worker, but that didn't mean Joe wouldn't give some to Darlene that night. He worked hard all day. Even though it was November the days were still warm and rings of sweat grew underneath his arms long before lunch came. When the clock hit noon he pulled his mask off and put the torch down. He bought a couple of donuts and a cup of coffee from the snack truck and sat in the cab of his truck. He couldn't get enough of that truck; he loved sitting in the cab even when he wasn't driving, loved putting his head back and just smelling it. It was the kind of bad-ass truck he'd wanted ever since he was in high school, the kind of truck the rich kids all had, the ones whose daddies owned the John Deere place and the car dealerships. Those kids looked down on him like he wasn't worth a shit. But someday he'd slide over there in his truck and just let them see it. They were still there, he knew, running those same businesses they'd inherited from their daddies.

He turned on the radio. It was playing some singer he didn't know, probably one of those faceless kids with the big hats, the ones you'd hear about for a week and then they'd be gone. They looked like those fags on the TV, with their long hair and soft faces. Most of the radio stations were just as bad as the TV shows for that. He went through the stations until he found George Jones singing "He Stopped Loving Her Today." Now there's the real thing, Joe thought. Then they played Merle Haggard and Johnny Cash and Kitty Wells, and it was getting time for him to get back to work when out of nowhere came the thought of that pinto horse again, and in less than a second those doughnuts felt like they were gonna punch in a round-trip ticket. His stomach heaved, and it was all he could do to keep them down. He didn't know why the horse came back into his mind. This time it wasn't Little Joe riding it, it was just out in a field or something looking straight at him. He closed his eyes and after a few minutes it went away. He wiped his face because sweat was beaded all over it. His stomach was still queasy, but when he went back to work after a little while he felt okay again.

Over the next couple of days the horse came back again, although after a while it didn't take as long to go away and didn't take Joe quite as much by surprise. He tried drinking more beer, but that didn't really help. He went to the Midnight Rodeo and shot pool a couple of times. One night while he was there he ran into a woman named Trish that he'd seen there a couple of times before. Usually she was with another pool player, and sometimes she and her boyfriend would take a break and dance. Joe watched her a couple of times while they scooted around the dance floor. This night he was shooting with some other guys and noticed her standing a few feet away, watching them, her hand wrapped around a bottle of Coors. He liked the way it slid into her mouth, and thought about how it would feel sliding his cock into her mouth. After the game was over he struck up a conversation. Joe knew how to flirt with a woman, some women at least, how to put them at ease. It didn't always work, but with this one it did. He asked her where her boyfriend was, and he could tell she was flattered that he'd noticed her in there before. She said the two of them had broken up, and that he had him a new girlfriend now.

"I had me a girlfriend looked like you do, I wouldn't even be thinking about breaking up," Joe said. He knew by the way her eyes lit up that he had hit the right chord with her. They chatted for a few more minutes, and he bought her a beer that she drank down. Then he suggested that they go someplace else, and she said how about her place. Joe followed her back to her apartment, and for a few minutes they chatted a little bit. They drank a couple more beers, Joe watching the way her ass swayed when she walked away into the kitchen. They talked for a couple of minutes, then he grabbed her wrist, pulled her to him and kissed her. Her hands were all over him, pulling at his clothes, yanking the tail of his shirt out of his pants and then they were in the bed, and he was inside of her, sliding in and out, and her fingers were digging into his back, squeezing his ass. He fucked her three or four times, until early in the morning, and finally she dozed off. He did too, and an hour later he woke up again, his cock starting to stiffen right away. He reached down and stroked it until it was hard, and he was about to roll on top of her again. That'll wake her up quick, he thought, but before he could start the image of that horse came into his head again, and his hard-on shrunk away in his hand. He started to get that sick feeling in his gut again and acid came up into his throat. He sat up on the edge of the bed, and Trish mumbled and turned over in her sleep. He looked at her and rage rolled up inside him, the rage and the sickness in a tie over which would come first. He wanted to hit her. He knew Trish hadn't done anything wrong to him, that whatever was going on wasn't her fault, but she was the closest person around, and somewhere inside Joe he knew he would feel better, would feel *something* if he could hurt her. He wanted to wake her up, to hit her in the mouth, to fuck her in the ass, to make her scream in pain, his hand over her mouth so no one would hear. He could feel the pain her teeth would cause as she bit into his hand trying to get rid of it. He could feel himself fucking her hard and slapping her, and as her pain increased so would his, as blood, his blood leaked from his hand—

She mumbled again in her sleep, and his nausea won out. Joe stood up from the bed and stumbled into the bathroom, shutting the door behind him, throwing up, trying to do it quietly so she wouldn't hear and come in, asking him what was wrong and wanting to take care of him. He finally finished, his stomach empty of all the beer he had drunk that night. He stood up and looked at his face in the mirror. Joe could see that it looked drawn, that his jaw line had lost some flesh. He splashed water onto his face, rinsed out his mouth, and opened the medicine cabinet. There was a bottle of green mouthwash in there, one of those little ones that you get free in the mail, or in a drugstore for traveling. Joe swished some around in his mouth and spit it into the basin. He looked at himself in the mirror again and saw that his face looked like shit. He couldn't figure out what was wrong with him, why he kept thinking about that horse and why it made him so sick when he did. Fuck it, he thought, maybe it'll just go away.

He turned out the light and opened the door. Trish was still in bed; he could tell by her regular breathing that she was still deeply asleep. He picked up his underwear and jeans from where he had dropped them on the floor at the foot of the bed. He had to reach inside the legs of his jeans and pull the socks out, and he didn't feel strong enough to put them on standing up, but he didn't want to sit on the bed and wake her up. He couldn't see a chair, so he finally leaned against the wall and put on his socks and jeans. He pulled on his boots and his shirt, not bothering to tuck it in, just letting it flap. Joe started to leave the bedroom and suddenly the air conditioner kicked on. He ducked his head and half raised his hand as if to ward off a blow, before he realized what it was. Shit shit shit, he thought. I'm getting just like a little candyass kid, scared of my own shadow. He heard a sound from the bed and looked over to see Trish turn from her back onto her side and shiver, as if someone had just walked over her grave. She took the other pillow, the one Joe's head had just been on, and hugged it to her breasts. He heard a little mewling sound coming from her, and he walked out of the bedroom.

Trish lived in a tiny apartment; the bedroom was just off the living room, and the kitchen was barely big enough for one person to stand in. He opened the refrigerator and took out the three remaining cans of a Schlitz six-pack. He closed the door quickly and glanced over his shoulder, to make sure that the light hadn't leaked into the bedroom. He started to pop the tab of a can, but at that moment all he wanted was to get out of there as fast as he could.

He didn't know what was wrong with him. He was acting like a pussy, running out of a woman's apartment, afraid she would wake up and what? Catch him? Yell at him? That was stupid shit to be thinking. If she said anything to him he could slap her around or fuck her, either one was all right with him. But still here he was sneaking out of the place, letting the door quietly shut behind him. He walked down a concrete path that led to the small swimming pool the complex had. The lights in the walls of it shone creepily up through the green water. He could hear crickets somewhere not far away. In one of the second floor apartments, a party was going on. There was laughter suddenly, a woman's high voice breaking through the air and several others, men's and women's, joining in. Over the laughter and conversation was the sound of loud rock music from the 60's. He looked back into the pool and saw a frog scissoring around in the corner, trying to get out, with no luck. He sipped from the beer can and then raised his head up and drained the whole thing in three long swallows. He wiped his mouth on his sleeve and flipped the empty into the pool. It missed the frog.

Joe found his pickup, parked next to Trish's little Escort. He looked from the truck to the car in disgust. He couldn't believe the same company had produced them; it was like a Great Dane and a Chihuahua, for Christ's sake. They didn't even look like they were both the same animals. He got into the pickup and started it up, cranking the engine. Fuck 'em, he thought. Fuck 'em all. Her and Darlene and that fucking horse and everything. He jammed the truck into reverse and pulled out of the space. Then he pressed the gas pedal, revved the engine, and pulled out of the parking lot, heading toward home.

Chapter 20

At some point after Stephen F. Austin led colonists into Texas and before sunny Californians began descending in droves on Austin, some wag came up with the adage that only fools and Yankees predicted the weather in Texas. Natives of the state had come to take a kind of perverse pride in that saying.

Sometimes the Panhandle would go for a year with no more than a trace of rain. The next year might see twenty inches of snow before November 1st, and a solid week of blowing sand and temperatures in the 20's. Once a decade, sometimes less often, the summer would be cool with rain, the plains a glorious palette of every shade of green. More often it would be hot and dry with no hint of moisture. Sometimes in those hot summers, with no warning the sky would grow purple and black with clouds until noon felt like midnight and the high plains would be drowning, strangling in a matter of hours. Caliche roads packed hard as concrete turned into quicksand, and ranchers driving four wheel drive trucks would count themselves lucky if they could reach pavement. The farmers praying for rain would curse, because the torrents destroyed their crops, beat them down and flooded them and uprooted them.

The week before Thanksgiving this year stayed unusually warm; the temperature touched 80 every day, and descended to the 50's at night. There was no humidity like there was down in Austin and Houston. The air felt fresh and pure, and the people counted themselves lucky.

At 3:00 a.m. Wednesday, a cold front swept down from the Rocky Mountains like a locomotive, picking up speed and force as it raged. When it hit Amarillo, among its freight were billions of grains of sand and dirt.

The morning commute was as slow as if the town were trapped in a blizzard. Drivers crept to work, their cars' headlights doing nothing to illuminate the murk. The thick blowing cloud made it difficult to see; it seemed ridiculous to use windshield wipers when it wasn't even raining, when there was just a sheen of dirt blowing across the glass, but without them vision was even more obscured.

All day long the citizens stared out the windows of offices and homes as the wind refused to abate, dreading the moment when they would have to face its fury. Some businesses began to let employees go early.

At 4:00 p.m. rain clouds formed above the sand, where no one suspected they would be hiding. In minutes it began to rain through the sand, great globs of mud splattering against the ground, the cars, and the windshields. Wipers did little good against this newest plague. The men and women who had promised to pick up last minute supplies for the Thanksgiving dinner cursed their luck.

The supermarkets were jammed with customers buying marshmallows to go on top of the sweet potatoes, crusts for pumpkin pies, olives and pimento cheese to stuff in the stalks of celery. Food Giant did its best business the whole year, even better than the Fourth of July or Memorial Day, when beer sales went through the roof. The clerks and the day manager were just the slightest bit nervous, remembering the Halloween robbery, and the night crew was terrified, as it had been for almost a month. Earl Waddell sighed deeply when he let the last clerk out at 12:30 a.m. The store would be open until noon on Thanksgiving Day. He would be home with his family, although he wished that thought would give him more comfort than it did.

The storm continued long after most people were clean and dry in their homes. Angel closed Bailey's at 7:00. There were only a handful of brave souls left, including Max. He stayed until she was finished, practicing shots, and they touched hands before they charged out into the storm, she and Bailey racing toward her truck, Max with his head down, fumbling for the key to his car.

Smith sat in the nursing home at his father's side, reading *Great Expectations*. The only good thing he could find about this ironic twist of fate was that he was getting a chance to read all the books that he should have in high school and never did. If this went on much longer, he figured he would be the best-read thief in America outside prison walls. Sometimes he asked himself what good he thought sitting here every day would do. He knew he ought to get a job because the money from Food Giant would run out soon. Usually though, if he waited long enough that question would go away. Something would distract him, and his mind would drift off. Tonight it was the sound of the wind that took him away, the hiss of the sand against the windows. When visiting hours ended he folded over a corner of one page and drove home.

Carl looked at Dolores and Nina in the kitchen; the girl was helping her mother, proudly reading off the ingredients and instructions for stuffing. Carl had taken a shower, trying to wash the dirt and grime out of his hair and off his body. His clothes were in the hamper. He felt fresh again, and as long as he didn't think about Freddie nothing seemed too bad. Dolores glanced at him, and for a moment there was no expression on her face. Then she smiled, not just a lifting of the lips that said oh, well. It was a genuine smile, and there was love in it. He started to go into the living room to watch TV but turned back into the kitchen. He put his hand on Nina's head and stroked her long, black hair. Then he put his arm around Dolores's waist. She leaned her head against his shoulder and the three of them stood there like that for a long minute, not talking. Finally Dolores broke away from him and went back to the preparation. Carl tried to help but found himself asking too many questions and realized that he wasn't any help at all. He sat down in the living room and turned on the TV, realizing that he had found an island of calm as long as he didn't think about Freddie. He wasn't looking forward to the dinner tomorrow; Dolores and Bernice, even Regina would try to pretend that everything was okay, just as they had for the past three weeks, but he could see ghosts in their eyes. The worst part was Maggie and Travis. They barely spoke and didn't play with Nina. They seemed gone, as if a part of them had just gotten lost. Carl couldn't look at them without feeling guilt. And that was something he didn't want to feel. He found a hockey game and started to watch it.

The storm stopped during the early dark hours of Thanksgiving, departing as suddenly as it had arrived. Dawn brought a silence that seemed eerily calm after the visual and aural onslaught of the last eighteen hours. The sky was clear, although red dirt and sand lay on every surface inside and out. Windowsills were coated with it, and few homes had doors that sealed tightly enough to keep the grit out of the entryways. Even before food went into the oven, brooms and vacuum cleaners came out of closets to eradicate the storm's remains.

Robin Green and Willie Stuart had been friends since the first grade, three long years now. They were getting kind of old for the Macy's parade, and the football games didn't start until later. Their moms were too busy cooking to pay them much attention, so it was pretty easy for Robin and Willie to get out of the house. They lived in a division that had grown up during the past ten years. Amarillo wasn't growing as quickly as Austin or Houston, Fort Worth or Dallas, but enough people left their small hometowns each year that Amarillo had to find places for them to live.

The boys' houses were three doors down from each other in a development of brick ranch-style homes. They had talked the day before on the phone and made a plan to meet on their bikes in the morning as soon as they could get away. When Willie wheeled his bike out of the garage onto the driveway, he saw Robin already sitting on his on the sidewalk in front of his house, shifting his balance from side to side, trying to stay on two wheels without putting his foot down. He was wearing brightly colored loose pants that his father referred to as "rapper pants," half in fun. Both the boys kept their hair an inch long on top and almost shaved on the sides and back. The day had dawned warm, and they both wore t-shirts.

Willie buzzed down the sidewalk, swerving at the last minute to avoid Robin, and swished down the driveway into the street. Robin took off without having to put his feet onto the ground, glanced into the street for traffic, and followed his best friend. They flew to the end of the block, gears clicking, turned two corners, and ended up at the edge of their still small division where it butted against the highway to Borger. They both brought their bikes to a skidding halt, standing up on the pedals. Willie's bike almost slid out from under him, and Robin slapped him on the shoulder.

"Way to go, doofus."

Willie glanced down the highway, checking for traffic. He hit his pedals hard, spraying gravel, and pumped furiously onto the shoulder with Robin right behind him.

The boys had been strictly forbidden by their parents to ride anywhere near the highway, let alone on the shoulder, but they knew that once they went out on their bikes they had almost exactly two hours before anyone wondered where they were. As long as they got back within that time, they were safe in going wherever they wanted to. And there was one place they loved more than any other.

Each month the boys looked in their biking magazines and got goggle-eyed over the courses big city kids got to ride on. Hills made of concrete, places that those guys could practice their moves without anybody hassling them. Some of them could take their bikes straight up into the air and land on both wheels, already rolling.

Willie and Robin could only dream of the day that they had a course like that. But still, theirs was almost as good. Not that the obstacles were anywhere close to being that challenging. It was just that this course was theirs alone. Nobody else ever went there during the daytime. They sometimes saw car tracks that were left during the night and used rubbers on the ground, which although they knew the purpose of in a broad sense, still left them mystified.

They rode the half mile to the dirt turn-in, hitting their brakes suddenly and producing a spray of gravel from their back wheels. They rode between the poles that held up the marquee and hummed across the rumbly cattle guard next to the seedy ticket booth. Sometimes when they got bored with jumping, the boys climbed through the window into the projection booth. The glass had long since been knocked out, but inside the projector still stood, focusing its cyclopean eye on the white screen. Once Robin had gone behind the screen to pee, and saw where someone had spray-painted "Please fuck me Lisa" in three-foot high letters. He started laughing so hard he almost peed his pants, and fumbled his fly open with seconds to spare. The moment he zipped up, he called to Willie. They laughed for five solid minutes, finally falling down onto the ground straight into a nest of grass burrs. That sent them immediately to their feet, with tears of a different kind.

Today they started right away with their favorite event, jumping their bikes over the mounds of dirt between the speakers. They rode hell bent for leather toward a mound, pulling the bikes straight up into the air, just like the guys in the videos they owned. Usually they landed on both wheels, but since the grass burr episode they made sure to wear long sleeves and pants, even in the hot weather. Willie started in the very back row and raced as fast as he could from the back to the front of the drive-in, hitting every hump of sand along the way. He judged his performance according to how high he flew on each row and how many seconds it took to complete the course.

Willie was in the air on the seventh row from the screen when he heard a screech of car brakes. He twisted around, looking for an intruder in their sanctuary, and as his wheels hit the ground the bike threw him into a sandy slide on his shoulder. It was only when he stopped that he realized a car's brakes wouldn't make a screeching sound on dirt, and besides that there wasn't a car in sight. He was trying to discover the source of the noise when he heard it again and realized it was coming from Robin, who was also lying on the sand. Except he still wasn't moving, and he was crying too, which scared Willie. He jumped on his bike and pedaled over to his friend. When he reached him, Robin's face was streaked with tears and he was shaking. Willie wanted to touch him, to see if he was okay, but he felt queasy about touching another guy, even if it was his best friend. "You okay?" he said, tentatively. There was no answer, and he tried another tack. "What'd you, see a big snake or something and get scared?"

Robin sat up suddenly. Startled, Willie jumped back and almost tripped over his bike. Robin wrapped his arms around his knees and started coughing. His face was bright red. He shook his head but kept on coughing. Willie pounded him on the back. "You okay?" he repeated.

Robin's coughing subsided, but his head was still shaking. He pointed his finger in front of him, and Willie couldn't figure out whether he meant the ground two feet away, or the mesquite trees which loomed over the plank wall fifty yards back. "What?" he said. Robin kept pointing, so Willie stood up and followed his pointing finger. He figured it couldn't be too far away, because Robin had fallen pretty close by. He was afraid it might be a rattlesnake, or something gross, like a dead dog. He walked forward, sweeping his eyes from side to side across the ground, but at first he couldn't see what Robin was pointing at. When he reached the first mound of dirt between the rusty, bent speaker poles he stopped short and stared.

A few years ago, before the place had closed up, he and his parents had seen a really scary movie there, one where zombies clawed their way out of a graveyard digging up through the wet earth with skeleton hands. Their faces had most of the flesh eaten away, and their jaws gaped open, making it look like they were grinning at something while they ate people's insides up. His mom didn't think Willie should be seeing the movie and told his dad to take them home, but he said Willie probably saw just as bad stuff on TV and wouldn't leave. His mom stopped talking to his dad, and later on Dad told him that was called the Silent Treatment, which was something women did to men mostly, and sometimes guys didn't mind it that much. Willie didn't think the movie was that scary most of the time, and some things in it were funny. He had an idea that it was a comedy for the most part, despite all the gross stuff.

But this wasn't funny at all. Willie looked at what he knew must be somebody's face grinning out at him from underneath that sand, and for a second he thought it must be that same movie he was watching, except that he was facing away from the screen, and it was daytime, and the drive-in had been closed for the past three years. He saw part of a shirt, and a shoulder, and that was all he could see except for the face, which was bad enough. Some of the skin was still on it, in little scraps, and one flap on the right cheek was waving very gently in the breeze. Most of the hair was still there, and it was light colored and curly, like Willie's own. As he stood looking at it, a cloud drifted from in front of the sun and a ray of sunlight shone on the yellow teeth. The jaws were wide open, grinning at Willie. He was afraid to look at the eyes, because what if they were staring straight at him, but he did anyway and they weren't. They were gooey and filled with dirt, and just as he looked at the left one, a little stink bug like he saw on the carpet at home sometimes crawled out of the eye socket and underneath the shirt.

Willie suddenly didn't know if he was going to be able to make it home to tell his dad and mom and have them call the police without peeing on himself, or maybe worse, because right now he was feeling pressure in front and back, and he couldn't see clearly anymore because tears were leaking down from his eyes. He didn't like to cry, but he was grateful because it meant he didn't have to look at that thing. He turned around and grabbed up his bike, got on it and was pedaling away before he remembered Robin. He looked over his shoulder and yelled for his friend, but Robin was already on his bike following him. Willie turned his head back in time to narrowly avoid hitting a speaker pole. They flew across the dirt, not trying to jump this time, not trying to do anything but get away, to get home. As Willie's bike whooshed over the cattle guard and underneath the marquee, he realized that he might get into trouble for going to the drive-in when he wasn't supposed to, but right now he didn't care. It might be good for him to stay away from it for a while, anyway. He'd heard about a course in a park somewhere in town, and he bet his dad would take him to it.

Cee Ross had just put his feet up on the footrest of his recliner, a can of Bud in his right hand, the remote in his left. He leaned the chair back and lowered the footrest just a smidgen, so he would be able to see the Cowboys over his socks. Cee figured everyone should have a tradition, and this was his. Every Thanksgiving morning he got up at 9:00, ate breakfast, and weather permitting washed his car (a blue Ford Taurus these last six years). Then he took a shower, watched the Cowboys or whoever else played at noon, and drove down to eat dinner at the Big Texan Steak Ranch. The Ranch was an Amarillo landmark because it offered a free 72-ounce T-bone to anyone who could eat it, a small potato, a roll, and a salad in one hour. Cee's record was fifty-seven minutes, nineteen seconds before he retired from the contest. It had taken him a while to get up to it; his first and second tries, where he was egged on by his whooping fellow officers, were failures. He went four and two minutes over, respectively. But that two-minute gap proved to him that he could do it, and his next three attempts were successes. He'd realized that the first two times, strange as it seemed, he had gone too fast. Slow and steady wins the race, like the old tortoise said.

At exactly 12:01 the Cowboys kicked off to the Patriots, and at precisely 12:02 his cell phone started vibrating. Cee closed his eyes as the crowd roared. No, he thought. It's a wrong number. Please let it be a wrong number. With a sigh, he shifted his weight onto his left buttock and pried the right out of the seat of his Lazy Boy, which seemed to become narrower with each passing year. He held the phone out in front of his eyes far enough to read it, which disturbingly seemed to be about two inches farther away than it used to. He set the beer can down on a coaster shaped like a Dallas helmet, pushed the "answer" button, sighed, and said "This better be important."

Three patrol cars and Champ Phillips' Chevy pickup were parked in the Comanche Drive-In when Cee pulled through the gate thirty minutes later. The midnight blue forensics van squatted about fifty yards in front of the blank white screen, its side door open. The crew was unloading equipment. Except for the van, the vehicles were all parked between pairs of speaker poles, facing the screen, as if the projector might at any moment decide to begin feeding loops of film through its gate. Cee chuckled to himself. No one likes to break the rules, he thought. Nobody except the bad guys. He parked in the middle of a wide lane between poles, perpendicular to the other cars. He saw Champ's cowboy hat bobbing around above the top of a patrol car and made his way over to it, his feet whispering in the sand and weeds.

Champ nodded at Cee. "How the 'boys doing?" he asked.

"Now how am I supposed to know, seeing as I only saw exactly sixty seconds of the game?"

"More than I caught of it. Probably miss the rest, too."

"What do we have here?"

Champ glanced at the hump in the earth where the techs were busily photographing and measuring.

"Body. Say a few weeks, maybe two to four. No signs of animals getting after him, so looks like maybe the sandstorm blew over, brought him up. Not too pretty anymore."

Cee reluctantly shifted a foot to the left so he could have a clear look at the body. He squinted his eyes and fought not to turn away. It always seemed like the corpses were staring at him, like one of those optical illusion paintings. He knew those deals just preyed on your own imagination, and the dead ones were the same way. In this case there were no real eyes left, just a couple of dirt-filled sockets above some exposed bones and patches of leathery skin.

"Not much to give thanks for here," Champ said.

"Who found him?"

"Couple kids, out playing on their bikes. One of them went straight over him."

"Good God."

"I don't think He had much to do with this one. Kids went home, and one of the parents called in. We have a couple of uniforms over there now, and then I'm going to talk to them."

"Make sure you take off that cowboy hat before you do. Thing still scares me, and I been looking at it for 20 years."

"You're such a comfort to me, Cee."

"And those mirror sunglasses, too. Look like you're the Lone Ranger." He glanced once again at the body. "Any ideas?"

"Not yet. They're still looking, so I don't know if he's carrying a wallet yet. Assuming he didn't take a nap here of his own free will, it's probably missing."

"Yeah, well you know what I always say. If they were smart, they wouldn't be criminals. Never underestimate the stupidity of a Texas punk."

Slowly and carefully, as if he was bringing to light a rare anthropological find, one member of the team brushed the sand off the corpse. He wore the standard white jumpsuit, but his blond hair was swept up into a pompadour, and his Buddy Holly glasses were vintage 50's. The other two, accompanied by two officers, slowly combed the ground in ever-increasing circles.

Champ gingerly stepped over to the corpse and kneeled next to it. He made a face and drew a handkerchief from his back pocket, pressing it over his nose and mouth. Cee, who didn't carry one, made do with his shirt sleeve.

"What color was his hair," Cee asked the technician, "sandy colored?"

The man, whose pocket had "Dan" stitched on it, said "Name me one thing in the Panhandle that ain't?"

"My ebony ass, which you're about to have to kiss."

"Sorry, Cee. Couldn't say no to that one. Yeah, looks like it. I'd call it dark blonde. Curly hair."

"Looks to me offhand like maybe thirtyish?"

"Thereabouts. Good head of hair, clothes don't look much older or younger than that. Off the rack at K-Mart, probably. Got that local look, a little too good to be homeless."

"Height?" Champ asked.

"Say five-ten. Weight maybe two, two-ten. Least he was a few weeks ago. Tip the scales a little lighter these days."

"Jeez," Cee breathed.

"Sorry again. I wouldn't be doing this if I wasn't a little weird. That's all I can say right now. Coroner's on the way, and they'll give you what you need in a day or two."

"Be nice if they'd give us the guy who did it."

"Hell, if they did, all you'd have to bitch and moan about would be the sorry-ass Cowboys. Guess that's not so bad, though. This fellow here probably wouldn't mind watching a ball game right now, if he had the choice. Ain't that right, Troy?" he said, straightening a wrinkle in the corpse's shirt.

"Dan, you are too strange for words. You ought to have some respect for the dead." Cee stood up to clear the smell of decayed flesh from his nose, knowing he'd have to take a shower the moment he got back home, ball game or not. Besides, in a rare moment of foresight, he had pushed the "record" button on the VCR before he left the house. Now watch this be the only one they lose this season, he thought. And I'll have captured it in all its glory.

He stood up and called out to the uniformed officers, "Finding anything?"

One of them looked up at him and lifted a hand to shade her eyes from the sun. "Nothing yet, except the usual junk. Just what you'd expect."

"All right." He turned back to Champ. "While you're talking with the kids, I'll get a team to start knocking on doors, see if someone might have seen something about—what, two to four weeks ago?"

"Yeah, give or take. I have an idea that trail's gonna turn up pretty cold. But you never can tell. When I get back to the office, I'll run a list of missings. If he's local, I think we'll get a tag on him soon."

A rumble of gravel signaled the arrival of the coroner's van. Champ took off his hat and thoughtfully tapped it against his thigh. Cee noticed that, as always, the crease on his khaki pants was razor edged. "Give me a call if you get anything on your canvas," Champ said. "I'll let you know if the computer turns up a hit."

Cee turned away from the body and crunched through the gravel toward his car. He glanced up at the mesquite trees ringing the drive-in, in some places starting to push in the boards of the fence like decayed teeth. Something was scrabbling around in his mind, and he couldn't quite get it in pinching distance.

A warm, dry breeze swirled some of the sand around a speaker pole and brought to him a whiff of cow shit from one of the feedlots to the south. Probably Hereford, he thought. Can smell that town fifty miles away, coming and going. What is it that I'm trying to remember? He opened the door of his Taurus and gingerly wedged himself into the seat. As he started to pick up his phone to call for assistance with the canvas, he glanced at the clipboard lying in the passenger's seat and picked it up. He thumbed the clip and loosened the stack of papers from it. Cee carried all of his case-notes on the board and had for nine years, once he figured out that the longest he ever kept one of those little spiral notebooks before losing it was about a month. He started through the stack, and just as he lay aside the first sheet he realized what it was that was itching at his brain. Dan talking to the corpse about watching football and calling the thing Troy. He had an idea that was accompanied by a bad feeling in his stomach.

There was a tap on his window, and he hit the button to lower it. Dan, the crime scene tech, was crouched next to the car holding up a wallet. "You interested in this?" he asked. He used a gloved finger to flip it open to the plastic window that held the driver's license. Cee blew away the dirt, read the name, and looked at the photo.

God damn it, he thought, as he pictured a crying widow sitting on a couch, a case of football trophies not five feet away from her. He shuffled through the stack of papers until he found his typed notes on the Freddie Odom case, where his mind was already headed anyway. Clipped to them was a copy of the photograph Regina had given him of Freddie and his little boy, Travis. Sweaty, probably just finished playing an hour or so with the football the little boy held. "Hello, Freddie," he said softly, almost with reverence.

Like a layer of frosting on a cake that's been sitting out for a week. It tastes real sweet on top, but underneath it's stale and almost sour. But everyone eats it and smiles, like everything is okay. That's what this is like, Dolores thought.

She and Regina and Bernice were bustling around the kitchen, trying to coordinate all the dishes for Thanksgiving dinner. The fragrance of turkey wafted through the entire house, along with the warm, yeasty smell of home-made rolls. A yawning bowl of sweet potatoes topped with gooey, crusty-brown marshmallows already sat on the table, side by side with plates of deviled eggs, stuffed celery, and cranberry sauce.

Dolores had no desire for any of it; her taste buds felt frozen. Regina and Bernice were chatting as they worked, but Regina's eyes perched above dark black circles. She had done her best to cover them with makeup, but three weeks of crying and lying awake staring at the ceiling had left her eyes swollen beyond any cosmetic assistance.

Dolores wiped her eyes on her sleeve and glanced into the living room where Carl sat on the couch, watching the Patriots gain nine yards against Dallas. Normally Freddie would be sitting on the other end of it, the two of them pretending, for the sake of the family, that they could stand one another. In the three years since Freddie started working for Carl, she had dreaded the silence between them that stretched tighter than a piano wire. She had hated seeing the anguish in Regina's eyes when Freddie tried to talk to Carl about work, about football, about anything at all, and got only curt responses. Dolores had talked to Carl about it, and he had always reluctantly promised to try harder next time, but he never did. But today, as painful as it always was, she would have welcomed the sight of the two of them on the couch like magnets that repelled each other.

They were already finished with dinner, and the football game was almost over when the phone rang. Dolores wondered for a moment who would call them on Thanksgiving; anyone who would was already there at the house. Everybody except one, she realized. She was putting dishes into the washer when the call came, and in the second that she realized it could only be Freddie, she ran to the phone nook, between the hallway and kitchen.

"Hello?" she answered, wiping her hands on a towel and slipping the receiver between her ear and shoulder. She imagined how it would be to hand the phone to Regina, to give her a big smile and say "It's him, Gina."

There was silence for a moment, the white hum of silence coming over the miles of lines. Then she heard background noise, like an office, and immediately her very practical schoolteacher's mind thought, What kind of office would Freddie be calling from, and on Thanksgiving, besides that? Then the voice started, and it sounded wrong and was saying the wrong things to her, talking not like Freddie at all.

She listened to the voice of the man who identified himself as Detective Ross, and she knew who it was now and why he was calling even before he told her. She knew it the way her mother Bernice had known when she heard a car door slam in front of her house one Saturday morning in 1972, when Dolores was just eleven years old and Regina five. Bernice always said she had known just from the sound of the door, but when Dolores grew up she thought that her mother must have glimpsed the uniforms through the lace curtains covering the diamond-shaped window in the pine door.

The detective was saying that he was especially sorry to deliver this hard news on such a day, but he had to do it. Someone had found a body that matched Freddie's description, and his wallet was in the pants pocket. He was saying that he needed some dental records, but he knew the offices would be closed and he'd call back tomorrow to talk more. Dolores kept the phone cradled tightly against her neck. Against all logic, all reason, she felt that the news wouldn't be official, be real, until she heard the phone disconnecting on the other end, heard the dead whine of the dial tone in her ear. The phone line clicked as Ross hung up, and after a few moments she did hear the line buzzing. She stood leaning against the archway into the living room, but everyone could see her, Carl on the couch, her mother and Gina and the kids in the kitchen. She wanted to make up a lie, to break the story gently to Regina, but she knew from reading her sister's face that it was too late. Gina's eyes widened, and her lower lip started to tremble. Dolores carefully put the phone back onto its hook, and said "Gina, honey, . . ."

Regina fell to her knees and started to sob, her small fists clenched tightly on her thighs. She started to beat them down onto her legs, at first slowly, then increasingly faster. Her sobs found a voice, and she began to scream "No, no, no," over and over again, the violence of her fists growing more frenzied as her voice rose.

Carl had come into the living room after Dolores hung up the phone, and he held Regina's left arm while Bernice took her right, gently lifting her to her feet. They guided her onto the couch where she sat, slowly rocking forward and back. Bernice slipped her arm around her daughter's shoulders, and a minute passed. Finally Regina's wracking sobs subsided to gentle weeping. She put her head on her mother's chest, and Bernice rocked her gently.

Dolores knew she would have to tell Maggie and Travis. They stood with Nina in the living room, starting to cry but not knowing why. If they were like she was when she was little, she knew that their fear was caused by Regina; there was nothing scarier to children than the grieved keening of an adult they depended on. All the structure of their world had suddenly dissolved, like an incoming wave steals the sand from beneath one's feet.

Bernice rocked Regina on the couch while Carl hovered helplessly around. He picked up the remote and fumbled it in his hand, pointing it at the TV but not pushing any buttons, unsure whether to turn it off, or whether the absence of it would cause a vacuum in the room that would be too stifling. He turned the sound down and finally hit mute. The light of the game, the brilliant green of the artificial turf and the blue and silver of the players, flickered over the two women on the couch. The furnace suddenly turned on and Dolores jumped, remembering what task it was now her duty to perform.

"Maggie and Travis, come here into the kitchen with me. You too, Nina." She guided them into chairs around the table and knelt down.

Before she could speak, Travis said "It's about Daddy, isn't it? He's dead, isn't he Aunt Dee?" His soft cheeks began to tremble, and his eyes pooled with tears. "What happened to him? Why did he go away?" Tears slowly slid down his face, and he wiped his eyes on his shirt sleeve.

Dolores stretched her arms out and drew the three children in close to her, holding them tightly as warm air flowed up through the grates and touched their skin.

Carl stepped back from the couch and opened the wooden door, slowly closing it behind him. He wrapped his arms around his chest and shivered. The night air was chilly, and in the west a thin band of blood hung over the horizon.

Chapter 21

Cee leaned back in his chair. He didn't have his own office, but by God he made sure he had his own chair. It was bigger and nicer than any of the others in the detective unit, all wood and leather. He would have snuck in a recliner if he thought the brass wouldn't have noticed. Instead, on the day he had made detective he had borrowed Champ's truck and brought this chair from home. It was his father's, used at the insurance company he had owned until he died. Nathaniel Ross had opened the company in 1939, when the Great Depression had the entire country in a vise grip and was squeezing the life's blood from it. The farmers from Oklahoma and Arkansas were pouring through Amarillo along 66 on their way to California. Nat's friends told him in the gentlest words possible that he was crazy, that if white people couldn't get enough to fill their bellies, then black folks surely shouldn't be opening businesses. Wait until this is over, at least.

But with his only training two years of high school accounting, he had started small and ended big. When he died in 1979, three days after Cee's twenty-first birthday, Nat had left his wife and only child with empty hearts and close to a million dollars. When Cee's mother died fourteen years later, she left her house to the Freewill Baptist Church and the money to Cee. He moved from the apartment he was living in to a nice little brick house in a decent neighborhood. He bought a state of the art lounger and a TV so big he could watch the Cowboys with nearly a 1:1 ratio. He took a few pieces of furniture to his home, and when he got his shield, moved his father's roll-top desk and soft leather office chair with wheels to the headquarters, where he now leaned back in it, tapping a pencil against his teeth, wishing it was a Tootsie Pop, and thinking about Freddie Odom.

The interviews with the boys and the canvas of the neighborhood had delivered squat. The boys hadn't known anything; they were just two kids who had, completely by accident, bought themselves a lifetime of waking from nightmares in sweat-soaked sheets. Although houses were creeping closer and closer to the Comanche, it was still isolated. Nobody had seen any activity there because no one had been looking at the old place. No reason to, God knows. No one much thought about it anymore, and soon it would probably be torn down to accommodate more ranch houses identical to their neighbors. Cee got lost for a moment in teen-age memories, then snapped back. There wasn't much anyone could say on the neighborhood canvas, and not much the officers could ask. The question "Have you seen any unusual activity at the drive-in in the past month?" usually elicited a look that translated as "What're you, an idiot?" The entrance wasn't visible from anyone's house, and if the guy who did it had half a brain he would have doused his headlights before he pulled in. Or the gal, Cee thought. Couldn't leave out the distaff side of life.

None of Freddie's coworkers seemed to know anything about what might have happened to him. Mostly they were just kind of blank where Freddie was concerned, not quite sure what to say. Some of them talked about a drinking problem, which was no news. Sometimes Cee thought half the folks in Amarillo had a drinking problem, and the other half were just kidding themselves. In a country where you could go from eighty degrees on Monday to a foot of snow on Tuesday, where sometimes it rained mud on your windshield, it didn't seem like an irrational response.

A few of the folks at the drapery company, when asked about Freddie, had kind of looked around suspiciously as if the place might be bugged, despite the fact that they were locked in the boss's office. These folks said they thought there had been problems between Freddie and Carl about job performance but hastened to add that they didn't think Carl would do anything about it. The profile of Carl that their cumulative words created was an okay guy who could sometimes be an asshole, particularly when he was stressed.

The most forthright of the group had been Sharon, the cowgirl glued into a lavender blouse with jeans and boots to match. "Yeah, sometimes Freddie would screw up and ol' Carl would get his dick in a wringer about it. He'd shoot lightning bolts at everybody for a few days, then he'd get back to being his usual grumpy-ass self." Cee, a lover of the English language, had never heard of someone's dick being in a wringer; he'd heard about tits being so caught, and thought of asking Sharon the derivation of the expression, but stopped himself, thinking it might not be a fitting topic to bring up during an interview. He filed it away for future use. "But I don't think he'd of *hurt* Freddie over it. And if Carl wouldn't hurt somebody over money, he prob'ly wouldn't over anything. Though God knows *I* want to shoot *him* sometimes for being so goddamn tight assed with the cash. Don't worry, though, I ain't about to. I don't even got a gun anymore." She flashed a glittering smile, and Cee let her go back to work while he pondered the difference between being tight-assed and tight-fisted with money. The former seemed much less sanitary, but neither was something he thought would be a good attribute to have.

The canvas at the pool hall where Freddie seemed to have a second home revealed about as much good information. The moment Cee and Champ stepped in, every eye in the room swiveled toward them. There were so many familiar faces he'd arrested that he might as well be looking at a video of mug shots. He figured they wouldn't get much information there, and his instincts were right on target. The first thing that happened right after they stepped in was that he almost had to remove a snarling wolf from his asshole. The second he saw it, he realized why the cops had never been called to Bailey's. If he hadn't thought it would spoil his credibility, he would have peed a puddle on the floor right then and there. The thing ignored Champ, probably because he ignored it.

The owner of the place gave them a wary eye before and after they identified themselves as police detectives. When Champ said they'd like to ask a few questions she said "It's a free country," as if their presence made her wish it weren't. Sure she knew Freddie, he was hard to miss, especially when he was the drunkest person in a room full of drunks, give or take. When she made that final statement, she flicked her eyes toward the right side of the room, over his left shoulder. She hadn't seen Freddie in a while; she couldn't keep track of every person who walked through the door. She didn't seem surprised or terribly sorry to hear that he was dead. A flicker of something approaching sympathy raced through her eyes when he said Freddie had left a wife and two little kids and was gone just as quickly. When they told her they were going to ask questions of her clientele she said "Go ahead," as if granting them her permission. Judging from the look she gave the wolf and the accompanying hand signal that clearly said "Stay put," she probably was. The wolf rumbled deep in its chest and flowed over the counter in one liquid leap. Cee hitched up his pants as if to show that he was still in charge and began to canvas the room. He looked in the direction that the woman had glanced and saw two men playing eight ball much better than he'd ever been able to, which meant they were actually getting the balls to go into the pockets other than by accident. One had long hair which, when he leaned down to line up a shot, fell over his shoulder and onto the felt. He straightened, reached into his pocket, and pulled out a rubber band that he used to tie his hair into a ponytail. He leaned back down again, connected with the cue ball, and sent the seven skidding into a pocket.

Cee couldn't quite put a tag on the guy, but his partner needed no introduction. His name was Danny Gonzales, and at six feet three inches and 250 pounds he towered over his partner. Cee knew Danny lived on a ranch outside of town, and every once in a while they'd get a call that he was in a fight in some bar or other, usually one of the scuzzy places on Amarillo Boulevard. When his name came over the radio the dispatcher would automatically call four units to go over there instead of the normal two.

He saw them approaching, and the tail of a smile curled around the toothpick that Cee had never seen him without, even when dead drunk. "Boys," he said.

"Hello, Danny," Cee said. "Long time no fights. You take early retirement from hell-raising?"

"Fellow don't want to get too predictable." Cee heard the faint jingle of spurs and remembered the rookie cop who'd waded in to put cuffs on Danny while two other officers pinned his arms. The kid had ended up with a ripped sleeve and a spur track down his arm, which meant he was luckier than most guys who had tangled with Danny. Cee heard he quit the force not long after that and took a job teaching science at Caprock High.

Champ nodded his head at Danny. The cowboy's toothpick wiggled when he smiled. "Lieutenant," he said. They were both cut from the same cowboy cloth, but beyond that and the thick mustache each boasted, they appeared to be from worlds alien to each other. Champ had a cool elegance and a smooth demeanor, while "getting cleaned up" in Danny's definition meant wearing a pair of boots not covered with manure. Tonight he wasn't cleaned up.

Champ looked at Danny's partner and smiled. "Evening, counselor."

Max nodded his head. "Howdy." He laughed, and Cee knew he was watching an inside joke being played out.

"You fellas prob'ly heard about Freddie Odom."

"Oh, yeah," Danny said. "Bad business. Y'all caught the sorry oscar who did it?"

"Not yet. That's what we're here for." They talked for a few minutes, Danny and Max resuming their game, answering questions as they lined up shots. They both remembered Freddie and knew him by sight but not by name. Danny hadn't been around Bailey's in a while, explaining that "sometimes it ain't good for my equilibrium," a remark which puzzled Cee. Since when had a place that served up cheap beer and pool disagreed with Danny Gonzales? Danny remembered Freddie playing with a Hispanic man whom the officers identified from his description as Carl Puente. Max had also seen them there together, and once with two other men, ones he couldn't identify and hadn't seen in a while. One of the men, he remembered, rarely spoke. Max remembered a short conversation with him one night when they left at the same time. He gave a brief description but could think of nothing he felt would be useful. The other he described as a "skell," which he had to interpret was New Yorkese for "scumbag."

"How so?"

Max nudged the eight-ball into a pocket and began extracting its comrades. He rolled them down to the other end of the table, where Danny racked them.

The lawyer leaned on his cue. "Drunk a lot, loved to goof on people, watch them squirm, but he didn't like it coming back at him."

"Sounds like most of the guys in here," Cee said, "present company excepted."

"Yeah, but there was something different about him. Most guys who drink a little, they get stupid. Try to act tough, then wake up hung over, go to work in the morning. This hoople, I think he'd sink a shiv in your back and then go home and jerk off to the memory. Sorry I don't know his name, but when I see guys like that, I tend to avoid them. Good talking to you."

Champ and Cee worked the rest of the room, not getting much more than Max and Danny had given them. Angel remembered all four of the players but not the names of the other two guys; she just knew Carl's and Freddie's, and "I tried not to learn them." Asked for a description, she provided a fairly in-depth analysis of their way with a stick, but couldn't remember height or hair color. "Bailey had to evict one of them a while back," she said. "Guy thought he had a pair of balls weighed a pound each. He hasn't been back since."

"I can't imagine why," Cee mumbled as he cast a wary eye on the wolf. He gave Angel one of his cards and asked her to call him if the guy ever showed up again.

Now Cee sat at his desk leaning back, gently rocking by pushing the toes of his sneakers against the floor.

"Don't fall asleep," Champ said. He had walked over from his desk and sat down in the chair Cee used for taking statements.

"I'm like the Mounties, Champ. Neither rain nor snow nor dog do-do will keep me from my chosen path. Or whatever that shit is."

"I think that's the mail carriers. The Mounties always get their man."

"Whatever."

"I assume you were in deep contemplation about getting our man."

"No, I was just contemplating my belly button."

"I guess you must miss it, long as it's been since you seen it."

"Hey, don't talk about my weight. I got a severe problem with my Twinkie gland."

"So, have you come up with anything?"

"The best thing we got right now is this 'skell.'" Cee rolled the word around his mouth. "My mind keeps coming back to that brother-in-law. Carl what's his name. If we think Mr. Skell might have something to do with it, Carl's the best one to talk to. He's had a few days now. I think we should pull him in and see if he can give us a name, or at least a better description. And there's something else that doesn't seem right about him. I can't say just what, but he strikes me as kind of snaky somehow."

"Hell, that's reason enough to bring him in right there. Let me run get a bulb for the lamp, and you see if you can find the rubber hose."

"I don't know why you're not in Vegas right now, Champ, funny as you are. I think we ought to run a check on Brother Carl. See if he's got a sheet."

"Sounds like a logical next step." Champ reached into his back pocket and slid out a single sheet of white paper, folded neatly in thirds. He laid it on Cee's desk.

"You want a sheet, one single sheet is what you get."

Cee leaned forward and picked it up, grunting as he did so. "You would put it out of my reach. How long were you going to keep pulling my chain?"

"It's the only exercise you get. You oughta be grateful."

"One hit. Armed robbery. Got fifty-seven dollars and twenty-nine cents. No wonder he quit, no better a robber than that. This was in 1972 March, Tricky Dick was still sliding his haunches into the big chair in the Oval Office. Piddly ass job, huh."

"Well, the country was in a depression."

"Nixon in the White House, I can understand why. I sure as hell was."

"You better keep it low, hoss. There ain't enough Democrats in this county to balance Rush Limbaugh on a see-saw."

"Hell, you're talking about a thousand right there, and me one of them.

Only reason that asshole ain't in the KKK is they can't find a sheet big enough to fit him. Carl said he was in on this deal with a cat named Smith Dixon, who couldn't be found. I wonder if he has a—" He stopped as Champ laid a manila file folder on his desk.

"This his?"

"Uh huh."

"Anything else you're not telling me about? You found the murder weapon? Know who waxed Freddie? He hadn't already been convicted or anything like that, has he?"

"You read that file, you'll know as much as I do."

"Just checking." Cee flipped open the folder and thumbed through the pages. "Damn." He whistled softly. "Man's got a sheet as long as my dick. You know, that's one of the parts I love most about this job. Getting to say things like that. He did a few piddly jobs here in Texas, but nothing after the date Carl says they broke the piggy bank at that gas station. Everything else is out of state for the next seven—no, eight years. Then he's out east, Beaumont and Texarkana. He ever get back this way?"

"Nope."

"Always had a driver's license. Guest of different states on a few occasions, but never for long. Maybe he just did it for spending money, maybe he never got caught for the big ones." Cee looked up at Champ. "You think he's involved in this?"

"No reason to think so. Gas station was what, '72? Doesn't seem like much to go on."

"You think we can use this record for leverage on Carl? Just bring it up, say it's no big deal, but let him know that we know? Maybe get him to give up the skell."

"Bat him around a little," Champ said. "Hell, I think it's worth a try. You want to call him?"

"No, why don't you do it. I want him to be a little scared. Not peeing his pants, but definitely squirming a little. And frankly, partner, I'm just not that scary."

Champ unfolded himself from the straight-back chair and walked slowly back to his desk, looking like one of the old Texas Rangers, the ones whose voices would never raise by so much as a decibel while they dispelled a crowd of a hundred. Cee wasn't normally a jealous man, but sometimes he wished he could turn people's blood to ice water just by putting on a pair of sunglasses and a cowboy hat.

He slid Freddie Odom into a mental file folder and worked on an assault case. Freddie's file would be opened up again soon enough.

Champ rested his right wrist on top of the steering wheel, smoothly maneuvering through traffic. He glanced in his rear-view mirror at the white Chevrolet a car length behind him. He wanted Carl to sweat a little, but he didn't want to get him lost. Champ knew that if somebody was invited to follow a police officer to headquarters, he damn sure would try to make sure he stayed in the same lane. Especially somebody like Carl, who had acted like a kid who'd got caught stealing the last cookie out of the jar. Champ wasn't sure just what Carl knew about Freddie's disappearance, but he felt damned sure that it was more than he wanted to let on. Maybe he and Freddie had tanked up that night and Carl left him somewhere without a ride. Maybe Freddie was going to shack up with another woman and Carl felt guilty because he didn't stop it. Hell, it could be anything. Maybe it wouldn't lead them straight to Freddie's killer, but if it helped them get a few steps along the path, he figured it was worth sweating Carl a little. He glanced up again at the rear-view mirror and smiled.

"Carl, how you doing? You may not remember me. Detective Ross."

Carl extended his hand. "Sure. I remember you. You came to the house after Freddie turned up missing." Ross watched him lick his lips. "I don't need a lawyer or anything, do I?"

"Why, you been cheating on your income tax? We usually let the federal boys handle that." Cee chuckled. "No, we just have a few questions for you."

Champ had nodded Carl into a chair next to Cee's desk and folded himself into one facing Carl. Cee turned his heavy wheeled chair so that Carl would form the apex of a small triangle. At 12:30 most of the detectives were at lunch or in the field. The room was comparatively quiet.

Champ stroked his left index finger over his mustache. "Mr. Puente, we really appreciate you coming in to talk with us, middle of your business day and all."

"What choice do I have?"

"Hell," Ross said, and ran his hand over his smooth scalp. "This is America, last I heard. You could have said no. We just want to get your perspective on this. See if anything has shaken loose for you. That will happen pretty often, when you get a few days away. Your mind starts to sort things out differently."

"Oh," Carl rushed. "I didn't mean it like that. It's—I mean, of course I'd come in. I want to do everything I can to help out, to find the guy who did this."

"You seem pretty sure it's a guy," Champ said.

"Well, I just meant—"

"We're assuming so, too. Most violent crimes—round here at least—are committed by men. Unless Freddie had something going on the side. I mean, that's not so uncommon. Happens to most of us, one time or another."

The telephone on Champ's desk rang, and he walked over to answer it. "Phillips. No, not yet, but I don't think it'll be long. Yeah. Sure are. Right now." He flicked a glance at Carl. "Yeah. I'll let you know." He replaced the receiver and walked back to Cee's desk.

"Let me guess," Cee said. "D.A.?"

Champ gave a nod. "Wanting to know about Freddie, as a matter of fact. She wants the guy who did it pretty bad. Might say she's protective of the folks in this town."

Cee glanced at the clipboard on his desk to help smother a smile. The well-timed call, usually from a detective in another room, was a common part of their interviewing technique. "So you told me that the night your brother disappeared—"

"Brother-in-law."

"Right, sorry. My mistake. Now when I was at your house, his wife said he was going out to the Pac-n-Sac for some beer, and then for a video. Is that still right?"

"Yeah, I mean I guess. You'd have to ask her."

Ross made a note. "See, the reason we're asking is that we couldn't find anyone at a Pac-n-Sac or video store who remembers seeing him that night. And not just in his neighborhood. I mean all over town. What would that say to you?"

Carl thought he was doing a good job of acting calm, but what he really wanted to do was slam the clipboard on that fat cop's head and smash his fist into the other one's face. Of course he'd never done anything even remotely like that in his life. Carl wasn't a violent man. The closest he'd come was twenty-seven years ago, and he hadn't even held the gun. He'd just stood there in the gas station trying not to pee his pants, while the clouds pounded the street with hammers of rain. He figured they had to know; they wouldn't have brought him in here if they didn't know the whole thing. Why didn't they just say it? Maybe he could cut a deal with them. He wasn't even there when Freddie got—when Joe killed him. Maybe they'd give him probation on Food Giant. He'd seen that on TV enough. But he already had a record. Would it still be there? Would they expunge it after seven years, like a credit record? No, that was only for kids. Well, he was nineteen when he went away. Wasn't the legal age twenty-one back then? No, that was just for drinking. Shit! He shouldn't have said anything about a lawyer; that was too fucking stupid. And if he asked again if he needed one, they'd lock him in cuffs. He knew that. Keep calm, he thought.

"I couldn't say, really. This is your area." He pressed his lips together. "I guess, either he went to meet someone or—or something happened to him on the way to the store."

"Like what?" Cee asked.

"What?"

"I asked first. Like what would have happened to him?"

"I don't know. Something obviously, since he—got killed. Died."

"One thing we do know," Champ said. "One of the last things he did before he . . . died, was he called me. At home. Why do you think he would have done that?"

"I don't know," Carl said. Joe was right, then. Freddie *had* gotten through to Phillips.

"Take a guess. You worked with Freddie, played pool together. What could he have been into that he would have called the police about, saying that he had something I wanted?"

"I'm sorry," Carl said. "I really don't know. I don't think Freddie ever would have, you know, confided in me."

Champ dropped his toothpick into the wastebasket and pulled a stick of Juicy Fruit gum out of his shirt pocket. He carefully unwrapped it, slid it into his mouth, and folded the foil into a small square. Cee waited. Champ was just letting Carl sit on the grill for a while to warm him up. Cee felt pretty sure that he wasn't their boy, but the technique was guaranteed to net something, because Carl was as nervous as an oil man at a solar power convention.

Champ chewed his gum slowly, his eyes fixed on the ceiling, hands crossed against his flat belly. "When Detective Ross interviewed you, you said that the last time you saw Freddie was when he left work that day. Is that still right?"

"Yeah. Nothing's changed. He took off. Asked me to shoot pool with him." The second the words slipped out of his mouth, Carl wished he'd clamped his teeth down on them good and tight. He had told himself not to mention the pool hall. It was too close.

Champ nodded. "And you didn't go because . . . ?"

"Well, because I was burned out on pool. Wanted to spend some more time with my family."

"Uh huh. So you didn't play pool. You think he might have anyway?"

"Maybe. Did you check down at the pool hall?"

"Said it had been a while since they'd seen either of you."

"Yeah," Carl said. A small breath of relief slid from his lungs.

Champ studied the piece of foil. "Same thing with those other two guys."

"What guys?" Carl said, too quickly.

"Your partners there. Quiet guy and an asshole, way we heard them described."

Carl made an effort to appear deep in thought. "I don't really remember that. I mean, sure, Freddie and I may have played a pick-up game, we did sometimes. But I don't really remember any of them. We usually played with each other—I mean, you know, by ourselves."

"Way we heard it, you got in a fight with one of them."

Cee was afraid that if Carl sweated any more, his clothes would slide right off of him.

"I don't—no, I didn't fight with anyone there. Where'd you hear that?"

"Remember the other guy getting bounced?"

"No. I don't."

Champ templed his hands together, and touched his joined index fingers to his lips. "Seems like it would be hard to forget. Too bad you did, though. We thought this guy we'd heard about might look good for the murder."

"Well, I'm sure you'll solve it anyhow." Carl's pulse had almost returned to its normal rate. "If that's all, maybe I can get back to work?"

"Yeah, I suppose so."

Carl stood up. He turned to go, and Champ said "Oh yeah, I do have one last question. How'd you ever get mixed up with a guy like Smith Dixon?"

Cee later thought Carl's face couldn't have gone whiter if Freddie himself had walked in at that moment and shaken his hand. His mouth opened and closed, and he was incapable of speech for several seconds. Then, expelling the words like a Heimlich-forced crouton, he said "Look, this is the first time I've seen him since back in '72, I swear to Christ. I just ran into him is all. I didn't have anything to do with it!"

He stood gasping, his chest heaving in and out. Champ and Cee turned to face each other. "Well, I'll be damned. It's like fishing for minnows and landing a five pound bass," Champ said. He turned to Carl. "Mr. Puente? Do you remember what you said about calling a lawyer?"

Chapter 22

Smith had barely locked the door of his cabin when he heard the gravel crunching behind him. Without turning, he knew it was the sound of cops and that they were coming for him.

"Smith Dixon?"

Still facing his door, staring at a ragged spot of flaking gray paint, he held his arms up and put them against the wall. He felt hands running up and down his legs, over his crotch, and under his jacket. "I ain't carrying," he said. The hands pulled his arms behind his back and clicked the icy steel handcuffs on his wrists.

They turned him around. An overweight black cop with a shaved head Miranda'd him. With a nod he agreed that yes, he did understand his rights. The cop made him say it out loud anyway. Another cop, a tall guy with mirror shades and a Stetson, opened the back door of the brown Chevy Celebrity. "You know what this is for?" he asked.

Smith shrugged like it didn't really make any difference.

He didn't make it difficult. They sat him down at a table in a small white room and trained a video camera on him. They told him that Carl had already given him up, and the best thing he could do was plead at the arraignment. If he turned over on Joe, it could go a lot easier with him. The D.A. would go along with it. Carl hadn't actually been there, and he couldn't testify to the murder itself. Smith was the only one who could tell what really happened. They couldn't get him off the hook completely; a guy with his record was going to do time, no two ways around it. If he worked with them, it didn't have to be that much.

He kept nodding, mostly. He felt like he'd already seen this hand anyway, and there wasn't even a pair of deuces in it.

The red-faced, sweaty supervisor at the job site said Joe hadn't been in to work for the past two days, and if he did show his ass up again, it'd be just long enough to get shit-canned. He wore a hardhat with "Duane" printed in black plastic letters on the front. "I need men who show up and work," he blustered. "I pay a decent wage for hard work. If he don't like it here he can kiss my ass. What he do, anyway?"

"He didn't do anything." Cee thumbed a business card from his shirt pocket and handed it to the man. "But if he does show up, don't let on that we know he didn't do anything. Just call me."

Duane squinted at the card like it was an eye chart. "I'll call all right, but I'm gonna take a piece of his butt first, I guarantee that."

"Leave some for us, is all we ask. Catch you later, Duane." Cee nodded at him, and climbed into the driver's seat.

"Smart ass," the man mumbled. He turned back to the steel girders, trying to see what those dumb asses had screwed up in the five minutes that had been stolen from him.

Champ reached over and turned the air conditioner up a notch. It was 78 degrees by the Amarillo National Bank sign downtown. "Think we should try his house again?" Cee asked.

Champ shook his head once. "I put a couple guys in an unmarked on the block. I imagine the only thing they'll catch is his wife, if she hasn't found the sense to leave him."

"You don't think he took off, do you?"

"I don't think he's got the sense for that. Probably on a bender. Way I imagine him, he may not even get that he's really done anything wrong."

"Basic barnyard variety sociopath?"

"What'd the lawyer man call him?"

"A skell?" Cee said.

"Yeah. Maybe it's the same thing, but I kind of like the word anyway."

"What about that pool joint? You want to put somebody there?"

"We can drop in, see if she's heard anything, maybe show his picture around."

"You think that woman'll call if he comes back?"

"I got an idea she'd be glad to get rid of him. Trick is getting her to call us before we have to pry that guy's pecker out of her dog's teeth."

Cee nodded. "That reminds me. My mouth's been watering for some barbecue sausage lately. You interested?"

"You're a sick man, Cornelius."

"Thank you, Harvey. Coming from you, I take it as a true compliment."

They drove back to the police headquarters and worked their other cases.

Danny worked the toothpick around in his mouth, sizing up his best shot. "So anyway," he said. "We's all a little tight—"

"Isn't that like saying Amarillo's a little flat?"

Danny's laugh rumbled deep in his chest. "And I was tighter than the rest of them by about .1 blood alcohol." Danny tried to bank the four-ball and slide it into a pocket but missed by half an inch. Max stepped around the table, looking for a shot. He and a middle-aged woman with tall hair and wide hips at the next table unconsciously avoided one another. "One of the guys we'd been drinking with wasn't a cowboy, just some old slick who'd bought a pair of those elephant hide boots, he got to his car and tried the handle. Locked. He pats around for his keys for five minutes or so, realizes he ain't got 'em. Kind of looks around at us. Walks over and says, 'My keys are still in my car. One of you fellows know how to get into a locked car?'

"'Hell I'll do 'er,' I say. 'I walk over to the driver's side, cup my hands around my eyes against the window, see them keys dangling in the ignition. They're in there, sure enough. Try the door. Then I step back about a foot, reach into my jacket and pull out a *pistóle* of about a .44 caliber, point it right at that window. Boom! Sounds like a cannon going off. Glass shatters all over the parking lot, inside of the slick's car, it's a Mercedes with that leather interior. That old boy goes from drunk to dry in two seconds flat. I look around, say 'Anybody else got something they need opened?' I was serious, too. The rest of them scattered like the four winds, and the next thing I knew it was just me and the slick standing out there."

"No offense intended chief, but I'm glad I didn't know you back then."

"Sometimes I wish I hadn't either."

Max was wondering what was up. When he came in at 7:00, Bailey had seemed tense. Instead of lying behind the counter with her front paws crossed, she was sitting up, her golden eyes glowing. "Everything okay?" Max asked Angel.

She filled a glass with ice and sprayed Coke into it. "Far as I know," she said as she slid it across the counter to him. "She's been a little uneasy for the last hour or so." Angel pushed her hair behind her ears, an unconscious gesture.

Max leaned over the counter. "Bailey," he said softly. She rolled her eyes up at him. "You okay?" She responded with a barely audible chuff. Her head didn't move, but her eyes flicked from side to side and her black nose opened and closed as delicately as a butterfly's wings.

Danny was already playing when Max got there, his John Deere cap shading his eyes. He nodded at Max from their regular table. Max was at Bailey's more often than not on most evenings, and Danny joined him every Thursday. Sometimes they ran into each other at the 5:30 meeting and walked down the street to Bailey's. Tonight Max had worked on some cases for the next morning's arraignment. He had a client who had been picked up for prostitution, and Jeff Skeffington, who was becoming a regular. Danny didn't really care what time he got there; he knew that Max would either show up or call and say he wasn't coming.

They had played one game of eight-ball which Max won, and a round of cutthroat with Frank Vaughn, whom Max had helped with more parking tickets. Now they were playing nine-ball. The place was filling up with its usual mix of Thursday night regulars and students from Amarillo College or West Texas A&M University down in Canyon. Max had just kissed the nine-ball into its pocket; he was still leaning over the table, and when he glanced up from the ball his sight line led him straight to the door when Joe Wagner walked in. He straightened up slowly.

"Holy Jesus," he said to Danny, who followed Max's eyes to the door.

One of the stranger phenomena that Max had witnessed since he came to Amarillo was the great number of what he thought of as AIDS cowboys. They didn't really carry the HIV virus, or at least he didn't think so. But they looked like they did. He'd see them coming in and out of small claims court, of divorce judgments, of drunk and disorderly sentences, of child custody cases, with eviction notices and decrees in their hands. The women with them were often overweight, looking like gravity was slowly dragging them down until one day they would simply disappear into the hard red earth. The men were painfully thin, emaciated, as if the weight their wives were carrying had been stripped from them, from the layer of flesh that was supposed to separate their skin from their bones. Their leather-brown faces were seared by the Texas sun, and their jeans always looked three inches too big in the waists. The wrists sticking out from their pearl-snap shirt cuffs were as thin as match sticks.

But Max knew they weren't really like the thin, wandering men he had become used to seeing in the West Village, the men whose lives and bodies were slowly being eaten away by a virus no one seemed to understand. The men he saw in Amarillo were disappearing from a virus of the soul, a virus of hopelessness and pain.

That was how Joe Wagner looked when he walked through the door of Bailey's. He had lost at least twenty pounds since Max had last seen him there, his face caving in around its cheekbones like he was wearing a pair of ill-fitting dentures. He was no longer the good-looking but cruel cowboy with an arrogant swagger; now he walked through the door on pipe-cleaner legs. Angel gave him a rack of pool balls, and Joe's eyes flicked behind the counter. Max knew without seeing her that Bailey had stood up and fixed Joe with her cold stare. Joe looked back at Angel, took the balls and lurched to an empty table in the back right corner. He made his way through the room without looking at any of the other players. When he brushed by Max, he exuded a smell of sour sweat, beer, and tobacco.

"You ever met that guy?" Max asked as his eyes tracked Joe across the room.

"I've seen him a few times when I was out there, drinking and fighting in one bar or another."

Max nodded. He glanced at the counter and saw Angel with the telephone receiver cradled on her shoulder, drawing a beer for a customer as she spoke. She collected the money and made change, her eyes never leaving Joe. When she replaced the phone she glanced at Max and raised her chin slightly.

Max walked to the counter and leaned over it to Angel. "Did you call Phillips?" he asked.

"Yeah."

Max waited a beat, his elbow on the counter. "So are you going to tell me if you actually reached him?"

"He's on his way. Smart ass Yankee lawyer," she added.

"He's always seemed pure Texas to me," Max said. "And I think he's a cop, not a lawyer."

"Go back to your table."

Max did as he was ordered. She didn't seem particularly nervous about having someone arrested in her place. He wondered if it had ever happened before. If not, it probably wasn't for lack of opportunity. Some nights he figured that half the customers there had outstanding arrest warrants. Max had met several of his clients in Bailey's during the last month, but none of them had ever been accused of murder. Max's criminal clients were strictly small time, and that was the way he liked it. The idea of sitting in a courtroom next to a guy who may have chopped up his entire family on a whim and trying to prove he didn't do it wasn't Max's idea of the high life. Of course, the streets of New York and probably Amarillo were filled with men and women in thousand dollar suits, driving around in cars worth eighty times that much, who paid for their lunch defending guys who had as much conscience as a tree. But then, they weren't usually murderers; on the economic ladder, murderers were usually hanging on desperately to the bottom rung. It was your starched white-collar clients who brought in the money: lawyers, doctors, stockbrokers. Unless you landed one of those violent criminals whose crime was so grotesque, so startling, that they became celebrities. Then half the lawyers in town, who normally would go racing for the hall when the joker came up for arraignment, would be stepping on each other's hands and feet to get a chance to defend him. It didn't matter how many people the guy had shot, sliced, or bombed; a practice thrives on publicity. Cynical? Not me, Max thought.

He went back to his game, occasionally watching Joe, whose movements were jerky, like he was attached to a set of marionette's strings that he couldn't get rid of.

It was just under ten minutes when Champ Phillips and Cee Ross cautiously walked into the place. Champ glanced at Angel, who pointed her chin toward the back right corner. They walked quietly between the tables, even Cee moving with purposeful grace.

The room didn't get deathly still like in the old western movies, but the noise level did decrease. The players continued with their games, but they kept their eyes on Joe's table. Half of them knew that the same two cops had been looking for a guy the other night.

Joe had on a pair of faded jeans and a denim shirt with the tail hanging down over his belt. When he bent over they saw that he wasn't carrying a piece in the small of his back and figured if he was playing pool he didn't have one in front either. Still, Champ and Cee kept their hands lightly on their gun butts.

Joe didn't look up when they approached his table, didn't make any sign that he knew they were there, but a line of sweat beads mustached his upper lip. Cee raised his eyebrows at Champ, who nodded. "Joe Wagner?" Cee said. Joe didn't say anything, didn't look up. Cee glanced at Champ again.

Champ took the toothpick out of his mouth and settled his other hand tighter on his pistol. "You need to answer up when we talk to you, son," he said in his softest voice. "Are you Joe Wagner?"

Joe paused, still lined up over his stick. He turned his eyes up to them. They were shot through with red. "What the fuck you want to know for?"

"You can't talk that way to an officer of the law," Champ said, reaching with his left hand for the handcuffs on his belt.

Cee was ready to move before Champ reached for his cuffs. He knew exactly what was going to happen, could have described it in detail before the action began, like a favorite movie he'd watched a hundred times. He knew that when Champ went for his cuffs Joe would straighten up, grabbing the narrow end of the cue stick in his fists, pulling his elbows back in a batter's stance, ready to hit whichever head he could reach first. Cee had his pistol out, and was ready to put Joe's head down hard on the green felt while Champ snapped his wrists into the metal loops. There was just one thing that the film in his head didn't contain.

When he had time to think about it later, after the cops were gone and the players had settled back into their routines, Max decided that it was two tables and not one that Bailey had jumped over. Danny said Max was full of shit, that even Bailey couldn't clear two tables, but Max knew that his eyes hadn't played a trick on him. When Joe went into his swing, Bailey, who had been watching from atop the counter, gathered her haunches underneath her and sailed into the air, a grey-white cloud with gold eyes and flashing ivory teeth. She hit the floor and in two long bounds was on Joe's back before he could even cock the stick up over his shoulder, before Cee could get his pistol to Joe's neck, before Champ could get his handcuffs off his belt. Joe lay flat on the floor, his nose slammed into the beery sawdust, the wolf's front paws on his shoulders, her saliva dripping onto his neck. The officers both had their guns out, unsure of where to point them, swinging back and forth between the man on the floor and the animal pinning him there.

Angel vaulted over the counter, a police baton in her hand, and raced between the tables to the back, running on the toes of her cowboy boots. "Take your guns off her!" she yelled at them.

"Make it back off," Cee said. "We're not going to arrest your dog, lady. Just back it the hell off!"

"Bailey," she said, and the dog's eyes flicked up at her. Angel cocked her head minutely to the side, and the dog carefully stepped off Joe's back. Champ bent down and yanked Joe's wrists behind him, snapping the cuffs on them. "On your feet," he said.

Joe struggled to his feet, glowering at everyone in sight. "What're you arresting me for?"

"We're taking you into custody for the murder of Freddie Odom," Cee said. "Lady, we could arrest you too, for interfering with a police officer in the line of duty. And I bet there's a law against keeping wolves domestically. That thing's too dangerous to keep here, or anywhere."

Max was standing behind Angel, his fingers resting lightly on the felt curb of a table. "Look I know that this isn't my business, but I think a good lawyer would probably make it more trouble than it's worth to you to follow that charge up." He and Danny had moved in close when Champ snapped the handcuffs on Joe.

Cee desperately wanted to get out of this redneck zoo. "Just make sure you keep that thing in line."

"Bailey's not a thing, and she never gets out of line," Angel snapped.

"Yeah, yeah," Cee mumbled. "All right, let's go," he said, and he and Champ each took one of Joe's arms.

They hustled him through the knots of gawking players and out the door.

Angel stared after them, the billyclub hanging from her left hand, her right automatically kneading Bailey's ruff. The dog rumbled deeply, her eyes closed. "I never should have let him in here," Angel said.

"How were you supposed to know he'd kill anyone?" Max asked.

"I couldn't have. But I knew he was a scumbag. I should have trusted Bailey."

"From where I'm standing, it doesn't look like anything bad happened."

"Besides the feeling in my gut when they had those guns pointed at Bailey? If they would have hurt her, then what?"

"I see what you mean," Max said.

"Do you? Cause if they had, I would have had to do something that would've landed me in jail. Opened one of their heads with this stick, or grabbed the gun and shot that Joe asshole through the head like he deserves."

Max felt a cool finger trace its way along the back of his neck, and he shuddered. "Is that what you think?"

Angel turned her eyes to him. "I don't know. Maybe not. I was never much of a Bible fan, but I kind of believe in that eye for an eye thing. Somebody does something bad, they deserve it back in kind. What do you think?"

"I don't know," he said. "It's one I've turned over and over for years, but I never have gotten a good glimpse of it."

She looked to the front, where a college kid stood looking around the room. "I got a business to run," she said.

As the last customers were straggling out, Max hung around and brushed the tables. Angel locked the doors and counted her takings. Bailey slept behind the counter, the necessity for alertness fading now that the place was empty.

"I'm ready," Angel said, and raised the gate in the counter. "Thanks for your help."

"You're welcome."

"You want to have breakfast in the morning?"

He thought it over for a brief moment. "Yeah. I have an arraignment at ten. Just name the place and time."

"Well, that's the thing," she said. "I was thinking maybe we could do it at my place, but it's kind of complicated to find. It might be easier if you just came out there with me tonight." Her arms were crossed against her chest. "What do you think?"

"I love it when you get shy," he said.

She laughed, and her cheeks turned red, making the dusting of freckles show up even more. "I'm not too good at this kind of stuff, I told you that."

"I think you're pretty good," he said, and stepped toward her. They wrapped their arms around each other and stood for a moment, swaying back and forth, taking comfort in the warmth of the hug. From behind the counter came a low "uff."

Max woke up at 6:30 a.m. For a moment he wasn't sure where he was. Whenever he experienced that, waking up in a strange room, there was always a moment of panic. When he was drinking it wasn't that uncommon to come out of a blackout in a completely unfamiliar place, and no matter how long he had been sober, it was always his first thought. He rubbed the sleep from his eyes and looked around the room. The walls were made of adobe, with heavy wood furniture. It felt like a man's house, solid and—he looked for the right word. Horsey, that was it. Like the house on *Bonanza*, but not as big. It wasn't like any woman's space he'd ever been in before, but then Angel wasn't like any other woman he'd known. Max was alone in the bedroom and he heard no noise in the house, although the smell of coffee tickled his nose.

Last night it had taken half an hour to get to her house on a dirt road in a rare grove of trees. He was afraid his car would bottom out on the rough gravel road. When the truck's headlights caught the trees circling the house, he thought of a joke Danny had made one night. "Here in the Panhandle, we like to say there's a pretty woman behind every tree." Max hadn't gotten it for a few minutes, until he realized that the Panhandle was the most treeless land he'd ever seen outside of post-nuclear nightmare science fiction movies. When there were trees, they were usually in parks or lining riverbeds that actually ran with water an average of about two weeks a year. The trees surrounding Angel's place were cottonwoods with a few mesquites mixed in here and there, she had told him. He hadn't seen much of the place last night; once she extinguished the headlights there was no light at all except for the sea of stars flowing overhead.

Angel had opened the front door and said "You can come in, you know. That was kind of the point."

"I know. Let me just look for a minute." He stood still and lost himself in the expanse of the stars. He realized that no matter how long he lived here, he would never get tired of the simple act of looking at the sky.

After a few minutes he followed her inside and admired the simple elegance of the house, the hundreds, probably thousands of books snaking their way along every wall surface, spines perfectly aligned against the edges of the shelves. She had turned on some more country music, but none of the raucous stuff she played at the club, with its strutting, drunken bravado. This was music he'd never heard before, country music that talked of pain and its flipside, redemption, as well as any of the folk singers he'd heard in the little clubs scattered around the Village. After they sat and talked, she took his hand and gently pulled him in the direction of the bedroom. He followed her to an antique bed with a canopy, with tiny lights in the shape of stars strung along the four edges.

They slowly undressed. Angel's body was lean and muscular, with full breasts and slender hips. Max walked to her, and put his arms around her waist. He kissed her softly, and she put her hands on his lower back. When the kiss stopped, she said "What's that?"

"What's what?"

She moved to his side, and her fingers traced a small jagged line above his waist.

"Oh," he said. "That's what convinced me to stop drinking."

She leaned her head against his shoulder for a moment and they held each other, then she turned down the quilt on her bed. "Come here," she said.

They made love, with no small amount of fear in both of them, and fell asleep with their arms around each other.

When he woke up the next morning, Angel's side of the bed was empty. Max stood up and dressed. A delightful chill flowed in from the half-open windows over the bed. He drew back the curtain and looked out. Twenty yards away was a small barn, hay poking its way out of a loft on the upper level. The trees gently circled the north side of the house and barn. Max leaned his face closer to the window and breathed deeply of the morning air. He closed his eyes and felt the chill on his skin. He heard a noise and opened his eyes, prepared to see Angel. Instead, he met the gaze of two golden eyes surrounded by gray fur the color of cold ashes, perched just above a grinning yaw of teeth.

"Shit!" he said, and stepping back, pressed a hand to his chest. "I'm having a heart attack here!" Bailey's head and paws disappeared from the window, and in a moment he saw her loping easily toward the corral attached to the barn. She ducked under the bottom rail, never breaking her stride, as Angel pushed open the barn door. The horses crowded past her, Summerlea bumping her head against Nightfall's. Nightfall blew air through his lips and pranced in joyous acknowledgment of his own beauty. Angel went back into the barn, and when Max walked out the back door of her house, a steaming mug of coffee in his hand, she was emerging with two flakes of hay and two grain buckets. She threw the hay onto the ground and hung the buckets from hooks on the top rail of the corral. She was wearing a flannel shirt and a red down vest with her habitual jeans and boots.

"Hey," she said. "Did you sleep well?"

"Yeah. How about yourself?"

She nodded.

"Last night I was afraid maybe I'd forget what to do or something," he said. "It's been a while since—"

"I don't want to do that," she said.

"What?" he asked, thinking that she meant she didn't want to have a relationship with him. He felt crushed.

Angel saw the disappointment in his face. "No, that's not what I mean. I mean I don't want to talk about the past, who we were with and how long, and all that. I'm not hiding anything, I just don't want to get into it."

"Okay."

"Besides, knowing that you were with one of those gals with the tall hair, tight yellow pants and spike heels would be more than I could handle. My disappointment would be too overwhelming."

Max laughed, relieved. "You mean a Guidette? Forget about it."

"A what? What did you say?"

"A Guidette. You know what a Guido is?"

"Why don't you tell me."

"A Guido's a guy who wears the gold chains around his neck, hair perfectly coifed and lubed. Wears a guinea t-shirt in the summer, you know the kind with straps? When he's going out on the town, it's a too tight shirt, silk or something that looks like it, probably still wearing a Miami Vice jacket, or maybe a real suit, but not a tie because you've got to see the chain. So the Guidette's the woman on his arm. She's the one you were describing, with the big hair, not that Texans have any room to talk, and the spike heels and pedal pusher pants, and layers of make-up. They're always arguing with their guys about cats and dogs, nickels and dimes, something. And they'll be looking at him with this look that says 'Just try it, and see what happens.' Doesn't matter what 'it' is. If his eyes stray it'll be 'What're you looking at huh for? What, I ain't good enough for youse no moah?' And of course he'll say the wrong thing, something like 'I wasn't looking,' because it's never a good thing to contradict her. And you know when they get home that night there'll be dishes thrown and in a year they'll laugh about it, calling it their best fight ever. So that's what a Guidette is, and if I'd been with one of them I'd be pretty disappointed with myself too. Which I wasn't, so don't worry. And that's my last word on that subject."

Angel said nothing.

"What?"

"That was pretty amazing."

"What, my powers of anthropological observation?"

"That too, but I meant the way you never took a breath. That first night you came into the bar, I never would have dreamed you could talk that much."

"That's because I was scared to death you might shoot me if I said anything."

She gave him a sideways glance. "You really thought I would?"

"With no second thought."

"Huh. If it's any consolation, I've never shot anyone in my life. I don't even own a gun. With Bailey around, I never figured I needed one."

"Good point."

She slid her arm around his waist, slipping her hand into his back pocket. "How about some breakfast? Do you eat bacon?"

"No."

"Is that a Jewish thing?"

"No, it's a vegetarian thing."

"A vegetarian who doesn't drink. Yeah, I was right. Texas is the place for you. Come on, let's fix some eggs. You do eat those, don't you?"

"Absolutely."

"Orange juice? Coffee? Are you concerned about all those oranges giving up their lives? Those poor peasants down there getting paid a penny a pound for picking coffee beans?"

"Yeah, but not enough to quit."

Chapter 23

Judge Edward Bruce was in his mid-sixties with a fringe of white hair cradling his shiny pate. If he sometimes seemed asleep on the bench, it was because he occasionally was. Bruce only napped when he knew the case in front of him was being handled by two competent attorneys who would need little direction from him and who wouldn't do anything outrageous enough to warrant a mistrial or reversal. If he was faced with a lawyer of known incompetence or a case of a convoluted nature, he was always alert.

Although he appeared grumpy, he actually enjoyed the job to which he had been appointed by President Gerald Ford, an act Judge Bruce considered perhaps the only significant action taken by the president who was a lame duck the moment he was elected. He especially enjoyed arraignments for the variety of entertainment from both clients and attorneys. For his money, it was more entertaining than a starlet at a Mensa convention.

He sat in his leather armchair, chin cradled in one hand, watching the two attorneys and one felon facing him. Jack Ogan was sweating despite the gentle temperature of the day. His collar was too tight, and Bruce was afraid if he sweated any more he might pass out right over the prosecution's table. Ogan had a swipe-over, a dozen lank hairs oiled down over his scalp. Edward Bruce believed that was the difference between criminal and civil law. The corporate types could afford a decent looking rug, while the criminal attorneys had to settle for a tube of Brylcreem and a prayer that the wind wouldn't pick up. In Amarillo, that was about as likely as finding a client who truly hadn't done it.

Ogan was trying to manufacture some moral outrage for the woman standing six feet to his left, behind the defense table. "Your Honor, now we really need to insist on a heavy bond on this woman. She's continually appeared before this court, never showing remorse or even holding out the faintest indication that she intends to stop selling herself to the good people of Amarillo. We need to send a message to—"

Judge Bruce cut him off. "Send a message" was a catch phrase that was irritating him more and more each time he heard it. "Maybe if the good men of Amarillo would 'send a message' that they're not in the market anymore, she would change professions." He waved his hand to quiet Ogan's tired sputter of protest. "Mr. Friedman? Anything you want to say about bail?"

"Thank you, Your Honor." Max knew his words came out "yeronnah." "The defense believes that ten thousand dollars is a usurious sum for my client. Ms. Wynn doesn't even own a car, and therefore her chances of flight are nonexistent. I request release on her own recognizance."

"Mr. Friedman, it's too early in the day for that. I need one more cup of coffee before I can get irritated at you. Is that her family in the third row?"

Max glanced back at the crying, overweight woman whom he knew to be Glenda Wynn's sister. "Yes, Your Honor."

"I doubt they walked here today, and I don't see any wings on their shoulders. Let's assume that they own a car. Bail is set at five thousand dollars, trial for December 14 at 9:00 a.m. Next."

The bailiff, a genial retiree with a Donald Duck tie under a burgundy jacket, stood up and announced "87946, State of Texas vs. David Spearman, how do you plead?"

Glenda was escorted away from the bench. Max touched her elbow. "We can probably have you out before tonight. Let me talk to your family about it."

"Okay." She lowered her white-blond curls and glanced up at Max. "Can you ask Mama to cook baked chicken and dressing?"

"I'll see what I can do." He turned toward the family, behind the rail. "What am I, a fucking waiter?" he mumbled to himself.

He had just elicited a promise from his client's sister to secure the bond before 5:00 p.m. when Bobby Turner and Sonny Tarleton scuttled up to him, briefcases swinging at their sides.

"Hey Max, did you hear?" Bobby said.

"What about?"

Sonny had a voice that sounded like a rusty file being honed. "Scuttlebutt this morning says that there's some kind of hairy murder coming up for arraignment. Word is that Diane herself is coming over for the plea."

"Color me thrilled, guys. Then tell me exactly what it has to do with yours truly."

"Oh, nothing. Just something to talk about," Bobby said. He and Sonny glanced at each other and smothered smiles.

Max narrowed his eyes. He knew something was going on, but he wasn't quite sure what. He turned back to Glenda's sister.

The double doors into the courtroom swung open and Diane DiAngelo stalked in, looking icy in a salmon colored suit. Moments later a door on the side of the courtroom opened and Joe Wagner, between two guards, entered the room. The guards pointed to a bench, and he sat down.

The bailiff stood up and announced "87949, State of Texas vs. Joseph Randall Wagner."

A guard prodded Joe's elbow and he rose to his feet, the chains on his wrists clinking. He looked around, unsure of where to go, and the guard pointed him to the defense table.

Judge Bruce opened his mouth to speak but stopped when he saw Diane striding down the aisle, heels clicking rapidly on the wood plank floor. She passed the railing that separates court officers from the spectators, made a sharp right turn behind the prosecution table, and elbowed Jack Ogan to the right chair. "Do you think you could have been any later?" he whispered.

Bruce looked at the assemblage over his half glasses. "So nice of you to drop by, Ms. DiAngelo."

"Thank you, Your Honor."

Sarcasm is so unappreciated, he thought. "What's the charge?"

"Murder, assault on a police officer, and resisting arrest," the bailiff intoned.

"Mr. Wagner, where's your attorney?"

Joe's head jerked up toward the judge. His hair was plastered to his skull with sweat, and the circles under his eyes and his limp skin made Bruce wonder if he was a junkie.

Joe's eyes flicked around the courtroom, from the judge to the bailiff to the prosecutors. He looked desperately behind him at the spectators, as if searching for a familiar face.

"Ain't got one," he said.

"Do you plan to hire someone?"

"How'm I supposed to pay for it?"

"We can help you with that," the judge said, and started looking around the room.

The moment Joe was escorted in, Bobby Turner and Sonny Tarleton snatched up their briefcases and raced for the door. Despite his considerably greater bulk, Sonny reached the door a briefcase's breadth ahead of Bobby.

Max sensed motion between himself and the door, but the two attorneys were already gone before he lifted his eyes from Glenda Wynn's sheet. He went back to her papers for a brief moment when he heard his name spoken in a loud voice. Max looked up again, glanced around the courtroom, and saw that

Judge Bruce was leaning forward on the bench, his right elbow planted on the top, looking straight at Max and crooking his finger.

"Sir?"

"Your presence is requested by the sovereign state of Texas," he said, smiling at Max.

What now, Max thought. He pushed the files into his briefcase and hurried up to the defense table.

"Yes, your honor?"

"Meet your new client," the judge said and nodded at the man next to Max.

It took a moment before Max recognized the face of the man standing next to him, and when he did his stomach sunk into his testicles. It was the asshole redneck from the pool hall, the guy Bailey had bounced and who had been arrested by the two cops the night before.

"On the charge of murder, Mr. Wagner, how do you plead?"

Joe glanced at Max. "I ain't done shit."

Out of the corner of his mouth, Max said "Not guilty."

"Not guilty," Joe said.

"Recommendations for bail?"

Diane drew a deep breath. "Your Honor, the crime this man is accused of is monstrous, and—"

The judge waved his hand at her wearily. "Save it for the trial, please."

"Five hundred thousand dollars, Your Honor."

"Mr. Friedman?"

"Your Honor, my client is not a wealthy man." He glanced at Joe, and said "Right?" under his breath. Joe nodded. "This amount of bail is again, usurious. Why doesn't the State ask for a million?"

Diane leaned forward and glanced across Jack. She gave Max her most dazzling smile. "Fine. We're agreed then? One million it is."

Max drew in his breath to respond. "Children, children," the judge said. "Perhaps you're confusing me with my wife. *She's* the kindergarten teacher. Now I understand why she's taking early retirement. Bail is set at fifty thousand dollars." He banged his gavel and called for the next case.

The guard started to lead Joe away. "Man, I didn't do nothing," he said.

"Don't say anything to anyone. I'll come to the jail tomorrow morning, and you can tell me the whole story."

"Tomorrow? What's wrong with today?"

"Tomorrow morning. I'll see you then."

Joe looked over his shoulder as the guard took him away. "Man, you better get me off this. I mean it."

Max managed a nod at him. He decided to leave the courtroom before the judge brought in Charles Manson looking for counsel. He yanked one of the double doors open, and as he entered the corridor a voice behind him on his left said "You get a good one there, Max?" Bobby Turner swung in front of him, a grin stretching his face.

From his right side Sonny Tarleton said "Yeah, you keep grabbing up all the good clients here, the rest of the lawyers may have to make a protest to the Bar Association." He emitted a raspy laugh.

"Is this what they mean by Texas hospitality? Well, my friends, you are both cordially invited to eat shit and die."

They whooped with laughter as Diane DiAngelo emerged from the courtroom. She walked quickly past the group, not even pausing when she gave Max a superior smile. Sonny clapped him on the back and said, "Go get 'em, hoss. And remember, they're all equal in the eyes of the law."

Their teary laughter was starting to wind down by the time Max stepped into the elevator.

"Isn't there anything you can do about it? How about saying no?"

"Can't do that, Danny. I mean yeah, theoretically I could, and I wouldn't go to jail, but you just don't. A judge tells you to defend an indigent defendant, you do it. It's just basic back-scratching."

Max was stretched out on the couch, the cats asleep on his chest.

"So it sounds like you got a couple choices on this deal," Danny said.

"And those would be?"

"You can defend our little buddy and not worry about it, just give it your best."

"And option B?"

"You'll still defend him, but you can lay up at night in your bed thinking about it, losing sleep, pissing off your friends, probably lose that good-looking girlfriend who never looked twice at any cowboy who walked into that place of hers until you, and maybe eventually go to some shitty little dive of a place and pick up a drink, and end up in a hospital or a long box."

Max gently rubbed Mayella's ears as she purred ecstatically.

"You still there?" Danny said after thirty seconds had passed.

"Still here, chief. So what you're saying is that this is one of those 'wisdom to know the difference' deals" he said.

"Sounds like you're powerless to change it."

"Yeah."

"Just my curiosity Max, but you gonna put your all into it?"

"I got no choice, Danny. I don't put on a good defense and he's found guilty, it could get reversed on appeal. That wouldn't do anybody any good."

"That the only reason?"

"I think you probably know that answer. I have to defend him to the best of my ability."

"Integrity?"

"Yeah. If I don't, then I'll probably end up in that shitty little dive anyway."

"Don't you hate that?"

"Sometimes. Other times it's okay."

"Yeah. Well buddy, I got some steers to move early in the morning, and it's best to do that when you're awake. Anything else?"

"I could probably talk for hours, but no. Not now."

"All right then. Thursday night at the meeting?"

"Yeah."

"Catch you later."

"Thanks, Danny."

Max hung up the phone. "Hey guys," he said to the cats, "what are the chances of you getting up so I can make it to bed?" They paid no attention, so he carefully stretched his arm out to the coffee table and picked up the police report about the death of Freddie Odom.

Dolores reached down and picked up the remote. Very deliberately, she pointed it at the television and pushed the power button. The TV's image receded to a minute point of light. Carl looked up at her.

"I want to know what's going on." She paused. "Do you plan to tell me?"

"I don't really know what—"

"Carl, please don't lie to me." She sat down on the couch next to him. He was amazed at how calm she was, at how hard she was trying. "Every time you lie to me, it's like you've punched me in my stomach."

"What do you want, Dolores?"

"You've been a wreck since yesterday, Carl. I didn't know what it was. Then I found out this morning that they'd arrested that man for killing Freddie. I would think you'd be happy or something close to it. Instead you've been like a ghost all day. Carl, do you know anything about this? About what happened to Freddie?"

Carl picked up the remote. It was all he could do not to push the power button. He rubbed his thumb over it lightly. "Dolores, I can't talk about it. I mean I would, but I've been told not to until this is over."

Dolores sighed. She felt her heart turning to stone as she sat on the couch next to Carl. "I can't imagine that you had anything to do with it. All day long I've been thinking, trying to figure out the best story. I finally decided that you knew the man who killed Freddie, that maybe he was a customer or something, maybe a friend of yours, and finally you took your suspicions to the police. That would be okay, Carl. You didn't want to get your friend in trouble, but finally you had to do what was right. I'm trying not to think that you might have known who killed him for sure and for some reason wouldn't tell. I don't think that you'd put Regina—all of us, through that pain."

Amazingly to Carl, she reached out and put her hand on his. "What I want is the truth."

"Dolores, believe me, I—I really can't talk about it. When all of this is over, then we can . . . ." His voice trailed away.

She looked at him for a long moment. "Carl, I'm going to take Nina and go to Regina's house. We'll stay there until this is over." He heard a catch in her voice and saw that her eyes were moist. "If you were some way involved in this, if you knew what happened to Freddie and let us all go on like this, in all this pain—" She stopped for a moment. "If that's the case, we're not going to come back. I couldn't live with you anymore."

"Dolores, I—"

"I really don't think I can listen right now. I'm going to get Nina ready, and we're going to leave." She stood up and walked out of the living room down the hallway toward Nina's room.

Carl turned the remote in his hands, rubbing his fingers over the buttons.

He heard Dolores talking to Nina back in her room, in a low voice. He pushed the power button and quickly hit the mute before the sound could leak out of the living room. He slid around the channels to the closest football game, Carolina and New York.

He thought about the plastic bag that had been in the desk in his office. He could feel and hear the crinkle of the plastic as if it were still in his hand, the solidity of the money the way it had been when he used to check it twenty times a day, before they had come and taken what was left away from him. He remembered seeing a cop show on TV one time, where a guy had committed a murder and stolen thousands of dollars. Then he told the cops that he wanted to use the money to hire a lawyer. They smirked at him, of course, and Carl did too. But now he knew the feeling. The money was his, it had belonged to him, and they came and took it out of his desk drawer, those two cops. They did it after the store had closed, so at least the workers hadn't seen it. But he still felt powerless, like when he was a kid and some asshole stole the candlestick he'd made in shop class and there wasn't anything he could do about it. Or like the way he felt when he knew that Smith Dixon had skipped town and he couldn't. He had to stay there because of his family, and he knew that the cops would find him. Smith Dixon, he thought. It's all his goddamn fault, all of this is. He talked me into it, he brought that fucking mad dog in, none of this would have happened otherwise. It was my money and now it's gone.

He stared at the game, barely noticing when Dolores and Nina left.

Chapter 24

It's not as bad as Rikers Island, Max thought. That was the jail in New York where he had spent too much time—mostly looking in, but once or twice looking out. He always reassured himself that the Amarillo jail wasn't quite as bad every time he had to go into it to visit a client. But no matter how much brighter or cleaner it was, it still had the same purpose, and every time he felt the steel reverberation of the bars it was all he could do to keep from shivering. He always felt the same as he had the first time he'd ever been picked up, when he was sixteen years old, for being drunk and disorderly in Thompson Square Park.

He had to walk through a metal detector, and when it beeped a guard whisked him aside and went over him with the wand. Max had already dropped his keys and change into a white plastic tray. When the wand passed over his chest it started chirping insistently, and Max reached under his shirt and showed the guard a medallion. The man lost interest, and Max slipped the medal back against his skin. On the silver disc was a triangle inside a circle, the symbol of Alcoholics Anonymous.

The guard let him into a windowless interview room. Max sat down on one of four little interview chairs facing a wire screen. He opened his briefcase, a gift from his cousin Mort when he graduated from NYU Law. Mort was one of the few family members whom Max had stayed in touch with through the years. The briefcase was ready for retirement, but Max wasn't quite ready to part company with it. He had a problem ending relationships, whether it was with a city, a third-hand car, or a leather bag.

He took out a yellow legal pad, uncapped a red pen, and set a mini-cassette recorder on the ledge. At the top of the page he wrote "Interview with Joe Wagner—December 7."

Pearl Harbor day, he thought automatically. The curse of the history major. No matter what the calendar date, he automatically tried to attach a significant date in history to it. He even did it with cash register totals. $10.66. $14.92. $15.64, the price of Shakespeare's birth. Jesus, he thought. Whatever normal is, I'm not it. Whatever compulsive is, I am.

He tapped the pen against the wooden tabletop and glanced at his watch. The depressing funk of the jailhouse slipped in through his nostrils. He realized he had been breathing shallowly, trying to keep it out. It was a mixture of bleach, depression, fear, and male body odor. Like the smell of a school locker room. He felt his throat start to swell with vomit and swallowed it back as he heard a steel door snick open on the other half of the room.

A guard led Joe to a stool at the screen opposite from Max and stepped back against the wall, his face turned away. Joe wore orange coveralls, his hands chained to a leather belt on his waist.

"How are you?"

"I feel like shit. I don't think I've slept in about three days. You bring me any cigarettes?"

"No."

Max smelled the sour breath he blew out. "Man, what kind of a lawyer are you? Ain't you supposed to take care of me?"

"The kind of lawyer I am is a good one, and it's my job to put on the best defense I can so that maybe you don't have to spend the next forty years in a place even worse than this. You need cigarettes, I'll ask your wife to bring some."

Joe nodded. "You think you can get me bail?"

"To get you out on bond, we need to come up with five thousand dollars. Do you have it?"

"Shit, no."

"Do you own a house? Can you put it up?"

"Belongs to my wife's folks. They sure as shit wouldn't agree to it."

"Okay. It doesn't look like you're getting out unless we can do it at the trial. So you want to tell me what happened?"

Joe closed his eyes and squeezed them in concentration. "You know about that grocery store?"

"Why don't you tell me?"

"Me and these three other guys done it. Then Freddie, he was gonna go to the cops. I figured I'd scare him."

"Did you intend to kill him?"

"Hell no. I ain't stupid. I just thought I'd scare him a little."

"Whose idea was the robbery?"

"Smith's, I guess. I'd been a security guard there, told him it would be easy. Then he planned it out, he brought in the two other guys. That's where our problems started."

"Tell me more about that."

"Well shit, we could have done it easy ourselves, without them. Look, I'm not an expert at this kind of thing. Fact is I've never done it before. But it seems to me, less people you got the better. Less chance of fucking up."

"So did the job get fucked up?"

"No. I mean it went okay, everybody done what they was supposed to. Just Freddie started going squirrely."

"What does that mean?"

"That night, few days after we did the store, I went out driving. Had a new truck. So I'm driving down Western, and I see him in his car. I don't know why, but I start to follow him. I see him pull up to the Pac-n-Sac, and I decide to stop, see what he's up to. He doesn't go into the store, just goes right up to the phone, so I figure shit, he's got a phone at the house, what's he doing this for? Hoping maybe he's calling his wife cause he forgot what he come for. But hell no, he gets on the phone to that cop, and that wasn't happenin'."

"What did you do to keep it from happening?"

"I hang up the phone, make him get in the truck. He's sweating sure enough, and I don't say a damn thing 'til we get out to the old drive-in."

"Why did you go there?"

"We'd met there before, and it was the first place I could think of."

"So you get out there," Max said. "How did he end up dead?"

"When we get there I make him stay in the truck, and I smoke a cigarette. Smith pulls up a couple minutes later, and Freddie gets out of the truck. He starts arguing with me, acting like a little asswipe, and then he fucking jumps me! I get him off me, and he's calling me stuff, and he hits me again, and then I don't—I see him standing there, then he's on the ground, and that little pinto pony wasn't running no more either, and—and then . . . ."

Joe's voice had grown quieter during the last words, and finally it trailed off completely. Max waited for him to continue. But Joe just sat, his eyes staring at the steel mesh like dull gray marbles, as dead as the eyes of a shark.

Max glanced at the recorder and saw the steady red light. "Joe," he said, but Joe didn't move. "Joe!" He put his hand up to his side of the screen and rattled it.

Joe didn't move, but his eyes flicked up at Max. "What?"

"Are you okay?"

"I guess so."

"What did you mean when you said 'that pinto pony wasn't running no more'?"

Max saw the blood drain from Joe's face. "I didn't say nothing about that."

"Yes you did. I have it on the tape here."

"Uh uh. No, I didn't."

Max wrote "pinto pony" on his notepad. "Okay. You said Freddie was standing there and then he was on the ground. Was he dead?"

"Yeah, I guess so."

"Who said he was?"

"Smith and Carl."

"Wait a second. Back up. When did Carl get there?"

Joe thought. "I don't know. He wasn't there, then he was."

Great, Max thought. Carl's a magician. "Didn't you see him drive up?"

"No. He must have come up while we was fighting."

"You said that Freddie was arguing with you. He got out of the truck, started arguing, and then he jumped you. That doesn't really sound like the kind of thing Freddie would do, does it? He doesn't sound like a very aggressive kind of guy. What did he say when he started arguing with you?"

"You know, just shit, trying to get under my skin."

"No, I don't know. What kind of shit?"

"Oh, he was calling me stuff, you know." Joe cleared his throat. "You know, stuff. Faggot. Like that."

"Why would he call you that?"

"Man, I don't know! We was arguing, that's why. He called me a lot of stuff."

"What else?"

"Like I said, calling me a faggot and like that. Queer."

"Why did he jump you?"

"I don't know."

"What I'm trying to get at here is that he didn't seem like the type to—"

"I don't know, I said! Fuck, dig him up and ask him if you want to know. You're supposed to be my lawyer, so help me!"

"Okay, okay. So he jumped you and the two of you fought. When did you pick up the bowling pin?"

"I don't know. Sometime while we was fighting. I was playing with it, tossing it around before Smith got there, then when Freddie went at me I fell on it. Killed my back. I guess I picked it up then."

Max pressed the palms of his hands together and took a deep breath. "Okay Joe, here's the deal. Our best chance on this thing is to plead self-defense. I'll have to take a deposition from this Smith Dixon, see if he can back it up. But to do that, we have to make a case that Freddie was trying to hurt you, that you were in fear for your life. Now, is that what you were feeling? That you had to defend yourself from him?"

Joe nodded his head. "Yeah. Like I said, he jumped me. But man, he was calling me a faggot and all that too. Calling me a queer. Just tell the jury that. Smith'll back me up. They got to let me off then, right? That ain't right, to call somebody a queer. They'd understand that."

"I don't think that we can build a case of second-degree murder on that," Max said. He turned off the recorder and put it into his briefcase. He reached for the legal pad and stopped. "Joe?"

"What?"

"What about the pinto pony?"

Joe's face had regained some of its color, but at the mention of the pony it drained again.

"What do you mean? What're you talking about?"

"A few minutes ago, you were talking about when Freddie died, and you said something about a pinto pony. I just thought you might have remembered something."

"No." He glanced around at the guard. "Look, next time bring me some cigarettes, all right? We about done?"

"Yeah, I think that will do it for today." Max stood up and put the recorder and legal pad back into his briefcase as the guard led Joe back to his cell.

Smith Dixon had the practiced look of a man who was used to jail, who knew exactly what to do and when to do it. He almost flowed into the room, chatting with the guard in a low voice. He didn't have to glance at the wire mesh, trying to figure out what it could possibly have to do with him, and what he was supposed to do with it. He already knew. His eyes found Max and he sat down opposite him. The guard withdrew into his corner.

"Mr. Dixon, my name is Max Friedman, and I need to—"

"How's Bailey's?"

"Good. I wasn't sure if you'd remember me," Max said, surprised.

Smith closed his eyes for a moment. "You like to play nine-ball, but just to break up games of eight-ball. Your english is a little too low sometimes, so the cue ball doesn't have quite enough push to get your target into the pocket. You like to go for the shot at the moment, but if you sacrificed sometimes, thought more about your next one you could win more games. But you're still a hell of a player, and if you weren't honest you could hustle a few. You play with a big Mexican cowboy, and that Angel woman has a serious crush on you. I haven't been there in a while, but if you're smart and lucky it's more than a crush now." He opened his eyes.

"So. Sherlock Holmes is alive and well and living in Texas. I have, by the way. Worked as a pool hustler."

"Me too. Not much of a retirement plan. I don't guess you came down to hear me critique your game, so I figure you want to find out what I know about Joe." He saw Max's expression, and said "Not much you can't find out in here." He glanced at the guard.

"Tell me what happened."

"Joe called me, said Freddie was gonna go to the cops. He'd caught him calling, something like that. He wanted to meet at the Comanche Drive-In, on the Borger Highway. I got there as fast as I could. Freddie was in the truck, scared out of his mind, and Joe was walking around. I get there and try to smooth things out, but it was too late for that. Joe pulls Freddie out of the truck, starts after him—"

"What do you mean?"

"Joe's usual shit. Calling him a faggot, all that. He slapped him on the face. I tried to get in between them, trying not to make it worse, but Joe pushed Freddie down."

"He didn't hit Joe?"

"Freddie? Christ, no. Not 'til later. Joe was running his faggot string again, and Freddie was on the ground. Then—I don't know just what happened to him, but Freddie came up off the ground and hit Joe with a body block, knocked him down. Then Freddie turns it around on him."

"Meaning what?"

"Starts calling Joe a queer, asking him why he doesn't have any kids, like that. I could tell it was gonna be real bad then. Joe got up from the ground and went for Freddie. I tried to stop him, but he threw me down and I landed on my wrist, gave it a pretty good sprain. Joe starts kicking Freddie's ribs in, really whaling on him. Freddie gets up, and Joe's got his hand on an old bowling pin that was laying there. He slams it into Freddie's head, and Freddie just stands there for a second, and then he hits the ground."

"DOA?"

"Yeah. I went to him, checked to see. No breath, no pulse, no nothing."

"What was Joe doing?"

"Nothing. First thing, after he hit Freddie, he said 'I didn't go to kill him.' Then he sat down by one of the speaker poles. Carl came up then, and tell you the truth, I kind of forgot about Joe for a while. Carl and I talked a bit about what to do. He was for calling the cops, but I said it wouldn't be smart."

"Did Joe have any part in that?"

"No. He was out of it."

"What do you mean?"

"Just sitting there, not saying anything. Had his head resting on his knees. Finally, when we're talking about what to do with Freddie, he comes around, says he can get rid of the car. He digs a hole and we bury Freddie, then he starts talking about how Freddie called him a faggot, and all that. Seemed like he was back to himself."

Whatever that is, Max thought.

"Is there anything else you remember? Doesn't matter if it's important or not."

"Not really. But it seemed strange, him just sitting there. It's about the only time I ever seen him with his mouth shut. Usually he's swinging his dick around, telling everybody how it's going to be. But after he hit Freddie, he just sat there for a while. Didn't say a word."

"Anything else?"

"No, not really. Except uh, you know I'm on the D.A.'s witness list."

Max nodded. "You going to tell me the same story as you do them?"

"I only saw it once."

"It won't make a difference that they're giving you a deal?"

The shake of his head was barely discernible. "I don't know if there'll be much of a deal. I guess you know that D.A.? The blonde woman?"

"Yeah, I've met her a few times."

"I think she wants to send me away for a while on this one."

Max didn't know what to say. "Well, it's hard to see the big picture when it's stapled to your face. Maybe things will turn out differently."

"Stapled to your face. I'll have to remember that one," Smith said. "Anything else I can do for you?"

"I don't think so. If there is, I'll get in touch."

"I'm sure I can fit you in." He stood up and glanced at the guard, who slid off his stool.

Max opened his briefcase and started to put away his recorder and notepad. Just before Smith reached the door, Max said "Hey. Take care of yourself. Okay?"

"Doing my best." He walked out the door in front of the guard.

Max sat on a rickety porch swing, slowly pushing himself back and forth with the balls of his feet. The chains were rusty, and each swing elicited a slow squeak. Before he sat down he had surveyed the eye-screws that held the chains into the ceiling of the porch and tentatively decided it was worth a try. Now, briefcase by his side, eyes closed, he leaned back and tried to empty his mind. Through his years as a lawyer he had found that when working on complicated cases, he needed to clear his mind between interviews. He remembered seeing *Julia*, the movie about Lillian Hellman and her childhood friend. Lillian had been amazed when Julia's wealthy grandparents served sherbet between courses of a meal to "clear the palate." For Max, even a few minutes of meditation served the same purpose. It helped him to prepare himself for someone else's perspective on the same events, a perspective that might be very different than what he had already heard. It was the reason he taped his interviews, so that he could go back and hear exactly what a witness or defendant had said without having to reconstruct it from his faulty memory. Taping the conversations and clearing his mind also had another use. He had once heard someone at a meeting talk about the need to rid one's mind of harmful voices from the past. "It's no good to let those fuckers live rent-free in your head," she had said, a pissed-off sixteen year-old girl chain-smoking in her black leather jacket, her hair half shaved and dyed fuchsia, mascaraed eyes both much older and much younger than her years. She wasn't talking about law clients, but Max didn't want Joe Wagner bouncing around in his head if he could help it.

He heard a car pull into the cracked cement-slab driveway. The door shut and footsteps scuffed their way to the wooden steps. He opened his eyes, glancing at his watch. He stood as a young woman walked up onto the porch. She fumbled with her keys, and he awkwardly realized that she hadn't yet seen him. He carefully cleared his throat and said "Mrs. Wagner?"

She jumped and gasped, fear sparking in her eyes, her hand at her throat.

He kept his distance and quickly said, "It's okay. I'm Max Friedman, your husband's attorney. I called you last night, remember?"

She glanced vaguely at the driveway and said "I didn't see your car . . . ."

"No, it's on the street, right there," he said, pointing at the red Honda.

"Oh. Well, I'm real sorry I'm late. Uh, would you like to come in?"

"That would be good, thanks." He gave her a moment to unlock the wooden door and walk through it before he crossed to the screen door. She was already a few feet into the room when Max entered, and he kept enough distance for her to feel safe. He looked around the room as if asking permission to sit.

"You can sit on the couch if you want," she said.

He smiled and sat down, busying himself with his briefcase. "Thank you. If it's not too much trouble, Mrs. Wagner, do you think you might be able to make a cup of coffee for me? I'm slowing down a little bit, and that might pick me up."

"Why, sure," she said. "I could use some myself. Be a couple of minutes."

"Take your time."

She walked through an arched doorway into the kitchen, where Max could hear her running water in the sink. He looked around the room. It was neat and clean, but not kept up. It needed paint, and there was an absence of light. He glanced at the window and saw that the curtains were drawn. The walls had a yellowish tinge to them, and Max was suddenly reminded of his parents' apartment in Park Slope, Brooklyn, the four rooms where he had lived until he was sixteen. The house felt just as absent of care, of love, as had the place that Joseph and Norma Friedman had called home.

In a few minutes Max smelled the comforting aroma of coffee wafting in from the kitchen. He really did want some, but he also wanted Darlene Wagner to get used to the idea of him, to know that he was safe before she had to actually sit and talk to him.

She leaned her head and shoulders around the doorway and said "You like anything in it?"

"No, just straight." In a moment she walked back into the room, carrying a mug in each hand. She carefully placed his on a crocheted coaster on the coffee table in front of him and sat in a faded floral pattern wing-back. Max picked up his coffee and blew on it.

"I have one of those that will pause when you pull the thing out, the what's it called—?"

"The carafe?" Max suggested.

Two furrows appeared between her eyebrows. "Is that what's it called? That doesn't seem right, for some reason. I want to call it a coffee pot, but that's not really right either." She grew silent. Max thought she looked young, but the circles under her eyes and her solemn expression made her seem older. She wore a knee-length skirt over stockings and flat brown shoes. She was pretty in a small-town, shy way. He wondered if anyone had ever told her that. He sipped the coffee.

"This is good," he said, not lying.

"Thanks." She looked down into her own mug of the black liquid, steam rising up from it.

"I have a few questions for you, Mrs. Wagner, if you're ready."

She glanced at his eyes and then down at the floor. "I guess I am. I don't know if I'll ever be ready to answer questions about did my husband murder somebody."

"I understand." He unsnapped his briefcase. "Do you mind if I record what we say, just so I can remember it?"

Her nod was barely perceptible. Max set the recorder on the coffee table. "Mrs. Wagner, did you know Freddie Odom?"

"No, sir. I hadn't heard of him until he come on the news. His name, I mean."

"Do you think he was one of your husband's friends?"

She cupped both of her hands around the mug and pulled her shoulders in closer to her body. "I don't know if Joe really has any friends, sir."

"You don't have to call me sir." He realized that the woman he was talking to was trying her best to hide from him, and at the same time wanting to answer his questions. "When you say you don't know if he has any friends, can you explain for me?"

"Joe doesn't really talk much. To me. We don't really go out or anything, you know. I mean, he goes out a lot, but I'm not sure where or what he does. Sometimes he'll say something about being at Bailey's—that's a pool hall—or one of the dance places, but he doesn't really talk about anybody."

"How about when he's at home? Does he get many calls?"

"Our phone don't ring much."

"Have you ever heard the name Smith Dixon?" She shook her head. "How about Carl Puente?"

Her eyes lit up for a moment. "My folks got him to do some drapes for them when I was in high school."

"Has Joe ever talked about him?"

"No," she said. "Why would he?"

"When your parents hired Carl, was that before you met Joe, or did you already know him?"

"No, I didn't yet. I grew up over in Claude. That's a little ways out on the highway. I met him after I was already out of the house."

"How about Joe's family, Mrs. Wagner? Do you know them? Did they come to your wedding?"

She cleared her throat and turned it into an embarrassed laugh. "Oh, we didn't really have a big deal. Just went down to the courthouse, and had the J.P. do it. He wore a suit, Joe did, and give me a ring. We had a couple of friends there with us."

"Your families?"

Darlene tugged the hem of her skirt down and straightened it. "My family doesn't much care for Joe. They didn't come."

"Why don't they care for him?"

"Oh, when I took him out there a couple of times, back home I mean, they never warmed up to his ways. He and Daddy got mad at each other one time, and Joe wouldn't go back and Daddy told me not to bring him."

"What did they get mad about?"

"Joe was talking about how the valves on Daddy's truck didn't sound right. He said it must've been a piss poor job of working on them, and Daddy said oh yeah, it was him done them, and it went worse from there. And then a couple of times Joe went to jail for fighting, and I called them up for money to get him out. Daddy said they'd give it to me if I'd leave him. I said no, but they give it to me anyway. But they haven't talked to me since then, neither. You want some more coffee?"

"If it's no trouble." She stood up and took the mug into the kitchen, returning a minute later.

"How about Joe's family?" Max said.

"His folks are dead. That happened before I met him. He's never talked about them other than to say that."

"Any brothers or sisters?"

Hey eyebrows furrowed again and she cocked her head. "Now isn't that funny? I haven't thought about her in a while."

"He has a sister?"

"Yeah," she said slowly. "One time we was over at Whistler's to get a hamburger, they got real good ones there, and I saw that Joe had a real funny look on his face. He was looking off behind me, and I saw this woman. She was dressed real nice, had short hair you could tell she put money into coloring it and everything. She kind of looked funny too, but she came over to our table. Joe, he kind of nodded his head at her, but it was like he didn't really want to look her in the eyes. He was looking everywhere but at her."

"Did she say anything to him?"

"Yeah. She said 'How are you Joe?' something like that and he said okay. She was a real pretty woman, and I thought she looked real sophisticated. She said 'I haven't seen you in a long time.' He didn't say anything, and then she said 'He's dead, you know that?' Joe looked at her real quick and said 'Yeah, I heard.' She said 'I'd like to see you some time.' He didn't say anything, just nodded his head, and she kind of just walked away. When she'd left I said Joe, who was that, and he just looked down at his plate and said that was his sister."

"Did she say anything to you? Look at you at all?"

"No. I think she was crying when she left. A few nights later, though, she called while Joe was out. I told her who I was, that I was his wife, and we just talked a little bit. Seemed like she was really uncomfortable."

"Do you know her name?"

"She told me her name was Evelyn Morton."

"Did she tell you where she lived?"

Her eyes squinted in concentration. "I remember when Joe and me were first together, he used to talk more. He never talked much about his childhood, but I remember him saying he was from Loving. I don't think she said so, but I got the feeling that she was living back there."

"Is that a town?"

"Uh huh. It's out west of here."

"Did Joe ever say anything about a pinto pony? Does that mean anything to you?" She thought for a moment and slowly shook her head.

"No," she said. "My uncle had a couple of pintos, but a lot of people do."

"What exactly is a 'pinto' horse, Mrs. Wagner? A child's toy, something like that?"

She smiled, genuinely, for the first time since he had surprised her on the porch. The years flew from her face. "No. It's you know, a horse with spots. They're white with brown spots or brown with white spots. Sometimes black. That's all it is."

"Ah." Max sighed, embarrassed. An image of Angel's horse Nightfall entered his head, and he reminded himself to look in the dictionary before he asked another stupid question.

"Mrs. Wagner, is there anything you can tell me that might help? Do you have any idea why Joe might have killed a man?"

She shrugged her shoulders and picked at the crocheted doily her coffee cup rested on.

"Any reason at all, Mrs. Wagner?"

She glanced up at him and back down at the table. "If he got mad enough, is all I can think of."

Well, that's a reason, Max thought. And a not uncommon one at that.

"I think that's about it for now," he said. He picked up the recorder and put it into his bag. "Thank you for the coffee."

She nodded. He glanced at her face and could see that she was trying to form a question. "Is there something else?" he asked.

"Not really. I mean, I was wondering, how'd you come to be his lawyer? We don't have any money we can pay you."

"You won't have to, Mrs. Wagner. I've been appointed by the court. The county pays me."

"To keep him from going to jail?"

"That's my job, yes."

She pursed her lips together for a moment and looked at him. "How hard are you going to try?"

The air was still warm when he walked out to his car, Darlene Wagner standing on the porch and watching him go, obviously because it was the polite thing to do. It wasn't that she didn't like him; he could tell that. She just didn't know what to do with him. A long-haired lawyer with a funny accent sitting on her couch and asking why her husband might have murdered someone was not her typical evening's activity.

The sun was completely gone when he pulled into the parking lot of the Pac-N-Sac, and when he opened the door he was surprised to feel a nip in the air. The weather would keep surprising him here as long as he stayed. He reminded himself that it was December already, despite the temperatures each afternoon near seventy. The sun was at rest every day by 6:00, and it didn't take long at all for the cold to follow. Some nights it was reaching down to the mid-thirties, a change of almost forty degrees in less than twelve hours. He reached into the back seat of the Honda, grateful that he had remembered to bring his windbreaker.

At the corner of the building, to the right of the door, a lone pay phone hung on the brick wall. He walked over to it, knowing that he wouldn't find anything important. He stood by the phone, picked up the receiver, and put it between his shoulder and ear. He wondered if Freddie Odom had faced the parking lot. Probably not. It was more likely that he would try to hide, and Max turned his body to face the chain-link fence on that side of the store. Joe could have walked up behind Freddie with no warning that way.

Max had talked to Champ Phillips, who although clear on the details of the conversation couldn't provide much. The phone call had been too brief, Freddie just saying that he had information for him. The call had ended abruptly. Max knew that was when Joe had put his finger onto the depressor.

Max walked into the store under the garish green and yellow neon lights. It was like any of the other convenience stores that seemed to be on half of the street corners in Amarillo. They weren't even much different than the ones scattered around Brooklyn, Queens, and New Jersey. The color of the kids working in them was usually different, but Max felt the same desperation in them, as though it was perpetually 3:00 a.m. inside, no matter that the sun might be shining on the parking lot.

He glanced around the aisles, all four of them, and his eyes were caught by a coffee machine, the pots sitting seductively on their burners. He was still warm from the coffee Darlene Wagner had served him, but another cup would never hurt. He walked to the stack of cups and saw something that startled him. It was a small machine with three buttons over plastic tubes. The letters at the top of the machine said "Cappuccino," and underneath the letters was a photograph of a cup of that same delightful concoction, complete with foam and a cinnamon stick.

Max had drunk an ocean of cappuccino during the past ten years, after he had stopped drinking alcohol and went to school. More than an hour of studying his textbooks or listening to a professor was bound to send him into a doze, and he always made sure to have a cup of coffee with him before entering class. Often when he studied he sat at a corner table at La Lanterna di Vittorio, a coffee house on McDougal Street. It was quiet, and he liked to watch the seasons pass through the postage-stamp garden in back. He sat by the window in spring when the aroma of the carefully tended herbs wafted in through the window and mated with the strong smell of cappuccino and espresso. In the winter he often lost himself in the snowflakes that drifted down onto the garden. The cappuccino came from a huge copper octopus of a machine, its arms steaming and sizzling every time the waiter placed a white porcelain cup underneath.

So how could they sell cappuccino from a box of a machine with three small white plastic spouts? He took one of the cups, held it under a spout, and pressed the button. What foamed out into his cup looked more like hot chocolate than cappuccino, and when he sipped it, the sugary liquid burned the top of his mouth and coated his tongue. He almost spit it onto the front of his jacket and closed his mouth, burning it even worse. Still, some of it dribbled through his lips and he glanced around. No one had seen. He took a napkin from the metal dispenser and wiped his mouth and chin. He made a mental note: never buy cappuccino from a gas station, no matter how authentic the photograph looks.

He talked to the clerk, a lanky white kid who looked like he might be a college basketball player. When shown a photo of Freddie, he remembered seeing him in the store "a hell of a lot. He'd usually come in and gas up, get some chips and beer—you know. Usual stuff." He couldn't remember if Freddie had been there on November 4th. Joe's face wasn't familiar to him.

Chapter 25

Bailey's was bustling but not frantic. The room was three quarters full with a mix of regulars and college kids. Angel offered a smile to him along with the rack of balls she placed on the counter.

"Hey," she said.

"Hey yourself."

"How's your new client?" She pushed her hair behind her ear.

"As sunny and pleasant as usual."

"Are we likely to see him back in here any time soon?"

"I guess that depends on how good a job his lawyer does."

"How good do you think his lawyer's going to do?"

"His very best, I would think. Equal protection, and all that."

"Well, speaking for all of us at Bailey's, as concerned citizens of Amarillo, we'd like to see him not come back in here for the next hundred years or so."

"Speaking as a Bailey's regular, I'd like the same thing. Speaking as his lawyer and a vow-taking upholder of the Constitution, I'm going to give him the best defense he can possibly have."

Angel set an iced glass of Coke in front of him. "How good is that defense going to have to be?"

"Funny, but his wife asked me the same thing not two hours ago."

"He's married? If I had a prayer list, I'd put her on it."

"Maybe you need to make one just for her. By the way, do you know where Loving is?"

"Yeah, it's a little town west of here, toward New Mexico but not near as far. How come?"

"That's where he's from. I'll probably have to go up there to get some information."

"Lucky you. Kind of ironic, don't you think?"

"What do you mean?"

"Joe Wagner being from a place called Loving."

"Ah."

Angel reached under the bar, and her hand came back with a cue ball. She cupped her palm around it and rolled it against the counter.

"Can I ask you a question?"

"Of course."

"Is this something you really have to do? Defend him, I mean."

Max leaned his arm on the counter and glanced around at the tables. "I probably could have said no. It's not unheard of. But it's kind of an unwritten code. You just don't do it. There are a lot of ways a judge can use that as an excuse to get you by the short-hairs in future cases. I don't know that this particular judge would have done it, but . . . . Long story short, I guess I think Joe needs a good defense. As much as we all think he's an asshole and want to say good riddance, I can't let that cloud the fact that the law guarantees him one."

Angel cashed out two college guys. "You'd better be careful of the way you talk. Don't want people thinking you're a liberal, or something."

"A little too late for that, I'm afraid."

"Got that part right."

He nodded. "So what kind of a name is Loving for a town? Who thought it up?"

"Named after an old cattle baron, Oliver Loving. He and his partner, Charles Goodnight, even got a trail named after them. The Goodnight-Loving Trail. They both got towns, too, that come close to blowing away every time there's a sandstorm." She looked around the room. "When're you going?"

"Tomorrow, I think."

"You want me to go with you, kind of be an interpreter?"

"No, I think I'll do okay on my own. I've been learning the language pretty well lately."

"Drive my truck, if you want. It could give you some authenticity."

"Probably what it would give me is a sentence for auto theft. No way they'd ever believe I had it legally."

"Well, at least I made the offer. Which I think was pretty big of me, considering who your client is."

"Thanks," Max said.

"Think fast," Angel said, and leaning toward him, brushed his lips lightly with hers. Then she glanced around the room to see if anyone might have noticed.

"And thank you again," Max said. "Aren't you afraid of hurting your reputation?"

"Hell, if anybody saw it they'll be too damn scared to say anything. I might eighty-six them, and then what would they do every night? Stay at home with their wives, or maybe study for their classes? Fate worse than death."

"The thought makes me shudder," Max agreed.

The next morning, after Max had carefully extricated himself from the sleeping cats in his bed, he showered and drank half the pot of coffee that had started brewing fifteen minutes before he woke up. He ran his finger around the edge of his coffee mug. In a few minutes he heard the slow clicking of nails on tiles, and saw the two cats drifting sleepily into the room. Jersey announced his presence with a short "yerp," and jumped from the floor to a chair to the table. Mayella followed him and sniffed at the coffee. When Jersey moved next to her to inspect the strange smell, she gave him a warning swat and he skittered away, startled and offended. When he got a foot away, he started methodically licking himself as if he wasn't the least bit intimidated and had forgotten the whole incident anyway.

Max rubbed his hand thoughtfully over Mayella's long silky fur. Underneath her left arm he found a sizable clump of matted hair and made a reminder to himself to trim it later that night, when he got back from Loving.

Loving. He realized that was the reason that he wasn't already out the door, why he was dawdling over a cup of coffee. Despite his belief that Joe needed a defense, Max wasn't enthusiastic about the prospect of tracking down his life in some little town. He had grown comfortable in Amarillo, although sometimes the stare of a tall cowboy with unconscious anger etched into every line of his face made him feel very vulnerable and in danger. He realized he was scared. He thought of calling Angel and asking her to go with him, but he didn't know how long he would be gone and knew that she would have to find someone to open Bailey's for her. Or just open late, as she sometimes did. Max realized that he didn't want to ask her because he didn't want her to think less of him. He tried to evict the thought from his head, telling himself that it was ridiculous, calling it stupid macho bullshit, but the voice remained. He picked up the phone and called Danny Gonzalez, but there was no answer.

Screw it, he thought. What are they going to do, string me up? Throw me in jail? For Christ's sake, I can call another lawyer and be out by nightfall. I can—he laughed, realizing what he was doing. Living in the wreckage of the future, trying to make up shit that probably wouldn't happen. Trying to create a crisis when there was none in sight. All he had to do was drive out to this little town, ask some questions, and listen to the answers.

Max made sure the cats had enough food and water and put on his jacket. Picking up his briefcase, he stepped out of the front door and onto the narrow balcony. A cold wind whipped around the corner of the building, stinging his cheeks and eyes. He locked the door and went down to his car.

The easiest route from Max's apartment to Loving was Amarillo Boulevard, which cuts through the northern part of the city before turning to the south and joining I-40. The Boulevard was part of Route 66, the road which brought the residents of the Dust Bowl from the blowing sand and dirt that was all that was left of their farms, to California, the land of opportunity. Max didn't know what it had looked like then, but he suspected that some of the motels, most of them closed now or home only to vagrants, were thriving businesses when the stream of cars started cutting the Panhandle from east to west. Now the street was Amarillo's Skid Row, littered with convenience stores, strip joints, body shops, tattoo parlors, greasy spoons, liquor stores, ramshackle houses, cigarette shacks, and tamale trailers. With more frequency than he would have thought, he saw Vietnamese restaurants, often next door to chili or barbecue joints whose signs featured cowboys dressed in bandannas, wearing stupid grins and holding bowls or plates of food. It was strange, Max thought, that the city's oldest and newest cultures lived side-by-side in its most run-down section. If time were money, the cowboys would be living in mansions, not subsisting in a ghetto. He wondered how they felt, living next to people who not so long ago were considered enemies of the country, people whom they would eagerly have killed in the name of patriotism.

Max stopped for a light and saw a twenty foot long piece of yellow plastic tape dance across the road in front of him. "Police Line—Do Not Cross," it read over and over. On the right side of the street was a strip joint called The Crystal Pistol. The faded, weathered sign showed a cowgirl dressed in fringe and little else blowing the smoke from her gun, staring seductively at the passers-by. The crime scene tape was blowing from that general direction, and Max wondered if there had been a shooting or stabbing in the parking lot. He knew from arraignment days it wasn't an uncommon occurrence; at least twice a month a man would appear before the judge, head hanging, staring at his feet, and either plead innocent or guilty of shooting, stabbing, or beating someone else, no doubt equally hangdog, at the Crystal Pistol. They were invariably drunk at the time, invariably desperate, invariably poor.

The light turned green, and Max slowly cruised through it. A woman wrapped in layers of rags picked through a dumpster, occasionally placing an item into the already laden shopping cart by her side. He still found it disconcerting, seeing homeless people in Amarillo. They had been a fixture of New York's history for centuries, perhaps from the beginning of the city itself. But it was another of those myths he had believed about the West. Texas, he had thought, would have no homeless populations. Neither would Arizona or

New Mexico. Los Angeles certainly had the homeless, but in his mind it wasn't the West. It was a country of its own definition, and no more a part of the real West than was New York. Max laughed to himself, remembering a college literature class where he discovered that Cooper's novels of the West were set in New York State. Probably the only constant in the world is our misconceptions, he thought, and the inevitability of them.

After a few minutes he left behind the sagging excess of the Boulevard for the flat winter grayness of the plains. He had never been this way from the town before. He and Angel had made a couple of trips into the Canyon, and his work had taken him north and east, but not west. After a few miles the flatness gave way to some rolling hills and arroyos. He saw a few rabbits hopping away from the road, and once, just heading over the top of a hill to the north, he thought he glimpsed a deer.

Thirty-five miles west of Amarillo he turned north on a state highway. According to his directions, Loving was about fifteen miles along this road, a lonely two-lane. Occasionally another car or truck passed him heading south, and once he thought he would have a heart attack when a big diesel pick-up truck smoothly cruised around him, going at least eighty. Max hadn't seen it in his rear-view mirror, hadn't even been aware that it was within fifty miles of him until it passed. The driver glanced over and nodded his head once. Max nodded back.

In a few minutes he saw the outline of a small town in the distance. If this had been New England, it wouldn't have appeared until he was practically upon it, but here there were precious few trees to conceal its existence. Max passed a faded wooden sign that depicted an old-fashioned tramp clown of the Emmet Kelly variety. He had a silly grin on his face and was lying on the ground, a bottle in his hand. At the bottom of the sign was painted "Final Product Of the Brewer's Art."

Can't argue with you on that one, he thought. In another mile was a sign that said "Loving, Texas: Let Us Into Your Heart."

Just past the sign, to the right of the highway, were a dozen old house trailers. None of them were new and few looked livable, but there were cars around most of them, and they did not strike him as abandoned. Max wondered what the collective noun for trailers was. A scattering? A rusting of trailers?

There were three traffic lights in the town, and they wobbled in the grasp of the north wind. Max drove around the little town and located the small Art-Deco county courthouse.

He wandered the corridors until he found the County Clerk's office. On his way down the hall he passed a tall, lean man who was close to 60 and obviously the county sheriff. He had the raw, sandpaper skin that most of the area's lifelong residents seemed to get by the time they reach that age. The man's khaki uniform was immaculately pressed, and on his right hip rode a leather holster that was threaded through the loops in his belt. In the holster was a pistol that looked to be a .38 caliber. The man nodded at Max.

He spent twenty minutes in the clerk's office. The clerk herself was working the counter and was more than happy to help him. Max had been concerned that she would freeze up at the sight of his ponytail, but she smiled graciously, treating him as if he were a lost little puppy. When he left he had a short stack of papers to peruse.

He stopped at the sheriff's office and spoke to the receptionist, who told him that the sheriff was in the courthouse across the street and would be back soon. Max had barely finished inspecting the photographs on the walls, a gallery of grip-and-grin poses with local dignitaries, when the man he had passed in the courthouse opened the chrome and glass door. He smiled at the receptionist, who glanced in Max's direction. The sheriff offered him a smile and a handshake.

"Yes sir, can I help you?"

Max told him that he was trying to do some background research on a client, Joe Wagner, and wondered whether Sheriff Hoskins might be able to help him.

"Joe Wagner, huh? Don't know if I can help you much, but I'll be happy to talk to you. Step into my office." Max thought it was the first time he'd heard anyone say that about a real office; usually it meant "walk over here and we'll talk in private."

The sheriff's office was decorated with more photographs and two deer heads, their eyes staring dully at each other across the room.

The sheriff reached behind him and pulled a glass coffee carafe from its burner. He raised his eyebrows at Max, who said "Please." As the sheriff poured, he said "This is about that business over there in Amarillo?"

Max nodded.

"I figured. Afraid there's not much I can say that will help you there. By the time I was elected, Joe was already gone. I was working in private business then, managing the phone co-op here, so I never had much truck with him."

"Did he have any kind of reputation? Good, bad, troublemaker? Arrest record?"

"I'll have Dana run up his record for you. When he got arrested on this deal I looked it up. Wasn't too much there. Mostly piddly little fights. Couple vandalisms, stealing hubcaps, drunk and disorderly, stuff like that. He didn't graduate high school, and I think he left town before he was eighteen. Most people said 'good riddance,' I gather."

He leaned back in his chair and craned his neck so that he could see into the outer office. "Dana, could you run me a record for Joe Wagner?"

Max faintly heard her say "Yes sir."

"I also understand he has a sister here in town," he said.

The lines between the sheriff's eyebrows wrinkled. "Is that right?"

"I believe her name is Evelyn Morton."

The sheriff put a hand to his head and lightly scratched his widening part. "You sure you got that name right?"

"Why?"

"Well, it just don't seem like—damn, I wouldn't have thought, ... I guess if he told you that he'd be the one to know, but it just doesn't seem likely. Her husband is the president of the city credit union. She teaches business classes over at the high school. You wouldn't want to meet a more professional-looking woman. Looks like she could be a banker herself. Huh. Seems like if she had a brother I'd have known it. Course I'm older than them, but you think I'd have known anyway."

The front door of the office opened, and a voice said "Morning, Dana." Max heard the dispatcher say "Hi, Paul. You get it taken care of?"

A deputy walked into the sheriff's office, and said "Yeah, sure did," before he noticed Max. He took off his dark gray cowboy hat, and said "I'm sorry, I didn't know you had—"

"That's okay," the sheriff said. "Relax. What was it you were working on?"

"Little fender-bender on the Dalhart highway. I just need to write it up."

"Paul, this is—I'm sorry, I'm terrible with names."

Max stood and extended his hand. "Max Friedman."

"Deputy Paul Hunter. Good to meet you."

"Paul's daddy was sheriff here for only about thirty years, and looks like Paul will follow in his footsteps if I ever retire or he runs against me." Max nodded and smiled at the small talk. "Say Paul," the sheriff said, "did you go to school with Evelyn Morton?"

"Sure."

"Did you know she had a brother?"

Hunter's face had been open and friendly, but it instantly turned guarded. "I bet you're an attorney from Amarillo."

"That's right."

"It's funny, but I'd kind of forgotten about it. Joe and Evelyn being brother and sister. I graduated twenty-three years ago. She was in the same class. When I saw about Joe being arrested, a couple of days later I ran into her in the Cashway supermarket. I asked her if she'd known Joe Wagner, and a real funny look came over her. It took me a couple of seconds to remember that he was her little brother. I'd really put my foot into it, I guess."

"Why had you forgotten?"

"You never would think of them as being related. She has some class, and that's one thing you never would've said about him. Course, back then she didn't have the money and the clothes she has now. She was poor, but she wasn't trashy, like he always was."

"Did you say she teaches at the high school?"

"Yeah, she's been over there for oh, I'm gonna say at least ten years. Maybe more."

"Do they have any other relatives here in town? Parents, cousins?"

The sheriff looked at his deputy, who slowly shook his head. "No, I don't think so," the sheriff said. "Seems to me their folks are both gone. I don't really remember anything about them, anyway."

Max glanced between them. "Is there anything else you can tell me about Joe that might be important? Anything at all?"

The sheriff thought for a moment before he said "No, that's about it."

"Deputy Hunter?"

The deputy shook his head. Max stood up and shook hands with them.

"If I think of any other questions, can I call you?"

"You bet," the sheriff said, and slid a business card out of a ceramic holder decorated with a cowboy hat and boots. "This is our number here; just call anytime you need to." He smiled. "You may not find many folks around here very interested in helping out Joe Wagner. Well hell, you know him. He ain't the friendliest type."

Max nodded. "The record for him . . .?"

"Oh yeah, Dana will have it for you up front." He stuck out his big hand toward Max. "Good to meet you, Mr.—don't tell me now." His brows furrowed. "Mr. Friedman?"

Max smiled and nodded again. "Good," the sheriff said. "Maybe I'm not getting as old as I think sometimes. You take care now, and let us know if there's anything we can do."

"I will. Thank you, Sheriff." Max left the office, glancing at a cluster of darts circled perfectly, like a bouquet of flowers, in the center of a red and black target opposite the sheriff's desk. He wondered for a moment if the man had thrown them all that perfectly and decided it was impossible. On his way out he picked up the arrest record from Dana and looked at the phone book. He wrote down Evelyn Morton's address and phone number and the address of the high school.

Max pushed through the glass doors. The day was bright, and he turned his back to the sun, a gesture that was unnecessary in Manhattan, but now was becoming second nature. The report was two pages stapled and revealed nothing more than the sheriff had said—possession by a minor, fighting, breaking out the window of the Western Auto store and tripping the alarm. He was arrested after the doctor who treated his cut hand called the former sheriff. There were notations in his report about fights in junior high and high school— not criminal offenses, but signs to the sheriff that he was someone to keep an eye on.

Max found his way back to his car and drove to a convenience store where he slid a quarter into the pay phone slot and pushed Evelyn Morton's number. He called on the off chance that she had stayed out of school for the day, but a machine picked up and he didn't leave a message.

Max drove slowly around the streets. The town had two banks, one of them called the Cattlemen's First National. The downtown consisted of three blocks; half of the storefronts were empty, and he noticed there were no competing stores. Each business was the only one of its kind. One auto store, one lumberyard. A drugstore. A department store. A barber shop. One pool hall that looked much less inviting than Bailey's. The windows were dirty, and the letters that said "Pool Billiards Foosball Air Hockey" were faded almost to illegibility. Max wondered how often businesses had to repaint, with the gritty sand working away at them during the winter and spring.

The only businesses with more than one representative were restaurants and convenience stores. Max realized that he was hungry and glanced up and down both sides of the three blocks. One Mexican restaurant, something that looked like a doughnut shop, and a small storefront whose sign read "Renee's Roundup Café." He was afraid that if he ate Mexican food in a small town he would suffer from grease overload for a week, and he needed something more substantial than donuts. He glanced ahead and in the rearview mirror, and the closest car was a block away. He made a U-turn and slid into an angled space in front of the café.

A cowbell over the door jangled when he opened it. Five brown leatherette booths lined the right side of the room, and down the center was a row of tables and chairs that might have lived a previous life in a seafood restaurant. The tables were empty except for three that were pushed together in the center of the room. Nine men sat around them, a wreath of cigarette smoke hovering above their heads. Cowboy hats were settled onto most of the heads, although several bore feed-store caps. They all stopped talking when Max entered, and their eyes tracked him toward the back booth where he slid in facing them. They began to glance away and resumed their conversations. Two menus were stuck between the wall and the condiment holder. He took one out and scanning it, decided to order pancakes. A waitress appeared next to him and without asking poured coffee into the thick, white china cup.

"You know what you want yet, hon?" she asked.

When Max ordered the pancakes, she said "Oh, now have you ever tried 'em with pecans?" He admitted that he hadn't, and she said "Well, that's about to change. Anything else? Some grits?"

Although Max had heard of grits he really had no idea of what they were, but before he could tell her that she scribbled something on her pad and went away. Ten minutes later she returned with two pancakes that, sewn together, could have made a slip cover for a bowling ball. The grits steamed in a small white bowl. Max tentatively dipped the tip of a spoon into them, and when the grits touched his tongue he closed his eyes and smiled at the thought of himself, a New York lawyer, eating a quintessential Southern dish in a cold, dusty, Texas Panhandle town, and feeling at home.

As he worked his way through the pecan pancakes and grits, he read the papers the county clerk had copied for him. Joseph Randall Wagner was born on September 24, 1964, the son of Samuel Payton "Buddy" Wagner, and his wife, Helen Joy Stokes Wagner. The couple had a daughter, Evelyn Marie, born March 17, 1958. The family lived on 125 acres nine miles west of town, where Buddy raised cattle and grew sunflowers. A charge of child abuse against Buddy was dismissed on July 19, 1969. No reason listed. Buddy sold off small pieces of acreage over the years, until at his death in 1985 only thirty-five acres were left. His wife died two years later of heart failure. Buddy Wagner's cause of death was listed as testicular cancer.

The court record didn't say which child he was accused of abusing before the charges were dropped, or what form the alleged abuse had taken.

"You look like you're studying for a test." The waitress topped off his cup of coffee.

"Just doing a little research."

"On what?" She craned her neck to look at the papers.

"A man named Joe Wagner, who used to live here."

"What are you studying him for?"

"Do you know him?"

"It's a small town, hon. You live here long enough you know most of the folks."

"You're too young to have lived anywhere a long time."

"I don't know if that's a compliment, but I'll take it anyway. Besides, I'm only fourteen years old." Her face was deadpan for a moment, before a wry smile broke out. "Times three."

"Are you Reneé?"

"I wish. If I owned this place, I sure wouldn't be workin' in it. My name's Wanda." She wiped her right hand on her jeans, and extended it. "Hang on a second, let me put this down." She crossed to the kitchen, disappeared with the coffee pot, and returned in a moment with a full cup. "Mind if I sit down?"

"Please. But what about your other customers?"

"Those old goats will sit here all morning and tip a quarter each, if they're feeling rich. They can pour their own coffee." She slid into the booth. "So what're you taking a test on Joe Wagner for?"

He smiled. "Not a test, exactly, but I am studying him. I'm representing him in a trial."

"Kinda figured that was it." She poured sugar and cream into the cup and blew on it gently.

"What do you remember about Joe?"

"Being scared of him. Not wanting to ever be alone with him."

"Why not?"

"You're his lawyer?"

Max nodded.

"You've met him, then. You can answer that question yourself."

Max sipped his coffee and took a bite of the pancakes. One of the farmers at the table looked in their direction and held up his cup. She ignored him, and soon he creaked from his chair and poured his own.

Wanda wrapped her hands around the cup, absorbing its warmth. "Joe was always wanting to be a tough guy. Always wanting to pick fights, calling the other kids fags and queers, picking on little kids. I know I'm from a small town, but I don't like that kind of talk. I believe in live and let live, you know what I mean?"

"Sure. Do you know his sister?"

"Mrs. Evelyn Morton?" She smiled wryly. "Yeah. I knew her when she was Evvy Wagner, too."

"Do you ever see her?"

She smiled again, and this time the wryness was ironic. "She and I don't move in the same circles, if you know what I mean. She doesn't come in here." Her eyes took in the homey but sad furnishings. "I bet when she goes out to eat she drives to Amarillo or Clovis."

Max got back in his car and drove slowly down the main street of the town. All three traffic lights swayed in the wind that was blowing from the north. He found the high school without much trouble, and parked in a space marked "visitor." The school was low-slung and long, perched at the top of a hill—the only one Max had seen in the town. The windows were all enclosed in a way that didn't blend with the beige brick the building was made of. It was obvious that a contractor with no imagination had installed air-conditioning.

He asked a young girl in the office, a student helper, if Ms. Morton was available. Looking with obvious fascination at his hair, she shook her head. "No, sir. She's already had her conference, and she ain't going to have any free time until after school."

He asked if there was somewhere that he could find a collection of school yearbooks, and she directed him down the hall to the library. It was sparsely occupied by five students, a middle-aged librarian shelving books, and a man who looked like a teacher asleep in a great leather chair. Occasionally he waved his hand near his face as if attempting to swat a fly, and then mumbled to himself too low for Max to hear.

He asked the librarian where he could find the yearbooks, and in a few moments had seven of them spread out on the table in front of him. The first was for the 1972-73 school year. He looked up Evelyn Wagner in the back of the book and found her listed as Evvy. Her only activities were Choir and Art Club. There were three page numbers next to her name, and Max marked the index with his finger and flipped backward to page 71, the first of the references. The page consisted of freshman class photos. The students were still adolescents, fourteen or fifteen year old. The boys were smooth-faced, some chubby with baby fat, and some gawky with Adam's apples that their faces had not yet caught up with. The girls looked more mature as a rule, in the way that girls grow up more quickly than boys. He ran his finger down the list of names, many of them Hispanic, and the rest ones that would seldom be found in the Brooklyn neighborhoods Max had grown up in. Magby. Kimbrough. Buckner. Kimmel. Wagner. Evvy's name was third in a list of five, and he glanced over to the third photograph, barely the size of a postage stamp. The girl who stared out at him seemed much more mature than her fellow freshmen. Her hair was light brown or dark blonde, as far as the black and white would allow him to imagine. She looked straight into the camera, seeming neither happy nor sad but just neutrally gazing at the lens, the slightest hint of a smile curling her lips. She was a little heavier than average, though not fat. He glanced back at the index page and found the two other listings for her. In one she was bent over an art table with a set of watercolors, her hair—Max could see now that it was long—hanging over her face, obscuring her expression. The third photograph was of the choir, Evvy standing on the second of three tiers. She's tall, Max thought. Taller than the other girls and most of the boys, but not for long.

Max set the book aside and picked up the second volume. Evvy Wagner was on four pages this year. Her sophomore class photograph was similar to the previous year's. Her hair looked not quite clean, and she stared at the camera with the same blank eyes and slight smile. She might have been wearing the same blouse. Max couldn't tell. She was still in the Art Club, but this time absent from the choir. Instead, she appeared on the page designated for the Future Homemakers of America, and in a shot of a pep rally. She stood surrounded by other girls, with no boys near the clique. Max looked at the photographs once more and shut the book. As he reached for the next volume, the pounding of feet sounded in the corridor outside the library. In the distance Max could hear a marching band play a song he couldn't make out. It was a steady thrum of percussion and a metallic blare of horns. In the corridor the voices grew louder in the cadence of chants. The five students in the library stacked their books together and left. On the way out, one of them touched the sleeping man on the shoulder and dashed out. He stirred awake and looked around, rubbing a hand over his forehead and down to his chin. He took Max in, obviously wondering what time it was, and why a stranger with long hair was sitting at a table that should contain only students. "Pep rally," he said, by way of explanation. Then he pushed to his feet, his hands braced against the chair's arms, and shambled into the hallway. Only the librarian and Max were left.

He opened the third yearbook. Evvy's life had changed very little, it seemed. She was still in FHA and Art, and this time there was a photograph of her on the bus on an Art Club trip to Galveston. She and three other girls mugged for the camera, large grins on their faces, index fingers held to imagined dimples in their cheeks, as a way of saying "Aren't I cute?" They were, he thought. Evvy showed more personality than in the other photographs; there was even a sparkle in her eye. Another showed her on the beach in a modest one-piece bathing suit. She was still tall, but the boys had caught up with her and her height would not be thought unusual.

Max closed the book, put it to the side, picked up the next year's volume, and Evvy was—gone. No trace of her. He looked in the index and found no mention of her name. He looked through the senior class portraits, the Art Club page, the FHA. The choir. Evvy Wagner had disappeared. He dug under the stack of books and found the county records he had copied at the courthouse. Buddy Wagner had died in 1985, and Helen in 1987. Evvy should have still been in school, in fact should have graduated in 1976. She could have dropped out—after all, hadn't Max himself done that? But it didn't seem to fit the image he had formed of the well-dressed business teacher the sheriff and Wanda the waitress had described. Nonetheless, she was simply not in the yearbook. He put it aside and picked up the volume marked "1979-80."

There was one reference for Joe Wagner, his freshman portrait. The school had brought in a photographer who took everyone's photo in one day. They were not imaginative or professional, as were the ones of the seniors who had gone to outside studios. Joe's photo was just a younger version of the man Max had encountered in the pool hall two months before—sullen and angry, but at that time barely shaving the cheeks that held an outbreak of acne. There was not, as in his sister's photo there had been, a hint of a smile.

The next year Joe had raised chickens for the Future Farmers of America, and in the group photo he looked as if he were rehearsing for the mug shot that he had earned after his arrest for Freddie's death. His sophomore portrait was even more like a booking photo, as it captured him by himself staring into the camera.

During his junior year Joe was no longer in the FFA, but his photo did show up in the Rodeo Club, roping a calf from a white-colored horse. His acne had cleared up by the time he sat in front of that year's portrait camera, and he had started to display the arrogant good looks that some women apparently found so attractive. There was a cockiness in the wounded eyes this year.

Max picked up Joe's senior yearbook, and like his sister he had disappeared. This time Max wasn't surprised; the sheriff had told him that Joe was a dropout who had left town before his 18th birthday.

He stood up and had an idea. Max found the shelf where the librarian had shown him the yearbooks and randomly picked one from five years ago. In the index he found "Morton, Mrs. Evelyn," and turned to the page. It featured photographs of the business teachers, and he saw a well-dressed woman with short stylish hair, a world apart from the girl she had been two decades earlier.

Max asked the librarian's permission to photocopy the pertinent pages and offered to pay for the copies, but she waved a hand at him and gestured him into her office, with its small copier. He finished, returned the books to her, and left the library, his briefcase thicker by a few sheets than when he had entered.

A few students and teachers were still straggling into the gym for the pep rally, and Max glanced briefly through the double doors. The band played the theme from *Rocky*, the cheerleaders danced and turned flips, and finally the football players walked out onto the gym floor while the students went wild.

Max, who had dropped out of a high school that didn't even have a football field, had trouble relating to the excitement. In the writhing throng of several hundred students and teachers, trying to find Evelyn Morton was useless. He walked down the empty hallways; lining the walls were large framed collections of the portraits from each senior year. Or at least all the graduates. Max knew that neither of the Wagners would appear there. And the question he needed an answer for was why? Especially Evvy. Why had she dropped out during her senior year before reappearing a dozen years later as a schoolteacher? Why did her brother Joe drift up to Amarillo and eventually murder a young man named Freddie Odom? He glanced at his watch and saw that he had at least an hour to kill before he could expect to catch Evelyn at home. He walked out into the bright, cool sunlight. As he unlocked his car he could feel more than hear the beat of the band and the yelling of the students.

On Main Street (Max was amazed that it was really called that), he found a Dairy Queen and bought a Coke. He drove aimlessly around the town, killing time. If he drove more than three minutes in any one direction he would be out of town. As he drove north he passed the city limits sign and in about two miles saw a sign that said "FM 2122," and that number sounded vaguely familiar to him. Max pulled onto the shoulder of the road and shuffled through his papers a moment before finding what he was looking for: the Wagner farm's address was 10800 FM 2122. He pulled onto the road, which after 10 yards traded in its asphalt for gravel and dirt.

The addresses began in the 7000's. He had to watch carefully for the signs, which were usually either small or non-existent. About five miles out on the road he started seeing 11000 without ever finding the address he was looking for, so he turned back around and drove slowly the other direction. Eventually he found 10200, and once again turned around. There was only one dirt lane leading off the main road between here and 11000, and when he arrived back at it he pulled his car between two lines of fence. The car rumbled across a pipe cattle guard. Fifty yards down the gravel driveway Max saw a weathered building which was clearly abandoned. In places the boards were hanging off the walls, and the windows had not seen a curtain in years.

Max pulled the car in front of the small two-story house. It looked fifty or sixty years old and might once have been attractive, but it was years past its last residents. The front porch sagged almost to the ground in places, the screen door hung off its hinges, and the porch was scattered with trash. He stepped up onto it, carefully avoiding rotting boards, and looked through the doorway. The wallpaper was a rose pattern now barely discernible, and it reminded him of the walls in his Aunt Dodie and Uncle Nate's apartment in Crown Heights. He shivered and stepped down off the porch. He walked around the house, peeking in windows, seeing an old kitchen with yellowed counters and an ancient gas stove. A bathroom with rusted fixtures. The living room where dust motes floated in shafts of light. The upstairs, he imagined, contained bedrooms for the small family.

Twenty-five yards from the house, across a crop of weeds, stood a run-down barn that leaned precariously to the left. In a few years, a decade at most, it would be just a heap of boards. Max walked to it and gingerly touched the large doorframe. It seemed firm enough, and he stepped out of the light into a cool, stuffy darkness through which large, blue flies buzzed lazily. On the right were several stalls for horses or cows, he imagined. On the left was a long workbench with a few rusty tools still lying on top: two hammers, a box of nails, a scattering of horseshoes, a broken block and tackle. In a loft he saw old hay and heard a skittering in it. He had spent too many years in New York not to recognize the sound of rats chasing each other. He walked further into the barn, glancing into stalls scattered with moldy straw. Max reached the last stall. As he had walked farther along, a tension had grown in his gut that he couldn't identify, and all he knew was that he needed to leave right then. He turned toward the light at the barn door, and became very aware of the dim corners of the stalls behind him. He walked faster, almost trotting, and looked over his shoulder before bursting into the daylight. What kind of shit is this, he thought. There's nothing in there; if there were I would have seen it going in. The warm sun felt good on his shoulders, even as he felt an involuntary shiver go from his crown to his toes. He looked around from the house to the barn and back again. Twenty yards past the barn was a small outbuilding, and he walked to it. It was empty inside but for a shovel with a broken handle, a hammer, and some rusted nails. A tool shed.

Max looked at his watch. It was 3:45, and he stood a good chance of finding Evelyn Morton at home now.

He started back toward the house and had barely taken three steps when he tripped on something hard. It felt like a shovel handle, or maybe an old tree branch, although there were few trees around. Max looked down and saw immediately that it was a bone he had stepped on. Cold sweat trickled from his armpits. The bones were too big to be a small animal, and at first they looked big enough to be human. Examining them closer, Max saw that they were the bones of a larger animal, a cow perhaps. He found the skull, and it didn't look like a cow, but he was no expert. The closest he'd ever come to seeing a cow skull was on a movie screen, and none of them looked like this. The skull was long, not triangular, and had large protruding teeth.

Screw it, Max thought. What do I know? Maybe it *is* a cow. What else could it be? Some other work animal, a horse or something. Maybe a deer that ventured too close to the house, and Buddy Wagner had blasted it from one of the upstairs windows. It could be anything.

Chapter 26

Evelyn Morton's address wasn't hard to find. The town was set up numerically one way and alphabetically the other. It wasn't like New York, where streets were built on old Indian trails, or as happens in the West Village, West 4th Street intersects West 10th Street.

The address seemed to be in one of the tonier neighborhoods in town. The grass was still green even in December, and it was neatly trimmed. The front walk to the one-story brick house had little lights installed along its length.

He rang the doorbell and waited only a few moments before it was opened.

Evelyn Morton was forty-one years old. Before Max dropped out of high school, he had thought there were two kinds of women teachers: the ones you thought were impossibly old and ugly, and the ones you fell helplessly in love with. Evelyn Morton was one of the latter. But she probably wasn't the teacher the athletic kids fell for; she was the kind who would break the hearts of the intellectual boys, the ones like Max himself who now found himself staring at her.

She was slender but more Sigourney Weaver than Michelle Pfeiffer. There was a beauty to her that was hard, and very carefully maintained. Her hair was salt-and-pepper, cut close to the head like the business women Max used to see in Midtown, Lexington Avenue in the 40's. He expected steel in her voice, and a quick attempt to dismiss him, but instead she tilted her head to the right and said "Yes, may I help you?"

"Mrs. Evelyn Morton?"

"That's correct," she said. "Is there something that . . . ?" Her voice faded away as she waited for Max to explain why he was there.

"Mrs. Morton, my name is Max Friedman, and I'm an attorney representing Joseph Wagner."

"Ah. Yes," she said, as if he had just told her that her dry cleaning was ready to be picked up.

"Mr. Wagner is your brother, is that correct?"

"Yes," she said, still smiling.

"I'd like to talk to you, Mrs. Morton, and ask you some questions about him. It might be helpful in his defense."

"Yes, of course. Oh I'm sorry, please forgive me. I haven't even invited you in." She stood aside and opened the door wider. The entry hall was a rich cream color, and an antique table stood against the wall. There was nothing on it except a plate with a painting of Jesus praying in the Garden of Gethsemane. It was the Jesus Max remembered seeing on the walls of the bodegas in Brooklyn, the little delis and candy stores. Jesus had medium brown hair, a sharp beard, a contemplative expression, and the requisite white robe.

He followed Evelyn down the hall to a living room that contained more antiques. She motioned him to a sofa. "Would you like some coffee?"

Max nodded, and she returned a few minutes later carrying a tray with two china cups, a cream pitcher, a bowl of sugar, and another small bowl laden with packets of Equal and Sweet and Low. She set the service on a small coffee table and handed a cup to him.

"You might notice there's no television in this room," she said. "I find there's too little time for the real necessities in life—contemplation and grading my students' work. Do you know that I'm a teacher? Yes? So much of what is on television today is just awful—but I suppose it's always been that way, wouldn't you say? I like to spend my time in service—to my students and to the Lord. My husband has a television in his study, but I find I don't need to see it myself. So much of it is just tawdry and awful." She paused to take a breath.

"Mrs. Morton, I'd like to talk with you, and ask you a few questions about your brother, if I could."

"Oh, I'm sorry. Yes, of course. You're his lawyer, is that correct?"

"Yes," he said carefully. "I've been appointed to defend him. Have you read in the paper about his situation?"

"Very little. My—" she faltered for a moment "—husband has told me some things about it. Of course it's been on television I'm sure, but I don't watch—" The smile that she had been wearing since she opened the door faded for a moment, but returned instantly. "I said that, I think."

"Mrs. Morton, your brother has killed a man, an acquaintance in Amarillo. There's no doubt that he killed him, but my job is to defend him. Some of your brother's behavior puzzles me, and I'd like to talk to you, to see if you can shed any light on why he did this."

She crossed her ankles and sipped from the cup of coffee. "I certainly am willing to try, Mr.—I'm sorry, but I've forgotten your name."

Max gave it again.

"Mr. Friedman. I'm not certain that there's much I can tell you that will be helpful. Joe was always—well, troubled is a good word, I suppose. From the time he was very small he cried, he was very angry. He would hit at me for no reason. I was six years older than he, and as a toddler, two or three years old, he would just run up to me and start hitting me on the legs. He was always so willful and angry."

"Did your parents try to do something about this?"

"Yes, of course. They would be strict with him, but kind. They would tell him no, and make him sit in a corner. None of it did any good at all, I'm afraid. He could be very sweet and charming sometimes, but he was usually just so angry and spiteful."

"Did your parents try to find professional help for him?"

She smiled. "I assume you mean a psychiatrist? No. I don't believe that there are any here in town today, let alone thirty years ago."

"Maybe in Amarillo there would have been—"

"You're not from here are you, Mr. Friedman?"

"I'm from New York."

"People here are hesitant to—"

Max thought she was about to say "air their dirty laundry."

"—go outside of the family or church for help. Instead, we would rather pray for God's intercession."

"Is that what your parents did?"

"Yes, of course."

But it doesn't seem to have worked, Max thought.

"Did your parents do more than put him in the corner?"

"What do you mean?"

"Did they use corporal punishment?"

"I see. They gave him spankings occasionally when he misbehaved, as they did me. It never seemed to work for him. He became even more willful and angry."

"So did it just go on like that? Nothing ever seemed to change once the pattern was established?"

"I can't say that it changed, no."

"It must have been difficult living in the house, if it never changed."

"It wasn't that way every moment, of course. There were times when Joe was not quite so angry. We sought refuge in the Lord when times were bad."

"Mrs. Morton, do you have any idea why Joe might have acted that way? Do you have any memory of what might have happened to him?"

She pursed her lips, as if in concentration, then picked up her coffee cup and turned it slightly on the saucer.

"Mr. Friedman, I teach high school, as I believe you know. Most of the children are quite good, if a little high-spirited. They get away with what they can, but they almost always respond to discipline. There are others, a very few, who are—unteachable. One can do nothing with them, and they typically leave school before graduating. I harbor no notion that anything was 'done' to them, at least not by any person. They are in the hands of the devil, Mr. Friedman. Oh, I know this may sound 'old-fashioned' to you, but it is true. It may sound cruel, but I think it is realistic. They are beyond help, and we only destroy ourselves trying to save them. This is what my brother Joe is like. I could see in your eyes when I told you I was only vaguely aware of him that you were surprised. This is why, Mr. Friedman. He will pull down anyone who tries to help him. I'm sorry, I have some papers to grade. Do you have any more questions?"

Max wondered if he had heard what it sounded like. Evelyn Morton thought her brother was in the hands of the devil? He shuffled through his notecards.

"Yes, as a matter of fact. I do have two. You didn't attend Loving High School your senior year. Where were you?"

It was her turn to be taken aback. "Why do you say that?"

"You weren't in the yearbook."

Her face seemed to relax. "During the summer between my junior and senior years, I was called out of town to help with an ailing aunt in Euless. That's near Fort Worth. She was a widow with no children. My parents thought I was mature enough to help her. She still wasn't well by the time school started, so I enrolled there and graduated."

Max scratched a note about that. "Just a couple of more questions, Mrs. Morton. In my interviews with your brother, he mentioned a 'pinto pony.' Do you know what that means?"

Her face didn't change. "No, I'm sorry. I don't know what that means." She sat with her hands in her lap, composed and patient.

"And one more. Several years ago, you saw your brother and his wife at a restaurant. You went up to their table, and you said 'He's dead.' Mrs. Morton, whom were you talking about? Was it your father?"

Evelyn looked at Max. He waited for her to reply. She kept looking at him, and he felt suddenly that he was looking at a mask of her, not the woman herself, but a smiling mask, beautifully painted and perfectly cast.

"Mrs. Morton?"

Slowly the mask moved, and a shadow crossed her eyes. Then they cleared and she was looking at him again. "I'm sorry, Mr. Friedman. I did see Joe and his wife. Seeing him was very painful for me. I really don't remember anything I said. I just wanted to say hello to him."

"When was the last time you had seen him before that?"

"I hadn't seen him since I left Loving."

Puzzled, Max checked his notes. "But Joe was ten years old when you left. You never saw him again? Didn't you come to visit your parents?"

Evelyn Morton rose elegantly to her feet. "Mr. Friedman, I expect James, my husband, home soon, and I need to start preparing dinner for him."

"Mrs. Morton, why didn't you go back to see your family?"

"I'm sorry, but I need you to leave now."

"Evvy—"

"Don't call me that."

"Your brother killed a man. Do you understand that? I don't know why he did it, and I'm trying to find out. It's the only way I can defend him. Why won't you help me?"

"Mr. Friedman, I have answered all of your questions to the best of my ability. I am not responsible for what my brother has done. Now please leave before my husband gets home, or I'll call the police."

Max surrendered. He picked up his briefcase and allowed her to escort him to the door. When it closed behind him he breathed deeply of the cool twilight air. He had been so close! What kind of a woman wouldn't go back to see her own family? And more to the point, why? He had left his own family, but there were reasons for it. What were hers? Goddamn it! Why wouldn't she talk? He knew she was lying. Knew it.

He got in his car, trying to think of what questions he would ask her the next time. He would be better prepared, he knew that much. As he pulled away from the curb, he saw a car turn onto the street behind him and into the Morton's driveway.

Sitting behind the wheel for a moment, leaning back against the seat with his eyes closed, Max blew out a long, slow breath. He put the car in gear, turned on the lights, and found his way to the highway.

He passed the Dairy Queen, a Pizza Hut, and a Golden Fried Chicken, but he wasn't hungry. At least not for what they were offering.

A quarter of a mile past the city limits, Max's rear view mirror exploded with red and blue lights. His entire body jerked. His foot didn't know whether to hit the brake or slam down on the gas, so for a moment he did neither, while the police car continued to glide behind him with its lights swirling. Finally Max touched his brake and eased off onto the side of the road. He could feel sand slide beneath his wheels as they eased off the pavement.

Max had watched this scene in a hundred movies: the city boy who goes out to the country and gets pulled over by the local police. He was usually found in a gravel pit months later, if he was found at all. It didn't matter what he was doing in the country—registering black voters, visiting his new girlfriend, or investigating a crime. His end was always the same.

The blue and red lights turned off, and in his rear-view mirror Max saw the door of the police car open. The dome light came on and the door shut, extinguishing the light. He heard gravel crunching, and then a figure was standing at his window. Knuckles rapped on the glass, and Max rolled it down. He looked up into the face of the deputy, the man whom he had met earlier in the day. What was his name? It was too dark to read the nameplate over his pocket.

"Mr. Friedman? I hope I didn't put a scare into you. It was the only way I knew to get you to stop."

"No, not at all."

"Good. I'm Deputy Paul Hunter. We talked earlier today over at the sheriff's office?"

Max nodded.

"I've got somebody who'd like to talk to you before you pull out of town. Maybe it has something to do with your case, or maybe not. But I've been thinking it over all day, and you might ought to give it a few minutes, if you can spare them."

"I can, sure. Can you tell me who we're going to talk to?"

Deputy Hunter cleared his throat. "Yes, sir. It's my daddy. Why don't you just follow me?"

The deputy drove to a small white house in a neighborhood much different than Evelyn Morton's. There would be no hidden sprinkler systems here; the yards were hard packed dirt, raked with precision. When Max stepped out of the car he smelled sharp spices drifting through the air. Deputy Hunter stepped up beside him and put a hand on his elbow, guiding him toward the front door. He opened it, and Max was struck by his courteous, almost courtly behavior.

The room he entered was small. An overstuffed couch and chair took up one wall, and against the other was a 32" floor model television. In the middle of the room a man sat in a wheelchair. He wore a plaid robe and a blanket over his lap and legs. His torso was broad and powerful, his hands as large as catchers' mitts.

The deputy stepped between them. "Mr. Friedman, this is my daddy, Elvin Hunter. He was sheriff here for thirty years. Daddy, this is the man I told you about. The lawyer from Amarillo."

Elvin Hunter raised a hand to his mouth and coughed softly. "Thirty-one," he said. "Just to keep the record straight."

Max shook his hand and glanced down at the blanket over the man's legs.

It took a moment before he realized that the legs ended above the knees. He glanced up and saw the former sheriff's blue eyes holding his.

"I'm sorry," he said.

"Diabetes. Would have kept on running for sheriff as long as they'd keep electing me, if it wasn't for that. But I just couldn't do it anymore. Take a seat."

Max sat on the couch, and the deputy took the chair. He reached for the remote control and silenced the television.

Elvin Hunter turned the wheelchair to face Max.

Max opened his briefcase and held up the recorder. "Do you mind if I tape this?"

The man shook his head and waited until Max had set it down and turned it on. "Paul came by this afternoon to check on me. His mama passed seven years ago. I got day-care people come by, but he checks on me. He mentioned that you were in town and what you were doing."

Max nodded.

"I never had much use for Joe Wagner. He was a mean little son of a bitch the whole time I knew him. I stopped him for stealing hubcaps, pulled him over for speeding. He always had one ol' rattle-trap pickup or another." Mr. Hunter reached down beside the wheel chair and picked up a coffee can into which he carefully spat tobacco juice. "Sometimes I'd throw him into a cell, trying to scare him if nothing else. Never much worked."

He cleared his throat. "Son, could you get me a glass of water, please?" The deputy stepped into a small kitchen, and Max heard the sound of running water.

"I've lived here all my life, you know. Went to school with Joe's daddy, Buddy. Joe was nothing compared to him." He paused, as if waiting for Max to say something.

"What made him worse?"

"He was the kind of a kid who would kill something for fun. I don't mean going duck hunting, or deer. Everybody'll do that. I mean killing dogs in the neighborhood for fun."

Max felt a chill move through his spine.

"Everybody knew he'd do it. Couple of times fellers would beat the snot out of him for it, but he'd always get back at them. Cut their tires, smash their windshields. They'd leave him alone then. Couple of times I think he raped girls. Back then you'd go on a date with a girl it wasn't like it is now, they talk about date rape. But I tell you what, these two girls went out with him and afterwards they didn't talk much. Eventually they just kind of slipped away."

"Did he go to trial? To jail?"

"Nah. No charges were brought. Oh, he went to jail for a few little things, just like with Joe. It never helped with him neither."

"Did he ever leave here? Move away?"

"No. He stayed here, started farming his daddy's land for him. Eventually he married Helen Stokes. She was a few years younger than him, maybe eight or ten. Sweet girl, too. Wasn't too long before you'd see her out somewhere, in the grocery store maybe, her eyes was just blank. Like a doll or something. He could do that to people."

"Did he do that to the kids too?"

"Oh, yeah. Evvy and Joe both. She was already in school when he was born, seems to me like."

"She was six then."

He nodded. "I don't ever remember seeing that little girl happy. You'd see her sitting in the little seat in her mama's shopping cart, and her eyes had nothing in them. She didn't laugh, didn't cry, didn't show anything at all that I ever saw. Just blank. It'd break your heart."

"She seems okay today."

"You went over to her house?"

Max nodded. "According to her, her parents were saints."

The sheriff grunted in bitter amusement. "I tell you what, I was surprised when she moved back to town. First time I heard who that gal was, I like to peed my pants. Mrs. Evelyn Morton don't bear no more resemblance to Evvy Wagner than I did to Cary Grant on the best day of my life. I haven't seen her in a long while." He glanced down at his legs. "Don't get out much anymore. But I've seen her with her hundred dollar haircuts and fancy dresses. The Evvy Wagner I knew barely had about two dresses, and her mama just sat her down at home on a kitchen chair with a pair of scissors. Paul can tell you."

The deputy nodded. Max said "Sheriff Hunter," and he saw a pleased flush flow over the old man's face, "did you ever see any overt signs of abuse? Ever arrest Buddy Wagner for child abuse? Was there ever anything that would appear in the criminal court records?"

Elvin Hunter paused a moment before he shook his head. "Never arrested him. I knew he was treating those kids awful bad. Didn't need to catch him at it. All you needed was to see that blank look in their eyes. Sometimes I'd hear something. Kids would show up to school with bruises on them, and I'd go out there to the house and talk to them. Helen of course, she'd try to act cheery, like nothing was wrong. Say oh, it wasn't nothing. Evvy fell down off a chair reaching into her closet, Joe got knocked down by one of the cows or horses. Something like that. Buddy, he wouldn't even make any excuses. Just look at me with those flat eyes of his, like he was daring me to accuse him of beating those kids."

"Why didn't you?"

"Back then it wasn't so easy to bring charges as it is today." He paused, and his eyes found the flickering images on the silent television. "One time when Evvy was oh, about ten I guess, I was down at the West Plains Clinic— the hospital, and one of the nurses took me aside and told me that Helen had brung Evvy in there that morning with a busted arm. They'd had to put it in a cast, and she just wanted me to know. Of course, what she wanted was for me to find out what had happened. I went out there, and it was like usual. Ol' Buddy, he wouldn't even talk to me. Said he had too much work to do, and caring for the kids was Helen's business. Helen said Evvy fell off the porch. I brought charges on him, but they was dismissed. No proof."

He glanced back at the television. "Mr. Friedman if you was to run a report on the accidents those kids had, the odds'd be about a million to one. I can't tell you the number of hours I've set here in this chair thinking about how chickenshit I was not to have done something, anything at all. Talk to the kids. Hell, they probably wouldn't have said anything. Throw Buddy's ass in jail. Get me three or four big sons of bitches, go out there to his place and kick the holy shit out of him until he told me the truth. Seems like there was something I could have done to help them, but I never. And I'm still living with that. I don't know much about what Joe done, or what they say he done. Killed a man, I know that. I figure he probably done it. Prison is probably the best place for him to be. But I felt like maybe I should say something to you about this. Tell you what I know."

The pauses between his sentences had grown so long that Max waited for him, to see if he needed to say something else. Max glanced at the deputy, whose eyes flicked back at his father.

"You okay, daddy? You need anything?"

The old man's head shook briefly from one side to the other.

Max leaned forward and said very quietly "Sheriff Hunter?" The man glanced at him, and Max saw two lines of tears shining in the light from the television. "In one of my interviews with Joe, he said something about a 'pinto pony.' Does that mean anything to you?"

It was a long time before he answered. "Going back about oh, twenty-five years or so. I remember driving out there for one reason or another. Their house, I mean. Probably because of another complaint. About the only reason I ever went out there. There was this little pony out there by the barn, and it was a pinto. Mostly white, with a few big brown spots on it. Grazing out by the fence. That was the only time I ever recollect seeing it."

The old sheriff went quiet again. Paul Hunter cocked his head and got Max's attention. He nodded at the door. Max quietly packed up his recorder and put it into the briefcase. He stood up and said, "Thank you, Sheriff Hunter." The old man didn't acknowledge him. The deputy walked Max to the door, but just before they reached it he heard the sheriff's voice, weaker than it had been before.

"Mr. Friedman?"

"Yes?"

"You go over there to Evvy Wagner's house and ask her how she busted her arm. You just go over there and tell her I said to ask her. See what she says then."

The deputy walked Max back to his car. "I think he's been holding this inside him for a long time. Tell you the truth, though, I'm not too sure how I feel about you using this to help Joe Wagner. I'm kind of like daddy, prison's probably the best place for him."

"I'll be honest with you," Max said. "I'm not too sure how I feel about using it to help him either. But I have to."

The deputy shook his head. "Yes, sir. I know." He extended his hand. Max shook it. "I appreciate you listening to him, Mr. Friedman."

Max got in the car and pulled away from the curb. Deputy Hunter stood watching him, his hands in his uniform pockets.

When Evelyn Morton opened the door she didn't recognize Max for a moment, but when she did her face became wary. "Yes, Mr. Friedman, wasn't it? Is there something else I can do for you?"

"There is, Mrs. Morton. You can tell me how you broke your arm when you were a little girl."

Her lips moved as they tried to invent a lie, but she was not fast enough. It had been too long since anyone had asked her that question, and her mother was no longer there to tell her what to say. Evvy Wagner tried a moment longer, then opened the door wider, and Max walked in.

When they finished talking he was too tired to drive home, so he found a motel room for the rest of the night. He slept fitfully, and when he woke up he could smell the odor of manure drifting from the feed yards outside of town.

Chapter 27

Christmas Eve brought snow with it. On December 23 it was 68 degrees at 3:00 p.m.. During the night a cold front blew in, freezing the water in ponds and birdbaths all over the city; in the country, stock tanks formed a layer of ice. Max spent the whole day in the courthouse, emerging only at lunchtime for a sandwich at the Snazzy Pig. At 5:00 when he walked out of the building, an inch of snow lay on the streets and sidewalks, muffling the sound of traffic. It was wet and clung to the lines of garland that crossed the streets of downtown. It settled into the cornices of the county courthouse and onto the shoulders of the statues in the parks.

It kept falling all night. Max spent Christmas Eve night at Angel's house, and in the morning the presence of a certain light and an absence of sound told him that the snow was deep. He molded his body against hers, shifted the long red hair away from her neck, and nuzzled her cheek until she woke up. She smiled sleepily. "Hi," she said.

He kissed her, and said "Well, this must be real. We're past the 'oh, we can't kiss until we've brushed our teeth' stage." She kissed him, and they made love, then drifted back to sleep.

When Max awoke again she was gone. He got dressed and found her outside, leaning her forearms on the top rail of the corral. Summerlea and Nightfall played with each other, feinting and nipping, suddenly turning their back legs and throwing a kick, then chasing each other in circles before skidding to a halt and reversing.

Max heard a whispering sound to his right and turned to see Bailey plowing through the snow, which hit her at the tops of the legs. She suddenly stumbled, sliding on her side for a few feet and righted herself. She snapped up a mouthful of the snow, furiously slung it in her mouth a moment and released it, the snow flying from both sides of her head. She ducked under the bottom rail of the corral and joined the horses' wild dance, her tongue hanging out.

Max slipped his arms around Angel's waist and she leaned back against him.

"I never asked if you do Christmas," she said. "I hope so, because I have a gift for you."

"My policy is to never let religion get in the way of a good holiday," he said. "I have something for you, too." They watched the horses and the dog for a few more minutes before they went into the house.

Max made waffles while Angel built a fire. When they had eaten and settled down in front of the fireplace she gave him a box two feet by two feet and six inches deep. "I figured if you were going to hang around here you might need these," she said. He tore off the wrapping paper and opened the box. Inside was a pair of black cowboy boots with the red initial "M" on the right one and "F" on the left.

"I assume this doesn't stand for 'motherfucker,'" he said.

"You would be assuming right."

He slid the boots onto his feet, feeling the smooth calf skin brush against his own calves. "You might need to borrow some of my boot socks until you can get to the store," she said. He stood up and walked around the living room. The boots felt unfamiliar but strangely apt.

"I guess I'm an official Texan now," he said. "If I leave, they'll revoke my passport or something."

"How quickly you see through my little plan." She tried to use the accent of a German spy, but her Texas twang got in the way and made him laugh. He handed her a long, narrow, shallow package. She removed the paper and inside was a wooden case. She opened it and slowly lifted out a blood red pool cue with "Angel" written in the same script that "Bailey's" was written in on the front window of the club. She looked at him and this time it was she who laughed. "Look at us," she said. "If these aren't the coolest, weirdest, Christmas presents in the whole Texas Panhandle, I'll salt them and eat them right now."

"We may very well be the coolest, weirdest couple in the whole Texas Panhandle," he said.

Later, they saddled the horses and went riding through the snow. The horses' breath fogged in tremendous clouds in the frigid air, and Max remembered his first ride with her, on that chilly morning barely two months ago.

After they had ridden a mile across country, the horses' legs little bulldozers in the snow, Bailey roaming in and around them, they stopped. Angel reached her hand out to him and he clasped it in hers, their gloved fingers twining together.

"I like being here with you," she said.

"The feeling is mutual."

"I'd like to continue being here with you." He squeezed her hand.

That afternoon Max drove into town and fed his cats. They sulked for a few minutes because he had left them alone over night. He sat with them on the couch while they purred and marched around his lap, reclaiming their property. "Okay troops," he said, "we're going to try an experiment." He put them both into their carriers and loaded them into the car.

Two hours later Angel and Max snuggled together on the couch in front of the fireplace. His right arm was around her shoulders, and her head leaned back on his arm. Her hand rested on his leg.

"It's okay," she said. "They're fine. They're around here somewhere, and they can't get into too much trouble. They're just hiding."

"I know, I know. I just worry is all."

"Too much, maybe."

"It's my nature. Max the worrier."

"They'll come out before morning."

"So you say."

When Max opened the cage the cats had carefully crept out, their slinking bellies dragging the ground. They did well until Bailey rounded the corner from the kitchen into the living room, and then they disappeared. They didn't just streak away. One moment Angel and Max were looking at them, and the next they were gone and had not reappeared since.

"You like the boots?" Angel asked.

"They're me, I think."

"I don't know much about it, but I think the ability to clonk in the courtroom is important. For women it's heels, for men it's boots."

"I'm sure you have a point."

"Speaking of the courtroom . . . . "

"Yes?"

"How's the case for your favorite client going?"

"I think it's going well, considering that I didn't want it in the first place, still don't want it, and don't see the situation changing anytime in the near future."

"Do you have a defense for him?"

"I've got one. I don't know how good it is, but I've got it. It's not going to make anyone happy, including my client."

"What is it?"

Max considered carefully. He had wondered if he wanted to tell Angel about it, to go over the details of his defense with someone.

"I think," he said, "that I'd rather keep it to myself for now. I don't want to jinx it."

She turned her head so that she could look up at him. "For real? You sure this isn't about us?"

"Not about us. I'm just not wanting to talk about it. Maybe I'm thinking if I don't tell people, it'll mysteriously go away or something. Joe will go away."

"Any chance of that?"

"Not much. It's pretty much the way I spent my whole life, though. Hoping my problems would just considerately disappear on their own. That's why I drank so much. If they wouldn't go away, the drink would make me think they had."

Angel looked into the fire. She could feel Max's head turning, looking around the room. She slapped him lightly on the arm. "Stop looking for the cats. They'll turn up."

"I know. Like I said—"

"You're a worrier."

"My middle name."

"If you do want to talk about it, that's okay," Angel said. "I'm not saying I want you to, but if you need to bounce ideas off somebody . . . . " He squeezed her shoulders and didn't say anything.

January 19, the first day of Joe's trial, fell on a Tuesday. Max had spent the weekend in his apartment rehearsing his opening remarks and reviewing his witness notes. The cats sat on the couch with their legs tucked under them, their heads swiveling as they watched him like spectators at a ping-pong match. The prosecution's witness list was short, and in fact its whole case was brief. He had interviewed all their witnesses. The forensic evidence would be simple. Cause of death was blunt trauma to the left side of the head. Diane DiAngelo might try to introduce the crime-scene photographs of Freddie's body as evidence, and if so he would fight it. She would call Champ Phillips, the police lieutenant, to testify about Freddie's phone call. The call would portray Freddie as an innocent, someone who was trying to extricate himself from the evil web that had been woven around him by three hardened blah blah blah. She would call Carl Puente. Diane probably didn't even need him because he wasn't at the drive-in when Freddie died. However, lawyers liked to tie things up in neat bundles, in the mistaken belief that life worked that way. She would ask Puente questions about what Joe was doing when he arrived and to confirm that Freddie was dead. She would try to squeeze every drop of tragedy that she could out of his death.

Max dropped down between the two cats, startling them out of their hypnotic trances. Jesus, he thought, it *is* tragic. Sometimes he thought he'd been a lawyer too long. A man was dead, and it was his charge to defend the man who had done it. He would do it to the best of his ability, and he had a good case. But if he lost sight of the fact that something horrible had happened that night three months ago, he would be no different than all the other lawyers who made the jokes about them a favorite national pastime.

He closed his eyes and put his hands out, finding the two cats. The moment he touched them they started purring deliriously. Max thought every attorney should be required to have cats. There was no way to be dishonest when your hand was resting on a purring cat.

That afternoon he met Darlene Wagner at her house and went through her and Joe's closets. He found some jeans, several dressy cowboy shirts, the kind with pearl snaps, and two sport jackets in a western style, with arrow pockets and a yoke on the back.

Darlene insisted on ironing the jeans and the permanent press shirts and made a pot of coffee. She chatted to him about nothing consequential while she dragged the iron over the clothing. She was lonely, Max knew, and welcomed having a man in her home, even if he was a little different than the men she had grown up around. When she handed him the unwrinkled clothes she shook his hand. Max asked if she would be at the trial. "It would look good to the jury if you were there," he said. She nodded quickly and said that she was taking personal leave from work.

"He'll appreciate that, I'm sure," Max said, knowing as he said it that it was probably a lie.

That night he went to Bailey's, wondering about the wisdom of hanging out at a pool hall the night before his first day of a trial. He decided that he had done all he could on the case. He had rehearsed his opening until the cats had gone to sleep and thought about any possible ways that Diane DiAngelo could surprise him. Of course there were probably many, but he had prepared for every scenario that occurred to him. Her witness list told him that she considered the case open and shut. The four men robbed Food Giant. Phillips would confirm the phone call; Dixon would testify that Joe said he had found Freddie on the phone and taken him to the drive-in, and that Dixon had seen him swing the bowling pin. Carl was required on the stand only to confirm Smith's testimony. She apparently didn't consider the trip to the drive-in kidnapping, because she wasn't pushing for capital murder. She had dropped the charges of assault on a police officer and resisting arrest, and Max doubted that the prosecution's case would take more than two days.

He played by himself tonight, practicing shots. Mondays were slow, almost as slow as Wednesdays. Getting out of the house on a Monday was a little too soon after the weekend, he supposed. The feelings of guilt over Sunday morning hangovers were too fresh. The college students stayed home, probably studying to make up for the weekend. He glanced at his watch just as Angel brought a glass of Coke to the table. Nine-thirty. He thanked her and sipped from it, the cold glass soothing on his lips.

"You ready for tomorrow?"

"I think so, yeah." He sipped again. "We'll see."

"You think you'll get him off?"

He rubbed chalk onto his cue. "You mean will he walk out free? I doubt it. I think I'll just settle for telling the truth."

When Max finished the Coke, he went home. He slept fitfully that night, sometimes waking up repeating his opening remarks in his dreams. Whenever he woke up he was aware of the cats curled together at the foot of the bed.

Chapter 28

When the alarm went off at 6:00 a.m. he stroked the cats, found the shower, shaved, and flossed. His one suit hung in the closet, wrapped in a dry-cleaner's plastic cocoon. He pulled his hair back into a ponytail, put on the suit and a tie that was decorated with Shakespearean quotations, and walked to the door. He stopped before locking it and leaned back in. "Wish me luck, guys," he called out to the cats, still in the bedroom. As far as he could tell, they hadn't moved since he got up.

Max drove to the Snazzy Pig for a breakfast of oatmeal and toast.

The trial was being held in the old courthouse, the one with the bas-relief of cowboys, Indians, and hardy pioneers cut into its exterior. Across the street the newer courthouse squatted like an interloper. Its hallways looked like the hallways in an airport, long and wide and without character.

At 8:45 Max walked into the courtroom and took his seat at the defense table, on the left facing the judge's bench. He nodded at Diane DiAngelo, seated at the prosecutor's table. She nodded back at him.

Five minutes later two sheriff's deputies escorted Joe in through a side door next to the judge's bench. They brought him to the defense table and unlocked his cuffs. Joe looked better than when Max had seen him the day before, when he brought the clothes. Despite his weight loss, the clothes looked good on him and restored some of the rakish quality that he had possessed when Max first met him at the pool hall. Rakish wasn't exactly good, but respectable and well-groomed helped. Joe was clean shaven and his hair was neatly trimmed, a little oil slicking it back.

Max put a hand on Joe's shoulder as he sat down. "How are you?" he asked in a low voice. Joe shrugged. He rubbed his wrists. "Them things hurt," he said.

"Well, you won't have to worry about them until lunch," Max said.

"I ain't worried about them. They just make me sore."

"Let me go over what I said yesterday. The prosecutor's going to start off first with her case. She'll open the trial by talking, then I'll talk. She's going to say a lot of bad things about you. She'll say you're a murderer. She'll say you're cold-blooded. But it doesn't matter what she says. I just need you to not react to it, okay? We don't want the jury to have a reason to not like you. If they hear her or any of the witnesses say you're a bad guy and then they look over at you and see you looking pissed off, or smiling, or anything other than neutral or sincere, then they'll believe the witness. That's the way it works. I want them to look over here and see a man who's innocent. That's all. You can do that?"

Joe nodded.

"Good. After she talks, then I'll go. I'll lay out our case. Then she brings out her witnesses. It'll take a couple of days. She'll call Champ Phillips and a couple of other police. People who found the body. She'll call the medical examiner. She'll call Dixon and Puente, and probably some of the family members. I'll cross-examine most of these witnesses. Then I think she'll wrap it up." He heard a noise at the prosecutors' table and saw Jack Ogan sit down next to Diane. Interesting. He couldn't imagine Diane letting anyone share the spotlight with her. Probably Jack was there just to show some balance, so that the table wouldn't appear so empty on one side. She was hoping that the jury would see on her side two good lawyers, on his side two dirtbags, one a lawyer and the other a criminal.

He took two seconds to process that and turned back to Joe. "After she closes her case, then I'll open ours. It'll take about two days as well."

Joe glanced over at Diane and licked his lips. Not looking at Max, he said "That's when I'm going to go up there, right?"

"Say again?"

"You're going to call me up then for a witness, right? To tell what happened?"

Jesus Christ. So far Max had avoided explaining his defense strategy to Joe, hoping that he wouldn't ask. "I'm not sure that would be a good idea," he said.

"What do you mean? Why the fuck not? I've gotta tell what happened!"

"Joe, if we put you on the stand, then that means the D.A. can question you, too. She's tough and tricky, and there's no way I can prepare you for what she'll ask. Her business is confusing witnesses, asking questions fast and quick."

"But it's the only way I can tell my side of the story. What are those people gonna think of what happened if I don't talk? If I get up there and tell them about him calling me a faggot, then they'll see that I had to do something! I couldn't let him call me a queer. I mean, yeah, killing him was wrong, but I didn't mean to. I just got mad, you know. They'll understand that if I tell it."

Max glanced up at the bench. No judge or jury yet. Diane wasn't looking their way, and neither was Jack Ogan. "Joe, you've got to let me argue this case. We're going to tell your side of the story, but we have to tell it in the best way possible. I don't think it's going to help us to put you on the stand."

Joe started to speak again, but the door on the left side of the bench opened and the bailiff stood up. "All rise," he said. Judge Edward Bruce came through the door in his black robe and took his seat behind the bench. "Be seated," he said in his gruff voice. "The State of Texas vs. Joseph Randall Wagner on the charge of murder. How does the defendant plead?"

Max stood up. "Not guilty, your honor."

The judge looked at the prosecution's table. "Is the State ready?"

"Yes, your honor." Diane stood up, smoothed the skirt of her lavender suit, and buttoned the jacket. She glanced once more at her legal pad and stepped out from behind the table.

She focused on the jury, taking a moment to make eye contact with them all. Then she flashed her prize-winning smile. "Good morning. My name is Diane DiAngelo, and I am the District Attorney for Potter County. I am here to represent you and the interests of the state. Now, in an ideal world we wouldn't even need a job like mine. In an ideal world everyone would treat each other with kindness. Any conflicts would be solved with logic and reason, and without violence."

She touched the jury rail with her fingers, lightly brushing them along it for several inches.

"However, as you know, this is not an ideal society. Every day our newspapers carry articles about tragedy. Some of those tragedies are beyond our ability to control. Earthquakes. Fires. Floods. They are acts of God, and hence beyond our ability to understand. But there are other occurrences that are not acts of God. They are acts of men. Perhaps we cannot control them or understand them either. But it is my obligation, as given to me in a sacred trust by you, the people of Amarillo, to deal with the aftermath of these acts."

Diane stepped back to the table and poured a glass of water from a pitcher. She took a sip and looked back at the jury.

"It is because of such an act that we are here today, ladies and gentlemen. We are here because a man named Freddie Odom is dead. A man in the bloom of youth, a husband and father of two, will never again walk this earth, will never again collect a paycheck, will never again play football with his son in the park. He is dead because he was manipulated by three criminals into helping them commit a crime. Yes, he does share some of the responsibility for the crime. But of the four participants, he alone tried to do the right thing when it was over. Overcome by remorse, and attempting to return to the path of a law-abiding citizen, he called a police officer. He dialed the number of Lieutenant Champ Phillips, a man many of you are probably familiar with from your newspapers and televisions. In order to protect the feelings of his wife and children, he decided to make the call from a pay phone. And that decision cost him his life. Because before he could complete the call and bring the forces of justice to his side, he was seen by one of the true criminals in this case, the man sitting at the defense table. Joseph Randall Wagner. Please look at him. He is the face of evil. He is the man who stole Freddie Odom from his wife and children, from his future. Mr. Wagner took Freddie Odom from the convenience store where he was making the call, took him to an abandoned drive-in theatre where, in the presence of one of the other criminals, he murdered him. The three conspirators buried him under a foot of dirt and sand, and forgot about him. He was discovered by two children, high-spirited boys celebrating Thanksgiving Day, and perhaps the experience has marked them for the rest of their lives.

"Before the prosecution rests its case you will hear from Lieutenant Phillips and the medical examiner, who will explain the circumstances of Freddie's death and the discovery of his body. You will hear from Mr. Wagner's criminal partners of the murder itself. And you will hear from his grieving widow, Regina, who along with her children, Travis and Maggie, are as much victims of this savage violence as is Freddie himself. The prosecution will show you how a good man who made one wrong decision was made to suffer the ultimate price solely because he decided to do the right thing. We will show you how he was savagely murdered by a man who has no right to walk free on the streets of Amarillo or any other city. He has forfeited that right. It is up to you to ensure that he will be very old before he ever again walks the streets as a free man. At the conclusion of this trial, ladies and gentleman, I will have demonstrated beyond a reasonable doubt that Joseph Wagner murdered Freddie Odom, and I will ask you to deliver the harshest penalty permitted by the laws of the state of Texas. Thank you."

She walked quietly but purposefully back to the prosecution table, smoothed her skirt, and took her seat. She was respectful, not arrogant, but secure in the righteousness of her position. A good performance, Max thought.

Judge Bruce slowly turned his sleepy eyes to Max. "Defense?"

Max stood up, glanced at his legal pad, and ran his finger along the first three lines. Then he turned his eyes to the judge. "Thank you, your honor."

He stepped out in front of the defense table, glancing at Joe as he went past. He saw in his client's eyes not the arrogance typically there, but fear. It seemed, perhaps, that Joe finally understood where he was and why he was there.

At Max's first step he was surprised by the sound his new cowboy boots made on the wooden floor. When he walked into the courtroom some of the observers had been talking quietly, and the bailiff was holding a conversation with a guard. It was not loud, yet it had apparently covered the drumming sound the boots made when they touched the wooden planks. Now they thrummed, and Max was momentarily disconcerted by the sound, as if everyone in the room would suddenly jerk their heads up at the disturbance. But no one seemed to notice; their eyes were on him. Maybe, he thought, Angel was right and clonking was an important part of being an attorney. Somehow the sound was satisfying.

He looked to the jury members and swung his gaze to the gallery of observers. The room was half-full, divided like a wedding into partisan groups. On the left side of the aisle as he looked at it he saw Freddie's family—his wife and sister-in-law, their mother with her mouth turned grimly down. The wrinkles that fell into place on each side of the frown told Max that the expression wasn't entirely a result of the trial. It was habitual. On the right side of the aisle sat Darlene Wagner, a few reporters, and some other faces, both familiar and unfamiliar. A few were regulars from Bailey's. His eyes continued and found Angel in the back row. She looked strangely unbalanced without Bailey by her side. For a moment he thought of Angel in a pair of dark glasses, pretending Bailey was her seeing-eye dog in order to sneak her into the courthouse, and he had to suppress a smile.

Then he walked to the jury box, already almost used to the sound of his boots. "Good morning," he said. The jurors, a mix of working people, retirees, and professionals, nodded at him pleasantly. "My name is Max Friedman, and I am the attorney for Joseph Wagner, the defendant. You might be able to detect from the way I speak that I'm not from around here, and I hope that you don't hold that against me." He smiled to let them know that he believed they were impartial people with no prejudices, that he was only teasing them.

"I'm still learning how things are done here in Texas, but I bet there's one thing that's not very different between New York and Amarillo. Back in Brooklyn we used to sit out on the stoops in the evening and tell stories." That wasn't exactly true; lots of families did, but Max's parents mostly sat in their apartment and drank and argued while he barricaded himself in his room or wandered the streets.

"One of the things I always noticed is that people remembered stories differently. Not entirely different, of course. They generally agreed on the plot of a story, but the details were often very different. I remember Mr. and Mrs. Weinstein; they could never get through a story, because one of them was forever interrupting the other one. 'Feh, Sadie, what are you, crazy? Here's the way it really happened. What do you know from Rachel's bat mitzvah?'" Max was good at copying other people's voices, and the jury members smiled.

"Ah," he said, "I don't see any Moishes or Sadies in the jury, but I bet you've had the same conversations, sitting on the front porch drinking iced tea and watching these beautiful Amarillo sunsets.

"Something similar is going to happen here in the next several days. Ms. DiAngelo is going to tell you a story, with the help of the witnesses she calls up to the stand, and I'm going to tell you a story that starts and ends the same, but there are going to be a lot of differences. Sometimes you might scratch your heads and say 'is this the same story?' Well, it is and it isn't. It will and it won't be. Because each person sees events differently. Ms. DiAngelo has interviewed a number of people in preparing her case, and she has a story to tell. I have interviewed those same people and a few others, and my story is going to have different details.

"Now, let me tell you one of my secrets. When I was in college I studied a lot of literature. I hope you don't hold that against me." Several of the jury members smiled, but as Max made the statement he looked right at the pleasant, middle-aged woman who taught Honors English at Amarillo High School. "The Greek playwright Aeschylus portrayed Athena, the goddess of wisdom, as the one who introduced logic and reason into the courtroom. But I'd like to suggest to you that the first true juror, the spiritual grandfather of Judge Bruce, of Ms. DiAngelo and myself, of you twelve, showed up a little earlier than that. We Jews like to claim him, but I think he belongs to all of us. That man was Solomon. Do you remember him?" He glanced at the building contractor who was the leader of his Bible study class.

"I bet you do. He was the very wise man who, when two women came before him claiming to both be the mother of the same baby, had to make a decision. Now I told you that I studied literature. I kind of nodded off during biology classes, but the last time I checked, I think it was still impossible for two women to give birth to the same child." All the jury members smiled. "So Solomon proposed to cut the child in half and give half to each woman. When he said this, he knew immediately from one woman's grief that she was the true mother. In this trial, ladies and gentleman, you have inherited the cloak of Solomon. You must listen to both sides of the story Ms. DiAngelo and I are going to tell, and decide which side makes sense to you. It is the job of the prosecution to prove beyond a reasonable doubt that Mr. Wagner did what Ms. DiAngelo claims he did: that he willfully murdered Freddie Odom, that he intentionally took his life, and deprived a beautiful woman and her two children of their husband and father. If you believe the story that Ms. DiAngelo tells you, then you must find for the State.

"However, I'm also going to tell you a story. I'm going to tell you how I believe the events unfolded. If you believe my story, then you are solemnly obligated by the law to find for the defense." At those words all the smiles were erased from the jury members' faces, as if the word "solemn" would be betrayed by any hint of levity.

"Ms. DiAngelo and I each believe what we're going to tell you, with all our hearts. But ultimately, when we have rested our cases, it will be up to you to decide which of us you believe. You will go into the jury room and use your intellect and your emotions, which we both trust completely, to decide whether the State has proved its case beyond a reasonable doubt." Max slowly turned his back on the jury box and started to walk back to the defense table. Halfway there he turned back to the jury and offered them his best serious smile. "Thank you," he said.

Judge Bruce sighed and rested his chin in the palm of his right hand. "Ms. DiAngelo, are you ready to call your first witness?"

"Yes, your honor. The state calls Regina Odom."

Hushed whispers raced through the observers as Regina squeezed the hands of her mother and sister, then stood and walked to the witness box. She was wearing a knee-length black dress, and her dark hair fell loosely to her shoulders. The bailiff swore her in and when he asked her full name, Regina said "Regina Ann Schell Odom, sir," with her right hand raised into the air.

When Regina settled herself into the witness chair, Diane said "Thank you for coming in, Mrs. Odom. I know this is difficult for you." Regina nodded.

Like she had a choice, Max thought, and immediately dismissed it as petty.

"Mrs. Odom," Diane said, "can you describe to the jury your experience on the night of November 4th last year, and the following day?"

"On that night," Regina said carefully, "I was at home with my husband Freddie and our children. It was about 8:30, and I was helping our son with his homework and getting our daughter ready for bed. Freddie said he was going out to rent some videos. He said he'd be home in about half an hour."

"Mrs. Odom, did your husband return in half an hour?"

"No ma'am."

"When did he come home?"

Regina started to speak, but tears ran from her eyes and she took a tissue from her purse. She dabbed at her eyes and finally said "He didn't. Come home."

"When your husband didn't come home that night what did you do, Mrs. Odom?"

"I waited up for him for a while, but finally I went to sleep. The next morning when I woke up he wasn't there either, and I was really worried. I called his work, but he never came in. I didn't know what to do. There had been a couple of times that he hadn't come home until—until later, and I kept waiting at home, hoping he'd walk in. But finally I had to call the police."

Diane looked into Regina's eyes, brimming with tears. "I know this is difficult, Mrs. Odom. I thank you so much for being here just a few more minutes. Did the police find your husband?"

Regina's lower lip started to tremble. "No ma'am, I mean yes, but not right away. It was a few weeks later. We hadn't heard anything from them, but on Thanksgiving Day, after dinner—" Her voice broke. She lowered her face, and the tears dripped into her lap. She wiped her eyes carefully with a handkerchief. "After dinner we got a call from the police. He said that they had found Freddie at a drive-in theatre north of town, that he was—oh, God!"

"Just another little minute, Mrs. Odom, please."

"The man said that he was dead out there."

"Thank you, Mrs. Odom. Your honor, those are all the questions I have."

The judge looked at Max. "Mr. Friedman?"

Max half rose from his chair. "No questions of this witness, your honor."

"You may step down."

Regina stood carefully, her hand on the witness box rail, and walked down the aisle to her seat between Bernice and Dolores.

When she was seated, Judge Bruce said "Please call your next witness."

"Yes, your honor. The State calls Dr. Charles Block."

Dr. Block, the medical examiner, was a business-like man whom Diane took through a detailed description of the remains of Freddie Odom. He established that the victim, a white male, approximately 25-35 years old, was found at the Comanche Drive-In Theatre. The cause of death had been trauma to the left side of the skull.

"Can you tell us, Dr. Block, what might have caused such an injury?"

"I can't tell you exactly what object would have caused it, but it was most likely large and heavy, wide rather than narrow, certainly a piece of wood, perhaps a baseball bat. There were splinters present in the skin, and small traces of white paint."

Max noticed the English teacher on the jury wince.

"Dr. Block, do you think that a bowling pin might have caused the injury that you are describing?"

"I think that would be very consistent with the injury, yes."

"Thank you. I have no more questions."

The judge raised his bushy gray eyebrows at Max. "Defense?"

Max half rose in his chair. "No questions, your honor."

Joe whispered to Max, "Why ain't you going to ask any questions?"

"Not worth it," he whispered back. "We're agreeing with what he says."

"Call your next witness please," the judge said.

"The State calls Harvey Phillips."

Champ Phillips rose lankily from his seat and slowly made his way up the aisle. He wore his standard uniform of white shirt and khaki pants but had added a bolo tie out of deference to the court's formality. His badge hung on his belt, and he had taken off his gun. He held his gray Stetson in his left hand as he took the oath. When asked he gave his full name, Harvey James Phillips, which few in the courtroom had ever heard.

He sat straight as the pharaohs' statues, knees together, the hat hanging on his left knee.

Diane walked to him, a smile on her face. "Sir, will you please tell us what you do for a living?"

"I'm a Detective Lieutenant with the Amarillo Police Department."

"Thank you for taking the time for us today, Lieutenant."

His lips curved slightly, and he smiled.

"Detective Phillips, please tell the court the circumstances surrounding the first time you heard the name 'Freddie Odom.'"

He nodded. "I was at home on the night of November 4th, when the telephone rang. A man's voice said that he had some information for me."

"Did he say information about what?"

"No ma'am. He seemed very nervous to me, and wouldn't give me his name at first."

"Did he seem nervous, or did he sound scared?"

Max glanced at the judge. "Objection, your honor. I think this calls for more information than the witness is able to provide."

Judge Bruce, his chin still in his hand, considered for a moment. "I'll sustain that objection," he said.

Diane gave Max a hard look that the jury couldn't see and turned back to Champ. "You said the defendant was nervous, Lieutenant?"

"Yes ma'am."

"Were you ever able to ascertain what the caller wanted, or who he was?"

"I was finally able to get his name, which he said was Freddie Odom. It seemed like he was about to tell me more when the line went dead."

"He hung up?"

"No, I didn't get that impression. He was still talking, and suddenly the connection was gone. I got the impression that he didn't hang up, but that the line went dead for some other reason."

"What kind of reason might that be?"

"Maybe someone else cut the line off."

"Objection, your Honor, that calls for speculation," Max said.

"Sustained. Ms. DiAngelo, that is conjecture."

"Thank you, your honor. Lieutenant, you said that the line went dead while Mr. Odom was speaking?"

"Yes."

"What did you do then?"

"I tried Mr. Odom's home number, which I found in the telephone book, and a woman answered and told me that he wasn't home."

"Lieutenant, did you ever have reason to trace the call that you had received that night?"

"Yes. About a month later I ascertained that the call had come from a pay phone at a Pac-n-Sac store."

"When was the next time that you heard the name Freddie Odom?"

"About three weeks later, on Thanksgiving Day, I received a call that a body had been found and I was needed to investigate it. I drove to the old Comanche Drive-In Theatre on the Tascosa Highway. Two boys had found a body buried there, and they called 911. When I arrived, the crime-scene unit had unearthed the body. There was a wallet with a license in the name of Freddie Odom. My partner confirmed that the remains bore a similarity in height and hair color to a missing person case he was investigating. We obtained dental records, which were a match."

"Lieutenant Phillips, just a few more questions. You said that the body had been found by two boys. Is that correct?"

"Yes, it is."

"Can you tell us about the circumstances?"

"They were out playing on their bicycles, jumping over the little hills out at the drive-in, when they found it."

"Did you speak to them personally?"

"Yes, I did."

"Lieutenant, is it true that the boys' parents have entered them into counseling?"

"Objection, your honor. Relevance."

"Sustained."

Diane walked to the exhibits table. "Your honor, at this time I'd like to introduce into evidence photographs taken at the crime scene."

Max stood quickly. "Your honor, I'd like to ask that these photographs not be introduced. The defense doesn't contest the—"

The judge crooked his finger at them. "Step up, please." They walked to the bench and Judge Bruce covered the microphone. "Mr. Friedman?"

"Your honor, the defense doesn't contest the location of the body, or its condition. The photographs are purely prejudicial. There's no substantive purpose for introducing them."

"Ms. DiAngelo?"

"In order for the jury to understand the entirety of the case, it is essential that they be able to see the crime scene—"

"Your Honor," Max said, "I have no objection to taking the jury to the drive-in in order to view the scene."

"Mr. Friedman, don't interrupt. It's very rude. I'll allow the photographs. Step back, please."

"Thank you, Your Honor," Diane said.

"Don't thank me. Next time it'll be you."

Diane stepped back to the exhibits table and produced two packets of 8x10 glossy color photographs. She dropped one in front of Max at the defense table and approached the jury.

"Ladies and gentlemen, in order for you to more fully understand the scene that greeted Lieutenant Phillips when he arrived at the Comanche Drive-In on Thanksgiving Day, I introduce into evidence these photographs."

Max looked through them as they passed slowly among the jury members. He'd seen them before in the evidence file, but the impact of crime scene photos never faded for him. He wondered if police officers felt the same. Did the photos somehow lose their power? Did an investigator look at a photo of a murdered and raped child, an old woman beaten pulpy for fifteen dollars in crack money and think of it as just another body?

In front of him Freddie Odom lay under the sand at the Comanche; what skin was left peeled back from the bones, and was already almost mummified from the dry ground. The shirt he had worn when he left home to get beer and videos was still intact, although his skin wasn't.

Max glanced at the jury. Some of them were trying to appear stony, but he knew it was an act. It always was. Some jury members thought their duty of impartiality was to act emotionless. Other members were showing their revulsion, and one woman had tears streaming down her face.

Max spoke very quietly to Joe, but not out of the corner of his mouth, which would have looked like they were both guilty. "Look at the photos, but don't make an expression. Just look at them. Not revulsion, not a thing. Just be serious, and then look back up."

Joe did it, glancing at the photos as Max moved them from the top of the stack to the bottom. When they had gone through all of them, Max placed them carefully back into the folder. The photos made their way to the final juror, who handed them back to Diane. She laid them on the prosecution's table.

"Lieutenant Phillips, were you present when these photographs were taken?"

"Yes, I was."

"Do you believe that they accurately depict the condition of Mr. Odom's body at the time of its discovery?"

"Yes."

"Your honor, I have no more questions for this witness."

"Mr. Friedman?"

Max rose and walked toward the witness stand.

"Lieutenant, I may have missed something in your testimony, so please let me ask you a couple of questions just to be sure."

Champ nodded.

"Can you tell me why Mr. Odom called you that night?"

"We didn't talk long enough for me to tell, but he said 'I've got something you want.' I assumed he had some information for me."

"But beyond that, you don't really know why he called, is that correct?"

"Yes."

"No more questions at this time."

"You may step down," the judge said.

Champ rose from his seat, walked through the swinging gate in the rail, and down the aisle through the courtroom doors. He looked to Max like the consummate Texan, a man's man. Even the way he pushed open the little gate, he could have been walking through the swinging doors of the Long Branch Saloon.

"Prosecution, call your next witness."

"The State calls Smith Dixon."

"Son of a bitch should keep his mouth shut," Joe mumbled.

"Knock it off," Max mumbled back.

There was a pause of twenty seconds before Smith entered the courtroom between two police officers. He was dressed in neatly pressed jeans, a white cowboy shirt, and the corduroy jacket he had come into town wearing four months earlier.

"State your name, please."

"Smith Dixon."

The bailiff looked at him suspiciously as if he were already telling a lie before the oath had been administered. "Full name, please."

"That's all there is."

"Do you swear to tell the truth, the whole truth, and nothing but the truth, so help you God?"

"I do."

"Be seated."

Smith settled himself into the witness chair. His wrists chafed from the handcuffs the officers had removed just before they brought him into the courtroom. No matter how short a time they were on, they always felt bad. Especially this time, when he had sworn to himself that he wouldn't ever have to wear them again. He wanted to rub his wrists, but he would let them itch before he did it front of this court.

Diane looked at him sternly. "Mr. Dixon, do you remember where you were and what you were doing on the night of October 31 last year?"

"Yes ma'am, I do."

"Will you tell the court, please?"

"That night I was in the Food Giant on Georgia Street."

"What were you doing there?"

"I was robbing it."

"Who was with you?"

"Carl Puente and Joe Wagner."

Among the rows of observers, Smith saw the women he knew were Freddie and Carl's family. Regina Odom's eyes were brimming with tears. When he said Carl's name he saw the other two women flinch, and then their faces became stony. Jesus Christ Carl, he thought, you didn't tell them, did you?

"Is that all?

"Freddie Odom drove the car for us, but he didn't come into the store. He was outside the whole time."

"Whose idea was it to rob the store? Was it Freddie's?"

He smiled, his lips curving just slightly. "No ma'am. Joe said he'd worked there, and he thought it would be easy."

"What'd I tell you," Joe mumbled to Max. Max didn't say anything.

"So you're saying the idea to rob the store came from the defendant, Mr. Wagner?"

"I think it was my idea. He just suggested the place."

"How did Mr. Puente and Mr. Odom get involved?"

"I knew Carl needed some money. I heard him talking one night. Freddie found out about it and wanted in too."

"Did the robbery go off as you expected?"

"It went fine."

"How much money did you make?"

"Came out with almost sixty-three thousand."

"Split four ways? That's a lot of money."

"Freddie got two thousand, and we split the rest."

Although her expression didn't change, Smith saw tears begin to stream down the face of Regina Odom, who had just discovered the price of her husband's life.

"Did you seen any of these men again?"

"I wish I hadn't."

"Can I take that as a 'yes'?"

"If you want to."

"Mr. Dixon, just answer the question please," the judge said.

"I saw them all again, yes."

"Describe that occasion, please."

"It was four nights after the robbery. Wednesday, November 4th. I got a call that night from Joe, said he needed to talk to me, to meet him at the Comanche Drive-In."

"Why did he choose that spot?"

"We'd met there once before, to talk it over."

"The robbery?"

"Yeah."

"Did the defendant say why he wanted to see you?"

"He told me that he'd found Freddie on a pay phone, calling the cops."

"Mr. Dixon, Lieutenant Phillips of the Amarillo Police Department has testified that he received a call from Freddie Odom that night. Do you believe that this is the call Mr. Wagner was referring to?"

"Seems like it."

"What did you do then?"

"I drove out there."

"Will you tell us what happened at the drive-in, to the best of your memory?"

"My memory's pretty good, ma'am." Smith couldn't be sure, but he thought he saw the long-haired defense lawyer suppress a smile. "I got out there about 9:15, and Freddie was in Joe's truck on the passenger's side. Joe was outside, and he told me that Freddie was going to call the cops and give us all up, that he'd heard Freddie on the phone."

Smith glanced at Joe, sitting at the defense table, and looked back at Diane. "What happened next?" she prompted him.

"I tried to get him, Joe, calmed down. Wasn't going to work. He pulled Freddie out of the truck, starting roughing him up."

"Can you explain that, please?"

"Pushing him around, calling him names. Threatening him. You know."

"Did he hit him at that point?"

"No. Mostly he called him names and he pushed him down. Then it was funny what happened. Freddie, he kind of got up and was giving it back to Joe."

"What do you mean?"

"Freddie stood up to him. Joe'd been calling him a faggot, a queer, and Freddie started doing the same thing. All of a sudden he just ran at Joe and knocked him down. Joe came right back up, ready to fight hard this time, and I tried to separate them. I had my back to Joe and he knocked us both down. I sprained my wrist. Joe went to hitting Freddie and kicking him in the ribs."

Diane turned to the jury with a look that said, do you see what this man is? This animal who is on trial?

"After the defendant had Mr. Odom on the ground, kicking him in the ribs, what happened?"

"They both got up. I was still down, hurting, and I saw Joe had something in his hands. I could tell he was going to hit Freddie, and I tried to stop him, but it was too late. I took the pin away from him, threw it away. But Freddie went down, for the last time."

"Mr. Dixon, you just used the word 'pin.' What do you mean?"

"Joe had a bowling pin that had been laying there. He'd been jacking around with it earlier, throwing it up in the air, and then he picked it up and hit Freddie with it."

"Was Mr. Odom dead?"

"I ain't a doctor, but it seemed like it. Joe hit him pretty hard, and when Freddie went down he didn't move. I checked his pulse and his breathing. There was blood coming out of his ear, and I took all that as him being dead."

"What happened next?"

"Right then Carl showed up. He and I talked for a while."

"What was the subject of your conversation?"

God, Smith thought, deliver me from this as soon as you can. "Carl saw what had happened and wanted to call the police. I talked him out of it, told him Freddie was dead, and it would be best for everyone if we didn't call."

Max heard stifled crying and knew that it was coming from Freddie's family. There was more than one woman crying now, he could tell.

"I told Carl that he needed to stay out of prison, he needed to take care of his family and Freddie's."

"How did Freddie Odom end up buried in a foot of sand and dirt?"

Smith started to speak, but his voice caught. He cleared his throat but still couldn't manage to find a word to begin with.

"Mr. Dixon?"

"We—I told Carl I thought it would be best if we buried Freddie out there. Joe dug the hole, and that's what we did."

"And then you left?"

"Yes, ma'am."

"I have no further questions for the witness at this time."

The judge looked at Max. "Mr. Friedman?"

"Just a few, your honor."

Max glanced at the legal pad where he'd been taking notes during Smith's testimony. He knew all the questions he wanted to ask already, but he'd found through the years that juries thought lawyers should ask questions that they came up with during the testimony. Perhaps it fed their sense of drama, the belief that an attorney's case could suddenly change in the middle of a trial, like it did in *Law and Order*. He found that in principle, the more a jury believed you competent and up to their expectations, the more willing they were to trust you and side with you. He picked up the pad and walked over to the witness box.

"Mr. Dixon, I'd like to explore some of the answers you gave to Ms. DiAngelo, and ask some questions that I didn't hear her address. Okay?"

Smith nodded, glad that the blonde D.A. had finally sat down. Smith didn't much trust lawyers, but he knew this one shot a damn good game of pool, and that made him admirable, if not trustworthy.

"Good. Now you said a short while ago under testimony that Mr. Wagner was 'pushing Freddie around, and calling him names.' Have you spent a lot of time around men who like to fight, who act like bullies?"

"I guess so."

"Did you feel at the time that the defendant was pushing Freddie Odom that there was a likelihood of violence, the kind that would result in death?"

Smith hesitated. "It didn't seem likely to me, tell you the truth. Joe always kind of struck me as, kind of all hat and no cattle. I didn't like him, but I didn't think he'd kill anyone. It seemed to me like he was going to try to scare Freddie a little. If he'd wanted to kill him, there'd be no reason to have called me."

Max wished he could see Diane's face, to see her reaction to her own witness scoring a point for the defense. "So when, in your opinion, did a scuffle turn into a violent fight that led to a man's death?"

Smith thought for a moment, staring down at his knees. "I think it was about the time that Freddie started talking back to Joe. At first he was real scared, but then he started talking back to him, and then he just flat out hit him, ran him straight over. That's when it changed."

"Now you said in your testimony that in addition to pushing Mr. Odom, Mr. Wagner had been 'calling him names.' Can you elaborate on that? What kind of names?"

"Well, Joe was always calling people stuff like faggot and queer and like that. Whenever he'd tell stories that's always what it was, 'faggot' and 'queer.'"

He'd done that to Carl one night in the pool hall where we hang out too."

"You said that then Freddie Odom started 'giving it back to Joe.' Can you explain what you mean by that?"

"He started up calling Joe a faggot and a queer. Saying other stuff like that."

"What other stuff?"

Smith's eyes flicked to the jury, then to Diane, and finally to the judge. He licked his lips. "I don't know if it's something I should say."

Judge Bruce looked down at him. "I'm sure we've all been around the block a few times, Mr. Dixon. Please answer the question."

"Well, Freddie started calling Joe a faggot and a queer, like I said, then he said Joe was the one who's a queer, said why are you always talking about sucking dicks—" He coughed as if to clear his throat. "Freddie said I've got kids and you don't, you know, so you're the one who's a faggot."

"Would you say at that moment Freddie Odom was acting aggressively toward Joe Wagner? Acting in a hostile, violent manner?"

"Objection," Diane said. "He's leading the witness."

"Sustained," the judge said. "Rephrase, please."

"Mr. Dixon, how would you characterize Mr. Odom's behavior at this point? Was it different than it had been before?"

"Yeah, I'd say so. Freddie was acting pissed off, like he was mad at Joe."

"Did you think the anger might become violence?"

"Well, it did a little when Freddie knocked him down. Joe came up real hot, and then he really went kind of crazy. Knocked me down when I got in his way, kicking Freddie, and then he hit him."

"Mr. Dixon, here's one of those questions that Ms. DiAngelo didn't ask you. After the defendant hit Mr. Odom that final time, what did he do?"

"I thought it was funny. Not ha ha funny, but strange. He didn't do nothing. I looked over at him, and I don't know, but it looked like he was crying. Then he just kind of sat down with his back to one of those old poles the speakers was on."

"Mr. Dixon, was this typical behavior for Mr. Wagner?"

Diane was on her feet in a moment. "Objection, your honor. The witness is not in a position to judge what is typical for the defendant. He's not a family member."

Max looked at the judge. "Your honor, Mr. Dixon spent quite a bit of time with the defendant over a period of a month or longer. I think he's qualified to say what he observed."

"Overruled. Answer the question, please."

"I wouldn't say it was typical, no. Kind of strange for him. Usually he'd be talking more."

"How long did this strange behavior last, Mr. Dixon?"

Smith thought for a moment, putting himself back to that night. "Maybe twenty minutes, half hour maybe. Carl showed up about the time Joe sat down, and we talked for a while. Then Joe started to come around, become his old self again."

"How would you say that he became 'his old self again?'"

"Started talking to us. He said he'd get rid of Freddie's car. He uh, he started digging, you know, for a place to put Freddie. Then in a little bit he started talking about how Freddie had called him a faggot, and how he—"

"Thank you. I believe those are all the questions I have for you." Max took two steps back toward the defense table, then stopped and quickly turned to face Smith again. "I'm sorry, I did have one more, Mr. Dixon. You said that after Mr. Odom called the defendant names, including 'faggot' and 'queer,' and attacked him, that they fought. You said that Mr. Wagner struck him, and then was quiet for about twenty or thirty minutes. Between the time of the fight and when Mr. Wagner started to speak again, did you hear him say anything?"

"Yeah, I did."

"What was that?"

"He said something like 'I didn't go to kill him. He should have shut up.' That's pretty close."

"'Go to kill him,'" Max said. "Can you tell me what that means to you?"

"Means he hadn't meant to kill him, you know. He wasn't trying to."

"One more question. You said that Mr. Wagner didn't speak for twenty or thirty minutes. When he did, what did he say?"

"Me and Carl were talking about what we could do with Freddie's car. Joe said he could get rid of it. Then he looked at Carl, and he said 'When'd you get here?

"How long had Mr. Puente been there?"

"He got there right after Freddie went down, so you know—twenty minutes or a half hour."

"Were you and Mr. Puente talking quietly?"

"Well, a little. You know, the place is kind of isolated, but we weren't yelling or anything."

"Were you talking loudly enough for Mr. Wagner to hear you, in your opinion?"

"Sure. He was right there."

"Thank you, Mr. Dixon. Those are all the questions I have, your Honor."

Judge Bruce said "The witness is excused for now. However, please remember that either side has the right to recall you to the stand."

"Yes sir," Smith said. "Your Honor." He stepped down and immediately a sheriff's deputy came to his side, escorting him down the center aisle. The deputy opened the door with his left hand and putting his right between Smith's shoulder blades, guided him through the doorway.

As soon as they got out into the corridor, the deputy said "All right, hold 'em out." Smith put his wrists in front of him, but before the officer could snap the handcuffs, a voice said "Hold off a second."

Smith looked across the hallway and saw Champ Phillips leaning against the wall next to a water fountain, one lean leg bent up, the boot against the marble wall, gray cowboy hat hanging loosely in his left hand. He slowly unfolded himself and ambled over to where they stood.

"I need to talk to this one for a while," he said.

"But I'm supposed to—"

"I'll take care of him when we're done," he said. "You're officially relieved of duties."

The young deputy still looked suspicious. "Tell you what," Champ said. "He tries anything, I'll just shoot him. That okay with you?" he said to Smith.

Smith shrugged. "I'll take that as a yes," Champ said, turning to the deputy. "Really. It'll be okay."

"Yes sir," the deputy said, and walked down the hall. He looked back over his shoulder once, as if to be sure Smith was still there.

"We going to need cuffs?"

Smith shrugged his shoulders again. "I'll take this one as a no. What I told that boy was true, though. I wouldn't hesitate to put a hole in you, although Maintenance would give me hell about the mess. You read me? You can talk, right?"

"Yeah."

"Good." He put a hand on Smith's shoulder. "I'm about to die for a cup of coffee. You?"

"Be okay."

No one gave them a look on the way to the cafeteria. Champ bought them each a cup and they settled into a small table away from anyone else. The coffee was served in thick porcelain cups on saucers. Champ lifted his and blew on it, the hair in his thick, salt and pepper mustache lifting slightly, then relaxing. Smith sipped from his.

"It okay?"

Smith nodded.

"I like these cups," Champ said. "Reminds me of when I was a kid." He took another sip. "I got a call this morning, over at my office."

"Yeah?"

"From that nursing home."

Smith sipped the coffee, and when he put the cup back on the saucer there was a little rattle. "He okay?"

Champ shook his head.

"Shit."

Champ took his handkerchief out and handed it over to Smith. "You want to talk about it?"

He shook his head. "Not much to say, I guess." He wiped his eyes, embarrassed. "He ever wake up?"

Neither of the men looked into the other's eyes. "No," Champ said. "They said he stayed in a coma until the end."

"I guess it's just as well. I'd have hated for him to woke up, seen me in all this again." He looked toward the cafeteria line. "You think the state of Texas could afford to buy me a piece of pie?"

"Oh, I don't know about that. Things are pretty tight down here, what with the price of executing people every month or so." Smith had to look at him to see if he was joshing, and he still wasn't sure. "If the state can't I will. Just don't run off, though," he said, patting his pistol significantly. "You wouldn't believe the paperwork when you shoot someone."

He handed Smith a five dollar bill and watched him buy a piece of chess pie. Smith glanced over at Champ as he put the receipt and change on his tray next to the pie. Goddamn cop with a sense of humor.

He sat back down and carefully forked a narrow slice of the pie into his mouth. He finished it one small bite at a time and wiped his mouth with the brown paper napkin.

"You think they'll let me have any of that supermarket money back so I can bury him?"

"Offhand I'd say don't count on it."

"Yeah. I got a couple dollars of my own left. You know how much it is to cremate him?"

"Not for sure. I got a couple favors owed me here and there. I might could call one in."

"What for?"

"Get me a good place in line on Judgment Day, I guess."

Smith got up and refilled both their coffee cups. "Don't shoot," he said when he sat down, putting Champ's cup in front of him.

"She offer you any kind of a deal?" Champ said.

"Oh, yeah. She said I might get out before I turned ninety, and if I was real good she wouldn't cut my dick off."

"That right. Have you pled yet?"

"Not yet."

"Might be with the right lawyer, you could cut a better deal, seeing as you cooperated and everything. Might could get a few years shaved off."

"You talking about a lawyer works for money? Cause like I said, there isn't much."

Champ brushed his mustache gently with his forefinger. "Could be you could find a lawyer who appreciates a man that plays a good game of pool. One who wouldn't mind taking on the D.A. again. Who knows, with a few people in your corner, maybe the parole board would let you out a little early. If you was to come back to Amarillo, try to settle down here and give up your wild old ways, you can't tell what they'd do."

They drank their coffee. "What are you wanting out of this?" Smith said.

"I don't know. Nothing, really. Maybe I'm getting sentimental in my old age, but I like to see a man go right when he's offered the chance."

"Most people wouldn't consider me much of a good man," Smith said.

"When we searched your place, must have been a hundred books in there. Most people never even buy a book during the course of a year, you know that? Or at least that's what I heard on the radio one time. It said over half the people don't even read a book the whole year long. Me, I read a lot of them."

Smith thought for a moment. "That lawyer from Bailey's, the one defending Joe?"

"Couldn't hurt to ask him. Maybe I could plant a burr under his saddle too, if I was to see him."

"I'd appreciate that."

"Yeah, well. I guess we'd better quit lollygagging here before they call out the cops on us. I need to get you back to the jail and get going on a stack of folders on my desk."

They stood up and bussed their table, then made their way out into the corridor. Champ found a passing deputy and turned Smith over into her custody. She snapped her cuffs on him, and as she started to take him away Smith glanced over his shoulder. "Thanks, Lieutenant."

"De nada," Champ said. "Just don't disappoint me."

Chapter 29

Carl Puente sat on the witness stand watching the D.A. approach him. Keep calm, he told himself. She said if he testified against Joe she'd make sure that he could plead guilty and get a suspended sentence. It wasn't like he'd planned it or anything. Besides, he had a wife and daughter to take care of, and Regina and her kids would need help. You're an upstanding citizen, not an asshole criminal like Joe and Smith, he kept telling himself. You'll get through this.

"Mr. Puente," Diane said, "will you tell us where you first met the defendant, Joseph Wagner?"

"Yes, of course," he said. "I can't tell you exactly what date, but it was in late October, I think, at a pool hall called Bailey's." He glanced over her shoulder, and as he did he saw Angel sitting at the back of the courtroom. He hesitated, lost in that moment, and realized he was hearing the D.A.'s voice.

"—tell us about that night?"

"I'm sorry?"

"What can you tell us about that night?"

"I was there shooting pool, with my—with my wife's brother-in-law, Freddie Odom. A man I'd known in high school, Smith Dixon, came up and asked if he and his friend could shoot a game with us. Wagner was his friend."

"What happened that night?"

"Wagner was causing trouble, trying to make me lose my temper."

"And how was he doing that?"

"He was talking about a Hispanic woman he liked to have sex with." Carl felt sweat creeping down his sides from under his arms, remembering Joe's voice that night, the fear he had felt, and hating himself for it. "He was doing it to make me angry, trying to start a fight."

"What happened that night? Was there a fight?"

"No. He got bounced out of the place before it could happen."

"Mr. Puente, did you feel that, before the defendant 'got bounced,' that it was likely he would attack you?"

"I felt sure of it."

"Did you believe that you were in danger of injury?"

Carl remembered the way he had felt that night, intense pressure in his bladder and his bowels, feeling like he was a little kid on the playground again, waiting for the second-grade bully to come for him.

"I felt sure of it, yes."

"When was the next time that you saw the defendant?"

"I can't remember the date exactly. About two weeks later. Smith Dixon and him were together, and Freddie and me. We got together to—" he paused, "to discuss something we were going to do."

"To discuss the four of you robbing the Food Giant supermarket?"

Goddamn bitch, Carl thought. "Yes." He had so far succeeded in not looking at Dolores and Regina and Bernice in the spectators' seats, but now he glanced at them anyway. Regina's face was in her hands and her shoulders were shaking. Bernice stared through him with frozen contempt. Dolores was slowly shaking her head, a single line of tears crawling from each eye, looking like someone had just kicked her in the stomach.

"Mr. Puente, can you describe Mr. Wagner's behavior at that meeting?"

"It was typical. He threatened Freddie."

"What was the nature of his threats?"

"He pushed him, and might have gone further if Smith hadn't stopped him."

"Thank you. When was the next time you saw the defendant?"

Carl felt more sweat rolling down his sides. "On Halloween night last year, at the Food Giant store." He realized that this was the first time, outside of being grilled by the police and the D.A., that he'd actually said the words since it had happened. He'd talked to no one since then, hadn't heard the words leave his mouth, and now he was telling not only a whole room full of people, not only that smirky ponytail attorney and Angel, but Bernice and Dolores and Regina, too. His guts started to roil again, and he prayed for this to be over with quickly.

"We met there that night," he said. "Freddie stayed in the car."

"And what did you do?"

"I went in with Smith and—" he poked his chin at Joe.

"Does that mean that you and Smith Dixon and the defendant robbed the store together?"

He cleared his throat. "Yes, it does."

"Did Mr. Wagner do anything that night that you would consider violent?"

"He stepped on the manager's ankle, when the man was trying to trip the alarm. I heard on the TV he broke some bones. Then it seemed like he wanted to rape one of the store clerks, but Smith stopped him."

"Is there anything else?"

"When the manager was tied up on the floor, Wagner stuck the shotgun to his head, like he was going to shoot him. He pulled the trigger, but the gun was empty. I think he did it just to scare him."

"Mr. Puente, please tell us about the next time that you saw Joe Wagner."

"Three or four days after the—after we were at the store, I got a call late one night from Smith Dixon. He said there was a problem, and that we had to take care of it. He told me to meet him at the Comanche Drive-In."

"Did you meet him there?"

"Yes."

"And when you got there, what did you find?"

Carl coughed. "When I got there, Smith was sitting on the ground. Freddie was laying in his lap, and—" his voice caught and he cleared his throat again. "Freddie was dead."

He dared a glance at the women of his family, and saw Dolores stand up and walk down the aisle to the courtroom door. She silently passed through it.

"Did you know who had killed Freddie Odom?"

"I just kind of assumed. I didn't think Smith would have done it, and I assumed Wagner had."

"Why did you assume that?"

"I never saw Smith as being a violent guy, but every time I saw Wagner, he was threatening somebody. Threatening to hurt them or kill them. I just figured he'd done it."

"What did you do then, Mr. Puente?"

"I wanted to call the police, tell them about everything, but Smith talked me out of it." He looked straight at Bernice and Regina, pleading. "He said that my wife and family needed me, and that Regina and her kids would need me to help out, too." Regina started to cry even harder, still silently. Bernice held her hand.

Diane turned to face the jury box. "After you decided not to inform the police about this crime, Mr. Puente, what did you do?"

Carl tried to think of something, anything he could say in his own defense, but there was nothing. "Smith and Wagner buried him, and then we left."

"You left Freddie Odom at the Comanche Drive-In Theatre?"

He expelled a long breath. "Yes."

"Thank you, Mr. Puente. Those are all my questions."

Judge Bruce looked at his watch. "Mr. Friedman, I'll give you the choice of proceeding now with your questioning, or breaking for lunch and resuming afterwards. Do you anticipate a long examination?"

"I think I can conclude before lunch, your honor."

"Good," the judge said.

"Mr. Puente," Max said, walking halfway to the witness stand, "let me clarify something I'm unsure of. Have you ever seen my client commit an act of violence?"

Carl thought for a moment, his fingers gripping the handrail of the witness box. He knew this slick guy from Bailey's and didn't trust him. Max was a lawyer, and Carl damn sure knew it was his job to make the state's witness look stupid. He thought for a moment longer and smiled. "He stepped on that man's ankle, and hurt him," he said. "I guess that was pretty violent."

"Okay," Max said. "Let's review that. He stepped on Mr. Waddell's ankle when he thought the manager was going to trip a silent alarm, is that correct?"

"Yes."

"And he did so during a robbery that you yourself participated in, isn't that also correct? Weren't you and Mr. Wagner there for the same purpose, to rob the store?"

God damn it! "Yes, but—"

"So let me ask you this. As a private citizen, you can decry Mr. Wagner's injury of Mr. Waddell as an act of violence. However, as a participant in the robbery of Food Giant, wouldn't the tripping of an alarm have been dangerous to you?"

"You've got to—"

"Please answer my question, Mr. Puente. Wouldn't it have been dangerous to you if the alarm had sounded?"

"Yes, but—"

"So essentially, Mr. Wagner's action was in the best interests of you and Mr. Dixon, and by extension Mr. Odom. Wouldn't you have tried to stop the manager from signaling the police if you could have?"

"I wouldn't have—"

"Just an answer to the question, please."

"Not in that way!"

"Of course, you could have asked him to stop. But if he didn't, wouldn't you have taken immediate action to stop him?"

"Yes, but—"

"What would you have done?"

"I wouldn't have hurt him! I would have told him that—"

"You would have threatened him?"

Diane rose to her feet, her right hand flat on the table top, her cheeks red. "Objection, your honor! Mr. Friedman is badgering this witness!"

The judge looked at Max with his sad, beagle eyes. "The objection is sustained. Counsel, you've made your point. Move on."

"Mr. Puente, besides the incident at the grocery store, when Mr. Wagner acted quickly to protect the interests of all of you—"

"Your honor!" Diane shouted.

"Mr. Friedman," the judge said, "although I've never spent the night at our county jail, I can almost guarantee you that the mattresses are not as comfortable as yours at home. Move on, please."

"I'm sorry, your honor. Mr. Puente, besides the incident at Food Giant, have you ever seen Mr. Wagner perform an act of violence?"

"I told you he pushed Freddie at the drive-in."

"The first time you met there, is that correct?"

"Yes."

"Was Mr. Odom injured that night? Did he fall down, get hurt?"

"No."

"All right. What other acts of violence have you seen Mr. Wagner commit?"

"At the pool hall," Carl said, sullenly.

"I'm sorry, do you mean the first time you met him? I understood from your testimony to Ms. DiAngelo that he insulted you, but I don't remember him acting violently."

"No."

"So, did you leave something out? What violent act did he commit?"

"Nothing, but—"

"So you have no knowledge—firsthand knowledge—of any violence committed by Mr. Wagner?"

Carl knew that the lawyer had done it. He'd made him look like a fool in front of everyone. His family, the judge, D.A., potential customers. A fool.

"I suppose not, but I knew that had the potential for it."

"Probably all of us have the potential for violence, Mr. Puente, but there's a big difference between having the potential to do something and actually doing it, isn't there? In most cases that potential will lie dormant, until something causes it to surface."

The judge turned toward Max. "Was that a question, Mr. Friedman?"

"No, your honor."

"In that case, do you have any more?"

"Not at this time, your honor."

Judge Bruce turned his face slowly to take in the entire courtroom. He rubbed his crown of white hair, followed it with his hand from one side of his head to the other. "In that case, the witness is excused. And we're breaking for lunch."

Carl tried hard to keep from trotting down from the witness stand and through the rail. Bernice had her back to him when he passed her, thank God, with her arm around Regina's shoulder. He walked down the aisle, averting his eyes when he saw Angel, although he could feel her staring a hole in his back. He opened the heavy door to the corridor and glanced around for Dolores. A young kid, probably a college student, walked up and stood right in front of him. The kid was tall, and Carl was craning his neck to look around him when he realized that the boy was saying his name.

"Mr. Puente?"

Carl finally focused on him.

"Yes?"

"Carl Puente?"

"Yes, I said that! Look, I've got to find some—"

"I have something for you, sir," he said, and thrust a thick envelope into Carl's hand.

"What's this?"

"I just deliver them, I don't read them," the kid said. "Hey, do you have that drapery business, over behind Western?"

"Yes," Carl said, his face automatically moving into business mode, his mouth bending into a smile. Then he realized where he was, and the smile faded.

"Yeah, we came over there one time, when my parents got new drapes for the house. Anyway," he said, starting to inch away, "sorry."

Carl was starting to rip open the envelope when he heard what the boy said. "What do you mean, 'sorry?' You said you didn't read them."

"Well, it's usually not good news," he said, and drifted into the crowd of people now filling the corridor.

Carl looked down at the papers, and the first words he saw were "dissolution of marriage." Then he saw his name, and Dolores's. He took a step backward, heard an angry "Hey!" when he stepped on a foot, and found his way to a bench against the wall. He tried his best to make sense of the words scattered on the paper, but it wasn't until that night, alone in the house, that he finally understood them.

He sat in his chair in the living room that night, a bottle of Pearl beer on the small table next to him, right beside the remote control and phone. He leaned back in the chair and took in the words on the paper. They told him, essentially, that Dolores was suing for divorce and taking Nina with her. After he left the courthouse he went to the store to see if anyone had managed to screw up anything, and then he went home to find all their clothes gone. Nina's closet was empty, and all of Dolores's stuff was gone from theirs. He microwaved some leftovers and thought about calling Dolores at Bernice's house, but he just wasn't up for it. In the morning, before work, he'd call her and see if maybe he couldn't talk some sense into her. After all, he didn't have to sign the goddamn papers, did he? He had a choice in this. She couldn't take his daughter away without his permission, could she? He needed to call a lawyer, and if she kept on with this shit in the morning, he'd do just that. After he finished eating he sat in his chair, his bare feet resting on the hooked rag rug, then he pulled out the papers again and looked through them. It was all that legalese crap, but it didn't take much effort to see what it was all about. Finally he put the papers aside and picked up the remote, hitting the mute button to bring back the sound. He idly flipped through the sports channels. The Super Bowl was already gone, so football was over until late summer. The Lakers were kicking somebody's ass, oh yeah the Knicks. He watched for a few minutes then flipped again to a hockey game, then a car race, then some cigarette boats zipping around a lake. He switched again, and the channel slid to a guy in a dress coat and a funny hat jumping a horse over little brick walls. He ended up at the Lakers and Knicks again and picked up the sports section of the *Globe News*. He looked over the schedule for the next few days and picked up the phone, pressing in a number he'd sworn he'd never call again. After three rings he heard the answer on the other end.

"Hey, Bobby," he said. "Yeah, that's right. Carl. You got a good ear. No, no, just a little while. Thought I'd knock off for a bit after we settled up, you know. Give it a rest. Say, what do you have on the Spurs tomorrow night? Uh huh. Yeah, I think I can do some of that. How about a hundred? Yeah, I'm good for it, no sweat there. I got the other stuff taken care of. Oh, you heard about that? Yeah, it's no big deal. Everything's great now. Yeah. Yeah. Me too, Bobby. We'll see how they play tomorrow night, I guess. I got my hopes up high, though. You're gonna be a little short after the horn blows on that one. Okay, you just watch. Yeah, thanks." He thumbed the off button on the phone and sat with it in his hand for a while, not really looking at it, but contemplating what he had done. Finally, he put the phone back on the table and picked up the packet of papers again. He took them out of the envelope, paused, and slid them back in. I'll look at them in the morning, he thought, maybe with the lawyer. Can't understand all that mumbo jumbo anyway. Goddamn lawyers. He turned the volume up on the Lakers and took a sip of his Pearl.

"How'd it go today?" Danny gently clicked the cue ball against the five, nudging it into the left side pocket. He was wearing what Max thought of as his dress-up clothes, meaning that his shirt was clean and he wasn't wearing chaps. The rest of his clothes, including the manure-caked boots with spurs that seemed to be a permanent part of the design, were the same as always. He nudged the toothpick from one side of his mouth to the other while he contemplated the logistics of his next shot.

"Oh great, wonderful," Max said. "I've got a client who thinks all I have to do is put him on the stand to tell his side of the story, and everything will be copasetic. He thinks all he's got to do is just tell the jury that Freddie called him a fag, and they'll understand."

"'He needed killing,'" Danny said.

"Run that one by me again?"

"Time-honored Texas defense plea. Surprised you could pass the bar without knowing it. All you gotta do is say 'he needed killing,' and the jury shakes their heads, the judge hits the gavel say three times, and it's all she wrote. Case over. Everybody go home."

"I guess I got version Y instead of Version Z of the exam, and they didn't cover that one," Max said. "I've got to admit though, it would help out the docket quite a bit. Maybe those poor judges would have a chance to play golf more than once a week, and us poor defense lawyers wouldn't be so overworked and underpaid."

Angel walked over to their table. "But really, how are you doing?" she asked. "I mean I know how you're doing in the courtroom, which is really good, but how are *you* doing?"

"Let me tell you something," Max said. He watched Danny narrowly miss sinking the eight ball. He chalked his cue and walked around the table, assessing the placement of the balls. "Danny, you're a cruel man."

Danny laughed, the rumble of thunder. "Is that what you had to tell me? It ain't exactly news."

Max smiled and made a complicated bank shot. "On the way from the courthouse to my apartment tonight, there was a car stopped next to me. Two blonde girls in it."

"Uh huh," Danny said.

"This isn't going to be a blonde joke is it?" Angel asked.

"You're a redhead," Max said.

"Yeah, but just on principle."

"No blonde jokes."

"Okay."

"Can I go ahead now?"

"Shoot."

"So they're both in the car, talking away. The driver's got a cigarette between her fingers, gesturing with it, blowing smoke out of the corner of her mouth, you know how that looks."

"Charming."

"And I'm getting more and more pissed off," Max said. "I mean she's right there in the next car, smoking, and who gives her the right to do that?"

"Makes sense," Danny said. "You being pissed off about it, I mean."

"But no, there's more. She rolls the window down, and just drops the butt out. Still smoking, onto the street. So what do I do? What anybody would."

"Do you need a lawyer?" Danny asked.

"No. I get out of the car, walk around to hers, I pick up the butt and tap on her window. She hits the button, lowers it about two inches, because I don't look *that* crazy, and I say 'Miss, you dropped this,' and I just toss it through the window."

"Like I said, makes sense," Danny said. "I mean, who wouldn't have done that?"

"I go back to my car, she's screaming for no reason, because it's not really on fire anymore, and she had it in her mouth a second ago, so it's not like a flying roach or something, yelling that she's going to call the police. I get back in my car, the light changes, I go home and change clothes, feed the cats, come over here. So I think that's the answer to your question, how am I doing."

"Now I ain't for sure," Danny said, "but I think over at Fresh Air, in that other room off the main one, they hold Al-Anon meetings there. I mean I can't confirm that for myself, but rumor has it that there's some of those folks that hang out there and talk about us drunks and how bad we are. Talk about how they're powerless over making people behave the way they want. I think they've even got an 8:00 meeting there."

Max crouched down so he was eye-level to the table and raised up a few inches higher. He carefully sighted his cue, hit the pure white ball, and knocked the eight into a corner. "And you're trying to say what?"

"Nothing. Just saying that they got those meetings over there, if a fellow wanted to go to one, if he got to feeling like he was powerless over other people. You know, people who smoke, or people he ain't got no choice about defending." Danny walked around the table, rescuing the balls from their pockets and rolling them back on top. Angel picked them up and, without looking, expertly nestled them into the rack.

"You think they hold those meetings over there, huh?"

"Rumor has it."

Angel lifted the rack from the balls as carefully as if she were placing a dozen eggs on the green felt.

"You ready for another one?" Danny said.

Max studied the pool-playing dogs for a moment. "No, go ahead. I think I'm going to take a little walk. Get some fresh air."

Danny nodded. "Never hurt anybody, far as I've heard."

Max slipped his jacket on and left.

Chapter 30

Diane arrived in the courtroom five minutes early the next morning. She wore a navy blue suit over a white silk blouse and a string of pearls. Jack wasn't there yet, but Max Friedman was, and for some reason the fact that he had gotten there earlier than she irritated her. It made her look slack, unprofessional, to let this lawyer who didn't understand how the game was played beat her to the counsel table. She shook her shoulders slightly, trying to unseat the feeling of irritation.

Diane was happy with her case; her only regret was that she couldn't have finished it with Regina Odom. If she had called Regina as her final witness, it would have left the jury with the memory of a good man, a husband and father, struck down by the defendant. They would see the emotional distress Wagner had caused in the distraught widow. But if she had called her last, there wouldn't have been any real justification for it. Any testimony she could impart had already been described. Yet Diane needed her in front of the jury to put a face on the crime. It was very important that the jury see Freddie Odom as a real man, and the best way for them to see it was by meeting his wife. Ultimately, it probably didn't matter that Diane didn't finish with Regina. She had started her case with the grieving widow. The jury had seen her dressed in black, a tragic color for such a young, beautiful woman to wear. They would know it was Wagner's fault that she was wearing it. It's all that would matter in the end.

Diane waited impatiently for Jack Ogan to appear and made a mental note to tell him the importance of being on time—no, of being early. She glanced at Friedman, and he smiled at her. She nodded curtly and looked away quickly. He just irritated her, that's all there was to it. Maybe it was his long hair, which he refused to cut, or that New York smirk he always sported. And Champ liked him, which irked her even more. She didn't know what he saw in Friedman. She admitted Friedman was a good lawyer; there was no doubt about that. But having good technique didn't mean you were meant for it, didn't mean that you had what it took to last, especially when you were as sore a thumb in Amarillo as Max Friedman.

She shook her head, as if trying to send him flying out of her thoughts. All this didn't matter. What mattered was that the jury would look at her table and see her and Jack Ogan, solid lawyers who had proved murder beyond a reasonable doubt; at the other table they would see a redneck criminal and his sleazy lawyer, and the choice would be simple. Convict the criminal. Send a message to the lawyer that he wasn't wanted here. She would make it happen.

"Mr. Friedman, call your first witness, please."

"Thank you, your honor. The defense calls Dr. Robert Vermazen."

A man rose near the back of the courtroom and walked to the front. He paused a moment before pushing his way through the rail and faced the bailiff, who today wore a Winnie the Pooh tie. He swore in the doctor, a small man with a trim moustache. Robert Vermazen was in his late fifties and bore a strong resemblance to Edgar Allan Poe. The doctor wore a pinstripe charcoal suit with a subdued burgundy tie. Diane noticed the glint of cufflinks peeking from the sleeves of his jacket.

Max glanced at his legal pad and said "Dr. Vermazen, will you tell us your occupation, please?"

"Certainly. I'm a professor of psychology at the University of Houston, and I'm also a psychiatrist in private practice."

"Doctor Vermazen, were you offered money to testify in this trial?"

"Well," the doctor said, "you told me you could pay me twenty-nine cents a mile, which I believe is below the IRS standard, but I accepted nonetheless."

A wave of muffled laughter washed over the courtroom. The judge leaned forward and banged his gavel once, then settled back with eyes closed. "You can laugh outside all you want."

"Is that the only compensation you received?"

"Yes, it is. I have family in Spearman, and I'm going to visit them as well."

"Dr. Vermazen, will you please tell me what your specialty is?"

"As a teacher, I concentrate primarily on early childhood trauma as a source of adult dysfunction. In private practice I often work with children or adults who have undergone childhood trauma."

"Can you tell us just what this means, perhaps give us an example?"

"Yes. In my teaching I discuss with my students the ways that experiences traumatic to children can affect their ability to live a healthy adult life. Let's say, for example, that a child loses his parents violently, in a car accident or fire. That child, if untreated, will undoubtedly carry that trauma with him or her throughout life. The experience will change the way that he or she treats her own children. Someone who has suffered a loss like that might be more possessive, less willing to allow children to take normal risks, such as playing sports."

"Thank you. Does your teaching ever involve adults who were the victims of trauma not caused by nature, for instance traumatic violence or sexual abuse?"

"Yes, it does."

"Would you tell the court, please, how such trauma might affect an adult?"

"In many different ways. One adult who is a survivor of violence might withdraw, becoming very shy and protective. Another might try to replicate the violence, in other words to take revenge on other people for what was done to him. Studies have shown, for instance, that most people incarcerated for violent crimes were themselves victims of violence in childhood."

"Some would say, Dr. Vermazen, that prisoners might learn to give the answers that they think researchers want."

" I'm sure that certainly does happen, but in many cases someone's account can be substantiated by x-rays of broken bones, by scarring, by social workers' reports. Although there most likely is some room for error or deliberate falsehood, I don't think it would be greater than in studies of other groups."

Max stepped back to the defense table and glanced at his legal pad another time. He wanted to let the jury know that there was about to be a slight shift in his questions, from the general to the more specific, and that they must be ready for it.

"Dr. Vermazen, you also said that your teaching and private practice include work with men and women, adults, who have experienced sexual trauma during their childhoods. Is that correct?"

"Yes."

"What can you tell us about that work?"

"It's very similar to the results of acute physical abuse. Sometimes, of course, in children sexual abuse results in physical damage. At other times there is no overt damage, or what there is, is more difficult to discern."

"Dr. Vermazen, I know in matters of psychology it's often difficult to generalize. However, would you say there are particular patterns that children of either sex who are abuse survivors might follow?"

"Yes, I believe it is possible to make some general statements. For instance, some females who have been sexually abused might react by gaining weight. The underlying belief is that they will be safe from men if they are unattractive. The extra weight acts as a literal and figurative cushion against the sexual attention of men. Other women might perhaps go in the opposite direction, intentionally making themselves as attractive as possible, and in some cases engaging in sex with multiple partners. This establishes that they, and not their abusers, are in charge of their sexual life."

"Dr. Vermazen, can you tell us what reactions male survivors of sexual abuse might have?"

Max glanced at Joe from the corner of his eye. His client was doing remarkably well. His right foot, wearing a black cowboy boot, was jiggling furiously, but otherwise he showed no reaction.

Before the doctor could speak again, Diane said "Your honor, may I request a sidebar?" The judge nodded his head and beckoned them both to the bench. He covered the microphone with his hand and raised his eyebrows. "And?"

"Your honor, I think this line of questioning is getting ridiculous. I've allowed it to go on, but—"

"You've done no such thing, Ms. DiAngelo. I do the allowing in this room. What's your objection?"

"Your honor, this sounds like it's heading in the direction of recovered memory, or something similar. That's a defense that's been thoroughly discredited in courtroom after courtroom. I want to know where he's headed with this."

"Mr. Friedman?"

"It should be obvious where I'm headed. And it's not recovered memory. Just keep listening."

"Kindergarten, Mr. Friedman. I don't like it. Keep going in this direction, but plan on a quick arrival please. Ms. DiAngelo, please take your seat."

She stalked back to her table, arching her neck in a way that gave Max a crick just looking at her. Arrive quickly but cautiously, he thought.

"Dr. Vermazen, you were about to address my question of typical behavioral patterns for adult males who are survivors of sexual abuse."

"Yes. Thank you. Again, there is no one typical behavior. Each individual can manifest the results in a unique way. However, there are patterns. For example men, who are by nature more aggressively sexual than women, might seek more sexual encounters than a typical female survivor. A male survivor might engage in numerous sexual relationships, for instance, a behavior that has historically been more acceptable than it has for women. Conversely, as in the case of many women, some men might become sexually anorectic, going for years without any kind of healthy sexual contact."

"These behaviors sound sad, but fairly benign. Are they all that way?"

Diane said automatically, "Objection, your honor. Leading question."

"Sustained."

"Dr. Vermazen, what other types of behaviors have you observed in your practice or in clinical studies?"

He crossed one leg over another and straightened the material of his pants. "In some men we observe a unique behavior. For instance, men who have been sexually abused by other men may become very violent, as a way of denying fear of homosexuality. Although they may be heterosexual, their memory of the abuse makes them feel weak, something that many heterosexual men associate with homosexuality. So by acting violently, they feel that they are denying the possibility that they might be homosexuals. This is behavior often characterized as 'gay bashing,' in which heterosexual men harm and sometimes kill gay men. Often these acts are initiated by the attackers' fears about their own sexuality."

Max glanced at Joe, who narrowed his eyes, trying to get his attention. Perfect, he thought. Just what I need right now. A client conference.

"Dr. Vermazen, is it possible for someone to commit an act of violence without realizing that he is doing it?"

Vermazen glanced at the jury, then at Diane before focusing back on Max.

"That is possible, yes. The word 'dissociation' means that a person can be temporarily unaware of where he or she is at the moment, or what he or she— please forgive me, but I'm going to be terribly ungrammatically correct, and mix singular subjects and plural pronouns."

Max took in the observers, the jury, and the prosecutors. "I'm fairly new to Texas law, but as far as I know incorrect grammar isn't prosecutable." The English teacher smiled. "Please continue."

"'Dissociation' means that a person can be temporarily unaware of where they are at the moment, or what they are doing."

"Can you give us some examples, please?"

"Of course. Normal dissociation at its mildest can describe highway hypnosis as a result of driving a long distance—something I felt, for instance, on my drive here from Houston. Anyone who has ever become so enthralled in a book that they look up hours later to discover that the sun has set without their knowledge and the room is now dark, experiences it. This is an example of normal, mild dissociation."

"Can you give me an example of a more serious type of dissociation?"

"There is a fairly wide spectrum. At the most extreme end of it is Dissociative Identity Disorder—formerly called Multiple Personality Disorder—where a person can literally separate into two or more separate personas, each quite distinct from the others in terms of personality, age, even gender. The personas are created in order to protect the base identity from the pain of the abuse."

"Can you move a little farther back along the scale? Describe symptoms of dissociation that, while serious, are not as radical as DID?"

"Yes. Dissociation can manifest as depression, as an inability to completely function in life, a wide variety of addictive disorders, such as alcoholism, bulimia, sex addiction. Patients who suffer from dissociation often have trouble sleeping, keeping jobs, and generally functioning."

"Is it possible that a person suffering from dissociation might not know where he is at the moment, that he might lose the knowledge of who is around him?"

"Yes."

"Is it possible that someone might commit an act of violence against another person, believing that person to be someone else entirely?"

"Yes."

"What would that diagnosis be called?"

"Certain types of psychogenic fugue could appear that way, as could DDNOS."

"And what does that term mean, DDNOS?"

"Dissociative Disorders Not Otherwise Specified. It is a phrase used to describe a behavior that does not fit perfectly into another of the diagnoses."

Diane hastily scribbled on her legal pad. "Can you believe this bullshit?" she whispered to Jack out of the corner of her mouth.

"So, Dr. Vermazen, let me be sure I'm hearing you correctly," Max said. "In your experience, which I believe is based not only on years of study but on many actual cases that you have worked on, it is possible for a person to commit an act of violence without knowing exactly why he is committing that act, or against whom?"

"While experiencing an episode of dissociation, yes, that is certainly true."

"Doctor, can you please tell us again just what are considered to be the typical reasons that a person would suffer from dissociation?"

"Of course. Dissociation other than those mild forms caused by weariness or a moment's disorientation is almost always the result of some type of trauma. This trauma is commonly, although certainly not always, a result of childhood abuse. When it begins in adulthood it is often a result of experiences in war, or other types of emotional or physical violence. Rape, for instance."

"And how might it begin in childhood, Doctor?"

"It is typically a result of violence or traumatic abuse of some other type. Children who have been sexually abused, for instance, have a high rate of dissociation."

Max said "Thank you, Dr. Vermazen. Your Honor, I retain the right to recall this witness at another time if necessary."

The judge acknowledged his assent with a wave of the fingers on his right hand. "Ms. DiAngelo?"

"Your honor, we'd like to request a slightly longer lunch break today, in order to prepare our cross."

Judge Bruce's gaze swept slowly around the room like a turtle's. "Court will resume at 2:00," he said.

Max walked back to his table. "What the fuck was all that about?" Joe asked.

Max didn't look at him, but instead stacked his legal pads together and put them into his briefcase. "It's about trying to keep you out of prison," he said.

"But what was all that shit you were asking him? Dissoc—whatever the fuck you said. Violence and sexual abuse. What's that all about?"

Max stood up just as the deputies arrived to escort Joe to his cell. "Just trust me." He picked up his briefcase and hung the strap over his shoulder. "I'll see you after lunch," he said.

Max glanced at the women in Freddie's family, his widow and her mother and sister. He nodded to them and quickly walked down the aisle. When he reached the back of the room Angel emerged from the back row and fell into step beside him. "I brought some lunch. You want to join me?"

"I'd love to." They walked quickly down the hallway and the stairs. The day was warm for January in Amarillo. They walked across a grassy acre of park to where her truck sat at the curb. She took a paper sack out of the passenger's side and unwrapped two egg-salad sandwiches and a bag of Fritos.

"Fancy," he said.

"I'm a hell of a cook."

Angel took out a thermos of coffee and poured them each a cup. "Where you going with all that?"

"Why don't you stick around and see?"

"I'm going to. Just thought I could get a preview."

"I think I'll hold onto it for right now. Superstitious, I guess. Don't want to jinx anything. Is that okay?"

"Yeah, I guess so. It's not like it's a secret or anything." She took a bite of the egg salad, and a small piece dribbled down her chin. She looked around for a napkin, realized she didn't have one, and wiped her chin on her sleeve. "You didn't see that," she said.

"See what?"

He finished his sandwich and opened the bag of Fritos.

"So what happens next?"

"The DA grills my guy and I call my next witness."

"Who's that?"

Max looked down the block and squinted his eyes. "Hang on a second." He slid down off the hood of the truck and brushed off the back of his pants. "Be right back," he said, turning back to her but still walking. Nice boots, Angel thought.

She watched Max half walk, half trot down to where a woman was standing uncertainly, having just gotten out of a gold Lexus. Angel wondered briefly if she should feel jealous, then dismissed the thought as quickly as it had come. A man climbed out of the driver's side and joined them. Max talked a few minutes to the couple. In her years at Bailey's, Angel had become a fair judge of body language, and neither the man nor the woman looked very comfortable. They walked toward a coffee shop across the street, and Max came back to Angel.

"Everything okay?"

"It's good."

"More witnesses?

"Yeah."

Angel looked at a bank of clouds moving in from the north. She closed her eyes, and to Max it looked like she was smelling the air with her face. After a few moments she opened her eyes and said "Snow's coming."

"You got that off the Weather Channel."

"Don't have cable."

"The newspaper."

"Don't read it."

"You're telling me you know it's going to snow just by looking at the clouds and closing your eyes?"

She shrugged and stared off into the distance. "I think you've got to be a Texan," she finally said.

"Sometimes you guys piss me off so much."

She glanced at him out of the corner of her eyes and leaned gently over to kiss his cheek with lips that breathed out the rich smell of coffee.

Chapter 31

The bailiff smoothed Winnie the Pooh down over his large belly and reminded the court that Dr. Robert Vermazen was still a sworn witness.

Diane stood up, consulted her notes, and with both hands pushed her shoulder-length blonde hair behind her ears. Max recognized it as her "earnest, no nonsense" gesture. She kept studying her notes for a moment longer and looked at the witness.

"Good afternoon, Dr. Vermazen," she said pleasantly.

He nodded at her. "Good afternoon."

"You and Mr. Friedman have the court at a disadvantage, sir," she said. "You know why you're here, and Mr. Friedman knows why you're here, but the two of you have decided not to inform the court why you're here as of yet."

He smiled pleasantly.

"Dr. Vermazen, you and Mr. Friedman talked about something called 'DDNOS.' Do I have the acronym correct?"

"Yes, you do."

"And that stands for—" she searched her notes, and in a show of confusion that impressed Max, said "I'm sorry, I can't find it. Would you tell me again what it means, please?"

"Certainly. It means 'Dissociative Disorders Not Otherwise Specified.'"

"Yes, that's it. Can you tell me again what that means?"

"It describes a type of dissociative behavior that does not fit into other categories."

"'A Type of dissociative behavior that does not fit into other categories.' So in other words, it's a catch-all? Is that what you're saying?"

"No ma'am. It is a psychological diagnosis for a type of dissociation that does not easily fit into another diagnostic category."

"I'm sorry Doctor, but that still sounds like a catch-all to me. How would you feel if an oncologist told you that you had a type of cancer that 'does not easily fit into another diagnostic category'?"

"I would believe that my physician was a qualified professional who was operating under the most current medical definitions."

Good, thought Max.

"Dr. Vermazen," Diane said, "isn't it true that DDNOS is a fairly meaningless 'diagnosis?'"

Max could hear the quotation marks around the word.

"No, it's not. In psychology, as in any field of medicine, discoveries are constantly being made. New diseases develop, and professionals define them as quickly as they can. For instance, AIDS was unknown when it started to be noticed by the medical community in the early 1980's. Physicians did not know what to call it. It was several years before they decided on Acquired Immunodeficiency Syndrome. The fact that it did not initially have a name did not mean that it didn't exist."

Diane shook her head. "I'm sorry, Doctor. I feel like we're having two conversations here. You're discussing a disease that clearly existed, and was clearly diagnosed. From what I understand of DDNOS, it is *not* clearly diagnosable, but can be whatever anyone decides at the moment that it might be. Frankly, sir, it sounds like an excuse for sloppy medical practice." She waited for him to respond, but he gazed at her patiently.

"I'm sorry, I was waiting for a response from you, and it didn't come." She turned to the jury, including the observers with a gesture of her arm. "Or perhaps you did respond and I was unaware of it. I must have been suffering from a touch of DDNOS."

Laughter rippled through the observers, and from the corner of his eye Max saw a couple of the jurors smile. "Doctor, let's get honest with each other. What is DDNOS other than an example of sloppy psychology, a way that a doctor can escape from doing his or her, or should I say *your* job? Wouldn't it be more honest to just say 'I don't know,' than come up with some convoluted 'diagnosis' that is completely meaningless?" She stopped on the side of the witness stand near the jury, so that they could see her contemptuous expression.

She stared at him, and finally said "Do you plan to answer my question?"

"I'm sorry, it sounded rhetorical to me. The answer to your question is no. DDNOS is a legitimate—"

"Oh Doctor, come on. It has absolutely no mean—"

"Your honor," said Max, rising to his feet. "Ms. DiAngelo is badgering the witness."

"Cease and desist, counselor," Judge Bruce said. "If you have a question, please ask it. Otherwise, release the witness."

"I will release him," she said, "but if I need to recall him I can always plead DDNOS, can't I Doctor?"

Max, still on his feet, said "Your Honor!"

"Counselor, if you want to get on my bad side, feel free to continue in this vein."

"I have no desire to do that, your Honor." Diane smiled sweetly at him. "I have no more questions," she said.

"You are excused, Dr. Vermazen. Mr. Friedman, please call your next witness."

Max stood and said "Your Honor, the defense calls Evelyn Morton." He sat down again. It took a moment before Joe recognized the name. He grabbed Max's arm and whispered, "What are you talking about? That's my fucking sister! She ain't got nothing to do with this! She don't know nothing about it! Don't call her up there, you hear me?"

A guard at the back of the courtroom opened the door a few inches and leaned his head through it. In a moment he opened it wider, and Evelyn Morton walked through. She was dressed in a blue suit with a white blouse, and black shoes with medium heels. Nice, Max thought. She looked as classy as Diane, without the sorority cheerleader slant. She looked serious and respectable, conservative. A good witness.

The bailiff extended his hand in the direction of the witness chair and she stood in front of it. "Raise your right hand, please." She did, and he said "State your full name."

"Evelyn Marie Morton."

He rattled off "Do you swear to tell the truth, the whole truth, and nothing but the truth, so help you God?"

"I do."

"Please be seated." She sat down, carefully smoothing her skirt against her thighs.

Max walked slowly toward her. "Good morning."

Her smile was noncommittal. "Good afternoon."

"Sorry, my mistake. Good afternoon." Max knew she would correct him but in a very kind way, and he knew it would give the jury a good impression of her—precise, truthful, and polite. He needed all three of those qualities to be obvious to the twelve jurors.

"Ms. Morton, are you married?"

"Yes, I am."

"So when you gave your name as Evelyn Marie Morton, that wasn't your maiden name, is that correct?"

"Yes."

"What was your maiden name, please?"

She hesitated only a moment before she said "Wagner."

"Mrs. Morton, would you please look at the defendant, the man seated at the table, and tell us if you know him?"

"Yes, I do."

"How do you know him?"

"He's my brother."

Diane stood up quickly and said "Your honor, a sidebar please."

Judge Bruce gestured at both of them. "Approach." Diane strode swiftly toward the bench, her heels clicking angrily on the wooden floor, and Max crossed the few short steps from the witness chair. The judge covered the microphone with his hand. "Go ahead."

"Your Honor, unless this woman was at the scene of the murder and can offer direct testimony on what she saw, I don't care if she's the Queen of England's sister. She has no place on the stand."

Judge Bruce thought for a moment. "I think the Queen's sister's name is Margaret, so that's a moot point. Mr. Friedman, what do you have to say?"

"Your Honor, we're not here to determine whether Mr. Wagner struck the blow that killed Mr. Odom. We're here to determine whether or not any action of Mr. Wagner's can be considered murder. Those are entirely different things. This witness will give testimony that relates to Mr. Wagner's state of mind at the time of the murder."

"Your Honor," Diane interrupted, "she *wasn't there*. There's nothing she can say about his state of mind at the time of the murder! This is another bullsh—another scheme of the defense to confuse the jury!"

"I'm so glad you didn't curse at my bench, Ms. DiAngelo. I don't take that lightly. Mr. Friedman?"

"Your Honor, my previous statement will serve. Mrs. Morton's testimony is essential to the defense's goal of introducing reasonable doubt."

The Judge closed his eyes for a moment and stroked his moustache. "Ms. DiAngelo, I'm going to allow the questioning. Mr. Friedman, get to the point.

If you dilly-dally around you'll get a judicial wedgie very quickly. You understand?"

"Yes, Your Honor." A judicial wedgie?

"Ms. DiAngelo, you may take your seat. Mr. Friedman, please continue."

"Mrs. Morton, do you and your brother keep in regular contact?"

"No, we don't."

"Until today, how long had it been since you'd seen him?"

"About five years, I believe."

"Can you describe that occasion?"

"I saw him at a restaurant."

"Did you speak to him?"

"Yes, briefly."

"And before that, the time in the restaurant, when had you last seen him?"

"It was when I was seventeen years old."

"And can you tell us please, what the age difference is between you and your brother?"

"Six and a half years."

"So before you walked into the courtroom just now, the last time you saw your brother was five years ago. And before that it was—I'm sorry, but I'm going to have to break the time-honored Southern rule against revealing a lady's age. How long ago was it that you last saw your brother before that?"

"It was twenty years."

Max performed one of a lawyer's stock in trade acting tricks; he started to proceed, and then stopped in surprise at an answer he already knew. "You hadn't seen your brother in twenty years?"

"No."

"Mrs. Morton, how old were you when you left home?"

Evelyn hesitated a moment, then breathed a low sigh that only Max could hear. "I had just turned seventeen."

"So am I correct in assuming that you hadn't finished high school before you left?"

"Yes."

"Mrs. Morton, why did you leave home?"

She hesitated again and said "I felt that it was in my best interests to leave there."

Diane stood up. "Your honor, I must ask—" Judge Bruce waved his hand, gesturing her back into her chair.

"Mrs. Morton?"

"I felt that it was unsafe for me to remain there."

"Unsafe in what sense?"

"Physically unsafe."

"Tell us why, please."

Evelyn smoothed her skirt down again and shifted slightly, glancing at the judge.

"My father was a very angry man. He did the best that he could, but—"

"Mrs. Morton, were you scared of your father? Is that why you left?"

Diane raised her head but stayed in her chair. "Objection, your honor.

Leading the witness."

Max changed the question. "Mrs. Morton, why did you leave your home?"

"I was frightened of my father."

"Why?"

"He was very angry, and I was afraid of what he might do."

"Were you afraid that he might hurt you physically?"

"Yes."

Max crossed to the defense table and picked up several pieces of paper.

"Mrs. Morton, I have a hospital report here dated August 12, 1969, from the West Plains Medical Clinic. Your name is written in as the patient, and it says that you sustained a 'severe break in your right radius,' which if I remember correctly from science classes, is one of the bones in the forearm. How old would were you then?"

"Eleven."

"Mrs. Morton, do you remember breaking your arm?"

She said quietly, "Yes, I do."

"Will you please tell us how it happened?"

"Yes. At that time it was my job to set the dinner table and to clear it off. That night I was feeling sick, and after dinner I didn't clear off the dishes as quickly as I usually did."

"Why were you feeling sick?"

She cleared her throat as if it were sore, and said "I was having menstrual cramps. It was my first time I'd had my cycle. It was really painful, and I didn't know what it was."

Max looked into her eyes, and said in a voice loud enough for the jury to hear, "Thank you. So you didn't clean the table off as quickly as you were used to, and what happened then?"

"My father came into the dining room, and he started yelling at me."

"What did he yell at you?"

"He, he started calling me stupid. He called me a stupid little—a stupid little bitch."

"Where was your mother?"

"She was in the kitchen."

"Did she hear what your father was saying?"

"He was in the next room and he was yelling, so I would say yes, she did. I never asked her."

"Your father was yelling at you, and what happened then?"

"I tried to tell him that I was sick, and I started moving very quickly, stacking up the plates, trying to show him that I was doing what he wanted." She paused, and Max could see a glimmer of tears forming in the corner of her eyes.

"And then?"

"I was holding a stack of plates and he was standing over me, yelling at me and laughing at me at the same time. I was crying harder and harder, and I let the plates tip. Two or three of them fell to the floor and broke, and the silverware. My father grabbed my arm, and he wrung it, then he pushed me against the wall." Unconsciously she rubbed the healed right forearm with her left hand. "I hit the wall really hard, and I started screaming. He told me to shut up, that I wasn't hurt, and to stop crying like a 'little pig.' My arm hurt so bad, and I knew it was broken."

Max spoke as softly and kindly as he could, while still letting the judge and jury hear him. "Mrs. Morton, the hospital report said that you were admitted at 9:03 a.m. Yet you said that you were clearing the supper dishes. Is that correct?"

"Uh huh."

"If you were injured at night, why was it morning that you were taken in?"

"Mama—my mother wanted to take me in that night, but my father wouldn't allow her to. He said it wasn't that bad, that I was just faking it, that in the morning I'd get bored with it and quit. The next morning it hurt worse than ever, so when he went outside to work, she took me in."

"Mrs. Morton, where was your brother Joe when this happened, when your father broke your arm?"

"He was sitting in his chair at the table."

"Did he see what your father did to you?"

"Yes. He was crying, still sitting there when I went up to my room."

"So he watched the whole thing and no one took him out of the room?"

"No."

Max walked back to the defense table, not making eye contact with Joe, who was desperately trying to talk to him. He heard Joe's urgent whispering but kept his eyes down on his tablet of notes. He didn't need to consult anything; he just needed to give the jury a few moments to absorb what they had heard.

He turned his back to Joe and the defense table and faced Evelyn again.

"Mrs. Morton, you've just told us that your father physically abused you to the point that he broke your arm and refused medical help for you. In addition to the physical damage, did he ever abuse you verbally?"

"Yes, he did."

"Can you describe that, please? What would he say?"

"He'd always call me bad names. If I didn't do something the way he wanted, he'd say 'you little bitch,' things like that. He'd always tell me that I wasn't good for anything, that I was lazy and worthless. He'd call me a lazy bitch a lot."

"Did this abuse extend to your brother, too?"

"Yes."

"What kind of things would he say to your brother?"

"He'd call him stupid when he did things wrong, like he did me."

"Was there anything else?"

She coughed into her hand. "A lot of times, especially when Joe got a little older, he'd call him 'queer' and 'faggot.' Things like that."

Max looked incredulous. "He called his own son 'queer' and 'faggot?'"

"Yes."

"You said 'when he got a little older.' How old was your brother when your father called him those words?"

"Eight or nine."

"Mrs. Morton, you told the court that the last time you saw your brother before the time in the restaurant was when you were seventeen years old. Why was it that you didn't see him after that?"

She replied in a voice too low for anyone but Max to hear, "I left home."

Max glanced at the judge, who said kindly, "Could you say that a little louder, please?"

She cleared her throat, as if a catch in it had prevented her from speaking up. "I left home."

"Why did you leave?" Max asked.

"I got married."

"At age seventeen? Is that typical?"

"It's not too uncommon. A few—several girls in my class got married at that age or younger."

"Did they quit school and move away, too?"

"No, I think they—stayed, I believe."

"Mrs. Morton, was your marriage planned out for a long time?"

"No."

"Did you elope?"

"Yes."

"Where did you go when you got married?"

"To Euless. That's up near Ft. Worth."

"How long did you stay married?"

A tear slowly made its way out of her right eye, and down her cheek.

"About six months."

"Did you obtain a divorce?"

"No. I had the marriage annulled."

"Did you then live on your own?"

"Yes."

"Graduate from high school?

"No. I took a secretarial job and I got my GED."

"You went to college then, didn't you?"

She dabbed the tear from her cheek with a tissue.

"Yes. I went to college at nights; first Tarrant County Community College in Ft. Worth, then TCU. I began working in businesses."

"You got married again?"

"Yes."

"How long have you and your husband been married?"

"Sixteen years."

"How did you meet him?"

"We were in graduate school together at SMU."

Diane chose a warm tone to cover the sarcasm of her words. "Your Honor, I'm sure Mrs. Morton's biography is fascinating to us all, but is it relevant to the case?"

The judge looked at Max with his beagle eyes and said "Mr. Friedman, please move on."

"Mrs. Morton, did you ever return to your hometown?"

"Yes, I did. I moved back in 1985, and I've lived there ever since. My husband is president of the credit union, and I teach business classes and accounting at the high school."

"This is in Loving, is that correct?"

"Yes."

"Mrs. Morton, were your parents alive when you returned to Loving?"

"My mother was. She passed away in 1987, two years after we moved there. My father had already passed away."

"When did that happen?"

"My father's death?"

"Yes."

"Shortly before I returned."

"How shortly?"

"Six weeks."

Max walked back to the defense table and glanced at his notepad. Joe was furiously trying to get his attention with his eyes, cutting them up at Max, but keeping his body still.

"Mrs. Morton, you said you saw your brother about five years ago in a restaurant."

"Yes."

"Did you say anything to him?"

"I spoke to him for a moment, yes."

"Do you remember what you said?"

She sighed. "I don't remember exactly, but I told him that our father was dead."

"And did he say anything?"

"He said he knew."

"Did you say anything else to him at that time?"

"No."

"Have you ever talked to him again?"

"No."

Max walked a few feet away from the witness stand in the direction of the defense table but did not arrive there before he turned around.

"Mrs. Morton, I'd like to take you back into your past, to 1975."

Her mouth tautened, and she nodded curtly.

"Did you have a horse when you were a child, a pet?"

She nodded again. "We had a small pinto horse, a pony really. He was more my brother's than mine."

"What was the horse's name?"

"Cocoa."

"How long did you have the horse?"

Her eyes focused on a place above the observers' heads. "About six years, I believe. I think Joe was about four when he came."

At the defense table, Joe's face had drained white, and his eyes got very still.

"Did your parents buy the horse for your brother?"

A thin smile appeared on her lips. "Daddy wasn't much on buying stuff for us. Either of us. I think somebody—someone gave him Cocoa. Joe had to feed the pony himself."

Max turned, surprised. "At age four he had to do that?"

"Daddy said it would teach him responsibility. There wasn't much to it. Just put some hay in his stall and grain in the bucket."

"Mrs. Morton, can you tell me the circumstances under which the horse died?"

She cleared her throat again. Pain rushed across her face. "Do you need a glass of water?" Max asked.

"Yes, please."

The judge poured a glass from his pitcher and handed it to Max, who gave it to Evelyn.

"Thank you." She drank from it, and looked for a place to put it, then held it in her hand.

"Mrs. Morton?"

"Yes." She took another drink of water. "One morning about a month after my birthday, my daddy called Joe outside. I was hanging out wash, and Mama was upstairs. Joe was on the back porch, I think, and Daddy called him around front."

"Mrs. Morton," Max interrupted, "how old was your brother at this time?"

"He was ten."

"Please continue," he said as kindly as possible.

"Daddy called Joe out to the front and told him to go get his gun."

"What kind of a gun was it?

"It was a shotgun, I think a 12-gauge pump. Joe went and got it, and—"

"Did he ask why?"

"You didn't question our daddy. Joe got the gun, and Daddy asked if it was loaded. Joe said it was." She stopped, and tears began trickling from both eyes.

"Mrs. Morton," Judge Bruce said, "do you need a recess?"

She shook her head, and tears flung from her cheeks.

"Daddy took Joe by his arm, and pulled him real hard over to a little corral we had where we kept Cocoa."

"What happened next?"

"I was still at the clothes line, watching them. I could hear Daddy was yelling, but I couldn't hear what he said, 'cause there was a little breeze."

"What did you see?"

"Joe was carrying the gun, and Daddy pulled him out there with him. I saw Daddy point at Cocoa. Cocoa was acting kind of skittish because he could tell something was wrong, I guess. Joe put the barrel of the gun down, and Daddy jerked it up. He hit Joe on the side of the head real hard. He yelled at Joe, and Joe put the gun up to his shoulder." Her voice broke and Max waited for her to continue. She took a long drink of the water, the smooth skin of her throat sliding with each swallow. She put it back down on her knees. It was empty, and Max took it from her and set it on the defense table. He turned to face her again.

"Mrs. Morton, what happened next?"

"Joe pointed the gun at Cocoa, and he shot him."

The spectators knew what was coming, but the words caused a ripple of exhalations to race through the benches.

"Was the horse dead?"

She shook her head. "No, not yet. He had been moving, and the gun was too heavy for Joe to control, so he just shot Cocoa in the neck. I could see blood spurt out in the air, and he went down like he had slid in the mud or something, but he didn't get up like a horse would if it'd slipped. I could see him through the rails of the fence, thrashing around on the ground, and Daddy, he grabbed Joe's arm and pulled him between the rails. They went over there and Joe pumped the gun, pointed it at Cocoa's head, and shot him again. Cocoa stopped moving then."

Sitting four rows behind the defense table, Darlene Wagner sat with her head bowed, tears falling onto her lap. Freddie Odom's family sat on the opposite side of the aisle motionless, their faces frozen. In the last row Angel's face was drawn with rage. Diane DiAngelo looked at Jack Ogan, wondering whether she should try again to shut this testimony down, wondering what the consequences would be in the jury's opinion, knowing that they wanted to hear the story finish, knowing that if she did ask, Judge Bruce would deny her request.

Max said quietly, "Mrs. Morton, do you need some more water?"

Evelyn was crying quietly. Her face was red, and tears streamed freely down her cheeks. She nodded and Max filled her glass from the pitcher on the defense table. He handed it to her, and once again she set it on her knees. Max saw a damp spot there where it had sat earlier, and she very precisely placed it exactly where it had been before.

"Mrs. Morton, after your father forced your brother Joe to kill the pinto pony, Cocoa, what happened?"

"Daddy, he took the gun from Joe and pulled him back up to the house, to the front porch. Joe had blood on his face, a little spray of it. Daddy told him to go in and get cleaned up. He come—came over to where I was standing there by the wash line. He looked at me and he said 'You see that?' I said yeah. He nodded, and went into the house. A minute later he come back without the gun. He put a chain around Cocoa's body, hitched it to the truck, and dragged him out behind the barn."

"Did he bury him?"

She shrugged her shoulders.

"You don't know?"

"No."

"Why not?"

"I never went to look. I left that house and that town a week later."

"Is that when you got married?"

She nodded her head, staring down at her lap.

"And today, in this courtroom, is the second time you've seen your brother since that day, is that correct?"

"Yes."

The word was murmured, and the judge said "Mrs. Morton, can you make your answer a little louder, for the benefit of the court reporter?"

She raised her head and said "Yes."

"Thank you."

Max walked back to the defense table, where Joe was no longer trying to get his attention. He simply stared straight ahead, his face thin and white.

Max turned back to his witness and addressed her from the table.

"I'm going to ask you to tell us one more thing today, before the State questions you. Are you ready?"

"Yes." Her eyes were red, but for a moment the tears were stemmed.

"Thank you. Mrs. Morton, do you have any idea of why your father killed your brother's pony?"

"I think I have an idea, yes."

"Will you tell us what that was?"

She nodded. "The day before my father—did what I just described, it was a Saturday. My brother and I were home from school, of course." She coughed softly. "My mother and I were going to go into town, and Joe was going to stay at home. Momma wanted Joe to go, but Daddy said he had some things for him to do. I wasn't feeling good that day, and I decided to stay. I was in the house when Momma left. I heard the car start up, she had a brown Ford LTD, and I saw her drive off toward the main road. I was in the kitchen putting up the lunch dishes, washing them you know. A few minutes after she left, I looked out the window and I saw Daddy and Joe going toward the barn. Daddy had his right hand, he had big hands, he had it on the back of Joe's neck. I could tell that Joe was struggling, trying to get loose, and Daddy wouldn't let hold of him."

She stopped a moment, and for the first time since she had identified him, her eyes glanced at her brother's face. He wasn't looking at her.

"I was afraid that Daddy was going to hurt him. Sometimes he used to beat Joe real bad. He'd take a belt and hit him all over, on the back and butt, 'whipping him' he called it. It was always real bad. Sometimes when he'd go after Joe I'd try to distract him, make him stop quicker."

She stopped for a moment, and Max asked "How did you do that?"

"Usually I'd tell him to stop."

"Did that work? Did he stop?"

"He'd stop hitting Joe."

"What would he do then?"

"Start hitting me."

"Mrs. Morton, after you saw your father taking your brother into the barn, what did you do?"

"I went outside. I went in and looked at the chickens to see if any of them had laid eggs. I'd gathered them up that morning, but I looked anyway. There weren't any, so I came back out. Cocoa saw me, and he ran over to the side of the corral and put his head between the rails, wanting me to come talk to him. So I did, I rubbed his nose and he pushed his head up against me like a horse will do when he likes you." Tears still streamed down her face, but she continued, unaware of them. "I rubbed his nose a little while, and then after a couple of minutes I started hearing a peculiar noise." She stopped and, becoming aware of the tears, wiped them away with the back of her hand.

"What kind of a peculiar noise did you hear, Mrs. Morton?"

"Oh, it sounded kind of like it was a kitten that was hurt or something. We had a bunch of cats that lived around the house, you know, and I thought maybe one of them was stuck or having kittens or something like that. I didn't want to go into the barn, that's where the noise was coming from, but I thought maybe that little cat needed my help or something.

"I walked a little closer to the barn, and the noise got louder. If it was a little kitten I didn't want to see it being in pain or anything, but I thought maybe I'd need to help it out, so I kept going closer until I got to the doorway.

"When I got there I could still hear it, so I walked a few feet into the barn. It was April, but it was already a hot day, and I started to sweat in there real bad. I looked around a little bit and I didn't see anything, but the noise was getting louder, so I kept going and then—then I saw—" She stopped talking and simply sat, thick tears sliding down her cheeks.

Gently, Max said "Mrs. Morton you kept going and then what happened?"

"There was—were some stalls there like for horses, at the back, and I kept walking real slow. I got closer, and oh please I can't say this, sir, I just don't think I can—"

Diane, knowing that what was to come would not help her case, said "Your Honor, if the witness is saying that she can't answer, defense should—"

The judge looked at her and shook his head sharply. He rolled his hand at Max, the universal gesture for "go on."

"Mrs. Morton, just a few more minutes, please. What did you see?"

"I saw my daddy and Joey, and he had him there in that stall, and I saw that Daddy, he always wore these overalls, and he had them down, and had Joe across a barrel in there, and he was you know, he was having sex on him, Joey was just a little boy, and I never knew anybody could do anything like—he was his own little boy!"

She looked at Max and he mouthed "thank you" to her. He was about to ask one final question when he heard behind him a voice begin to raise, a voice that could at first only utter unconnected words. The voice sounded like it was drowning in acid, being torn apart by razor blades.

"You goddamn, fucking you can't, ain't," Joe said, as he slowly rose to his feet. "You can't—that ain't true, you goddamn bitch, you can't say that, ain't none of it true!" His eyes focused on his sister, and his arms started to pinwheel aimlessly. He tried to move toward her, but the table blocked his way and he seemed unable to understand that it was there. He kept pushing his hips against it, as if it were water he could walk through.

The judge banged his gavel. "Mr. Wagner, sit down please!" Joe didn't react, but his voice kept getting louder and louder.

"No, goddamnit!" he said. "That ain't true, you can't say that, ain't none of it happened!"

"Mr. Friedman," the judge said, "please restrain your client!"

"With all due respect, your honor, I don't think I can."

The judge nodded his head toward the deputy on duty, who was already poised to move into action. He stepped toward Joe and quickly put his hands behind his back, securing the handcuffs around his wrists. He tried to get Joe to sit down, pushing on his shoulders, but Joe started to resist, trying to hit him with the cuffed hands. He was thrown off balance and fell onto the defense table, striking the water pitcher which fell to the floor, shattering and spreading water in a five foot radius.

The deputy looked at the judge, who said "Remove the defendant from the courtroom, please!" By that time three more deputies had come running through the courtroom door and down the aisle. They lifted Joe up and took him through the prisoner's. The judge rubbed his hand over his bald head, and said "The court will take a fifteen minute recess. Mr. Friedman, you may remove your witness until we reconvene."

Max put his hand under Evelyn's elbow and guided her to her feet. Her husband met them at the rail, his eyes drilling into Max with hatred. He put his arm around his wife's shoulders and guided her down the aisle and out the door. The judge gestured at Max and Diane. "Let's have a conference in my chambers, please." He stood and walked through the door to the right of the bench.

Diane barely looked at Max as he held the door for her to enter. He closed it behind him. The judge sat down behind his desk in a dark brown leather chair and rested his head against the back of it, his eyes closed. Max glanced at Diane and pulled out one of the guest chairs opposite the judge.

"Don't sit down, please. We won't be long enough for that." He expelled his breath in a long sigh. His eyes still closed, he said "I have a witness in my courtroom who appears ready to shatter into pieces right before my eyes. I have a glass pitcher, which actually did shatter into pieces, and finally I have a defendant, the witness's brother, who doesn't seem to be in one piece either. I don't like messes. I'm too old for them, and I never liked them when I was young. Mr. Friedman, how much longer do you need with this witness?"

"Your honor, I honestly think I can finish with her in less than ten minutes."

"Since you're an attorney, Mr. Friedman, I think that 'honestly' should be a redundant adverb. Ms. DiAngelo, how much of the witness's time do you desire?"

"Your honor, if I ask one question of that woman beyond the time of day and temperature, I'm going to look like the Marquis de Sade." She turned to look at Max. "I assume you're going to call Vermazen back again?" He nodded after a moment. "I don't believe most of what she's saying, but I don't doubt that she believes it. Your case is going to rest on what that quack says, so I'm going to cross-examine the hell out of him." She turned and looked back at the judge.

"Mr. Friedman," he said, "I'll need you to restrain your client."

"Your honor, I don't think I can."

"I'm ready to put him back in cuffs if I have to. I'll be very happy to chain him too, if you can't impress upon him the importance of acting like a normal human being. Have either of you ever been to Cozumel?"

Max and Diane glanced at each other. "I have," she finally answered.

Max shook his head.

Judge Bruce looked at her. "Is it nice?"

"I like it, your honor."

"Nice snorkeling?"

She nodded.

"I've always wanted to learn now to snorkel. I think after this I may put in for vacation."

Trying not to look at the pale skin on his head, she said "It's nice. Just be careful of sunburn."

He nodded. "I'll do that. Sunburn. With your help, I'd like to get this case finished as expediently as possible. Do you think you can do that for me?"

"Yes sir," Max said.

The judge glanced at Diane, who nodded vigorously.

"Good. Mr. Friedman, please collect your witness." He glanced at his watch. "It's 4:00 now. Ten minutes, Mr. Friedman?"

"Yes, your honor."

"Ms. DiAngelo, no cross?"

"No."

"We'll begin ten minutes from now. By 5:00 I want to be at home, reading my newspaper and wearing house shoes. Please don't disappoint me. I'll see you both in ten minutes."

Chapter 32

Max found Evelyn and James Morton sitting by themselves on a bench on the second floor of the courthouse, a floor below the courtroom where she was testifying. Max guessed that James was fifteen years older than his wife. He had thinning light brown hair and gold-framed glasses. He held her left hand in both of his, stroking it gently. Neither of them noticed Max until he stood next to them and cleared his throat.

James glanced up and his eyes, soft with love and concern for his wife, turned hard immediately. He was protecting his wife out of his love for her, and Max liked him for that.

"Do you think you can finish?"

She nodded.

"It won't be much longer," Max said. "In half an hour, you should be on your way back to Loving."

James Morton's lips were tight with the rage he felt. "I know you're doing what you think you have to, Mr. Friedman. Your job is to defend Joe. But making Evelyn sit up there and tell that was—" he paused, searched for a word. "It was unconscionable." Max's heart ached for him. "I think there will be a special place in hell reserved for you, sir."

"There may well be, Mr. Morton, but not for this, I don't think. I'm very sorry that your wife had to tell that story, but it was true and it—"

"But what good will it do?" James cut in. "Telling it won't do one bit of good. He killed that man, and you're not even disputing it, but you had to drag my wife through the memory of that, and what will the other teachers and students think when—"

Evelyn put her hand on his. "Shh, shh, darling. Please. It's fine. It will all be fine." She patted his hand.

Max looked down at his boots, embarrassed. "I'll see you in the courtroom, then." He turned away, but Evelyn's voice stopped him.

"Mr. Friedman?" He looked back at her. "I would like you to know that since I left the courtroom, I feel better."

"How?"

"I'm not exactly sure. Lighter? That feels right. Yes, lighter. For many years I tried not to remember what had happened then. I loved my mother, but I tried to forget about my father. I wasn't completely successful, but there were months sometimes, perhaps years, when I didn't think about him or Joe at all. When we moved back to Loving, it was more difficult. The streets, the buildings were all familiar, so it was harder. Sometimes I would wake up crying in the night, remembering."

Her husband nodded, looking down at their clasped hands.

"Why did you stay after your mother died?" Max asked.

She looked thoughtfully at a place in the air a few feet in front of her. "I was tired of running. And I know this sounds unusual, morbid perhaps, but it was my home. That town was my home. I'm proud of the work that I do there with the children.

"When you came to see me, I was caught by surprise. I had heard about Joe's arrest but chose not to think about it, chose to believe it had nothing to do with me or our family. I was wrong. I'm sorry I deceived you when you first came. I don't believe in deception or lying, but in some ways I think I've been deceiving myself for twenty-five years.

"So yes, I feel lighter, as if by having told someone about this, perhaps I can sleep easier now. I wish that I had been able to choose whom to tell, and not forced into it. But in some way I feel I need to thank you."

Max nodded, unsure if she was actually thanking him or not.

"When you came to our house, Mr. Friedman, I told you that my brother was in the hands of the devil. I said that nothing could be done with him, that he was lost to all good. I think you were shocked by that."

Max nodded.

"I still believe that," she said. "I believe in Satan, and the power he has to thwart God's plan for the world. Unfortunately, Satan doesn't wear a red suit or have horns and a tail. It would be easier for us if he did. In the case of my brother, Mr. Friedman, Satan came disguised as our father. What happened to Joe is not his own fault. He was taken by evil, by Satan, and now I believe he is beyond redemption."

"But—"

"I think that you are a good man, and you only want the truth to be told. I agree with you. It should be. I feel better having told it, having unburdened myself. But don't think that you're helping Joe. You're not. I remember him when he was a boy. He was full of fear, but he still had some love in him. He loved me, he loved my mother. He loved Cocoa. But that boy is gone. The man who sits in the courtroom no longer contains that boy. That man is now just another suit of Satan."

"Mrs. Morton—"

"It must be time for us to go back. We'll be there in a moment."

Max felt like he had been dismissed from the court of a queen and dutifully turned away. This time she did not call him back.

Evelyn settled herself back into the witness's chair. Joe sat behind the defense table once again, his hands cuffed, held on his lap underneath the table. His face was expressionless once again. The judge said, "Mrs. Morton, please remember that you are still under oath."

She nodded. "Yes."

Max rose from his chair. "During your testimony you recounted several incidents from your childhood. You told us of how, in front of your mother and young brother, your father broke your arm and refused you medical treatment until the next day."

Evelyn nodded.

"You also told us how, when you were seventeen years old and your brother ten, your father forced your brother to kill the pony whom he was responsible for, whom you both loved. You told us how your father made your brother raise a shotgun to the pony's head and shoot him, and how later your father simply dragged the body behind the barn, not burying it.

"Then you told us how, the day before that, you found your father in the barn, raping your brother." Max glanced toward the defense table. Joe did not move or change expression.

"Mrs. Morton, what happened after you saw what you did in the barn?"

Evelyn was composed again, the woman she had been the first time Joe ever saw her, the woman he had just talked to in the hallway

"My father didn't see me. His back was to me, and I walked out as quickly as I could, walking backwards to make sure he didn't see me. When I got outside of the barn, about two feet, I turned to run to the house and tripped over a plow point, an old-fashioned one that he didn't use any more. I got up and ran as quickly as I could to the house. By the time he came out of the barn I was already inside, watching him from behind a second-floor curtain, in my bedroom."

"It would have taken you at least a minute to pick yourself up, to run to the house, open the door, and go upstairs to your room. Why did it take your father so long to reach the doorway?"

"When I saw him come out, he was hooking the straps on his overalls. It must have taken him that long to arrange himself."

"Did your father see you, Mrs. Morton?"

"I don't believe so."

"What did you do then?"

"I hid under the bed until my mother came home."

"Did your father know that you had seen him?"

Diane rose to her feet. "Objection. Calls for speculation."

The judge shook his head at her. "Overruled. Answer the question, please."

"I don't think that he saw me, but I believe that he knew I had caused the sound he heard. My mother had gone into town, and I was supposed to be with her. I believe that's why he chose the time he did, because he expected us both to be gone. He didn't see me, but I think he knew that I might have seen him."

"Mrs. Morton, are you aware of your father doing this to your brother at any other time?"

"No."

"Do you believe that it was the only time?"

Diane stood again. "Objection! Leading the witness."

"Sustained."

"Mrs. Morton, you've told us that you eloped a week later, and never returned until your father was dead. Is that correct?"

"Yes."

"One last question, and then I'll turn you over to the District Attorney." Max said this knowing Diane would decline to question her, but he wanted it to sound as if the hands of the District Attorney were a dangerous place to be.

"Do you believe that the killing of the horse had anything to do with what you saw the day before?"

"Your honor," Diane said, "once again Defense is asking the witness for speculation."

"I believe he's asking the witness for her opinion about the meaning of an event she saw. I don't believe it's speculation. I'll allow it. The witness will answer."

Evelyn said, "I believe that my father made Joe kill Cocoa as a warning to my brother and to me. I think he wanted me to know that, if I had seen him and I told anyone, this was what would happen to me. I think he was saying the same to Joe. What happened to Cocoa could happen to either of us."

"Mrs. Morton," Max said, "thank you for your very difficult testimony today. I appreciate your honesty and courage. I have no further questions."

Judge Bruce raised his eyebrows at Diane. "Your witness, Ms. DiAngelo."

She stood and said "We have no questions at this time."

"In that case, court is adjourned until 9:00 tomorrow morning." He banged his gavel on the bench and disappeared into his chambers.

Chapter 33

That night Max decided not to go to Bailey's. About 10:00 he realized that it was very quiet outside his apartment, and when he opened the living room blinds he saw that Angel had been right. Snow was falling silently, muffling the sounds of the traffic. He sat on his couch with his stocking feet tucked under him. Jersey sprawled across his lap, and Mayella snuggled against his leg, her tiny pink tongue sticking out of her mouth. He read over his notes for the next day. His final witness was Dr. Vermazen, and he knew that Diane would try to tear his testimony apart. There were holes in it, he knew, but he had never heard of a case that was perfect. He thought the case, and his closing argument, offered more than a good chance that the truth would be heard. Max didn't think Joe Wagner should go free any more than Diane did. He just wanted a chance to tell the story. Evelyn had given him that, even though she hadn't spoken to him when she left the courtroom. She glanced his way when she was released from the stand and offered him a wan smile before she disappeared with her husband down the aisle. They would have been safe back at their home in Loving long before the snow began its quiet dance.

Thirty minutes after he noticed the snow he called Angel at the pool hall, but she was too busy to speak more than a minute. He felt lonely when he hung up and remembered one of the great pieces of AA wisdom: to never let yourself get too hungry, angry, lonely, or tired. HALT was the shorthand. He realized he was feeling lonely and very tired. He wasn't angry or hungry, but he could still be on the edge of danger. He hoped that Angel would call back, but the phone didn't ring, and hadn't by 11:00 when he went to bed. He reminded himself that he was as powerless over her or any other person as he was over alcohol. He thought of calling Danny, but realized that the hard-working cowboy would no doubt be asleep. Long before midnight he was too, with Jersey draped across his shoulders and Mayella curled up on his legs.

As Max waited for court to convene the next morning, he noticed that Angel had entered and sat again in the back row. She was wearing jeans, boots, and a snap-button cowboy shirt, but out of deference to the court and the weather, she was also wearing a brown suede jacket. He went back and sat beside her for a moment, touching her hand with his. She held his for a few moments, apologizing for not being able to talk the night before. She seemed distant to him, but he was glad she was there again.

Diane had already been there when he arrived and shot him a smug look, as if she had something up on him. He shook off the feeling of mild irritation.

At 9:00 a.m. Judge Bruce entered the courtroom. When everyone sat down, Max said "The defense calls Darlene Wagner."

"Darlene Wagner," the bailiff called, in an example of redundancy that Max had never understood.

Darlene rose from her seat on a bench two rows behind Joe. She was wearing a navy blue dress, and her pretty chestnut hair was pulled back and held with a clip. The bailiff swore her in, and she sat down with her knees together and her back straight.

Max walked toward her with his hands in the pockets of his suit pants. "Mrs. Wagner, you are the wife of the defendant, Joseph Wagner. Is that correct?"

"Yes sir."

"How long have you been married?"

"Five years."

"Mrs. Wagner, I'm going to ask you a few questions about your life with your husband."

He saw her eyes flick toward Joe, terror in them. Max moved subtly so that he was standing between them.

"Mrs. Wagner, does your husband sleep well?"

She shook her head.

"Can you answer out loud, please, just so it will be on the record?"

"No sir, he doesn't sleep well."

"Will you tell us why you say that?"

"Joe, he uh, lots of times he'll have trouble sleeping at night. He'll be okay for a while, then he'll start to twitch and jerk you know, his arms and legs.

He'll start to mumble, and it sounds like he's in pain."

"Objection," Diane said. "The witness cannot testify to the defendant's physical or emotional state."

"She said it 'sounds like' he is in pain, counselor," the judge said. "That's an opinion I can allow."

"Go on, Mrs. Wagner," Max said.

"Well, like I say he'll twitch and jerk. It gets worse and worse, and sometimes I'm afraid he'll hit me or kick me or something."

"What happens to stop this?"

"Sometimes he'll stop without waking up, but usually when it's that bad he'll wake up. Sometimes he'll fall out of the bed or hit the wall with his arm, and that'll wake him up. A lot of times he gets up and doesn't come back to bed again. He might go to sleep on the couch. Sometimes when I leave for work he'll be asleep, but I'll see a bunch of beer bottles on the porch, and it seems like he'd sat out there for a while. Sometimes he's gone all together, and won't come back until night."

"Mrs. Wagner, you said that when your husband has trouble sleeping he might mumble?"

"Yes, sir."

"Does he say words that you can understand, or is it just noises?"

"He says words sometimes."

"What does he say?"

"Sometimes things like 'no, don't,' or 'stop.' Stuff like that." Her voice had grown very low, until the jury and judge were leaning forward to hear her.

"Mrs. Wagner, I'm not asking you to say how your husband was feeling, but I'd like to get your impression of how he sounded. If you heard someone else talk in the tone of voice he was using, saying the same words, what would you think?"

"I'd think they were scared."

Max looked at the judge. "I have no more questions for this witness," he said, and walked back to the defense table.

The judge raised his eyebrows at Diane. "Ms. DiAngelo?"

"Thank you, your honor," she said, standing. She walked to Darlene, not her hard, powerful striding walk, but slower, the walk of a friend.

"Good morning, Mrs. Wagner."

Darlene glanced down at her lap. "Hello."

"Mrs. Wagner, have you ever had nightmares?"

"Yes, ma'am."

"Do you always remember what they were?"

"Not a lot of times."

"When you do remember them, what are they?"

"Oh, just usual stuff, I guess. For dreams, I mean. Being chased by monsters, or being in trouble. Sometimes I have one where I'm on a Ferris wheel, like at the carnival, but instead of the little cart I'm just on a piece of wood, with no rails or nothing to hold onto. It's real high and fast, and whenever it starts on the way down I'm afraid that I'll get thrown off of it."

"That sounds pretty scary."

"Yes ma'am, it is."

"Has it ever woken you up?"

"Sometimes. I'll wake up and realize I'm not really on it, and be relieved."

"Do you go back to sleep right away?"

"Not always. Sometimes I'll be up for a little while, get a drink of water or read a magazine or something."

"That sounds like something we all do at one time or another. Mrs. Wagner, have you ever had a nightmare that's exactly something that you went through in real life?"

"No, ma'am. Sometimes people will be in my dreams—Joe, or my family or friends, but never something exactly."

"Thank you. I'm going to ask you a couple of harder questions, and then I'll let you go. Okay?"

Darlene nodded at the rhetorical question.

"Is your husband a violent man?"

"Well, he. . . ." She looked over at Joe. Diane, exactly as Max had, moved between Darlene and her husband.

"It's okay to answer."

"Sometimes he is. He's gotten into trouble before, for fighting. He's been in jail a couple of times."

"Three times, actually, for fighting in bars."

"Okay."

"Mrs. Wagner, has your husband ever turned his anger on you?"

"Well, he—"

"Darlene, has he ever hit you?" she asked quietly.

"Uh," Darlene cleared her throat, "sometimes he has, you know."

"Tell us about that, please."

"Well, he gets mad, and sometimes he's you know, he's hit me."

"How did he hit you?"

"How?"

"Did he slap you, punch you, push you? Ever break any bones?"

"Yes ma'am."

"All of those things?"

"Uh huh."

"He broke bones?"

"Yes."

"How did he do that?"

"He grabbed my finger one time, and twisted it until it broke. It didn't take much, it's a little bone."

"When he hit you, punched you, pushed you, broke your finger, did he have a reason for it?"

"Ma'am?"

"Did you do anything to make him hurt you?"

"Your honor," Max said, jumping to his feet, "I object to this!"

"Your honor," Diane said, "this will take one more moment, and it's very important."

"Overruled. Please continue."

"Please answer the question, Mrs. Wagner. Did you do anything to make him hurt you?"

"No! He'd just get mad at me for no reason at all, for little stuff like not having the supper made in time, or telling him no, or something like that. Nothing I ever done."

"So are you saying that in your experience, your husband becomes violent with no provocation, that he needs no reason to hit you?"

"Um, yeah. Yes. He doesn't really have a reason. Not a good one."

"One last question, Mrs. Wagner. Does your husband drink?"

"Yes, ma'am."

"Does he drink to excess?"

"What do you mean?"

"Does he drink every day? Is it common for him to be drunk?"

"Yes, ma'am."

"Does he become more violent when he's been drinking?"

"Usually that's when it happens."

"Thank you, Mrs. Wagner. Those are all the questions I have."

She took her seat, and Max called Dr. Robert Vermazen back to the stand.

The doctor walked quietly but confidently, settling easily into the witness chair.

"Good morning, Doctor," Max said.

He nodded. "Good morning." He crossed his legs at the knee and settled his hands palm down, one over the other, on his thigh.

"Dr. Vermazen, have you examined the defendant, Joseph Wagner?"

"I have spoken with him."

"How many times?"

"Twice, and I've spoken with his wife once, and his sister once." Max heard a hard exhalation of breath from the defense table.

"Doctor, are you familiar with the testimony given by the defendant's sister, Mrs. Evelyn Morton, in this courtroom yesterday?"

"Yes, I am. I read her testimony from yesterday last night, and I have also listened to her story, essentially the same one she described here, at another time."

"Doctor, what are your conclusions, based on your interviews with the defendant and his sister, and on your reading of the testimony?"

"Objection, your honor. That's a vague question."

"I agree," the judge said. "Objection is sustained. Be more specific please, counselor."

"Dr. Vermazen, based on your interviews with the defendant and his sister, and your reading of the testimony, are you prepared to offer a diagnosis of the defendant?"

"Yes, I am." He turned his torso toward the jury. "Please understand that the visitors' room at the jail is not the ideal condition in which to conduct an interview. However, based on the interviews, I did complete a diagnosis."

"And what is it, please?"

"I believe that Mr. Wagner is suffering from post-traumatic stress disorder and Dissociative Disorders Not Otherwise Specified, or DDNOS."

"Can you tell us on what you have based this diagnosis?"

"Certainly. My interviews with Mr. Wagner and the testimony of his wife indicate that he has great trouble sleeping, particularly since the death of Mr. Odom. He experiences what are called 'body memories' at night—this is a phenomenon that occurs when the body involuntarily reenacts the experience of abuse, normally without the person realizing what he or she is experiencing."

"Can you describe what this is like?"

"It can manifest as simple shivers, when something usually unknown reminds us of the abuse. The shiver might last only a few moments. In other cases, someone experiencing body memories might lie for hours curled in the fetal position on the floor, unable to move."

"Dr. Vermazen, what causes 'body memories?'"

"They are caused by extreme trauma."

"Can you tell us more about this, please? What kind of 'extreme trauma?'"

"Soldiers who have served in very harsh conditions have been known to have body memories. We also see it typically in survivors of rape and childhood abuse."

"Dr. Vermazen, you have read the testimony given by Mrs. Morton. In your opinion, could the abuse suffered by Mr. Wagner at the hands of his father have caused body memories such as the ones described by Mrs. Wagner?"

"Yes, it could."

"In your interviews with Mr. Wagner, did you ask him about his relationship with his parents?"

"Yes."

"How did he describe it?"

"He showed a contempt for his father bordering on hatred. He called him an 'asshole.'"

"Did you ask him if his father ever beat him?"

"May I refer to my notes?"

"Certainly."

The doctor reached into his inside jacket pocket and withdrew several sheets of paper folded vertically.

Max turned to Diane. "Would the State like to review them?"

Diane shook her head.

Dr. Vermazen slid a pair of glasses from the same pocket and put them on. He turned to a page and read from a highlighted section, "When I asked if his father ever beat him, Mr. Wagner said 'no more than anyone else gets beat.'"

"Doctor, did you ask Mr. Wagner about what happened the night that Freddie Odom died?"

"Yes, I did."

"Was there anything unusual about his memory of that night?"

"Objection, your honor. Leading."

"I'll rephrase the question. Doctor, what were your observations about what Mr. Wagner told you regarding the death of Mr. Odom?"

"Mr. Wagner's memory of the night was clear, up until the fight with Mr. Odom. At that point, however, he seemed very vague about how Mr. Odom had actually died. He said that they were fighting, that Mr. Odom was calling him names, and then he was on the ground, dead."

"He had no memory of hitting Mr. Odom?"

"No, he did not."

"Did you draw any conclusions from this?"

"I believe that Mr. Wagner truly does not remember hitting him."

Max turned to the judge. "Your honor, I'd like to read a short bit of testimony from Smith Dixon. I think it would be easier for the court for me to read it than to recall Mr. Dixon, although I would be happy to do that if you'd like."

Judge Bruce glanced at Diane. "State? Any objections?"

"No, your honor."

"Please continue, Mr. Friedman."

"Mr. Dixon testified that after Mr. Odom fell down, Mr. Wagner said 'I didn't go to kill him.' When I asked if Mr. Wagner had any part in deciding whether to call the police, Mr. Dixon replied 'No. He was out of it . . . . Just sitting there, not saying anything.' Mr. Dixon also said that Mr. Wagner suddenly became aware that Carl Puente was there, although they had been talking for at least twenty minutes in voices loud enough for Mr. Wagner to hear them."

"Dr. Vermazen, can you draw any conclusions based on this testimony?"

"I can state my opinions, yes. It is my belief that Mr. Wagner was unaware of his actions when he hit Mr. Odom. As I testified earlier, it is possible for a person to function but to be totally unaware of his or her surroundings. This is typical in Dissociative Identity Disorder, or DID, in which a person has several very distinct personalities, one of which may emerge and subside, leaving the person with a blank memory. However, I see nothing in Mr. Wagner that would lead me to believe that he suffers from DID. I do believe that he suffers from Post Traumatic Stress Disorder and DDNOS."

"Doctor, based on your own expertise, the interviews with Mr. Wagner, his wife, and his sister, and on the testimony offered here in the courtroom, can you offer a scenario that might have led to the death of Mr. Odom?"

Diane stood. "Your honor, I object."

"Grounds?" the judge asked.

"On the grounds defense counsel is making a specious request designed only to give credence to his own scenario of the events leading to the murder of Mr. Odom. I believe that his 'expert witness,'" she said, her voice dewy with sarcasm, "is prepared to parrot whatever Mr. Friedman tells him to say."

The judge closed his eyes for a moment. He didn't turn his head toward the witness stand as he said "Dr. Vermazen, are you planning to repeat a scenario dictated to you by Mr. Friedman?"

"No, your honor."

"Ms. DiAngelo, both the State and the defense have a right to present witnesses, both eyewitnesses and experts. I have no reason to believe that Dr. Vermazen plans to serve as a mouthpiece for the defense. I believe that we can trust him to uphold the tenets of his profession. Your objection is overruled. Reporter, please repeat the question."

The reporter immediately read back Max's last words.

The doctor said "I believe that the sexual abuse suffered by Mr. Wagner at the hands of his father made him react by bullying other men, often in a sexual way. Some men who have survived such abuse react during adolescence and adulthood by becoming homophobic. This is what Mr. Wagner did. As most of us know, the most common reaction to a bully is to acquiesce, to give in to him.

"Based on the testimony offered here and my interviews, I believe that Mr. Wagner took Mr. Odom to the drive-in theatre only for the purpose of scaring him into not going to the police. Mr. Wagner is a bully, and he used emotional and physical intimidation to convince Mr. Odom. However, Mr. Odom did something that few people ever had. He turned the tables. He started calling Mr. Wagner those same words—'faggot' and 'queer.' I believe that the words Freddie Odom called him essentially put Joe Wagner back into his childhood. In his mind, he was once again a little boy, being brutalized by his father. However, he was no longer a child, and his adult's body did what an adult will instinctively do when attacked. He defended himself, in this case by hitting the man whom he felt threatened by. I believe that in Mr. Wagner's mind it was his father he was hitting, in revenge for sexual abuse and verbal humiliation. The testimony given here indicates that after hitting Mr. Odom, Mr. Wagner was in a fugue state, where he did not know where he was, similar to an alcoholic in a blackout. His statement that 'I didn't go to kill him' indicates that he didn't intend to kill Mr. Odom."

Max turned to the judge and jury and said "Your honor, I have no more questions."

"Ms. DiAngelo?"

Diane stood, picked up her notepad, and took a step toward the witness stand. Then she turned and tossed the pad back onto the table, a gesture which said that she needed no notes to quickly take apart the witness.

"Dr. Vermazen," she said, "to the best of your knowledge, is Freddie Odom dead?"

"To the best of my knowledge, yes."

"And to the best of your knowledge, who killed him?"

"That is a question that is not so easy to answer—"

"Of course it's easy to answer, Doctor. Let me guide you through the process. Joe Wagner and Freddie Odom came to the Comanche Drive-In together, but only one of them left, because Freddie Odom was dead. Now, based on the testimony you've read and the witnesses you've interviewed, were you able to determine who held the weapon that killed Mr. Odom?"

"Your honor," Max began, but the judge waved him down and said "Ms. DiAngelo, I have little tolerance for sarcasm. Please rephrase your question."

"Yes, your honor. Dr. Vermazen, whom do you believe wielded the weapon that killed Freddie Odom?"

"Mr. Wagner," he said, with a nod at the defendant.

"Thank you. Now was that so difficult?"

"Ms. DiAngelo," the judge said.

"I'm sorry, your honor." She turned her back to the bench and offered the jurors a slight smile.

"Dr. Vermazen, you testified that what you call 'body memories' are sometimes manifested as 'simple shivers, when something usually unknown reminds us of the abuse. The shiver might last only a few moments.' Am I quoting you correctly?"

"Yes."

"Doctor, have you ever experienced shivers?"

"Yes."

"Were they caused by childhood trauma being remembered when you were an adult?"

"No."

"What were they caused by, not turning your furnace up high enough?"

"Your Honor!" Max protested.

"Ms. DiAngelo," the judge said, "are you taking my warnings against sarcasm lightly?"

"No your honor. Please forgive me. It's just that some statements are difficult to take with a straight face."

She turned back to the witness. "Have you ever had bad dreams?"

"Yes."

"Have you ever had the kind of dream that makes you suddenly startle yourself awake, almost fall out of bed?"

"Yes."

"I think that all of us have, including myself, the jury members, the defense counsel, and the judge himself. Does this mean that we're all survivors of childhood abuse and just don't know it?"

"No, but I—"

"Thank you. Doctor, you've made some conjectural statements about Mr. Wagner's motivation in killing Freddie Odom. Can you prove any of them?"

"They're my professional opinion."

"Yes, that's exactly what they are—an opinion."

"However, I would like to point out that they are based on years of research and observation."

"I'm sure that's true, but the fact remains that there is no way to prove your opinions. We have heard the testimony given by Mrs. Morton about her brother's unfortunate abuse at the hands of her father. However, isn't it beyond the ability of anyone in this courtroom, you included, to know exactly what was in Mr. Wagner's mind when he murdered Mr. Odom?"

"Objection, your honor," Max said. "A determination of murder has not been made by the jury."

"Sustained."

"The truth is, Doctor, that none of us know what Mr. Wagner was thinking on the night that he killed Freddie Odom. We can postulate and deduce all we want about 'Post Traumatic Stress Disorder' and 'Dissociative Disorder Not Otherwise Specified,' but we cannot know why Joe Wagner killed Freddie Odom. We can only know that he did, and for the purposes of this court, his guilt has been determined." She turned her back on the witness and strode back to her table, accompanied by the rapid-fire clicking of her heels. When she arrived there she said "Your honor, the state is finished with this witness," and sat down, smoothing her skirt.

Judge Bruce said "Mr. Friedman, please call your next witness."

"Your honor," Max said, rising slightly, "Dr. Vermazen was our final witness, and with him the defense rests."

The judge glanced at the clock on his bench. "It's 11:30 now. I'd like to break for lunch. Do you think that you can be ready for closing arguments this afternoon?"

"Yes, your honor," Diane said.

"Mr. Friedman?"

"Defense will be ready."

"Good. We'll reconvene at 1:00 p.m." He banged his gavel once and disappeared into his chambers.

Two sheriff's deputies gently lifted Joe by the elbows. As they started to lead him away, he said "Hey" softly to Max. The guards stopped a moment.

Joe said "Ain't no call for you to have said them things about Daddy. I'd as soon go to jail as have you say all that shit. Evvy, she never give a shit about me, and I know you don't neither, but you was supposed to defend me, tell how it really was, that I had to do it. I told you that back in the jail, just tell that Freddie called me a faggot and a queer. You shouldn't have put in all that other stuff. That wasn't right, man. If I go to prison, it's you put me there. You and her and Smith, and that pussy Carl, and that fucking woman with the dog." Max tried to keep his face blank, but Joe saw the anger and fear. "Oh yeah, I figure it was her who called the cops on me that night they come for me. Y'all are all to blame for it. You remember that." He turned his back, and the guards led him to the door that would take him to the jail.

Most of the spectators were gone from the courtroom, as were Diane and Jack. Max put his notes into his briefcase, shut and latched it. When he looked up to find Angel, she was already gone.

He looked for her in the hallway but couldn't find her there either. He thought about going to the Snazzy Pig for lunch but didn't feel like seeing any of the courthouse crowd at the moment. Instead he put his briefcase in the car and walked, his boots plowing twin paths in the ten inches of snow the sky had deposited the night before. The sky was still overcast, and the weather forecasters were predicting more snow tonight. The fact that he could see stretches of undisturbed snow amazed him; even in the most residential parts of any borough in New York, fresh snow didn't last long except in the aftermath of a blizzard. He remembered a Sunday afternoon when he wasn't yet sober but wasn't drunk at the moment; he and a group of friends had walked down the middle of Third Avenue, normally one of Manhattan's busiest thoroughfares. The streets were almost empty of cars save the occasional brave cab that plowed slowly through the knee-deep snow, beeping its horn to warn the walkers. New York for once was quiet and beautiful, and strangers began impromptu snowball fights.

Max finally settled onto a park bench. He brushed the snow off it and made sure his overcoat was between the remaining powder and his suit pants. His toes were beginning to tingle, but it wasn't exactly painful. Sometimes pain reminded him that he was still alive and still sober. For many years he had drunk as soon as he felt a twitch of pain. By the end of his drinking days he started long before the pain did, knowing that it would come. It was usually emotional pain rather than physical, the bar fights excepted. The way he dealt with it was by staying drunk most of the time.

Sometimes the urge struck him again, like now. He felt that Angel was avoiding him, and he didn't know why. Of course his mind could come up with a thousand reasons. He talked funny, he was too short, his hair was too long, he was going bald, he wasn't a cowboy, he was too smart for her, too stupid, too something. She had come to her senses and realized that he'd never be able to ride a horse, or look good in cowboy boots, or make love the right away. Of course she'd never said any of these things, or even intimated them. She said she loved his hair, found his accent funny but sexy, was the smartest man she'd ever known, even though he tried to analyze country-western songs, and satisfied her sexually in ways she'd never thought possible. But all that aside, it was easy for Max to convince himself that he was doing something wrong, something that made him deserve to be ignored and abandoned.

Which she wasn't doing, he reminded himself. She was just less available than she usually was, and that probably had nothing to do with him. He knew that all he really needed to do was ask her about it and tell her how he was feeling. As a recovering alcoholic, the easiest thing was often the last tactic that came to his mind. He determined to ask her when he saw her again outside of the courtroom. He hoped it would be tonight.

Max tilted his head up and gently blew out his breath, watching it form clouds in the cold air. His toes were starting to get bitingly numb, so he stood up and began to walk again, eventually making his way back to the courthouse in time for the warm hallways to thaw them out before the court convened again.

Chapter 34

Judge Bruce banged his gavel once and said, "The court is now in session. Ms. DiAngelo, are you ready to begin the state's summation?"

"I am, your honor."

"Proceed."

Diane stood and strode toward the jury, a study in self-confidence. "Good afternoon, ladies and gentlemen. The lunch break probably wasn't long enough for you to have forgotten who I am, but let me reintroduce myself. I'm Diane DiAngelo, the District Attorney for Potter County, and I work for—" she paused and swept her gaze quickly over each face, "—you. I represent you. At the beginning of this trial, you heard Judge Bruce say 'the State of Texas versus Joseph Randall Wagner.' You are not here to do my bidding. No. I am here to do yours. Under the laws of the state of Texas, someone who commits murder must be punished for it to the full extent of the law. 'The full extent of the law' in this case means life in prison. There will be no justice unless that man over there at the conclusion of this trial and sentencing, is taken to prison and never gets out again." She turned and pointed her finger, arm extended to its full length, at Joe.

"I was going to start out my summation by thanking you for your patience.

But to tell you the truth, this trial hasn't taken very long, has it? The reason for that is because it's a simple case. I've tried cases, even murder cases, that were much more complex. Each and every single one I've prosecuted is tragic, and this one is no exception. It's an aberration of God's law, the laws of the United States, and the laws of the state of Texas. But it's not complicated.

"You might remember that Mr. Friedman, in his opening argument, said that he and I were both going to tell you a story. That may be the only thing he's been right about during these past several days. No, one more thing. He said that you twelve men and women are the inheritors of the cloak of Solomon, and that you will intuitively know which story to believe. I agree with him up through those points, and that's where we depart. We have both told you stories, but with one very big difference. Do you know what it is?"

She had walked close to the jury. Now she rested her left hand on the rail, her perfectly manicured and polished nails tapping once on the heavy wood. She leaned toward them, a confidante speaking to her peers, and said "Only one of them is true. Guess which?" She watched their faces a moment. "I think you know the answer to that, don't you? The story told by the State, your employee, these past several days, is the true one. Four men decided to rob a grocery store. Well, three men, actually. The fourth man made a very unfortunate choice to participate, but he didn't actually rob the store. He sat outside in the car, and waited. Now I am not by any means excusing what Freddie Odom did. It was a wrong choice. He had hoped to make money from doing this. But he didn't. Instead, he ended up paying. The price he paid for this very bad choice of throwing in with three hardened criminals was the ultimate one. He paid with his life. Of the four, he was the only one with enough conscience to finally do the right thing. He decided to call a police officer, and throw himself on the mercy of the court system. I don't know what would have happened if he had succeeded, but I suspect that the court would have been lenient with him, would have forgiven him for this one mistake that he wanted so much to undo. But he didn't have that chance, because before he could complete the call, he was discovered by the defendant, Joe Wagner. Joe Wagner is a man with no sense of right and wrong, only a sense of himself. And he saw in Freddie Odom, this inherently good man, someone who would stand in the way of his scheme. So to Joe Wagner, the answer was simple. He took Freddie Odom to the Comanche Drive-In Theatre, he terrorized him, brutalized him, and murdered him. That is the story that the state has told, and I implicitly trust that you will recognize the truth in it."

She turned and gestured contemptuously toward Max. "But as the defense attorney promised, he has told you another story than the State. It is a story so patently ridiculous that it would be laughable had not the conclusion been so tragic. Mr. Friedman told you that when Joe Wagner stole Freddie Odom from the side of his wife, from the future of his children, he was acting in a condition of 'Post Traumatic Stress Disorder,' and 'Dissociative Disorders Not Otherwise Specified.' Ladies and gentlemen, if any of you believe that pile of—" She stopped, as if afraid to say the word. "I'm sure Judge Bruce would be very displeased if I called it what it is in his courtroom. Let me put it this way. When the wind is right, blowing from the feedlots of our good neighbors in Hereford, you can smell it. I will put DDNOS right in that same category. If I had a truckload of it I bet my garden would grow very well next year. And where did this story come from? A psychologist who walks in with a ridiculous theory designed only to assure that the murder of a good man goes unpunished, and a bad man goes free. Maybe it works down in Houston or over in Dallas, but here in cattle country we know it for what it is."

During the last minute a smile had been playing on her lips, but now it was gone, her face suddenly as solemn as the ones on the bench where Freddie's family sat. "The defense's other witness was one for whom I feel nothing but the most profound sympathy. Mrs. Evelyn Morton, the defendant's sister, lived through a childhood that no one of us should ever be asked to experience. The stories she told of her father's cruelty baffle the imagination of compassionate people. I must admit, ladies and gentleman, that when I heard her describe the cruelties perpetrated on her and her young brother, I felt a moment of sympathy for him. Perhaps more than a moment. The cruelty that she described is unfathomable. But let me be very clear with you." She said the next sentence very carefully, almost pausing between each word. "It is no reason to murder a fellow human being. I hope that none of you have ever suffered cruelty this monstrous. Now, I'm not a betting woman, but I'd be willing to wager that some of you, some of the other people in this courtroom, have endured tragedies. The death of children and spouses due to accident and disease. Bankruptcies. Divorce." As she said each word, she looked at a member of the jury whom she knew had gone through it. "But all of you, all of us, are honest citizens, working hard to make money the way we were taught, not blaming our problems on other people, but taking responsibility for our actions. There's one person in the courtroom who has not done that."

She turned and looked at Joe. "That man there, Joseph Wagner. The rest of us live through hardships and work hard to become responsible citizens. He didn't. Instead he stole money that wasn't his, and when one honest man tried to stop him, he murdered him in cold blood and buried him in a hill of sand for two young boys to find. I'm sorry for what happened to Joseph Wagner when he was ten years old, but no amount of pop psychology will change the fact that he murdered Freddie Odom."

She walked to the State's table, and Max knew that she would pull one of the time-honored ploys of prosecutors. She would produce The Photo. And she did, reaching for the frame that had until now been lying face down next to her briefcase.

She picked it up and held it in her hands, slowly showing it to Max, Joe, Judge Bruce, and the entire courtroom before turning it to the jury.

"This is the man whose life was stolen. This photo must have been taken on one of the happiest days of his life, don't you think? He was playing with one of the three people he loved most in this world: his son Travis. It must have been taken after a wonderful afternoon of football. This is the face of Freddie Odom. And do you know what was the last thing Freddie saw before he was catapulted into God's hands, so long before his time?"

She turned and pointed once again at Joe Wagner. "That face," she said quietly. "The man in that chair is the last thing Freddie ever saw. His murderer.

Now when I am finally taken from this world, I hope, I pray that it is not in the bloom of youth. I pray that I will be surrounded by my family and loved ones, and that their faces will be the last things I see before God takes me. I want you to just take a moment to imagine what it was like to have this man's face be the last thing you ever saw in this world. The leering, evil face of the man who has just struck you on the head hard enough to kill you. The face of the man who has just made sure that you will never again lie in your partner's arms. That you will never help your children celebrate another birthday, will never walk down the aisle of a church and give your daughter away to the man she loves. Will never watch your son carry a football across the goal line. The face of Joseph Randall Wagner. If you do your duty and send him to prison for life, you will ensure that he will never murder anyone again."

She placed the photograph back on the prosecution table and very slowly laid it face down again. She stared at it a moment, and then looked up at the jury. "Thank you," she said.

"Mr. Friedman?" the judge said.

"Thank you, your honor." Max stood up. "Along with my colleague, Ms. DiAngelo, I thank the ladies and gentlemen of the jury for the duty that you have performed in this trial. Are you surprised that I called her my colleague? You shouldn't be. Because that's what she is. We're both officers of the court, and our duty is to tell the truth in this courtroom. It's her responsibility to prove guilt beyond a reasonable doubt, and my job to introduce that reasonable doubt. But it is not her responsibility to find him guilty, or mine to find him not guilty. That duty is yours, and to be quite frank, I'm glad I don't have it on my shoulders. It must weigh heavily right now. No. Our only duty is to tell the truth. And you know what? I think we both have. I know that sounds strange, because as she just reminded you, I promised that we would both tell different stories. And we have. So you might say 'okay, I want you to explain to me how two such different stories can be true.' We can't. That's because we both believe them with all our hearts."

He walked toward the jury, his hands in his pockets, his jacket pushed casually back to accommodate them. "I wonder if both women who came to Solomon believed that the baby was theirs. We always think that one was simply lying about it. Have you ever thought that maybe she wasn't, and she really thought the baby was hers? I don't know. What I do know is that you have heard two stories and you have to choose between them. But even though we both believe our stories, I think there's one very fundamental difference between my colleague and me. She sees life in black and white. I see all shades of gray in between. This is a case where the truth lies in the shades of gray. For Ms. DiAngelo, it's simple. Four men went to the drive-in, and three left. Mr. Wagner did it, and because he did it he should go to prison forever."

He stopped a moment and gazed around the courtroom. Angel was in her back row seat again.

"But it's not as simple as that, is it? You heard the testimony given by Mrs. Evelyn Morton yesterday. The first time I heard it, I wanted to put my fingers in my ears and refuse to listen. I wanted to become a child again, before I knew that there was such evil in the world, in my world. When I thought things were black and white, that the bad guys were somewhere far away, and the good guys were right here with me, and I would be protected forever. But ladies and gentlemen, the truth is that we aren't protected. Freddie Odom wasn't protected, and Joe Wagner wasn't protected.

"Ms. DiAngelo feels free to throw around the word 'murder' in this courtroom. Well, let me say 'rape.' Because that's what happened to Joe Wagner. You see in front of you, sitting at the defense table, a grown man. Imagine for a moment this man when he was ten years old. He was raped in body, mind, and spirit. Can you imagine what life must have been like for him after that? I would think that the only way to deal with it would be to put it away from you. To refuse to remember it. Is that possible? I think so. I think it's possible to consciously forget something traumatic. Maybe it surfaces occasionally. Perhaps it comes to you in the middle of the night, completely unbidden. So what do you do? Do you wake up, look in the refrigerator for a bottle of beer to push it away? That's what Mrs. Wagner said her husband did. Can you blame him?

"I don't condone the act of robbery committed by these four men any more than Ms. DiAngelo does. They chose to act outside the boundaries of decent societal behavior. They took what did not belong to them. And she's right—only Freddie Odom had the courage to try to make things right. But did Joe Wagner take him to the Comanche Drive-in Theatre and murder him in cold blood? If you believe in black and white, that's the only choice left to you. But let's look at the gray."

Max walked closer to the jury box and glanced briefly at each member. "I'm going to ask you to do something difficult," he said. "I'm going to ask you to put yourself into the defendant's shoes. Or, because this is Texas, his boots. Even I'm wearing boots these days." A chuckle fluttered through the courtroom, and several jurors smiled.

He waited for it to die down before he spoke again. "Imagine yourself as a ten-year old child, betrayed by the person who should love you the most in your life. Your father. The man who should show you how to grow up straight and tall. The man who should protect you from the bullies, teach you how to shoot a gun, how to shave, and drive a car. Imagine that this man is himself a bully, and worse. Imagine that he takes you into the barn and commits an act against you that God in his heavens could never imagine, that only the evil in a man's soul could invent. Then the next day, rather than teaching you how to shoot a gun, he makes you pick it up, point it at the beautiful pony whom you love so much, whom you are in charge of caring for, and slaughter the animal. It doesn't die, so your father makes you put the gun to its head and shoot it again, splattering its blood on your innocent face. Your mother doesn't interfere. She never tries to protect you, perhaps out of fear for her own life. The only other person who loves you, your sister, leaves home a week later and never comes back, never calls you.

"I don't know what Joe Wagner's life was like before and after those two days we have heard about in such graphic detail. I shudder to speculate. But one thing we do know is that his father didn't just abuse him physically. He abused him verbally, calling him a 'faggot' and a 'queer.' Was Joe called those names on a daily basis, for his father's amusement? I wouldn't doubt it. Think of what that would be like. Some men might grow up terrified of life, of every shadow. Many might not grow up at all; they might exit life by their own hands. But some would have grown up angry, unconsciously taking vengeance against the world for their own pain. You might do that. Would you know what you were doing? Could you say 'well, my anger is a result of what my father did?' Of course not, because if you did you would stop. Now imagine that you feel you have a sense of control over your life. You're so angry that everyone knows not to mess with you. You use the same horrible words against other men, to protect yourself, that your father used against you. 'Faggot,' and 'queer,' you call other men, to make them scared of you. Until one day you fight with a man who turns the tables. He calls you a faggot and a queer, and questions your manhood, much like your father did so many years ago. Do you think you would be capable of clear thinking? Or would you strike out at the man calling you those names? Would you strike at Freddie Odom, or at the ghost of a man already dead?

"Smith Dixon and Carl Puente have told you that after Freddie Odom died, Joe Wagner was 'out of it.' Mr. Dixon said that immediately after Mr. Odom died, Joe Wagner said 'I didn't go to kill him,' and for perhaps twenty to thirty minutes, he was unaware of their conversation, until finally he came back. Came back. Where do you think he was during that time? Does this sound like the behavior of someone who set out to commit a murder? Or does it sound like the actions of a man with no sense of reality, of the very ground he was sitting on?

"Let me ask you this question again. If you had been brutalized by the very man who was supposed to protect you, who constantly called you cruel names, and you had fashioned your life in such a way as to deny those very memories, what would happen if someone else broke through that protective shell, reminding you of the very man who had so terrorized you? Would you strike out at him, either in anger or defense?"

Max put his hands into his pockets again and walked halfway between the jury and Joe. He glanced at Regina, Dolores, and Bernice, and then at the jury. "What happened to Freddie Odom was a tragedy, and I feel only sympathy for his family. You can put Joe Wagner into prison for the sake of revenge, put him away for the rest of his life so that you will feel safe at night.

"But if we really want to punish the man responsible for Mr. Odom's death, the attempt will be fruitless. Why? Because he lies in a grave in the Loving County Cemetery, next to his wife, the mother who was afraid to stand up to him and protect her own children. If you want to exact vengeance, drive out there and rail at a man named Samuel Payton Wagner, who was responsible for unspeakable cruelties to his own son. He's the man you want, the one who started the long road that led to that tragic night at the Comanche Drive-in Theatre. You can send Joe Wagner to prison forever, or you can give him what his father never did: a chance.

"The decision is yours. I know that you will do what the evidence, and your conscience, tell you is right." He paused, searching for anything else to say, then said simply, "Thank you."

The judge looked at his watch. "It's 2:45 now; we'll break while I prepare my instructions to the jury. Let's reconvene in one hour." He rapped his gavel once and retreated into his chamber. The courtroom stirred and stretched to its feet. The deputies stepped closer to Joe, who didn't look at Max or anyone else.

Max glanced at Diane, who was huddling with Jack. He looked at Freddie's family. Dolores had her arm around Regina's shoulder. Bernice caught his eye and glared at him. He found Angel in the back row and slid in beside her.

"So how do the instructions work?" she asked.

"It's not too hard. The judge tells the jury that it's their solemn duty to make a decision in this case, and then he instructs them on the points of law involved. That's mostly the choices of what they can convict him of. Or of course they can find him not guilty."

"Do you think they'll do that?"

"I don't think there's much chance of it."

"Good."

Max didn't say anything.

"You don't want him to get off, do you?"

"I feel like you're giving me some kind of test here, and I'm afraid of failing."

She sighed and reached for his hand. "I'm sorry, Max. This isn't a test. I just don't like the idea of him going out onto the streets again. I don't want him in my club, and if he shows up there again Bailey will bounce him in a flat second. But I don't want him in anybody else's club either. I just don't like him. The fact that he's even alive kind of pisses me off."

"Sometimes the fact that he's alive amazes me, given what his life was like."

"I guess. You remember that movie *Lone Star*? Like the bartender in it, I'm as liberal as the next guy, given that in Amarillo the next guy's probably a redneck. In New York I'd probably be a conservative—"

"You'd be surprised."

"—and I know what happened to him is bad, but I can't see it excusing what he did. I mean lots of people have had problems. I have. You have, for Christ's sake. Lots of us. But we don't go around killing people because of it."

"I know, I know. Look Angel, I feel pretty much the same. I don't like the guy either." He was speaking in a very low voice, close to her ear, but he looked around to see if anyone could hear. No one was close by, or paying attention. "It's just—when I heard Evelyn's story, I just couldn't let go of it. I couldn't help but think it had something to do with the killing."

"Who came up with the theory that you used?"

"I did. I thought about it a lot, did a lot of research, talked to some psychiatrists. Dr. Vermazen was the most helpful, and he came up with possibilities that I hadn't. But you know, Angel, I really think it's true. I don't think it excuses what happened—"

"The murder, you mean."

"Yeah. But I think it explains it. You said before that other people have had bad things happen to them. That's true. Lots of people have been raped. But lots of them got help. I did, and I just would like for him to get help too. I've seen people in meetings with stories as bad as his, who seemed that low-bottom, but they came back. I came back. Why shouldn't he have that choice?"

"But Jesus Christ, Max, is he the kind of guy who can make that choice? You were smart, and you knew what you were doing was fucked up!" Her voice, although still low, was becoming very intense. "I don't think he's had a coherent thought in his life!"

"Yeah, but how could he? Maybe he did before his father raped him! Before he hit him the first time! What he was like then?" He saw Angel's eyes glancing over his shoulder, and looked back to see Bobby Turner standing respectfully a few feet away.

"Hi, Bobby. What's up?"

"Sorry to interrupt, but . . ."

"It's okay," Angel said.

"I heard you were on break, and I just caught a case I think maybe you can help me with. You interested? I think you'd be good for it."

"Maybe. What is it?"

"Kidnapping case, but not the dad. It's a mom, and she says the dad is neglecting and endangering the kid. She's hired me, and I think I could use your help."

"You need to talk now?"

"If you can, that'd be good. Yeah."

"All right. Give me a second."

Bobby went back into the hallway.

"Look," Max said to Angel. "I'd like to talk to him about this, and I think you and I have some things to say that this isn't the best place for."

She sighed. "I agree. Look, Max, I don't want to come off as belligerent. I've just got a lot of opinions about it."

"I know. Can we talk tonight? After you close?"

"Yeah. What happens now with the trial? I mean after the instructions?"

"He gives the case to the jury, and it's all in their hands."

"You think they'll have a verdict today?"

"I doubt it. My best guess is tomorrow morning."

"Is your part pretty much over?"

"I'll barely say a word from now on."

"All right, I'm going to leave then. If anything does happen, you can tell me tonight."

He leaned over and gave her a light kiss on the lips. She pulled him close and kissed him on the cheek, and they both slid off the bench and into the hallway. Bobby saw them and waited until Angel had disappeared down the hallway with a small wave; then he stepped close to Max with an open manila folder. "Okay, here's what we got. Divorced two years, little girl's four, dad twenty-four, mother twenty-two."

They huddled together on a bench.

At 3:45 precisely, Judge Bruce walked back into the courtroom and reconvened the proceedings. He instructed the jury for thirty minutes, explaining that they must consider only the evidence and testimony offered before them in rendering their verdict. They could not consider any stricken questions, nor could they base their decision on the opinions of any friends or relatives. He told them that if they found that Joe had "intentionally or knowingly caused the death of Mr. Odom, or intended to cause serious bodily injury or committed an act clearly dangerous to human life" that caused Freddie's death, they could convict him of murder. If they found that Joe had "acted under the immediate influence of sudden passion arising from an adequate cause," they could find him guilty of second-degree murder. He explained that adequate cause meant "that which would commonly produce a degree of anger, rage, resentment, or terror in a person of ordinary temper, sufficient to render the mind incapable of cool reflection." If they believed Joe had "recklessly caused" Freddie's death, they could find him guilty of manslaughter. Max wasn't sure how many people "of ordinary temper" with minds "capable of cool reflection" he'd ever known. Not that many in the AA rooms he'd inhabited for years, and certainly none before that. Of all the people he'd known, Joe Wagner was probably the person who would least fit the description of having an ordinary temper and a mind capable of cool reflection. He doubted that someone who did possess those qualities would let being called a faggot or queer push them over the edge. Joe certainly hadn't acted in self defense; after all, he had attacked Freddie. The truth was, what the jury did now was a crapshoot. They could find him guilty on any of the verdicts, and not one day of Max's three years of law school or Diane's either could influence what the jury would do now.

The judge asked the jury to begin deliberations and said that if they had not reached a decision by 6:00 p.m., they would begin again the next morning.

Max looked over the file Bobby had given him and decided that they could make a strong defense on the kidnapping charge. She suspected abuse and neglect, and had gotten into the habit of driving by his house during custody hours to see if he was at home. She thought he was leaving their daughter by herself while he went barhopping. Sure enough, she found the little girl crying and sitting in the living room with a video playing, the husband and his truck nowhere in sight. She took the girl to her aunt's house and refused to give her back when the ex came pounding on the door three hours later.

At 6:00 Max was interrupted when Judge Bruce announced that the jury had not yet reached a verdict and would begin deliberating again the next morning at 9:00. He banged his gavel and disappeared into his chambers.

Chapter 35

Max packed his briefcase and went home, where he took off his suit, covered himself with a blanket, and fell asleep on the couch until 8:30. The cats were sprawled across him, and they grumbled sleepily when he gently pushed them off. He put on jeans and a flannel shirt, walked into the kitchen, and peered at the remnants of a salad in the refrigerator. It looked like it was good for one more portion before he declared it over the hill. He finished, washed the plate, put on his heavy insulated boots and leather jacket, and left for Bailey's.

When he walked in, the acrid smell of cigarette smoke slipped into his nose, and the warmth replaced the cold outside so swiftly that he had to take his jacket off and hang it on one of the hooks nailed into the wall. Hank Williams decried the lovesick blues that his baby had given him. Behind the counter Angel flashed him a quick but genuine smile.

"Howdy stranger," she drawled. "Care for a cool sarsaparilla?"

"Sure," he said, in his best Brooklyn accent.

"Sorry, fresh out. Coke do?"

"Hey, it's the real thing."

"Say that again and I'll shoot you. Anything happen after I left?"

"Judge sent us all home."

"You think they'll have a verdict tomorrow?"

"I don't think it'll stretch past a day. I'd guess tomorrow, sooner rather than later. I don't know why, exactly. Call it lawyer's intuition. Maybe some putz will hang it up, but it'll fall between manslaughter and murder. I'm guessing the former, or maybe second degree."

"Either one okay with you?"

"I guess it'll have to be, won't it?"

"What's second-degree, anyway?"

"What they used to call 'voluntary manslaughter.' Means yeah, he did it, but he had a reason. Not necessarily a good one, but still it's one that all right-thinking people could recognize."

"Sure. That's the 'needed killing' defense Danny told you about one night."

"Ah! A mystery explained."

Max glanced around the tables. "Seen him tonight?"

"No."

"I think lots of times on cold nights he has to check on stock."

"That's not a life I envy," Angel said. "The only way I touch cattle is on my plate or coming out of a chute."

"Chute?" Max said, puzzled.

"Yeah, I rope sometimes. Didn't I tell you that?"

"What's that mean?"

"What's what mean?"

"Rope."

"You don't know what roping means?"

"You mean like in a rodeo? Chasing a cow and throwing a rope around its neck?"

"Or its heels, yeah, but that's the concept."

"They let women do that?"

"Let us?"

"Sorry, I mean—"

"For your information, mister New York Lawyer, there used to be all-women rodeos. I don't do it much anymore, but sometimes I'll show up at a little roping get together and keep my hand in."

Max shook his head. "If I keep learning things like this every day, I hope God never lets me die."

He leaned over the counter and saw Bailey on the floor with her paws stretched out in front of her, the left delicately placed over the right. Her eyes were closed, but when Max said hello she let out with a small "ufff."

He took a rack of balls and a cube of chalk, picking a table close to the counter. Angel joined him when she didn't have a customer. The other players had grown used to seeing him trading shots with her. At first they had thought it strange, that this tough woman whose typical wardrobe consisted of Wrangler jeans, cowboy boots, and pearl-button shirts with the sleeves ripped off was playing with the man whose accent and hair set him apart from the cowboys, students, yuppies, bikers, and recalcitrant husbands who peopled the place. But they respected his game, and after a while he was just the lawyer to them, or the Yankee, or sometimes Max. He answered to them all.

At 11:00 Angel flicked the lights on and off. "Everybody out!" she yelled. "We're closing early!"

There was a wave of muttered "shits," "fucks" and "what the hell for's?" around the room, but no one tried to question her. They all knew that the place closed when Angel and Bailey said it did, and bitching would only gain them a too-close glimpse of white teeth and golden eyes. They all started racking their balls and putting sticks away, draining beers and bringing it all to the counter. Angel gathered their money, put it into a zippered bank bag, and started washing beer mugs while Max emptied the ashtrays and swept the tables and floor.

"You ready?" she said, and he nodded.

"Why'd you close early?"

"Two reasons. There's something I want to ask you about, and I want you to spend the night. That means either you go home and get a change of clothes now, or you get up early and do it then. I want you in bed with me in the morning as long as I can have you, so that means I close up early." She put her arms around his neck and kissed him, her lips brushing his lightly.

"I can't argue with logic like that."

"Sure you could. You're a lawyer, after all. It's your job to argue with logic. You just know I'd whup your ass if you did."

"And take great pleasure in it, I'm sure."

Angel drew her arms back from his neck and said "Bailey, let's go."

Bailey rose to her feet and leaped over the counter. Angel stuffed the bank bag into the floor safe and turned off the lights. They put on their jackets, and when they went out Angel locked the door behind them.

Max drove to his apartment, wondering all the while if he should be looking for anything in Angel's remark about logic. It seemed to him that she was hitting it a little hard on the lawyer remarks lately. He didn't know if he was imagining it, or if she was somehow letting her anger at him for defending Joe come through. Mayella was curled up in a ball, and Jersey was lying on his back, the white spot on his belly almost perfectly circular. He poured a few crunchies into their bowl and let them sleep. He picked out a shirt and tie, and brushed the cat hair off his suit. He had toothpaste, razor, and shaving cream at Angel's house, a sure sign that they were having a serious relationship. He was glad that she wanted him to stay the night but wondered what the question was. He was tired of talking about Joe, tired of seeing Joe every day in the courtroom and was afraid that she wanted more justification about it. "I had to, okay?" he said to himself as he locked the apartment. Yet he didn't think that's what she meant, and his stomach felt faintly nauseous as he thought about her "question." What the fuck is that about, he thought.

When he got out of the car by her house he heard the horses nicker a greeting to him from one of the barn's cozy stalls. It was still cold, and his breath fogged in the dim light of the stars.

He went in, and Bailey uffed at him from her place in a deep leather chair, her golden eyes never leaving him as he went to find Angel. The only light on was in the kitchen, where she was standing at the sink finishing the dishes, hot water steaming up from the stainless steel.

"You hungry?" she said without turning. He wondered if, like Bailey, she had intuitive eyes in the back of her head.

"No, thanks. I ate before I came to Bailey's."

He put his hands tentatively around her waist, and she leaned back against him, her head on his shoulder. "Mmm, that feels good."

"I'm glad."

"Give me a second, okay? Otherwise I'll be standing here all night with chapped hands."

"Sure." Max sat down at the kitchen table and watched her head move to the music drifting from the stereo in the living room. It was a song called "Spring Wind" by Greg Brown, a favorite of his from the folk clubs in Greenwich Village. When he showed surprise that anyone in Amarillo had heard of him, she tipped her head and narrowed her eyes. "Ah, then New York is the repository of all that's good in culture, is that it?" He surrendered, and she told him that she'd heard the singer on *A Prairie Home Companion*, and yes, Amarillo and Lubbock both had National Public Radio stations.

Angel turned off the water and wiped her hands on the seat of her Wranglers. She leaned against the counter and looked at him for a long time, both of them silent. Finally a smile curled her lips and she nodded her head in the direction of the bedroom, taking his hand as she walked past him. Max walked beside her into the bedroom, turning off the kitchen light on the way. On the night table was a lamp with a base made from an old piece of cactus. The shade had drawings of horses that the light shown through. She flicked it on and put her arms around him. She kissed him, sliding her tongue into his mouth. He reached around her and put his hands into the hip pockets of her jeans and squeezed her gently. Her hair smelled of strawberry shampoo, and he realized that she must have showered before he got there, to get the smoke out of it. It was still slightly damp, and the dampness and freshness of it made him want to never let her go.

Angel always wore men's shirts with pearl-snap buttons; until he moved to Amarillo, the only place he'd ever seen them was on cowboys in TV westerns, the ones from the 1950's. Clint Eastwood would never wear something like this, but Roy and Gene used to. The only style change Angel observed was that when it was cold her shirts were flannel, and when it was hot the sleeves were ripped off of them. Max took one side of her shirt in each hand, and slowly unsnapped it, one at a time. Every time he did this it made her even sexier to him, and once again he was struck by the absurdity of the turns his life had taken. This Jewish attorney from New York was making love to a cowgirl from the barren plains of Texas. He reached the waist of her jeans and pulled the shirt out, unsnapping the last few buttons.

Max was always surprised by the size of her breasts. Angel was a slender woman with lean muscles. She often wore a vest over her Western shirts, so to anyone who wanted to look, and most men at Bailey's wouldn't last long if she caught them, she might seem to have small breasts.

He unbuttoned her jeans and slid his hands beneath them and her panties, cupping her ass tightly. She put her arms around his waist, and for a moment they swayed as if slow dancing. He reached up with his left hand and softly caressed her right nipple, rolling it between his fingers. She slowly slid to her knees and unbuttoned the Levis he'd started wearing as an attempt to fit in. She slid her hand into his underwear.

"Hey there," she said. "How about a kiss?" She put her mouth on him, drawing her tongue along the underside where his foreskin had once been attached, wrapping her lips around him.

"If you keep doing that while I'm standing up, broken bones might result," he said.

"Then lay down," she said. They took off the rest of their clothes and held each other on top of the blankets. It was chilly in the room, but soon they were sweating. They lay on their sides, caressing and kissing. She hooked her right leg over his, and he slowly pushed inside her. She was warm and wet, and as he pushed all the way in she gasped. "God! I thought it was in Texas that things were supposed to be bigger." He pushed into her even more and started stroking back and forth inside her. He bent his head down, and putting his hand on her right breast, he drew the nipple into his mouth, sucking on it and teasing it with his tongue and lips. She rolled him onto his back and leaned low over him, her breasts in his face, her long strawberry hair tickling his nose. She put her hands on either side of his shoulders, and raised and lowered herself onto him, stroking him, doing pushups on him. Max put his hands on her ass and they found a rhythm together, working in tandem until he exploded inside of her and she came in great shuddering waves, beyond the point of speech. She collapsed onto him, covering his face with her hair. He gently brushed it off onto her shoulders and wrapped his arms around her back. She breathed into his ear, and in a few minutes said "I have *never* felt anything like that in my life."

After a minute he said "Good. However, it's my duty to assure that you most definitely will again. Very soon, I think."

She bit his earlobe. "Your license to talk like a lawyer stops when you reach my bedroom door."

They drifted into sleep, and Max woke up when she slid off and snuggled against him. He glanced at the alarm clock. 1:20 a.m. Her green eyes were wide open now. She wrapped a tendril of his hair around her index finger.

"You feel like talking for a little bit?"

"Have we arrived at the time that you ask the question?"

She didn't say anything for a minute. She touched his chest, his lips, his cheeks with the tips of her fingers.

"You said something in the courtroom earlier that I wanted to ask you about."

"What was it?"

"You were talking about why you wanted to help Wagner. You said—" she paused, her brow knitted, remembering. "Something like 'other people have had bad things happen to them' and 'a lot of people have been raped, but they got help.' Then you said 'I did, and I want him to get help too.' That's as close as I can get."

Max brushed his fingers over her breast, then down her side to her ass. "I said that, huh?"

She pulled him a little closer and nodded.

"Maybe I was talking about being a drunk, and going to meetings, getting help there."

"Could be. Just the way you said it though, it didn't feel like it to me. Still doesn't."

He nodded and turned onto his stomach, facing the headboard, his hands folded under his chin.

"There's a good reason for that. I wonder what old Freud would say about it?"

"Who cares? I don't trust men who smoke cigars."

"Good idea." She stroked his hair and traced her finger along his triceps.

"I think I told you that my parents didn't pay much attention to me. They drank, not really falling-down drunks but more maintenance drunks. They drank enough to take the edge off things. You've seen those t-shirts that say 'Everyone should believe in something. I believe I'll have another drink.' That one?"

"Sure."

"That was them. Mostly television and drinking enough to keep the buzz going. So I was kind of on my own, even before I stopped going back there at night, before I hit the streets. I had to do a lot to cross their radar. I needed attention, and not the kind I got at school. Half the kids there hated me because I was smart, and the rest because they thought I was a geek, and I was easy to pick on.

"I wasn't any good at stuff other than English and math and history. We had shop classes. Forget about it. I'm lucky I didn't cut my finger off. Then we had gym class too. I was even worse at that. That stupid fucking rope we were supposed to climb up, but some of us couldn't do it and the other kids mostly could, and they laughed at the rest of us. I couldn't play volleyball, basketball, anything like that. The gym teacher we had was a creep. We had him in sixth and seventh grade. He was a yeller. Too fat to do anything himself, so he just stood in one place. He left, and we all breathed a sigh of relief.

"The next guy we got, eighth grade year, was a lot better. His name was Richard Weinglass. I'll tell you right now that his name had nothing to do with me being an alcoholic. Beer and whiskey were more my style. That's a joke, in case you missed it." He laughed nervously. "No, this guy seemed okay. He was young, nice-looking. He was in good shape, wasn't fat. Sometimes he'd play the games with us, and if we didn't do well he didn't yell at us or anything. Everybody liked him. He was a married guy, had a wife and a couple of kids, I think.

"And the great thing was, he liked me. He didn't make fun of me, and he'd actually go out of his way to talk to me. I wasn't getting any attention at home, and this felt good. It wasn't like my other teachers ignored me or anything. I mean, they liked me, I was smart, and I talked in class when asked questions. But this guy was different. It felt more like, like I was a guy. I don't know if this will make any sense to you, but being bad in gym when you're a boy makes you feel like less of a man. It feels like there's a sexual content to the other kids' harassment. Like because you're not athletic you're less masculine. So this guy made me feel good when he talked to me.

"I had a habit of hanging out on the streets after school with my friends, or going to the library. Sometimes the movies. I'd get home in time to eat, and then I'd read in my room, do homework until it was time for bed.

"So one day this guy, Mr. Weinglass, asks during gym class if I'll help him with something after school. He said that he needed to inventory the equipment, and he needed some help with keeping things organized, writing it down, just to generally keep him company. I said sure."

He was silent for a minute. Angel rested her chin on his shoulder blade and stroked his back.

"You sure you want to hear this?" he asked.

"I don't like the way it's going, but I think I need to hear it."

Max nodded and after a few moments continued his story.

"The place where they kept all the equipment was in the back of the locker room. It was kind of a cage, like a jail cell. Wire mesh, with a locking door. There were baseballs and bats in there, basketballs, volleyball nets. They even had some fencing equipment. Foils, masks, vests. You know.

"So that's where we went that day. I had a clipboard, which made me feel very official. He went through the equipment, and I had to mark down how many of what we had, whether anything needed to be scrapped, write down how many new ones to order. Like that.

"We worked forty-five minutes or so, and then he had to go to the bathroom. He said he'd be back. What we were doing didn't require Einstein, so I kept going. After a while, I don't know how long, I heard his voice behind me. It scared me, because I didn't know he was back. He was close, too, so he must have come in very quietly. I told him what I'd been doing and he seemed nervous, like he wasn't listening. I noticed then that he'd changed clothes. Before he had shorts on, and now he was wearing sweat pants. I could see a bulge at his crotch, and just then he reached into the pants and pulled out his cock. He came toward me and I backed up, but there wasn't far to go. We were in the cage.

"He told me he really liked me, that I was a good kid. He said I was better than all the other kids, nicer. Stuff like that. He said that he wanted me to put my mouth on his cock.

"I can't tell you how scared I was. I didn't know what to do. He was between the door and me, and as far as I knew there wasn't anyone else left in the school. Yelling wouldn't do any good, and I knew I couldn't outrun him."

Max was silent for a minute. He was still lying on his stomach, and he could feel the point of Angel's chin resting on his back.

"So I did it. I hated every second of it. But in some really strange way, I liked that he was paying attention to me. No one else did. My parents barely knew when I was home. That's what sexual perps depend on, some of them. Not Joe's father. He wasn't like that. But this guy was.

"It didn't take too long. I didn't know what to do, but it didn't really matter. After a minute he came on me. I turned my face away, because I didn't want it in my mouth, so it was all over my cheek. He handed me a towel that he'd brought with him for that purpose, and I ran out into the shower room and threw up. I couldn't even make it to the toilet. The sink is as far as I got. After a minute he came in, and he told me again how much he liked me, how I was 'different' than the other kids, smarter and nicer. I said 'thanks' because I didn't know what else to do, and I was a polite kid. I got out of there and didn't go home until after dark. I went straight to my room. If I'd eaten I would have just thrown it up again."

"The next day I skipped out of school, went to Prospect Park, and hung out by myself. I went to a movie. *The Omen*. It was scary, but nothing like what had just happened to me. That was a Friday, so I was safe until Monday. I went back to school then.

"I had gym class, but I was safe because there were other kids around. But as I was leaving he came over and said 'Max, I need you to help me again. We didn't finish on Thursday, remember?' And the fucked-up thing is, after school I went back again. Pretty much the same thing happened, but this time he didn't bother pretending to work. It didn't take very long before I had my head over the sink again."

Max stopped. "You okay?"

He felt Angel's face nod slightly against his back, felt her hair graze him up and down. "You want me to stop?"

Her hair brushed side to side.

"He didn't say anything for a couple of days. Just ignored me. Part of me was glad, but that fucked-up neglected part wondered what I'd done wrong. That's why he chose me in the first place, because he could see that vulnerability in me.

"Thursday came around again, and he told me he needed to see me. I thought of running away, but I was afraid. Afraid he'd tell someone. I know that makes no sense, that of course he wouldn't have, but I was just a kid. I was afraid I'd see the other kids looking at me, laughing. Calling me 'faggot' or 'queer.' Afraid no one would pay any attention to me at all. At least when he was doing his thing to me I knew I existed.

"So Thursday I went there again, and this time it was different."

He stopped again. His throat felt raw from telling the story.

"What?" Angel said.

"Give me a second."

He breathed deeply, waiting until he could talk again. He felt her shift her head, her hair tickling him.

"This time he had a tube of cream. He told me to lean over a rack of weights—dumbbells. I said no, I wouldn't, and I tried to get past him and out of the door, but he grabbed me and put me over them, and he sodomized me. I've been hit in my life, been cut with a knife, been kicked, and this pain was right up there with it. The humiliation was even worse. I don't know how long it lasted, but when it was over he stroked my hair and thanked me. 'Don't ever tell anyone about this,' he said. 'Nobody will believe you if you do, but just don't. Let's keep it between us. I'd hate for either of us to get hurt.' I was trying not to look at him when he said that, but I could read his eyes. 'I'll hurt you if you tell,' was what he was saying. At least that's what I heard.

"I went home late, my mother asked where I'd been, I said the movies and she said okay. Went back to the TV and her glass of something. The next day I skipped out again. Went to the park, rode the F train into the city and hung out on St. Mark's Place in the East Village. Went home, stayed in my room, just sneaking out to get something to eat, but I couldn't keep it down. I must have lost five pounds in a week, and I didn't weigh much to begin with.

"Monday morning I took my books, but I didn't go to school. I hung out wherever I could that I felt safe. The candy store. The library at Grand Army Plaza, hiding in the shelves. The Brooklyn Museum. I did that all week long.

"Finally, about 4:00 Friday afternoon, I was walking along Prospect Park West, and I heard somebody yelling my name. I looked around, scared for a second, and saw that it was Jimmy Giordanella, a kid in my grade. 'What do you think?' he said, and of course I said 'about what?'

"'About the fag gym teacher, moron, what do you think?' I started to sweat, because my first thought was that someone had seen us, and now everybody in the school knew. But after a second I realized that if that were true, Jimmy would have wasted no time in calling me a queer. So I said I hadn't heard, that I'd been out of school sick that week. He said 'Yeah, you look sick,' to let me know that he knew I was skipping, then he told me that Weinglass had been caught in the locker room after school, in his words 'buttfucking' a sixth grader, a kid named Ronald Abramson. I didn't really know him, I just knew his face. Jimmy told me that a janitor had been cleaning up in the gym after school the day before, and he was checking the doors to make sure they were all locked when he heard some strange noises coming from the locker room, and he saw Weinglass and Ronald in the cage. He yelled at him, and then threatened to hit him with the mop wringer. The coach ran off, and the janitor took care of Ronald, called the principal. Ronald said he didn't want to see a doctor, didn't want to see anybody. I could understand that. The cops were trying to find Weinglass, but he wasn't home. His wife and two kids, a son and a daughter were, but he wasn't. They finally found him the next week, in a bus station in Buffalo. He was about to go to Canada.

"I heard later that he pled guilty. There wasn't a trial, so Ronald didn't have to testify. I don't know if there were other kids or not. Knowing what I do about perps, I suspect there were, but nobody ever heard their names. Or mine. I never told anybody. My parents, any of the teachers, nobody. I just kept it inside me. There wasn't any permanent damage to me physically. That was before AIDS, and the guy must have been clean of VD. It hurt me, but he used lubricant, so it wasn't as bad as it could have been. Physically, I mean. Emotionally it was indescribably bad. Spiritually. I wasn't too great in the self-esteem department before that, but now I had absolutely nothing. I couldn't stop thinking about what had happened. I'd rerun it in my head all the time, trying to figure out what I could have done differently. I blamed myself. If only I'd gone home that first time, told him 'no, I have to be somewhere.' Anything like that. I asked myself what I did to make it happen, maybe I really was gay. It just went on and on for weeks.

"Finally, one night I was at home, reading in my room. I wasn't studying, because after that my class work went straight down the crapper. Most of the time I didn't go to class. I got truancy reports, but I lied to my parents, told them that I'd gone to the bathroom when the teacher took the roll, that I was in the library, anything. They seemed to believe it. So I was reading one night and my parents had already gone to bed. I went into the living room and very quietly opened their liquor cabinet and took a belt of scotch. I can remember exactly how it felt. It was like someone had dropped a beautiful, purple velvet curtain inside of me. It flowed down slowly, calmly, covering my insides, protecting me, cutting me off. I felt better instantly. I could still remember Weinglass, but suddenly it didn't seem to matter as much. So I took another drink, then a third one. I was only fourteen years old, so by then I was drunk, but I managed to negotiate my way back to my room without falling over, holding onto the wall. I went to sleep right away and woke up the next morning with a monster headache and a dry mouth. Some water and aspirin took care of them both after a while, and Weinglass was more in the past than he'd been the night before. It didn't feel like he could hurt me anymore.

"So I started drinking every night. I started going back to school, too, but then soon the summer came, and I spent a lot of time at the library, or at the swimming pool in Sunset Park. On August 12, I turned fifteen. I was more confident, somehow, a little louder, more popular. There weren't a lot of kids who were smaller and weaker than I was, but I found a few, and I bullied them. With the help of other kids, of course.

"When school started in September I was in the ninth grade, in high school. Every once in a while some kid would mention Weinglass, but he was last year's news. The funny thing was I didn't think about him much. If I did, it was easy enough to pick up a drink. Sometimes I'd wake up at night in a sweat, and I knew it was about him, but a drink cured it.

"I didn't pay attention in school. I couldn't. I made it through that year with lots of D's and F's, and the next year I didn't go back. I didn't really go back home either. I went there less and less, and finally not at all. My parents raised a minor fuss about it, but they were too far gone.

"I moved into Manhattan. I was sixteen years old. I lived on the streets sometimes, but not much. I was always good with words, and I could manage to talk myself onto someone's couch or floor. I'd get a group together, a few guys who would share a sublet for a few months. One year I lived in five different places. I had about twice as many jobs some years. Minimum wage stuff. I worked at a Communist bookstore on West 13th street, took tickets at most of the movie theatres in the Village, Chelsea, and all points south of 59th street. I worked the counter in a pet food store, a vitamin joint, video houses. I hustled some bucks playing pool. The best job I had was as a bike messenger. Even in the winter, it was strenuous enough to sweat the alcohol out during the day. The high of it kept me from thinking about stuff too much. Screaming in and out of traffic, trying to make too many addresses on one run, something that we all competed for. Drinking lots of water. It paid pretty well, too. Not the base, but there were bonuses sometimes and lots of times I'd talk the yuppies into giving me tips. Mostly it was secretaries, so all I got from them was a smile—"

"I hope that's all you got," Angel said.

Max smiled. It was good to hear her voice. "Sometimes the account execs would be up front, sweating matzahs—"

"I think 'bullets' is the correct word."

"—waiting for their precious package, and I'd let them know I almost got clipped by a truck or cab or something, and they'd pass me a yuppie food stamp—"

"What's that?"

"A twenty. So I did okay at it. But really, I was just treading water most of the time. The years slipped by. I mean it. I'd get drunk on New Year's, and it seemed like two weeks later everybody would be tooting horns and popping corks again, and yelling 'Happy New Year' again. A year had passed, and I had no notion of where it had gone or what I had done. None at all.

"I spent my nights hanging out in bars or drinking at home. I'd sit in an espresso shop with a shot of something in my coffee, so I could think I was coolly Continental and not just a drunk. I'm amazed I never got a job tending bar or working the counter at a liquor store. Used to be if you worked the counter they might as well paint a target on your chest, but then they installed these Plexiglas booths that the customers stand in to make it a little harder to kill the clerks."

He reached up onto the nightstand and took a drink from the glass of water he kept there. "Sometimes when I hung out in bars I'd get in fights. I wasn't really a belligerent drunk, but a lot of them are, so I was in a few. Usually it was just a couple of drunk guys pushing each other, but a couple of times it was worse. I smashed a bottle on a guy's head one time, and took a couple myself. Then one night I must have said the wrong thing to the wrong guy, because he waited for me a few doors down and took a knife to me."

Angel's fingers went to the scar on his back that wound around to his right side.

"Thank God he missed my kidney. That's when I ended up in the hospital. The doctor there told me I would die if I didn't stop drinking, and I thought he was full of shit. I was there a couple of days, forced to be sober, and guess what happened?"

"Weinglass?"

"Yeah. I started remembering. It's not like I had totally forgotten him. Every once in a while there would be a dim awareness of him, of what had happened. But I took it in a very antiseptic way. 'Oh yeah, that,' I'd think, and pick up a drink. He'd go back to wherever he was living again. But when I was in the hospital he was really back. Without the drink, I couldn't get rid of him. So I went to a few meetings there, and when I got out it was too much for me to do sober, and I'd drink again. That happened four times before I was finally able to quit. So far I haven't picked up the first one. I got my GED, which wasn't very hard, and somebody at a meeting told me that NYU had free tuition if you worked there. I got a job in the Registration office. They also had benefits, which thank God covered psychiatry. I lucked out and found somebody who knew about sexual abuse and alcoholism. I knew if I didn't get rid of that fucker I'd never stay sober."

"And have you? Gotten rid of him?"

"I don't know that I ever will completely. But I have enough to stay sober and not let the memories kill me. When I get depressed he comes back, or when I'm afraid. It was hard when I first moved here, but now it's okay. When I first got sober I'd have these perfect sense memories—I'd remember exactly what it felt like to have his cock inside me."

"Whatever happened to him?"

"I don't know. I haven't exactly kept up. I hope he's dead. But my guess is that he got paroled, and probably did it again to some kid."

"I hate that it happened to you. I hate that it happened to Wagner too, as much as I can't stand that bastard. I can't believe there are people sick enough to do those things to kids."

"The sad thing," Max said, "is that it's not that uncommon. When I was taking a sociology class for my B.A., we all had to give an oral presentation on some social problem. One woman gave a report about child abuse. I'll never forget her name. Susan Taylor. Beautiful woman. Redhead too, not that I noticed or anything."

Angel pinched the soft skin on the inside of his thigh.

"Hey, that hurt!"

"Good. I meant it to."

"Anyway, Susan Taylor gave a report on child abuse. She made the strangest statement. She said that anything that can be done to food has been done to a child. I thought my head was going to explode when she said it. Then I realized that lots of things you can't do to food have been done to kids, too."

"Jesus."

"Yeah."

She rubbed her hand over his back. "You really think this is why he acts the way he does, why he killed Freddie?"

"Yeah, I really do."

"The same thing happened to you, though, and you didn't kill anybody."

"Other than trying to kill myself, no. But I was angry. I fought, struck out at people. I've used my tongue as a weapon sometimes."

"I like the way you use your tongue."

"Gee, I could never tell." He was silent for a few moments.

"I think the one Joe hates the most is himself, just like I did. I would have been different than Joe no matter what happened. I think a lot more than he does. He's been trained since his birth by his culture not to. And we know his parents didn't help. Sometimes I think of Danny, and what he must have been like. He probably wasn't that much different than Joe when he was drinking. Now he's a great guy. Compassionate, intelligent. I think Joe has the ability to be like that too, somewhere in there. The question is, can it ever get out? I hope that in prison, maybe he'll go to meetings, figure things out."

They didn't talk for a few minutes. Angel's head still rested on Max's back, and he felt dampness on his skin.

"Max," she said, "I'm sorry that happened to you."

He reached back and stroked her smooth hip. "Thank you."

His lids got heavy, and before he went to sleep he heard her say, "I love you."

"I love you too, Angel." It was the last thing Max remembered before he woke up in the morning.

Chapter 36

When his eyes opened, Max was pressed up against Angel's back. He touched her breasts, brushing his fingers lightly over her nipples. She rolled over to face him and kissed him. They touched each other's bodies; then she not quite gently put her arm around his waist and drew him on top of her.

When they finished making love Max dozed for a few minutes with her arms around him before he slid out of bed. He put a cup of coffee in a big earthenware mug on the night table next to her and took a shower.

He drove to his apartment and checked on the cats before driving to the courthouse. He ate breakfast at the Snazzy Pig and was in the courtroom by 9:00 a.m. The room was close to empty. The bailiff, wearing a green jacket and a Tweetie Bird tie, told him that the jury had just reconvened.

"Thanks," Max said. "Nice tie, by the way."

"Why, thank you," the bailiff said, genuinely pleased. "Not many folks seem to notice."

I doubt that, Max thought as he walked away. He sat in the hallway reviewing cases and making notes on a yellow ledger. He lost track of time and didn't notice any of the passersby until he felt a hand ruffling his hair.

"Hey," Angel said. She was wearing jeans and a long-sleeved shirt, but the sleeves were rolled to her elbows and she didn't have on a vest.

"Getting warmer?" he asked.

"Yep. Fifties already. It's pretty slushy now, but in a few days it'll be gone, unless it'll all freezes over. This is Amarillo, after all."

"Give the folks in church something to pray for," he said.

"Other than the souls of heathens like you and me, you mean? That's a full-time job right there." She sat down next to him. "No word from the jury?"

"Not yet. What time is it?"

"Ten-thirty."

"I didn't know if you were coming."

"Hey, there's only a certain number of hours of beauty sleep I can get."

"You don't need many."

"Flatterer."

"That's me." He leaned his head against the marble wall.

"Working on your next case?"

"Yeah."

"You do lot of child-abuse work, don't you?"

"Like Danny says, you've got to ride your horse in the direction it's going."

"A horse doesn't know where to go unless the rider touches the reins."

"I'm getting confused. Maybe I should relate it to the subway system."

"Maybe you should just answer my question."

"Yeah, I do a lot of those cases. Sometimes I feel like I'm the only one sticking up for them. The parents are too shocked, usually, or they take it out on the kids. Sometimes they get too overwhelmed by their own guilt to do anything. The parents get frozen, and the kids get lost."

"I'm glad you're doing it. Just take care of yourself, okay?"

"I do." He reached out and took her hand. "But thank you."

She squeezed her fingers around his.

"Sorry to interrupt, Mr. Friedman."

Max looked up to see the bailiff leaning around the door. "No, it's okay. Are they ready?"

"They'll be back in about fifteen minutes."

"Thank you," Max said, and started putting his files and pads back into his briefcase.

"Where does he get those ties?" Angel asked.

"I'm guessing grandchildren," Max said.

"I suppose so. They've got to be good for something."

Max sat down and was barely in the chair before the deputies brought Joe in and unlocked his handcuffs. "Hi," Max said.

Joe nodded at him. "They about to come back?"

"Yes," Max said.

Ten minutes later Diane came into the courtroom with Jack Ogan and sat at the prosecution's table. She glanced at Max for a moment. It was just a few minutes before the jury returned.

Max looked at them. In the movies and books the lawyers all seem full of wisdom about the jurors' behavior. If they look at the defendant, they've found him not guilty. Or maybe if they look at him it means a guilty verdict. None of the writers could get it straight. As far as Max was concerned there was no rule. They could look or not, and it had nothing to do with the verdict that they came up with. The client would be guilty or not, and there was no need to second-guess the verdict. They all filed in and took their seats.

Judge Bruce looked at the building contractor who had been chosen foreman, the one who taught Sunday School. "Ladies and gentlemen of the jury, have you reached a verdict?"

The man nodded seriously. During the trial he had dressed in short sleeved shirts with no tie, but today, out of respect for the solemnity of the occasion, he wore a tie and jacket. Max wondered if the shirt had short sleeves.

"We have, your honor."

"Bailiff?"

The bailiff walked ponderously over to the juror, who accepted the piece of paper extended to him. He handed it to the judge, who read it and without expression handed it back.

"Will the defendant please rise?" he said. Max and Joe stood up as the bailiff lumbered back to the jury box and took his position next to the judge, his arms crossed. The foreman stood for a moment until the judge said, "Will you read the verdict, please?"

The foreman unfolded the paper and in his most serious voice said "In the state of Texas versus Joseph Randall Wagner, we the jury find the defendant guilty of second-degree murder."

Max heard a loud cry from Freddie's family. He didn't know if it was the widow, her sister, or her mother, and he didn't turn to look. Instead he looked at his client.

Joe leaned against the table, his hands placed flat against the top. He didn't say anything. Max hadn't known how Joe would react, and he had been nervous. He didn't know if Joe would attack him or Diane or maybe the judge. But he did none of those. He just stood with his head bowed. Maybe, Max thought, all his rage had come out during his sister's testimony. Maybe he had none left to give.

"Thank you," the judge said. "Before I relieve you of your duties, you have one more service to perform. You must convene as a jury to determine the sentence. Are you prepared to do that now?"

"We are, your honor," the foreman said. They filed back out through their door to the jury's chambers once again.

Max said "It's not too bad, you know. They could have gone for murder, but they didn't. Manslaughter was too much to ask, given the testimony, but I think this means they heard what we were saying."

"What you were saying."

"Well, yes, what I was saying."

"'Cause I didn't get to talk, to tell what really happened."

"Joe, I just think it was too risky."

Joe nodded.

"But," Max continued, "I think this sounds good. It's very possible they'll come up with a light sentence."

When Joe laughed it sounded like a cough. "Yeah, but it ain't you who's gonna do it. I mean, who are you to say what's light and what ain't?"

"That's true, but—"

"Look, I don't want to talk no more. Just leave me be, all right?"

"Sure, of course. I'm going to check on a few things, and—" He stopped when he saw that Joe wasn't listening.

Max found Angel at the back of the courtroom in her usual seat. He glanced at her as he went by, and she gave him a light smile. Max went into the hallway and sat down on the bench, leaning over his knees. "God," he prayed to himself, "Grant me the serenity to accept the things I cannot change, the courage to change the things I can, and the wisdom to know the difference." He sat there until his neck began to hurt, and when he sat up straight again he felt better. He glanced into the courtroom and saw the bailiff walking heavily down the aisle toward him. The man looked relieved when he saw Max and reversed his course

That sure didn't take long, Max thought.

The jury filed back in, and when the judge asked if they had arrived at a sentence the foreman straightened his tie, coughed, and announced that the defendant, Joseph Randall Wagner, was sentenced to serve no less than five and no more than ten years in a Texas Department of Criminal Justice facility.

Joe closed his eyes. "Five years," he said.

"Yes, but that doesn't mean five. You keep straight while you're in there, and you can be out in less than two," Max said.

"Whatever. It's still two, and that's a goddamn long time."

"Look," Max said, "I'll come see you before you go. You can get help in there, in prison. There are people who can—"

Joe cut him off. "Far as I know, you was the one supposed to help me," he said. "If they can't do no better than you did, fuck 'em." The deputies led him away.

Max picked up his briefcase, but before he reached the rail veered to the left, toward the prosecutor's table. He offered his hand to Diane, who hesitated before she took it. Max shook Jack's hand too.

"Creative defense," she said.

"Thank you. I also think it's true."

"It was effective. You ever think about switching sides?"

"Working for the State, you mean?"

"Yes."

"I'm okay where I am now, I think. Thank you, though."

"Well, you're good," she said. "I hate to see it get wasted on crap like this." She nodded abruptly and walked back down the aisle, Jack trailing behind her.

Max swung open the rail in the gate and walked through. Angel was waiting for him at the back, standing next to her usual bench.

He was passing the third row of spectators when he heard a steely voice. "I just want to know how you do it."

He turned and saw Bernice Edwards. She and Dolores Puente stood with Regina Odom between them.

"Pardon me?"

"I want to know how you stand up in front of God and the whole world and defend trash like that. He murdered my daughter's husband, and he practically gets away scot-free."

"He was sentenced according to the law."

"You know that sentence was nothing. How long before he gets out?"

"Probably not less than a year and a half."

"Oh," Bernice said, "that's harsh. A year and a half for murder? How dare you say that to me, as if it's a real punishment? My daughter is a widow because of him, and my grandbabies won't have a father for the rest of their lives! And you say a year and a half is enough for him. He should go to the electric chair, and you too."

"There's no electric chair in Texas anymore," Max said.

"Don't be smart with me," Bernice said. "You know exactly what I mean."

"I'm sorry Ma'am, but I have to go. I'm very sorry for your family's loss." Max walked away before she could say anything else.

"Trouble?" Angel asked when he reached her.

"Just another satisfied customer," he said. He was silent while they walked out of the building and into the surprisingly balmy air. She guided them toward her truck. Finally he said, "That woman has a point, after all. Her loved one was murdered, and the killer gets a year and a half. She decides it's wrong, so who does she blame? Me, of course. I got him the sentence. Now if she looks in the paper and sees an article about a child who's been abused, she'll say 'Somebody ought to do something about that.' Well, someone does. I do. The judges do. We do the best we can. But to her, I'm the enemy. And why? Because I defended Joe, told the truth as I see it, and to her that means I'm 'on his side.' Half the time I'm ready to just say fuck it, you know?"

They reached her truck and he leaned against it. "How long does it take to be a cowboy? Maybe I can start over."

She laughed. "You can call yourself a real cowboy the first day you sincerely regret it. Danny would probably tell you that. And that day would probably come the first time you broke your leg, or a calf kicked a hole in it, or a horse made a sandwich of itself, you and the ground." She put her hand on his arm. "You do good work, Max. Maybe the adults don't know it. Maybe even the kids can't realize it. But you're helping them."

He nodded. "I know."

"You feel any better?"

"A little bit."

"Good. It adds up."

"Thank you."

She watched a patch of blue among the cloud. "Are you done with Joe?"

"Almost. I want to go talk to him before he transfers to prison."

"When will that be?"

"I don't know. A week, maybe. I'm not looking forward to it."

"Him shipping out?"

"Talking to him."

"Do you have to?"

"No, but I should."

"Why?"

"It just seems right."

"You can't save him, you know."

"What are you, my sponsor?"

"No, I'm your sweetheart, and if you talk to me again like that I won't be for long."

Max blew out his breath in a long, slow sigh. "I'm sorry. Yeah, you're probably right. I keep thinking that if I say or do the right thing, it'll fix him. Take away his pain and anger, something. Suddenly make his dad not a sexual psychopath. God, can you imagine what he went through? I don't even mean being raped. I mean being forced, as a ten year-old boy, to kill your own horse. I can't even think what it did to him."

"You know what it did to him, Max. But I'll tell you something else you already know. There's nothing you can do about it. You can't fix him, and you can't make it not have happened. You can't get rid of Weinglass, either."

"I know."

"You do great work, Max. Sometimes that just has to be enough."

"What day is this?"

"Thursday."

"You know what I'd love to spend the weekend doing?"

"Stripping stalls at my barn? If you really want to be a cowboy, it's a necessary skill."

"Let's compromise on stripping you in your bedroom."

"That can be arranged. After the stalls, as a reward."

"And second, not to be a lawyer until Monday. Joe's not going anywhere before then."

"Sounds like a hell of an idea. How about right now you munch down some sad-ass soybean thing disguising itself as meat while I let the juice from the real thing drizzle disgustingly down my chin?"

"That sounds very unlawyerly. You just made yourself a deal."

On Monday morning, Max went to the jail to see two clients. Joe Wagner refused to see him, according to the guard. The second client was Smith Dixon, whom Max assured he would do his best to get the lightest sentence possible.

Over the weekend he had retrieved messages from Smith and from Champ Phillips, who said he thought Smith might just be ready to follow a new path, and that he wanted to help out a fellow reader. He thought Max might, too. Smith's message said that he wanted to hire Max as his attorney, but he didn't have any money because the state took away what he had stolen, and every dollar to his name had gone to have his father's remains cremated. He couldn't promise when he would pay Max, only that he would someday.

Max believed him. He requested a bench trial for Smith so that the sentencing would be left entirely to a judge. He did that when he found out that Edna Gandy would be presiding. He knew that she was tough, but he believed her to be fair.

Smith pled guilty to aggravated robbery, a first-degree felony. In the sentencing phase, Max told the judge how the defendant had been a key witness for the state in The People vs. Joe Wagner. He called Champ Phillips, who admitted that he felt intuitively that Smith was, finally, a good prospect for going straight. Diane, who handled the questioning herself, hammered away at Champ's intuition, something she had greatly relied on in the past. Max made sure that the judge couldn't see him smiling. When he asked what he thought should happen if Smith broke the law again, Champ brushed his thick mustache for a long moment and said "I hope he'd never see the light again. This is his last chance."

Smith told the judge that he had come to Amarillo to start again and had gone astray. He didn't blame Joe, he said, but he felt desperate and he robbed a store. The judge asked what would happen if he got that desperate again, and Smith said "I'd go buy a gun and kill myself. But I'm not going to steal what ain't mine again."

The judge took a day to decide that she would sentence Smith Dixon to three years in a state prison. Diane fumed, Max smiled, and Smith said "Thank you," before the deputies led him away. He was sent to the Clements unit, close to Amarillo.

Carl Puente pled guilty to aggravated robbery and was given three years in prison, sentence to be suspended. Max did not represent him. The lawyer who was representing him in his divorce proceedings did double duty.

Max regretted that he hadn't been given one more chance to talk to Joe Wagner before he was sent across the state to a prison in Bowie County, close to the Arkansas border. Whenever he mentioned it, Angel told him again that he couldn't save Joe. Max knew it was true, but it still ate at him sometimes.

Chapter 37

Spring was heralded, as it always is in the Panhandle, by the coming of the sand storms. Max learned that an autumn sandstorm like the hellish one he arrived in was a rarity, but in the spring they were commonplace. The wind blew throughout the month of March, carrying small objects and some large ones with it. One Friday afternoon when he was driving north on Interstate 27 from Lubbock, he felt the right wheels of his car lift slightly off the pavement as the wind buffeted it. When he told Angel and Danny, they dismissed it. Anyone who lived in the Panhandle for very long had seen much worse. They horrified him one night at Bailey's by telling wind stories almost nostalgically. Danny topped Angel's story of a Fed Ex truck blowing over into a ditch with a description of a wind that ripped out a poorly secured gas pump, setting the whole 7-11 parking lot on fire moments later.

In April the wind stopped and the cool plains air, which normally held not a drop of humidity, brought light rain. Every plant came back to life, and the land was gloriously green.

The temperatures reached over 100 nineteen days in July and August, and the only reason Max could stand it was the low humidity. It didn't seem to bother the natives, although the ones who traveled for business or pleasure to Dallas, Austin, or Houston complained about the heat "out there," and couldn't wait to get back where it was "cooler." Max made a note never to go to those towns in the summer.

On August 14th he tore himself away from the air conditioner to answer the phone. It was a woman in the Criminal Justice program at Amarillo College, asking if he would be interested in teaching a class called Fundamentals of Criminal Law. She said that he had come recommended by the person who had taught the course for the past three years.

"And who might my benefactor be?" he asked.

"Pardon me?"

"Who recommended me?"

"Oh, Diane DiAngelo," the woman said. "She's in the District Attorney's office, but she couldn't teach it this year and—I'm sorry, but did I say something funny?"

"No, not at all," Max said. "Just an inside joke, I guess. You had to be there."

He agreed to teach the class and on the first day was surprised at the beauty of the campus. It actually looked like a college. NYU hadn't; it was just a collection of buildings in Greenwich Village. This place was more like Columbia, but on a smaller scale. Young people who could be nothing else but students walked in pairs or groups between the buildings, backpacks slung by one strap. At NYU it was hard to tell some of the students from the office workers or the slackers who endangered lives with their skateboards in the dry fountain of Washington Square. Or for that matter from the pushers who seemed to be carrying on a one-sided conversation as they mumbled their wares to passers-by.

As he made his way through the roll sheet on the first day of class he thought a woman on the back row seemed familiar, but he couldn't quite place her. He thought he might have seen her at a meeting or in a courtroom until he reached the final name on the sheet, which was "Wagner, Darlene." He looked at her in surprise, and she smiled shyly then looked down at the desk. When the class was over, she stood up and started out with the other students, her notebook and text held tightly to her chest.

"Darlene!" he called, and she hesitated, unsure whether to come up front or wait for him. Then she walked up to him.

She looked much different than when he had last seen her. Her hair was longer, and she had put a perm in it. Her eyes no longer had dark circles under them, and although she was still shy she no longer looked scared.

"It's nice to see you," he said. "Is this your first semester?"

She nodded. "Yes, sir."

"Why are you taking Criminal Law? Thinking about law school?"

"Oh, I don't know about that," she said. "I was reading an article a couple months back about people who help other folks through the courts—you know, women who have been raped, kids who have been hurt. Like that. I thought it was something that maybe I could do."

"I think that's a great idea. You *would* be good at it."

"Thank you, sir," she said, and a slight flush spread across her cheeks.

"You don't have to call me sir. Just plain old Max will be fine."

"Okay."

He put his book into his briefcase. "How's Joe doing?"

She looked at the floor, and her face lost its sparkle. He was sorry he'd asked.

She shrugged her shoulders. "I don't know. I wrote to him a couple of times, but he's not the kind to write back. It's a long trip out there too. I ain't— I've never been anywhere by myself, and my folks, they wouldn't want to go, any more than they liked him." She looked up at his face, finally. "Tell you the truth, Mr.—Max, I've filed for divorce. I would have done it before all that mess last year, but I was too scared. Now I figure I can." She paused a moment. "You think I was wrong to do that?"

"No, I don't think so. I think you'll be better off."

"That's what I think too."

There was nothing else to say. "I'm glad you're going to be in the class," Max said, and started walking toward the door.

She fell in beside him. "I'm kind of nervous. I mean, I've never taken a college class before."

"What a coincidence. I've never taught one. So we'll learn it together."

Then he saw Darlene do something for what may have been the first time in years. She smiled and was suddenly beautiful.

Darlene Wagner received one of the five A's in the class. In December, Max was hired to teach the class again for the spring semester. At the end of the month, he and Angel celebrated their second Christmas together. By now the cats were almost used to Bailey; when she chased them they came out of hiding in less than two hours instead of disappearing for an entire day. On Christmas Eve Angel closed the club early, much to the chagrin of the customers. For Christmas she gave Max a tooled calfskin briefcase, and his gift to her was a hand-made bridle carefully decorated with hundreds of multi-colored glass beads and tassels of horsehair. "It's supposed to be a Nez Perce design," he said, "which is perfect for an Appaloosa. But what do I know? I'm from Brooklyn. It could be anything."

They sat on her couch in front of the fireplace, and Max had never felt safer or more loved in his life. He had grown to love waking up in the middle of the night and finding Angel's smooth skin next to him. On the nights that he spent in his apartment, he missed her and slept fitfully.

Max's practice grew slowly but steadily, and he rented a small office downtown. He didn't have a receptionist, or for that matter room for one, but he had a telephone with voicemail, a desk, one chair for himself and two for visitors, and a file cabinet. He felt prosperous.

On February 3, a little more than a year after Joe's trial, Max and Angel drove to the Clements Unit, where Smith Dixon was up for parole. He sat in front of the three members of the board and told them that he had truly changed his ways and was now ready to become a productive member of society.

Max said he believed him. Angel said that when he ended his parole she was prepared to offer Smith a job at Bailey's doing general custodial work and helping out behind the counter.

"Will he be allowed to handle money?" the middle-aged woman with seniority on the board asked.

"When hell freezes over," Angel said. "He even looks at the money, I'll set my dog on him and send what's left back to you."

The board conferred for fifteen minutes before deciding that they would grant parole to Smith Dixon. If he comported himself and checked in regularly with his parole officer, then he would finish in three months. They also told him that if he ever committed another crime or failed to report one, as he had done with the death of Freddie Odom, it would be his final act as a free man. He would never see the outside of a prison again.

The three of them slid into the seat of Angel's pickup truck.

"How do you feel?" Max asked.

For almost a minute Smith stared out at the passing fields, which in several months would be crowned with white cotton.

"Grateful," he said.

They took him to a halfway house where he was required to live during his probation. His few books and pieces of clothes were in cardboard boxes stored in Angel's barn. They brought them to him the next day, and he arranged them as well as he could. That afternoon he took a job in a mechanic's shop, waiting until he could go to work at Bailey's.

On August 30th, Diane DiAngelo went through her mail, as she did every morning. She slit the flap on an envelope with a letter opener that matched the pen set on her desk. Inside was only a newspaper clipping. What the hell is this, she thought. She unfolded it and saw that it was a photograph of her that had appeared in the newspaper a week earlier; she had given a press conference on the courthouse steps after successfully prosecuting a hospital administrator accused of fraud. A *News-Globe* photographer had taken the picture. It was a clipping from the paper, just like any other, with one exception: her eyes and mouth had been very cleanly cut out. She looked at the envelope without touching it. It was hand written, with no return address. The postmark was yesterday. After clinically observing all this, she stifled the urges both to curse and cry, and picking up the phone, dialed a four-digit extension. "Champ?" she said. "I need you in my office, right now."

Dolores Puente could never figure out why Nina just couldn't go to the same school as her mother taught at. But no, that would make too much sense. It made much more for her to have to drop Nina off and then race over to her own building two miles away, then go to pick her up after school. She was sure that some administrator in the AISD offices could explain it to her, but she'd hate to have to ask Carl for bail money.

After school when she pulled up to the curb in her car, Nina almost trotted up to the door. She opened it quickly and got in. She was very quiet. Usually she greeted her mother with news of the projects she had worked on, of what she'd learned. After the separation, Dolores had to coax it out of her for a while, but now Nina was mostly back to her old self. Not this day.

Dolores waited a few blocks before she asked if everything was okay. Nina just nodded yes, but she was still quiet. Dolores got them both safely home, and it wasn't until she started making dinner that Nina came quietly to her. "Momma," she said, "why would a friend of Daddy's talk to me at school?"

Very quietly, Dolores put down the spoon she had been using to stir pasta sauce. Trying not to change expression, she said "What do you mean, honey? What friend of Daddy's?"

"At lunch today I was on the playground, and a man called to me from the fence."

"Which side of the fence? Your side or the outside?"

"Outside. He didn't say my name. He just said 'Hey, little girl. Is your daddy named Carl? Cause he's a friend of mine.' I didn't say anything, Momma, because he scared me. I just went inside right away."

"Did any of the teachers see him, Honey? Did they say anything to him?" She smoothed Nina's long bangs away from her face.

Nina shook her head back and forth. "Just me."

Dolores glanced a moment at the bubbling pot, then turned the heat down. "I'm glad you told me, Honey. Next time make sure you tell a teacher right away, okay? Not that it'll happen again, but if it ever does. Now can you do me a favor, please? Can you just sit right here at the table? Momma needs to make a phone call."

Dolores walked out of the room and down the hall before she let out her breath, which she had almost been holding all during the exchange. She fought down the urge to vomit, then she was flooded with anger, and she made two phone calls: one to Carl, and one to the police. She had planned to take Nina to a movie that night, but they stayed at home.

Carl was watching a football game when she called, in the small house he had bought after the divorce was final. His leg was draped over the arm of his easy chair, and he reached for the phone without looking away from the screen. When he heard Dolores's voice at first he thought Jesus Christ, what is it this time? She already has custody because I have a criminal record. Is she going to try to take away all my visitation rights? Dolores explained what the problem was, and he put both feet on the floor and hit the mute button on his remote. He listened carefully until she was finished and sat in his chair in stunned silence, the game forgotten. He had been sitting there less than half an hour when the phone rang again.

"Yeah?"

He got there in five minutes, covering a route that normally took him fifteen. From two blocks away he could see the smoke rising up from his store. Three crews of firemen held the hoses that spewed water at the ruin of his business. Here and there small flames still flickered. He got out of the car, and a fire fighter moved to stop him.

"Sorry sir, you can't—"

"This is my place, I own it!"

"Sorry sir. Are you Mr. Puente?"

"Yeah, that's right."

"You'll still have to stand back here with me. There's a lot of damage, but it's not completely burned. It's mostly the front of the building that got the worst of it. The structure in the back looks pretty intact, although you'll need a lot of smoke and water repair. We can't help that, but they got the fire pretty quick. The call came in before it had gotten too far."

Carl squeezed his eyes shut against the pain. First Nina, and now this. "Any idea what happened? The inspectors came a couple of months ago, and they—"

"Oh, no question there. You could smell gas back to the sidewalk when we got here. It's arson."

"Arson? Jesus Christ, who'd want to—" He stopped when he realized that there could be no coincidence. His daughter stalked at school by a stranger who said he knew him and now his store burned. It had to be the same person. But who would do that?

"I think it's winding down here, Mr. Puente. Why don't you go on home and get some sleep. In the morning, you can call your insurance agent, and he'll come look it over. There's nothing you can do tonight." He put his hand on Carl's shoulder sympathetically.

Carl stumbled back to his car, and on automatic pilot he found his house again. He watched the rest of the football game without seeing it. Still in shock, he finally went to bed.

The phone rang at 8:30 that night, and when Angel answered it no one was there. She slammed it down into the cradle. "Assholes," she said to no one in particular. Twenty minutes later there was another call. "Excuse me," she yelled out, "is there a Mr. Friedman here tonight?"

Max looked up from his game. Sometimes he got calls at Bailey's, usually clients, but they asked for "Max."

"I don't know," he said, chalking his cue. "Did they say 'esquire'?" He barely dodged the cube of chalk she threw at him and walked to the counter. Propping his elbow on it, he said "This is Max Friedman."

There was a moment of silence, and then a woman's voice said "Hi, Mr. Friedman, Max, um this is Darlene. Darlene Wagner."

"Hey, Darlene. How are you? I saw you at the courthouse the other day. Is the job going okay?"

"Yes sir, real good. Oh, sorry. Max." She paused again. "I feel a little scared."

Max focused his attention immediately. "What's wrong?"

"Well, probably nothing. I don't know. Just a couple of times tonight my phone has rung, and it wasn't a wrong number or a marketer or anything. Somebody was there but didn't say anything, you know? I said hello a couple of times, and after a few seconds the line went dead again."

"You think it was Joe?"

"I'm afraid of it."

"Do you know if he's out?"

"No, but I wouldn't have heard."

"Look Darlene, I'm sure it's all fine, but if you feel scared maybe you have someone you could call and spend the night with? If not, just make sure everything's locked up."

"I think I'm okay. I just wanted to let you know too, just in case."

"Thank you, Darlene. Anything else?"

"No."

"You know, if you call the police, I bet they wouldn't mind making a few extra drives down your street tonight. They're good about that."

"That's a good idea. Thank you."

She hung up. Max didn't have to ask her "just in case" what. He knew. Just in case Joe Wagner was back. Just in case he hadn't learned a fucking thing in prison. In the morning he'd make a couple of calls and find out, although Joe being out this early would have meant good behavior in prison, something he doubted his former client would have been capable of.

Smith Dixon waited until Max was off the phone before he drifted up to the counter. On most nights when he wasn't working he was there at Bailey's anyway, playing pool. He was responsible for emptying the trash and sweeping up at the end of the night. He put the cues away and made sure each table had a bridge hanging underneath it. He walked around among the tables to see if anyone was getting too drunk, but the presence of Bailey was usually enough to ensure that no one got out of hand. It was a humbling job, but it felt good to have his own place to live, even if it was just a studio apartment. His collection of furniture and books grew slowly but steadily, and soon he would have to move to a bigger place. He had a 12 year-old Buick that he had bought from Frank Vaughn, who always seemed to be juggling several used cars at once. He tinkered on it himself before work and on weekends, and it was probably running more smoothly than it had since the day it rolled off the line.

"Everything okay?" he asked Max.

"I think so. Ghosts from the past. That was Darlene Wagner, Joe's wife. She was afraid maybe he was back in town. She got a couple of hang-ups. They could just as well be wrong numbers."

Smith nodded and leaned his elbows against the counter, surveying the room. "Probably. I'd like to think I've heard the last of him." Angel drew a beer and set it in front of him. "Appreciate it, boss," he said, a wink in his voice.

"Know what he told me one time?" he asked Max.

"I might run out of guesses before I got it."

"Said he didn't use his turn signals because he didn't want the government telling him what to do. 'What right they got to tell me what to do?' So there you have a refusal to use turn signals as a form of civil disobedience. That's enough to make Thoreau proud, ain't it?"

"It takes all kinds, I suppose."

"You ever heard of anything more ignorant in your life?"

"When I was in college," Max said, "I was in the lobby of a building at NYU. Right off Washington Square, in the Village. I'm standing there, and the elevator doors are just closing when a woman runs in from the street. She starts yelling, 'Hold the door, please!' except her tone is completely devoid of 'please.' By the time she gets to the elevator it's already on the second floor, which anyone can see who bothers to look at the numbers that are lit up."

"They ain't got them arrows that move, like in the movies?"

"No not anymore. Just the numbers."

"Huh."

"So there she stands, and she slaps her hand against the door, and says 'Hell-lo-oh!' Like they're just waiting there behind the door, and they'll open up and let her on. Meanwhile, they're on the fifth floor. That's ignorant."

"No, I think that's arrogant," Angel said as she finished with a customer.

"You've got a point," Max said.

Smith continued to survey the room. "Sometimes there's a real fine line."

At midnight Smith flashed the lights and the customers starting putting up their cues, placing the balls and chalk back into the trays. They formed a line at the front, turning in the balls to Smith and paying Angel, while Bailey sat next to Angel's feet.

When the customers were all gone, Max locked the door and brushed the tables while Smith swept the floor and dumped all the trashcans into one big plastic bag. He took it out the back door to the dumpster in the alley.

"How'd you do?" Max asked Angel, who was counting the money.

She finished putting fifty one dollar bills into a stack, counting silently to herself, before she answered. "Yet another banner night at Bailey's." At the sound of her name, Bailey gave a small "chuff."

"Who was that woman who called for you before?" Angel asked.

"Jealous?"

"Need to be?"

"No."

"Then I'm not."

"It was Darlene Wagner. She got a couple of hang-ups tonight, and she was feeling scared."

She looked up at him, and pushed her hair away from her eyes.

"Hang-ups?"

"Yeah. Why?"

"We did too."

"What, at Bailey's?"

"A couple of times tonight. Phone rang, and nobody was there."

"Nobody there at all?"

"What'd I say?"

"But I mean, could you hear breathing, background noise, anything?"

"With the noise in this place, I have trouble hearing voices sometimes. But no, there wasn't anybody there."

Max was silent for a moment.

"You think there's something going on?" Angel's voice was quiet, and Bailey heard the apprehension in it. She stood up, her ears at attention, and moved so that her head touched Angel's hand.

"I don't know. Maybe we're just spooking ourselves."

"Max?"

"Yes?"

"Where's Smith?"

"He went to—" he said, and stopped.

"That was five minutes ago. How long does it take to dump the trash?"

"Shit." Then he laughed. "Look at this. We're spooking ourselves. It wasn't five minutes, was it? It was less." He glanced at the back door. "I'll go check."

"You're not going by yourself. We'll all check."

Angel lifted the gate in the counter and walked through, Bailey padding quietly at her heels. Max walked beside her, threading through the tables, and in seconds they were at the back door. A small wooden wedge had been shoved between the door and the jamb to keep it open half an inch. It was what they always did to keep from being locked out. Bailey put her nose to the crack and immediately her hackles stood up and rumbling growls started deep in her chest. Suddenly she flung herself at the door, slamming it open. Smith was lying face down in the alley. They only saw him for long enough to recognize that there was a wet spot on his head over his ear before Bailey leaped at Joe Wagner, who was standing with his back against the alley wall. He stretched his hand out, and Angel screamed "Bailey, no!" when she saw the flash of metal at the end of it.

It was too late. Bailey was still in mid-leap when Joe pulled the trigger and the gun fired. The bullet hit Bailey, and she crumpled to the ground at Joe's feet. Angel cried out in rage and grief and bent down to touch Bailey.

"You do that and I'll kill you right now, lady, I swear to God. Stand up!" Angel did it, slowly, murder on her face.

Joe Wagner was dressed in a denim jacket and jeans, and he was no longer the empty shell that Max had last seen. The wasted-away prisoner in the courtroom was gone. Joe was his old self again, a smirk on his face, his voice arrogant and taunting.

"I knew you two were stupid enough to do it," he said. "All I had to do was take out your pal there, and you'd come looking for him. You both thought you were so smart, didn't you? Well, look where it got you. Your buddy and your fucking dog are dead, and the two of you will be too, soon enough. Mr. Smart Prick Lawyer, and his cunt girlfriend. The two of you will look great dead, won't you? Enough talking. Come on, let's go." He waved the gun toward the opening at the end of the alley.

"Go where, Joe?" Max asked.

"What the fuck do you care? It don't matter to you, cause you'll be just as dead no matter where you are."

"You take us somewhere and kill us, Joe, and that'll be kidnapping and murder. They'll get you for capital murder, and that means the needle. You want to chance that?"

"That's assuming I'm dumb enough to get caught, which I ain't. I kill you two, and I'm gone. Nobody's ever gonna find me again."

"Where are you going?" Max asked.

"Fuck you. Wouldn't you like to know?"

"If you're going to kill us, what does it matter?"

"You ain't playing your lawyer word games on me, the way you did my sister in the court. Getting her to say all them lies. You just shut the fuck up and move."

Joe stepped back to let them pass. Max looked at Angel and shook his head. She took her hand in his, and together they walked past Joe, facing him and giving him plenty of room. Angel looked back at Bailey. She and Smith were still lying on the red bricks of the alley, and Angel couldn't tell if they were alive or dead. She kept her eyes on them until she was at the end of the alley, when Joe stuck the gun into her spine, and said "Turn your goddamn head around! They ain't goin' anywhere, I promise you that. I been owing it to you and that mutt ever since what you did to me in there. You got no right to treat me like that, throw me out of the place in front of everybody. Now we're gonna see how tough you are. I bet you bleed just like anybody else, like that goddamn Smith and your fucking dog. You ain't so tough, I bet."

They reached the end of the alley and Max, his hand still in Angel's, turned to look back. Joe shoved Max with his free hand, and he almost sprawled onto the pavement, catching himself at the last moment.

"Where's your truck?" Joe asked Angel. She glared at him. He grabbed her arm and savagely twisted it up behind her back. "I said where's your goddamn truck! I ain't fuckin' with you! Where is it?"

Max turned and threw his fist at Joe's head. Joe saw it coming and pushed

Angel from him suddenly. She landed against the brick side wall of the club, and Joe swung the gun at Max's head, clipping him above the eye. Max didn't go down, but the blow stunned him.

"I ain't planning to kill you right here, but you try any of that one more time, and I will. I don't give a fuck. Now where's the goddamn truck?"

Angel told him it was parked at the end of the block, and Joe pointed the revolver at them. "Get going then." They walked in front of him until they reached the truck.

"You got the keys?" he said to Angel. She nodded.

"You're driving, then. You get in first. Then you right behind her, lawyer. You try to make a smart move and you'll be wearing each other's brains, you hear?"

Angel slid behind the wheel and craned back, trying to see the alley. All she could see was the mouth of it; Bailey and Smith were too far back. Max got into the passenger's side and Joe pushed in against him, the gun jamming painfully into his ribs.

"Get on the interstate and go east," he said. "And don't start any shit, or I'll shoot both of you, and be out of the truck and gone before a cop can even get close. You got me?"

Neither of them said anything. Max glanced at Joe's face, sickly green in the lights of the dashboard. Joe smelled of sweat and alcohol—both at the same time. Sometimes when people drank a lot of anything, it didn't matter whether it was whiskey or beer, they would smell of it. The alcohol would come oozing out of their pores, sickly sour. That's what Joe was doing now. For all his macho bravado, Max could tell he was scared, and he knew that scared men were more dangerous than any other kind.

Angel eased the truck up onto the access road and then the interstate. After two miles, Joe told her to turn north on 287. Max knew where they were going, had suspected it before Joe forced them into the truck.

They passed by Wonderland, an aging amusement park. Whenever Max drove by it he was reminded of Coney Island, which he had often visited as a child. It had the same seedy feeling, and the roller coaster was more than a little spooky.

After a few minutes the traffic thinned out, and the houses grew sparser.

"Ain't none of it true, you know," Joe said.

Max didn't take the bait.

"You know what I'm talking about," Joe continued. "All that shit Evvy said in court. She always was a lying bitch. The old man was an asshole, and Ma was a sack of shit, scared of her own shadow, but none of that happened. He whipped me with a belt, but that's it. I don't even remember being in the barn, but if I was, I was just getting a whipping. And that shit about the horse was a lie, too. That horse just died one day, I don't know of what. It was probably old when he got it, and it just died."

Max glanced at Angel's face, but it was a mask of rage, grief, and pain. She didn't look at him.

"You should've let me talk," Joe said. "I told you that back then. The jury would've listened to me, and I would've walked away, instead of going to prison for a year and a half. It wasn't so bad, though. I just did like they said, and the only reason I could do that was so I could get out again, and come back here. Worked in the woodshop there, making furniture that they probably sell for a lot of bucks. Rest of the time just hang out in the yard and lift weights. I'm in a lot better shape now than I was before I went in. Lots of niggers and Mexicans in there, you know. I just stayed away from them, and out of trouble. It was all worth it, so I could get out. Bet you two didn't think you'd see me again."

Max and Angel were still silent, and Joe continued "Y'all ain't the only ones I got plans for. That whore wife of mine divorced me while I was in there, you know that? She should've known she—"

"Joe," Max said, "at the risk of you shooting Angel and me right now, and crashing the truck into a fiery ball, I have to ask you to just please shut the fuck up. I'm tired of hearing you. I'm sick of hearing you whine, and I'm fed up with your goddamn threats. So you want to shoot, go ahead."

To Max's surprise, Joe just laughed. "You fucking pussy, you'll get it soon enough. Both of you." He stopped talking, and they drove for five more minutes before he said "You see that stand of trees there on the right? Turn in to the gravel road."

Max would have known without looking where they were, but he looked anyway and saw the splintered, falling down hut where the cashier used to sit at the front of the Comanche Drive-In Theatre. Seventy yards beyond it the ghostly white screen, sections of the paint almost peeled off, stood sentinel over the metal poles.

"Cut your lights and pull in," Joe said.

Angel turned off the headlights, and the truck rattled across the pipe cattle guard through the sagging wooden fence at the front of the drive-in. Max glanced through the windshield at the poor figure of Quanah Parker on the sign.

The truck was halfway to the screen when Joe said "This is good." Angel braked, and the truck stopped. Joe reached behind him for the door handle and backed out. He jerked his head at Max. "Get out real careful. You just got a few minutes left, and you oughtn't to waste them." Angel started to get out of the driver's door, and Joe said "Nah, you come out this way too." She slid across the seat behind Max.

A light breeze had picked up, and Max could smell the scent of rain. Thunder rumbled a few miles away, and the leaves of the poplar trees meant to mask the screen from the road started to flutter.

Joe backed away from them and moved to the side. He waved the revolver at Max. "Y'all stand next to each other," he said. "You're so in love with each other, you might as well go out together. Your pal Smith and that fucking dog are already dead, so you might as well be. Hey, tell me lawyer, is that how you got Smith to lie about me, settin' up a deal to get him a job? You bribe him?"

"Smith was the prosecution's witness," Max said. "I didn't have anything to do with his testimony."

"Yeah, but he helped put me away, didn't he? Him and Carl and my goddamn sister. I'm still trying to decide if I'm gonna do something about her. I don't know. I'm gonna tell you one thing, though. When I finish with you two, I'm gonna go visit Darlene for a while. I ain't gonna kill her but I'm gonna give her a taste of what she's been missing the last couple years. She's probably got her another man by now, that fucking whore, but she ain't had me.

"All right, I'm tired of messing with you. Y'all go over in them trees there. I ain't got time to bury you. Come on, now."

Angel glared at Joe. "Screw you," she said. "You want to kill me, do it right here. I'm tired of taking orders from you."

Joe's eyes narrowed and the mocking smile he had worn disappeared. "Get into them trees," he said.

"She's right, Joe," Max said. "There's no profit in it for us. You want to kill us, do it now."

Max looked at the space between them. It was about ten feet, and he knew that if he charged Joe, he couldn't get to him before he was shot. Maybe though, just maybe he could distract Joe long enough, get him to change the angle of the gun, so that Angel could do something. He glanced at the ground. There were rocks there, and some were sizeable enough to do serious damage. If he provided a distraction, Angel could scoop up a rock and bash Joe's head or his nuts with it and buy herself some time. Max knew that he would die; being shot point-blank offered no other outcome. He thought of trying some cheap trick that always worked in the movies, like picking up sand and throwing it in his face, or saying "Joe, behind you!" but those only worked in comedies and stupid action movies. He doubted that they had been tried with any success in real life. Joe was a few bristles short of a broom, but Max didn't think he could be tricked that easily.

Joe raised the gun and pointed it at Max's head. "You're first, lawyer," he said, and thumbed the hammer back.

Max heard a voice from somewhere yell "Hit the ground!" and he reached out to grab Angel's shirt and pulled her down.

A shot pierced the thick air of the night, and Joe Wagner fell backward like a hammer had hit him in the shoulder. He landed on his back, his arm outstretched but the revolver still in it. It moved feebly, and Angel scrambled on her hands and knees across the rocks and sand, reaching her feet halfway to him.

Max looked behind him and saw Champ Phillips, his service pistol still in his hand, running toward them. Twenty yards behind him Cee Ross opened the door of his car and swung out with surprising speed for a man his size. He pulled his weapon and ran after Champ.

Max heard a howl of pain and turned to see Angel, her boot clamped tightly on Joe's wrist. She reached down and pulled the gun from his hand, then moved her foot away. She very deliberately pointed the gun at his head. Max could see that her arm was steady.

"I'm not going to," she said before Max could beg her not to do it. "I could kill him without a second thought, but I'm not that stupid. I just wanted to see what it was like to have him in my sights." She tucked the gun into the back of her jeans, then pulled back her boot and kicked Joe in the ribs as hard as she could. "You killed my dog and you killed my friend, you stupid motherfucker," she said through gritted teeth. Joe screamed, a circle of blood slowly spreading from his shoulder into the sand. Angel kicked him again.

Max wrapped his arms around her from behind, pinning her arms down. "No, no, no," he whispered. "Come on, that's enough." He could feel the cold steel of Joe's revolver pushing against his stomach.

"Just one more, Max. Come on."

"No. He's not worth it. I don't want you to be arrested for assault. I couldn't defend you, because it would be a conflict of interest."

Slowly he felt her relax in his tight hold. He released his arms; then he took her hand and pulled her gently away.

"I didn't see any of that," Champ Phillips said. He still held his pistol in his hand, but the barrel was pointed down to the ground.

"See what?" Ross said.

Max felt a drop of rain hit his forehead, and above the poplar trees a streak of lightning stabbed the sky. In the distance a siren's wail came closer.

"Cee, you got this until EMS shows?"

"Got you covered," the big cop said. "You better get some rest, all them reports you'll have to be filling out tomorrow."

"And thank you for reminding me." He turned to Max and Angel. "Y'all mind following me?"

"Sure," Max said. "You'll need us for statements, right?"

"Eventually."

Max put his hand on Angel's back, and they walked over to the truck.

"You mind driving?" she asked him.

He shook his head and took the keys. He had never driven the big diesel truck before and felt a little intimidated, but he opened the door for her and then climbed into the driver's side. He fired the truck up and Champ pulled out of the drive-in ahead of them. When Max swung in behind him, Champ hit the flashing lights and took off at least twenty miles over the speed limit.

"What the hell?" he said, glancing at Angel. She shrugged her shoulders listlessly. Max pressed the accelerator, keeping a safe distance behind Champ. He reached across the seat and took Angel's hand.

Fat drops started to splatter the windshield, and Max saw tears trickle down Angel's cheeks. She wiped them away on her shirt.

Champ kept up the same speed as the houses grew more and more dense. There was almost no traffic on the streets, so when he came to a stop light he slowed down enough to check for anyone coming, then flew through.

Angel stirred from her downward spiral and looked at him. "Where do you think he's going?"

"I don't know. At this speed though, it won't be too long before we find out."

Champ slowed down long enough to get on the entrance ramp to the interstate and exited on Georgia Street. They passed Dunevin Circle, where Bailey's was two blocks away. Angel averted her head as they went by.

Champ started to brake eight blocks later in front of a green and white sign reading, "AM/PM Pet Hospital—Open 24 Hours."

"Oh my God," Angel whispered, so low that Max could barely hear her. She was out of the truck and pulling open the glass doors before Champ

Phillips' boots touched the asphalt. Max clambered out and followed her into the waiting room. It was empty.

Angel ran to the counter and craned her neck to see if anyone was in sight. The sound of a door opening yanked her attention toward it, and Smith Dixon, a gauze bandage on his head seeping a little bit of blood, stepped out.

"Smith," Angel whispered. She walked slowly to him and looked straight into his eyes. "I thought he killed you."

"He did too, that little son of a bitch," Smith said. "And I didn't know if I was ever going to see either of you again." His glance took in Max, who was now at Angel's side. "God damn, it's good to see you." His arms reached out and around their shoulders, pulling them in close to his body. The three stood there for a moment taking comfort in each other.

Finally, Angel pulled away and stared straight up into his eyes. "You have to tell me, Smith. You don't tell me now, I'll fall to pieces right here. Is she dead?"

"She—" He tried to speak, but the words wouldn't make their way out. A tear trickled from the corner of his eye.

"Oh, please don't say—"

He shook his head rapidly. "No," he managed to get out. "No, she—she's going to be okay, they think. They've got her on the table right now. She's got a good chance."

Angel's bottom lip started to tremble and tears flowed down her cheeks. Max put his arm around her, and she pushed her face into his shoulder. "Goddamn it," she finally managed to say, "y'all better not start thinking I'm an old softie, or I'll kick your asses, both of you."

"No way I'd ever think that," Smith said.

A gentle voice said "Excuse me," and they saw Champ Phillips standing politely a few feet away, his gray Stetson held in his hand. "I'm glad to hear the news," he said.

"Oh my God," Max said. "I'm sorry. Please forgive me. We owe you big-time for this, Lieutenant."

"At the risk of sounding clichéd, Counselor, I was just doing my job." His mouth under the thick moustache smiled. "The person you really owe a debt to is that fellow right there," he said, and nodded at Smith.

Max and Angel turned to look at him, and Champ said "He was the one called me, said Wagner had taken off with you."

"But how did you know where to go?" Max said.

Smith shrugged and looked slightly embarrassed. "I guessed, pretty much. I didn't figure Joe had that much imagination. He's a dumb bastard, and I thought he'd probably take you back out to the Comanche. Figured he'd find it funny in some kind of sick way. When I came to I went back inside and made the call, praying that I'd be right. Then I picked her up and got her here as fast as possible."

He glanced away from them. "What about him? He dead?"

Champ shook his head. "No. He'll be out of commission for a while, but I didn't shoot to kill. He'll probably have to recover in prison. D.A. will charge him with aggravated assault, unlawful possession of a firearm by a felon, kidnapping. Maybe making terroristic threats and arson too, we'll see. Carl Puente's place burned down tonight. Before he gets out this time, he'll have a lot of the vinegar taken out of him."

"I don't want him to get out," Angel said. "If he does, I'll track him down myself and—"

"If I were your attorney, I wouldn't recommend saying anything further in the presence of an officer of the law," Max said.

"Funny thing is," Champ said as if he hadn't heard, "He helped save you. I knew I had to make my move when he cocked the hammer. I guess he didn't know he was holding a double-action. Or maybe he was just being dramatic."

"Jesus Christ," Smith said. "Thank God for small favors and dumb rednecks." Even Angel managed a small laugh.

"At the risk of sounding like a naïve Yankee," Max said, "You're going to have to tell me what you're talking about."

Angel rolled her eyes. "Sorry," she said. "A double-action revolver means when you pull the trigger, it cocks the hammer and releases it with the same movement. A single-action means you have to pull the hammer back and then pull the trigger. What he's saying is that Joe pulled the hammer back when he didn't have to. He could have just pulled the trigger, but that gave the lieutenant time to warn us."

"Hang on a second," Max said. "If you only have to pull the trigger, why isn't it called single-action, because that's all you have to do? A double-action should mean you have to do two things instead of one. But that's not the way it is, right, because the double-action does it all at once, which is only one action."

"Max, it doesn't have to make sense. It's like when you asked why the defense team can't knock down the kicker when—"

"Right, when the whole point of football is lots of big guys knocking down lots of other big guys. I mean, how does that make any sense?"

"It doesn't, that's the thing. It's football. It's Texas. It's just the way it is."

"I still don't understand."

"I know you don't, and I love you anyway."

"Good."

"This is getting too deep for me," Champ said. "I'm going to start on that paperwork. Your friend should be at the hospital about now, and then on his way to the crossbar hotel." He started for the door but turned back. "Piece of advice, counselor?"

"Sure."

"Let somebody else defend him this time."

"Thanks, Lieutenant, but that had already occurred to me."

"Good." He put his hat on, touched the brim, and walked out the door and into the light summer rain.

They all looked at each other.

"So," Angel said. "What do we do now?"

Smith glanced at the closed doors leading back into the clinic. After a few moments he said, "Wait?"

Smith had been staring at the same page of an old *Sports Illustrated* for half an hour when the door opened. Angel was sitting at one end of a long bench staring at nothing. Max's head rested in her lap, his arm covering his eyes.

When the knob turned, Max sat up quickly and they were all on their feet in seconds. The doctor, a tall slender woman in operating greens, smiled at them. She walked over to Smith and gently examined the bandage on his forehead. "Not bad for a vet," she said.

"I'm fine. What about Bailey?"

"Come on." She inclined her head toward the open door, an examining room. There was another open door at the back, and she led them through it. Halfway across the large back room was a steel table, and on top of it Bailey lay on her left side, her ribs rising and falling gently.

Smith and Max stood back and let Angel walk toward the table. "Can I touch her?"

"Sure," the doctor said. "She's sedated right now, so she won't feel it, not physically I mean. But I think she'll know you're here. She'll feel it in some way."

Angel gently ran her hand over the silver fur, stroking her ears and chest. She gently kneaded the thick ruff.

An IV line ran from a stand down into Bailey's front left leg. A white cloth covered her ribs on the right side.

Angel glanced at the doctor. "This is where . . . ?"

The doctor nodded. "The bullet caught her here, went in between two of her ribs and lodged in the muscle there. No ribs broken, no organs damaged. She lost some blood. It's good that you got her here quickly," she said to Smith. "How'd you know about us?"

"Just seen the sign, I guess."

"I'm glad. She's a tough lady, but still—timing was everything."

Angel walked back to Smith and gave his bicep a hard squeeze.

"We'll be here all night," the doctor said. "She won't wake up until morning, so you can go home and get some rest if you want."

"What time do you think she'll wake up?" Angel asked.

The doctor glanced at the clock. It was shaped like a black cat with a white belly, the tail and eyes moving from side to side as the seconds ticked by. The clock hands on its belly pointed to 2:30.

"Figure about 8:30 she'll wake up. She'll be groggy, but that won't last long. We'll have to give her some painkillers, but I think she'll be able to stand up. If I'm right, she's the kind of dog it'd be hard to stop. You think you can be back by then?"

"I'd be hard to stop."

The doctor laughed. "Yeah. I think she'll make it just fine." A bell sounded from the waiting room, signaling a new patient. "If y'all will excuse me, we're going to need our space here. This late at night, it's always an emergency."

"Thank you, Doctor," Max said, and touched her arm.

They walked out through the same examining room in time to see the doctor and a young teary-eyed woman disappearing into another of the rooms. The woman held a towel in her arms.

"Call me hard-hearted," Angel said, "but right now I don't even want to know what she's got in that towel."

The three stood in the parking lot for a few moments, awkwardly letting the rain dampen their hair and shoulders. Finally Smith said, "I reckon one us of in the sick ward is enough. I'm going to go home, catch some sleep."

"Smith," Max said. "You saved our lives tonight."

Smith shrugged his shoulders, embarrassed. "Phillips did it."

"No. If you hadn't made the call, he would have heard about it tomorrow, along with everybody else. Or whenever they found our bodies."

"I was thinking earlier, while I was waiting for you. Didn't know if you were dead or alive. I was thinking—" His voice broke and he stood for a moment, head down. Finally he said "I wondered why he didn't shoot me. He could have killed me easy."

"Maybe he didn't want the shot to warn us," Angel said.

"Maybe it was the grace of God," Max said.

"I could use some more of that," Smith said. He got into his car and left for home.

"You got the keys?" Angel asked. Max handed them over, and they drove to Angel's house nestled in the cottonwood trees. They slept deeply for four hours until the alarm clock went off at 7:00 a.m. Max cooked breakfast, and they both showered. The rain had stopped, and the air was fresh and warm. They fired up the truck and drove back to Georgia Street to the animal clinic.

A receptionist greeted them with a yawn and woke up quickly when they told her why they were there. "Just a second," she said, and disappeared into the back. A moment later the examining room door opened, and the doctor stepped out, looking tired but happy. "Hi, y'all," she said. "Come on back."

"She's not awake yet, but I expect her to be pretty soon. She had a good night after you left, been sleeping the whole time." Her own face and jaw clenched and her eyes closed, the yawn of someone trying to stifle it. "Sorry. You can stay in here, unless someone else comes in. Usually when it gets past dawn, we just have calmer stuff, check-ups and shots. I've got another hour to go, and if there's anything you need, just holler."

The doctor walked out to the front, and in a few minutes they heard a puppy's bark coming from behind the closed doors of one of the examining rooms.

Angel stood by the table, rubbing Bailey's fur and massaging her large, pointed ears. She whispered to her, and Max gave them some space.

At 8:45 Max said "Any signs?"

"Nothing yet," Angel replied, and a moment later the hand she leaned on the steel table in front of Bailey's head received a very soft, wet lick. Angel looked at Bailey's face, right into her golden right eye, which was blearily open. "Max!"

He rushed over and Bailey glanced up at him. A low, scratchy "chuff" came from her dry throat. Angel buried her face in Bailey's neck fur and cried until she was empty, while Max stood next to her and caressed her shoulder.

Bailey convalesced at home for a week before she was well enough to come back to the club. The patch the vet had shaved during the surgery had already half grown back. Angel took the piece of lead the doctor dug out of her side and mounted it on a square of wood with the words "Bailey's Bullet" burned into it. She hung it on the wall behind the counter.

At 9:30 on Bailey's first night back, Angel decided that her friend was getting tired. "You ready to go, sweetheart?" she asked, and Bailey stared into her eyes before rising carefully.

"Hey, Max. We're leaving. You want to go?"

Max and Danny Gonzalez were playing a game of eight ball. "Since Danny just successfully sank the eight, I think this would be a good time for me to gracefully exit."

"Hey Smith?"

Smith Dixon was drawing a beer for a customer. "Hang on," he said, as he topped off the mug, handed the beer over, and accepted the payment. "What's up?"

"We're going to call it a night. When you close up just count the cash and put it in the safe. Here's the combination." She wrote the numbers on a pad and handed it to him. He glanced at it, then tore it into tiny pieces and threw it into the trash.

"Thanks, boss."

"De nada."

"No, for once you're wrong. It's something, all right. It's everything to me."

"See you tomorrow, then."

She and Max and Bailey walked out the doors side by side into the warm, dry, West Texas night.

Made in the USA
Charleston, SC
18 November 2014